# the elemental war

academy of magical creatures book five

MEGAN LINSKI & ALICIA RADES

We the authors acknowledge that the United States of America is a country formed on stolen land. We respect and honor the indigenous peoples who have lived here for centuries, and we recognize there is still much work to do to make reparations and heal the damage caused to the many indigenous nations who were first here, both in the past and today.

May we remember the atrocities once committed, create a better world in the present, and look forward together for our future.

A special thank-you to our sensitivity reader Kris Riley of the Cherokee tribe for her invaluable feedback on indigenous life and culture, as well as her commentary on living with chronic illness.

This book features conversations in American Sign Language (ASL). ASL is a unique language that uses hand gestures to communicate. ASL has its own rules for grammar and syntax, and does not follow the same rules as English. However, all conversations in ASL (shown in italics) have been translated to English for ease of reading. In the United States, approximately 48 million people are affected by hearing loss.

# Liam

## ONE

*S*on. *You need to open your eyes.*

Everything ignited. The landscape around me dipped and folded. Each tree and plant had been demolished to cinders. There was nothing left around me but an empty desert that went on for miles and miles, far past the horizon. The ground was cracked, raw and devoid of life except for the ashes that littered the area. Blackened, charred ground met with an orange-yellow sky. The smell of smoke and fire was everywhere, surrounding me and closing in. It was suffocating me, and my throat gasped for air.

Breathe. I needed to breathe.

*It's okay, son.* Hands reached out and steadied me through the blazing darkness. Once they touched me, the smoke scattered and dispersed in columns that went rushing upward. The harsh sunset illuminated a tough face and a grim exterior.

My entire body quivered with relief as I recognized the stern expression and familiar features that were so much like my own.

"Dad," I choked out. Relief rushed through my veins like a harsh stream. I never thought I'd see him again. Ancestors, I missed him so much.

I reached out for him, but my hand glided straight through his spirit. He could touch me, but I couldn't touch him. Horror grew in my lungs, and I took a breath to let out a scream. The twilight welled, and the temperature shot up several degrees. We were standing at the cusp of the Ancestral Lands, and he was on a plane of existence I couldn't reach.

Because I wasn't dead. *Why* wasn't I fucking dead?

Dad reached out and put his hands on my shoulders. *Listen to me,* he said roughly. *There isn't much time. You need to get Sophia to a safe place.*

"Where?" I asked. "Where is safe anymore?"

*She has to come first now. Do you understand?* Dad's eyes bored into mine with an intensity that I'd never seen before. *You protect her with everything you have. You need to be her leader and guide. If you don't, everything's at risk. Your whole life has come down to this.*

"I'm trying," I pleaded. "I'm trying so hard."

*I'm sorry, but you don't have time to fall apart,* Dad growled. *Your family is counting on you. Be there for them, Liam. They're your responsibility.*

"I don't know what you mean," I stuttered. "What am I supposed to do?"

Dad said nothing more— just vanished. I stumbled forward, and his spirit melded into the colors of the sky, a grizzly bear running with the vibrancy of the wind.

"Dad? Dad!" My voice grew into a panic as I searched for him. "Dad, don't leave me! I need you!"

It was too late. He was gone again.

I had to find him. I was nothing without him, without his guidance. I couldn't face this world alone. I couldn't be the man of the family. That was his job, not mine.

I started running. I bolted through the desert as fast as I could. My body couldn't labor me here. I was merely spirit energy, so I didn't feel any pain. But no matter where I ran, it seemed like I remained in the same spot.

The ground beneath my feet began to split. Large, cavernous holes opened up in the earth, and lava bubbled at the bottom. I looked down and saw with a horrible fall of my stomach that the pits beneath were five-hundred foot drops... and they were growing around me, leaving me nowhere to go.

I wasn't in the Ancestral Lands at all. I was in *Aiya Nocshun...* the Mighty Darkness. The Hawkei's literal hell. I'd been sentenced here because I'd failed to save the people I loved. My ancestors had turned their backs on me. I had committed too many sins. I was no longer worthy to join them in the afterlife.

A wretched screeching caught my attention. A red baby dragon, no longer than my forearm, was running from the caverns opening up in the ground. He slid as the rocks tilted backward, chirping for someone to save him.

My heart plummeted. Julian had been damned along with me? Ancestors, what had I done?

"Julian, come here!" I called out to my dragon.

Julian spotted me on the edge of one of the caverns and gave a cry of relief. Julian ran, avoiding the gaping holes in the earth that were threatening to swallow him whole, and leapt into my arms. The newborn dragon shook as he cuddled against my chest, burying his head in my jacket.

"It's all right," I forced out as I stroked the dragon's back, but I was certain it was a lie. The lava pits were closing in, and any second now I'd tumble into them, sending Julian and I headfirst into eternal torment.

We had to move. There were small round platforms of earth, around five feet across, that I could jump to in order to escape the caverns and get to the other side safely. I leapt from platform to platform, avoiding the lava and keeping Julian close to my chest. I didn't want him getting hurt. I needed to get him out of here. If I couldn't save myself, there had to be a way to save my dragon. I wouldn't let him suffer because of me.

Finally, I reached solid ground, and I staggered away from the bubbling pits. Eventually, Julian and I made it back to... somewhere... and the lava pits behind us disappeared.

I trembled as I clung to Julian. Water. I wanted water. Just a drop. I wanted to use my powers again, one last time.

I wouldn't get it. I was being punished. I'd never be able to use my element again. I'd be stuck in this horrible world of flame, constantly scared and uncomfortable as I was beaten down and tortured by my opposite element.

"Liam!" A deep voice interrupted my alarmed thoughts, and I spun around. Fear pierced my chest as I saw Jonah on his knees, his hands and ankles bound with noxite cuffs. True fear shone in his eyes as he cried out for me.

No. No, this couldn't be happening! I couldn't have *dragged* my friends down here with me!

"Help me!" Jonah cried. "Why aren't you doing anything?"

I completely froze. Julian scrambled in my jacket, his nails tearing at my shirt. Jonah struggled as he tried to get out of his cuffs, but he couldn't break free.

"We need you!" Another voice broke into my mind. Imogen had appeared beside Jonah. She too had noxite cuffs binding her limbs, and she couldn't move.

I glanced behind them and saw the lifeless bodies of Squeaks and Sassy.

The hippogriff and fox lay immobile, bodies broken and shattered as they stared out into the endless night. Jonah and Imogen hadn't noticed their Familiars had been killed— all they had eyes for was me.

I still couldn't move. I was too afraid. I was a coward, and that's exactly what had gotten us down here. It was all my fault.

"You're supposed to be our *leader*! Do something!" Jonah barked. Their faces tightened with rage as I remained passive.

I couldn't. I was wholly incapable. I couldn't be the leader my father demanded I be. I wasn't half the chief he was. *Helpless* felt like a term of strength, compared to how weak I was in that moment.

It was then that two spears came flying out of the black clouds. The first one pierced Jonah's neck. It severed his spine and punctured his throat, ending all hope of life. He fell to the side, and his body landed with a sick *thud.*

The second spear sliced Imogen's chest. She gave a few ragged breaths, and tears of blood fell from her eyes as she stared up at me hatefully.

"You've killed us, Liam," Imogen whispered in a dying breath, then she slunk forward. The spear stuck out of her back as she collapsed forward and didn't move again.

I'd killed them. I was a *murderer.*

I had to get out of here. I ignored the wild protests from Julian inside of my jacket as I sprinted, trying to get away from this nightmare. As I did, I passed mountains of bodies. Mom's face stared out at me in a blank expression. Her body was draped over Maddie's and stuck full of arrows, as if she'd been trying to protect her. Maddie was already gone, her throat cut and insides opened up. A cockatrice fed on her remains, its beak dripping blood as it gave me an ominous warning to stay back.

I could hear my other siblings crying somewhere, but no matter which direction I turned, they weren't there. I didn't see Katie, Christian, or Jackson, though they screamed for me relentlessly.

The scariest thing of all was that I could neither see nor hear Ezra. I searched everywhere for him, but I couldn't find my little brother. I didn't know what had happened to him, and the fear of what he could be enduring broke me.

Without warning, the mountains of bodies vanished. All the corpses disappeared, and I was left by myself in the twilight, desert landscape, only the smell of death for company.

"Julian?" I looked inside my jacket, but he was gone, too. He'd been stolen away from me. A lump grew in my throat at the prospect of being totally alone in this land, forever.

Death was a total ending. And here I was. I'd earned every bit of it.

"Liam!"

My heart simultaneously leapt with hope and clenched in fear as I heard the most beautiful voice in the world behind me. It was Sophia who had shouted my name. Her arms were wrapped tightly around her stomach. Her face appeared horrified, a torturous reflection of my own terror. Esis wasn't with her. I had no idea where he'd gone, but I hoped he was safe. I didn't want Sophia here with me— didn't want her to experience this world — but at least I hadn't been abandoned completely.

"*Pawee*," I wept. I surged forward and wrapped her in my arms. I held her tightly and rocked her back and forth as I cried. Sophia hugged me back and rested her head on my shoulder, a light smile on her lips.

She didn't smell like herself. She didn't *feel* like herself. It was like I wasn't even touching her, though she was right here in my arms. Something was way off.

"Sophie, you need to get away from me," I begged. I forced myself to let go of her, and although it was painful, it was the right thing to do. "I'm no good for you. If you stick with me, you'll end up like everyone else."

"It's going to be okay. We'll make it through this together," she insisted. She put her forehead to mine and brushed the hair back from my face before she took a step back.

"I have something to tell you," she began. "I'm—"

She never got the words out of her mouth, because an ax came swinging downward. The blade wasn't held by anyone or swung by anything, but it met its target. It sliced through Sophia's neck, decapitating her and severing her head right off her shoulders.

Her blood splashed onto my face, and I gave a wailing cry of grief. I fell to my knees as her headless corpse crumpled against the ground. I watched as her head went rolling away, coming to a stop several feet away. She still wore a shocked expression, mouth open in surprise.

I put my head in my hands and rocked back and forth. I didn't want this to be real. It couldn't be real.

*This isn't real,* a low, kindly voice growled. *You need to wake up.*

I knew that voice like I knew the sound of my own. I refused to raise my head out of my hands, but I felt a wet nose nudging at me, and saw black fur from between my fingers.

*Liam, you don't have time. The Task Force is coming. Your family is in danger,* Nashoma growled. *Wake up!*

I was aware of someone's hand on my shoulder, shaking me awake, and the sound of my name as the hellish landscape faded from my sight.

As my eyes opened once more, I took in a gasp of breath. Reality crashed upon me like a wave, but what I'd experienced stuck with me as I came back to the land of the living.

I was afraid of hell... but it was already here.

TWO

A heart-wrenching scream tore through the tent and startled me awake. I shot upright in my sleeping bag, my heart hammering. It took me a second to realize the scream had come from Liam, who lay beside me.

"Liam!" I cried. "Liam, wake up!"

My stomach plummeted to my toes as I shook Liam to get him to awaken. Heavy tremors rocked his body, and his eyes moved rapidly behind his lids. Beads of sweat dripped down his forehead. No matter how hard I shook him, he wouldn't wake.

Esis scurried on top of Liam's chest, working his healing magic. My Familiar's face knitted together in concentration. At Liam's feet, Julian— the baby dragon who'd hatched last night— spun around in circles and let out a high-pitched wail.

"Imogen! Jonah!" I yelled. My voice cracked as I called out my friends' names.

Jonah had already kicked his sleeping bag off and knelt at my side. His broad shoulders blocked my view as he crouched beside me. "Liam," he gasped. "Bro, wake up!"

Jonah shoved Liam hard in the shoulder, and Liam's eyes shot open. He sprang upright, sending Esis flying off of him. Esis landed on top of Julian, and the two rolled into the side, colliding with Squeaks— who insisted she had to sleep with us in the tent last night, even though it left us with no room.

Liam's chest rose and fell rapidly. He stared straight forward, as if his vision was blurred. Across the tent, Imogen lunged for my bag, her short strawberry blonde hair flying in all directions. She scurried over the sleeping bags, nearly squashing Sassy, and shoved Liam's inhaler in his direction.

"Breathe, Liam!" she demanded.

Liam grabbed the inhaler, but he didn't get it to his lips before his face paled.

"What's wrong—?" Jonah started, but he was interrupted by Liam flinging his arm out and pushing him out of the way.

Liam lunged forward and grabbed for the tent zipper. He opened the tent so fast it sounded like he ripped the fabric. Liam stuck his head out the door and began retching. The smell of vomit filled the tent.

Jonah, Imogen, and I all shared a look of concern. This wasn't good.

I inched forward toward Liam and pressed a hand to his back to let him know we were all here. I grabbed his water bottle and handed it to him.

Liam groaned and lifted his head. He wiped his mouth with the back of his hand. When he looked at us, his eyes had cleared, and color had returned to his lips. He wore an expressionless mask, but it wasn't fooling any of us.

If he thought he could convince us he was fine, he was dead wrong.

"We have to move," Liam said before taking another swig of water.

"Wait, Liam," Imogen insisted. "You're not feeling well."

"Yeah," I agreed. "We should at least get you breakfast before we go."

Liam's lips tightened as he placed the cap back on the water bottle. "There's no time. The Task Force is coming."

With that, Liam stood and stepped out of the tent. He was shaky on his feet, but I could tell he was trying not to let it show.

"Hold up!" Jonah called after him. "How do you know that?"

Liam ignored the question. "Let's hurry up."

Jonah lowered his voice. "It's not like he's a *naderei*. He probably just had a nightmare or something."

"It doesn't matter. I'm not taking any chances," Imogen said. She quickly began gathering our sleeping bags, and Jonah started helping her with our things. Sassy and Squeaks joined in.

I stood and followed Liam out of the tent. It was early morning, and the sun was just cresting over the horizon. Liam had gone to the other side of Jonah's truck where I couldn't see him. When I stepped around it, I found him sitting on the ground, his head between his knees.

"Liam?" I asked as I cautiously stepped toward him. The sound of crunching leaves came from behind me as Esis and Julian followed.

"I just need a minute, *pawee*," Liam whispered.

I ignored his request. Instead, I sat beside him and wrapped an arm around his shoulder. Esis and Julian both came up to him. He sat straighter to cradle them both in his arms.

"Liam, I need to know you're going to be okay," I said. "I know we can't go back to Kinpago, but we need to find *some* way to get your meds."

Liam stroked Julian's scales. "Don't worry about it, *pawee*. I'll be fine without them. It was just a bad dream."

My lips tightened. "Liam, we agreed not to lie to each other anymore. Don't tell me you're fine when you're clearly not."

Liam finally lifted his gaze to meet mine. "I don't want to lie to you, Soph."

"Then what happened in this dream? How do you know the Task Force is coming?" I asked.

Liam took a deep breath. "Because Nashoma told me."

My eyebrows knitted together. Liam had been sleeping— he could've just imagined the whole thing. Ancestors knew we'd been through one hell of a night.

But I also knew that ancestors sometimes visited in dreams, and I wasn't willing to take the risk that this was just a conjuring of Liam's imagination. If Nashoma had really came by to warn us, we needed to listen to him.

The sound of the doors opening on the other side of the truck startled us both. We could hear Imogen and Jonah shoving supplies into the backseat.

"Chop, chop, people!" Jonah called.

I sighed and rubbed Liam's back. "I won't question Nashoma. Let's go."

I helped Liam to his feet, and we climbed into the back seat together. It was crowded with all our supplies, since we didn't have a chance to put anything away properly, but it didn't matter. Esis and Julian both insisted on sitting on Liam's lap. Squeaks climbed into the bed of the truck, and Jonah quickly tied down a tarp over the top of her to keep her hidden. He left her head uncovered, but she ducked down low so she couldn't be seen.

"Liam, lie down," I encouraged. He was really freaking me out. I'd seen him sick before, but this was *different*... in a way I couldn't explain.

He groaned, but he eventually caved and leaned against the pile of sleeping bags.

Within minutes, we were all packed up. Jonah put the truck in reverse and drove backward until the trees had cleared enough that he could turn around.

Imogen stroked Sassy's red fur and turned around in her seat. "Is anyone going to explain what just happened?"

Liam sounded irritated when he answered. "Nashoma came to me in a dream, okay? I don't want to talk about it."

Liam pressed his hand to his forehead and closed his eyes.

Imogen frowned. "I'm going to go out on a limb and say that Liam's condition isn't going to get any better, considering we don't have all his meds. We need to figure out what to do about it."

"Agreed," I stated firmly.

"What all does he have?" Imogen asked.

"Guys," Liam protested. He tried to sit up, but I pushed him back down onto the sleeping bags.

"Rest, Liam," I demanded, before turning back to Imogen. "We have his inhaler, his blood pressure meds, and his lung pills."

Imogen frowned. "Which means we're missing the painkillers, digestive medication, and antidepressants."

"We can stop somewhere to get the painkillers over the counter," I suggested.

Liam scoffed, though he didn't open his eyes.

"What?" I asked.

"Good luck," he grumbled. "I need more than ibuprofen."

"It should help," I argued.

Esis chittered and pointed to his chest.

"And Esis can help, too," I added.

"We can get meds when we stop for gas," Jonah offered.

Liam caved. It was like he didn't have the strength to argue his needs weren't important. "Fine," Liam said. "I'll take whatever you want me to."

I groaned. "Come on, Liam. Don't do that."

"It's not like it's going to help anyway," he said under his breath.

I wanted to say more, but it wasn't going to help right now. We were all still on edge after everything that happened last night. Truth be told, I didn't have the best dreams, either. I couldn't get the images of the battle of Orenda Academy out of my mind— how my grandparents had been gutted right in front of me. I probably never would. Just thinking about it made my chest feel hollow and heavy all at the same time. Tears rose in my eyes, and I wanted to cry again— but we'd already cried far too much in the past two days. I could grieve once we got to a safe place.

The silence in the car was deafening, but no one dared to break it. Eventually, we made it out of the forest and back onto the road. I held Liam's hand and watched out the window, keeping close watch for the Task Force. I saw nothing.

Hours passed, and no one spoke. Imogen kept shooting me these skeptical glances. I could tell we were thinking the same thing, that maybe Liam's dream was just that— a dream. Part of me hoped so. Another part of me worried about him if that were the case.

Finally, Jonah spoke. "Guys, Squeaks needs to stretch her wings. We're going to have to stop somewhere."

Imogen looked out over the landscape. We were far away from home, and the snow-capped mountains of Kinpago were far behind us. Still, dark clouds loomed overhead— as if the terror of the previous night's battle had come to follow us. We weren't taking the main highway, in an effort to lose the Task Force, so there was nothing but empty road ahead of us.

"I think it should be safe to stop," Imogen said. "We haven't seen any sign of the Task Force, so we must've lost them. I saw a sign back there for a rest stop ahead."

"Okay," Jonah replied. "We'll stop there."

A few minutes later, Jonah pulled off into a rest stop. It was quiet, and the bathroom facilities looked a little run down. There weren't any other cars around, so we wouldn't be seen with our Familiars.

As everyone piled out of the car with their Familiars, Liam stirred from where he slept beside me, though he didn't wake.

Imogen and Jonah took the Familiars to the edge of the parking lot to go to the bathroom, while I went inside to use the restroom myself. When I stepped back outside, I stopped in my tracks.

My heart lurched into my throat as a black SUV tore into the parking lot, and the tires squealed to a halt behind Jonah's truck. Jonah was ushering Squeaks back into the bed of the truck, and Imogen was climbing into the passenger seat with Sassy in her arms.

Inside the vehicle, Liam shot upright in his seat. Esis and Julian perched on the middle console.

Everyone froze at once as four Task Force members jumped out of their vehicle. They wore their usual black uniforms and helmets, and each of them held a noxite gun.

I gasped. The Task Force pointed their guns toward Jonah.

"Put your hands up where we can see them!" one of them shouted at him.

I had no intention of my friends being captured. They hadn't seen me yet, so I threw my hands outward, intending to throw a fireball at each of their heads and catch them off-guard.

But no Fire came out of my palms. What the hell?

Jonah took a step back and slowly raised his hands. He glanced around and noticed me standing far behind him. His gaze darted from me to the truck, as if trying to tell me to make a run for it. "Hey, we don't want to cause any trouble. We just want to—"

Jonah swiped his hands through the air, and a bolt of lightning came down from the sky at his command. It cracked against the pavement, and the deafening sound of thunder boomed over the rest area. At the distraction, Jonah ran for the door.

Noxite darts shot toward him, but I thrust my arms out and willed my Anichi force field to protect him. The darts slammed into my invisible shield and fell to the ground just as Jonah jumped inside the truck.

The engine roared to life, and I sprinted toward Imogen's open door. I jumped inside just as Jonah threw the truck into reverse. I was crammed in the front seat with Imogen and Sassy, but we managed to get the door shut as Jonah pressed on the gas. Esis and Julian scurried to the back seat beside Liam.

The earth rumbled beneath the car, and the pavement cracked as dirt upheaved around us. Imogen screamed and used her powers to reduce the impact.

Rain came pounding down hard on the car from the Toaqua Task Force members. It was so thick that we could hardly see out. Jonah tore out of the parking lot and back onto the road. Liam gritted his teeth as he pushed the water away from the truck with his magic. The vehicle began to shake violently as Air rushed past us. If Jonah's truck weren't so heavy, the Air magic might've knocked us straight off the road. Esis squealed.

"Jonah!" Imogen screamed.

"Fuck!" he cried. "I'm driving, here!"

Squeaks lifted her head in the bed of the truck. Wind whipped through her feathers, and she opened her beak in a scream as she tried to control the air around us, but the car continued to shake.

I tried to push my force field outside the truck to block the wind, but my heart was pounding so fast that I couldn't concentrate. When I'd protected Jonah earlier, it was in the heat of the moment. Now I couldn't get outside my own head to push my force field outward.

"Jonah, *do* something!" Imogen screamed.

"I can't drive *and* use my element!" he yelled back.

"Then let me drive!" I cried, my pulse quickening.

Jonah let go of the wheel, and I leaned over to take it. Jonah kept his foot on the gas, but he closed his eyes and took his focus off driving while I steered for him. Imogen pushed me off of her, and I had to climb over the middle console to sit on Jonah's lap. My grip tightened around the steering wheel. I could barely see out the window past the dirt flying past and the heavy rain.

Jonah gritted his teeth. "Hang on."

"They're getting close!" Liam shouted.

I glanced in the rearview mirror to see the SUV was following close behind, just outside of the air tunnel whipping past our vehicle. Liam used his water magic to push back the rain onto the Task Force's car. They swerved, like they couldn't see out their window. Liam gasped, like the effort to use his magic was draining him— he hadn't had enough time to recover last night, and now his powers were weak.

"Im, get ready," Jonah warned.

"Ready!" she replied.

"Now!" Jonah shouted.

He thrust his arms outward, and the air around us split in two directions in an instant, clearing a path for us up ahead.

At the same time, I heard the squeal of tires behind us. My eyes darted out the back window. I gasped when I saw a tall wall of earth behind us. The pavement had been heaved up from where Imogen had controlled the earth to create a barrier. All I saw was the top of the Task Force's SUV stopped behind it. Pavement crumbled and flew in all directions as the Nivita Task Force tried to flatten the wall of earth, and failed.

The air and rain stilled, but Imogen's face was contorted in pain. She fought against the Task Force to keep the wall steady so they couldn't pass.

Jonah sped so fast that we soon reached the range of Imogen's powers. But it was enough to get away. With a look behind, I saw that the Task Force hadn't followed. The four of us breathed a collective sigh of relief.

"I've got this, boo." Jonah grabbed the wheel again and I climbed into the back seat, my heart rate finally slowing. Jonah took another turn, and he didn't slow until we couldn't see the Task Force anymore.

Liam slumped in his seat. "I think we lost them."

He looked more tired than ever. I knew using his magic must've taken a lot out of him.

Imogen pushed the hair out of her eyes. "How did they find us?"

"Better yet, why are they wasting their resources on four fugitives?" Jonah pointed out. "There's enough going on in Kinpago right now."

"Isn't it obvious?" Liam said harshly. "They're afraid of us. Oleander only kept us alive as long as he did to keep an eye on us. He must've thought we were more use to him alive than dead."

"Yeah, until he decided to execute you and Sophia!" Imogen cried.

"We outlived our usefulness," Liam said. "Oleander hadn't learned anything about the prophecy from watching us, so he decided we were better off dead. Now I bet he's scared we might be planning to retaliate."

"Fuck," Jonah breathed. "I just want to *live*."

"Agreed," I stated before turning to Liam. "I get Oleander's scared of us because I'm still the chosen one, but it's kind of dumb that he's being this persistent, isn't he?"

"You don't get it. You're *still* the prophesied one. People think you're special," Liam said. "You stood up to Oleander when I was about to be executed. People will follow you if you ask. You've become a symbol of rebellion, Soph. Oleander can't let you live. It gives people hope."

My mouth gaped. "But I don't want to be a leader!"

"It doesn't matter. You're still a threat," Liam countered. "That means the Task Force isn't going to stop hunting us until we're dealt with."

"That still doesn't answer Imogen's question. How'd they find us?" Jonah asked.

"Oh my gosh!" Imogen yelled, as if she'd just realized something huge. "Jonah, your phone!"

His face went pale. "Do you think they have hackers?"

"They must. Nothing else makes sense," Liam said quickly.

"Fuck this shit." Jonah dove a hand in his pocket, then tossed his cell phone out the window. I watched as it shattered on the side of the road.

"Whew," Jonah said. "Crisis averted!"

"Hardly," Imogen grumbled. "Now they're close enough to tail us. We can't go to my house now."

Jonah glanced to her. "What do you mean?"

She was still trying to catch her breath. "It's supposed to be our safe house. We can't risk the Task Force following us there."

"Where else are we going to go?" Jonah asked, sounding a little peeved.

"I don't know," Imogen snapped back. "But we have to throw them off our trail somehow before we head there."

"We could go to my parents' house in Utah," I suggested. The words slipped out before I really considered the offer.

Imogen turned in her seat and furrowed her brow. "But your parents aren't there."

"Right," I said. My stomach sank as I thought back to the letter Amelia had left for me after we found her apartment raided. She said she was with my parents, but I had no idea where they'd gone. My teeth gritted as I thought about how they'd left me behind— how they'd left *all* of us behind. Imogen's family had done the same. They said they'd come back for us when it was safe, but it *never* was safe.

Maybe they were never coming back...

I tried to keep my voice steady as heavy emotions settled in my gut. "The house is still there, though. Or... I assume."

Fuck, if my parents sold their house, I didn't know what we were going to do.

Imogen bit her lower lip. "Well, I guess it *would* throw the Task Force off..."

"I think it's our best option," Jonah said.

All eyes turned to Liam. We needed his leadership at the moment— like we were all waiting on his approval. But Liam was slipping, and it was clear to see.

He considered it a moment, then said, "I agree. We can't go to Imogen's right away. We'll stop at a hotel tonight, then go to Sophia's parents'. Once it's safe, we'll head to Imogen's house."

*Once it's safe...*

The words echoed in my mind.

We were fugitives. We must've been wanted for at least a dozen crimes. We'd just escaped execution!

We'd never be safe.

❧

"LIAM, YOU NEED TO EAT." I held out a piece of pizza to him. Our order had come to our hotel room an hour ago, and he still hadn't taken a bite.

Liam shook his head. He'd barely moved since we'd arrived. He lay on his stomach on the bed with his face pressed into the pillow. It was like he was trying not to scream. I'd managed to convince him to take some ibuprofen we'd picked up at the gas station earlier, and Esis had done all he could. He and Julian were even massaging Liam's back. And still, Liam wouldn't move. His body shook with painful tremors as he clung to the pillow in agony.

A rock settled in my stomach. I felt totally helpless. This was why I didn't want to leave Kinpago. I knew Liam wouldn't be able to handle being on the run. We'd only been on the road for a day, and already, it was taking its toll on him.

No one spoke much. Imogen was curled up with Sassy on the opposite bed, her eyes staring blankly at the wall. Jonah was outside, looking for a place to hide Squeaks in the nearby woods for the night. The TV was on, but that was the only sound in the room. It was more or less on to make noise.

The more I watched Liam, the tighter my chest became. I'd never felt so stressed in my life, and it was giving me a horrible headache. But I didn't care, because nothing I felt right now even compared to how Liam felt.

I closed my eyes and rubbed my temples, but all it did was bring back horrible images. Every time I closed my eyes, I saw the flames consuming Orenda Academy. I saw the lifeless look in Liwanu's eyes. I heard Alric's screams as he was burned to death by Doya's magic. I saw my grandmother's intestines being ripped from her abdomen by Renar's cockatrice, and the blood spilling from my grandfather's chest.

I tried to push the images out of my mind, but the more I pushed, the quicker they came rushing in. I hadn't had a chance to cry since everything happened. I'd held it in all night in the tent, and the entire ride in the car. But seeing Liam suffer like this— it was the last straw. I couldn't take it anymore.

I jumped up from the bed and ran to the bathroom. I barely held myself together before I'd shut the door behind me. Once I was in the privacy of the bathroom, I slumped to the floor and buried my face in my hands. Tears streamed down my cheeks, and sobs bubbled up from my chest.

I bit down hard on the sleeve of my shirt to keep from making any noise. I didn't want my friends to worry.

A light knock came at the door. "Sophia?" Imogen asked gently.

"I'll be out soon," I told her, but my voice cracked. I couldn't hide it any longer. An audible sob bubbled out of my chest.

"Sophia, I'm coming in." The doorknob turned, and Imogen opened the door a crack. She peeked inside. Her face fell when she saw me sitting on the floor. She didn't say anything as she stepped into the bathroom and sat on the cool tile beside me.

I leaned my head against her shoulder. Tears slid down my face and onto her shirt. Imogen immediately placed her arm around me and pulled me closer.

"I get how you feel, Sophia," she whispered. "I feel the same way."

That only made me sob harder. "Imogen, why did they leave us? Why didn't our families take us with them?"

Imogen swallowed. "I keep asking myself the same thing."

Imogen and I sat there for at least ten minutes without saying anything, just holding each other. We could hear Sassy and Esis scratching outside the door, but we didn't let them in. We just sat there, sobbing as we took in the heavy weight of the last few months. It was unbearable.

Finally, I drew away and wiped my eyes. "Imogen... I have to tell you something."

She reached over to the toilet paper roll and pulled off a few squares to blow her nose. "What is it?"

I glanced down to my open palms. "Something happened back at the rest stop. I tried to summon Fire, and I... I couldn't."

She tilted her head to the side, looking confused.

"Does that have anything to do with being away from Kinpago?" I asked. I shuddered at the thought. We had to be able to defend ourselves from the Task Force.

She shook her head. "Your magic should act the same no matter where you are. Unless..."

She pressed her lips together thoughtfully.

"Unless what?" I asked.

Imogen took a deep breath. "Unless you didn't *want* to summon Fire."

The words felt heavy, but they hung in the air.

I blinked a few times, contemplating what she'd said. "I *did* summon my force field. I used my Spirit magic. Just... not Fire. So my powers must still be working."

I closed my eyes, and the fiery images of Orenda Academy returned. "You might be right, Imogen. Fire's just so... destructive. I don't... I don't..."

I swallowed the lump in my throat as I looked down at my hands. I hated how much damage they could do— how many people they could hurt. It was like my grandfather had said— Fire was made of anger and deep emotions. My Anichi power, on the other hand, was made of peace and protection.

"I don't want to be Koigni anymore, Imogen," I admitted. I hadn't realized it was true until I said it out loud.

Imogen furrowed her brow. "Sophia, you can't just *stop* being Koigni."

"I don't care," I said. "I don't want to be associated with Fire anymore. There's more to me than that."

"You mean..." Imogen trailed off as she looked down to my hands.

A bright white glow came off of them as a sense of peace settled in my heart. I realized what I had to do now.

I sat up straight and held my glowing hands out in front of me. "I'm going to find my parents, Imogen. And I'm going to become a real Anichi."

&

IMOGEN and I snuck our Familiars into our coats, and we headed into the forest behind the hotel where Jonah was hiding Squeaks. Julian had stayed behind with Liam, who hadn't even responded when we told him we were leaving the room.

"Jonah!" Imogen hissed through the darkness.

A light breeze brushed through my hair, and I turned in the direction of it. "Jonah, is that you?"

A loud squawk came from twenty yards away. "Shh..." Jonah hissed at Squeaks.

At the sound of Squeaks' voice, Esis jumped out of my coat and bounded over to her.

"What are you two doing here?" Jonah whispered through the dark as we met up with him and Squeaks. They were both sitting on the ground, looking like they were having a personal conversation.

"Sophia wants to work on her Anichi magic," Imogen announced. "We didn't want to disturb Liam."

Jonah sat up straighter. "Well, have at it. I'd like to see these powers in action."

Imogen set Sassy on the ground, and she went over to Squeaks and Esis to cuddle up with them. Imogen sat beside Jonah and faced me. I could barely see them through the darkness. "Okay, Sophia. Let's see what you've got."

I stood in front of them and swallowed. I wasn't sure I was ready to *present* my powers yet, but I needed to practice them if I was to master them— just as I had with my Koigni lightning.

My guts sank. *Koigni lightning.* Everything the Koigni made was destructive. I didn't want that anymore. I wanted beauty and light in my life when everything else felt dark.

I cleared my throat. "What do you want to see first?"

"What's easiest for you?" Imogen asked.

"Light," I answered automatically.

Imogen nodded. "Okay, then we'll start there."

I lifted my palm and conjured my Anichi light, but it was dimmer than any light I'd conjured before. It was nothing like the glowing light I'd created in the bathroom minutes ago. It was dim, like the light of a dying flashlight. I could feel the block within me, like my peace was waning.

"Whenever you're ready," Jonah said.

My shoulders fell. "I'm trying."

The more I tugged at my magic, the more my Koigni heat flared in my bones. I pushed that aside and buried it deep down within me. I didn't want to feel that anymore. It was just a reminder of all the pain and suffering I'd gone through the night the fire consumed my home at Orenda Academy. I pushed those images aside and tried to focus only on the peaceful Soul magic flowing through me. But the more I tried to connect to it, the dimmer the light became.

Imogen popped up from the ground and took my hands. The light faded completely. "What are you thinking about, Sophia?"

"Um... my magic," I said.

"And what are you *feeling*?" she questioned.

That was a tougher question to answer. I couldn't put a name to the heaviness in my stomach.

"I feel heavy," I admitted. "I feel blocked and tense. It's like every time I try to forget about what happened, it makes it worse."

"Maybe don't try to forget about it," she encouraged. "Face it, and work through it."

"Face it?" I balked. "Imogen, thinking about what happened isn't going to bring me any sense of peace."

Imogen shot a look at Jonah, like she needed help explaining what she meant.

"Well, you know, you just..." He shrugged, unable to find the words. "Think of man butt?"

Imogen elbowed him in the side. She turned back to me with a sigh. "Okay, let's try something else. Two nights ago, we lost everything."

"Imogen!" I protested. "Not helping."

She held a hand up. "Hold on. I'm not done. Look, I get it, Sophia. I feel like I've lost everything, too. Kinpago isn't the home it used to be. Orenda Academy burned to the ground. My family left ancestors know where without me, and I don't even know if they're alive anymore."

"Im!" Hot, heavy tears rose to my eyes as she reminded me of all the horrible things we'd recently faced.

Imogen squeezed my hands, and her voice cracked. "But despite all that, I'm blessed. I am *so* blessed. And so are you."

I blinked a few times, shocked by her words. "Blessed? Imogen, my grandparents died in front of me. If anything, I'm cursed."

"No, Sophia," she pressed. "You think you've lost everything, but you haven't. See, you still have me. You still have Jonah and Liam and Esis. All of us and our Familiars are alive. And your grandparents... they're gone, but you know what? I bet they're in the Ancestral Lands right now looking down on you and feeling *proud*."

I swallowed the lump in my throat. "I guess you have a point. I mean, at least I got a chance to get to know them. But Im—"

"No buts," she said firmly. "Focus on me, Sophia. The rest is in the past and can't be changed. But I'm here right now. Jonah is here. Be grateful for that, because I'm so grateful that I still have you guys. You two are my best friends in the whole world, and by the ancestors, if we can stick together through this, we can stick together through anything."

Jonah sniffled, and it was the first time I'd noticed he'd stood up. He pressed his hand to his heart. "Ancestors, Im. Are you trying to make us all cry?"

A sob broke out of my chest, and I gestured for Jonah to come closer. "Get in here, guys!"

Jonah scooped Imogen and I into a tight hug. Soon, our Familiars all came to surround us, and I was packed into the middle of the biggest, tightest group hug of my life. The only one thing missing was Liam.

"Ancestors!" Imogen gasped.

I had my eyes squeezed so tightly shut that I didn't see what she was talking about at first. Jonah dropped us both, and I took a step back. I gasped when I lifted my palms. Inside my right palm was a tangible, glowing orb the size of a baseball. It hovered above my hand like a fireball, only it was made of Spirit magic.

"Oh my God," I breathed. "I did it!"

"What *is* it, though?" Jonah asked, stepping closer to get a good look.

I poked it with my left hand. It was solid and warm, but I didn't know its purpose. My grandfather had never mentioned this when he gave me lessons on the Spirit Totem.

"I don't know," I admitted. "Imogen?"

She stared down at the orb in awe. It was so bright it lit up her entire face. "I have no idea, either. But whatever it is, keep it, Sophia."

I closed my palm, and the orb disappeared inside of it. My chest filled with a bright sense of hope. "I will."

"Well," Imogen said. "It's getting late, and we told Liam we wouldn't be gone long. We should probably head back."

Jonah didn't move. "Squeaks and I are going to camp out here for the night."

"Are you sure?" I asked. "There's a nice warm bed up in our hotel room."

"Squeaks is too big to sneak in, and I don't want to leave her alone," Jonah said. "We'll walk you to the tree line, though."

We started back toward the hotel. "I'm really proud of you, Sophia," Imogen said while we walked. Sassy strolled alongside her. "I think you're going to do really great things with your Anichi magic."

"Thanks, Im," I said, snuggling Esis closer to myself in my arms. "I feel a lot better now—"

Jonah grabbed me and Imogen by the shoulders and dragged us behind a tree just as we reached the edge of the hotel lawn. My pulse quickened as he placed his index finger to his lips. He pointed toward the parking lot, and my stomach plummeted to my toes. A black SUV sat parked near the entrance. Four men in black moved quietly like shadows through the night toward the door.

*Shit.*

The Task Force was back— and Liam was all alone.

# Liam

## THREE

I liked the quiet around me. I hadn't been alone in days, and I needed time to just... settle.

I remained face down in the pillow, trying not to lose it. Leaving those painkillers behind was a heavy blow. The sensation of a thousand tiny knives pricking my body, slowly slicing off my skin and muscles layer by layer was agonizing. It hurt to have anything *touch* me. Even lying in bed felt like I was extended on a row of spikes. Every part of me was sore, like I'd just completed a triathlon and then had the shit beat out of me at the end of it.

With a fucking hammer.

When I moved, my eyes watered, so I tried to stay as still as possible. Julian was on my back. The hatchling was curled up at the base of my spine, and his body gave off a warm glow. It was almost like he was trying to act as a heating pad.

One of the reasons I'd kept my face in the pillow was because I didn't want Sophia to see me like this. We all knew I wouldn't last on the road, and she'd been right, but this was worse than we'd all expected. The fact that I hadn't had time to pack my pills, hadn't gotten any rest, and we'd been constantly forced to move every few hours after I'd barely escaped execution and survived one of the biggest battles of my life equaled total chaos for me. As a result, my body decided to give a giant *fuck you* and decided to *make me* slow down one way or the other.

Even if that resulted in me feeling like someone was punching me over and over and wouldn't stop.

Maybe a bath would help. I forced myself to get up, though it felt like my joints were being ripped apart as I did so. Julian slid off my back. He hopped off the bed and followed me as I staggered to the bathroom.

I began filling the tub up with water. As the tub became halfway full, Julian squealed. He perched on the edge of the tub and jumped in, splashing water everywhere. His wings spread out on the surface to keep him afloat. His tail sent water droplets flying as his tiny paws paddled around the tub. He made small growling noises, like he was thrilled to have his own personal pool.

"Hey jackass, this bath's for me, not you," I countered.

He dove down, scooped up a bit of water in his mouth and shot it on my face.

I laughed and wiped off the water with a nearby towel. "You're such a little shit."

He peeped in response. I couldn't help grinning. At least Julian could make me smile.

Smiling itself felt weird. It didn't seem right to smile when I knew what was going on back home, and how many people were suffering. It didn't feel okay to crack a grin when my family was out there somewhere, not sure if I was dead or alive— or if the opposite was true, and I was the only one left.

I didn't like smiling when my dad was dead. It felt wrong.

Julian wailed. He didn't like it when he didn't have my full attention. I reached out and stroked his scales, running my hand over the spines on his back. He cooed and arched in the water.

Well, despite all the bad shit that had happened, I was still glad to have Julian. I didn't think I'd be lucky enough to have another animal companion after what happened to Nashoma. I didn't think I was worthy. Still didn't.

But Julian had chosen me. Which meant I was going to spend the rest of my life taking care of him, in every way he deserved. He was a dragon— he deserved respect and care. No matter the reason he'd imprinted on me, he needed me, just like I needed him.

Julian was my second chance. I'd never thought I'd get one, and this time, I was determined not to mess it up.

Julian screamed again. I shushed him and grabbed the soap on the cusp of the bath. I began washing his scales. "If you don't shut up, we're going to be found out. Then I'll have to explain to a bunch of humans why dragons exist."

He gave a shrill cry, and I said, "How did this turn out to be for you?"

The dragon's eyes half-closed in relaxation as I bathed him. It felt good to focus on Julian. I hadn't had a Familiar to tend to in so long, and it gave me a distraction from the pain. For once, I felt like I had a creature who could help share my burdens, and Julian was there. He was strong enough to take them all.

I hoped we made it to Imogen's house soon, and that she'd been smart enough to buy a place that was secluded as fuck. Julian was going to get really big, really fast. He'd be big enough to ride by the fall. I didn't know where we were going to hide him. I didn't think he'd be a small dragon, like Aisha or Eirakari. Sophia had told me dragons of his type grew monstrous within a year of hatching.

Fuck, it was a good thing we had somewhere to go. I was so grateful we had Imogen. If she hadn't been smart enough to purchase a safe house for us months ago, we'd be totally fucked.

Julian's head went sharply up, and he became alert. In his throat was a low growling that didn't seem friendly.

He was trying to warn me about something. I paused and listened.

There were voices outside. I heard several males speaking in low tones, and my blood ran cold.

The sound of wood breaking shattered the room. The door was busted open, the lock blown to bits by elemental magic.

*Dammit! How did they find us?*

I wasn't sure how they knew which room we were in— unless they'd watched us come in and out. Four Task Force members stormed into the room, noxite guns raised. I spun around, and Julian leapt out of the bathtub. He bared his fangs beside me and hissed as the Task Force approached.

"Hands up!" one of them shouted. "Or we'll shoot."

I didn't make a move to obey. Would we ever be rid of these assholes?

"Where are the others?" another demanded. "Cooperate, and we'll spare your life."

That was a fucking lie. No way was I going to tell them where Jonah, Sophia and Imogen were. Through clenched teeth, I said, "I'm not telling you a fucking thing. You can go to hell."

"This is your last warning! Where are they?" the cop threatened again.

My last nerve finally broke. I didn't feel well, my family was missing, and I'd lost the only home I'd ever had. I hadn't had a spare moment to grieve the father I'd lost, and I couldn't sleep because every time I did, the dreams I had always became nightmares, and ended with Sophia losing her head.

And it was all because of the Task Force. Now they wanted to cause even more trouble.

I'd had enough. I was officially *pissed off*.

Fuck how I felt. It was time to kick some ass.

"You've messed with the wrong Toaqua." Before anyone could fire, I shot out my hand. Four streams of water came out of the tub behind me and knocked the noxite guns out of their hands. The water wrapped around the guns and drew them backward, behind me and out of their reach.

One of the Task Force reacted. A fireball formed in his hand, but I quenched it with my magic and delivered a kick to the face. My foot hit his helmet and he went staggering backward into the nearby wardrobe, where he slammed against it and slumped to the floor. The wardrobe itself tilted, making a smashing sound as it crashed onto its side.

The others reacted. Another cop attempted to blast me backward with Air magic, but the water created a shield around me, protecting me. The Yapluma cop ran forward, intending to break through my defenses. I made ice daggers out of the shield and shot them like bullets at high speed toward the police.

All the others ducked, but the Yapluma caught the daggers in the chest. They pierced through his armor, and blood splattered everywhere. He went down, clutching at his injuries as blood poured out of them.

"Sergeant!" his teammate replied. He was Toaqua, and lifted a hand to combat my Water shield, but his magic was pitiful next to mine— even with how weak I was, he couldn't break through my powers. I formed the rest of my shield into water whips and shot them out at the Toaqua cop. He put his arms in front of his helmet to protect himself while I began a relentless assault. I knocked over a lamp and bashed the TV sideways before a side table near one of the beds went crashing to the floor.

The Koigni in the corner was slowly coming around. He noticed the Yapluma was down and crawled toward the sergeant. He lifted the man onto his back and began retreating out of the room, crying, "Fall back!" The Toaqua followed, glad to get away from my magic.

The last Task Force member was huge in stature— probably a Nivita. And he wasn't going to give up, even if it meant disobeying orders. He ran through my Water whips like it was nothing, and I barely had a chance to get my shield back up again before he put his hands on me. The Nivita was inches away.

To protect me, Julian gave a scream and charged at the remaining Task Force member. He sank his teeth into the man's leg, and the cop gave a scream of pain. He kicked Julian off, and my dragon went rolling to the floor, gasping as he landed on his wing.

Rage boiled inside me when I saw that the Nivita had hurt Julian. *Nobody touched him.* My water shield fell to the floor, soaking the carpet as I raised my hand and channeled every inch of fury and frustration I had felt over the past few days into the Nivita's body.

The Nivita didn't even have time to cry out. He slumped to the floor in a pile, and didn't move again. The other three Task Force members had gotten away, but this one wouldn't follow.

He was already dead. I knew. I'd felt and savored the feeling as his heart stopped beating.

I immediately rushed to Julian, who was curled up on the floor and whimpering. "Jules, you okay?"

I picked him up, and he cooed. I checked his wing. He'd landed on it wrong, but it was fine. He'd be okay.

I cradled him to my chest. That had been so scary. And not because my life was on the line. I had worried that Julian would get hurt.

More footsteps approached. I readied myself, preparing to kill whoever walked through that door, but my hand dropped when I saw that it was just Jonah, Sophia and Imogen. Esis was curled up in Sophia's arm, but Sassy and Squeaks were nowhere to be found. Their faces drained of color as they took in the mess around the room.

"Liam, what the hell happened here?" Sophia asked, her jaw dropping open.

"I'm done, Sophia. I'm just so fucking done," I raged. I held Julian closer. I thought taking my anger out on a couple of goons would help, but apparently, all it did was make my wrath worse.

"There's blood all over the place!" Imogen shouted. Jonah cringed and stepped around a puddle of red the Yapluma cop had left behind.

Everyone's eyes fell to the corpse on the floor. Sophia's hand covered her mouth. "Liam... did you...?"

"I killed him before he could do the same to me," I snapped. "It was self-defense."

Sophia didn't say anything more, but her expression appeared vaguely sick. Esis jumped down from her arm and put his paws on the Task Force member, like he thought he could heal him.

Didn't work, obviously. Esis' face contorted. I don't think he grasped what death was. Such a thing seemed impossible for him.

In a rage, Imogen began rushing around the room in an aggravated fashion, straightening things out that had been knocked over in the fight. "Liam, this is a crime scene! We have to clean this up."

"Easy." I lifted my hand, and the blood that stained the carpet, the beds, and the walls lifted up. I levitated the blood to the tub, where I dumped it and turned on the water. All the evidence went rushing down the drain, like it was no problem at all. I had trouble getting blood out of the carpet last semester, but it was easy now.

Something had changed in me over the past few days. I was afraid of the dark side of me before, but I fucking welcomed it now. Blood and gore no longer scared me. I'd accepted that it was part of my life.

I was no longer worried about becoming a monster and losing myself. It was worth it to protect the people I loved.

Jonah righted the wardrobe by himself before Imogen picked up the lamp and Sophia straightened out the TV. Imogen began shoving the few things we had into Sophia's backpack, while Jonah stooped down beside the corpse of the Task Force member. With a grunt, he hefted the body over his one shoulder and stood.

"What are you doing?" I asked.

"We have to get rid of the body," Jonah shot back. "We can't just leave it here."

Fair point. Jonah gestured toward the door and said, "You guys cover me."

"I can't believe we're really hiding a body," Sophia mumbled under her breath.

The three of us clustered around the door. Imogen, Sophia and I kept watch while Jonah slipped outside into the hall, then carried the body down the stairs, which were only supposed to be used for an emergency exit. Sophia used her Anichi light to shine into the cameras as we passed so they wouldn't catch Jonah getting rid of the evidence.

We slipped into the woods outside the hotel. Jonah walked as far as he could, until he was out of breath. He slipped the body to the ground and breathed, "Here."

We didn't even have to discuss this. It was just what had to be done. And it was fucking freaky. Imogen waved her hands over the earth, and the dirt began moving of its own accord, piling up and creating a hole six feet deep.

From the shadows, Sassy and Squeaks emerged. Their eyes were wide and glinting, like they couldn't believe we were really doing this.

I couldn't believe it, either. This was a first for the Reject Team. When had we gone from making stupid jokes and dancing in the Commons like idiots to covering up a murder?

A murder that I had committed. Not the first one, either. And if I was being honest with myself, it wasn't completely an act of self-preservation. I could've defended myself without taking the Task Force member's life.

I just didn't want to.

"Help me, man," Jonah said. He grabbed the cop's ankles, and I moved to take his wrists.

We threw the Task Force member into the hole. Imogen moved the dirt back over the body, and Julian gave a low note from my shoulder.

It was quiet for a long moment. The wind whistled by, and the darkness seemed harsher than what it was a second before. We stood over the freshly turned earth and stared at what we knew was beneath it.

"Should we say something?" Sophia asked quietly.

"*Say something?* He tried to kill me," I spat. I crossed my arms and held myself tightly. "I don't think he deserves any words."

"I know, and that's terrible, but..." Sophia trailed off. "Don't you think he has a family too, just like us?"

I made a scoffing noise. "Yeah, well, if he didn't want to be separated from his family, he shouldn't have gotten involved working for the Elders."

"Maybe Oleander forced him."

"He could've stood up and said no. This is on him."

The bitterness was evident in my tone, but I didn't care. Jonah was sending me a disapproving look that I ignored.

After a few minutes, it became clear that no one was going to say anything, so we just left. We got in the truck, and Jonah drove for a few more hours to get the Task Force off our trail before we stopped for the night.

We set up the tent. By the time I collapsed beside Sophia in my sleeping bag, I was almost out of it. Julian curled up against my chest, and I put an arm around him as I closed my eyes, ready to dissolve into another fit of nightmares.

❦

THE NIGHT PASSED. My dreams were full of death and horror, but this time, the Task Force member we'd buried was in them, and I'd killed him over and over. Sophia's head went rolling off her shoulders, and I'd watched my friends die over and over, all in equally horrible ways. I woke up the next morning feeling sick, but at least I didn't throw up again.

As we started packing up, Sophia shoved Esis into my arms. "Liam, you need a treatment," she demanded. "You're barely staying on your feet."

I noticed Jonah and Imogen eyeing me. I took Esis into my arms, though it elicited a jealous squeak from Julian, who was sitting in the bed of the truck. Esis put his paws over my heart and his blue eyes narrowed in concentration, but as his healing powers worked, I only felt a small twinge of fatigue ebb away. Esis' teeth gnashed together, as if he was frustrated. He returned to Sophia's arm, chattering away sounds that seemed like swear words.

"Did it work?" Sophia asked hopefully.

I shook my head.

She gave an angry noise. "Why aren't Esis' powers working like they used to?" Sophia asked in frustration.

"Soph, you've asked him to do a lot in a few days," I pointed out. "Everybody's magic has its limits."

"Yeah. He basically restored Liam's skin in seconds after you toasted it off," Jonah subbed in unhelpfully. "And Esis did a lot of healing besides that. His powers aren't unlimited."

*Thanks, Jonah, for bringing that up.* I'd tried to put the memory of Sophia burning me out of my mind forever. It was my own fault that she'd had to do it, but still.

Sophia's eyes watered, and she whispered, "I'm sorry. I wish I could take that back."

"You had to. It was the right decision," I responded monotonically. "I don't hold it against you."

She looked away. "I know Esis needs time to recover his powers, but we can't wait that long. If one of us gets hurt— I don't even want to think about it."

Esis' ears drooped, like he was afraid of letting Sophia down. I reached out and scratched his head. "It'll be okay, Soph. We're almost to your parents' house, and there we can take a break. We just have to learn not to rely on him so much."

Wasn't easy for me to say. I depended on Esis for survival.

"Well... I'll just have to figure out this healing thing, then," Sophia said stubbornly. "So it's not all on Esis."

"We've already tried that, and it didn't work," I said.

"I can develop my Anichi powers. I've been practicing," she countered. "I'm sure I can figure it out soon."

I frowned. "Don't get your hopes up."

Sophia's expression dropped. She turned away from me, clearly hurt. Normally something like that would bother me, but it didn't. I worried I was losing the ability to feel anything at all.

I didn't want to be unsupportive, but also, I didn't want to give false hope. I didn't want Sophia to face one more disappointment.

"Let's go," Imogen said. Squeaks climbed in the back, and Jonah covered her up before he took the driver's seat and we headed off.

After a half an hour, Jonah spoke up through the silence. "You know, this isn't *all bad*," Jonah started. "We did talk about taking a road trip this summer."

"This is hardly my idea of a vacation." I slumped against the seat and stared out the window. Julian sat on my lap. He was playing tug-of-war with Esis. The two of them had a cloth between them, Julian holding in his mouth and Esis with his paws, and were tugging it back and forth. Sophia watched them and giggled. Julian gave a final tug, but he stumbled forward and Esis yanked. Esis won, holding the cloth like a victory flag.

"Um, Sophia, you should take that away from him," Jonah started as he glanced back. "That thing's been used for some, uh, *unmentionable activities*."

"Ew, gross! Jonah!" Sophia squealed. She pulled the cloth out of Esis' hands and tossed it on the floor, kicking it under the seat. "Just how many guys have you had in here?"

"I like to keep that information classified," Jonah replied.

Sophia wrinkled her nose. "That's just great. My Familiar had a jizz-rag all over his paws."

"How do you think I feel? It was in Julian's mouth," I grumbled.

Just then, Julian crawled up my shirt and licked my face. I gave a disgusted noise, and everyone else laughed.

"Jonah's right," Imogen added. "We can make this fun. We've gotta stop to get gas and let the animals run anyway. Let's pick up some snacks and make this the best escape-for-our-lives trip ever."

"Please." I needed to go to the bathroom and wash my face, stat.

We dropped the Familiars off by an empty rest stop near the woods, so they could stretch their legs in the trees and hunt for food, while Jonah took the rest of us to the gas station a mile up the road. It was risky with the Task Force on our tail, but we didn't have much of a choice. I worried about Julian, but the older Familiars would keep an eye on them, and they knew well enough to make sure they weren't seen.

Imogen, Jonah and Sophia stormed into the gas station and began snatching snacks off the shelves. Jonah grabbed a large coffee, complaining loudly they didn't have pumpkin spice, even though it was the start of summer, before snagging a bag of cookies, three boxes of cupcakes, fruit-flavored rainbow candies and an apple for Squeaks. Imogen's arms were piled high with pretzels, small chocolates, and chips that had flavors like salsa, pizza, and hot wings.

Sophia got Esis two hamburgers and held on to a giant blue raspberry Slurpee for herself. She had a basket full of popcorn, licorice, and peanut butter cups.

Peanut butter everything, actually. She had three different types of candy that had peanut butter in it.

"Going a little overboard with the peanut butter, aren't we?" I asked as I peered in the basket.

"I just have a craving." She looked at my hands and made a face. "Liam, that is *not* appropriate college road-trip food."

I had jerky and a wrap for Julian, along with trail mix and protein bars for myself, and a water.

"What?" I said defensively. "This stuff is good for you."

Sophia laughed. "Well, at least you're eating something."

"If you haven't noticed, my tastes are pretty particular," I said.

"Believe me, I've noticed." She rolled her eyes. "Feeding your picky ass after we get married is going to be the biggest challenge of my life."

"I'm not that bad," I objected. "I just don't like preservatives. They're gross."

"Come on. There has to be *one* thing that's bad for you that you like," Sophia objected.

My eyes wandered. I broke down and said, "Okay... I might have a weakness for cheese puffs. And nachos. You know, those chips with the really nasty processed melted cheese on them—"

"Done." Sophia shoved the basket toward me, then grabbed a bag of cheese puffs before she poured cheese from a machine onto a tray of chips from the concession. Imogen paid for the items, and we were on our way.

I didn't feel relief until Julian was back in my arms again. Squeaks gave a happy buck when she saw Jonah coming with the apple. She and Sassy had been hunting, but she was excited about the treat. She jumped up and snagged it out of the air as he tossed it to her, while Sassy wagged her tail as she chowed down on the hot dogs Imogen had bought.

Julian practically sang when I showed him the wrap. He scarfed it down in seconds, then chewed on the jerky while eyeing Esis' hamburgers. Which didn't last long, by the way. Esis snatched them out of Sophia's hands and gobbled them up quickly. Sophia laughed and tickled Esis' chin, and he chortled happily.

As we got back on the road, I begrudgingly ate the nachos and took down half the bag of cheese puffs. Which were *so good*, by the way. I hadn't allowed myself to have them in years. A little bit of my sickness abated. Though my nausea pills were gone, I knew part of the reason I felt so shitty was because I hadn't eaten much and was refusing food.

Sophia watched me carefully. I think she felt relieved I was taking down anything at all.

"We need some music up in this bitch," Jonah announced, and he turned on the radio.

Imogen gave a happy scream, and Sassy barked as Jonah cranked the stereo to full blast. Sophia smiled, and my heart felt a little lighter. Already, some of the heaviness from the previous night was fading away. This felt normal. Like we were actually taking a fun road trip instead of fleeing for our lives.

Didn't last long, though. A few hours later, we'd crossed over the Utah state line, and I was *this close* to losing my mind.

"Is there *anything* on this playlist that isn't Taylor Swift?!" I shouted as I scrolled through Jonah's music player. It was connected to an auxiliary cord that went to the stereo, and had been blasting nothing but mindless pop songs forever. I was at my wit's end.

"That playlist is golden. Sophia and I made it ourselves," Imogen objected.

Julian chirped and danced on the seat between Sophia and I with Esis, jiving to the beat.

"How about we play something we all like?" I objected. "My ears are starting to bleed."

"Hey, nobody wants to listen to your music," Sophia objected as she chewed on a licorice strand. "It's all punk rock emo bands and alternative West Coast songs about California, with a bit of screamo thrown in."

"And what's wrong with that?" I asked.

"Babe, I love you, and I get that *My Chemical Romance* is your favorite band, but if I have to listen to *Helena* one more time, I'm going to scream," Sophia objected. Esis bobbed his head enthusiastically.

"It's good music!" I objected.

"Yes, you listen to good bands, but we're trying to feel *happy*, not remind ourselves that life sucks," Jonah argued. "It's all about the mood."

"I'll give you a mood," I growled.

"Oh my gosh, Sophia *literally* wouldn't stop singing this when you guys broke up, and you *totally* got back together. So lame," Imogen said as yet another boppy break-up song blasted through the speakers.

"So sue me." Sophia threw a licorice at Imogen, and she squealed. Esis darted to the front seat, nabbed it where it had landed, and started chewing on it.

"You know what? Liam's right, guys." Jonah turned the volume down from full-blast to mildly fucking tolerable. "I'm all for this girl-power playlist, but it's getting a little stale. We need to get *spicy*."

"We could play a game," Imogen suggested.

"Ooh, road games. I love those," Sophia gushed.

"What should we play?" Imogen asked.

"I've got one," Jonah burst. "We used to play this in the Yapluma dorms. You're supposed to guess the size of the biggest dick you've ever had."

Imogen and Sophia made noises of approval, while I rolled my eyes. "Come *on*, guys. Is that all we ever talk about? Sex?" I groaned.

"Yes," Imogen, Jonah and Sophia said at the same time, and they laughed.

"Well, I'm obviously not playing," I pointed out.

"Why not? You could've had a secret gay past none of us know about," Jonah teased.

"Thanks, but the only dick I've ever seen is my own," I said. "I'm out."

"Fine. I'll go first," Jonah said. "So, ladies, how big do you think I've gone?" His eyebrows waggled.

"Um..." Sophia tapped her chin with her finger. "Nine inches."

Imogen snorted. Jonah gave Sophia an endearing smile before he said, "You're so innocent. Baby, dicks don't usually get that huge. Unless you're exceptionally gifted."

"Really?" Sophia's eyes widened. "I mean, I know I've only seen one, but I thought all guys were that big, typically."

Imogen scoffed. "Okay, Sophia, just because *you're* used to Liam's monster cock—"

I gagged on my water. Sophia's mouth dropped open and she said, "Imogen! You weren't supposed to tell the guys we call it that!"

"*Excuse me?*" I asked.

"Monster cock, eh? I like it." Jonah winked at me in the rearview mirror.

"What the fuck do you two talk about when I'm not there?" I asked, looking at Imogen and Sophia.

"Oh, she tells me everything," Imogen said with a wave of her hand. "I probably remember more details than you do."

"Of course you do." Girls were weird. I didn't give Jonah a play-by-play every time Sophia and I decided to get it on.

Sophia was slightly pink. Esis gave a squeak. Imogen started forward and said, "Anyway, back to the game. Jonah, I'm calling you've had... seven inches."

"Nope." Jonah shook his head. "Maybe I shouldn't have started this game. It's kind of embarrassing."

"Why?" I asked. "I thought you slept around last semester."

"Um... okay, maybe I exaggerated about all those dudes. We messed around, but I never went all the way," Jonah confessed. "Renar was the only one I ever had sex with, and therefore, he's the only one that counts for the game."

"I really don't want to hear about Renar's dick." I scowled, and Julian copied me. It was funny to watch, his little face scrunching up into a sneer.

"Okay, so if we're talking Renar, I say five inches," Sophia said, ignoring me completely.

Jonah shook his head sadly as he unwrapped another cupcake. "Nope. Not even that."

"Okay, so we lose the game," Imogen said, and she opened another bag of chips. "Tell us."

"Renar had a micro-dick. It was like, four inches, tops," Jonah mumbled through the cupcake in his mouth.

"Wow," Sophia gasped. "I can't even imagine."

"Thank me for that," I responded, and she elbowed me. I couldn't resist giving a snicker.

"That is so sad." Imogen patted Jonah on the shoulder. "I hope your next boyfriend is better endowed."

Jonah snorted. "Yeah, well I hope my next boyfriend is better *everything.*"

Amen to that. Sophia leaned forward and said, "Im, it's your turn. Now we get to guess."

"That's not fair! You already know all the answers!" Imogen protested.

"Wait. I thought you and Cade never actually banged?" Jonah said.

"We didn't have sex, but we fooled around," Imogen said. "I definitely saw what he had to offer."

"What about Sam?" Jonah teased. "I know you two were dating for a few weeks."

Imogen shook her head. "We never got farther than first base. I kissed him once, but I felt guilty after..."

She didn't need to finish that sentence. I knew kissing Sam had probably made Imogen feel remorseful about Cade. Imogen and Sam weren't exactly perfect for each other, but they might've worked out if Imogen could've moved past her grief.

"Okay, so anyway, I'm calling six inches," Jonah said. "Cade seemed like he was a decently sized fellow."

"Six and a half," Imogen said proudly. "And I loved every inch of it. He used to do this thing where he'd use his magic to make the ground vibrate—"

"Ancestors, spare us no details, Im!" Jonah burst, giving a loud laugh.

Sophia howled with laughter. "Are you going to tell them about the vine thing?"

"You tell them!" Imogen went red. "That was *not* my idea! Cade came up with that one!"

The four of us laughed— even me. Julian copied me and let out a few laughs of his own, complete with puffs of smoke, even though I didn't think he understood what we were talking about.

Something crossed my mind, and I learned forward. "Im, you're fine with talking about this, right?" Every time Cade had been brought up before, it had nearly made her dissolve into tears.

Her expression didn't falter. "No, it's okay," she said brightly. "It sounds weird, but talking about him... it actually makes me feel a little better, you know? Like he's still with me."

I was glad. Imogen seemed like she was finally recovering from what had happened last year. Maybe it was a sign we could leave all that bad stuff in the past and put it behind us.

We finally pulled into Sophia's hometown late that night. By this time, it was dark— which was a good thing, because I didn't want us to be spotted.

We parked the truck in the garage, and Squeaks was able to wiggle out of the bed. Sophia used a key hidden in a toolbox in the garage to open the door. After a bit of shoving, we managed to get Squeaks inside before the rest of us walked in ourselves.

Since the Henleys were missing, I had been dreading a gruesome scene inside like when we'd walked into Amelia's apartment. But that wasn't the case. The house was clean and spotless. There was no evidence of foul play, or even a sign that anyone had been here in months. The electricity didn't work, so we figured it must've been shut off. Sophia found flashlights in the closet for us to use as we swept the house, checking for Task Force members hiding in the dark. We surveyed the kitchen, but there was no food in the fridge, or even any canned goods in the cupboards. Everything had been cleaned out. There was a thin layer of dust on the furniture, and a book placed hap-hazardly on the shelf, but besides that, there was no indication that whoever had lived here had been in a hurry to leave at all.

That meant the Henleys absence was planned. It had been their choice to leave Utah. Good news, but confusing.

"Most of my parents' clothes are gone, along with a few other things they wouldn't have left without," Sophia said as she returned from their bedroom. "It doesn't look like anything's been stolen."

"I think this is evidence your parents weren't taken. They left of their own accord," I said as we were done sweeping the house.

"Okay, but where? Where did they go?" Sophia asked.

"Hopefully the same place my family and Liam's went," Imogen responded. "This is good news, Sophia. It means your family and Amelia are probably in a safe place."

Sophia nodded grimly. "You're right." She dropped her voice to a whisper before she added, "I just wish they would've told us where first."

Squeaks and Sassy were in the kitchen. They dug through the cupboards, looking for clues, while Esis opened and closed the fridge over and over, obviously upset there was nothing to eat. Julian gnawed on a chew toy that had been left behind by one of the Familiars without a care in the world.

"So where are we crashing?" Jonah asked. "I'm beat from driving all day."

"Um... Liam and I can sleep in my parents' bedroom. You and Imogen can decide between mine and Amelia's," Sophia suggested.

Imogen and Jonah eyed each other. Reluctance was in their gazes. I knew what they were thinking. Despite this being a hopefully safe place, we still didn't know if the Task Force was nearby, and therefore, didn't want to separate— even if it was in rooms that were just down the hall.

"I think we'd all prefer to stay together," I offered. Squeaks chirped— she had a blanket in her beak that she'd found on the floor, and Sassy had dragged in a pillow from another room.

Sophia smiled. "Well, I guess we can crash out here."

"Sleepover!" Jonah cheered. Sophia gave him an affectionate look. We began piling the cushions from the furniture onto the floor. The Familiars brought the pillows and blankets from the other rooms into the living area, and soon, we had one big pile. Jonah jumped into it with a whoop. Squeaks circled a few times before she lay down, and Sassy plopped down next to her, lying a head on Squeaks' hoof.

"Are you sure you don't want to take the couch?" Sophia questioned me, eyes narrowing in concern.

"I'll be fine, *pawee*." I wasn't taking the couch when everyone else was sleeping on the floor.

"I'm surprised you're not bitching about this," Imogen said, with a wayward look at me as I climbed onto the pile and pulled a blanket over me.

"I've seen enough of you people this is no longer weird." I yawned. Everyone needed to shut up so we could get some sleep. "I'm not cuddling, though."

"You'll cuddle with *me*," Sophia said as she snuggled up to my side. Esis lay next to my head. Julian curled up beside him, so they could share body heat.

"Of course." I put an arm around her and pulled her to me. I buried my face in her hair and inhaled. As much as I hated to admit it, sleeping together like this made me feel safe. And having Sophia close to me was the safest feeling in the world.

"This is like the Elemental Cup, except a lot more comfortable," Imogen said.

"Yeah, and I'm not freezing my balls off," Jonah protested. "Also, that burrito I had earlier isn't going down well, so sorry in advance."

Sophia giggled. She ran her fingers down my chest, and I shivered as she said, "Goodnight, you guys. I love you."

"I love you too," Imogen piped up, and Sassy gave a loud snore.

"Love you more, bitches," Jonah chimed in.

"Goodnight, you crazy assholes." A slight grin managed to creep its way onto my face as I tucked Sophia to my side and went to sleep.

I was the first to get up the next morning. The sun hit my face through the open window, breaking through my nightmares, and I stirred. Sophia was still tucked closely next to me, her breathing gentle and at ease. Esis was still sleeping, but Julian stared at me with bright eyes, his tail wagging.

I stared at Sophia for a moment, watching her sleep. She looked so peaceful— something I'd missed over the past few months. I allowed my fingers to drift through the tendrils of her hair. When I touched her, she smiled and moved closer to me in her sleep, like she could sense I was near and my presence was what she needed to maintain a quiet night's rest.

I loved her so much. I'd live for her. I'd *die* for her. There wasn't a single thing on earth I wouldn't do for this woman. I knew the Task Force was after us because of her, but I didn't care. I'd fight the whole fucking world if it meant giving her one more day. She was my everything, and I needed to protect that.

On the other side of her, Jonah and Imogen slumbered on. Jonah had Imogen wrapped in his arms and was squeezing her tight. Imogen clung to Jonah, her mouth in a frown and eyes shifting behind her lids, like she was experiencing some kind of bad dream. Squeaks' head rested on Jonah's hip, while Sassy lay on her back and whimpered, waving her legs as she dreamed of chasing rabbits.

I got up slowly, so as not to disturb anyone. I whispered to Julian, and he jumped into my arms as I started toward the kitchen.

I checked the clock. It was already noon. We really were exhausted from our trip. I rummaged through the cupboards one more time and found coffee grounds, but we couldn't make any, because the coffee maker wouldn't work without electricity and the gas had been shut off to the stove as well.

I hoped the water would still be running so we could grab showers, but when I tried, it was a no go.

We couldn't stay here long. We didn't have the needed amenities. A few days, at most.

A half an hour later, the others began to stir. They came into the kitchen just as I'd finished searching through the cupboards for medicine and found nothing.

"So guys, how long until we throw the Task Force off our trail?" Sophia yawned and rubbed her eyes. Esis copied her, appearing a particularly sleepy baby.

"Um... two days should be enough," Imogen suggested. "If we leave on the ninth and nothing happens until then, I think it's pretty safe to say we've lost them."

"Well, we need to eat something. We're out of supplies and there's nothing here," Jonah pointed out.

"I don't suggest we use the car," Imogen said. "It should stay in the garage so there's a lesser chance it'll be recognized."

"We can go to the grocery store later. It's not far from here. We can walk," Sophia suggested.

"Maybe tonight," I offered. "But I don't think it's a good idea to spend more than an hour outside the house until we know for sure we haven't been followed."

Sophia stroked Esis' ears. "The coffee shop down the street sells sandwiches, and we can get them to go. You remember it, Liam. We met up there the night you took me to Orenda Academy."

I vaguely recalled the place.

Jonah patted his stomach. "So what are we waiting for? Let's get some eats."

"It'll be safer if we go together. We risk attracting attention, but it's not for long," Imogen said.

Nobody liked the idea of leaving the Familiars at the house, but it wasn't like we had a choice. We walked down the street to the coffee shop, keeping our eyes open. We jumped every time a black SUV passed us by or a loud noise sounded off, but nothing ever came of it.

We were totally on edge, but it was pointless. It was obvious the Task Force hadn't come here, to a small town outside Salt Lake Valley. This seemed like a safe place to stay for now.

The smells of coffee and baking bread hit my nose as we walked into the shop. I observed the green walls and wooden tables with a slightly prompted familiarity. Now I remembered. I'd been sitting at a table and checking Sophia out when she'd walked in.

If I could go back in time and tell myself what would become of Sophia and me, the old Liam wouldn't have believed me. If I had told him Sophia and I were engaged, he would've scoffed and said I was nuts, even though he was secretly hoping for everything I now had.

I could still recall the thoughts I had the first time I set eyes on her. *Holy shit, that's* her? *She's the prophesied one? She's the sexiest fucking girl I've ever seen. She's gorgeous! Ancestors, I hope I don't look like shit. I probably look like shit. Why is she so damn beautiful?*

I'd barely composed myself in time to tell her what I'd been sent to do. We'd come a long way since then. Two years wasn't a long time, but so much could happen in that short span.

It was mostly empty inside the shop. They were having a slow day. Sophia went up to the counter and placed our orders. Jonah kept his eyes on the window, scanning for Task Force members, and we clustered around the delivery area as we waited for our food to arrive.

The bell chimed as the door opened, and someone else walked in. He was definitely a human. Gangly and tall, with a long face and a pinched nose. He had short hair, and acne peppered around his chin. He was probably our age. I didn't consider him a threat, so I ignored him.

Sophia's eyes contracted. "Oh, no."

She ducked behind me. Her head lowered, and she stared at the floor. It was like she was trying to hide. She pulled on Jonah's arm, trying to get him to block her, too, but he was oblivious so he didn't notice. Her cheeks were tinged with embarrassment.

"What's wrong?" Imogen asked when she noticed Sophia's cowering. She looked at the guy with a weird expression.

"It's *Blake*," Sophia hissed.

I didn't recognize the name, but Imogen's gaze soured. She knew him, apparently.

"Who?" The tone in my voice made it obvious she needed to answer me. I turned to face her, and she moved so I was blocking her again.

"I told you about him," she mumbled. "That first night at the waterfall."

I pieced things together quickly. Wait a minute. This was the *prom guy?* The fucking asshole who'd assaulted Sophia in the back of a limo in high school?

I'd prayed for a chance to meet this motherfucker one day. Looks like the ancestors had acknowledged at least one of my requests. I couldn't wait to pound this dickhead into the dirt. There weren't enough names on earth I could call this scum.

My knuckles cracked as I bunched my hands into fists. Sophia saw.

"Liam, don't do anything," Sophia pleaded. "Let's just hope he doesn't notice me."

But he did notice. He'd caught the sound of Sophia's voice and looked up. A nasty grin spread across his ugly mug. I noticed he had crooked teeth. Honestly, Sophia had been into *him?* I was starting to doubt how I looked when I saw what her type used to be.

"Hey, Henley!" he said. "Haven't seen you in a while. Where've you been all this time?"

Sophia forced a polite grimace. "I'm in school. I transferred to a university in California."

She shrank several inches as Blake's eyes roved over her. He had the *audacity* to let his eyes linger on her breasts for a moment. I would've pummeled him right then and there if Imogen hadn't grabbed the back of my shirt and yanked it, as a reminder to behave. Jonah didn't know what was going on, but he noticed Sophia was uncomfortable, so he pressed in behind her for support.

"California, huh? That's pretty far." He frowned. "But not so far away we can't keep up. You haven't been responding to my texts. Why'd you ghost me?"

"Sorry. I don't have a phone anymore." Sophia shrugged. "It's not allowed at my school."

"What kind of lame-ass college do you go to?" Blake laughed. "That's kind of a shitty excuse, Sophia. Everyone has a phone. If you don't want to hang out with me, you don't have to lie."

"I didn't lie," Sophia snapped. "Those are just the rules."

"Yeah." Blake scowled. "Okay."

He was checking her out again, which was un-fucking-acceptable. I put my arm around Sophia's shoulders, and Blake noticed. His eyes narrowed, but he didn't say anything.

*Yeah, back off, douchebag. She's mine.*

"So... you back for good, or...?" Blake's voice trailed off. He'd definitely noticed I'd been giving him a death glare.

"We're in town visiting my family," Sophia lied. "We had to tell them the good news."

Sophia flashed her engagement ring. Blake's mouth opened, and Sophia said, "Blake, I'd like you to meet Liam. He's my fiancé."

She looked up at me, and I was pleased to see a gaze of adoration crossed her features.

Blake's eyes widened. He glanced at me before giving a short, harsh laugh. "Are you kidding me? You're engaged to *this* guy?"

"Yep. We're getting married," I said loudly, before Sophia had the chance to respond.

"Hm." Blake frowned. "Don't take this the wrong way, but he doesn't really seem like your... type." His attention drifted to Imogen and Jonah. "New friends, too? Not your usual crowd."

Disbelief and a bit of resentment echoed in his voice. Sophia raised her voice and said, "Actually, they are. I found out I'm part of an Indigenous tribe. That's why I go there. It's a college on the reservation."

"Ah, that's probably why I haven't heard of it," Blake quipped. His words implied that the school we went to was shit. "But I always thought you'd go to a *good* college, you know? You're too smart to go to a school on a reservation."

I wasn't the only one struggling to hold it in. Imogen was fit to bursting, and Jonah stiffened behind me. Sophia let his words roll off of her and said, "I'm glad I'm Native. We're a proud people, and we have a strong history."

"Come on, Sophia. You're totally white." Blake snorted. "You can obviously see that these guys are... you know... not *our* people."

His gaze locked on mine. Oh, great, he was racist, too. How predictable.

Sophia's tone hardened as she said, "I'm not the same person I was in high school. I know that's hard for you to believe, but maybe you didn't know me as well as you thought you did."

"That's not true," Blake countered. "We haven't talked since graduation, and we used to talk every day. What changed?"

"I grew up," Sophia said harshly. "I stopped being a little girl who needed attention."

Blake threw back his head and gave a cruel laugh. "Really, Sophia? You *always* needed attention, and you loved it when I gave it to you. And everyone at school eventually found out what a slut you are."

I started forward, but someone held me back. Jonah had put a hand on my shoulder to stop me from murdering Blake. I remained on the spot, but it took all my free will to do so. The only thing holding me back from kicking the crap out of Blake was the fact that we were on the run, and we couldn't afford drawing attention to ourselves. Otherwise, this guy would already be a bloody mess on the floor.

"That was all you, Blake. You started those rumors," Sophia seethed. "You know I didn't touch you."

"Yeah, but I touched you, didn't I, baby? Does your *fiancé* know that?" Blake said lowly.

"Don't react," Jonah pleaded from behind me, but I barely heard him. I was seeing red right now. I almost thought I'd turned Koigni, for all the rage boiling underneath my skin.

"As a matter of fact, he does. He knows everything about me. I've told him more about myself than you will ever know," Sophia responded coolly.

"That's not an accomplishment, sweetheart." Blake's tone dripped with indignation. He'd lost Sophia, and he obviously wasn't getting her back, so he held nothing but contempt for her in response. "Too bad you don't realize you lost your chance with a real man."

"Let's face facts, Blake. You didn't give a shit about me. All you cared about was getting in my pants," Sophia snapped. "Now you're trying to do it again, and I'm not interested. I never will be. So you can go fuck yourself."

"Wow. The Sophia I knew would never talk like that." Blake shook his head, like a woman swearing was some horrible thing. "You really have changed."

"You're damn right I have. So leave me alone." Sophia's voice shook, but she was serious. She was just as close to losing her temper as I was.

I couldn't let her endure a second more of this. It was my job to protect her, and even though Blake was as big a threat as a wet noodle, he was making her upset, which was a no-go in my book. I stepped in front of Sophia and blocked her from Blake's view.

"You need to fucking leave," I said. I made it clear I wasn't playing around.

"Yeah? And what the hell are you gonna do about it, you drunk Indian?" Blake snarled.

I hit him. I fucking hit him. My fist collided with his cheek, and he went down. The employees behind the counter screamed. Our food had just arrived, and they'd seen me punch Blake just as they were putting it on the delivery table. Jonah hurried to grab the sandwich bags as I stood panting over Blake. He looked up at me in total fear, like he couldn't actually believe I had the balls to hit him. His one hand was clapped over his face, and a trickle of blood leaked through his fingers.

"Liam! Come on, let's go!" Sophia yanked on my arm. I came back to reality, and we high-tailed it out of the shop.

We ran all the way back to Sophia's house. Jonah put the food on the table, and Sophia locked the door behind us. We drew the shades and clustered around the kitchen, trying to catch our breath. The Familiars watched us from the living room, heads tilted as they tried to figure out what we were running from.

"Did anyone see us?" Jonah breathed.

"No," I gasped. Fuck, that was stupid. I shouldn't have done that. It wasn't worth the risk, but still, it was satisfying all the same.

"Do you think he'll show up here?" Imogen asked. She was practically shaking in fear.

"No. He knows where I live, but he's a total wuss," Sophia replied. "He'll be too scared to bother me again now that Liam put him in his place."

Sophia's words shone with gratitude, but Imogen stepped forward. She quivered in anger as she shouted, "Liam, that was totally unacceptable! We can't risk you getting arrested on an assault charge!"

"Blake won't report it to the police," Sophia objected. "He's had a few bad run-ins with the cops. We don't have to worry about him."

"Okay, so what if he goes around town saying that Sophia Henley's boyfriend punched him in the face? Don't you think that'll get the attention of the Task Force if they show up here?" Imogen spat.

"That would make him look like a little bitch," Jonah argued. "He won't."

"We *don't know* for sure." Imogen slammed her palm on the table. She rounded on me. "I get that he deserved it, and this situation was hard—"

"Everything about this situation is hard, Im!" I threw my arms wide. "So what if I just couldn't take *one more* thing? I can't stop the Elders, but at least I could teach that fucker a lesson!"

"Liam, I'm *sorry* your dad died." Imogen's eyes beaded with tears. "And I'm sorry we're in this situation. But you can't lose your temper anymore. It risks exposing us, and if the Task Force finds us again..."

Imogen trailed off as she noticed my expression. When she mentioned my dad, my throat got tight, and my eyes burned. I wasn't sure I could argue further without breaking down.

Being hurt was tough. Being angry was easier. I rolled my eyes and turned my back on her. "Whatever. I won't do it again."

"I sure the hell hope not. You can't go around punching people," Imogen snapped.

I ignored her. I headed to the back yard to get some space, and slammed the door behind me. I took deep breaths, trying to calm down.

Soft mews were at my feet. Julian had followed me through the dog door. We were exposed, but there was a fence around the property and nobody was around, so I didn't care.

I bent down and picked up my dragon. He nuzzled against my neck and licked my cheek with his forked tongue.

"Good thing you weren't there, huh, Jules?" I asked lowly. "You would've roasted him."

Julian growled in agreement, though he wasn't sure who I was talking about.

The door opened and shut behind me. It was Jonah. I resisted the urge to bite his head off and asked, "What?"

Jonah took a deep breath. "Dude, I'm sorry, but you're being a fucking prick."

"What'd you just say to me?" I whirled on Jonah. Julian hissed, but Jonah didn't flinch.

"You're not gonna like this, but you need a reality check," Jonah whispered. He was keeping his voice low so the girls didn't hear us. "You've been acting like the world is against you since we left, and it's not helping."

"Look around you! The world is against us. We can't catch a break," I replied.

"I know it's frustrating. I'm right there with you," Jonah replied. "But you're supposed to be the boss, and you're falling apart. As far as your *leadership* goes, you're getting an F."

I seethed. "Maybe I don't want to be a leader anymore."

"Doesn't matter. You don't have a choice. No one holds the group together like you do," Jonah countered. "I've been trying, but this isn't my forte, man."

"Jonah, do you realize I don't know what I'm doing?" I used my free hand to rub my eyes. "I can barely keep my head straight. It feels like I'm underwater with no way up."

"I'm sorry you feel that way. I know it can't be easy with you being sick. And I miss your dad, too." Jonah's voice broke. "But we gotta focus on the people we've still got. And you've gotta start taking responsibility and stepping up, bro. We can't have you out for the count like this. We're never gonna last."

"Is it too much to ask for a few days of reprieve?"

"Yes. There's no time for it." Jonah shrugged. "I don't know what else you want me to say. You're acting like your old self, and to be honest, it's kind of pissing me off. I thought you weren't going to go back there."

That stung, and he knew it. "I'm sorry I disappointed you," I replied. "I'm not giving excuses, but try to put yourself in my shoes."

"Look, bottom line, we need you to start giving orders and start taking control around here. I know it sounds counterintuitive, but nobody knows what to do if you're not in charge."

Jonah's words were full of disgust as he continued. "It didn't help that you acted like a sociopath after you killed that guy. You showed no remorse at all. You acted like you *enjoyed* it."

I wanted to reply with, *so what if I did?* But that really would make me sound like a sociopath, and Jonah had a good point. I didn't like the man I was becoming. Not one bit.

"I just need a break. My dad's been gone for *three days*," I argued. "I'm worried about Maddie, and I don't know where Ezra is, or if Mom got the rest of the kids out—"

"We're all worried. But you and I need to stay strong for the girls. Imogen puts on a brave face, but she's slipping," Jonah argued. "Sophia is obviously looking to you for guidance, and you're fucking failing her."

Nothing he could've said would've hurt me more. He delivered a harsh blow right to the core of me. But that was Jonah. He was my best friend, and he knew me better than almost anyone else. He knew what to say to get me to wake up.

I was silent. Jonah clapped me on the shoulder and said, "Just think about it, man. The team really does need you."

Jonah left me alone. Julian chirped, and I felt a sinking feeling in my gut. As much as this situation sucked... Jonah was right. No matter what I was going through, I couldn't afford to fall apart now. Not when other people were depending on me.

I went back inside and climbed up the stairs. I saw Sophia in her bedroom, sitting on the edge of her bed. She was going through a scrapbook that she'd found. Esis sat on her shoulder, brushing her hair.

I sat down beside her. Julian crawled onto a pillow. The corners of her lips turned up as she said, "Hey."

"Hey," I replied. I leaned in to look. The scrapbook was full of photos of her and her sister. "Missing Amelia?"

"Yeah. I miss her so much." Sophia closed the scrapbook and held it to her chest. "I wish she was here right now. Maybe she could tell us what to do. Being here, in this place with so many memories... I don't know how to handle it."

My heart twisted. Jonah had been spot on. Sophia really did feel lost. "We know what we're going to do. We'll go to Imogen's house and figure out what to do from there," I replied. "Our families can't be lost forever."

"I hope so." Sophia set the scrapbook aside and faced me. "Thanks for sticking up for me back there," Sophia said quietly. "I know it wasn't the right thing to do, but it made me feel a little better to see Blake get some payback."

"You don't have to thank me. I'll always be there for you."

She leaned forward and placed her head on my chest. I wrapped my arms around her and held her tightly. Esis grumbled that I was messing up Sophia's hair.

Sophia sat backward. I pulled her onto my lap, and I leaned against the wall as she curled into me.

"Do you think they're still out there?" she whispered. "That they're even alive?"

"They have to be," I murmured back. "We'll find them, *pawee*. I promise."

I hoped that wasn't yet another promise I'd be forced to break.

# sophia

## FOUR

Returning home was a painful reminder of my family. Though I didn't let it show, they hovered in the back of my mind every second of the day. I knew Amelia had said in her letter they were safe, but I wouldn't believe it until I saw it with my own eyes. Liam had tried to reassure me by pointing out that my parents obviously left on purpose, but it didn't help. All that did was open up this gaping hole in my chest that reminded me they'd left me behind.

I woke the next morning on the living room floor, Liam's arm draped around my middle. Esis and Julian were curled together at our feet. A terrible sinking sensation entered my gut, but I couldn't pinpoint why, until the dream I'd just woken from came rushing back.

*I stood in the Great Hall at Orenda Academy. The tapestries around me burned, filling my lungs with choking smoke. I held my hands up and tried to control the flames, but the more I struggled to subdue them, the worse they got.*

*Shadows blurred across my vision as three figures walked down the grand staircase. A horrible sense of dread overcame me when I realized it was my parents and Amelia. Their Familiars were nowhere to be seen.*

*"You have to leave!" I shouted to them.*

*"Oh, honey," Mom said gently, reaching her hand out to me. "Don't you realize? We already have."*

*A burst of flames shot up from the floor, and they disappeared from view. I screamed, but when the flames died, my family had vanished completely.*

*My stomach dropped as panic set in. I whirled around, looking for my friends— looking for anyone. I longed to hear the cry of Esis echoing down the hall.*

*But I was all alone.*

I curled in on myself as I replayed the dream in my mind. *It wasn't real,* I told myself. And yet, everything the dream made me *feel* was real. I had my friends, but without my family, I didn't quite feel whole.

Beside me, Jonah was snoring, and Imogen was still as a log. Liam was sound asleep, so he didn't notice when I pushed his arm off and tiptoed out of the room.

I went to my parents' bedroom and crawled under the covers. Tears pricked at my eyes, and I buried my head into my mom's pillow. I took a deep breath and inhaled her scent. It still smelled like her.

The knot in my belly tightened. I wasn't sure whether to miss them or be mad at them. It was a little of both.

As I wiped my eyes, an unexpected thought cut through. *My real parents would never do this to me.*

I felt sick the second I thought it. How could I be so mad at my parents when I was so worried at the same time? And how could I *really* know if my birth parents wouldn't do this? They'd given me up. There was no way to know for sure unless I found out who they were and asked them. But it wasn't like I had a birth certificate lying around that listed their names.

I sprang straight up in bed. Holy shit. I had to have a birth certificate! It could tell me who my real parents were.

I threw the blankets off myself and scrambled over to my parents' closet. I tried not to make any noise as I pulled the door open and began rummaging through the boxes inside.

"Please let it be in here…" I whispered under my breath.

I found nothing, but I went through it again to be sure. When I didn't find anything, I started pulling open their drawers, but they were mostly empty, except for a few articles of clothing left behind.

I gritted my teeth. The more I looked, the more frustrated I got. My parents were liars, and right now, I hated them for it. They lied to me about being adopted. They never told me I was Elementai. They wanted to keep me out of Orenda Academy. They never admitted who my real parents were. They'd just repeated the same lie my grandparents had. They left and didn't tell me where. What else were they hiding? And *why?*

I went out into the hall and started throwing open drawers in the computer desk.

"Where is it?" I mumbled.

Heat flared in my cheeks. I couldn't find it. I'd never figure out who my real birth parents were.

*Fuck my parents! Fuck my grandparents! Fuck everyone who lied to me!*

I kicked the computer desk drawer closed, and it slammed shut with a loud *bang*.

"Ancestors!" Imogen cried as she startled awake.

"It's okay, guys!" I called down the hall. "It's just me—"

Liam stumbled into the hallway. He gasped as he tripped and caught himself on the wall. He looked startled and out of breath.

"Liam!" I screamed.

He landed on the floor, inhaling deep breaths. "*Pawee*, you okay? I thought—"

"I'm fine," I assured him. I leaned down and helped him to his feet. I knew how shitty he felt in the morning and how stiff he got after he slept. For him to get up that fast, especially without his meds, was nothing short of a miracle.

Esis and Julian came rushing behind him. Jonah poked his head into the hall. He only looked half awake. "What's going on?"

"We're fine," I told him, before turning back to Liam. "You should lie down."

Jonah rubbed his eyes and headed back to the living room. Liam sucked a sharp breath as he took a step down the hall. He tried not to let it show, but I could see he was in pain.

"Let's go to the bed," I suggested. "You'll be more comfortable there."

Liam followed me into my parents' bedroom. I helped him down onto the bed, then sat beside him. Esis and Julian jumped beside him and cuddled close. Liam groaned, but it was mixed in with a pleasant sigh— like he was happy to lie down on a comfortable mattress again. I wish I'd insisted he sleep there the last few nights. He'd probably feel a lot better by now.

Then again, he still didn't have his meds, so it could've been just as bad. I worried it wasn't just messing with his body but seriously screwing with his mood. *Is this the real Liam? The one who murders Task Force members and punches ex-boyfriends in the face?* Was I only in love with the drugged-up Liam?

*No*, I told myself. I refused to believe that. He was just under a lot of stress. We all were. Hell, I'd done a lot of shit I wasn't proud of recently, too. I'd burned him, for ancestor's sake.

Liam took my hand in his. "What's on your mind, *pawee*?"

I shook my head. "Nothing."

Liam frowned. "No lies, Soph. Remember?"

It seemed like we were always reminding each other of that. "I just meant... nothing you need to worry about."

Liam didn't look convinced. "What were you doing in the hall?"

I hesitated a moment. For some reason, I couldn't tell him how mad I was at my parents. It made me feel guilty just thinking about it. I couldn't say it out loud.

"I was trying to see if I could find my birth certificate," I admitted.

Liam sighed. "Soph, they probably took it with them, along with all their other important files."

My shoulders fell. Of course they took it with them. Why would I think otherwise?

"Sophia, if you want help finding your birth parents, I'll do whatever you need to help—"

"Shh..." I silenced him by placing a hand on his chest. "I told you, Liam. It's nothing you need to worry about."

His brow furrowed, like he was offended. "Why wouldn't I worry about you, *pawee*?"

He lifted my hand to show me the ring. "You're going to be my *wife*. I'm allowed to worry."

The knot in my stomach eased a little when he called me his wife. It was the one good thing in this whole mess.

"It's not a big deal," I lied. "You have bigger things to worry about."

"Oh yeah?" he challenged. "Like what?"

I bit my lower lip. I knew this was Liam's way of saying I was the most important thing to him, that there was nothing worth worrying about more — but he was also waiting for a real answer.

"You need to worry about yourself, Liam," I whispered.

"Pft," he said, leaning his head back against the pillow. "You do enough of that for the both of us."

"Do I?" I replied, harsher than I intended. I quickly softened my tone. "Liam, I can't help you if you don't want to be helped."

His jaw dropped, like he was really offended. "What makes you think I don't want help, *pawee*? I've been going to therapy every week since we got back together. I haven't missed a single session."

"Yeah," I said. "But that was before..."

He raised an eyebrow. "Before?"

I swallowed the lump in my throat. "Before the battle of Orenda Academy. Before you lost your meds."

His lips tightened. "Soph, that was only days ago. I've barely had a second to grieve."

"Because you're not letting yourself!" I burst.

My guts sank when I said it. I was one to talk. I hadn't faced anything that happened that night, either. I was still a walking shell of a being— like I was trying to convince myself it never happened and my grandparents were still waiting back in Kinpago for me.

I was stupid.

I took a deep breath. "Liam, I'm sorry. I didn't mean—"

Liam yanked his hand away from mine. "You don't think I'm trying?"

Tears welled in my eyes. "I just... wish you could talk to me about it. We haven't talked about your dad at all."

Liam pushed himself to a sitting position, but I could tell by the way he winced that it hurt. "Soph, you don't get it. I'm not like you. I'm not in touch with my emotions in the same way. Talking about things just makes it worse, so I deal with it on my own. I don't do it to offend you or because I don't love you. I just... need time."

I sniffled and wiped my nose. "We all do. I just wish... I wish we could do it together. I'm just worried you blame me."

His eyes widened. "Blame you? *Pawee*, why would I do that?"

"Well, because... because..." I choked up and couldn't get the words out. *Because I kept you from saving your dad to save the rest of us.*

But I couldn't say it out loud. What I'd done was horrendous. He should've broken up with me on the spot after what I did to him.

The tension in the air was palpable. I was sure he could feel what I was about to say. But he didn't push me, so instead, I said, "Because I didn't pack your antidepressants."

Liam wrapped an arm around me and pulled me close to him. "Soph, we left in a rush. That's the furthest thing from your fault. I'll be fine without them."

"Will you?" I drew away to look him in the eyes. "You're not acting like yourself lately. And I know you've been having nightmares. You haven't said a thing about them to me."

Liam looked on the verge of tears. "I can't, Sophia. Every night in my dreams, I see you..."

He shook his head, like he couldn't stand to picture it. "It's not something I want to think about when I'm awake. Because when I'm awake, you're here, and you're real. And I thank the ancestors every damn second that you weren't killed on that execution block. You're still here with me, and *that's* what matters."

I was so touched by his words, but at the same time, I knew it was his way of side-stepping the issue and pushing the conversation in a new direction.

"I'm grateful for that, too," I said. "But maybe I can help."

I wanted to. I wanted to help *so badly*, but I felt bad even suggesting it. *I* was the one who'd been having recurring nightmares since the New Year's riots, and though they'd slowed down, I hadn't gotten rid of them completely. I was a total hypocrite. But I really, *really* wanted to help Liam.

"You want to know the truth, Sophia?" Liam asked bitterly.

I was taken off guard by his tone, but I nodded anyway.

"The truth is... each night, I find myself in *Aiya Nocshun*," he admitted.

"The Mighty Darkness?" I whispered. "You mean, like... hell?"

He nodded solemnly. "Each night, I'm faced with losing you again. Over and over. And Soph..." His eyes glistened with tears. "I'm *so* afraid I'm going to."

I pressed a hand to the side of his face. "No. The ancestors haven't separated us yet. They wouldn't let that happen."

"But it's going to happen eventually, *pawee*."

A heavy weight landed on my chest. "W-what do you mean?"

"Sophia, you're such a pure and kind-hearted soul," he began.

I resisted the urge to snort. I was a sinner just like him.

"It's obvious you're going to end up in the Ancestral Lands," Liam said. "But me? I'm already damned."

I gasped. How could he believe that? He was being absurd. Liam couldn't be damned to hell. He was kind, and sweet. He loved harder than all of us and always put others first. That was the last kind of person that was going to hell.

My hands shook as I squeezed his tighter. "You're not damned."

He stood and began pacing around the room, even though I could tell the last thing he wanted to do right now was walk. It was like his way of punishing himself.

"I've killed people, *pawee*," he reminded me.

"In the name of something good," I shot back. "What happened with that Task Force member, you did it to save us."

"But I could've— I should've—" Liam balled his hands into fists.

"You can't change what you did," I said, stopping him. "But you have to understand that you're not a bad person for it. You have a good heart, Liam. And that's why the ancestors would never damn you."

"You don't know that," Liam said quietly.

"Neither do you!" I snapped. "Is this why you won't take care of yourself anymore?"

He raked his fingers through his long dark hair. "I told you I'm trying."

"But you haven't *shown* me," I emphasized. "Liam, it's gotten so bad even Esis can hardly heal you anymore. We agreed that when you got out of the hospital, you'd do better."

He scowled at me. "A lot has changed since then."

"I know," I said softly. I stood from the bed and reached out to him. I half expected him to pull away, but he didn't. Instead, he relaxed into my embrace. "Our lives have changed so quickly. If we're going to get through this, then we need to change, too. Together."

Liam pressed his nose into my hair and took a deep breath. For a moment, I thought he wasn't going to say anything. Then he whispered, "Okay, *pawee*. We will."

❧

LIAM and I both meant it when we promised each other we'd work through our issues together, but it was like there was an unspoken agreement between us that we'd start as soon as we felt safe and not a second before. Everyone was still on edge— as if waiting for the Task Force to burst into my parents' home and attack us again.

By the time Thursday arrived, though, nothing had happened.

"I think it's safe to say that we lost the Task Force," Imogen announced that morning as she handed out breakfast sandwiches she and Jonah had gone out to get. "We should be safe to leave."

"Yeah, and I'm dying for a shower," Jonah said as he sniffed his armpits.

Imogen twisted her nose up at him. "Yeah, seriously. You stink."

"I guess we should pack up," Liam suggested.

While everyone worked on packing the bedding and Imogen raided the bathroom for toiletries and other supplies, I went to my bedroom. I'd lost almost everything that was important to me when we fled Orenda Academy, but there were a few things at home I didn't want to leave behind. I took a few pictures of Amelia and my parents off my bulletin board and gathered some of my old clothes.

While I was digging through my dresser, I found something I'd forgotten I had. My friends Emily and Leah had given them to me for my sixteenth birthday as a gag gift. I never thought I'd be the kind of girl to use them, but the thought had me excited. *Finally, a bit of good news.*

I slipped the gift into my bag where Liam wouldn't see. I wanted to surprise him.

Finally, I went into Amelia's room and pulled one of her hoodies from her closet. I still had her jeans she'd given me, but the hoodie smelled like her. It wrapped around me like a warm hug. It was hard to stay mad at her when I missed her so much.

Esis tried to crawl into one of her shirts, but it drowned him. I giggled and curled him in my arms, then went over to set him on the bed. "If you want something to wear, buddy, try this."

I reached for one of the bears in Amelia's endless stuffed animal collection and pulled the rainbow t-shirt off it. Esis put it on, and it fit him perfectly. He ran over to the mirror and modeled, looking pleased. I snickered. He brought me so much joy.

"Sophia?" Liam called down the hall, his voice filled with concern. He barely let me out of his sight these days.

"In here!" I shouted back.

Liam poked his head into the room, and Julian peeked past his feet. "You ready to go?"

I grabbed my backpack and swung it over my shoulder. "Ready as I'll ever be."

The drive to Imogen's house was long. The house was located in Southern California, and we still had to get out of Utah before we crossed the rest of the state. We had to stop for the night, but nothing happened like last time. I think all of us wondered if the Task Force was fucking with us or if we'd really lost them, but by the time we got to Imogen's house the next day, it felt like we could actually breathe.

I gasped when we drove into Imogen's driveway. Her house was nestled between the mountains, next to a national forest. Evergreens bordered the property on all sides, and though she had a couple of neighbors, they'd never see anything past the tall fence at the front of the property. The house itself was small— nothing more than a little cottage— but it looked cozy and safe. The outside was painted a light green for Nivita.

"Imogen," I breathed. "It's gorgeous."

"I know." She blushed. "Wait until you see the inside."

Jonah drove to the back of the house, where we couldn't be seen. When we stepped out of the car, the air was nice and warm, and I could hear the sound of water trickling through the mountains.

"Water!" Liam cried. "I feel water."

Imogen chuckled. "I knew I couldn't buy a property without water. There's a river behind the house."

Liam rounded the car and looked down into the ravine behind the driveway. A rocky little creek cut through the trees and twisted around the back of the property.

"Thanks, Im," he said. "You're the best."

She shrugged. "I try. So, who wants the grand tour?"

"Girl, I've already started," Jonah said from the deck. He and Squeaks were already investigating.

Esis jumped out of my arms and hurried up the stairs to join Squeaks. She nudged at something I couldn't see, until I climbed the stairs and saw there was a hot tub on the porch. She was trying to slip the top off to climb inside.

"Imogen!" I cried. "You have a hot tub?"

"What?" Liam asked. His eyes brightened suddenly. He came up behind me with Julian in his arms, and the little dragon leapt out of his arms to land on the hot tub cover. "Oh, this is *sweet*. I call dibs."

Imogen rolled her eyes as she passed. Sassy hurried to the back door and scraped on the glass with her paws. "You can use it *after* you shower. Besides, it hasn't even been turned on yet."

"Turn it on! Turn it on!" Jonah jumped up and down.

Imogen pointed a finger at Jonah. "You're definitely getting a shower first. I don't need your nasty ass contaminating my hot tub."

Jonah's shoulders fell. "Fine."

Imogen unlocked the door, and we all followed behind her. Inside, the house was decorated like an old country cottage. I never thought that'd be Imogen's style, considering the white walls and light-toned accents. I was expecting more bright colors and flashy posters, but it actually suited her well. Downstairs was a living room with a fireplace, a fully-stocked kitchen, a laundry room, and a bathroom with a walk-in shower. Upstairs, there were two bedrooms. Imogen pointed Liam and me to the one with the queen bed, while she and Jonah took the room with two twins across the hall.

"Ugh," Jonah groaned. "I thought you promised me a full-sized bed, Im. I'm too big for that thing. You expect Squeaks to sleep on the floor?"

Imogen placed her hand on her hip. "Do you *want* to know how much this place cost? Because if you wanted to contribute the entirety of your Cup winnings, we could've upgraded a few hundred square feet and gotten you a full-sized bed."

Jonah's shoulders fell. "I hear you, Im. This will do."

Jonah went into his room to set down his bags, but Liam stopped in the hall. "Thanks for doing this, Imogen," he said. "We all really appreciate it."

She shrugged. "Yeah, well, it's the least I could do. Who wants their clothes washed? Sassy and I are going to do a load of laundry."

"You can take mine right away," I said. "I'm going to take a shower."

Imogen pointed to the closet in my room. "There's a robe for each of you in there when you're done."

"Thanks, Im," I said. As soon as she went back downstairs, I turned to Liam. "You're invited to join me."

His face remained passive. "Maybe another time, Soph."

"Come on." I tugged on his hand. "There's no bath for you to relax in. I can help you wash up."

Liam sighed. "Okay," he agreed reluctantly.

We changed into our robes. Our Familiars stayed behind in our room as we went downstairs to put our clothes in the wash, then got into the shower.

Liam tilted his head back as the warm water rushed over him. He looked like he was really enjoying it when I rubbed suds all over his body. But when I touched his dick, he didn't even get hard.

It was kind of like a slap in the face. "Liam, what's wrong?" I asked.

He snapped back to attention. "Nothing. Why?"

"You're basically unresponsive," I said.

"I didn't mean to be."

I ran my hand back over his dick. "We're safe now. Don't you want to fool around again?"

"Of course I do," he said, and I felt his dick begin to harden. "What do you want to do, Soph?"

What do I want to do? He never asked like that. He just read my signals and went for it.

This worried me. It was just another sign he wasn't quite himself lately. All I wanted to do was make him feel better.

"Well... I kind of have a surprise for you, but it's upstairs," I admitted.

He looked intrigued. "We better hurry up, then."

Liam ran the soap over me, paying particular close attention to my breasts and my ass. I could tell he was starting to cheer up, because he grew harder and harder.

I stood on my toes and kissed him on the lips. He ran his hands down my wet hair and moaned. It felt so good to feel his body against mine again. It was like in these simple stolen moments, I could believe everything was going to be okay. And I didn't want it to end.

I couldn't lie. I was more or less screwing around because I wanted to forget. As much as I wanted this to be romantic, it was more of a distraction.

Liam drew away. "What's the surprise?"

I bit my lower lip. "Well, it's more for me."

He shrugged, staring down at me with smoldering eyes. "I like pleasing you."

For the first time in what felt like forever, I cracked a smile. "Then you're going to like this."

"Show me," he said. "I want to see."

"Okay." I turned the water off and climbed out of the shower.

Liam smacked my ass, and I giggled. We dried off and put our robes back on, then snuck upstairs into our room. Esis and Julian were playing somewhere downstairs with Sassy, so we had the room all to ourselves.

My heart hammered as I dragged him over to the bed. I was already wet as I anticipated what was about to come. I pushed Liam down onto the bed, and he relaxed into it, eyeing me curiously.

I liked the way his eyes locked on my body. Slowly, I tugged on the tie of my robe, and it dropped open. I let it fall from my shoulders, until I was fully exposed in front of him. Liam straightened a little on the bed.

I smiled. "You like what you see?"

His gaze roamed my body. "I always love looking at you."

"Aww," I swooned, my heart lifting in my chest. "Thank you. Now wait right here."

I went over to my bag and dug to the bottom, then pulled out the package I'd hidden in there earlier. Liam tilted his head to the side, like he couldn't tell what I had in my hand. I walked over and handed it to him. He eyed it for a second, then laughed.

"Nipple clamps, Sophia?" he laughed. "Wow. Of all the things you could've packed, you packed fucking nipple clamps."

I swatted at him. "No! I found them at my parents' house."

His face fell. "Ancestors, are these Amelia's?"

I laughed. "No. They're mine. My friends bought them for me as a gag gift years ago. I forgot I had them."

He looked up to me. "You're sure you want to use these?"

A blush rose to my cheeks, but I nodded. We'd messed around with toys in the past, but this was a step up.

"Then I'm all for it." Liam opened the package, and my heart slammed against my rib cage. He pulled out two tiny clamps that opened when you pinched the ends together. Each one was covered in a soft rubber tip, and they had diamonds dangling off the ends.

I crawled on top of him and straddled him.

"Excited, huh?" he teased.

I reached up his robe and ran my hand over his cock. "You, too?"

He smiled. "Oh, yeah."

Liam placed the clamps on my nipples, and I gasped as he tightened them. Nerve endings in my nipples ignited. Oh, my God. They felt so good. I moaned.

"That good?" Liam asked. He ran his hands down my hips, then slipped one hand between my thighs. Tingles spread down from my nipples to my most sensitive area as he brushed a finger up against me.

"Yes," I breathed.

Liam tugged lightly on the clamps, and I gasped again. He put a finger inside of me and began moving it as the clamps tingled against my nipples.

"I want you so bad right now," I told him.

"I'm all yours."

Like an animal, I ripped his robe open, then lowered myself on top of him. Liam tilted his head back as he entered me. His hands settled on my hips as I started riding him.

Liam moaned, and it only turned me on more. I started moaning along with him as he hit my g-spot. I felt intense pressure increase as his dick rubbed against the tender spot again and again. It almost felt unbearable. I bet our housemates could hear us, but I didn't care. Right now, I just wanted to forget everything and live in this moment with Liam.

I moved my hips over him and he thrust upward, moving with me in perfect synchrony. Over and over again, he moved into me, his dick pushing up against that sensitive area. He closed his eyes, and his hands traveled upward to my breasts. He gasped, like he forgot the nipple clamps were there, then relaxed back into the pillow as he squeezed my breasts.

"Oh God," I moaned. This was amazing. I'd never been so sensitive to his touch. It was like every nerve was firing off, making the feelings ten times more powerful. I quickened the pace of my hips... and spiraled into a mind-blowing orgasm. As I cried out his name, Liam flipped me over and thrust into me, intensifying the orgasm at the same time he reached his peak.

It was another half hour and two orgasms later before we finally slumped onto the bed side-by-side. We were both breathing really hard, but it'd been totally worth it.

I turned my head to look at Liam. "Liam?"

He relaxed into the bed and let out a blissful sigh. "*Pawee?*"

"I like Imogen's place already," I said. "I think we're going to be happy here."

Liam took my hand and squeezed it to his chest. "Wherever you're at, *pawee*, is where I'm home."

I HADN'T BEEN LYING when I said we'd be happier at Imogen's, but over the next two weeks, it felt like we were playing some sort of charade. Everyone was quiet and worked on their own things to occupy their minds.

Liam and I had promised each other we'd work through our issues together, but it was like neither of us wanted to bring it up— like we were worried talking about our problems would shatter this beautiful, perfect picture we had where we were safe and comfortable. The nightmares continued to assault me, and though Liam tried to hide it, I was pretty sure he was still having them, too.

*I was back inside the burning castle, but instead of my family walking toward me down the grand staircase, it was my grandparents.*

*"Sophia!" my grandfather called. "You must come with us."*

*"But the fire!" I screamed back. "We have to put it out."*

*"There's no time," my grandmother insisted.*

*Before I could blink, Esis squealed at my feet as a large winged creature swooped out of the air. It was a cockatrice, and its razor-sharp talons were aimed straight at my grandparents.*

*"No!" I screamed, but it was too late. The cockatrice's claws sliced straight through the two of them in a single swipe. Their bodies crumbled to the ground, and they fell down the stairs, organs peeling out. They came to a stop at my feet, their lifeless eyes staring up at me.*

*I threw my hands over my mouth and started crying as my knees buckled beneath me. "Grandma! Grandpa!"*

*I shook the both of them. I didn't expect them to move, but a second later, my grandfather's eyes shot open. I jumped back.*

*"Sophia," he strained. "Sophia, you have to come back!"*

My eyes shot open, and a horrible nausea slammed into my gut. I jumped out of bed and raced down the stairs, stomach reeling.

I barely made it to the bathroom before last night's dinner flew out of my mouth and landed in the toilet. I gagged for a few minutes longer before I finally stopped retching.

"Ugh," I groaned as I sat down. I was already starting to feel better now that I'd thrown up. I hated to admit it, but the stress was really starting to get to me.

Esis ran into the room behind me and jumped into my lap. He pressed his paw to my face, and the nausea subsided. I sat there for a few seconds longer until I heard the sound of soft footsteps padding in the hallway.

I looked up to see Imogen and Sassy at the door. Imogen pushed it open a little wider, revealing the sullen look on her face. "You okay, Sophia?"

I swallowed, though it tasted horrible. "I'm fine. Just a bad dream."

Imogen sighed and stepped into the room. Sassy nudged my hand with her nose, until I moved it aside and let her snuggle into my lap with Esis.

Imogen crossed her arms and leaned against the vanity. "Sophia, I know I haven't said anything, but I'm really worried about you."

"Don't be," I told her. "It's nothing."

"That's not true," she said. "You've been having these nightmares all year, and they've gotten worse since we left Kinpago. Don't you remember what Hattie said?"

"The tarot card reader?" I asked. Honestly, I hadn't really thought about the tarot cards since we'd gotten that reading.

Imogen nodded and knelt on the floor so we were at the same level. "Remember? She drew the Devil for you."

"Imogen, those were just cards," I argued. "They didn't mean anything."

"But they did, Sophia," she said. "The Miriamic Coven has magic, and witches use tarot cards to show the way. Hattie is half-witch, so what she said has to be true. She said that to move on, you have to face your demons. Are you facing them, or ignoring them?"

Silence hung in the air for several seconds. I dropped my head, because what she said hit too close to home. It was stupid, because this was exactly what I told Liam he had to do, and I couldn't even do it myself. How was I supposed to help him if I couldn't help myself?

"I wouldn't say I've been ignoring them," I said, but I could hear the lie in my own voice.

Imogen sighed. "Look, it's going to be hard, Sophia. But if you let me, I want to help."

"Im, I don't think you can."

"Just let me try," she begged.

I contemplated her words for a few seconds. It *would* be nice to stop feeling this way all the time— like I was trapped in my own body and couldn't even breathe.

Finally, I nodded. "What did you have in mind?"

"I thought we could talk about it before the guys wake up," she suggested.

I really didn't want to, but Imogen was right. I had to face my demons at some point. And if I tried helping myself before helping Liam, maybe it'd go smoother when we finally opened up to each other.

"We can try," I agreed.

Imogen took my hand and helped me to my feet. She led me into the living room and told me to lie down on the couch. Esis and Sassy curled up by the fireplace, even though there was no fire going. Imogen sat in the chair next to me and crossed her legs, like she was a therapist or something.

"Sophia," she said calmly. "I want you to close your eyes and think back to the night of the riots."

"You mean the night at Orenda?" I asked.

"No," she replied. "Return to the night of the New Year's Powwow, in the Kinpago town square."

I swallowed the lump in my throat. Fire flashed behind my lids, and my heart started to race as I saw images of lifeless bodies all around me. I could still hear the crunch of bone as Ben and Marcee were dropped out of the sky. I winced.

Imogen touched my shoulder. "It's okay. I'm right here."

I grabbed her hand and squeezed it tight. She gasped, but I didn't loosen my grip. When I thought back to the riots, images started assaulting me from all angles. I saw the manticore above me as it tried to kill me, and the Blessing Tree alight in flames. I saw the Task Force ripping mine and Liam's Spirit Art in half. I saw the Great Hall crumbling to pieces, and Chieftess Annette shoving an arrow into Liwanu's heart. I heard the cries of Alric as he was burned to flames and saw my grandparents being torn to pieces in front of me.

"No!" I shouted, shooting to my feet.

Water dropped from my face and onto my nightgown. I didn't even realize I was crying until then.

Imogen's face paled. "Sophia, I'm only trying to help."

I wiped the tears from my eyes. "I know, Im. I'm just not ready yet, okay?"

She stared at me, shell-shocked. "Sophia, I'm only trying to get you to face what happened. It's a part of your life that you can't keep shutting out. You need to find a way to accept it so you can move on."

I stared at her, trying to keep the lump in my throat at bay. "I will. Just... not now."

The stairs creaked above our heads, and Jonah came into view. He stretched and yawned really loudly. "What's going on down here?"

I put on a passive face and said, "Nothing."

I scooped Esis up and went straight for the back porch, where I could cry by myself and didn't have to admit to anyone that I still didn't have it together.

❧

"Imogen, you have the *best* taste in houses," Jonah said one morning while Imogen and I were eating breakfast on the deck. We sat on the patio furniture, a pan of scrambled eggs and bacon between us on the table.

Jonah was sitting in the hot tub with his arms up on either side of him. Squeaks looked like she wanted to get in, too, but she was too big. Julian and Sassy stood on the edge and splashed in the water, but Esis stayed put at my side. I think he was scared of the water, since he couldn't swim.

Liam was upstairs sleeping. He did that a lot these days.

"I *know* I have great taste," Imogen said proudly as she popped a bite of toast in her mouth. "It's who I am."

"Yeah, but this hot tub, these trees..." Jonah gestured around him, then closed his eyes and inhaled deeply. "This air..."

"I know, it's great," Imogen said. "You better enjoy it while it lasts."

"While it lasts?" Jonah asked. "I'm staying here forever."

I snorted. "No you're not. There aren't enough hot guys around willing to screw you."

Jonah chuckled. "True that."

We were all getting cabin fever. We'd left a few times to buy food, but we tried to keep our trips into town as minimal as possible. Imogen had been working on fashion projects to occupy her time, or trying to help me with my issues, though it hadn't helped much at all. Jonah had spent most of his time practicing his soccer kicks in the driveaway with our Familiars, working out, or watching sports. When Liam wasn't sleeping, he was weaving baskets from supplies he found in Imogen's craft room, or reading. I spent a lot of time soaking in the hot tub, studying up on photography, or practicing my Anichi magic.

As nice as this was, it was starting to get boring.

I poked my food on my plate, but Esis snuck up between my arms and snatched a piece of toast off me. He ran away and stood at the steps and shoved it in his mouth. At least *he* was eating. I didn't have much of an appetite this morning.

"Speaking of leaving," I began. "How long do you think we'll be here?"

Imogen took a long, contemplative breath. "I'm not sure. We've been here six weeks already. Eventually we're going to have to go looking for our families."

Jonah climbed out of the hot tub and wrapped a towel around his waist. "This again? Im, we don't even know where to start."

"But we have to try," she snapped.

Jonah sat down beside us and started filling an empty plate with scrambled eggs.

"Jonah's right," I said. "We have no idea where to begin, and we can't go back to Kinpago and wait for them. Not when the Task Force is swarming town and wants our heads."

Imogen bit her lip. "I know. I'm still working things out."

I pushed my plate away from me. "While you work on that, I'm going to practice my magic some more. Esis, do you want to help me?"

Esis looked up to me with an expression of complete guilt. His cheeks were stuffed so full that crumbs were falling out of his mouth.

I stepped off the deck and stood in the driveway. It was completely bordered by a forest of thick trees, so I never felt unsafe when I practiced my Anichi powers outside. That was the one good thing about having so much free time at Imogen's house. I'd had lots of time these last few weeks to practice my powers. It was really helping to calm me, too.

I took a few deep breaths, then tugged on my Anichi magic and brought it to the surface. I thought of Liam, and a hundred memories flashed through my mind— the day he took me up the mountain to teach me of my heritage, the time we screwed in the Toaqua dorms, when we'd gone bungee jumping... amidst all the chaos since I'd learned I was Hawkei, there'd been some really good times.

I settled on the memory of fooling around in the Commons, when our relationship was still forbidden and Ezra almost caught us. It was before everything in our lives took a shit. Looking back on it filled me with warmth.

Light glowed in my palm, and I swirled my hands around each other until the light formed a solid ball. Last week, Jonah had suggested I try throwing it to see what it'd do, but every time I tried, it just fizzled out. This time, I'd get it.

I aimed my focus on a nearby tree, then shot the ball of light outward. It flew through the air, but it only made it halfway to my target before it disappeared.

"Whoa!" Jonah cried. "Sweetheart, not so close to the truck."

Imogen ignored him. "You're doing better, Sophia."

Esis jumped in front of me and clapped. I bent down to his level and ran my hands across his horns, which were so big by now it was hard to think of him as a baby anymore. He'd kind of bulked out, too. I had a sneaking suspicion he'd been watching Jonah work out and was trying to copy him. Last week, I saw him helping Jonah pile wood for the fireplace. It was funny, watching him pick up tiny sticks and little logs, but he did his best to help.

"Why don't you give it a shot, buddy?" I asked. "Grandpa said you should be able to do it, since you're Anichi. You can heal, so you've got to be able to produce light, too."

Esis chittered proudly and reached out his paws to me. Nothing happened. He glanced down at them like he was shocked. He shook his head and clapped his paws, like banging on them would make them work.

I chuckled. "We'll work on it, buddy."

The sound of the sliding glass door met my ears, and Liam stomped onto the deck. Jonah opened his mouth to say something, but Liam breezed right past him. His eyebrows were knitted together, and his lips were tight. In his hand, he held a notebook.

My stomach dropped.

"Why didn't you tell me about this, Sophia?" he demanded, shoving it in my direction. "I thought we weren't keeping secrets anymore."

I took it from him, but I'd otherwise totally frozen up. "W-we're not," I replied. How did I even begin to explain this to him?

Imogen rushed over to us. "What's going on?"

I ignored her and looked to Liam. "What were you doing going through my stuff?"

"I was double checking to see if I had any meds left," he said. "It fell out of your bag."

"And you just thought you'd read it without asking?" I huffed.

"The pages fell open," he snapped back.

I tried not to get mad, but I wasn't sure I believed him. It was like he was purposely snooping through my stuff.

"What's in it?" Jonah asked. He reached out for the notebook, but I snatched it away.

Silence settled over the yard for a few moments. Everyone looked at me for an explanation.

"I'm not mad you want to do this." Liam's tone softened. "I'm mad you didn't *tell* me, Sophia. So why'd you hide it from me?"

My shoulders fell. "I didn't try to hide it. I just know it's never going to happen."

"What is it?" Jonah begged. He couldn't stand not knowing. "What's not going to happen?"

I sighed and turned to him and Imogen. "Before we left Kinpago, I came up with this plan— that we were going to get the kids out of those camps. I wrote down estimates on how many kids I thought were in the camps, how many Task Force members there would be guarding them, and how many people we'd need to break them out, along with some other stuff. I thought that after we left with Liam's family and were safe for a while, we could get a team together and save the kids. But then the whole execution happened, and we had to leave. I know we can never go back and save them, but—"

Liam's features softened. It was obvious he could tell how much this bothered me and understood why I hadn't shared it with him, not when we'd lost hope. He stepped forward and pulled me into a hug. "Don't say that, *pawee*."

"Say what?" I asked.

"That we can never save them," he stated.

I let out a breath of disbelief. "But we can't. I don't even know where to start anymore. We don't know what's been happening in Kinpago these last few weeks."

Liam took a deep breath. "I don't know how we're going to do it, Sophia, but if you want to break those kids out, we will. It might take some time, but we'll get to them... no matter what."

Tears pricked my eyes. "You mean it?"

Liam nodded. "I mean it. I know this is important to you. I'll make it happen, no matter what."

I was so happy and elated at his vow. It gave me hope that maybe things weren't as bad as they seemed, and we could turn things around.

But just that moment, a wave of nausea rolled over me.

I held up a finger. "Thanks, Liam, but if you'll just excuse me a second."

Liam didn't have a chance to respond. I ran into the house. I swung the bathroom door shut behind myself and knelt over the toilet, gagging. I wanted to puke, but nothing came out.

Shit. What was with these nausea spells hitting me all the time lately? And not just when I was stressed. It was when I was happy, too. It wasn't like I had freaking morning sickness—

My body stilled as the thought crossed my mind. Instantly, I started doing the calculations in my head.

*No. No, no, no, no, no.*

I hadn't been tracking my period since we'd left Kinpago. With everything else going on, it was the last thing on my mind. But I *must've* missed it by now... or maybe I'd missed it twice?

*Fuck!* I knew I always wanted a baby, but not now! Not when we were on the run. What would happen to a baby if the Task Force found us? I couldn't bring a child into this world right now, not when my world was on the brink of collapse.

*Don't jump to conclusions. It's just the stress,* I told myself.

I knew that could happen. Back in high school, my friend Emily had missed her period once when her parents were going through a divorce— and she was still a virgin.

But I *had* gone off my birth control after the pharmacy refused to fill Biyami prescriptions. Then again, maybe it had something to do with the hormones. They must've been all over the place now that I wasn't taking my pills— not to mention I'd been completely freaked out these past few weeks.

That must've been it. Because we all knew Liam was sterile. I knew I'd never have kids. So what was I worried about?

Nothing. I had nothing to worry about. This didn't even warrant a pregnancy test, because there was no chance in hell I was pregnant.

I closed the toilet lid and sat on it. My hand settled on my belly. A warm sensation settled in my heart when I thought of the possibility of carrying a child, but I quickly shut it down.

I couldn't do this. I couldn't work up hope only to be crushed by utter disappointment. I wouldn't be heartbroken again.

Liam and I couldn't have babies. I'd already had to accept that. I couldn't go back to thinking it might be a possibility, because it would only crush me all over again when I realized the truth. I'd never be a mother. I had to let that dream go.

A light knock sounded at the door, and Liam's voice came from the other side of it. "You okay, *pawee?*"

I wiped my nose with a tissue I pulled from the counter. "Yeah. I will be."

And it was true. Whatever happened next, I was ready for it. I had to be.

I didn't have any other choice.

# Liam

FIVE

I needed space— even from my friends. Being trapped in this little house was really starting to wear on me.

And though I hated to admit it, I needed space from Sophia.

Early the morning of May eighteenth, I walked beside the river until the house was mostly shielded by the trees and I felt like I could breathe. Julian soared behind me, diving around trees until I came to a stop at a wide expanse of the creek. He perched in the branches above and looked down in interest as I started manipulating the water. I played with it, absent of thought as I created thin streams that twisted in the air.

I didn't know how I was going to keep my promise to Sophia that we were going to save those kids. What she didn't know was those camps bothered me just as much as they did her. It was probably the cruelest thing the Elders had come up with. If I couldn't stop this war, I at least wanted to set those kids free.

But I didn't know how. I felt useless. I was just one man. What could I do against an all-powerful government, one that was willing to hurt the people I loved in order to suit its agenda?

I'd always promised myself growing up that if something terrible happened in the tribe, I'd do everything in my power to stop it. But I didn't realize what it would actually be like once the situation arrived. Most things were out of my hands. Anything I could do something about would most likely get me killed.

I needed help. Others needed to rise up. But Kinpago never would.

We'd relied on the people of the tribe to protest and get involved before things got this bad, but nobody did anything. The Defortai had sat back and watched as Biyami were tortured and sacrificed. Nobody had made a stand, and things couldn't change unless people were willing to sacrifice everything for what they believed.

I didn't know if I was willing to do that anymore. Fuck the Hawkei. They deserved what they got.

When I heard someone calling my name, I sighed and returned to the house. In the kitchen,

Jonah was making breakfast. All he was wearing were bunny slippers and tight-ass boxers with purple hearts on them that didn't fail to show everything. He hummed as he poured batter into the waffle maker and turned over the bacon, like some nineteen fifties housewife.

Jonah walking around mostly naked was something we'd all long gotten used to, but it didn't make it any less annoying. Squeaks lay on the kitchen floor, a collection of beer cans around her hooves. I scowled as I saw Jonah down a Budweiser.

"Do you *really* need a beer at ten a.m.?" I complained.

"It's a holiday, man. Party's gotta start early. Imogen, we need more beer!" he called out around the corner.

"I *just* bought a twelve-pack!" Imogen's indigent voice could be heard from a room down the hall, and Sassy gave a bark.

"Guess what day it is!" Jonah wiggled his eyebrows at me.

"I don't care," I grumbled.

"Happy Ancestors' Day!" Imogen cheered as she entered the kitchen. She seemed chipper this morning. She squeezed Sassy in her arms, and the fox gave a yip. Julian flew to one of the kitchen chairs and perched on it, waiting for me to sit down.

Sophia shuffled in. Esis sat on her shoulder, rubbing her neck. There were bags under her eyes. She looked really tired.

"Jonah, *please* put some clothes on." Sophia rubbed her face in exhaustion as she came into the kitchen. She sat at the kitchen table and put her head in her arms.

"No can do, babycakes," Jonah replied. He sat a full stack of waffles on the table. "Eat up."

Jonah cooked most of the time, with Sophia and Imogen occasionally subbing in to give him days off. Squeaks dug into her stack of twelve waffles, while Sassy politely chewed on one. Jonah and Imogen seemed more than happy to chat and get excited about all the Ancestors' Day traditions they still intended on following, but it was clear Sophia and I weren't in the mood to celebrate.

"Jonah, these waffles are amazing!" Imogen sang. "You're the best cook ever."

"Perks of having shit parents who make you fend for yourself," he replied with a full mouth.

I fed Julian bits of my waffle. He snapped them up, accidentally biting my fingers in the process.

"Ow. Watch it," I told him.

He gave a sorry coo and snuggled into my neck. I laughed under my breath. I loved him.

Halfway through breakfast, Sophia got up and opened the fridge. She rummaged through it before her face fell. Esis' eyes widened, like he could sense an impending storm.

"What's wrong?" I asked.

"There's... there's no orange juice left." Sophia's lip wobbled. I saw tears dotting the corner of her eyelids, and all I thought was, *what the fuck?*

"We can get more," Imogen offered, but it was too late. Sophia broke down into sobs. Imogen and Jonah's mouths dropped open in shock as they watched her bawl. Julian's wings sagged.

"*Pawee.*" I got up and wrapped her into my arms. She cried into the front of my shirt. Ancestors, she was acting like not having enough juice in the house was a major crisis— even though I knew that wasn't what this was really about.

"I just... I just can't take one more thing," she wept. She tore out of my arms, running out of the kitchen and onto the deck. I beckoned to Julian, and he flew off the chair and landed on my arm.

"What's with her?" Jonah thumbed in the direction Sophia had gone.

"It's just stress," I mumbled. I followed Sophia. Esis frantically wiped away her tears as she bawled.

"Sophie, it's time to calm down." I rubbed her back, but the tears didn't cease. She'd gone over the edge.

"I know. I'm being so irrational for no reason." She wiped at the tears on her face with the palm of her hand. "It's just... my emotions are everywhere lately."

"You've been through a lot. It's okay." *Though random crying spells aren't exactly reassuring me you're stable,* I thought.

"I don't want to be like this." She sighed, and Esis patted her cheek.

"I know it's hard, but you've gotta stop this. You've been making yourself sick. You throw up whatever you take down. Don't think I haven't noticed," I said.

She took a few deep breaths. "I know. It's over the top for sure."

"You need a distraction. How about we work on your Anichi powers?" *Anything to get her to stop crying.*

Sophia took a few quick breaths. "That sounds like a good plan." Her tears slowed, and she walked off the deck. I followed her into the woods, and she set Esis on a nearby branch as she faced me. Julian flew off my shoulder and perched next to Esis, where the two snuggled up close. They were best buds already and practically inseparable.

"I can expand my shield pretty far now," Sophia said. "Watch."

She raised her hand, and out of her palm bloomed a transparent shield that slightly shimmered in the spring sunlight. It grew until it encompassed the entire area, even the house. It had to have a circumference of fifty feet.

"How long can you hold it?"

"About five minutes." She let the shield drop. "Though I'm still having trouble enclosing my shield around other things."

She focused her attention on a boulder around twenty feet away. A shield wrapped around the rock, but it only held for a moment or two before it wavered and faded completely.

Her shoulders dropped. "I just can't get the hang of this."

"You've been practicing every day. It's not for lack of effort. Think of what you could do when you were just learning your Koigni powers. You could barely sustain a flame. You've only been working with your Anichi powers for a few months. It takes time."

I reached up and took Esis down from the branch, and Julian growled. "Maybe we should practice healing. Watch."

Esis laid his paws on my middle. I felt his warm magic work its way through my body, and the stiffness in my muscles ebbed as the pain gradually resided. The cough that had settled in my lungs this morning eased, and I visibly relaxed.

Sophia came close. "You seem better lately."

"I've been feeling a lot better since we got here," I said. "I've had some time to rest, and Esis' powers are finally strong enough to start working again. Now you try."

I extended a hand. Sophia took it, but when she tried channeling her Spirit into me, all I felt was a tingling sensation lingering at the top of my skin. It was like what I felt when Esis began the healing process.

"You're getting better. I can feel your magic trying to change my body," I encouraged.

"I can't seem to get farther than that." She scowled. "It's not like Koigni magic. The Fire just does whatever I tell it to. With Spirit, I can feel your Water magic fighting against mine, and I can't get past the barrier."

"Healing's the most difficult magic there is. It's beyond complicated to manipulate a supernatural's body system."

"You do it. You can stop someone's heart." She dropped my hand and looked up at me.

"It's easy to destroy things. It's infinitely harder to repair the damage after it's been done." I shrugged half-heartedly. "My Water has to overpower another person's magic by brute force. Healing isn't done that way. It's supposed to be gentle."

"I guess you're right. I just need more practice. I can do *this*, though." Sophia conjured a ball of light, then threw it. It sailed around the area in an arc before it returned to her hand. She tossed it at a nearby tree, and the light sailed through it, sending splinters flying as it made a baseball-sized hole in the center of the trunk.

"Impressive," I noted. Esis was wiggling to get out of my arms. I set him on the ground and said, "Do you think Esis has other Anichi powers, too?"

"That's what I've been wondering. We've been working on it." Sophia stooped down to the earth. "Okay, buddy, show Liam what you've got."

Esis' little face scrunched up in concentration. He rubbed his paws together and focused. A tiny ball of light, no bigger than an inch across, formed in his paws. His eyes lit up in delight, and he gave a warrior cry as he chucked it. It landed pitifully on the ground with a *plop* and vanished.

"Good job, Esis!" Sophia cheered. "That's farther than he's ever gotten."

"You're doing good, little buddy." I reached down and scratched him behind the ears.

Apparently, this was too much for Julian, because he leapt down from the trees and pinned Esis to the ground. The two of them wrestled back and forth, Julian slashing with his claws and Esis trying to choke him out. Julian opened his mouth and revealed his baby teeth, plunging downward to grab Esis' ear.

But before Julian could bite him, Esis *fucking vanished* before our very eyes. Julian froze, his tiny eyes darting this way and that as he looked to where Esis had gone.

"Esis!" Sophia screeched. "Ancestors, what happened to him?"

"Holy shit, where did he go?" I shouted. I turned on the spot, and Sophia frantically started rifling through the leaves.

Just as I was about to wonder if both of us were going nuts, Esis reappeared again, waving.

"What the hell?" I asked. Sophia ran forward and snatched Esis up. She snuggled him affectionately, though he shrugged, like he didn't get what the big deal was.

"What did he just do?" I asked.

As if in response, Esis vanished once again, so we couldn't see him anymore. Sophia's eyes widened.

"I can still feel him. He's in my arms, we just can't see him," Sophia said.

Esis reappeared again and flipped Julian off from where he sat. Julian hissed and stuck out his tongue.

"Invisibility must be an Anichi power," I marveled. "Soph, if you could do that, it would really help us."

"Why did Esis never disappear before?" she asked. "There were plenty of situations where invisibility would've helped him stay safe."

"Maybe he couldn't. He must be growing up. The older Familiars get, the stronger they become," I pointed out.

"That must be it." She bit her lip. "How'd you do it, little buddy?"

Esis chattered, as if giving instructions. He scurried up her shoulder. Julian, who was being a baby and wanted attention, wailed at my feet. I bent down and picked him up as Sophia tapped her chin.

"There has to be a method for it," I offered. "All elemental magic has steps to follow."

"Give me some time to think." She paced around the clearing, her brow furrowing in thought. Julian wanted to beat Esis up again, but I held him tightly so he couldn't move. He gave a few whiny puffs of smoke before he looped around my neck and shoulders.

After five minutes, Sophia's expression cleared. "I wonder..."

It was then she disappeared. Her entire body dissolved into thin air, as if she'd just slipped into a different pocket of reality. I knew it was coming, but I was still shocked. I staggered backward as I witnessed Sophia vanish entirely.

She was still there, though, because Esis was still there. It looked like he was floating in mid-air as Sophia became invisible. If I looked very closely, I could see the thin outline of her form shimmering, like her shields did, but if I didn't know what to look for, I could be fooled like she wasn't there at all.

Sophia reappeared moments later. A huge smile spread across her face. "I can't believe it! I did it!"

"How did it feel?" I asked curiously.

"It's hard to explain. It's like I'm here, but I'm not. I feel weightless, warm, and at peace. Sort of... cocooned by my light. I don't know if I really disappear— more or less just control the light around me so you can't see me." She moved Esis to her hands and nuzzled her nose against his. "Thanks for showing me, buddy. You're so smart."

"How'd you figure it out so fast?" I asked. I was surprised she'd managed to do it at all, and on her first try, too.

"I... don't know," she admitted. "Light is an Anichi power, so all I did was take control of the light and bend it around my body."

"You made it look so easy."

She scuffed her shoe on the ground. "I just had the thought that I really wanted to disappear. Forever."

Well, I didn't like that.

A smirk spread across my face. "You want to put that invisibility magic to good use, and play a prank on Jonah and Imogen?"

She gave a devilish giggle. "Would I ever!"

We approached the house, keeping quiet. Julian and Esis settled. Imogen and Jonah were on the porch. Imogen had gotten into the hot tub with Sassy, and Jonah had finally put on clothes. He was lifting weights while Squeaks sang obnoxiously to the music blaring from the speakers sitting on the table.

Sophia snickered. She disappeared. I saw footsteps appear in the dirt as she approached the patio.

Jonah put the weights down and stretched. "So anyway, for the cabaret costumes, I'm thinking black and green. Or maybe red and black?"

Ancestors, was he still talking about that stupid cabaret? We were in hiding. It was never gonna happen.

"Red and black, definitely," Imogen said. "It'll fit the theme better."

Jonah went to reply, but before he could, Imogen screamed. Water had come out of nowhere and splashed her in the face.

Jonah gasped. Seconds later, his workout shorts dropped to his ankles, like someone had yanked them down. I knew it was Sophia. I had to put a hand over my mouth to keep from dying as Jonah stood gaping in his boxers. Squeaks leapt to her feet in alarm, and Sassy floundered in the tub.

"Holy crap, this place is possessed!" Jonah wailed as he bent down to pull on his shorts.

"The realtor didn't say anything about the place being haunted!" Imogen complained.

"Well, they definitely lied to you. It's *obviously* haunted with a pervert who wants to fuck us," Jonah shot back. His expression changed. "On second thought, I haven't gotten any in a while."

He turned back toward the house and cupped his hands over his mouth. "Hey, ghost! If you're willing, I'm DTF!"

Sophia reappeared. She doubled over laughing, tears streaming down her face. Esis and Julian gave happy cries as they ran onto the porch. I had to grab on to the banister at the porch stairs to keep from falling over in laughter.

"Sophia, what the hell was that?" Imogen asked in astonishment. She drifted to the edge of the tub. Jonah made a double knot in the ties around his shorts, like he was worried she'd do it again.

"I've... got invisibility powers..." she forced out between laughs. "Esis showed me. It's an Anichi power. Watch."

Sophia vanished and reappeared again. Imogen clapped in delight, while Jonah seemed stunned.

"Sophia, that's great!" Imogen squealed. "Do you realize how we can put this to good use?"

"Wow. And you thought a *good use* of your new, fancy magic would be to expose me to the entire world?" Jonah shook his head, though the corners of his mouth switched. "Nice one, guys."

"Invisibility is easy for me. It's way simpler than other forms of Anichi magic," Sophia said. "It shouldn't take me long to learn how to sustain it for a long time."

"I swear if you prank me again, it's gonna start a war," Jonah warned. Sophia hissed with laughter.

Sophia practiced her invisibility until dinner time. I watched her, sitting on the deck and working on a complicated basket pattern while Imogen and Jonah prepared the complicated holiday meal. By the time they called us in for dinner, Sophia appeared accomplished. Her face was flustered, but her eyes were bright, which I hadn't seen in a long time.

"I think learning invisibility is going to help me with my other Anichi powers. It gives me a better understanding," she said as we entered the kitchen.

"That's good," I replied, but my mind was on other matters. My eyes lingered over the set-up Jonah and Imogen had made. There was salmon with pine nuts, bread made with mesquite powder, shellfish, steamed acorns with berries, and a buckwheat cake.

All the traditional Ancestors' Day food was here. It was just like my mother used to make.

It kind of made me sick to look at.

We sat in silence. The Familiars gathered around the table with us. Julian perched on my chair, and Imogen looked at Jonah. "Would you like to do the honors?"

"Of course." Jonah took Sophia and Imogen's hands to begin the prayer. Imogen and Sophia extended their hands for me to take, but for some reason, I didn't.

I don't know what was wrong with me. I felt frozen.

And angry. Very, very angry.

Sophia noticed the pause. Her eyes were pleading with me to go along with it and not make this difficult. Esis tilted his head and chittered, while Squeaks and Sassy both gave hurried noises— as if telling me to hurry up and say the holiday prayer, so we could eat. Julian sensed my hesitation and gave a supportive nudge of his head to my chin.

"Liam, come on," Jonah said when I hesitated to join hands. "Let's pray."

When I still didn't move, Imogen added, "We need to thank the ancestors before we begin the meal. It's tradition."

*Tradition.* That one little word set me off. I didn't want to ruin this meal that Jonah and Imogen had worked so hard on, but at the same time, there was something in me that was at an impasse. I just couldn't do this.

I shot up from the table. "No," I said indignantly. "No, I'm not going to *thank the ancestors* for something they should've provided in the first place. You want me to be *grateful* for this? No way."

"We should be thankful," Imogen insisted, and she pulled her hand out of Jonah's. "We have food, a safe place to stay, and each other. Do you know how many Biyami would kill to have that right now?"

"Im, we have this stuff because *you* made sure we did. The ancestors had nothing to do with it. We should be thanking you, not them," I spat.

"We *should* thank them! They helped me do this!" Imogen shouted. "They gave me the foresight to know we needed a plan, and I followed it."

"And what about all the other Biyami out there, huh? Why aren't they worthy to have shelter, or safety, or something to eat? Why aren't they worthy? Why do the ancestors favor us and not them? Why are so many of them dead, and why are we still alive?"

I crossed my arms. "I'll tell you why. Because we got lucky and you were smart enough to be prepared. That's the only difference."

Sophia didn't say anything. I could see in her eyes that she didn't want to upset me further, but that she agreed with Imogen. Jonah was still holding her hand. He gave it a supportive squeeze, as if telling Sophia he was sorry for how I was behaving. It just pissed me off more.

"This isn't the ancestors' fault. Or the Great Spirit's," Jonah said. "They didn't cause the Elders to do what they did."

"But they had to have seen it coming! They could've intervened, but they did nothing!" I insisted.

"Maybe what's happening is necessary," Jonah said lowly.

"Necessary?" I gave a laugh that almost sounded insane. "You think it's necessary for children to die."

"I didn't say that, but the tribe was at a point it needed to change. Maybe this was the only way," Jonah argued.

"I refuse to believe that." My voice was full of spite and hate. "Look, you guys, I don't want to make a big deal out of this, but I can't participate. Not this time."

"You don't have to. But we don't need to hear your rant on a day like today," Imogen insisted. She didn't need to tell me she thought I was ruining this, because I could see it written all over her face.

But the floodgates were already open. Now that the dam had broken, everything came welling up and tumbling out. "I think I'm finally seeing the light. Religion has caused a shit ton of problems for everybody in this world, including the Hawkei. Maybe it's time we just did away with our faith altogether. Look how the Elders used the ancestors to get the Hawkei to believe them. It's just a tool to control people."

"You think someone like *Oleander* has a spiritual bone in his body?" Imogen's voice began to rise. "He doesn't give a shit about the ancestors or the Great Spirit, only what their name can do to bolster his power."

"Exactly!" I shouted. "He said the ancestors were on his side, and clearly they are, because he's still running the show."

"I'm not going to blame a bunch of deities for something the Elementai did. Something the Elementai *chose* to do." Jonah's eyes narrowed.

"How do we even know the Great Spirit is even real? I've never seen him. Have you?" My tone was accusatory.

"Liam, we see our ancestors all the time. They arrive when we summon them. We have proof of our spirit guides," Imogen said, with a wayward glance at Jonah. Now she was making it sound like I was totally nuts.

"We have proof that *magic* exists. That's it. How do we know the rest of it isn't some big illusion? Some power we've tapped into to bring back memories of the past?" I questioned.

At this point, Sophia let go of Jonah's hand and slowly began to rise. "Liam, I know you're having questions, and it's okay to doubt." She took a deep breath. "But you're saying things you don't mean right now."

I gave a disgusted noise and shook my head. "I need some space." I hurried out the door. Julian flew behind me. I let the screen slam on the way out.

I went to the river. When I got there, I shot out my hand, and a burst of energy caused the water to splash over the sides and slam against a tree. It made me feel a little better, but ultimately did nothing. It wasn't until I looked at Julian, who appeared worried at my feet, that I realized what was *really* bothering me.

I was angry at Nashoma. And that was a weird feeling to have. He was an ancestor. He could've intervened in all this. He could've saved us, stop my dad from dying.

But he chose to stand by and watch.

Maybe he was mad at me, because I had Julian now. Maybe he thought I replaced him and didn't need him anymore.

That had to be it. There was no other explanation. I collapsed by the river and sat there for a while, watching the water rush by while Julian sat in my lap and cooed.

When it grew dark, I heard the sound of leaves crunching beside me. Sophia sat by my side. She'd left Esis behind. She remained at a distance as she asked, "Do you want to talk about it?"

"No," I scoffed. "Do I ever?"

"I think you should. You really hurt Imogen and Jonah's feelings."

My stomach dropped. I was such a prick. "I know," I said regrettably. "I'm sorry."

"What set you off?" Her voice was full of concern. "It's just a prayer."

"It's not that. It's the intention of the whole thing." I didn't know if I was explaining myself well.

"It helps me when we pray at dinner. My grandparents used to do that before we ate. It helps me feel close to them." I could hear the plain grief in her voice as she spoke.

My voice dropped. "Yeah, well, my family used to do that, too. But you know what? Praying hurts. It just reminds me that my dad is gone and I have no idea where the rest of my loved ones are. I have no idea if I'll ever see them again.

And I can't sit there and do something my family used to do together while having it shoved in my face that the ancestors see all of this and do nothing."

"That can't be true. There must be a bigger plan."

"Open your eyes, Soph. The Great Spirit abandoned us. I hardly believe he or the ancestors ever cared at all."

The hopelessness was evident in my voice. Fuck, I sounded like such a sad sack. I needed to get it together.

"You can't give up. That's not the Liam I know," she objected.

"Then maybe you don't know me at all." I didn't mean to say that— I didn't even think it was true— but for some reason, it slipped out.

Sophia got to her feet. Her face had turned slightly red, and her knuckles turned white as her hands became fists. "I can't fucking believe you," she snapped.

Great. She'd gone from gentle to *totally pissed* in two point five seconds. I couldn't handle this.

I got up, too. My temper was already sparking. "I know we're close, but you can't deny there's distance between us now. There's a wedge, and it's because..."

"Say it," she snapped. "Fucking say it."

"No." I refused to say what we were both thinking out loud.

"Then I will. You're angry at me because I burned you. You think if I hadn't stopped you, your dad would still be alive." A bitter tear ran down her face. "Well, let me tell you something. I wonder if I should've. Maybe I should've let you open that door, and the Elders would've killed us all. Maybe then we would've died where we belonged, in a place we *loved*."

"It doesn't matter! We're here now. We can't go back and change the past."

"But you wish we could," Sophia snapped. "I didn't know if I made the right decision, but I had seconds to decide! And in that moment, you had left me no choice. I either had to hurt you, or I had to hurt all of us. It was an impossible decision, but I did the best I could."

"We could've fought back! We could've saved him!" I shouted.

"I'm sorry, Liam, but you're in denial. There was no saving your dad," Sophia pleaded. "If we had intervened, we were all going to die, and he told us to run! He knew he was going to die! He sacrificed himself for you, to give us time to escape!"

I couldn't hold back anymore. "I'm sick of people dying for me. Maybe if you had practiced your shield magic more—"

Her face went pale white, and I regretted saying the words the minute they were out of my mouth. "*That's* what we're resulting to now? This is all on me?"

"No, that's not what I—"

"That's exactly what you meant," she snapped. She gave an angry noise. "You know what, Liam? If that's what you think, you can just take the ring back."

A horrified feeling caused my stomach to plummet. "Are you serious? What, so you don't want to get married now?"

She gave a hollow laugh. "Well, when your husband blames you for the death of his father, it doesn't say much for your marriage, does it?"

"I don't want to blame you! I don't *want* to be angry with you!" I shouted. "Logically, I know it's not your fault! You did the right thing!"

"But your heart tells you otherwise. You don't have to deny it, Liam. It's all over your face," she seethed. "You've barely *touched* me since we've been here! It's like you can't stand to look at me."

"That's not true! I just... need time," I offered, strained.

"You withhold from me when you're hurting. It's what you do. I can't deal with you acting like I'm not alive." She turned away from me and put her face in her hands.

Julian looked between us, not understanding what we were fighting about. He curled inward and sucked his wings to his body. He was acting like the argument was his fault, and I felt guilty about that, too.

"Soph, you use my body as an escape. And I'm fine with that, but you can't expect me to jump whenever you say so!" I objected.

"That's not the point! It's not about sex, Liam. I can deal with not getting sex, but I can't deal with you constantly pushing me away when you're hurting. I can't be ignored by you. You withdraw when you're upset. You run away and hide."

Sophia took a step away from me. "You shut yourself off from me, and then the intimacy is just gone. It's like when we make love, you're not even there anymore! You're somewhere else. I can see it in your eyes. And you won't open up and tell me what's wrong!"

"It's how I deal with shit. I keep people at a distance and learn to process. It's the only way I know." This whole argument made me feel like she blamed me for everything, and it really fucking sucked.

Sophia scoffed. "You put everything into a box until you self-destruct. Then everyone around you has to deal with the implosion. And though you're trying to protect everyone, all you're doing is hurting the people you love most."

That stung. Julian crept against the ground and rubbed against my ankle, like he was trying to get me to forgive *him*. The move broke my heart. "Stop acting like I'm the problem. We promised each other to work on our issues, and we haven't done a thing since we've gotten here."

Sophia shook her head. "I don't even know if you want to."

"I'm not the only one putting it off. You say I'm on edge, look at you! You're a complete mess!" My voice was starting to rise, but I dropped it. I could argue with Sophia, but I wouldn't full-out scream at her. That wasn't okay— no matter how angry we were at each other.

Sophia noticed the change in the argument. She stiffened, then took a few steps back before she said, "Maybe you're not the one who needs space. Maybe it's me."

"Soph—"

She disappeared. I turned on the spot, looking everywhere for her, but she'd turned invisible and left.

She'd just walked out on me. I never thought she'd do that. She wasn't that kind of person.

But apparently she was. We'd said some pretty awful stuff we couldn't take back.

The worst part of it was, it was all the truth. Both of us were being honest. At least it was out in the open and we didn't have to hide it anymore.

At least she hadn't taken her ring off and thrown it at me. Julian made a weeping sound. I picked him up and hugged him. "I'm sorry, Jules. Maybe this is all my fault."

He purred and nuzzled into my neck. I heard the sound of footsteps. My heart leapt, hoping Sophia had come back, but it wasn't her. It was Imogen and Jonah. Both of them looked miserable.

"We could hear you two all the way from the house," Jonah said solemnly. "Yelling at each other isn't okay. You guys gotta work out your shit, man."

I sighed. "Yeah. I know we do."

Imogen took a step closer. In her hand, she held a small bundle of white leaves, bound with a red thread, and a deerskin bag.

"This is all the white sage I have," Imogen said, and she pressed it into my hand. "You need it to perform the invoking ceremony and summon your ancestors. I don't have enough for all of us. You deserve it, Liam. It's yours."

"No, Im. You keep it." I tried to put it back in her hands, but she refused to take it.

"You lost your chance on Ancestors' Day to talk to Anna last year. You *need* to do this," Imogen insisted. She closed my fingers over the white sage before giving me the deerskin bag. "When you're done, come back and make things right with Sophia. We'll be waiting."

"Aren't you guys gonna stick around?" I asked.

"This is something you need to do for yourself." Imogen gave me a hug. "We love you, Liam. Please do this for us."

Jonah and Imogen left. By this time, it was growing dark. I reached into the deerskin bag and found flint. I made a small fire, then looked around for a flat rock I could use as an altar. I found one and carried it beside the fire.

I took a small bowl out of the bag. I drew water from the river, then placed it onto the altar. I lit the white sage and swept it around the area to cleanse the space before I placed it on the altar beside the water.

You were supposed to have something from one of your ancestors to place on the altar, but I didn't have anything. I'd lost it all when we fled Orenda Academy. Something personal could sub in its place, but I didn't have that, either.

Julian tugged on my arm. I looked down and saw that he was offering up one of his own red scales.

"Thanks, Jules." I placed the scale on the altar, then sat down and crossed my legs. Julian scrambled onto my lap. I closed my eyes and tried to open my heart up to the spirits, but it was hard. I really didn't want to do this, but I'd promised Jonah and Imogen. I couldn't let resentment get in the way. I cleared my soul out as best I could and tried to remain open as I uttered the summoning prayer.

"*Ei suma Anna Cedrick, andii au ei anichi un ama haq ina bian ei. Ei yoqua am naadu es ei deeyai te hode au ei inavita, un soqua am hadiple di hasincri ala-tione.*"

*I summon Anna Cedrick, blood of my spirit and mother who existed before me. I seek her guidance as I journey the path of my life, and ask she fill this sacred gathering.*

When I opened my eyes again, a figure emerged from the trees— a long-legged white she-wolf, her form shimmering and transparent. She was beautiful to observe, like she was made of nothing but starlight and colors.

The she-wolf sat by the fire, directly across from me. The wind rustled as a woman took her place. A beautiful brown-skinned girl, with a kind face and two long black braids, sat parallel to me with a welcoming expression.

It struck me then just how young Anna was. She'd died so early— in her twenties. Would that be my fate? Would I be dead before I hit thirty?

When speaking with your ancestors, it was best to communicate in Hawkei if you knew how. I abandoned English and turned to the language of the tribe. *"Welcome, Anna. I am open to your knowledge and what you have to say."*

Anna's eyes glimmered. She seemed even more alive than I was. *"I greet you, Da-ahi Mitoh Anichi, son of my blood. Do you know why I volunteered to be your spirit guide?"*

*"I supposed the answer was obvious. You were sick, like me,"* I offered.

She gave a hearty laugh. *"I was a lot like you. I am here to prevent you from making the same mistakes I once did,"* Anna said kindly.

*"Can you tell me more?"* I leaned forward. The shadows flickered off of Anna's face as she smiled.

*"My death was preventable. I did not have to pass so young, but the consequences are of my own design,"* she began. *"I did not accept that I was unwell. I fought against what I had, but in the wrong way. I did not tend to my body and my spirit, and it led to my downfall."*

*"So you didn't take care of yourself."*

*"No. I did not want to admit I was not like the others in the tribe, though my father tried to change my mind. I did not want to accept I was unwell."*

That did sound a lot like me. *"So even the Anichi couldn't do anything about our condition."*

*"Yes. Even the most powerful healers in the tribe could not heal me if I refused to heal myself,"* Anna stated. *"I passed from an influenza that swept through the area. It was devastating, but preventable. I would've lived on if I had accepted I needed more care. But I did not, and I left my son stranded as an orphan. You nearly made the same mistake mere weeks ago."*

Her situation sounded a lot like the pneumonia I'd had. I'd been lucky to get over it. *"So you ask that I take care of myself."*

*"More than that. You must accept your path. I know it isn't easy to live on in this way. But being angry that you are what you are will only destroy you,"* she said gently. *"You must come into the full of it and let your anger go. Your condition is a part of you, and fighting against it instead of learning to work with it is a battle you cannot win. It is not something I can explain until you experience it for yourself."*

*"How can I accept this?"* I asked. *"How can I come to terms that I'm not getting any better?"*

*"Your condition has improved your life in more ways than you know,"*

Anna said. *"It has brought great pain, and great sadness. But it has improved your capabilities as a leader. It has caused you to be more compassionate and understanding. Can you say with certainty that if you had not lost Nashoma, if you had not gotten sick, you would've been able to help Sophia with her journey? Would your friends be the same? Would your life?"*

I thought about it. If I wasn't sick and I still had Nashoma, I'd still be in the running for chief. I'd probably still be stuck in a miserable relationship with Mia. I never would've gotten close with Imogen, and would've eventually had to put Jonah at a distance. I probably would've gotten swept up in the Defortai business with the Elders. Hell, I might've even *become* one of them and started hurting people for the "good of the tribe."

And I never would've gotten the chance to love Sophia, which was the biggest consequence of it all.

*"Your illness is a great pain that has brought great joy. I failed to see this when I was alive,"* Anna stated. *"Your illness is not the end of your life, but a new beginning. One that you can even argue has changed your life for the better, even at the result of your suffering. Suffering is far from the worst thing we can experience in this world. It can even lead to good, and be a gift. The true agony is missing out on our calling, our true destiny. What would you have missed if you did not suffer?"*

Shit. I would've missed... a lot. Doing treatments, being ill, feeling like crap all the time wasn't easy. But it'd brought me closer together to the people I loved. When you were sick, you didn't have time to fuck around. What was important and what wasn't became instantly clear. Having a condition that could kill you didn't leave any room for keeping people at a distance, no matter how hard I'd tried.

Being sick had forced me to become vulnerable. And it had forged an unbreakable bond with my friends.

*"So what do you advise? Where do I go from here?"*

*"You must learn to be at peace with your illness, and allow it to become a part of your life once and for all. Not allow it to become who you are, but let it become something that is,"* she said gently. *"Then you will finally be free."*

*"But I don't know what to do. Jonah wants me to be strong, but Sophia wants me to open up. I can't do both,"* I said.

*"Yes you can,"* Anna insisted. *"You must be. All of us have decisions to make in this world. There is a time to be strong and a time to be open."*

*"I'm scared of making the wrong decision,"* I confessed. It felt like I was messing up everything in my life lately.

*"We will never always make the right decision. Even the best one will*

*always contain consequences. If I had not given life to my son, the disease would've died with me."* Anna shrugged. *"But then you would not exist, and neither would hundreds of others. Each crossroad on the path we take in our life affects so many."*

I dropped my gaze in defeat. *"I just feel so alone. I know you understand how I feel, but no one else does. No one knows what it feels like to carry a burden like this."*

*"You are not the only one. There are other Toaqua out there like you."*

*"What!?"* I started. Julian nearly fell out of my lap. *"You mean, there are other people living with my disease?"*

*"Yes. You will find them soon."* Anna's expression was warm like the sun. *"You will not have to endure this alone for much longer."*

My heart beat so frantically I thought it was going to burst. This couldn't be real. There were other people out there like me? It was wholly incomprehensible. I'd been suffering by myself for so long I thought I was the only outlier— a freak of medical science.

Anna's form began wavering against the night. *"My time with you is up, my son. Do not repeat the mistakes I made. Find the good in what's been given to you. Then the war inside yourself will finally end."*

Anna faded away. The white sage had burned out. Julian peeped in my lap. I sat completely still.

That experience had affected me on a profound level. I started scrambling for things. I shoved the remaining items in the deerskin bag and put out the fire before I raced back to the house. Julian followed, his wings beating frantically as he tried to keep up. I couldn't wait to tell the others what I'd experienced.

I flung open the door, but froze when I saw Sophia standing in the hallway. She'd been waiting for me to return. She was leaning against a wall and hugging herself nervously.

When we saw each other, we didn't even need words. Our earlier argument was forgotten and kicked to the side. I tossed the bag to the floor. Sophia ran into my arms, and I embraced her like I never had before. Julian curled around our legs, and Esis chirped happily from Sophia's shoulder.

"I'm so sorry," Sophia murmured. "I never should've threatened to give the ring back. I went too far."

"I forgive you. I said some things I didn't mean, either." I rubbed her arms before I bent down to give her a kiss. "Shit happens. We'll get through it together."

Sophia lifted her head. "Did you talk to Anna? Imogen told me she gave you the sage."

"I did." I took Sophia's hand. "I need to tell you guys everything."

We entered the living room. Imogen and Jonah were watching a fashion show, but looked up when we came in. Both of them looked relieved at the sight of Sophia and I holding hands. The two of us sat on the couch while Imogen leaned forward impatiently.

"So? What did she say?" Imogen asked.

"She... she said there were people like me out there." I said the words in a breathless rush. It felt foolish to say them out loud.

"What? You mean, with your illness?" Sophia's eyes widened.

"Yeah! Apparently, there are other Toaqua alive with Combined Magical Suppression Syndrome. She says I'm going to meet them soon. I mean, I feel bad for them because they have it, but at least I'm not alone, right?" I sounded so excited. It felt strange to feel something other than sadness again.

"Dude, that's great news," Jonah said. "I'm so happy for you."

I was happy for *myself*. Even though I didn't know them yet, the thought that there were people out there who could understand what I was going through was so insanely comforting to me. I had hope again things could get better.

For the first time since we'd left, things started to feel right.

ANOTHER WEEK AND A HALF PASSED. The end of May arrived, and things started to feel different in a way I couldn't explain. For the past few weeks, we'd been hiding— but after talking to Anna, hiding didn't seem like enough anymore. I had the itch to do something that I always got before the group went out to accomplish something important, and I couldn't shake it.

Sophia and I were washing dishes when Imogen and Jonah arrived, carrying grocery bags that they set on the table. Imogen looked thoroughly upset— her face was white, and her eyes were calculating. Sassy gave a curious peep as Imogen shakily sat down, while Squeaks rifled through the bags for alcohol.

"What's wrong now?" I asked as we finished up the last of the dishes. Imogen remained silent.

"Im's card was declined at the store," Jonah said. "It's the first time she's used it since we've been on the run."

"I *know* I have enough money in there!" Imogen burst. "I put enough away to get us by for at least a year after we left. I've budgeted it all."

"Okay. Maybe it was a mistake," Sophia said.

Imogen shook her head. "No. I think this was on purpose."

"You mean..." I put two and two together. "Oleander's probably shut down all Biyami bank accounts." I frowned.

"Yes!" Imogen burst. "I can't get access to our funds, because I'm betting the bastard closed my account and took the money."

"So what do we do?" Sophia asked. Squeaks sat on the floor and grumped there was no beer.

"We have enough cash to get us by for a few more weeks," Jonah offered. "After that... I don't know."

There was silence for a moment. I decided to take charge. "Guys, I've been thinking. We've been here for almost two months now. We have to start making a plan," I said. "I know we needed time to recover after what happened at Orenda Academy, but it's time to pull together. Our families are somewhere out there. We need to begin searching for them."

"Are we ready?" Sophia asked. "I mean, we just lost all our money."

"Maybe that's a sign we should start taking action," I suggested. "We can't stay here forever."

"Looking for our families feels too much like hunting prophecy pieces," Imogen whimpered. "I don't want to fail at that, too. I'm afraid of what we'll find."

I walked across the room and squeezed her shoulder. "I know you're scared, Im. I'm worried about what we'll find, too." The thought of figuring out the rest of my family was dead made my heart skip a beat, but I continued. "But what if they need our help? We need to find them."

"Liam's right. We should do something," Jonah said. "If Oleander shut down all Biyami accounts, he's closing in."

Sophia nodded. "I'll follow wherever Liam leads. Plus, if our families are in a good place, they can help us."

Imogen looked up. She seemed conflicted as she said, "I'm with you. I just hope this is the right decision."

"Then it's settled. We'll have one more day of rest, then tomorrow we'll start searching for our families," I confirmed.

That night felt good. It was nice to have a sense of direction once again. It was almost like we'd been lost ever since we'd recovered the Air piece and didn't know what to do next. We clustered in the living room together to spend our last night of recovery. Jonah sat on the carpet, leaning against

Squeaks and watching a sports game. Imogen worked on hand-stitching the dress she was making, while Sassy slept at her feet. Julian and Esis wrestled on the floor. I sat on the couch, weaving a basket. Sophia had her legs thrown over mine and was working on a sketch. We didn't talk, but it was nice to be together.

The team finally had a goal. We were unified on this. After so long, our lives finally felt normal—

An explosion rocked the house. The right wall blew out. Flames ignited and roared, claiming the drywall for its own.

Sophia and I were blasted off the couch and sent flying. Both of us smacked painfully against the opposite wall, and we cried out in unison. Imogen had been knocked from her chair. Sassy yelped in fear as the flames encroached around us, spreading faster than any normal flames had the ability to do so. Julian and Esis were sent tumbling, embers skidding sideways.

Jonah screamed in unbearable pain. I looked up through my dazed stupor and was repulsed to see half of his face had been burned off in the explosion. He'd been closest to the wall, and had taken the brunt of the hit. Beside him, Squeaks' body smoldered, several patches of her flank singed. She cried out in agony as the flames enclosed on us from all sides.

Esis darted across the room and laid a paw on Jonah's chin. His face healed and knitted back together, but not before we had a chance to run. As Esis worked on getting Squeaks healed, a battalion of Task Force members charged into the room. They ignored the flames enclosing in on the area and raised their hands, elements glowing within their curled fingers. Unlike the last brigade, all of them were Koigni. A demolition force.

"Shoot, damn you!" one of the Task Force growled.

Elements started firing everywhere. Imogen screamed. She ducked as Sassy changed into a kitsune and began lashing out with her vines. I wanted to help, but there was no water available. Jonah was just now helping Squeaks to her feet. I dodged the elements and ducked behind the upturned couch, grabbing Julian and pulling him to my side at the last minute. I yanked Sophia next to me just before a fireball went right through her.

"Sophia, control the fire!" I screamed, but she had frozen. All her eyes could focus on were the flames crawling up the edges of Imogen's house.

Imogen and Sassy dove behind the couch with us. Jonah sent a blast of Air at the Task Force members, knocking them off their feet. He ran to our side and crouched as he screamed, "I have an idea, but it's not gonna be pretty! We need a shield!"

"*Pawee,* don't dip out on us now," I begged. She didn't respond to my words.

"Sophia, *wake up!*" Imogen snapped. She slapped Sophia across the face.

I guess that got her attention, because suddenly, a giant shield bloomed around us and our Familiars.

"Hold on!" Jonah called. At that moment, a bolt of lightning struck the house. It was huge— several feet across and burning with heat. When the lightning bolt connected, it erupted in a huge detonation, one that ripped at my eardrums. The electricity bounced off Sophia's shield and created cracks in the dome, but it held.

The second explosion caused the house to crumble. It fell inward and crushed the Task Force members. The rubble overhead smashed against Sophia's shield, forming a dome around us. We could hear painful screams, and then silence as the Task Force bodies were swallowed up by the flames and broken concrete.

"We've got to get out of here." I tugged at Sophia's wrist. She kept the shield up as we moved, but remained shell-shocked as we crawled our way out.

A few moments later, we'd broken free and managed to pull ourselves onto the lawn. All that was left of the house— and everything we'd gained in the past few weeks— lay in a burning pile of wreckage and debris. The carport was still intact, thankfully, and we still had the truck filled with a few essentials, but everything else had been destroyed.

I couldn't believe this. After two months, how had they found us?

*Imogen's card.* They'd traced it to the area. There was no other explanation.

"My house!" Imogen sobbed. She'd fallen to her hands and knees. Sassy licked at her face for comfort, though it didn't seem to help.

"We gotta go," I said quickly. "If the Task Force showed up here, more will be on their way."

"Where are we going to go?" Imogen cried. "There's nowhere left!"

Ancestors if I knew. Sophia had slowly come back to reality. "The cave system under Kinpago," she blurted. "There's an underground river there. The Task Force won't expect us to be so close. It'll be easy to hide in plain sight. The camping stuff is still in the truck. We can make it."

We'd kept the car stocked with some supplies and personal belongings, just in case something like this happened. We never thought we'd actually have to resort to running once again.

"You want us to camp in *caves*?" Jonah's tone was dripping with resentment.

"I know you don't like caves, but we don't have a choice! We need to hide somewhere. We've got nowhere else to go!" Sophia shouted.

There was no better plan, and we had to leave immediately. I opened the truck door. The keys were still in there. "Get in the car. We're going."

When no one moved, I dropped my voice and growled, "*Now.*"

Imogen wept as she sat in the front passenger seat with Sassy. Julian and Esis hopped in, and Squeaks climbed onto the bed. She seemed petrified after the pain she'd experienced. Jonah rubbed her head and mumbled a few comforting words before he covered her up with the tarp.

"Where we at, Jonah?" I asked. "I know it's a twelve hour drive, but we can't stop."

"There's enough gas money in the truck to get us back to Orenda Academy," Jonah mumbled. "But after that... we're out, man."

"It's gotta be enough." We were living on a prayer right now.

We drove all through the night and early into the next morning. My body screamed for a break, but that just wasn't possible. If we stopped for more than five minutes to refill the tank, it'd increase our chances we'd be found again.

I didn't sleep at all that night. Imogen and Sophia eventually slipped into a sad unconsciousness, but my eyes were glued open. We'd been lured into a false sense of security. We thought we were in the free and clear.

We'd never be free.

Eventually, we ended up right back where we'd started. Jonah parked the car in the woods outside Kinpago, a couple miles off the reservation. We were so tired, but we forced our helpless bodies onward as our gazes scaled the woods for Task Force members. We didn't run into any, but it was a small comfort. I think we were almost hoping they'd spring upon us, just to end our suffering.

To lose everything once was demoralizing. To lose it twice... you didn't feel like a person anymore.

When the morning was still early, we came to a cave entrance. Jonah whimpered, but Imogen took his hand and dragged him inside. Sophia used her Anichi light to guide the way.

As we walked, the cave began to shimmer as crystals grew from the walls. Small cave dragons called dracaverns buzzed throughout the cave, giving welcoming noises. Julian jumped up to try and nab them, but they fluttered away from his teeth every time.

"Where are we going, Sophia?" Jonah asked grumpily. I knew he was pissed at us for dragging him down here.

"I learned in my Elementai Explorations class that the river here used to nourish the Anichi," Sophia said. "A group survived here for months during the last Hawkei war before the Koigni found them. They didn't need food, as long as they drank from the river. It'll keep us alive until..."

Her words dropped off. Until when? None of us knew.

I heard a tiny trumpeting noise. I looked down. Small creatures were at our feet. They looked like tiny elephants that were made of clouds. They hovered above the ground and made trumpeting noises as they dug in the dirt, for what, I don't know. Food, maybe. They seemed friendly, and cried a hello as we approached.

"Oh my gosh! Elepees," Imogen said. She stooped down to run her hand over one of the small elephants. "I can't believe it."

"What are elepees, Im?" I asked.

"They're Air creatures. They're supposed to be extinct, but it turns out they're just endangered. The Hawkei used them as cave explorers. Their eyesight and sense of direction are useful underground, and their trunks can make noises that can be heard for miles." Imogen stood. "Jonah and I found one once in the Anichi dorms. It was hurt. We brought it back to health, but it found a way out before we could release it into the wild. This is where he must've come from."

"I miss Alejandro," Jonah said with a wistful sigh. I shook my head.

"I bet these elepees can lead us to the river," Imogen said. "Go on, little guys. Show us the way."

The elepees raised their trunks and floated above the ground ahead of us. The cave grew dark, the path winding— the crystals became larger, and eventually, all light was lost as we relied on our ears to follow the elepees forward.

"I fucking don't like this," I heard Jonah mutter.

"I think I know where we are," Sophia spoke from up ahead. "Vanessa and I explored this tunnel last semester, but we went back after a while. We have to go deeper."

I didn't think we *could* go deeper, if not for the elepees. We would've gotten completely lost if not for their trumpets leading the way. The walls were so tight, it was a miracle we could slip through the crevices at all, especially with Squeaks behind.

Eventually, the cave widened. Hundreds of feet above us, there was an opening in the cave that gave light to the outside world so we could see. Sophia dimmed her magic, and I looked around in wonder. There were a few trees and bushes dotted throughout this cave, all clustered around a wide river.

The elepees and dracaverns weren't the only magical creatures down here. Moles the size of horses with fur that sparkled like the crystals dug holes in the ground, while white fennec foxes with wings for ears fluttered in and out of the hole in the ceiling. Deer that had crystals growing out of their backs rested beside the calm water, while a creature that looked half reptile, half cat slithered across the floor. I watched as the cat-reptile batted at the river, trying to catch the silver fish that glowed and swam beneath the river. The noise scared scaled rabbits with iron horns, sending them scurrying across the cave floor. Giant blue moths nested in the trees, giving the area a calming ambiance.

There were so many creatures down here I'd never seen before. It was a whole ecosystem living in the caves. This river was the stuff of legend.

"That must be it," Sophia whispered. The animals, including the elepees, charged toward the river. Squeaks splashed in, and Sassy drank deeply. Esis filled his little cheeks with water as Julian lapped. The elepees used their trunks to drink, squirting each other as they trumpeted.

Sophia knelt by the river and cupped her hand to take a drink. Her expression became amazed, and she said, "Liam, come taste this."

I knelt beside her. I took water into my own hands and raised it to my mouth. As I sipped it, I instantly felt full. What was more, the river seemed to have the same healing effects on me as Esis did. My tiredness faded, and the pangs radiating throughout my muscles ebbed away.

"This river is definitely magical. At least we won't have to worry about food," I said.

"Great. So we're stuck down here." Jonah threw the camping gear down. I sighed.

We sat by the water and watched the Familiars play. I'm sure I shared the same feeling of listlessness that my companions did. None of us knew how to proceed.

This was worse than the Elemental Cup. All we had to do during the tournament was get to the finish line, and the Elders would stop hunting us.

This never ended. There was no conclusion in sight. It just went on forever.

§

WE SLEPT through most of the day, and the night afterward. The elepee herd continued to stay. They and the other magical creatures were our only avenue of entertainment as we sat by the magical river and stared into its depths, trying to reason what to do now.

No one had spoken since we'd gotten here. It was eerie.

Jonah shifted from where he sat beside us. His hands buried in Squeaks' feathers as he asked, "So how are we going to search for our families now?"

Nobody said anything, because we knew the real answer. We couldn't. We were basically waiting down here to die.

Without warning, the elepees scattered. They hurried down the tunnel we'd come from yesterday, squealing and trumpeting. Esis perked his ears, mouth dropping as he watched them go. Both Sassy and Julian raised their heads.

"What's their...?" Sophia's words drifted away as we heard a soft, tinking noise behind us, like the sound of metal hitting stone.

We turned. A small, golden bell had fallen without explanation into the middle of the cave.

Without explanation, the golden bell broke open. A purple gas emitted from it and began spreading throughout the cave. It immediately entered our lungs and filled the area.

We all started coughing. Jonah retched, and Squeaks had a similar reaction. Sophia gasped for breath and tried to stand, but she fell immediately. I tried to get to my feet, too, but I couldn't. My limbs were made of lead. My eyelids felt like they had bricks attached, and my mind desperately longed for release. All I wanted to do was crawl into a ball and rest. I tried to resist, but the more I thought about resisting sleep, that's all I wanted.

"Imogen," I gasped, hoping for an explanation. She was breathing harder than most of us.

"A sleep hex," Imogen coughed. "From the Miriamic Coven."

That was it, then. They had us. Jonah and Squeaks were already gone, sprawled out on the ground with their eyes closed. Imogen succumbed, and she only had time to pull Sassy to her side before her eyes shut.

I reached for Sophia. My fingers grazed her hair as the four of us, along with our Familiars, slumped to the ground and passed out.

§

"JAKE, they're coming around. We'd better have a good explanation."

A voice I knew stirred me awake. I expected to be in a jail cell and separated from the others when I woke up. But that's not what happened. Julian was still tucked into my side, and so was Sophia. She was just coming out of it, Esis curled on her lap.

I realized we'd been placed on a couch. Jonah and Imogen were nearby, sleeping on opposite armchairs. Their heads stirred. Sassy and Squeaks both sat up from their places on the rug.

We were in another cave, though this one didn't look the one we'd come from. It almost looked like a... room. The floor was polished marble, and the walls had been sculpted to create a hollowed-out area you could stand in. It was well-lit, and there was furniture placed all around. I could see a dining room and a kitchen around fifteen feet away. The place looked well-lived in, and neatly kept. This was somebody's house.

There were two men in the room. The first was tall and broad, a giant that stood at six foot seven, long blond hair sprawled across his muscular shoulders. A dark grey hippogriff towered beside him.

I briefly recalled them. We'd only met them in passing, but they'd helped save our lives at the battle of Orenda Academy. Jakob and Sabor.

My attention turned to the second man, who had a colorful feline creature at his side. As my eyes adjusted, I realized I still had to be dreaming. No way could this be real. I'd watched his death with my own eyes.

Standing across from us was someone I never thought I'd see again.

Cade.

# sophia
## SIX

Nobody moved. We were completely frozen in shock at what we were seeing. Cade Garcia stood in front of us in the flesh. I couldn't believe it.

I *literally* couldn't believe it. That gas we'd inhaled must've been causing hallucinations, because Cade was dead. We all knew that.

My eyes darted to Imogen. Was she seeing the same thing I was?

Tears welled in Imogen's eyes, and her bottom lip quivered. A hundred emotions flickered behind her eyes, like she couldn't decide on just one. She looked directly at Cade and didn't take her eyes off of him. Sassy had a similar look on her face, only she was eyeing Arabelle.

Cade stared back at Imogen with relief painted on his features. "Im," he breathed.

Imogen swallowed, like she was having a hard time breathing. She stood on shaky feet and reached out for Cade's outstretched hand.

*No, Im!* I wanted to say. *It could be a trap.*

But I was still so shocked that I couldn't find my mouth. Cade and Arabelle had drowned in the Elemental Cup. Unless someone had summoned the ancestors, they shouldn't be standing in front of us.

Imogen ran her hand up Cade's arms, until her fingers settled on the side of his face. A single tear spilled over her lids, and she whispered breathlessly, "You're alive."

Cade ducked his head in shame, but the relief on his face didn't go away. He was obviously really happy to see Imogen. "I'm alive. I wanted to tell you, but—"

*Thud!*

Imogen's fist slammed into Cade's jaw, and he went stumbling to the side. My stomach lurched and I leapt to my feet, along with Jonah.

"*Imogen!*" the two of us shouted at the same time.

Imogen ignored us. She stomped right up to Cade and kicked him in the shin.

"Ow! Imogen!" he cried, landing on one knee.

Imogen smacked him, and he lifted his arms to protect his face. "How could you do that to me!?" she shouted. "I thought you were dead!"

"You have to understand—" he started, but Imogen cut him off.

"*I put you in the ground!*" she roared.

Sassy had shifted into kitsune form, and her vines twisted in the air in warning. Esis hissed at my feet and lowered his horns, like he was about to headbutt someone. Arabelle, Cade's *alebrije*, bared her teeth, jumping into defense mode to protect her Elementai, but it was only as much of a warning as Sassy's vines were. Neither of them struck.

Imogen didn't seem to notice. She kept slapping Cade and shouting things. "We held a funeral for you! I've grieved for months!"

She grabbed her short hair, which had barely grown past her ears now, and tugged on it. "I cut my hair for you!"

Jonah jumped in and grabbed Imogen around the waist. Liam had come up behind me and wrapped an arm around me like he thought I might try to get in the middle of it, too. Julian sat nuzzled in his other arm.

Imogen kicked her legs out as Jonah dragged her away, and the two hippogriffs in the room squawked. Jakob— Jake, Cade had called him— stood back, looking uncomfortable.

Tears streamed down Imogen's face as she struggled out of Jonah's hold. "You liar! You asshole! I hate you! I fucking hate you! How could you lie to me like this?"

Cade's face paled. He looked freaking terrified of Imogen right now. He'd never seen her like this before. She'd changed since his death.

Imogen's struggling did nothing but make Jonah hold her tighter. "Im, calm down," he insisted. "Let's be rational."

"Rational!?" she screamed. "Nothing about this is rational. He's supposed to be dead!"

At those words, Imogen gave up fighting. She threw her hands over her face, and her whole body slumped in Jonah's arms. Jonah lowered her to the ground and cradled her in his arms, rocking her back and forth. Imogen's shoulders shook, and Sassy finally backed down.

"I can't believe... you're alive..." Imogen sobbed.

My chest tightened as I stared down at Imogen. She looked so fragile right now. I wished I could do something to help. Liam must've felt the same way, because he pulled me closer and squeezed me tight.

I was still trying to wrap my head around this being real— that Cade was, in fact, alive.

Cade stood cautiously, never tearing his gaze off Imogen. "Im, please, let me explain—"

Cade didn't get a chance to say anything more as a pair of footsteps sounded down the hall. A guy rounded the corner. His feet nearly slid out from under him, but he grabbed the stone wall and righted himself.

"She's here!?" he asked Jake.

The stranger's eyes scanned the room frantically, until they fell upon Imogen. He stilled, and I finally got a good look at him. He was a few years older than me and pretty tall, with blond hair. Something about him looked familiar, but I couldn't place it, until a fennec fox followed him into the room.

I'd seen him in the caves! He was there the day my Elementai Exploration class went to see the dracavern, and Vanessa and I got lost going after Esis. But who was he? And what business did he and his friends have hexing us and dragging us here against our will?

Imogen's sobs ceased at the sound of the stranger's voice, but she didn't look up right away. It was like she was waiting for someone to make another noise— like she couldn't believe what she'd just heard.

Cade shot a soft look at the stranger, like the two knew each other. He stepped back, and the blond guy with the fennec fox moved forward. He walked straight up to Imogen and Jonah and knelt right beside her.

"Imogen?" he asked in a soft tone.

She dropped her hands from her face, but she kept her eyes squeezed tightly shut. She pressed her hands over her ears and shook her head back and forth. "No. No, no, no. This isn't real. You're not real. *Why are you doing this to me!?*"

Her pained cry was heart wrenching.

"Imogen, please look at me," the stranger said. He reached out and touched the bottom of her chin, then forced her face upward to look at him.

Slowly, Imogen dropped her hands from her ears and opened her eyes. Her whole face was red, and tears streamed out of her eyes. Sassy nudged her with her nose, but Imogen didn't notice. She was so enamored by the stranger and stared deeply into his eyes. I had no idea who he was, but Imogen obviously knew him.

"This isn't real," Imogen whispered. "Even the ancestors can't bring people back from the dead. Please don't make me go through this again."

The stranger looked as if Imogen's pain had pierced him right through the heart. "It is, Imogen. I promise you."

Imogen sniffled and wiped the tears from her cheeks. "But you died in the tournament, Trace."

I inhaled an audible breath, but neither Liam nor Jonah looked as shocked as I was. They must've recognized him the moment he came in. But I'd never met him before.

It was Trace Ahnild— Imogen's older brother, the one who'd been buried alive in a cave-in during the tournament a few years ago. Except...

They never found the body. Or Cade's.

In fact, there were a lot of bodies that had gone missing in the tournament. They'd always been written off as victims of the elements— crushed by the land or taken out to sea.

Ancestors! This *was* real. Trace and Cade were still alive!

Relief swept through me. Imogen's breathing pattern changed. It was a mix of relief and anger all at once. She threw her arms around her brother's neck, and Jonah finally let her go. She squeezed Trace so tight that his face started to turn red.

"Imogen," he gasped.

"No," she replied without loosening her grip. "I just got you back. I'm not letting you go. Not now. Not ever."

"If you don't let go, I'm gonna pass out," he said through ragged breath.

Imogen finally relaxed her hold on him and pulled away. She wiped tears from her eyes and looked to Cade. He had this longing expression on his face, like he wanted to hug her, too. Imogen sighed and stood, then offered her arms to him.

Cade didn't hesitate a second. He wrapped her in his arms and pressed his nose into her hair.

"I missed you, Imogen," he mumbled as he drank her in.

She sniffled when she drew away. "I missed you, too. And I'm glad you're alive. But I'm mad at you." She shot a pointed look at her brother and added, "At *both* of you. Lying to me like this is bullshit."

"Believe me," Cade said. "I never wanted to lie to you."

Imogen crossed her arms. "Then explain yourself."

Jake finally stepped in. "You should probably sit down so we can explain."

The four of us exchanged a glance, like we weren't sure whether to trust Jake or not. But even though Cade faked his death and didn't tell any of us, we trusted him enough to stop and listen.

None of us sat, though. We were still on high alert after being kidnapped.

I curled Esis close in my arms. Squeaks sat next to Jonah, though she kept throwing glances at the other hippogriff. Sassy and Trace's fennec fox Familiar were sniffing each other.

Imogen petted Sassy on the head. Her voice came out dry, but she tried to be nice. "That's right, Trace. You haven't met my Familiar yet. This is Sassy."

Trace let her sniff his fingers. When she bowed her head, he scratched her behind the ears. "Hello, Sassy. I think you and Maxwell are going to get along great."

Trace turned to the rest of us. "If you haven't gathered, I'm Imogen's oldest brother, Trace."

He extended his hand to Jonah. Jonah shook it firmly, though he had this dark look in his eyes, like he was pissed at him for hurting Imogen. "I'm Jonah, the *best* friend. I'm the guy who will protect Imogen with my life."

Cade leaned in to add, "Don't worry. He's a sweetheart."

Jonah's lips tightened, and he shot a cold look at Cade. "When I want to be."

Trace turned to Liam and I and shook our hands. "You must be Sophia and Liam. I've heard so much about you."

I was wary to shake his hand, because I was mad at him. It wasn't fair what he or Cade did to Imogen.

Imogen sniffled. "So, if you're both here... is this where Mom and Dad went?"

My heart fluttered in my chest as I thought about being reunited with our families.

Trace looked at Imogen with a soft expression. "Yes. Everyone's here, and they're safe."

"What about my family?" I demanded.

"And mine," Liam added harshly.

Jake stepped in again and held up a hand. "They're all here. You don't need to worry."

"Well, take us to them!" I cried.

Jake didn't get defensive over my tone, but instead spoke calmly. "All in due time, Miss Henley. There's much to discuss."

Liam's features hardened. "We want to see our families. Who are you to deny us of that?"

"Yeah," Jonah added, though he looked more like he was drooling over Jake than angry at him. "Who exactly are you?"

"Forgive me," Jake said. He extended a friendly hand toward Jonah. "We met briefly the night of the academy battle, but we haven't been formally introduced. I'm Jakob Weatherby, leader of the resistance. You can call me Jake."

My eyes nearly popped out of my skull, and Liam stiffened beside me.

"Resistance?" I balked. "There's a resistance?"

"You're Jaymin's people?" Liam questioned.

Jake laughed. "Hardly. Though Jaymin is with us now, we do not sanction anything she or the Interhouse Alliance did. We are a separate group formed many years ago to fight against the Elders. It's like I said on that night at Orenda. I'm on your side."

Liam crossed his arms. He wasn't entirely convinced. "If you're on our side, why'd you drug us with an illegal hex to bring us here?"

Jake's eyebrows shot up, like he was impressed Liam knew the sort of magic he'd used. "That kind of magic is only illegal in Kinpago. The resistance makes their own rules."

Liam's features darkened. "That doesn't answer my question."

"No, I suppose it doesn't. I'm terribly sorry we had to knock you out." Jake sounded like he meant it. "We couldn't risk you running before we had a chance to explain. We couldn't lose you four again."

"Again?" I asked.

"We meant to bring you here that night we came to Orenda," Jake explained. "But you disappeared. Miss Henley's grandparents went back for you, but we found them dead with no trace of the rest of you."

"My grandparents were part of the resistance?" I asked. I tried to keep a level head, but it was just one more thing someone had lied to me about. It was hard not to feel bitter about it.

Jake nodded. "Yes."

Imogen narrowed her eyes. "How'd you find us in the caves?"

"We have magical creatures all around Kinpago, keeping watch for us," Jake told us. "Especially in the caves. The elepees work for us."

I wasn't sure I was buying it. He claimed they came for us that last night at Orenda, but why not sooner? "Why would you wait until we were about to be executed to get us out? We'd been treated like shit for months by that point!"

Jake had a deep look of regret on his face. "The Elders were watching the four of you very closely. We couldn't risk them finding us— or everything we'd fought for years would be lost."

"Where exactly are we?" Liam demanded.

"We're not far from Kinpago," Jake answered. "But we're outside the magical boundary that protects the city. We call this place *Hok'evale*."

It sounded like a Hawkei word, though with the little Hawkei language I'd picked up on, I couldn't translate.

"*Hok'evale*," Liam mused aloud. "Harmony Valley?"

"Peaceful Valley," Jake corrected. "It would be easiest to explain if I gave you a tour."

"Hold on," Jonah said, and Jake eyed him curiously. "There's something I've been dying to know. That night at Orenda wasn't the first time we saw you. We saw you coming out of Head Dean Alric's office a year ago. You two were fighting about something. Before we come with, we want to know what."

Jake's expression softened. "I was not an enemy of Alric's, if that's what you're thinking. In fact, I was a strong ally of his. If you must know, I was trying to convince Alric to join me here in *Hok'evale*. He wouldn't come."

Liam seemed to accept that. "How big is *Hok'evale*? I want to see it."

Jake gestured to the door. "Right this way."

We all exchanged a wary look, but Cade and Trace moved to follow Jake immediately, so we kept our Familiars close and followed behind. Jake led us past a large, modern kitchen that seemed to be built right into the cave. There were outlets in the rock wall, and running water. Next, we were guided through a fancy living room that was all straight lines and grey-toned decor, like it came straight out of an expensive condo magazine. A long wall of glass stood in front of us, looking out over a patio with ferns and other greenery all around.

A huge rock face was all I could see beyond that, but when we stepped outside, I got a better look at *Hok'evale*. The town was tucked tightly between two towering cliffs. Glass panes lined the walls of the rock in random intervals. I could see curtains over some of the windows or rooms beyond them. It was like there were apartments built straight into the cave system.

But those weren't the only houses. The canyon was huge— at least several hundred yards across, and so long that I couldn't see all the way to either side. There were clusters of thatch-roof cabins all around, and they seemed to keep going where the canyon twisted out of sight. Light chatter filled the air as people came and went from their houses. Huge Familiars like dragons and griffins walked wide trails and were careful not to step on the many garden plots that were arranged carefully between the cabins. Nivita tended to the gardens, growing plants and flowers I'd never seen before. I noticed a beautiful plant that looked like a transparent rose—almost like ice.

Elementai drove carts and carriages like back in Kinpago. One guy drove a cart led by a strange Familiar. It had the beautiful white body of a horse, but had the head of a lion and the wings of a dragon. His cart came so close that I could see that he was hauling boxes upon boxes of magic beans —the kind we used to eat at the dining hall that were said to be blessed by the ancestors.

Next, my eyes landed on a rainbow-colored sloth with a single golden horn growing out of his head. He walked slowly and carried a basket full of fruit. The uni-sloth walked straight up to us and held up one of the fruits in my direction. It was the size of an apple and yellow in color, with soft spikes all around it. I glanced uncertainly at Jake.

"Go ahead," Jake encouraged. "They're Anichi kiwis. They're delicious."

"Anichi kiwis?" I asked curiously as I took the fruit from the uni-sloth. He began handing them out to my friends. Though the river had kept us full, now, we were kind of starving. I wondered if it was some kind of trap, but to be honest, I was too hungry to care.

We each took a bite. Sweet flavors burst in my mouth, and the juice dripped down my chin. It tasted like a mix between a pear and a mango, but had the texture of a kiwi.

"Mm..." Jonah moaned. "This is really good."

Jake's eyes gleamed. "Yes. They're my favorite, actually."

The town was filled with joyous laughter that intensified as we followed behind Jake. My eyes darted every which way, trying to take it all in. A group of people our age sat around a daytime fire, watching as a middle-aged Koigni man manipulated the flames and told a story I couldn't hear. A few cabins down, a Nivita woman hung a wet sheet on her clothesline, until an older Toaqua man came over and sucked the water right out of it. She thanked him, and together they folded the sheet. Tiny Familiars fluttered around them. From this distance, they looked like butterflies that lit up and changed color.

Children sprinted past the woman and squirted the old man with water guns, but he held up his hand and caught the water mid-air. He splashed it back on them and laughed. They ran away squealing in exhilaration. The kids met up with several other children and a group of baby Familiars, who were dancing in a straight line down the street like a parade. Some of the children leapt and twirled, spinning multi-colored streamers above their heads. Others wore masks made to look like dragons and rode on the backs of magical creatures.

Three children spotted us and ran over, giggling. They held out beaded necklaces designed with the colors of all five Houses.

"For you!" a young girl said, before curtsying in front of me.

I was stunned, but I couldn't refuse, so I took the necklace she offered and looped it around my neck. "It's beautiful," I told her. "What's the occasion?"

The young girl gave a mischievous smile. "You don't need a reason to dance in the street."

She curtsied again before hurrying back to join the parade of children.

My eyes continued to scan the streets, but there was so much to take in. Two fox-like creatures galloped alongside each other. They were completely white in color, with fur so long it brushed the ground. Their legs were longer than their bodies, and each had a set of golden antlers growing out of their heads. They nipped and played with each other like they were engaged in a mating display.

Not far from them, I noticed a crowd of people dancing beside a street performer. The man played an upbeat tune on the flute. He was accompanied by a pink panda on the drums. Another creature danced to the music and encouraged others to move their bodies. It had the head of a wolf, the body of a deer, and the tail feathers of a peacock. Its entire body shimmered a beautiful blue and green.

"Ancestors! Look!" Imogen pointed upward, and we all looked to the rock face above us.

A giant mural had been carved out in the rock high above our heads. It was in the ancient Anichi form of art, and it depicted all different types of Familiars running alongside each other. The rocks moved, too, making it look like the creatures were running.

Jake smiled proudly. "It's infused with Nivita magic. The rocks move in and out to create the illusion."

Imogen turned to Jake. "How long has the resistance been around? This mural must be at least a century old."

"The resistance didn't create the mural," Jake explained. "The Anichi did."

"The Anichi used to come to this canyon?" Jonah asked.

"Used to?" Jake asked. "They're still here."

"The Anichi are *alive?*" Imogen squeaked. She sounded half shocked and half exhilarated. She was probably going to interview the first one she saw.

"They're alive, but without their magic," Jake explained.

"But... how did they survive?" Liam asked. "They were supposed to all die off after the Great War."

"Most of them did," Jake said. "But a few of them escaped. The ancestors led them to this canyon, where they've been protected for over a century."

"But they should still have their magic," Imogen argued.

Jake shook his head. "The ancestors took away their ability to bond at the end of the war, as a means to protect the last bit of their magic so the Koigni could not destroy what was left. Without their bond, the Anichi can't use their powers."

"I thought the Koigni killed all the Anichi creatures, to weaken their magic?" Liam said.

"They tried," Jake agreed. "But like the Anichi, a few survived."

Imogen tapped her chin thoughtfully. "So, if only their bond is broken, do the Anichi creatures themselves still hold power?"

"Good question," Jake said. "The answer is... complicated. The Anichi creatures have magic, but without Elementai to bond with, they aren't as strong. Some can create light, others minor shields. But healing magic is nigh on impossible without a bond."

"What about the river inside the caves, where you found us?" Imogen asked. "That has to have some healing powers."

"It does," Jake confirmed. "But only *inside* the caves. If we remove the water from the stream, it loses its magic. It has proved useful at times, but it is far from the magic Anichi needs. They've been waiting a long time to see their magic restored."

He shot a look at me, though I couldn't read what it meant. Did he know I was part Anichi and could use my magic? I honestly wasn't sure how I could do it myself. It had to be because I was mixed house, so I was able to bond from my Koigni side— though that still didn't explain how Esis, an Anichi creature, was able to bond with me if the others of his kind couldn't.

Holy shit. I was *mixed house*. I didn't know why it never occurred to me before. I obviously had Anichi blood, but I'd assumed it came from one of the last Anichi before they'd died off. Knowing they were still alive changed everything.

I whirled toward my friends, and my voice increased several pitches. "Do you guys realize what this means? That the Anichi are still alive?"

"Ancestors! Your parents!" Imogen realized.

"Exactly," I stated. "My Anichi side could be way closer than I thought. What if my real parents are here? What if one of them is Anichi?"

Cade furrowed his brow. "I thought your parents were the Greysons."

"We thought so, too," I said.

Jake pressed his lips together. "We're aware of your Anichi connection, but we haven't been able to track your lineage just yet. You can talk to Chief Cauac about it after our tour."

"I thought you said you were chief," Jonah pointed out.

"No, I said I was the leader of the resistance," Jake replied. "We live in harmony here with the Anichi tribe, but they still have their traditional council. Think of the resistance as... the Anichi's military."

Jonah drooled even more when Jake said that. I bet screwing a military captain was at the top of his bucket list.

"Anyway, there's much more to see—" Jake started, but the sound of a *baa* coming from the sky cut him off. We looked upward, and puffy white creatures with large, feathery wings came swooping down in a herd. It wasn't until they landed in the middle of the road that I realized what they were.

"Winged sheep!" I exclaimed. We didn't have any of those back in Kinpago.

A winged canine dropped from the sky behind the sheep. Its tongue hung out of his mouth, and he looked positively pleased as he ran circles around the herd. They took off into the air again, and the sheepdog followed.

"Come on." Jake cocked his head, while the rest of us were still trying to take it all in. "Let's take a walk."

Liam took my hand, and we walked side-by-side behind Jake. "*Hok'e-vale* is a very tight-knit community," Jake said. "We built our houses in the caves and in cabins because we want to be as connected to the earth as possible. We hold our native roots very dear."

I couldn't stop looking around long enough to really listen to him. There were so many Familiars I hadn't seen before, like a white koala bear with a mane around its face. It clung to the side of the canyon and looked as if it was sleeping. Esis squealed and pointed over to a group of lemurs swinging in a tree. They all had the same color of eyes as Esis did.

A moment of familiarity struck, and I slowed my step. "Wait. Hold on."

Everyone got this same worried look on their face when I stopped to turn in a circle.

"What's wrong?" Liam asked with urgency, like I'd just spotted something dangerous.

I held up my hand to tell him to give me a minute. Then it hit me. I'd seen all these creatures before, but they were only in drawings. Mixed among the familiar creatures like dragons and unicorns were Anichi creatures that were supposed to be extinct!

"Those are *Anichi* creatures! This could be where Esis came from!" I exclaimed, turning to Liam. I was so excited about meeting Esis' family that I could hardly contain myself.

But before Liam could respond, Jake frowned. "I'm afraid I'm not familiar with his species."

My head dropped. Esis grumbled in my arms, though I couldn't tell exactly what he was saying.

"Where did all these creatures come from?" Imogen asked thoughtfully. "I mean, I realize the Anichi creatures left with the tribe, but there are others here, too. You said we're out of the magical boundaries of Kinpago. How did all these Familiars get here?"

Jake took a breath. "That's one of the many secrets we've kept from you four, to avoid the Elders catching on. We've been smuggling creatures out of Kinpago for some time. I believe you're familiar with Professor Costas and Professor Fawn?"

Liam's face paled at the mention of Professor Fawn, and his tone became harsh. "We are."

Jake noticed Liam's hostile tone, but he shrugged it off. He had no idea what Liam had done. "I'm sure you remember they were caught smuggling magical creatures out of Kinpago."

"That was for *you?*" Jonah asked in astonishment. "But I thought they said they did that to create distrust in the Elders."

Jake shook his head. "That was only an explanation used as a cover-up. The truth is, they were bringing creatures here to bond with our people, as we had more Elementai than creatures at the time."

"But the professors took bonded creatures, too," Imogen pointed out.

"That was only a precaution to keep them from getting sick from the plague," Jake explained. "We had to take the vulnerable out of the equation to avoid further damage."

Jake quickly added, "But once the plague was cured, we returned those creatures to their rightful owners."

I still remembered when Essarae disappeared. Isabella was devastated that her filly-pixie was missing. It all made sense now. She was the daughter of Madame Laurel, one of the first Elders to get sick from the plague. A small creature like a filly-pixie was especially vulnerable to contagions, and she would've caught the plague for sure had the resistance not protected her.

I wasn't saying it was the right way to deal with things, but all the pieces of the puzzle were starting to fall together.

"How exactly does the plague tie into the resistance?" Imogen questioned.

Jake frowned. "I'm afraid what you know about the plague is true. Professors Fawn and Costas helped to implant the plague in Kinpago. We intended to use it to take out the Elders, and nothing more, but it got out of hand. Innocent people weren't supposed to get hurt. A miscalculation on our part."

A silent beat passed. No one wanted to relive all that.

"Let's keep moving," Jake said. "We've barely started, and there are people I want you to meet."

Jake led us to one of the nearest gardens, where a Nivita girl crouched in the dirt and made a flower bloom right before our eyes. Her back was to us, and her hair was tied up. I saw the filly-pixie land on her shoulder, and my jaw dropped.

"Isabella!?" Imogen squeaked.

Isabella glanced up, and shock immediately took over her expression. "Ancestors! Liam, Sophia, Imogen, Jonah! You're all back!"

Isabella jumped to her feet, and suddenly, it was like the entire block had gone silent. All around us, eyes turned from porches and out windows to look at us. The crowd over by the fire heard Isabella shout our names, and they all went silent. It was only when they got to their feet and looked over to us I realized I recognized them all. It was a group of twelve people we'd smuggled out of Kinpago— the ones Liam found marked as dangerous in the Elders' computer files.

Liam seemed to notice the same thing I had, and he turned to Jake. "You weren't lying about you and Alric being allies. You were working together the whole time."

Jake nodded.

Jonah slammed a fist into his open palm, like he'd just been hit with realization. "*This* is what Alric was hiding from us last semester! This is what no one would tell us about."

"Precisely," Jake said.

People started flooding out of their houses and began walking toward us at all angles. It was kind of weird, but welcoming at the same time. I recognized so many faces that I knew. I didn't think I'd ever been so relieved in my life. I saw Riley, and a few others who Jake must've got out the night of the Orenda Academy battle.

A girl with wild blonde curls stuck her head out of a nearby cabin door and squealed. "Aunt Kaye! They're here!"

Taylor came rushing out of the house, a shimmering red armadillo at her heels. She hadn't bonded before we'd helped smuggle her out of the castle, so she must've bonded after she arrived in *Hok'evale*.

"You finally made it!" Taylor exclaimed, pulling each of us into a hug one by one.

Taylor had been less than friendly to me in the past. It was strange to see her so nice.

"I can't thank you enough for helping me get out of Kinpago," Taylor said as she drew away from Imogen.

"You knew about *Hok'evale* all along?" Imogen asked.

Taylor shook her head. "No. After I left in the woods, I hitched a ride to my aunt's like I said I would. She brought me here."

She gestured to her aunt, who'd come up beside her and gave us a sweet hello.

"Who else is here?" Imogen asked, looking around at the welcome party.

"All of us!" Isabella said brightly. "Everyone you guys saved, and so many more!"

A group of four people stepped forward, and my jaw dropped. I hadn't seen them in over two years, but it was clear as day. It was the entire Yellow Team from our Elemental Cup. None of them had survived our first task in the water. We thought they'd drowned. But here they were— alive.

"Hold up," I said, pressing my fingers to my temples. It was all so much to take in at once. "How many people 'died' in the tournament but ended up here instead?"

Trace was the one to answer. He and Cade had been so quiet, I almost forgot they were there. "There've been dozens. We've been recruiting kids from the tournament for years. It's the best way to get people here without the Elders suspecting anything."

Liam pressed his finger to his lips in thought. "So, all that talk about the tournament getting more dangerous... that wasn't true. It just *looked* like it because of the people the resistance was getting out?"

Trace nodded. "Remember that huge cave-in that happened during the tournament last year?"

How could we forget? It'd been broadcast for all of Kinpago to see.

"Most of those people made it out through a special tunnel we'd directed them to," Trace said. "And the water task you lost people to your year? Our Toaqua got them out."

Imogen turned on Cade, though she didn't sound as mad as before. "That's how you survived," she realized. "There were Toaqua underwater who staged your death."

Cade nodded. "Yeah. It was the only way to get out without drawing suspicion. I'd planned on it for years."

Imogen's lips tightened. "You could've told me."

"No, he couldn't have," Trace snapped at her. He shot her this look that said, *We'll talk about it later.*

"I have so many questions," I stated. My head spun, and I didn't even know where to start.

"Same here," Liam said firmly.

"And I intend to answer them all," Jake said as a girl came up behind him, pushing a small cart. "But first, how about some Spirit Tea?"

"Spirit Tea?" Jonah asked, sounding intrigued.

"It's really good," Isabella said. "You have to try it."

Jake held an arm out to the girl who was pushing the cart. I recognized her from the Orenda Academy battle. She'd been there with Jake, but I'd barely seen her a minute. I didn't even know her name.

"This is my sister, Sarah," Jake introduced. "She's one of our generals."

Sarah gestured down to her cart filled with tea mugs and a steaming teapot. "I was going to bring this back to the house, but I see you're already giving them the tour."

Jake reached for one of the teacups. "Spirit Tea, anyone?"

Jonah reached for the first teacup after Sarah filled it. He took a sip and moaned. "Ancestors, that is heavenly."

Sarah passed out three more cups, and we each took a sip. It was warm and bubbly on my tongue. It was really sweet and flowed down my throat smoothly.

"What is this, exactly?" I asked.

"Spirit Tea is infused with Anichi magic," Sarah explained. "It has a magnificent calming effect."

"I thought Anichi magic wasn't working," Imogen pointed out.

"Oh, it's still out there," Jake responded, shooting a glance at me. "It's just not readily available to all. Creatures still have some magic, remember, and the kiwis you ate earlier grow healing properties."

Everyone seemed to like the Spirit Tea. Even Liam, who seemed a bit distrusting of Jake, took another gulp.

I lifted the cup to my lips again, but I stopped mid-sip. It suddenly occurred to me that I shouldn't be accepting unknown substances right now. I didn't know for sure if I was pregnant yet, but I *had* missed my period. It was best not to risk it.

I knew I should've taken a test when we were back at Imogen's, but every time I thought of going to the store to pick one up, I chickened out. I wanted a child with all my heart, but I thought that even if Liam and I had kids someday— or adopted— it'd be way down the line, not in the middle of a war. And certainly not here, in this strange place with these strange people.

Besides, I didn't even know if Liam wanted a kid— at least, not one he fathered himself. He had a hard enough time accepting his illness. What would he do if he passed it down to our child? He'd blame himself. And I couldn't put even more guilt on him than he was already experiencing.

The problem was... I really worried that might be true. Liam had said Anna told him he was about to meet other people like him with his condition. My first thought when he told me was that the person he was about to meet was his own child. But that only made me feel sad, because I knew Liam would be torn on having a baby if he thought his child would have his disease.

The truth was, I wasn't trying to hide anything from Liam, since I didn't know the truth for myself yet. So I decided I'd tell him only once I knew for sure. I'd wait until my next period to see if it came.

And it had to— because Liam was sterile. Even if I had this wishful thinking at the back of my mind that *maybe* I was pregnant, I knew I couldn't be. Not with Liam. It wasn't possible.

And yet, I put the Spirit Tea aside anyway... just in case.

We stayed another few minutes as the crowd around us greeted us, until Jake suggested we move on. "Let's continue the tour," he said.

We returned our teacups to the cart, left Jake's sister behind, then followed behind him. My breath caught when I noticed a woman standing at a man's door. There was a cart beside her, and she looked like she was delivering something. Dark brown, feathery wings the shade of her skin rose from her back. They were almost as tall as she was. I'd never seen anything like it.

I was just about to ask Jake about her when the man inside threw his head back in laughter. Long, pointed fangs protruded from his mouth.

The interaction didn't go unnoticed by my friends. "Did I just see a Celestial and a Midnighter?" Jonah asked under his breath.

"Yes," Jake answered. "*Hok'evale* is a neutral tribe. Though our main population is Elementai, we provide protection to other supernaturals who have left their own people. As long as everyone chips in, they are welcome here."

They let angels and vampires into the village? Interesting. It seemed like the population here was composed of the outcasts of society— which was appealing to me, because that's what my own little group was. The fact that the resistance was a city of rejects only made me want to open up to the possibilities here.

We continued on the tour. As Jake pointed out various things, I noticed Jonah couldn't stop staring at his ass. The houses gave way to a dozen open-air amphitheaters, all set throughout beautiful flower gardens. Each amphitheater was small, with a few wooden benches and a small stage. Most of them were full of people, but were spread far enough apart that one group wouldn't bother another.

My eyes roamed over the flowers we passed by on the path. There were so many I'd never seen before— like huge white puff balls that sang a pleasant tune. I spotted a cluster of multi-colored flowers that looked like they had tentacles. I reached out to run my fingers over the tentacles, and I felt a surge of magic rush up my arm— though I couldn't place what kind it was.

"This is one of our many schoolyards," Jake said, gesturing around at the full amphitheaters. "The children have a school building up the canyon, but our college-level classes are taught out here in the open air."

I looked from class to class to see what they were teaching. One woman stood on a stage and waved her hands in the air. The leaves beneath her twisted to her will and seemed to tell a history lesson I wasn't familiar with. The next group sat on the ground in an open classroom that didn't have any benches. They were weaving baskets and looked to be meditating. All the students were either our age or older.

My eyes fell upon the next class, and I stopped in my tracks. Two men stood on stage in front of a chalkboard. Their Familiars, a golden reindeer and a hound, were curled up next to the stage.

The older man pointed to a term written on the board. "Can anyone tell me what it means if I said the witness's affidavit was presented as evidence in court?"

Several hands shot up, but I didn't hear the answer, because Liam balked at my side. "Is that *Vanderbilt*? Our lawyer?"

He was hardly recognizable. He was well put together and looked years younger.

"Ancestors, it is," Imogen gasped. "And that's his son! I didn't even know they left Kinpago."

"Oh, yes," Jake said. "Ludwig joined us shortly after the riots in Kinpago Square. He got out with his son, Sean. They co-teach a college class on law together."

"How'd they even know about the resistance?" Liam asked.

I had the same question. If Vanderbilt knew, he never gave us any clues.

Jake shrugged. "Sean's been with us since he was a teenager."

"I thought he was adopted after the Elders found out he was mixed house," Imogen said.

"He was," Jake confirmed. "But once he came of age, he returned here in order to bond."

"He said at our trial he lived on his own in the woods when he bonded," I recalled. "He was really with you all along?"

Jake nodded. "Right. But he obviously couldn't tell the Elders that."

Liam eyed the classes as we passed. "How many people do we know came from here?"

"Not many," Jake said. "Most of our spies in Kinpago were born there. All except for Madame Wells."

"*What?*" the four of us squeaked in unison.

Liam composed himself first. "Madame Wells *came* from *Hok'evale*? She was born here?"

"Yes," Jake said. "She's half Anichi, half Toaqua. She moved to Kinpago years ago with the single goal to get herself on the Toaqua Elder Council, to infiltrate it. She was eventually able to convince your father to turn to the resistance, which was how we managed to ally with him after Oleander took over."

We exited the schoolyard and Jake gestured forward, where aisles upon aisles of vendors lined the streets. "This is our market, where we trade goods like food and clothing. We have more modern conveniences at the store around the corner—"

"SOPHIAAAA!!!"

I turned toward the sound of someone squealing my name, and my heart stopped. A girl with a parrot on her shoulder rushed over to me with her arms stretched out wide. The air knocked out of my lungs, and I was so struck with joy that I nearly dropped Esis. He jumped out of my arms, landing at my feet.

"Amelia!" I screamed, sprinting over to her.

Our bodies slammed together, and she pulled me into a hug so tight that I could hardly breathe. Her sweet apple scent filled my nose.

Amelia drew away and wiped at her eyes. "Ancestors, I can't believe you're here. We tried to go back for you, but you were gone."

I grabbed her face in my hands and looked her straight in the eye. "I'm here, Amelia. That's all that matters."

She wiped at the tears on my cheeks and chuckled, like she was so overwhelmed with joy to have me back. She took my hands in hers, and she gasped when she felt the ring on my finger. She looked down to my hand and squealed, "Great Spirit! You're engaged!"

Her eyes darted around the group, though I didn't know what sort of answer she was looking for. It was like she was asking if everyone else knew about this. Her eyes landed on Trace for a few seconds, then returned to me.

I sniffled. This wasn't exactly how I wanted to tell her, but I was just so happy to see her that I didn't care. "I am."

"Congratulations!" She threw her arms around me and squeezed me tight again, then turned to Liam and hugged him. He seemed a little surprised.

As she drew away from him, I noticed a tattoo on her forearm where her Biyami mark used to be. It'd been covered by an image of a feather.

"I'm *so* happy for you two," She gushed. "Liam, do you mind if I steal your fiancé for a while? You know, sister stuff?"

Liam glanced at me. He didn't look happy about separating in this strange place, but it wasn't like I was running off with just anyone. I trusted Amelia with my life, and I missed her *so* much. Sister time sounded perfect.

"I'll be fine," I said. "You guys go ahead. I'll catch up on the tour later."

Amelia squealed. "Yay! I have so much to tell you."

Liam handed Esis back to me. "Don't get her into any trouble," he warned my sister.

Amelia crossed her heart with her finger. "Promise."

Amelia grabbed my hand and dragged me away from my friends. We wove between vendors so fast I could hardly take anything in. Esis scurried to catch up behind us.

"Whoa, Amelia," I laughed. Her bright mood was infectious. I almost forgot I was mad at her for all the secrets. "What's up with you?"

"What do you mean?" she asked, slowing her step.

"You're like, so... happy," I pointed out, before quickly adding, "Not like that's a bad thing."

"I *am* happy," she said. "*Hok'evale* is amazing. It's so different from the *Hozho*. Everyone is so nice here."

"And...?" I sensed there was something more.

She blushed deeply. "And... I'm dating someone."

"Trevor?" I asked.

Her face scrunched up. "Ew. No. He was just my roommate."

"Then who?" I asked.

She didn't answer right away. Instead, she said, "Come on. There's something I want to show you."

Amelia led me past the vendors and toward the face of the cliff, far away from anyone else. We stopped in a secluded area brimming with beautiful foliage. A trickling waterfall ran down the side of the cliff and into a small stream, which disappeared into a wide cave opening. Beautiful ivy climbed the rocks, and the sunlight glistened off the wings of shimmering dragonflies.

"Amelia, it's gorgeous," I breathed.

Esis started batting at the dragonflies, chittering. They fluttered around him and landed in his fur.

"I know. It's probably my favorite place in all of *Hok'evale*," she said. "Have a seat."

Amelia led me to a park bench. We sat down facing the beautiful stream. She bounced a little in her seat and turned to me. "I have *so* much to tell you."

"You can start with your boyfriend," I teased. "Why won't you tell me?"

She bit her lower lip, like she was half-excited and half-scared.

I frowned, feeling my mood quickly shift. "Am, I'm sick of you hiding things from me."

"That's why I'm so excited you're here!" she exclaimed. "I don't have to hide anything from you now that you know about the resistance!"

If that was supposed to soothe me, it didn't. I was excited to see her for sure, but I wasn't thrilled that she'd lied to me or left me behind. "How long have you known about it?"

She dropped her head guiltily. "A few years. Before I even knew you were an Elementai."

"Ancestors, Am!" I cried. "I'm so sick of you lying to me."

"I had to!" she insisted. "Look, the resistance did everything to keep you alive, and part of that was not telling you about them. You were already a target. They were trying to keep you from becoming a bigger one. And to be honest, they had to protect everyone else, too. They knew the Elders would come looking for you once you fled Kinpago. We couldn't risk putting the resistance in jeopardy until we had no other choice."

"That's why no one told us?" I demanded. "You, Cade, Alric..."

"Exactly," Amelia said. "And no one could tell your friends, because they'd tell you, and then the Elders would find out. If the resistance was exposed before we brought you in at the proper moment, this whole thing would be over."

I pressed my fingers to my eyes. "I'm not even going to begin to *pretend* that makes any sense. You should've brought me here with you."

Amelia's features hardened. "Believe me, I wanted to. But the Task Force came for me so fast. Trevor and I had to leave."

"Why did they come for you?" I asked. "Amelia, I want to know everything."

"Okay," she said softly. "I'll tell you."

The tension in my shoulders eased as I settled into the bench and listened.

Amelia took a deep breath. "Let me start from the beginning. A few years ago, Trace and I... got involved."

"Imogen's brother?" I balked. "But you were *so* against Liam and I being in an interhouse relationship."

"Exactly," she emphasized. "Because it didn't work out for me and Trace. Not at first. We had to break it off for obvious reasons."

I shook my head, trying to absorb the information. "Wow. You and Trace... I didn't even know you two knew each other."

Amelia snorted. "I thought it was obvious. When you first told me about Liam, I accused you of running off in the woods to blow a Nivita guy. Remember?"

My jaw dropped as realization dawned. "Ancestors, you blew Trace in the woods!?"

"Shh..." Amelia hissed. She glanced around, but we were alone. "Anyway... yes. I gave him a blow job, big deal. Then we got together, and it was this whole big thing. Trace was the one who brought me into the resistance. But things had to end between us when he faked his death in the tournament."

"You sound bitter about it," I pointed out.

"I was," she admitted. "But I stayed with the resistance because I believed in their cause. They used me as a spy. That's why I took the job on the *Hozho*."

Realization hit me. "And that's why you kept your job after you were sorted into Biyami, even though you had all that money."

Amelia nodded. "Not that I have it anymore, thanks to Oleander."

I frowned. "He shut down Imogen's bank account, too."

"Anyway," Amelia continued, "I got caught spying. This bitch named Jill Larsen somehow found out and turned me in."

"Jill?" I squeaked. I remembered her. She was in my Hawkei Careers class and had been horrible. I remembered she'd talked about wanting to work on the *Hozho*.

"Yeah," Amelia said. "But she's old news, probably still working for the Defortai on the *Hozho* like some little pet. I'm glad we left, honestly. I mean, I regret leaving you behind, but I'm really happy here, and Trace and I are back together. I guess I have you to thank for that."

"Me?" I asked.

She nodded. "I never would've considered getting back into an inter-house relationship if it wasn't for you and Liam. Now that you're here, everything's just right."

"What about Mom and Dad?" I asked. "They're here somewhere, aren't they?"

"Yeah. They've been here for about a year now," she said. "They're working closely with Jake. They're actually the ones who created the communication system between the resistance and Biyami."

"What communication system?" I asked.

"The dracavern," she said. "We used them to send coded messages back and forth through the caves."

"Oooh," I said in realization. "*That's* why Alric always had cave dragons hanging around him last semester."

Amelia sighed in relief, like a huge weight had just lifted off her shoulders. "I'm so happy you finally know the truth."

"Me, too," I said. "I just wish you hadn't kept it from me."

"I had my reasons," Amelia insisted. "But you're here now. You're really going to like it. And you can train with the Anichi."

I furrowed my brow at her. "I never told you I had Anichi powers."

Amelia eyed me. "Seems I wasn't the only one keeping secrets."

My stomach sank. "No. I guess not."

"A few resistance members saw you use a shield during the battle of Orenda Academy," she explained. "I knew it must be the Spirit Totem."

I touched the totem lying beneath my shirt. Amelia and I had a long talk about the totem before she left for the resistance, about how the ancestors had her leave it in the cave for me to find.

"Anyway, do you remember sign language from that class you took in high school?" Amelia asked.

I furrowed my brow, confused by the sudden change of subject. "Yeah. Why?"

Amelia stood from the bench and held her hand out. "There's a friend I want you to meet. She's going to help you with your powers."

"My Anichi powers?" I asked.

Amelia nodded. "She's Anichi herself."

My heart beat wildly in my chest. I was going to meet my first Anichi—

And I'd finally become one of them.

SEVEN

Out of all the things I'd been expecting, this certainly wasn't it.

A lot of the people we thought were dead were still alive.

The Anichi hadn't died out— they were merely in hiding.

And by the ancestors, this place was incredible.

*Hok'evale* had so much to offer. Julian peeped in my arms as we took in the sights, Jake leading the way. The buildings that weren't built into the side of the mountains were constructed in Anichi-style, built out of stone with intricate carvings into their sides, vines wrapping up the pillars. Houses were made of wood with thatch roofs. We passed by a ball court, stone with sloped sides, where Anichi kicked a leather ball around in some sort of old game. Nearby was a large square temple to the ancestors, built upward in large steps like a pyramid.

The whole village reminded me of the architectural structures of indigenous South America. Statues were placed beside gushing fountains that represented Spirit Warriors of old, and the Anichi here dressed as if we were still living in ancient times. Men and women walked in brightly colored robes were sewn with beads around the shoulders and middle. All genders wore feathered headdresses, and some even wore masks that were painted with geometrical shapes in green, red, and yellow. Others wore necklaces that were made of bone, and had striped shawls that covered their bare chests. It was clear that *Hok'evale* was a place that was far more attached to the past than Kinpago ever could be.

I had to swivel my head from one direction to the other constantly to take it all in. Even though I'd come from a magical society, it was like we were walking into a brand-new world.

I noticed that Jonah stayed close to Jake, but Imogen had distanced herself from Cade. They weren't holding hands, or even walking close together. Cade kept sending desperate glances at Imogen, pleading her to acknowledge him, but she fixed her eyes everywhere but his face. Trace, who'd obviously gotten the message that Imogen needed space, kept away a few paces back.

I couldn't blame her. They'd put her through hell keeping a secret that I wasn't sure was worth the price.

Jake gestured to a restaurant that had sloping stairs built into the side of a mountain. People ate inside the carved hollow. I smelled spices, as well as fish cooking above. "This is *Falcon's Nest*. It's one of our main restaurants here in the village. You'll find a variety of traditional Anichi dishes inside, as well as entertainment. It's where many of the recruits come to take a break after training for the day. On the main level, you'll find *The Blue Rabbit*, the best ice cream shoppe in town— their dark chocolate and chili spice flavor is worth a try."

I wrinkled my nose. That sounded gross, but Jonah tilted his head in interest.

Jake pointed to the other side of the square, to a building that looked like it was a round, stone dome. There was the sound of an explosion, and the door bent. Green smoke slowly filtered out of it.

"*Rattlesnake Rarities*," Jake stated with a grim frown. "There, you'll find any potion or magical artifact you desire, Hawkei made or not. Though it sounds like the poor shopkeeper set something off again."

"You'll let any magical items into *Hok'evale*?" I questioned. Trade with other magical races was strictly regulated in Kinpago.

"Provided it isn't exceptionally dangerous and won't harm the cause," Jake replied. "In fact, *Hok'evale's* entire industry is based off trading with other supernatural races. Though resources are limited, the taxes on magical imports and exports ensure we have enough money to take care of our people and keep the resistance running."

"Isn't trading risky?" Imogen asked.

"Yes," Jake agreed. "We must be very careful not to expose ourselves, but our tradesmen are very good at keeping our location a secret."

We passed by a small building, where I could hear loud shouts and the sound of people typing furiously inside. Through the window, I saw that papers were flying everywhere. It was apparently a busy news day.

The door opened, and little newspapers folded up into origami birds floated outside, propelled by Air magic. The origami birds fluttered their wings on the wind and were blown down the street, probably to be delivered to people's houses. Sassy and Arabelle rose up on their hind legs to try and catch them, but they floated out of reach.

"We have our own newspaper, *The Armadillo*. It's not biased like the media in Kinpago," Jake added at my curious look. "The reporters are paid to only report the facts, and nothing else."

"Any particular reason everything's named after an animal here?" Imogen asked.

"Several types of creatures are very symbolic to the Anichi," Jake explained. "The other Houses understand that they are guests here, and these are primarily Anichi lands, so we try to assimilate to their culture as much as possible."

Jake handed me this week's copy of *The Armadillo*. It was a pretty funny paper. The columns were printed all different ways, so you had to tilt and rotate the paper in order to read it.

One of the main articles on the front page was the total death count of the battle of Orenda Academy. I wasn't sure I wanted to know, so I pocketed the paper and didn't bother handing it off to the others.

"Why show us all this?" Jonah asked aloud.

"We're doing our best to make sure you feel at home here," Jake said. "It's very important you feel like you're a part of our cause."

"And what is that?" I questioned. I didn't want us getting involved in anything that wasn't our fight.

Jake stopped and turned toward me. "Our one task— and it's always been this way— is to overthrow the Elders and find a way to restore the healing powers of Anichi. Our tribe deserves to be united. Every House has its place in our world. Our ultimate goal is to restore the tribe back to what it used to be. No more sacrificing children, no more separating people based on House lines— just a unified community, one tribe for all Elementai."

Sounded great. Didn't think it was possible. "Look, buddy, we're tired. We don't want to be involved in this war any longer."

Jake drew himself up. "I understand your concerns, but I think we both know that's not an option. Considering Sophia is the reason you're all here — and the one we've been waiting for— I'm sorry to say you don't have much of a choice. We won't force you. But we know you'll do the right thing."

Jake didn't say anything else on the matter, just kept walking. Jonah, Imogen and I shared a glance. What exactly were we signing up for, here?

"I know you guys don't understand," Cade began. "It'll take some time."

Imogen made a skeptical noise. "Must be a pretty important cause for you two to fake your deaths and cause pain to everyone you care about."

Cade blanched, but Trace didn't say anything. He seemed like he was sorry for the grief he'd caused Imogen, but I didn't see anything in his eyes that hinted at regret.

A pretty girl stood outside a candy shop, holding a tray of sweets. The sweets themselves were small blue butterflies that whizzed in the air. On closer inspection, I could see they were gummies. The girl with the tray had dark hair and eyes, though there seemed something... reckless about her that was different from any Hawkei.

"Meet Malwina. She comes from the Anichi tribe, but is part Arcanea," Jake said. "She owns the candy shop, *Jaguar Confections*. She enchants the candies with illusions to give them a more interesting experience."

One of the jelly butterflies flew toward Julian and landed on his nose. He snapped it up, and got a blue tongue for it.

I took one out of the air and tossed it in my mouth. It tasted sour and had a raspberry flavor that fizzed on your tongue. Julian darted up my arm and looked around for more sweets. When he didn't find any, he yanked my jacket hood over my head in disgruntlement. I laughed.

"I hope you enjoy the treats," Malwina said kindly. "Come by anytime and I'll give you a free bag of anything you like, on me."

I caught a thin Slavic accent peppered in her words, and she beamed a bright smile. Everyone was so nice here. This had to be a trap.

Jake tweaked Malwina's chin. "You still keep a jar of hippogriff gumdrops in the back?"

"For you? Always." Malwina batted her eyelashes, and Jake grinned.

Out of the corner of my eye, I caught Jonah scowling. Jonah seemed put off by how kind Jake had been to the girl handing out samples.

"She seemed *nice*," Jonah stated in a bitchy way as we left the candy shop behind. Ancestors, he was already jealous.

"Malwina and I are very close friends," Jake replied. "Have been for some time."

"I see." Jonah looked down at the dirt path and mumbled, "I hope she makes you happy."

"It's not that way between us. Women don't offer what I'm interested in," Jake said in a teasing way.

"Really?" Jonah's eyebrows raised.

Jake gave a laugh. "I'm gay, Jonah."

Jonah's eyes widened. "Oh."

"I've been single for some time," Jake went on. "I haven't found anyone who's quite what I'm looking for, but I'm hoping that's about to change."

Jake's eyes roamed up and down Jonah's form hungrily, and I saw Jonah visibly gulp.

Okay, *that* was an obvious hint. He was definitely hitting on Jonah. Talk about sex eyes.

As Jake moved on, Imogen eagerly started forward. She elbowed Jonah. "Did you hear that? He's on the market! And he's totally making eyes at you!"

"Shut up," Jonah hissed under his breath. His cheeks reddened. This was weird behavior for Jonah. Normally, he'd throw himself at any guy who gave him an ounce of attention. It almost seemed like he was... *shy* around Jake.

Totally weird. Imogen, who obviously needed a distraction from Cade and her brother, decided to meddle. "So, *Jake*, how did you get involved in the resistance?" she asked sweetly, trying to appear innocent. Jonah waved his hands frantically, trying to get her to shut it, but she ignored him.

"My parents were resistance fighters. They died a few years ago in the fight against the Elders." Jake frowned. "My sister was next in line to lead, but she turned down the position, so I stepped in."

"How old are you? You seem pretty young to be the leader of the resistance army," Imogen said.

"Twenty-seven. I graduated from Orenda Academy almost six years ago," Jake replied.

"Ooh, an *older* man," Imogen whispered. Jonah sent her the finger.

Squeaks and Sabor were behaving oddly. They were eyeing each other and taking tentative steps. That is, until Squeaks decided to get too close, and Sabor reacted.

Sabor gave a screech and lunged out at Squeaks with his beak. Squeaks jumped out of the way and delivered a hoof to his face. Sabor shook his head, shocked, before he rose up on his hind legs and beat his wings at her. Squeaks lowered her head and charged, knocking Sabor off his feet. The two of them battled ruthlessly, lashing out with their beaks and looking to draw blood. It didn't seem like they were trying to kill each other, but still, the battle was brutal.

Holy shit. Something similar had happened between Alvarice and Squeaks before. Was this a bad sign?

"Squeaky!" Jonah shouted. He ran forward to intercede, until Jake threw out an arm to stop him.

"Wait," he said. Jonah paused.

The fight continued, until Squeaks had the upper hand. She knocked Sabor on his back and put her beak to his throat.

Sabor heaved a few times, and Squeaks backed off. She let him onto his feet, and unexpectedly, the two hippogriffs started *cooing* at each other. Squeaks gave a low trill, and she nestled her head into Sabor's neck. The male hippogriff puffed out his feathers, like he was proud.

"What just happened?" I asked, feeling completely lost.

"Hippogriffs are noble creatures. When they first meet, they fight, to assume dominance," Jake replied. "Once the battle is over, they take roles and become friends. Squeaks won the fight, so Sabor will follow her lead from now on."

"Wow! How do you know so much about hippogriffs?" Jonah asked eagerly. He obviously found Jake's hippogriff knowledge another thing to swoon over.

"I majored in Breeding of Magical Creatures. I was going to be an expert in hippogriff behavior and reproduction," Jake replied. His shoulders dropped. "But the resistance needed me more, so I gave up that up."

Squeaks and Sabor were walking so closely together they were touching. In a quiet voice, Jonah said, "I hope you can get your dream back."

In a restless way, Jake gazed at Jonah and said, "Someday. Once this war is over."

His tone implied it might not ever be, which is what we were all worried about.

We left the center of town and edged toward the residential area. The shops ebbed away, until all there were around us were houses. Jake led the group and said, "I'd like to show you to your new living quarters—"

"Ezra!"

The sound of my brother's name cut off Jake's words. It was a young woman shouting it, though not a voice I recognized.

I turned just as a girl half my height slammed into me. She was a curvy girl, who looked Toaqua, and had to be nineteen or so. Her black hair was piled in a ponytail, topped off with a big pink bow. She giggled loudly.

Without explanation, the girl flung her arms around me and squeezed tight. Julian peeped in curiosity, and, before I knew what was happening, the girl planted a kiss straight on my lips.

*What the hell is going on?!*

I immediately pried my mouth off of hers. I didn't shove her away, but I took a few steps back. I was so shocked I couldn't speak. Thank the ancestors Sophia wasn't around. Somehow, I managed to stutter out, "Um... sorry, I'm engaged."

The girl's eyes widened as she took in my features. She yanked my jacket hood down and tilted her head when she saw my long hair. "Hey... you're not Ezra."

I gave a hoarse laugh. "No, I'm not."

"You must be Liam. My boyfriend told me so much about you." Her smile brightened. "I'm Stevie, by the way."

I opened my mouth to ask who her boyfriend was, when a voice I *did* know shouted, "Liam!"

I almost thought I was hallucinating, until I realized this had to be real. I spotted Ezra in the crowd, his features a combination of ecstasy and ease. He pushed people aside to get to me. His thunderbird, Dyami, gave a welcoming cry from where he flew overhead. Julian meeped and flew off my shoulder to greet him in the sky. I started forward.

"Ez!" I ran as fast as I could. When we met, we flung our arms around each other. I clung him to me as tightly as I possibly could. Ancestors, I never thought I'd see him again. I felt my knees go weak with relief as I held him. Fuck what anyone thought, I didn't care. My brother was alive, that was all I cared about.

Ezra's eyes were wet as his hands tightened on my shoulders. "Bro, I thought you were dead."

"So did I." I gave a half-hearted laugh and wiped at my eyes. "Is everyone—?"

"Mom and the kids are here. We managed to get half of Toaqua out, before..." Ezra trailed off. "Never mind. It's not important right now."

Ezra grinned. "Dude, you are a hard man to find. Do you know how fricking long we've been looking for you guys?"

"I assume the night we left, you came here?" I asked.

He nodded. "I knew about the resistance a couple months before everything went down. I tried convincing Alric we needed to tell you, but he didn't allow it. The night of the battle, Dad—"

Ezra broke off abruptly. At the mention of our father, I asked, "Does everyone know?"

Ezra sighed. "Yeah. We found out the next day. Did... did you see it happen?" he whispered.

I nodded slowly. Ezra's voice became choked. "I am so sorry."

"It's over now. There was nothing we could do."

Ezra shrugged. "There wasn't anything anyone could do that night."

Ezra's gaze shot to the side, and a smile brightened on his face. He reached out an arm, and the Toaqua girl slid into it. "By the way, this is my girl, Stevie. You guys had a pretty intimate first meeting."

Stevie giggled. "You can say that again. Sorry I kissed you."

"It's okay. Just don't tell my fiancé." I laughed.

"You finally popped the question, huh?" Ezra asked slyly.

"Yep. It was more of a, *will you marry me and go on the run,* kinda thing," I stated.

"That sounds so romantic, doesn't it, Ez?" Stevie asked sweetly.

"You know I'll do better," he replied.

She tilted her head up, and he kissed her in a way that was almost embarrassing to watch. Fuck, they were all over each other. When they finally stopped making out, Ezra held her even tighter.

Uh, what was going on? This was so weird for Ezra. I thought he'd never settle down. By the way he looked at her, she seemed different from all the rest. I got the feeling Stevie wasn't one of Ezra's rotating girlfriends. Maybe this one would stick.

I heard footsteps behind us. Jake and the rest of the group were looking onward in interest. "I think before we show you our living quarters, a few reunions need to be in order," Jake stated. "The Mitoh family is residing on the beach, while the Ahnilds can be found in the main town."

"Isn't it a little... strange there are no House neighborhoods or districts?" I asked.

"We don't do that here. We're an integrated community, not a divided one." Jake turned toward Imogen and I. "I suggest both of you meet up with your families first."

"Are you sure they *want* to see me?" Imogen crossed her arms and frowned. Cade looked uncomfortable, while Trace gave a long sigh.

"Your family would be delighted, I can assure you," Jake said, letting the jibe roll off. Jake turned toward Jonah. "I'm sorry to say the resistance wasn't able to locate your family, Jonah. The Chanees are particularly close with Oleander, and it was thought if we reached out, our cover would be blown."

Jonah shrugged. "The family I have doesn't give a shit about me, anyway. The people I care about are already here."

"That's too bad." Jake frowned and looked concerned. "In any case, would you like to continue the tour? There are still a few places around town I haven't shown you."

"Of course!" Jonah nearly jumped at the chance to go on a private walk with Jake.

Jake waved Trace off. "We'll meet back up in a few hours. Ezra, you know where to take him?"

Ezra nodded, and Jake replied, "Good. I'll give you some space."

The group split up. Imogen headed off with Trace and Cade, while I followed Ezra and Stevie, and Jonah went back into town with Jake. I'd normally be uneasy about splitting up like this, but the presence of my little brother had me at ease. If Ezra was here and he was okay with it, it couldn't be dangerous.

Stevie seemed a little pale. She walked slower than Ezra. I noticed he slowed his steps so she could keep up. Her breathing was a little ragged, though she acted like it was no big deal.

"Babe, you should go back home and lie down." Ezra frowned. "We've been running around all day."

"I'll be fine," Stevie protested, though she didn't look it. "I want to get to know your brother. It's nice to be around someone who finally understands."

I screeched to a halt. "Wait a minute. Did you just say...?"

"Oh, yeah. You've got it too, don't you?" Stevie shrugged before she dug in her pocket. She took out an inhaler and inhaled a puff before she said, "My little brother Teagan and I were both diagnosed last year."

Holy shit. Anna was right! "You have Combined Magical Suppression Syndrome?"

"Yepper. Royally sucks, doesn't it?" Stevie pocketed her inhaler and smiled. "But your brother, he's been so sweet. He knows exactly how to take care of me, because he has experience with you."

"You're perfect the way you are, babe." Ezra leaned over and kissed Stevie's forehead, and she giggled.

I had so much to talk to her about. "So, is it the same for you? Like, is your fatigue really bad and you've got this really intense pain in your back, and—"

"No energy, you catch everything that goes around, and every organ in your body pretty much goes to shit?" Stevie asked. "For sure, it's all there."

A warmth bloomed in my chest and radiated outward. Finally, someone who *got it*. My friends loved me, but they could never really understand what I went through on a daily basis and what hell it was.

"Um... not to point out the obvious, but the disease comes from Anna Cedrick's bloodline," I said. "Are you sure you two aren't related?"

"Hey, screwing your cousin is *hot*," Stevie cracked.

Ezra burst out laughing and he said, "No, not really. We've checked. Anna's son had two children. Stevie and I are from different lines. We're not into incest."

"I'd be into incest for *you*," Stevie joked. Ezra snickered.

"You guys are gross," I cracked, yet I couldn't keep the smile off my face. Stevie might be a stranger, but I immediately felt a closeness with her I never had with anyone else. *I wasn't alone.* The fact gave me such a sense of relief.

But one thing didn't make any sense. I had Esis, so I was still alive, but how were Stevie and Teagan around if Anichi couldn't heal anymore?

Stevie read the look on my face. "There is *one* healer left in the Anichi tribe," she admitted reluctantly. "She heals us and keeps us going. You'll meet her later. Meanwhile, Professor Perot's been treating us on the side, trying to find a cure."

I almost fell over in shock. "Perot? He's here?"

"Yeah. He lives just down the way," Ezra said. "We can visit him before we check in with Mom."

"That'd be great."

Ezra took a different path, and soon, we entered a small cottage. Dyami was so big now he had to wait outside. The cottage had a thatch roof, but seemed modern inside, with wood floors and working appliances. The cottage was small, only a one-bedroom, though it felt smaller because it was packed with alchemist bottles and dozens of potion ingredients.

A peacock rested on a perch above a bubbling cauldron. He sang a hello and stared curiously at Julian in my arms.

"Hello, Baxtor." I stroked his feathers, and Baxtor let out a low coo as Julian growled.

The backdoor opened. I marveled as Professor Perot strolled in with an armful of bottles. His expression brightened when he saw me.

"Liam!" he burst. "I am so thankful that you've finally joined us!"

"It's nice to see you too, Professor." Perot looked... different. Older than he had been when he'd left Orenda Academy. There were more wrinkles on his face than I remembered, and there was a sadness in his eyes that hadn't been there before.

I took a step forward and looked around. "So... this is where you've been."

A guilty visage crossed his features. "Yes. I apologize. I wish I could've told you more, but Caspian and I... we didn't agree on what to do."

Perot stumbled over Alric's name. He nearly flinched. It was clear the loss had devastated him. I said the only thing that might provide some comfort.

"I was with him, until the end," I commented lowly. "His last wish was to see you before he died. Until the last moment, he was thinking of you."

Perot turned his back to me and started setting potion bottles onto the table. "Well, that's something I can hold on to. Caspian and I had quite a disagreement before I left. I wanted him to come to *Hok'evale* with me, but he thought he could still change things in Kinpago. We... never got a chance to make up."

Baxtor gave a mournful cry. He appeared to miss Valda very much. Perot observed Stevie and said, "Miss Descheeny, you're looking a bit better. Finally got over that cold?"

"Thanks to your potions," Stevie replied brightly. "I think you finally found a recipe that worked."

"Stevie and Teagan have both been instrumental to my research," Perot informed me. "Now that I have a small population of people with your disease, Liam, I am finally able to test on a broader scale."

"He's honestly been a saving grace," Stevie said. "Teagan and I didn't have any idea what was wrong with us, until he showed up. Getting an answer was a miracle."

"You showed many of the symptoms Liam did, and your test results all came back the same. It was only a matter of making absolutely sure," Perot said.

I leaned against the desk. "So was the resistance your plan all along? How did you know about it?"

My question provoked awkwardness from Perot. He made a face and admitted, "This is where most of the teachers who fled Orenda Academy went. After your trial, and shortly before the deaths of Professors Costas and Fawn, Madame Wells came to the school and informed everyone she thought she could trust about the resistance. Caspian had already been told several years ago by Jakob. I found out by accident sometime sooner. It was never my plan to be here. I wanted to stay at Orenda Academy, but after your fiasco at the trial, I knew all hope was lost in Kinpago. If I truly wanted to make a difference, I had to come here and aid the war effort."

Perot looked down. "It was something Caspian refused to admit. He insisted on going down with his ship."

I put a hand on his shoulder. "Alric saved many lives. He helped us smuggle dozens of people out of the city. He sacrificed himself and did everything he could to stop the Elders. You should know his death wasn't a waste."

Perot gave a weak smile. "I know it. But it doesn't stop the grief."

Couldn't reply to that. Perot sighed and said, "I almost wish I had stayed. Taken up a spy position for the resistance, like Professor Cheveyo."

My eyes widened. Professor Cheveyo had been my teacher for Hawkei Leadership, as well as War and Negotiation. "Cheveyo works for the resistance?"

"Yes. He's still in Kinpago, doing what he can to keep an eye on Oleander. He works as intel for the resistance," Perot said.

Julian chirped. He flew away from me and onto the desk, where he nipped at Baxtor's feathers. Baxtor moved his tail away in disgruntlement, and Perot laughed. "Who's this little fellow?"

"Julian," I said. "He's my buddy."

"Ancestors, Liam, did you bond again?" Ezra asked in wonder. He reached out to scratch Julian on the back, and Julian's tongue lolled. "I didn't know that was possible."

"I didn't exactly bond, but Julian's my companion now. He hatched and imprinted on me," I explained.

"Extraordinary," Perot marveled. "This will make a difference in your treatment. That is, if you still want me to be your doctor."

Perot's tone was full of guilt. He really did feel bad for walking out on me.

"Of course I do. You were the best doctor I ever had," I said.

Perot's manner lit up. Ezra reached for something. "By the way, bro, here are your pills." He handed me a small brown bag that was sitting on Perot's desk. "The town's got its own pharmacy, so you won't have to do without."

Thank the ancestors. I pocketed the bag in my jacket and said, "We should probably get going. My mother's waiting."

"Goodbye, Liam. I hope to see you once you get settled in." Perot gave a nod, and I waved as we left the cottage. Dyami chirped and flew low as we exited. Julian pumped his wings and took to the sky behind him.

"*Hok'evale* is built in the safety of the mountain range, but the ocean is close by," Ezra said. "It's where most of the Toaqua village relocated, though some chose to mix in with the other Houses in town."

We walked for another mile or so, until the rocky ground leveled out. A beach came into view. Homes were dotted along the shoreline, most of which looked brand new.

As we came to the beach, a strange animal rose out of the waves and pulled itself onto shore. The front half of the creature was like a large bird. It had a beak and talons, with feathery ears, though the feathers coating its front half looked more like scales, shiny and iridescent. The back half of the creature was a long mermaid's tail, a fin that shimmered as the creature moved it back and forth. The animal let out a pretty cry like a siren as we approached, and Stevie brightened.

"This is Nihoni, my Familiar," Stevie said. She stroked the creature's scales, and it chortled pleasantly.

"She's beautiful. I've never seen a creature like her before," I noted.

"She's a cypher," Stevie replied. "Half-griffin, half-hippocampus. They're rumored to be extinct, but Anichi was hiding them."

"Did you bond when you came to *Hok'evale?*" I asked.

Stevie shook her head. "I've lived here all my life. I've never been to Kinpago."

"Trust me, man, if this babe was walking around back home, I would've noticed," Ezra purred. Stevie smiled.

Dyami landed, and he snuggled his head into Nihoni's feathers. The cypher nipped him playfully, and Dyami threw a wing over her body. Julian stared up at the cypher in wonder.

Stevie climbed onto Nihoni's back. "I should probably get going. I was supposed to be back by now. See you tonight, Ezra?"

"You know it, baby." Ezra gave her a wink, and Stevie let out a girlish laugh. Nihoni swam out to sea, then dove downward. Dyami hung his head, like he was sad she was gone.

"So how long is this one going to last?" I asked as we left the shore.

Ezra gave me a flat look. "Forever," he stated. "Stevie's awesome. She's been there for me like nobody else has."

"Are you sure this isn't another phase?" I teased.

"Nah, dude. She's the one. I can feel it." Ezra shook his head.

Wow. That was pretty intense, coming from Ezra. "You never liked being tied down. What changed your mind?"

"She's different. She gets me," he said. "The way I love her... I've never felt like that for anyone else."

"You two haven't been together that long," I commented, but I guess when you knew, you knew. I'd had a feeling Sophia was meant to be mine the first time our gazes connected. I hadn't believed in love at first sight until then, but hearing it from my brother was a little strange.

"Okay, we might've banged on the first day we met," he admitted, and he grinned wickedly. "The chemistry is off the charts. It's been pretty intense. But I'm telling you, she's the girl for me. I just know."

Thank the ancestors. Hopefully now Ezra would stop being such an insufferable man-whore.

Something crossed my mind. I'd been putting off asking this, because I was afraid of the answer. "Ez, where's Madeline?" I asked. "Did she make it here with you?" I prayed to the ancestors she'd made it out of Orenda Academy the night everything went down.

He paused, as if he hated to deliver bad news. "We don't know where Maddie is," Ezra admitted. "We haven't seen her since the night of the battle. She's missing."

My chest ached. "Do you think she's—?"

"No." Ezra shook his head. "We've had spies sweep Kinpago, and her name doesn't come up in any of the death counts. She's still alive. Most likely, Oleander's got her. We just don't know where he took her."

Fuck Oleander. He could go straight to hell. The moment I got my hands on him, I was going to make him pay. Painfully and slowly. "Do we have any leads?"

"We've got people looking. It's only a matter of time. There are only so many places he could've hidden her." Ezra scowled. "We can't find Drew, either. Most likely, they're together."

I hoped we'd find Maddie soon. There was no telling what Oleander was doing to her. She needed to be with her family. But even if we did find her, I worried she wouldn't come back without Drew... though I doubted he was still alive at this point. Even if they had been taken together, chances were Oleander had already killed him. He had no use for Drew like he did Maddie.

Except to torture him, so Maddie did what he wanted. The thought made me sick.

We approached the outside of a two-story home that was built on stilts on the side of the beach. Two kids were playing outside. A boy and a girl knelt by a long cylinder. The boy lit the cylinder with a match, and they ran away. The cylinder soared into the sky until it erupted against the clouds, sending sparks everywhere. The kids cheered and gave each other high-fives.

"Where did you two get fireworks?" I asked. They turned around, and their mouths fell open as they saw me approach.

"Liam!" they both screamed at the same time. Katie and Christian flung themselves onto me. I put an arm around each of them and lifted them up. They hugged my neck and squeezed until I could hardly breathe.

"You're alive!" Katie screamed. "I *knew* you'd come back! Pay up, Christian!"

Christian ignored her. "You're not toast!" he exclaimed. "I was dead wrong."

"That you were." I laughed and put them down. I ruffled Christian's hair and asked, "How do you like it here?"

"It's pretty awesome. Even the Koigni are nice!" Katie exclaimed. "They gave us these fireworks to play with for free."

She gestured to a large box sitting nearby. I grimaced. Whatever Koigni decided to give fireworks to a couple of pyromaniac nine-year-olds was probably an idiot.

"Yeah. And there are no stupid Defortai around to ruin everything." Christian wrinkled his nose. "We can do what we want."

I wanted to ask how they were doing after Dad died, but they seemed happy right now, and I didn't want to bring up things that would upset them. So instead, I asked, "Where's Mom?"

"On the porch with Jackson." Katie frowned, and she looked down at the ground. "She doesn't like leaving the house much."

"Or ever," Christian replied sourly. Apparently, Mom was a subject of contention for him.

"I should see her. Please don't burn your faces off," I said.

Both of the twins gave me eerily similar salutes. "Aye, aye, captain!" Christian barked.

Dyami stayed behind to watch them as Katie and Christian rummaged through the box of fireworks. "Are they okay?" I asked Ezra as we approached the house.

"For the most part? Yeah. As good as they can be, anyway," Ezra said with a sigh. "Christian's been a bit explosive, and Katie's somewhat sad, but there are a lot of distractions here for them, which helps."

After a beat of silence, Ezra added, "I feel most bad for Jackson. He's not gonna be able to remember Dad at all."

The statement made my throat get tight. It hurt that my Dad was gone, but Ezra and I were both grown. I felt worse for the younger kids who hadn't gotten as much time with him, especially my baby brother, who wouldn't have any memories of Dad except pictures we still had.

The house was quiet and clean. It didn't have much, but it was definitely still cozy. Mom had apparently done her work to make sure the rest of the family felt at home here.

"How's Mom doing?" I asked. I dropped my voice to a whisper, though I didn't need to. It felt almost sinful to raise my voice in such a subdued environment. Houses— even new places— took on a weird feeling once somebody died.

"Mom took it really hard," Ezra said quietly. "She didn't eat or come out of her room for three days after she heard the news."

Oh, no. Poor Mom.

"She probably needs time alone with you," Ezra noted. "I'll wait in the kitchen."

He gestured toward the screen door. Julian flew to the counter beside him, to stay behind. He knew I needed some space.

I headed toward the door, an impending feeling of dread working its way over my form. In a way, this felt worse than watching my dad die. I didn't know how I could face my mother again. How I could admit that I did nothing, that it was basically my fault?

I walked onto the porch and caught a slight ocean breeze. At first, I thought I saw my grandmother sitting in a rocker holding a baby, but with a jolt, I realized that it was my mom.

She looked like she'd aged years in a few months. Her hair was in disarray around her face, and she wore a shawl over a dress that hung loosely off her too-thin form. Her expression was drawn and tight. She kept her dark eyes, which were now hollow with loss, fixated on Jackson's face like he was the only source of comfort she had.

"Mom?" I whispered.

She slowly sat up. Mom silently rose from her chair as she turned to face me.

When her sight landed on me, her lip wobbled. She stretched out an arm and shuffled toward me. "My firstborn."

I hugged her. Jackson writhed at her side. I heard her give a sniff. This was harder than anything I'd had to do recently. Seeing Mom without Dad... it was like seeing the ocean without the waves. Unnatural. She didn't seem... I don't know... *there* anymore. I could only imagine how she'd screamed when she'd heard the news.

The happy, optimistic woman that was so full of life was gone. She'd been replaced by someone I didn't know. Nothing could knock my mother down in life— except this.

Mom brushed my hair back. "I knew you'd return." Her voice shook. "I didn't think the ancestors would be so cruel as to take you away as well."

"I wasn't going to leave you." I kept my hold tight on her. "I'm sorry. About everything."

Mom didn't respond. She only inhaled slowly, as if she was hoping I wouldn't vanish on her, too.

I tried turning the subject to happier thoughts. "Sophia said yes," I offered with a slight smile. "You have a wedding to plan."

Something small sparked in her eyes, though it wasn't the light I was hoping for. "I'm so happy for both of you. Sophia must begin her *shantee* training. I made sure the blanket you wove for her was one of the few things I took from the house."

"Thanks, Mom. That's going to mean so much to her."

"I'll make sure your ceremony will be beautiful. But your father won't be there to..."

A tear ran down her face. I quickly wiped it away and said, "His spirit will be there. That's what counts."

She gave me a watery smile. "You don't need to see me cry. It's time you moved on to your new home."

"I'm not staying here with you?" I asked.

"No." Mom shook her head. "You have a life of your own now that you need to begin with Sophia. I'll be fine. I promise you."

I hoped she would. Her fingers trailed away from mine as I left the porch, and she sat back down in her rocker again. She looked out at the sea like she could make herself believe Dad was out there waiting for her. She hummed a lullaby to Jackson, and he gurgled in her arms.

Dad had been the love of her life. She'd been with him for over twenty years— most of her life. Without him, she was lost.

When I joined Ezra, he appeared as hopeless as I did. "Worse than you thought, huh?"

I gave a helpless nod. It was all I could do. Julian hopped off the counter and planted himself on my chest. I held him, desperately wanting something happy to distract me from the darkness that was pressing in all around the house. As much as I hated to admit it, I didn't *want* to stay here. I didn't think I could handle my mother's grief on top of my own.

"Hopefully the wedding will give her a distraction," Ezra mumbled. "She doesn't do anything but sit there all day and look at the sea. She needs something to do."

I agreed. I worried Mom was going to lose her mind.

"So where are we going, anyhow?" I asked Ezra as we returned to the beach. Katie and Christian were setting off fireworks again, and Dyami was doing his best to outmaneuver them in the sky.

"Jake's put aside a house for the four of you in town," Ezra said. "We're to meet up there."

"Did you partake in the ceremony for the chief hood?" I asked Ezra.

He shook his head. "No. I was waiting for you to get back."

"You need to do it. Toaqua can't go on without a leader," I said.

Ezra's face remained passive. "Soon. After the funeral is over. We needed you to perform the rites, Liam. We couldn't move on until we were sure you were dead."

The mention of the memorial made my guts twist. I wasn't ready to say goodbye yet to all the people we'd lost. But it'd already happened. There was no choice but to move forward.

Dyami stayed behind, and Ezra led me back into town. By this time, it was growing dark. He took a long, winding set of steps upward that were carved into the mountainside. I followed, and eventually, we came to a door that was set into the side of a stone wall.

Ezra opened it, and Julian gave a gasp as we stepped inside. The area inside the mountain was carved out to look like an actual house. The kitchen was wide and vast. It had stone countertops and modern appliances. The kitchen opened up to a living room with designer couches and a large-screen TV. Every piece inside, from the rugs on the floor to the paintings lining the walls, was beautiful and spoke of craftsmanship. Some of the rock had been carved out into openings and lined with glass to make windows that velvet drapes covered. The Anichi had spared no expense in furnishing it.

Jake and Jonah were already inside, lounging on the couch in front of the TV. Sabor and Squeaks had curled up next to each other on one of the rugs. Imogen was sitting at one of the high-top chairs next to the counter, drumming her fingers and appearing irritated. Sassy lay in a surly way on the floor. Neither Cade nor Trace were with her.

She caught my curious glance. "I told them I needed space," Imogen said harshly. "From both of them."

From her tone, some sort of argument had obviously taken place at the Ahnild residence. There were dried tear stains on Imogen's face. Her attitude had totally changed from earlier. She seemed pretty pissed.

I averted my eyes and instead focused on Jonah and Jake. They were talking in low tones, and both of them were smiling. Seemed like they were getting along.

Seconds later, the door opened. I felt relief when I saw Esis skitter inside and immediately go to the fridge, so he could fling it open and rummage for food. Julian left my arms and flew to the countertop, where he and Esis argued over who had first dibs on the cupcakes the kurble had found.

Sophia and Amelia walked in. The tightness in my chest loosened. I knew we were safe, but still, I didn't feel at ease these days unless Sophia was in a place I could see her. She wordlessly reached out and took my hand, and my entire form relaxed.

At Sophia's arrival, Jake rose to his feet. "The Anichi Council would like you to know that everything will be provided for you here. All your needs will be taken care of by the tribe, and you are welcome to stay as long as you like. Before I leave you to get settled in, there's someone we'd like you to meet."

There was the sound of a lock clicking as a girl exited one of the bedrooms and ventured inside the living area. She was young, nineteen or so, and had tan skin with long white hair that fell all the way down her back. Her face was kind, and she wore a white cotton sundress that seemed to dance around her form. Bangles jingled around her ankles, complementing beaded moccasins and thick jewelry that hung from around her neck and earlobes. She almost twirled into the area. A twinkling set of bells hung loosely around her hips, like a belt.

A luna moth, bright green in color and no bigger than the girl's hand perched on one shoulder. Imogen's eyes widened when she witnessed the girl. She obviously appreciated the girl's sense of style.

Jake gestured to her. "This is Luana, and her Familiar Sierra. She is the firstborn daughter of Chief Cauac, the leader of the Anichi tribe. She's our resident healer, and our expert researcher to boot."

Luana bowed her head, then raised her hands. She pointed her thumb to her chin and held her fingers up while rolling her hand across her face.

Sophia's expression brightened, and she moved her hands in calculated motions. "You're so sweet! It's nice to meet you."

"Luana is deaf. She uses sign language to communicate, though she can read lips as well," Jake clarified.

"I took four years of sign language in high school," Sophia said. She continued to sign as she talked, so Luana could understand her fully while she was speaking.

Luana's expression brightened, and Jake added, "Quite an asset, Miss Henley. Luana will be your teacher here while you're residing with us. She intends to help you grow your Anichi powers."

Luana's hands moved quickly. She took a step forward, and Sophia looked at me as she said, "She wants to know if it's okay to touch you."

"Uh, sure," I said. I put out my hand. Luana took it— her hands were soft and cool. Esis gurgled from the kitchen, like he was envious.

Luana's eyebrows knitted together. She closed her eyes, and I felt a wave of serenity pass through me as warmth bloomed from her fingertips and rushed over my form. The exhaustion and pain from our flee from the Elders was whisked away and replaced with a pleasant buzzing. My mouth dropped open in awe.

Luana's healing powers seemed more developed than Esis' were. She dropped my hand and stood back with a smile, signing again to Sophia.

"She says... your vitals look good. And everything's working as it should," Sophia interpreted. "Though she also says you haven't been getting enough sleep. And if you keep refusing to eat, things are going to get worse."

Luana smirked playfully, while Sophia had this gloating look on her face that she always got when she was right. I gave a low snicker and said, "Well, doesn't look like I'll be getting away with much of anything with you around, will I?"

Luana let out a laugh. Her eyes wandered to Jonah before she put a hand to her head and pretended to tug at a few strands of hair with her thumb and forefinger. Sophia giggled and said, "She thinks you look fabulous, Jonah. Your hair looks really healthy."

Jonah shook his head. "Well, darling, some of us are just born to be pretty."

Imogen's cheeks reddened as Luana and Jonah shared a private laugh. Imogen seemed... I don't know, *jealous* of her? It was weird.

"So, Luana, I have a question," Jonah asked. "If all the Anichi lost their powers, why do you still have magic?"

"She's the only Anichi who hasn't lost access to her healing," Jake informed us. He began signing as well, so Luana wasn't kept out of the conversation. "She's the only reason our society has been able to be kept secret all these years. She keeps the shield around the community sustained at all times, so that the Elders cannot find us."

"Couldn't the Elders see the town from the air if they flew over?" Jonah asked.

Jake shook his head. "The shield extends higher than any Elementai or Familiar can fly."

"Doesn't that mess with the weather?" Imogen asked— a bit harshly, if you ask me.

"No," Jake answered simply. "Luana can let in air particles if she wants. Keeps our weather stable."

"The shield must be huge," Sophia said thoughtfully.

Luana shrugged, as if to say sustaining the shield was easy. She made swooping motions with her hands, and Sophia frowned. "She says that the ancestors permitted one female from the Anichi tribe, from each generation, to keep their powers so they would be able to teach the others how to use Spirit once the war was over and their magic was restored. The last Anichi to be able to heal was her mother, and her mother before her... though both died in childbirth at the arrival of their daughters."

Luana's expression became tight at the mention of her mother. I felt sorry for her. I knew what it was like to lose a parent.

Sophia put a finger to her lips, then began signing while she spoke. "Though if that's true, I don't understand why I can use Spirit magic as well."

"Maybe your mixed blood means you still have access, because you're not pureblood Anichi," I suggested. Luana read my lips and nodded.

"Luana is very special. She's been chosen by the ancestors as the one who will retain the knowledge of Anichi magic for the tribe, a *memularti*. It means *memory holder*," Jake clarified.

Luana's face grew unpleasant as she saw Jake sign the term, and the luna moth fluttered on her shoulder. If I had to guess, she didn't like being called special any more than Sophia did.

"We'll discuss more in the morning," Jake said, and he strode toward the door. Jonah's eyes were on his strides as he paused at the entrance. "I understand this is a lot to process, and you need time to recover."

"Yeah. My girl's waiting on me," Ezra added. He clasped my hand, and we bumped shoulders. "See you tomorrow, bro."

Luana waved a kindly farewell as she departed after Ezra. Imogen sent her a smoldering look. Sabor's giant hooves clomped on the floor as he followed his Elementai.

Before Jake could exit, Sophia touched his arm lightly and said, "What do we do now?"

Jake hesitated, then he replied, "The Anichi Council will summon you. We have to find stations for you here in the resistance."

"Stations?" Sophia blinked a few times. "What do you mean?"

"All of us have jobs here. It's crucial to keep our survival going," Jake replied. "As the prophesied one, you have the most important job of all."

"But the prophecy already came true," Sophia said in a rush. "I couldn't stop it."

"We have reason to believe that there's still hope. If you're as powerful as the prophecy mentions, we can still use your powers to turn this war around. This isn't over," Jake replied.

Sophia backed away and shook her head. "I don't know if I want to be involved in all that. My friends and I just need a place to stay."

"I don't believe you understand, Miss Henley," Jake said slowly. "The resistance has been waiting decades for your arrival, ever since the prophecy was first made. You're our last missing piece that we need to defeat the Elders and unite the tribe once and for all. Your participation is crucial. If you decide you don't want to be a part of this... it's over for good. Your training is essential to the survival of our people. Think about that before you meet the Anichi Council tomorrow."

Jake gently closed the door behind him, taking everyone but Jonah, Imogen, Sophia and I with him. The minute everyone else was gone and the four of us were alone, Imogen burst.

"Fuck this place!" she shouted. "I want to leave!"

"Im, are you crazy?" My eyes widened. "This is the first safe place we've found, and everyone we love is here. We can't go anywhere."

"They're up to something. I know it." Imogen crossed her arms.

Julian and Esis looked up from their place on the counter. They'd found a bag of chips and were devouring it quickly. Sassy and Squeaks looked on with longing eyes.

"What are you *talking* about? This place is awesome!" Jonah mumbled through a full mouth. He'd stolen a cupcake from Esis and devoured it in seconds.

"They got some cute guys here, don't they, Jonah?" Sophia teased. Jonah blushed.

"It's too perfect," Imogen protested. "They had everything here waiting for us. They obviously want something. They wouldn't be giving us a free house if there wasn't a price attached."

"Obviously, there's a price attached." Jonah rolled his eyes. "And we've got her, don't we?"

All eyes fell on Sophia. She sighed, and her shoulders drooped. "I don't want to become some kind of war puppet."

"But this is a *good* thing!" Jonah insisted. "You wanted an army to rescue those kids from the camps and get revenge on the Elders for all they've done! Now one's practically fallen in your lap. Are you going to turn it away?"

Sophia ran a hand through her hair. "No. I guess not."

"It depends on what they ask," I argued. "Maybe Jake is right and there's more to the prophecy than what we're seeing."

"You guys are missing the obvious. Everyone lied to us," Imogen hissed. "There was no truth whatsoever. We were kept in the dark for so long."

"It's not like they didn't have a good reason," Jonah pointed out. "The resistance couldn't bring Sophia in until they were sure the Elders weren't watching her, so she wouldn't expose their location. They couldn't just take Sophia and the rest of us until there was no other choice, because they knew the Elders would send people to look for her. If we knew about the resistance before we got here, we probably would've given it away. You guys know we can't keep our noses where they belong. We would've demanded to get involved, and it would've exposed the whole operation."

That was the most honest thing anyone had said all night. Jonah was right. The four of us had no concept of minding our own business. We would've blown the secret somehow, and ruined everything if we knew.

Imogen's glare demanded I back her up. "I've gotten over the fact everyone lied," I stated bluntly. "I'm more or less glad we're all still alive, and together."

"Well, I haven't. Relationships are built on trust. And there's none here," Imogen replied bitterly. "I know my family is here, but I don't care. I don't want to be around them if they can't be honest with me."

Sophia frowned. "I'm not happy with Amelia for keeping this a secret for so long, but... Liam is right. We have to forgive them."

"My boyfriend broke up with me by *faking his own death*!" Imogen screamed. "And my brother let me believe he was dead for years! Now my family just expects me to welcome both of them with open arms. Are you guys seriously okay with that?"

"I mean, it's not right, but you can't change the past," I said.

Imogen let out a frustrated noise and buried her face in her hands. Sassy gave a worried whine. "There are still too many variables we don't know about." Imogen shook her head. "How is the Anichi tribe going to get their powers back? And when? After the war is over and the tribe is united? Are the ancestors just going to stroll in and be like, *here you go, you can use Spirit magic now?* No one seems to know."

"Maybe nobody does. It's been years since they lost their magic," Sophia offered.

"Exactly! Another fucking mystery!" Imogen shouted. "Somebody has to know *something*. And I swear, if I find out one more person is lying to us, I'm going to cause an earthquake and make this entire place crumble to the ground."

"Im," Jonah said. He went to put a hand on her shoulder, but she wrenched away. His face fell. He was obviously hurt.

I crossed my arms. "Jonah, you once said that the only people you could trust were the three of us. Do you still think that's true?"

He was the only one who didn't have family here— he wasn't biased.

Jonah stroked his beard. "Hm. I can't say for certain. But I have a good feeling about this. It seems like this is the right place for us to be, at this time. And having an army backing us up is a hell of a lot better than continuing to be on the run."

"You're just saying that because you want to get a look at General Weatherby's dick," Imogen said nastily.

"I do not!" Jonah screeched. Squeaks' eyes narrowed, totally calling him out.

I reached out and put an arm around Sophia. "*Pawee,* I'm gonna leave this up to you." I drew her close. "If you want to go, we'll go, but if you want to stay, we'll stay. You're the one they want. If you want to join the resistance, and fight back, we'll be behind you."

Sophia took a few moments to mull it over. She pressed into me as she said, "If we want to rescue those kids, I don't think I have a choice. This is the right thing to do. For now, at least."

Jonah sighed in relief, while Imogen huffed and turned away. It was like Sophia was one more person that had betrayed her, though that totally wasn't the case.

"Let's get some rest," I suggested. "It's been a long day."

Imogen rolled her eyes. "Whatever." She stomped down the hall and wrenched a bedroom door open. Sassy barely had time to dart inside before Imogen slammed it behind her. A picture fell off the wall.

Jonah stared after her. "I guess she's taking that one."

I took Sophia's hands. "Come on, *pawee*. We need to sleep."

She didn't object. Esis and Julian remained in the kitchen, tossing popcorn between themselves to catch. When Squeaks jumped up and caught a kernel in her mouth that Julian threw, Esis raised his arms like she'd scored a touchdown. Jonah settled on the couch and turned on the TV, like he couldn't sleep and needed a quick distraction.

Sophia closed the door behind us. I swept her into my arms and laid her on the bed. It was so soft and comfortable. She hummed as I pulled her against my chest. Holy hell, for the first time in forever, it seemed... quiet. Not like a sound, but as if something drastic and terrible wasn't about to happen for the millionth time in a row. Maybe we could finally sleep without nightmares tonight.

Didn't know if I was that optimistic.

"I hope I'm making the right choice," Sophia whispered. Her words seemed uncertain.

"You did. There was no other choice to make," I replied.

I trailed my fingers down her spine and said, "I wanted you to know. I met someone with my disease today. She's Ezra's girlfriend. It was so incredible to meet someone like me. She's got a brother with the same condition."

"That's great, Liam." Sophia seemed relieved, though I wasn't quite sure why. It was like she was worried about what Anna had said for some reason.

She was already nodding off. "You okay, *pawee*?"

"I've been really tired lately." Sophia sighed. "More than usual."

"You'll get your strength back. We're safe." *For now.*

She didn't respond. She was asleep.

My mind wandered. The resistance was more than what we could've ever hoped for, but at the same time, Imogen's warning wouldn't leave my head. The Anichi Council wanted us here for a purpose; otherwise, they wouldn't have brought us in. We were welcome here, but our stay wasn't free.

I just hoped when the Anichi Council summoned us, we could give them whatever it was they were expecting.

# sophia

## EIGHT

I woke the next morning feeling more refreshed than I had in months. The four of us still weren't totally settled on this idea of hanging out with the resistance, but it was better than watching for the Task Force every two seconds. Though *Hok'evale* had this uncertainty around it, I felt safe from the Elders here, and that was a relief I wasn't sure we'd ever find.

I rolled over in bed until I was snuggled against Liam's side. He sighed and wrapped me tight to his chest. Esis and Julian stirred at our feet, but they didn't wake. A beam of sunlight streamed in from a small window in the corner of the room, lighting Liam's face at the perfect angle. I stared up at him. A sense of gratitude settled in my chest and filled me with warmth. We'd come so far, and after everything we'd lost, I was glad he was still here.

*Thank the ancestors,* I thought.

No, seriously. Thank the ancestors. Liam was still here because the ancestors wanted him to be. It was why he'd survived Nashoma's death. Everything that had happened since was to perfect design. Had Liam not come to take me to Orenda Academy, we never would've gotten together. If I'd bonded with anyone but Esis, Liam never would've survived this long. If I hadn't taken a walk that night and found him on the bridge... I couldn't imagine.

The ancestors wanted Liam alive.

I didn't know where all this was coming from. Maybe it was being here in this place, where the Elders couldn't touch us. But it was only hitting me

149

now as I stared into my fiancé's face while he slept. The ancestors had a job for Liam.

And the Great Spirit knew they had a job for me from the start.

But I didn't get it. We'd failed. We hadn't gathered the prophecy pieces in time. The prophecy had been fulfilled. Defortai had taken over.

And yet, I couldn't get what Jake had said out of my head.

*We have reason to believe that there's still hope. If you're as powerful as the prophecy mentions, we can still use your powers to turn this war around. This isn't over.*

It hit me in that moment. *We were still here.* Against all odds, the four of us had survived the night of the Orenda Academy battle. We'd escaped two separate attacks by the Task Force. Liam hadn't taken his meds in months. Showana told me I was supposed to die to fulfill the prophecy.

And. We. Were. Still. Here.

We should've died ten times over by now with all the shit we'd been through. And yet, we were still alive. All four of us and our three Familiars. Which only meant one thing.

The ancestors still had a job for us. The prophecy wasn't over. Jake was right.

It was like Showana had told me. Prophecies could be interpreted in different ways. They were always fulfilled, but it was the interpretation that mattered.

I thought back to the night I'd spoken with Showana at the Anichi temple. My mind raced through all the things she'd told me. I *could* be the prophesied one, but only if I wanted to be. But she said she'd *hoped* it would be me.

*"You are the first child with the tools to carry the prophecy out,"* she'd told me.

I didn't know what that meant. My power? The Spirit Totem?

I dug back through my memory more, trying to make sense of it all. *"You will understand when you are ready,"* she'd said. *"Once you find all the pieces to the prophecy— once you see what the future truly holds for your House— you will understand what has to be done."*

But I didn't understand. I didn't know what I was supposed to do. Unless there was a part of the prophecy we'd missed.

I inhaled a sharp breath as something else came back to me. I shot upright in bed and swatted Liam on the chest. He startled awake and grabbed the sheet, which caused Esis and Julian to roll off the end of the bed. Esis screamed as he went tumbling to the floor. Liam gasped and glanced around the room, but he quickly relaxed when he saw it was just me.

"Liam!" I cried.

"*Pawee*, what's wrong?"

"Liam, we forgot!" I said.

He furrowed his brow and pulled the blanket up higher on his chest. Esis and Julian jumped back onto the bed and fought for the prime cuddling spot at Liam's feet. "Forgot what?"

My breath wavered. "We forgot we haven't been looking at Koigni's full piece of the prophecy! There's more to it."

Liam tilted his head. "What do you mean?"

"My first semester here, Doya told me that I had to find a powerful item that would help fulfill the prophecy," I reminded him. "Showana said that was *part* of Koigni's piece, but a part they didn't share with everyone else. I can't believe we forgot about it!"

Liam rubbed his eyes, still trying to process what I was saying. "Wait... so you think we still have a chance because we haven't found this item yet?"

"Yes," I said brightly.

Liam pushed himself to a sitting position and groaned. "We didn't address it because we don't *want* to fulfill the prophecy," he pointed out. "We've been trying to *prevent* it."

"Maybe we don't have to," I said.

Liam looked at me like I was utterly insane. "Now you *want* to fulfill the prophecy? I thought we already had. *When fire blazes through the sky...*"

"But remember what Showana said?" I pressed.

Liam stared at me blankly, like he didn't remember much of what was said that night.

"She said, '*The prophecy is only a destination. But there are many paths to the end. Your choices will affect the outcome. You, Sophia, have the power to determine the fate of the Hawkei.*'"

Liam tilted his head. He still didn't get what I was going at.

"The outcome can be changed," I told him. "We just have to change the *meaning* of the prophecy."

Liam pressed his lips together thoughtfully. "Maddie said something similar. She said a prophecy can be good or bad, and there could be many different paths to take to the outcome, but it will be fulfilled regardless."

"Right," I agreed. "Liam, if there's still time, maybe we can change what the prophecy means."

Liam frowned, like he didn't believe we had time left— like he thought we'd already reached the end. "I hate to say this, Soph, but maybe your Spirit Totem had something to do with it. Maybe that was the object you were supposed to find, and now the prophecy's been fulfilled."

I shook my head. "No. I showed it to Doya. She didn't think the totem was it. Ancestors... she sent Naomi after Amelia because she thought she had something powerful. Doya was looking for this thing that's in the prophecy!"

"Doya never told you *what* you needed to find?" Liam asked. "Did she give you a name?"

I shook my head. "No, but it must be something more powerful than the Spirit Totem."

Liam looked deep in thought. "I don't know many objects that are more powerful than a Spirit Totem."

"I do," I stated.

Liam's eyebrows pinched together. "You do?"

"The *Azaimperiai*," I reminded him, and recognition fell across his face. "I thought about using it to contact the ancestors to get all four prophecy pieces, but what if it *is* part of the prophecy? What if that's what we've been looking for?"

Liam opened his mouth to say something, but before he could, a knock came at the door.

"Come in," I called.

Imogen stepped inside. She was wearing a new white top with multicolored threads through the neckline, along with a flowing skirt made of a rainbow of colors all swirled together. It looked as if she'd just gone down to the market to buy it. Her short hair was spiked up, and Sassy stood at her side with a rainbow bow around her neck.

Imogen glanced between the two of us on the bed. "I'm sorry. If you were having a moment—"

"No, it's okay," Liam assured her. "What's up?"

"This just came," Imogen said, holding up a small envelope. "The Anichi Council wants to see us."

"Thanks, Im," I said. "We'll be right out."

Imogen shut the door, and Liam turned to me. "The Anichi's going to want something from you, *pawee*. I can feel it. But before we give it to them, we need to get something in return."

"What's that?" I asked.

Liam took a deep breath. "We need to find out what they know about the prophecy."

❧

LIAM HELD TIGHTLY to my hand as we left our new house. Imogen was corralling all the Familiars, who had started a game of tag with one another, while Jonah was fussing with his hair.

"You look great, Jonah," I told him. "Jake's going to think you're *so* hot."

Jonah's eyes lit up. "You think?"

I looked to Liam, and both of us started laughing.

Jonah narrowed his eyes at me. "Oh, I see. You were being condescending."

"No," I assured him. "I just think you're worrying too much. Be yourself."

"Yeah, bro," Liam said. "You're the Storm Lord. There's no reason he shouldn't love you."

Jonah puffed out his chest as we walked down a dirt path. "You're right. I am the mother fucking Storm Lord. The One. The Almighty."

I snickered. "You might be getting a little ahead of yourself there, Jonah."

He pointed a teasing finger at me. "That's *my Lord* to you, missy."

I swatted his hand away.

"Julian!" Imogen cried as he jumped on Sassy's back. She scooped him up and brought the dragon to her chest. He was getting so big now he looked like a toddler in her arms. "Behave yourself."

Imogen tickled Julian's stomach, and he blew a puff of smoke. She turned back to us and waved a hand. "Come on, guys. The temple's this way."

We came to a stone temple built in the middle of town. It looked a lot like the abandoned Anichi temple we'd explored over a year ago, except it was smaller. However, it was a skyscraper compared to the houses built around it. It was made entirely of stone and built like a tall pyramid, with stairs going all the way up to the top and doors leading inside. Anichi symbols were carved into the sides, and tall statues of Familiars, some over fifty feet tall, were placed around its base.

Instead of entering through the front doors, Imogen led us around to the back, where there was a smaller stone building not far from the temple. It looked like a mini temple itself. Beautiful carvings of the sun and moon were placed above the door, and the most amazing windows were set into the side of the building. The windows were cut into pictures like stained glass, but the glass wasn't colored. The pictures were more or less carved into it, giving the glass ridges and valleys that formed images of magical creatures. It allowed the light to filter through without anyone being able to see inside.

"I thought we'd be going to the temple," I said.

"The temple is for sacred ceremonies and prayer," Imogen explained. "Even at the height of Anichi times, they didn't hold their council meetings within a temple. The letter says to meet here, which— if I'm not mistaken— is the Anichi headquarters."

The door to the Anichi headquarters opened. One of the last people I expected to see stepped out. His hair was gray as always, but I could've sworn his age lines had smoothed out, and he definitely looked in better shape than the last time I saw him. He actually looked in his proper fifties, instead of giving off the old-man vibe I always got from him.

Holy crap. Was it really him?

Baine kicked a door stopper into the door and didn't notice us right away. He wore a tank top, which I couldn't say suited him, but it was fair considering the heat. At least it wasn't a Speedo again.

Baine grabbed the hem of his shirt and pulled it up to wipe the sweat from his brow. I averted my eyes as his six-pack came into view, but Jonah's gaze locked tight on Baine's abs.

Imogen cleared her throat, and Baine looked up. Delight crossed his features as he dropped his shirt. He adjusted his thick-rimmed glasses, like he couldn't believe what he was seeing.

"Ah, my favorite students," he said brightly. "I heard you were back."

Jonah's jaw dropped, and his voice rose several pitches. "Baaaine?"

Baine furrowed his brow. "Yes, it's me, Mister Chanee."

Baine stepped forward to shake Jonah's hand, as if to prove he was there in the flesh. "You look surprised to see me," Baine remarked. "I got out of Orenda Academy with the others."

Jonah choked on his words. "No, not surprised at all. Just..."

Jonah eyed him up and down, but Baine didn't notice, because he'd moved on to Liam and shook his hand.

"Good to see you, sir," Liam said.

"And you." Baine gave a firm nod.

When Baine got to me, he pulled me into a tight hug. He was all sweaty, but it was hard to care when I was so happy to see him. Baine had been a really great mentor when we went through the tournament. I was glad he'd made it to *Hok'evale.*

Baine clapped me on the shoulder when he drew away. "All's good, Sophia? You're glowing."

"Yeah," I said. "Fine."

Baine turned to Imogen and sighed, then held his arms out wide. "Miss Ahnild, so glad you're back."

Imogen hugged him. "We're *so* glad you're okay. We were worried you didn't make it out."

I could've sworn Baine was blinking away tears, but it was hard to see behind his glasses. "Yes. The events of the battle were... tragic, to say the least. So, Miss Ahnild, how comes the research?"

"What research?" she asked.

"Oh, you know." Baine waved his hand. "You're always doing *some* sort of research."

While Imogen and Baine kept talking, Jonah nudged Liam in the side and muttered under his breath. "Holy ancestors, Baine's a total silver fox."

"What?" I hissed.

Jonah stared at Baine. "Yeah. He got totally hot over the summer."

"What are you talking about, Jonah?" Liam demanded.

"I'm saying, Baine's *fiiiine*," Jonah said. "If I didn't already have my eyes set on someone, I'd totally tap that."

"Ew, Jonah!" I punched him in the arm. It must've been pretty hard, because he scowled at me and rubbed his bicep. Squeaks shot daggers my way for punching her Elementai.

Baine's eyes brightened, and he gestured to the door. "Come, students. The council is waiting."

We walked forward, but Liam spoke before we reached the door. "I don't mean this to come out the wrong way, Professor, but what exactly are you doing at the Anichi headquarters?"

"Oh, I work closely with them when I'm in town," Baine explained. "I'm a Toaqua representative."

"We have representatives now?" Liam asked.

"For the time being," Baine said. "We're trying to build up House relationships."

"Hold on," I said, stopping outside the door. "What did you mean when you said *when I'm in town*? Where else do you go?"

"I'll explain later, Miss Henley." Baine gestured to the open door. "Right now, the Elders are waiting."

The word *Elders* made my guts twist, but I realized he meant the Anichi Elders. I didn't think we had anything to fear from them. Not yet.

Baine hesitated at the door. "Before we go in, you should know the Anichi greet their Elders with the Hawkei phrase *Ancestras benesod por ve*, or *Ancestors blessings to you*. I suggest you give them the proper respect."

I steeled my nerves and stepped inside. Four Elders and the Anichi Chief sat on stone chairs behind a thick stone table. Behind them, a complicated swirling design was carved into the wall. I recognized the symbol from the totem pole on the mountain where Liam had first told me about the ancestors. It was the symbol for Spirit.

Each of them had a creature at their side. I barely noticed most of them, as my attention was caught by the creature in the middle. It was a large white jaguar bigger than any feline I'd ever seen— at least the size of a brown bear and easily a thousand pounds. But it wasn't the size that shocked me. It was the mesmerizing blue lines that ran through its skin. The lines were the same color as its eyes. They cut through the white fur and created shapes that reminded me of Anichi art, but seemed to create an image I couldn't make out. Each line glowed, and there was an ebb and flow to the color that made the creature shimmer. I'd never seen anything like it.

Imogen leaned over and whispered to Baine. "I thought Anichi couldn't bond."

"They can't," he answered. "These creatures are merely companions. They serve the Elders, but are not bonded to them."

"Like Julian," Liam murmured, and the dragon at his feet chirped.

Before I could take another step, Esis jumped out of my arms and scurried to the center of the room. He stopped in front of the chief's chair and bowed so low that his nose touched the ground. Chief Cauac brought his hands together at his chest and bowed his head back at Esis. I was so shocked to see Esis take part in an Anichi custom I myself wasn't aware of.

Liam stepped forward and followed Esis' lead by bowing to the chief. "*Ancestras benesod por ve*," he spoke in perfect Hawkei.

Chief Cauac bowed back and repeated the phrase in a slow, calm voice. "*Ancestras benesod por ve*. Mister Mitoh, a pleasure."

"I'm very honored to meet you, Chief Cauac," Liam said.

It took me a few moments to tear my eyes away from Chief Cauac's companion before I could take in the chief himself. He was an older man, but his face was smooth of age lines. The wisdom in his eyes, however, spanned far past his years. White feathers had been twisted into his long dark braids. He wore no shirt, though his chest was covered by a thin white shawl.

The other Elders wore similar clothing. I noticed there were three women on the council and two men, unlike back in Kinpago, where each House was ruled by one sex or the other.

I stepped forward and bowed to Chief Cauac as Liam had. "*Ancestras benesod por ve.*"

"*Ancestras benesod por ve,*" Chief Cauac replied. "Miss Henley, welcome to *Hok'evale*. We hope your stay has been pleasant so far."

"It has, Chief Cauac," I said. "Thank you for the lovely accommodations."

Chief Cauac exchanged greetings with Imogen and Jonah as well, addressing each of them by name. When they'd finished, the four of us stood in line beside our Familiars, while Baine had taken a seat to the side.

Chief Cauac gave a polite nod to the four of us. "Welcome, fellow Elementai. You've been summoned here because we have business to attend to. *Hok'evale* is not like the Kinpago you're used to. Monetary exchanges are rare and reserved for luxury items. Everything else will be provided to you— so long as you do your part and provide for others within the community. Each of you will be assigned a job according to your skill set, assuming you accept your residency in *Hok'evale* and vow to abide by our rules."

"What rules are those?" Liam asked, using a diplomatic tone.

Chief Cauac took a breath. He seemed like the kind of guy who wasn't rushed by anything. He spoke slowly, like he had no concept of time and just went with the flow. "Simple, Mister Mitoh. We do not harm one another. We take care of each other."

Liam nodded. "We agree to those terms and accept our residency in *Hok'evale*— on one condition."

Baine held his breath, like he couldn't believe Liam had the gall to try making a deal. Chief Cauac's expression didn't falter, but there was something behind his eyes that suggested very few people had tried to negotiate on this before. Truth be told, the refugees here needed *Hok'evale* more than *Hok'evale* needed them.

"What do you propose, Mister Mitoh?" Chief Cauac asked curiously.

"Your people say we might be able to turn the prophecy around," Liam stated. "Which means you need us."

Chief Cauac shook his head, though he remained calm. "No, Mister Mitoh. We need *her*."

My tongue went numb as Chief Cauac gestured to me. For a brief moment, I couldn't find my words. After a silent beat passed, I realized people were waiting for me to speak.

I cleared my throat. "I won't go forward without these three and their Familiars," I said, gesturing to my friends at my side. "So, yes, if you want me, you need all four of us. Our proposal is simple— we will take the jobs you assign us and follow your laws, provided you tell us everything you know about the prophecy."

Chief Cauac didn't hesitate. Instead, he simply nodded and said, "Agreed. This arrangement will only work if we trust each other. But we need the four of you to be honest as well and tell us all you know."

I was a little taken aback by his kind nature. I was so used to Elders who lied to get what they wanted and twisted the truth to meet their own agendas. I didn't know whether I could trust him or not, but nothing suggested otherwise. The Anichi truly wanted to help us, because they believed we could all benefit together.

I glanced to my friends, and they all nodded in unison. If we were going to move forward, we had to trust the Anichi. I turned back to Chief Cauac. "We can agree to those terms."

"Then by all means, Miss Henley," he said, gesturing in front of him. "The floor is yours."

I came forward and told the Anichi Elders that we knew the prophecy had been split between the Houses, then recited what each piece had said. It didn't take very long— what the prophecy had spoken of had already happened, and it was easy to explain to the council the meaning of the different pieces with events from the past.

"What I don't understand is how we can change this," I concluded with. "Jake said there's still hope for the prophecy, but all the pieces have come true. Which makes us think we might be missing something, since we haven't found the object Koigni's hidden piece speaks of."

Chief Cauac looked deep in thought, like he was contemplating how all the pieces fit together. Something akin to realization crossed his eyes, like he had a missing piece and had figured it out.

And that's when it hit me.

Holy ancestors, why hadn't I realized this the second we were told Anichi was still alive? Showana said she split the pieces between the Houses, but she never specified how many there were! We'd assumed it was just the four— since we thought Anichi had died out. But *she* was Anichi. We thought she was one of the last, but she wasn't! What if she'd given a piece to Anichi?

"Chief Cauac," I said slowly as realization dawned. "Do the Anichi have their own piece?"

Imogen's eyes went wide, like she couldn't believe we'd never considered it.

Chief Cauac took a deep breath. "I'm afraid not, Miss Henley. At the time the prophecy was given, Anichi was dying out. If we'd have received a piece, it would've died with us."

"But you know something," Liam guessed.

Chief Cauac nodded. "You're looking at the prophecy wrong. You assume the Koigni piece comes first, but it doesn't. It comes last."

"Wait..." Imogen said. "We thought we'd reached the end because Yapluma's piece came true. But you're saying we still have another step?"

Chief Cauac nodded, but his eyes turned to me. "What do you think the Koigni prophecy means, Miss Henley?"

I mulled over what I knew. *The fated Koigni child, born in the Summer Solstice in the Year of the Dragon, shall bring glory to the greatest House.*

I hesitated, like he was looking for a specific answer. "Well, the Koigni child, that's me. Bringing glory to the greatest House... for a long time we thought that was Koigni, because they're the most powerful. But when Defortai took over, we figured it was them."

"And do you believe Defortai is the greatest House?" Chief Cauac questioned calmly.

I furrowed my brow, wondering what he meant by the question. "Well, they're the strongest."

"But are they the *greatest?*" he asked.

"That depends on your definition of *great,*" I replied.

"There you have it, Miss Henley," he said simply. "If you change whom you believe to be the greatest House, you change the prophecy altogether."

I looked to Liam, my heart pounding in exhilaration. It was true! The prophecy *could* be changed!

"So, what does it mean, then?" Liam asked Chief Cauac breathlessly.

"*Anichi!*" Imogen and I exclaimed together at the same time, looking wide-eyed at each other.

"Yes!" I cried. "Liam, it never was about Koigni or Defortai taking over. It was about Anichi."

Imogen whirled toward Chief Cauac. "You think Sophia can restore your magic and bring Anichi back?"

Chief Cauac nodded. It was weird he was being so calm when the rest of us were bursting with excitement. We'd spent so long trying to make sense of this prophecy, and it was finally coming together.

"With Anichi restored, their healing magic would be..."

I couldn't find the words. I just stared at Liam, mouth agape. With that kind of magic, Liam wouldn't suffer anymore. It'd be so much more powerful than anything Esis could do for him. "This is great!"

"But the Air piece..." Jonah cut in. "The fire in the sky... Hawkei's extinction. How does that *not* come last?"

Baine leaned back in his chair. "It's all about how you interpret it, Mister Chanee," he reminded him.

"I think that's pretty damn clear," Jonah said. "We saw the fire. The Hawkei are going extinct."

"And what definition do you give the Hawkei?" Chief Cauac added. "The residents of *Hok'evale* have not lived with the Hawkei for over a hundred years. Are we still one of them?"

All the pieces were coming together in my mind. "Wait a minute, so if the Hawkei refers to the Elders... and the greatest House is Anichi... that means we really *do* have a chance of winning this war. We can restore the tribe. You guys, the Orenda Academy fire wasn't a sign of the end. It was a sign of hope!"

"You must not forget the last piece of the prophecy, the missing piece from Koigni," Chief Cauac warned. "You must find a powerful object to fulfill it, Sophia."

"Right. The *Azaimperiai*," I stated.

"That is our best guess," Chief Cauac said.

I turned to my friends to assess their reactions. We were all so sick of fighting, but today, we'd been given renewed sense of hope. I could see in each of their eyes. If we had a chance to get rid of the Elders after everything they'd done and bring healing magic back to the tribe, we'd do everything in our power to obtain it. I hadn't felt this hopeful since before we found the Nivita piece.

"Then we'll do it," I told Chief Cauac. "We'll help you get your magic back."

A smile touched the corners of Chief Cauac's lips. "Bless the Great Spirit, Miss Henley. That is wonderful to hear."

I bit my lower lip. "We just... we aren't sure where to start with the *Azaimperiai*."

"Not to worry," Baine said. "I've been working on that."

Liam looked shocked. "You have?"

"We'll let you discuss the details with Professor Baine," Chief Cauac said. "But first, we must give you your assignments. Mister Mitoh."

Liam held his head high. He was obviously willing to do whatever job assigned, no matter how small, in order to help serve others.

"You will be serving as a teacher," Chief Cauac told him.

"A teacher?" Liam floundered. "I, uh, have no teaching experience."

"But you have *real life* experience," Chief Cauac reminded him. "Your magic is powerful and exceptional. You can use your prolific talents to teach young warriors how to use their magic in battle."

Liam seemed hesitant, but he didn't reject the offer. Chief Cauac turned to Jonah next, who had a proud smile on his face.

"Whatcha got for me, Chief?" Jonah asked. "Kick back, relax, you know, Storm Lord duties?"

Chief Cauac frowned, which was the most emotion I'd seen him show this whole meeting. "Not exactly. You will be training each day to grow your Storm Lord powers, Mister Chanee."

Jonah eyed him curiously. "Training with *who?*"

"With our commander, of course," Chief Cauac said.

Jonah's eyes lit up. "I get to train with *Jake?*"

The chief nodded, but he didn't seem to notice Jonah's excitement. "The Storm Lord's powers are truly unmatched. Jakob has personally requested you train to become his officer, and serve in the rebellion's army."

"*Personally* requested?" Jonah practically squealed. "You've got it, sir."

Jonah was more thrilled about his newly appointed position than I thought I'd ever seen him before. I knew it wasn't all just to show off his Storm Lord powers, either. He just wanted one-on-one time with Jake.

"Miss Ahnild," Chief Cauac continued. "You will be helping grow food in the Nivita gardens. Feeding the tribe is an exceptionally important job."

Imogen's face dropped. "That... that's it?"

"Well... yes." Chief Cauac sounded confused. "You are Nivita, correct?"

"Well, yeah, but I can help in more ways than that," Imogen said. She shot a glance at Jonah. I could've sworn I saw jealousy in her eyes, which was weird, because I'd never seen Imogen act like that toward him. It was like she couldn't believe he'd been assigned to the military and she was stuck growing pumpkins.

Chief Cauac pressed his lips together, as if wondering what they'd missed. "What sort of special skills do you have, Miss Ahnild. Are you a weaver? A seamstress?"

"No. I'm smart," Imogen snapped.

It was obvious the second she said it that it came out the wrong way.

Imogen pressed her fingers to her lips, like she couldn't believe she'd just spoken like that to a chief.

Baine jumped out of his chair and scrambled in front of her. "What she means, Chief Cauac, is she's very skilled in research and strategy. Miss Ahnild is one of the brightest students I've had the pleasure of mentoring, *and* she's had plenty of experience in combat. She might serve better in a role, say, working with the strategy team?"

Baine shot Imogen a glance, as if to ask if that was a good suggestion. Imogen gave him a subtle nod.

"Very well," Chief Cauac said. "Elder Baine, you may introduce Miss Ahnild to Carter Thompson, and we'll see how the arrangement works out."

"Carter's here?" Liam asked.

I hadn't really met Carter before, but I knew his story. He'd been injured during Flight class and held hostage by the Toaqua Elders in order to convince Liam they could bring people back from the dead. Carter had escaped Kinpago with his Familiar, Tiara, over a year ago.

"Yes, Carter's here," Baine confirmed. "He's one of our leading strategy officers within the resistance."

"I'm glad he's safe," Liam said.

His words left tension in the air I was sure we could all feel. We all knew what the Toaqua Elders had done to Carter— how they had kept him prisoner for so long.

"What about me?" I asked to break the silence.

Chief Cauac took a breath before answering. "For you, Miss Henley, we have no appointed position."

"What do you mean?" I asked, confused. I was the prophesied one. They wanted me to restore their magic. Shouldn't they have *something* they wanted me to do?

"Restoring our magic is the greatest gift you could ever provide the tribe," Chief Cauac said. "We don't want your focus torn by giving you more than you can handle. That is why we ask only one thing of you, Miss Henley."

"What's that?" I questioned.

"Grow," he said simply. "Learn your powers, and connect with the ancestors. My daughter, Luana, will assist you in your training. When the time is right and you are ready, the Anichi will reveal themselves to Kinpago, and we will go to war."

The thought of war left an unsettling feeling in my gut, but I knew it was necessary. Yet I couldn't accept this position without requesting one more thing from the chief. I'd been thinking about it since we got here.

"There's one thing that might help me," I said.

"Anything," Chief Cauac agreed.

"I don't know who my true parents are," I told him, before going on to explain. "I think one of them might be Anichi. Do you have any idea who they might be?"

Chief Cauac frowned. "I'm afraid we have no knowledge of this matter. However, we can provide you access to the Anichi Hall of Records. Luana can help you search for your parents."

I breathed a sigh of relief. At least I didn't have to figure this out on my own. "Thank you, Chief Cauac."

"No reason to thank me, Sophia," he said, catching me off guard when he called me by my first name. "All we ask is that you be ready when the resistance makes their move against Kinpago."

I swallowed. Something told me we didn't have much time left.

❦

"So, tell us more about the *Azaimperiai*," Imogen said to Baine once we left the Anichi headquarters.

Baine led the way down a dirt path that twisted through town and pointed toward the beach. "Where do I begin, Miss Ahnild? I've been researching the *Azaimperiai* most of my days. It is my life's work."

"You used to be an explorer for the Hawkei, right?" I asked.

Baine nodded. "Correct. I spent many years searching for the *Azaimperiai* under the direction of the Toaqua Council. I'm afraid I only hit dead end after dead end."

"Then what makes you think we still have a chance?" Liam asked.

"The Anichi have reawakened my hope, Liam," Baine said brightly. I'd never seen him look so happy before. "They have many insights I wasn't aware of before. It's kickstarted my research all over again."

"What kind of insights?" Imogen asked, sounding intrigued.

"Let's talk about it inside," Baine offered. He gestured to a small house along the beach. It was on stilts like the others, but was one of the smaller homes I'd seen. Baine led us up the stairs and opened the screen door for us.

Inside looked a lot like one of his classrooms. In other words, nothing spectacular. There was a small living room that sat across from an equally small kitchen, with two doors that led off to other rooms— the bedroom and the bathroom. The most notable feature was the wide window that looked out over the ocean, but it was hard to enjoy the beauty when his house was such a mess. There were dishes piled in the sink and papers spread all over the table, along with a pile of clean clothes heaped on the edge of the couch. The coffee table was over spilling with stones and old Hawkei artifacts, like a smudging wand and a miniature totem pole.

Esis and Julian ran forward. They both grabbed one of the stones off the table, then started fighting over a shiny one they'd uncovered underneath.

"Esis," I scolded, scooping him up and putting the stones back.

Liam took the other stone from Julian, then turned to Baine. "I see you've been cleaning up," he said, not a hint of sarcasm in his voice. He was actually being serious.

"Yes, I try to keep it neat," Baine replied.

My eyebrows shot up. *This* was Baine's idea of clean? I'd hate to see what his house looked like back in Kinpago.

"So what's all this?" Liam asked, gesturing to the coffee table. "Clues about the *Azaimperiai?*"

"No, no," Baine replied. He picked up a large piece of fabric that I was surprised to see was folded nicely. It had intricate stitching and colorful threads. Though I couldn't tell what the image made, it looked like it might be one of the tapestries from Orenda Academy. "This is what I managed to save from the castle. I tried to get as much as I could."

Imogen stepped forward and ran her fingers over a wooden carving of a kitsune. Tears welled in her eyes. I knew she'd taken it hard that all that history had been destroyed in the fire. Her voice cracked when she spoke. "At least you managed to save some of it."

"Yes, well, I wish I could've saved more," he said in a melancholy tone. "Now, about the *Azaimperiai*, Miss Ahnild…"

Baine walked to the kitchen table and pushed a stack of papers aside to reveal a book so thick I might've had trouble lifting it myself. He pointed to the page, and we all stepped closer to take a look. It showed a picture of a small ax decorated with feathers and symbols carved into the blade.

"*Azaimperiai* roughly translates to *ancestral control*," Baine explained. "This tomahawk would give the owner the power to control the ancestors. We believe this is the item that could win us this war."

"You've been looking for it since you came here?" Liam asked.

Baine smiled proudly. "Yes. It's why I'm in *Hok'evale* only on short stints. My assignment is to find the tomahawk and bring it back."

"So, you've been exploring again, and that's why you look like... that?" Jonah asked, eyeing Baine up and down.

"You noticed?" Baine's features brightened.

Jonah lifted his sleeve and flexed his bicep. "Let's compare."

Baine waved his hands. "Oh, no, Mister Chanee."

"Come on," Jonah encouraged, flexing and unflexing his arm.

Baine sighed. "Oh, all right."

Baine flexed his arm, and the two of them leaned close. I was actually surprised to see how buff Baine was. His arms were almost as big as Jonah's.

Imogen giggled, while Liam pressed his fingers to his eyes and groaned.

"Guys, can we get back to the *Azaimperiai?*" Liam suggested. "What have you learned since you came to *Hok'evale?*"

Baine relaxed his arm, and he turned back to the book. "For one, I've learned the history of this particular *Azaimperiai.*"

"There's more than one?" I asked. "If this one is lost, maybe we need to look for another."

Baine shook his head. "This is the last known one in existence. It's why I've been after it for so long. I've learned that this *Azaimperiai* was created by the Anichi at the end of their reign. In fact, it was created by Showana Harjo herself."

"Showana *made* an *Azaimperiai?*" Imogen balked. "How?"

Baine frowned. "Well, I don't know the exact magical theory behind it. That was knowledge lost when the Anichi fell. What I do know is that she created it hoping it would end the war. But it was lost before the prophecy was made."

"That's how it fits into the prophecy," I said thoughtfully. "As a *naderei*, she must've created it knowing it could end the war, but she didn't know until she made the rest of the prophecy that it wouldn't end it until..."

"Until you came along," Baine finished for me. He eyed me intently before snapping back to attention a few moments later. "Anyhow, the Anichi knows of hidden temples and cave systems that are unknown to the rest of the tribe. I've spent my months here exploring these areas, hoping it is hidden within these secret Anichi locations."

"What can we do to help?" I asked.

Baine shook his head. "Nothing, I'm afraid. I took a team with me on my first excursion, but..."

He got a faraway look in his eyes. "I prefer to work alone. But don't fret. I feel like I am getting closer every day. In fact, Thalassa and I will be leaving this week to explore an Anichi temple that was lost to the sea long ago. It will be quite interesting to explore underwater."

Baine sounded really excited. I was so happy he'd finally gotten back to something he loved.

Liam crossed his arms. "Are you sure there's nothing we can do to help? Didn't you say a while ago that the *Azaimperiai* might be calling out to Sophia?"

Baine pressed his lips together. "I thought it could be. But if it's protected somehow, then perhaps not."

"What about the missing Koigni piece? Can we start looking for that?" I asked.

Baine frowned. "I'm afraid that's a problem. We would have to gain access to a Koigni Elder— and none of them are willing to help us, seeing as how all of them want us dead. Not to mention that any clues we could find would be back in Kinpago, and it's not worth the risk sending you there to investigate. The resistance spies are stretched as it is."

A knock came at the door, and it opened. We all turned to see Luana standing there, her luna moth on her shoulder.

*My father said you'd be here*, Luana signed to me.

*Is it time for our lesson?* I asked.

*Whenever you're ready*, she replied with a smile.

I turned back to Baine. "Luana's come to get me for our lesson."

"That's fine," Baine said with a wave of his hand. "You should all be getting introduced to your jobs anyhow. Liam, how about I show you to the school? Miss Ahnild, I can take you to meet Carter."

"And I'll go looking for Jake," Jonah said, sounding overly eager. Squeaks shook her wings, like she was excited to see Sabor as well.

"We'll meet up for dinner, then?" I asked everyone.

"We'll see." Jonah winked. "Depends on how my training goes."

Liam rolled his eyes. "Slow down there, bro."

"Me?" Jonah joked. "Slow down? Honey, do you know me at *all*?"

"Yeah, which is why I'm warning you," Liam stated.

Jonah's jaw dropped. "Im, you don't think I come on too strong, do you?"

Imogen scrunched up her nose, and Sassy made the same face beside her. "I'm going to opt not to answer that."

Jonah huffed. "Fine. I'll see you guys for dinner."

I turned to Liam and pulled him into a hug. "I'm going to miss you."

He kissed the top of my head. "I'll miss you, too. Are you going to be okay on your own?"

I nodded. "I can handle myself. Besides, I'm really excited to learn more about my Anichi powers."

"Have fun then," Liam said, before placing a kiss on my lips.

*Ready to go,* I signed to Luana.

She smiled sweetly and gestured for me to follow her. Esis jumped into my arms, and we followed Luana back toward the middle of town. Esis kept his eyes on Luana's Familiar, like the glowing luna moth mesmerized him.

*You know Baine well?* Luana asked while we walked.

*He was my mentor,* I told her.

*That must've been fun.*

I shrugged. *Yes and no. He can be dull sometimes, but he makes me laugh.*

*He's funny?* She looked a little surprised.

I scrunched up my nose. *He tried to give me and my boyfriend sex advice once.*

*Liam?* she asked.

I nodded.

Luana started laughing. *Awkward.*

It was strange to have such a silent conversation with someone, but understand everything they were saying. I hadn't used sign language in so long, but it came back naturally.

*Liam seems nice,* Luana pointed out.

*He is,* I told her honestly.

*I like your other friends,* she told me. *Imogen's really pretty. I love her hair.*

*I'm sure she'd love to hear you say that. She cut it for Cade.*

Luana frowned. *I heard she was really mad about what he did.*

*Yes, but she's going to forgive him,* I signed. *I know it.*

*That's good. I know he missed her a lot.*

My heart sank. I felt bad for Imogen and Cade. I hoped they could make up. They always made a really good couple.

*Where are we going?* I asked Luana when we turned down a new path.

*To the caves,* she replied. *It's not far.*

Luana led me to a door set into the side of the canyon. I expected us to walk into a house like the one we were staying in, but instead, we came to a long, dark tunnel.

*Can you produce light?* she asked me.

I nodded, and she gestured ahead. I stepped into the doorway and took a deep breath. Light illuminated out of my palm, filling the tunnel. I couldn't see to the end, though, because it dipped down.

Luana stepped into the light. *This is where we will train. It's safe down here, and no one will interrupt us. Follow me.*

Luana's Familiar, Sierra, flew off her shoulder and led the way down the tunnel. After a minute of walking, we came to a cavern at least twenty-five feet across. There were lights all around the floor that illuminated the area, along with a beautiful waterfall that trickled down the cave wall. It gathered into a shimmering blue pool before disappearing into a hole in the wall.

The room housed a few plush chairs and various potted plants. A large shelving unit was stacked neatly with towels and pillows. Esis jumped out of my arms and bounded over to one of the chairs, where he settled in comfortably. Sierra fluttered over to him, and he touched her wings softly.

*What is this place?* I asked.

*It's a meditation space, but it's all ours.* Luana offered a kind smile. *Do you think you can show me what you can do so I know where to start?*

I showed Luana my light, then demonstrated throwing it across the room. It burst against the wall. I made a force field around myself, and she pressed against it with her hands to feel. Then I closed my eyes and focused on the magical buzz of light around me. I grabbed hold of it and shaped it to my will. I could tell when I disappeared, because I could feel the light wrapping around me like a warm cocoon. It felt good— like I was safe when I was invisible.

Luana clapped. When I opened my eyes, she signed, *You're much farther along than I thought.*

*I've been practicing,* I admitted.

*You're very good,* Luana complimented. *It took me forever to learn invisibility. All I want is for people to see me. Being mute, no one hears me.*

My stomach sank at the thought, and I felt really bad for her.

*I hear you,* I told her kindly.

She smiled.

*I thought invisibility would be hard, but it's easy,* I told her. *Do you think it's this?*

I pulled the Spirit Totem from under my shirt to show her. *It's a Spirit Totem.*

Luana's eyes went wide. She looked positively entranced. *I've never seen one before.*

*Do you think since it's Spirit it'd strengthen your powers?* I asked her.

She pressed her lips together in thought. *I'm not sure.*

*Should we give it a try?* I offered. I was so excited to have someone to learn from that I wanted to know everything.

Luana's eyes brightened. *I'd love to.*

I handed the Spirit Totem to her, and she placed it around her neck. Esis became immediately alert and raced across the room, planting himself between us. He growled at Luana.

"It's okay, buddy," I told him, pulling him into my arms. "She's good."

Esis relaxed. Luana closed her eyes and looked deep in concentration. I couldn't see her working her powers, but the look on her face told me she was trying something.

After a minute of silence, she opened her eyes. She pulled the totem over her head and handed it back. *It doesn't work for me because I'm not a Spirit Warrior.*

*What did you do?* I asked.

*I tried to expand my protection magic around* Hok'evale, she explained. *It didn't budge. I'm not sure your totem is the reason invisibility comes easily to you.*

*Any other ideas?* I asked.

Luana's face fell, and she hesitated. She signed slowly. *It's easy when you want to disappear.*

What? I didn't want to *disappear.*

Or... did I?

My stomach sank when I realized it for the first time.

*It's hard being the chosen one sometimes, I guess,* I told her.

Luana sighed. *I get it. In* Hok'evale, *I'm the chosen one. I'm the only one who can do Anichi magic, so people depend on me for so much. It can be a lot of pressure.*

*Thank you!* I chuckled. I suddenly felt a close connection to Luana. We both knew what it was like to have everyone looking to us for answers... and not always having them.

*If invisibility is easy because all I want is to disappear, why is healing so hard?* I asked her. *I really want to help Liam, but I don't know how.*

Luana frowned, and she reached out for my hand. I followed her lead as she took me to the shelf with the pillows. She handed me one, then took one for herself. She led me back toward the waterfall, where we both sat down on our pillows. Luana faced me and gestured to take a long breath, then let it out slowly. I followed her guidance and took deep breaths, letting my shoulders sag as hers did.

Luana held her hands out to me, and I placed my palms in hers. I was caught off guard when I felt the buzz of magic enter my skin. It was like when Esis had healed me in the past, but instead of settling in one area that needed healing, it filled my whole body with warmth. I wondered if Luana was trying to diagnose me, rather than heal.

When she dropped her hands away from mine, I signed, *I'm not sick. Nothing's wrong with me.*

*Not physically,* she agreed. *But there's a block in your mind. We must work to break it.*

I furrowed my brow. *How does that apply to my training?*

Sadness crossed Luana's face. *Because you can't heal anyone without first healing yourself, Sophia.*

Her words settled deep into my heart. All this time, I thought I was the only person relying on myself to heal mentally. But when she put it like that, I realized others needed this from me, too. I didn't want to let them down. I wanted to help.

I had to help myself. I had to get better.

*Healing magic comes from love. You can't love anyone if you don't love yourself first,* Luana signed. *You must work on forgiving the mistakes of your past if you're ever going to progress as an Anichi.*

There was a hard lump in my throat. I had made a lot of mistakes. Some I felt I couldn't forgive myself for. But I had to try.

She smiled. *Come on. We'll start with breathing exercises.*

The rest of my day involved meditation with Luana. I expected to feel frustrated because I didn't feel like we were making any progress, but slowly and surely, I felt my resistance ease. It wasn't gone, but I had an inkling of control over it.

By the end of the day, I felt this warmth in my heart that hadn't been there for a long time. Something about being around Luana was peaceful and encouraging. I was glad she was mentoring me.

On my way home, I stopped by Jake's to discuss a few things. I wanted to tell him my ideas about the child camps, as I felt it was something that couldn't wait. Unfortunately, he made it sound like getting in and out would be more difficult than I imagined.

"We need more intel," Jake informed me. "It's something we're working on, Sophia. We'll get those kids out. I promise you."

At least there was progress being made— though it wasn't moving as quickly as I'd hoped.

When I returned to the house for dinner, Imogen was at the stove browning meat in spices that smelled savory and delicious. Sassy and Julian were on the counter putting vegetables into a pot. Squeaks was supposed to be helping, but she was just eating the carrots instead.

Jonah and Liam sat at the table with a huge pile of rocks spanned out in front of them. Another guy sat next to them, though I didn't know who he was.

"Amethyst is probably my favorite," the stranger said. "It always holds my magic better."

At least... I *thought* he was a stranger. His back was to me, so I couldn't tell— until I noticed the sleeve of tattoos on each arm and the scorpion on his shoulder.

"Luca?" I asked. It was the tattoo artist from the Yapluma village, the one who'd done my flower tattoo on my shoulder and the Biyami tattoos on our arms.

Luca turned and smiled at me. "Sophia! Great to see you again!"

Esis hopped onto the table and wiggled his tail at Luca, then pointed to his butt.

Luca's eyebrows pinched together. "Um... what does that mean?"

I laughed. "I think he's asking you for a tattoo on his ass."

Luca laughed. "You sure about that, little guy?"

Luca scratched Esis under the chin, and he purred.

"How was your training?" Liam asked me.

"It was good," I told him as I sat. "I really like Luana. She's so... peaceful."

Imogen shot me a look from across the room, but I couldn't read it. I wasn't entirely sure she trusted Luana.

I turned back to the guys. "What's going on here?"

Jonah smiled. "We're practicing transference. Direct orders from the commander himself."

"Jake gave you homework?" I asked.

Jonah frowned. "It is not *homework*. It's a very important assignment. We're building up our arsenal so we have extra magic when we go against the Elders."

I picked up a white stone and flipped it around in my hand. "You know how to do transference, Luca?"

He shrugged. "I've done it once or twice."

I raised an eyebrow. "What made you become a tattoo artist?" He could've done so much more if he was that strong of an Elementai.

"I love it. It's my passion," Luca said. "That's actually why I came over — to see if you guys wanted your Biyami tattoos covered up. On the house, of course."

Liam and I exchanged a glance. He gave me this look as if to say it was up to me.

To be honest, I'd gotten used to all of us having matching tattoos. It was like a symbol of our bond after everything we'd been through.

"I sense hesitation," Luca said. "You don't want the Biyami mark, do you?"

Imogen had turned from the stove. She had a frown on her face, like she was thinking the same thing I was. I looked to Jonah. He seemed less than thrilled about covering up our tattoos, too.

"I don't know, Luca," I admitted, running my fingers over my tattoo. "We've kind of gotten used to them."

Luca's eyebrows knitted together in confusion. "You know what it symbolizes, don't you? You know what Biyami means?"

"We do," Liam said, his eyes shifting over the group. "But it serves as a reminder of what we survived. And maybe... maybe we can change the meaning."

Luca stared back at us like we were crazy, but a smile slowly crept across his face. "It's no wonder the ancestors chose you four."

I furrowed my brow. "What do you mean?"

"You're not like everyone else," Luca pointed out. "Everyone else wanted their Biyami tattoos covered up. But you guys... you see things differently. Be proud of that. It's the reason you'll save us all."

Luca stood casually, like his words hadn't meant anything. But to me, they hit hard.

"Anyway," Luca said, "I'm teaching art at the elementary school. If you ever change your minds, you know where to find me... though something tells me you won't."

Liam nodded. "We'll let you know."

Luca left the house, and the four of us looked back and forth at each other in silence. It was like we were all trying to weigh each other's reaction to know if we made the right choice.

"We aren't going to change our minds, are we?" Imogen asked. "I like matching you guys."

"Me, too," Jonah said. "Screw the Elders. I'm a *proud* Biyami."

"Agreed," I added.

"If we can change the meaning of the prophecy, we can change this, too," Liam stated.

"Reject Team for life!" Jonah cried, shooting to his feet and lifting his tattooed arm in the air in victory.

"For life!" Imogen laughed from behind the kitchen island.

We all joined in, and soon the Familiars were chuckling, too. Squeaks laughed so hard she started choking on a carrot, and Jonah had to slap her back until she coughed it back up.

Imogen turned back to the stove, taking deep breaths to calm herself. "Dinner's almost ready. Can you guys clear off the table and set it?"

"Sure," Jonah said as he started packing the crystals into a box. "I'll put them in my bedroom, since we won't get back to this until Sunday."

"What do you mean?" I asked. "What's happening tomorrow?"

Jonah's face fell, and he looked to Liam. Liam's eyes looked heavy, and he frowned. He stepped around the table and took my hand in his. My guts twisted, because I could tell whatever he was about to say wasn't good.

"Everyone's been waiting for us," Liam said softly. He took a deep breath. "They're all ready to say goodbye."

"Say... goodbye?"

I knew what Liam meant. I knew what had to be done. But I didn't know how anyone could be ready for this. I didn't want to say goodbye.

Liam nodded solemnly. "Tomorrow, we'll hold a funeral for the people we lost."

TEARS DOTTED my cheeks the next afternoon, and my bottom lip trembled. The house was quiet, since everyone else had already gone down to the funeral site after work. I'd purposely stayed with Luana longer so I'd come back to an empty house, because there was something I had to do before the funeral.

Grief twisted in my stomach. For the months we stayed at Imogen's, I could pretend none of it ever happened. I could imagine my grandparents were back in Kinpago and happy. At Imogen's, it was like we were in our own little world, where death hadn't touched us.

It was obvious I'd been avoiding this for too long. Now that we were back with our tribe, we had to face what happened. I had to accept that my grandparents were gone.

"Maybe we don't have to do this," I'd said to Liam last night while we lay in bed. We'd just gotten back from visiting my parents, and the funeral was weighing on me. "It's been so long already."

"We must, *pawee*," he'd replied while running his fingers through my hair. "If we don't, they'll get stuck here as ghosts. A Hawkei funeral is more than a funeral— it's a ceremony that sends our loved ones to the other side with the ancestors."

"If that's true, why aren't there ghosts everywhere?" I asked. "I mean, if you have to perform this ceremony so they can move on."

"Every culture's different," Liam explained. "Some crossover with angels, others with reapers... our people can only cross over when we let them go."

*I don't want to*, I thought, but I didn't say anything. I just leaned my head against Liam's chest and let the anguish silently build in my chest. It wasn't fair that my grandparents had died the way they did. *They should still be here with me.*

"At least they'll be in a better place," Liam had said, though his tone was stilted. "In the Ancestral Lands."

That was the only comfort I had in doing this. I didn't want to curse my grandparents to wander the earth forever.

Now I sat in my room, running my fingers over one of the last photographs I had of my grandparents. It'd been in my bag in the truck before we left Imogen's. Esis snuggled against my side, rubbing his paws over my leg to help me feel better. In the photograph, my grandparents were much younger, since I'd taken it from Lucy's scrapbook. It was one of only two photographs I had left of them.

And I had to let this one go.

"Bring something personal," Liam had told me. "You'll see why when the funeral starts."

I already knew. I'd been at Cade's memorial. I'd seen the things they'd burned for him. Now I had to burn the one thing I'd managed to save after all the wreckage. But it was the only way to set their souls free.

"Grandma... Grandpa..." I whispered. If what Liam said was true and they couldn't cross over until the funeral was performed, I had to believe they were here with me. "I've spent these last few months denying that you're really gone. You did so much for me. You gave me a family when I'd lost my own. You taught me to use my powers. You helped me find myself."

Sobs built in my chest, and I wiped the tears from my cheeks. "I bet you're ready to move on by now. I'm sorry it's taken me so long, but it's not fair to you for me to wait any longer. I bet you're waiting to see Lucy. I... I know she wasn't my mother, but I hope you'll tell her about me."

I let out a shaky breath. "I know you weren't my real grandparents, but you were the best grandparents I could've ever asked for."

I stood and walked over to the vanity, where a pair of scissors sat. Esis scurried up the chair and stood on the tabletop. He reached for the scissors and held them up to me. I sniffled and took them from his hands.

"Thank you, Esis," I whispered. "You miss them, too."

Esis gestured to my hair, and I nodded. "I know, buddy. It's time."

***

I DIDN'T KNOW what to expect when I arrived on the beach that night, but I didn't expect everyone to turn and stare at me.

Everyone else was already here. Liam's family stood around a stone altar next to the ocean. I noticed his mother's braid was missing, and her hair fell just above her shoulders. The rest of Liam's siblings had all cut their hair, and were staring at the ground with darkened expressions.

Behind the altar, a totem pole stood tall. It'd been carved into the shape of a bear. Ezra had made it— he said that totems were always constructed after the deaths of important people.

My chest tightened when I thought of Liwanu and his Familiar, Tatum. It was hard to face the totem, because I thought Liwanu might blame me for what happened. What if he was here and considered me his murderer?

Not far from them stood Imogen's family, along with Cade. They all had a solemn look on their faces that only made my grief churn faster in my gut.

Perot and Baine stood next to each other. Perot twisted something colorful in his hands, though I couldn't tell what it was.

Beside them were my parents and Amelia. I walked up to them first and pulled each of them into a hug in turn. Esis joined in on the hug from my shoulder.

"I'm so sorry for your loss," my mom whispered to me. "I know you loved your grandparents very much."

Dad squeezed me tight. "We miss them, too."

Sometimes I forgot that my parents had lived in Kinpago for so long and my dad had worked with my grandpa. Amelia ran her fingers through my hair when I hugged her. Her fingers stopped at the ends, which came right above my shoulder now. "I like your hair, Little Dweeb."

I sniffled. "Thanks. I cut it for them."

Amelia nodded, and her eyes glistened. She pulled her braid over her shoulder to show me it was shorter, too. "I cut mine for Alric. He was a really good headmaster."

I furrowed my brow. "I thought you already held funerals for everyone else."

Amelia shook her head. "Perot wasn't ready. But now that you're saying goodbye to your grandparents and Liam's dad, he figured he couldn't wait any longer. He's gotta crossover sometime."

"Yeah," I said softly, for a lack of anything else to say.

Amelia rubbed my arm. "We'll be right here, Sophia. Go join Liam."

I took a deep breath and turned to my friends. They were each dressed in the nicest clothes we had. Imogen's hair had been buzzed short again, and Jonah wore his hair down. It fell in waves just above his shoulders. Liam's dark hair had been cut to the same length. Each of their Familiars stood beside them with the same sad look on their faces. All held something in their hands— offerings to the ancestors.

Liam's gaze was the most intense. It was mixed with all sorts of emotions— some of which were impossible to read. The pain, though, was most evident.

Liam reached out to me. I took his hands, but I was surprised when he pulled me into a tight hug instead.

"It's going to be okay, Liam," I whispered, though I didn't truly feel it myself.

"I miss him, *pawee*," Liam said for only me to hear.

"I miss them all." I whispered.

Liam drew away and took my hand. "Let's get started."

Liam, Perot, and I stepped up to the altar, and our Familiars followed at our feet. I knew from Cade's ceremony that the closest living relative traditionally performed the ceremony for the dead. In Liwanu's case, it was his first born, Liam. My grandparents didn't have anyone but me, and Alric only had Perot.

"Remember," Liam said lowly, "don't speak the names of the dead. It might keep them from crossing over."

I nodded as we stopped in front of the stone altar. The light from the full moon glistened across the water. The beach was quiet, except for the waves lapping against the shore.

Liam looked up at the totem pole, and a single tear fell down his cheek.

*"Chifte au Toaqua, ei reldeya ve,"* Liam spoke in Hawkei. *"Deya naan un beingo te ancestras te Ancestra Teryah."*

*Toaqua Chief, I release you. Go forth and join the ancestors in the Ancestral Lands.*

Liam's mother stepped forward and held out a beautifully decorated headdress— the only thing she'd saved of her husband's possessions after she'd fled Kinpago. There were so many feathers I couldn't count them. Liam took his father's headdress from her hands. Before he stepped to the altar, he reached and drew his mother into a hug. Sobs rocked her chest, but she didn't make a sound.

Beside her, Katie and Christian were making enough noise. They held on to each other and cried. Ezra rubbed their shoulders, though he looked seconds from breaking down, too. Liam held his mother a few moments longer than normal, until she finally drew away and stepped back.

Liam swallowed, but he kept his features stoic, as if trying hard not to show emotion. I knew what he'd say if I asked him about it. *I have to be strong, pawee.* That was fine, because I was going to cry enough for the both of us.

Liam approached the altar and placed his father's headdress on it. He stepped back and reached out for my hand.

The photograph of my grandparents shook in my fingers, and my voice cracked when I spoke. I spoke the words Liam had taught me. *"Ei analia, ei reldeya ve. Deya naan un beingo te ancestras te Ancestra Teryah."*

*My grandparents, I release you. Go forth and join the ancestors in the Ancestral Lands.*

I stopped in front of the altar and held the photograph above it. I hesitated at the last moment. For reasons I couldn't explain, my fingers just wouldn't let go.

*You have to,* I told myself. *Otherwise, they'll get stuck here.*

I dropped the photograph and took a sharp breath as it landed on the altar. Tears streamed down my face, and I couldn't move. Liam had to wrap an arm around my waist and lead me back a few steps.

Perot approached the altar next. *"Ei pawee, ei reldeya ve. Deya naan un beingo te ancestras te Ancestra Teryah."*

*My cherished one, I release you. Go forth and join the ancestors in the Ancestral Lands.*

Perot set the beaded fabric he held onto the altar. It was only then that I realized what it was— a Hawkei collar, big enough to fit a dragon. It was Valda's, Alric's Familiar. She must've worn it during ceremonies.

Perot stepped back in line with Liam and me. Liam glanced between the two of us, and we spoke the words he'd taught me together. "*Aymare onus, veni naan un oblah ve coraj te ancestras.*"

*Loved ones, come forward and offer up your hearts to the ancestors.*

Liam held me close as we watched our family and friends come one by one to place an offering on the altar. Imogen was first, and she placed a beaded necklace on the altar.

"*Por te ancestras,*" Imogen whispered.

*For the ancestors.*

Jonah followed her and set a loaf of bread beside her offering. My family was next, and each gave a stone. More and more people kept coming, all placing food, jewelry, or other treasures on the altar— anything that would please the ancestors.

I prayed that more offerings would keep coming, because I wasn't ready for what came next. But all too soon, the altar was full. Everyone stepped back, and the beach went completely silent again.

"*Pawee,*" Liam whispered. "It's your turn."

It took me a few moments to find my feet. When I did, Liam and Perot followed me up to the altar. I held my breath and hovered my hand over the headdress. I couldn't take my eyes off the picture of my grandparents, though. My chest was so heavy that it felt like rocks were weighing me down.

"Ready?" Liam asked, squeezing my shoulder.

I squeezed my eyes tightly, and tears fell freely down my face. I had more to say before I was ready. I didn't know where it came from— whether I'd picked up on enough Hawkei by listening to Liam, or if my ancestral guides were speaking through me, but I found the Hawkei words slipping off my tongue with ease.

"*Ve ni aymare de all te adzil au Koigni, Nivita, Toaqua, un Yapluma,*" I said. "*Tahli an hok'ela, an nan ancestras.*"

*You are loved with all the strength of Fire, Earth, Water, and Air. Guide us peacefully, our new ancestors.*

Warmth rushed through my body, and the feathers of Liwanu's headdress lit up in flames. Perot gasped beside me, and Liam stiffened as the flames consumed the items set atop the altar. The fire blazed so hot that it felt like it was burning my face, but none of us took a step back. We watched in silence as the flames consumed our loved ones' personal belongings and the offerings our friends had shared. It seemed to take hours, but it must've only been minutes. Either way, it was over far too soon.

Perot waved his hands, and the wind swept up the ashes. They settled onto a large piece of driftwood placed beside the altar. Liam lifted the driftwood, cradling it close to his chest so that the ashes wouldn't fall. He stepped to the ocean and calmed the waves, then placed the driftwood into the water. The ocean current carried the ashes out to sea.

It was so quiet, so melancholy, until the sound of Haloke's voice cut through the silence.

"*Ancestras*," she sang, her voice cracking. "*Benesod an aymare onus...*"

*Ancestors, bless our loved ones.*

Imogen and Jonah joined in on the funeral song, and soon everyone was singing the soft, sad melody. I didn't know the song well, but I sang the words I did know. Liam pressed his nose into my hair and sang in a deep voice. Esis hummed in my arms, and Julian swayed at our feet.

Tears streamed down Haloke's face. She stepped forward, until the ocean waves washed over her feet. As the song grew in intensity, Haloke dropped to her knees in the water. Liam rushed to help her up, but she waved him off. She needed this moment to grieve.

Liam returned to my side. Imogen's and Jonah's voices grew louder as they came to stand next to us. Sassy curled herself around Squeaks' legs, and Squeaks nuzzled her beak into Sassy's fur. We all joined hands as the song grew in intensity.

Then, without any sort of warning, the ocean water spiraled up into a column as the piece of driftwood lit aflame. I gasped. One moment, the driftwood was floating peacefully out to sea, and the next, it was nothing but ash. The column of water crashed back down to the sea, and ashes rained down onto the water.

I glanced around at my friends, who had stopped singing out of pure shock. It was clear that wasn't a normal part of Hawkei funerals.

But Liam didn't seem at all concerned. From beside me, he relaxed. Imogen started up the song again, and I just *knew*. It was their sign that they'd crossed over. Liwanu, Alric, and my grandparents... they were all in the Ancestral Lands now.

For the first time all night, a sense of peace fell over me.

Liam tugged my hand. "It's time to cleanse the area, *pawee*."

Haloke handed me a bowl full of sage and pressed a smudging wand into Liam's hand. I lit the sage, and Liam used the feathered wand to spread the smoke and purify the space. It was a signal to the end of the ceremony, an assurance that the spirit that crossed over wouldn't stick around.

And I was glad for that.

At least if we couldn't move on, the people we'd lost would be free.

# Liam

## NINE

After we received the sign from those who'd moved on, it finally seemed like life could get back to normal. *Hok'evale* was starting to become our home, and though it couldn't replace what we left behind, it offered something better. *Hope.* We had another chance to figure out the prophecy, and save the Hawkei. All we needed to do was wait until Baine had a lead on the *Azaimperiai,* and we'd be able to end this war for good.

Even so... I sensed there was something... I don't know, *off* about things. Something that warned life would never be normal again— but in a good way. I didn't get how to describe it, as that's just how I felt.

My nerves were shot the first day I was supposed to instruct students. This was Jonah's thing, not mine. I didn't even know how to teach. I'd never done it before. My stomach was in knots all the way to the Anichi school.

Julian walked behind me. He'd grown exponentially in the past few days, and was too big for me to carry anymore. He held his head high as we wandered the village streets, like he knew exactly what he was doing.

Glad to see someone had some confidence around here.

"You did a good job teaching me Fire," Sophia pointed out. She was walking beside me, as she was meeting up with Luana nearby. Esis sat in her hood and chittered, waving to people as we passed them by.

"That's you, though. It's not a whole crowd of people." Ancestors, I was on edge. I didn't want to mess this up and get us in trouble with the Anichi Council.

"You'll be fine. I have faith you'll do great." Sophia gave me a kiss on the cheek and added, "They wouldn't have picked you if they didn't think you were a good leader."

That's what I was secretly afraid of. People always *told* me I was good at leading, but privately, I kind of thought I was shit. I hadn't been able to guide my team during the battle of Orenda Academy, and now I was being trusted with a whole classroom.

Sophia and I parted, and I left to go teach the class alone. After walking for fifteen minutes, I entered an open area underneath a rock formation. It was a clearing about twenty feet across, open to the air. There were elaborate fountains and other clearings nearby where classes were being taught.

Students were clustered around in a half-circle. Most were around eighteen, and looked Anichi, though there were some other Houses scattered here and there. Their conversation died down when I walked to the front of the group. Their eyes seemed curious, not doubtful like I expected.

I cleared my throat. "Uh, hi," I started. "Glad to see you all made it." I'd been expecting an empty class.

They blinked at me. It was like they were waiting for instructions on what to do. Julian headbutted my legs.

*Get it together, dumbass. Act like someone in authority.*

I forced myself to stand up straight. "We're going to start by learning a technique of magic I call *intrafusion*. Specifically, the definition of intrafusion is harnessing magic from sources other than your own body. It's the opposite of transference, which is channeling your power into another object that you can use later."

"Excuse me, what's the point in doing this?" an Anichi girl at the front raised her hand. "We can't do magic. Learning theory is interesting, but it's not going to help us fight, is it?"

"Well, no." I paused. "But I have an idea on how we *could* get you to access your powers."

Excited conversation broke out amongst the classroom, and a few people got wide-eyed.

I'd been thinking about this since I was assigned to teach. Baine had taught me intrafusion last semester, and I'd used it to draw energy from a magical creature in order to perform spectacular feats of Water magic. Anichi couldn't use their own magic, but what if they could perform healing spells by taking power from other sources?

"Settle down," I began. "It's just an idea."

"But if it works, it changes everything, doesn't it?" a boy near the back asked.

"It would, but you have to understand how it works first," I said. "An Elementai can summon power from their Familiars to charge their spells, but you don't have to be bonded to a magical creature in order to gather magic from it."

A girl at the front raised her hand. "Is that how people use their magic before they bond, if that's the science behind it?"

"Elementai gain their magic once they come of age, and once their Familiar is born," I explained. "An Elementai can still do magic even if they're unbonded because their creature is still out there somewhere, waiting to be found."

"That doesn't work for us, though," she objected. "The other Houses get their magic before they bond, but we don't have any Familiars. This isn't going to work for us."

"The other Houses have magic before they bond because their magic is predetermined. They draw from their Familiar even if it's far away. Your bond was severed by the ancestors, but you might still have the ability within yourself to draw from other things, like the earth," I explained.

The Anichi couldn't do healing magic because they didn't have Famil-iars, but what if their abilities weren't completely gone— just blocked by the severed bond? I'd discussed this in detail with Baine earlier, but he'd shrugged me off and insisted such a thing wasn't possible.

Yet I wasn't sure. I was almost convinced the Anichi still had their magic, it was merely obstructed somehow instead of gone completely.

"So you're saying we still might have our magic, we're just struggling to access it?" a student asked in excitement.

"Exactly," I said. "Think about what the ancestors did. You could still have access to your powers. The ancestors just blocked your ability to harness it in order to protect you, and protect your magical creatures, so the other Houses wouldn't go after your Familiars in order to destroy them all, and therefore, destroy you."

"So... the ancestors thought it was best to take away our powers in order to keep our creatures alive?" the girl questioned. "If that's true, how do we know we're drawing from another source besides our Familiar?"

I shook my head. "A connection with a magical creature is sacred. When you have it, you feel it. Taking power from something else, such as nature, feels different. It's like you can feel there's a limited source of power, instead of an endless connection that loops inward on itself."

They still looked confused. I rushed to explain. "A Familiar is an Elementai's soul, their life force. That life force is endless, because it's a consistent connection. When that life force is taken away, the body can no longer exist without it. That's why Elementai die when their Familiar does."

The girl at the front wiggled uncomfortably. "Pardon me for asking this, but how can you still do magic? Your Familiar... well, he isn't here. And you're still alive and using Toaqua magic stronger than anyone else in your tribe."

I was taken aback for a moment. "I... don't know. It's one of the great mysteries about me. So far, I've never gotten any answers."

"You must have some other life force driving you somehow," a boy suggested. "It's the only way you could still be alive."

I shrugged. "I don't know. Maybe."

I gestured to Julian. "Julian isn't my Familiar, but I can still harvest magical energy from him as a source. Though you don't have Familiars, the rest of you can still harness magic from the earth around you to fuel your energy. Watch."

I concentrated my focus on Julian. As I felt his magic flow through me, I took a breath. Holy shit, dragons were strong. There was enough power in Julian for me to level the place. I only had to take a small amount.

I sent Julian's power toward a fountain fifty feet away. The water in it erupted and spewed a hundred feet in the air, forming into the shape of a dragon before it splattered back down into the fountain, People oohed and clapped in response.

"Can we try it now?" someone burst. "It might be the perfect way to get our powers back!"

I hesitated. I was worried about teaching intrafusion. I'd been the only student in Baine's whole class to master it last semester. I'd suggested he try to teach it to the Anichi students, but Baine was so insistent this wouldn't work that he didn't even want to try. He feared getting their hopes up only to let them down.

I didn't know if any of these kids could pull it off, but I had to try. If they could use magic, it'd change the whole course of this war.

"Let's start by clearing our intention," I began. "Focus on the elements around you, and pick something you can pinpoint your attention to. A leaf, a rock, it doesn't matter, so long as it's elemental. It's similar to meditation. Let yourself become one with nature, and once you feel that connection solidify, pull on it and draw that power into yourself. Don't draw too much

— if you do, you'll kill whatever you're working with. You must form a connection with life around you, and realize that everything is connected, a constant moving form of energy. Once you do that, you'll be able to use your magic in any way you desire."

The Anichi students instantly quieted, and the area became silent. A Nivita girl concentrated, but as she attempted to channel magic from a rock, it broke in two. A Koigni guy scowled as he watched the leaf in front of him shrivel up and turn black as he sucked all the magic out of it without being careful to moderate what he took.

Minutes passed, and nothing happened. I was worried I was a shit instructor and this wasn't going to work. *This was a stupid idea.*

"I can't get it," one of the students complained. "I don't even know what magic feels like. How am I supposed to get this?"

"Magic is like... it's like breathing," I said. I felt like I wasn't explaining the process correctly. I was totally struggling with this. "All it is is a transfer of energy. When you use your magic, you're directing your intention and your will onto the area around you. You know it works because you'll be able to feel the magic shifting in your veins, almost like getting a chill."

Suddenly, the Anichi girl at the front gasped, and a small orb appeared in her hand. It was tiny— much smaller than the ones I'd seen Sophia make — but it was there. The small flower she'd picked had only slightly wilted in her lap.

"I did it!" she cheered. The orb vanished, but a huge smile lit up her face. "I did Anichi magic!"

"I can do it, too!" another voice at the back cried. A guy was creating a small beam of light to erupt from his fingers before it flickered out. Notes of astonishment and praise broke out amongst the classroom.

"Well done!" I felt euphoric. My plan actually worked! So the Anichi's powers weren't completely taken away— the ancestors had merely restricted their access. They could still use magic so long as they could siphon it from a base.

As time passed, more and more Anichi could use intrafusion to harness their blocked magic.

By the end of the class, Anichi students were creating light beams and making small balls of pure energy to throw around.

Only one Koigni and one Toaqua had managed to make intrafusion work, and only for a short time, but the Anichi kids were performing intra-fusion flawlessly. I didn't know if they had a closer connection to the earth or what. It seemed like Anichi had a sensitivity to harvesting energy and could do it much easier than all the other Houses could— which made sense, because the way I understood Esis' powers worked, he was able to manipulate a person's own energy for healing purposes. No wonder Anichi themselves had no issue moving magic from one source into another.

It still didn't solve the main problem. Anichi needed their own powers back, and they had to be able to channel the energy from themselves if they were ever going to restore their House to full power. Pulling magic from rocks and plants wasn't going to cut it. But at least it was a start.

I instructed several more classes throughout the day and got the same results. I felt exhausted, yet accomplished. Every Anichi student was able to master intrafusion. If Anichi could fight back, the Elders didn't stand a chance.

My friends and I had all agreed to meet up at *The Falcon's Nest* at the end of the day to recuperate. I'd never been there, so I didn't know what to expect.

I climbed the staircase and entered into a restaurant that looked like a jungle. Vines hung from the ceiling, and plants grew out of the walls that constructed the restaurant in a circular orb. Ivy wrapped around columns placed by the booths, and flowers bloomed from pots that were placed beside ferns larger than my body.

Animals were packed into the restaurant. Tropical birds, their feathers a multicolored rainbow, flew from branch to branch overhead, while sloths slept against tree trunks and monkeys ran along the floor. The ceiling itself was painted black, with tiny lights shining in the ceiling to represent a starry night.

In the middle of the restaurant was a large, circular aquarium that reached all the way to the ceiling. Schools of tropical fish swam amongst Anichi water creatures, like hammerhead sharks that glowed a pearly white sheen, and a white hippocampus who had pearls for scales lining her back.

Julian and I passed a small stream built into the floor. A white crocodile with feathery wings and a long white mane lining his back hissed as we walked by, sinking further into the coolness of the stream. Julian snapped at the crocodile, but I told him to leave it alone, so Julian merely let out a resentful flame before carrying on.

A kangaroo wearing an apron hopped after her Koigni Elementai, who was carrying a tray full of food. I caught sight of Sophia, Jonah and Imogen sitting at a circular booth in the corner of a room next to a waterfall. The booth looked big enough for ten people. Jake was with them, along with Luana.

Both Jake and Jonah must've just gotten off-duty. Jonah was sitting on the opposite side of the booth, in-between Imogen and Luana. Jake kept sending him grins, but Jonah was too shy to meet his eyes.

Imogen scanned the menu in front of her. "I don't know what to pick. Everything looks so good."

"Thank the ancestors," Jonah almost shouted. "I haven't gone out to eat in ages. It's nice not to cook for once."

The Anichi Council provided a monthly allowance to all its inhabitants so long as they contributed to the village. And thank the ancestors for that, because we'd been flat broke.

Sophia beamed as I slid in the booth beside her. "You look like you've had a good day."

"It was fantastic." Julian tried to squeeze his way under the table, but I told him no, so he stuck his tongue out at me and crawled away. He walked to a booth opposite ours, one made for Familiars. Sassy, Squeaks, Sabor and Esis were already sitting at the table. Julian nudged his way in, and it caused a shoving match between him and Squeaks that he obviously lost.

Julian grumbled as he took a spot next to Esis across from Squeaks. She chortled as Sabor looked on fondly. Luana's Familiar sat on Sassy's nose, calmly moving her wings, while Esis banged his menu on the table loudly in a rude attempt to get the waitstaff to hurry up and take his order.

"I heard you found a way to help the Anichi with their powers." Jake leaned forward on the table and cocked an eyebrow at me. "You've managed to do more than any of us ever had in less than a day. I knew Chief Cauac made the right choice assigning you to teach the Anichi students."

"What?" Imogen squeaked in surprise. "How'd you do that?"

"It's intrafusion. I told you guys about it before," I said. "The Anichi can't use their own magic, but they can take it from something else. It'll make a difference while we're searching for a way to bring their powers back for good."

"Liam, that's amazing," Sophia gushed. Luana signed on the other side of the table, and Sophia added, "Luana says what you did is incredible. If the Anichi can learn to heal for themselves, she can focus on teaching me, as all the burden isn't on her. She doesn't have enough magic for everyone to use, but if they can start harnessing power for themselves, who knows what they could do?"

"It was nothing, really," I said. "More luck than anything. I'm sure the Anichi tribe respects you for what you can do on your own, without intrafusion."

Luana frowned slightly. She signed again, and Sophia said, "Luana doesn't quite feel like people respect her. She's more or less just someone that's on the outside, because of what she can do."

"Oh, so you're an *outcast*," Jonah clarified. He threw his arm around Luana's shoulder. "That's perfect. You'll fit right in with us."

Imogen scowled, but Luana's whole expression brightened. It was then that a waitress came up to the table. She had long black hair and wore a navy t-shirt with the restaurant's name. There was a design like a tattoo across her cheek in tan ink— it looked like a constellation, maybe Scorpio, circled by strange ruins I didn't know the meaning of. A wombat waited at her side as she held a notepad to take our order.

"I'd like to introduce you to Lani," Jake began. "She's the owner of *The Falcon's Nest*, and also our local Astromancer."

Lani gave a scoffing noise and rolled her eyes. "Half-Astromancer, Jake," Lani replied.

"An Astromancer? So you're an enchanter. You can control the stars. That has to be amazing," Imogen said in interest, leaning forward.

Lani gave a small laugh. "I'm not quite that good. But yes, I do get my power from astronomy. It's very complicated magic."

"I'd love to sit down with you and learn all about it," Imogen gushed.

Lani frowned slightly, and she shared a glance with Jake. "I'd love to tell you about where I came from, but I'm not sure how helpful I'd be. Things have probably changed since I've been home."

"What do you mean?" Sophia asked.

Lani gave a sigh. "I've lived in *Hok'evale* for almost ten years. I had to run away a long time ago."

"Really? Why?" Sophia leaned close to the edge of her booth.

Lani frowned. "Astromancers are only permitted to be male. If a female is found having the powers of astromancy, the officials either forcibly take your magic away, or, if you refuse, kill you. I didn't want to give my magic up, so I had to leave my home."

Wow. That was terrible, and ridiculously sexist. "We're really sorry," I said honestly. It sucked to lose your home. We all knew how that felt.

"It's okay. I've found a place where I belong with Chanda now," Lani said, and she knelt down to pat the wombat on the head. "Besides. I always wanted to run a restaurant."

"And you do a fine job of it, Lani." Jake patted Lani on the arm, and Jonah's eyes narrowed.

Ancestors, it was too early for him to already be getting envious. Jake hadn't even asked him out yet. Which I was sure would happen soon. Jake obviously liked Jonah, and I knew Jonah was too big of a wimp himself to ask Jake on a date, so he'd have to make the first move.

*The Falcon's Nest* had a menu that was pages long, but we decided to try authentic Anichi food at Jake's suggestion. And he was totally spot-on, because it was *amazing*. The tamales and homemade corn tortillas that you could pile with every vegetable imaginable were fricken awesome. Across from us, Esis scarfed down his eighth taco while Sassy was nice enough to share her pork dish with Julian.

Sabor and Squeaks were tugging on a slab of boar meat between them. Squeaks ripped it away, only to bite it in half and share it with the other hippogriff.

Sabor coughed up a bit of his food and spat it on the table. Squeaks gobbled it up, her sights on Sabor the entire time. Sabor cooed in pride.

That was so fucking disgusting. "Gross." I wrinkled my nose. Jake laughed.

"It's typical hippogriff behavior. They feed each other," he explained. He looked over and grabbed a napkin. "Jonah, you have something on your face."

Jake reached across Luana and wiped a smear of hot sauce off the corner of Jonah's mouth. Jonah went utterly still, while Luana giggled.

Ancestors, they were making me sick, too. I noticed Sophia was picking at her chicken lime soup. Sophia had opted out of getting anything too out of the ordinary and ordered something bland, though it didn't look like she was eating it.

"Are you all right?" I asked. She looked up. Esis, whose cheeks were smeared with taco sauce, glanced at us with full cheeks.

"I'm okay. Just feeling a little nauseous." She pressed a hand to her stomach and grimaced.

I figured that'd be over with since we'd settled in. "You should probably eat. It might make you feel better." I knew I always felt ill whenever I didn't eat, and Sophia had been picking at all her meals lately.

"Maybe." She continued playing with her soup and took small bites. I kept my eye on her, wondering when this was going to end.

Luana shuffled through her purse and handed Sophia a bottle of ginger pills. "Thanks, Lu," Sophia said as she popped one. Luana gave her a kind smile. When Sophia tried to hand the pills back, Luana shook her head, as if to say they were for her. Sophia put them back in her purse, and Luana gazed at the two of us in a way I couldn't read.

Imogen stared into her drink. She threw heated glances at Luana every now and then, though she did her best to ignore them.

As we finished up our meal, the entrance to the restaurant slammed open. I tried not to pay attention, thinking it was just a creature trying to force its way in or whatever.

"Aw, hell no," Jonah said. I turned around. My stomach sank when I recognized the woman who'd just walked in. It was Jaymin Riske and a couple of her Interhouse Alliance members.

"Fucking *ew*," Imogen said. She didn't bother to keep her voice down. Jaymin caught it, and her eyes roamed our way. Jaymin's gaze narrowed when she recognized us, but she didn't bother to offer a greeting, just took a booth on the opposite side of the restaurant.

All the Familiars had stopped eating and were glaring at Jaymin in a clear warning to stay back... except for Julian, who didn't understand what was going on.

Jake glanced at Jaymin before dropping his gaze. Clearly, there were no feelings lost between Jake and Jaymin either.

"She bothering you?" Jonah asked. His tone had gotten deeper— like he was willing to deal with any issue that caused Jake's slight discomfort.

Jake's hand tightened on his beer. "Let's just say she's caused plenty of problems for the resistance since she's been here."

"Why don't you kick her out?" Jonah questioned.

He scowled. "Exiling anyone from *Hok'evale* would damage our mission of peace... and until she does something that truly threatens our tribe, it would go against our values to cast her out. Not to mention she's the type to expose us out of resentment."

Jonah wore an expression that clearly said Jake should toss her on her ass anyway. Sophia gripped my arm tightly. "Liam, I can't be around her," Sophia whispered. Her skin had turned a slight shade of green, like Jaymin's mere presence was triggering a whole lot of flashbacks she didn't want to get into.

I got it. It was totally upsetting to be around the woman who'd basically caused the Kinpago riots and started a night of hell.

"Let's get out of here." None of us wanted to be in a place where Jaymin was hanging around.

We paid for our meal and left to go back home. Sophia didn't relax until Jaymin was out of our sight. Her body eased underneath the arm I'd wrapped around her waist. She clung to Esis, who was trying to clean his fur but only spreading the taco sauce around.

When we got back to the house, Sophia immediately headed to the bathroom. I wondered if I should follow her... she still looked kinda pale... but figured it best to give her space. Seeing Jaymin was enough to make anyone puke.

Jake leaned on the kitchen counter as Jonah opened the fridge to start handing out drinks. "You know, I hear you're the Storm Lord, but I haven't actually *seen* you in action." Jake's eyebrows waggled. "I'd like a demonstration of what you can do."

It sounded like he was talking about way more than conjuring lightning. Jonah leaned on Squeaks. He was trying to be casual, but it was so utterly awkward to watch. "You got a place for me to practice? I can go all day."

"I bet you—"

Jake's words were cut off as Sophia came rushing into the living room. She held a bottle of lotion in her hands, but her fingers looked sticky— and full of goo.

I realized what had happened and barely held in a snicker. Jonah took one look at Sophia holding the lotion bottle and completely lost it.

"Jonah! Did you *really* replace my lotion with lube?" Sophia screamed.

Jonah couldn't answer. He was laughing too hard. Sophia rolled her eyes, but she couldn't stop the grin that spread across her features. "I can't believe you. That is so childish."

"Hey, you started it. You pulled my pants down and exposed my beautiful boxers for the world to witness," Jonah combated.

"I would've liked to see that," Jake teased, and Jonah turned fucking red.

"Oh, this prank war is *on*!" Sophia laughed. "I'm totally going to get you back!"

"You can try, baby, you can try. But I'm a master prankster. You'll never win." Jonah shook his head.

The corners of Jake's lips twitched. Imogen's mouth remained flat as she sat at the table, drumming her fingers.

"We were just seeing if the *Storm Lord* here could give Jake a demonstration of his powers," I added. "Why don't we go down to the beach and see if we can make a lightning storm?"

"Sure. I could use a refresher," Sophia said. "Just give me a minute to get all this shit off my hands."

Jonah hissed in glee. Sophia stuck her tongue out at him.

Storm clouds had already gathered over the beach when we arrived, making the entire landscape dark. Jonah rubbed his hands together eagerly.

"Hold on to your panties, boys and girls, because things are about to get *spicy*."

Jonah flung a hand toward the sky, and a lightning bolt crackled across the clouds instantly. I rolled my eyes. Squeaks cheered in delight, and Sabor let out an awed coo.

Lightning balls flew from Jonah's fists as he fired them across the ocean. As he swirled his hands, a windstorm whirled around him, and the hippogriffs had to flatten themselves to the ground so they wouldn't be in danger of being carried off. Julian was blown backward, but I knelt to the ground and held him down. He gave irritated growls as Jonah increased the intensity of the windstorm, directing his magic at a tree so that the wind whipped it out of the ground. Above him, lightning ricocheted across the sky, making the heavens above crack into a million pieces. He wasn't even breaking a sweat.

Jake sat on a flat boulder and watched, clearly impressed. Jonah sent a small tornado twisting across the beach before giving a quick glance back at Jake.

Okay, Jonah was totally showing off to impress Jake. It was *so* obvious.

Sophia set Esis on Julian's back before she walked toward the shoreline. She concentrated, her one hand holding the Spirit Totem as a lightning bolt flickered out of the sky and connected with the ocean. It wasn't as strong as Jonah's, but to be honest, I was relieved that she could still conjure lightning at all. I worried she'd all but lost the ability after the riots. Sophia cast a few more lightning bolts, but they seemed timid and unsure.

As Sophia and Jonah worked, Imogen sat by herself and stroked Sassy's fur, staring out at the water. What was wrong with her? She'd barely spoken at dinner, and now she was acting like a loner.

When the windstorm died down and Jonah was busy conjuring larger and larger lightning bolts for Jake's entertainment, I walked toward Sophia.

"You seem to be conjuring lightning just fine," I told her. "Why are you still struggling with making flames?"

She'd used Fire at the funeral, but that was different. I'd seen it in her eyes.

"Lightning doesn't feel like Fire. I know that doesn't make sense, but it doesn't seem as destructive," Sophia explained.

I nodded. Jonah hovered several feet in the air around the lightning storm he created before he landed next to us, and the bolts died down.

"You know Sophia, I wonder if we could channel lightning together," Jonah suggested. "It would be really helpful if we could shoot lightning back and forth during a fight. You know, like share it, instead of having to conjure it every time we need to."

"I don't know if it works like that," Sophia protested. "I thought you said only a Storm Lord can control lightning."

"We don't know until we try." Jonah took a wide stance. "I'll call it down, then I'll try to send it to you. You catch it, okay?"

"Okay..." Sophia prepared herself, and I backed off. As Jonah's attention turned toward the skies, Luana's eyes grew wide, and she shook her head *no*, though Sophia didn't see her.

"Soph, maybe we should reconsider," I blurted out. Her eyes flashed to me, then to Luana. She hesitated, and Jonah noticed, though he was already channeling the lightning— and it was too late to recast the spell.

"Shit!" I heard Jonah shout, then everyone screamed as the lightning bolt crashed down from the sky and collided with Jonah's body. He immediately went rigid. As the lightning absorbed into his body, he collapsed onto the beach limply.

It happened in less than a second. The lightning was gone, and the clouds had cleared, but Jonah was unconscious. His clothes were singed, and a smoking smell filled the air. Harsh burns covered Jonah's skin, from his face all the way down his arms and torso.

"Jonah!" Imogen had jumped up and ran to him. She fell on her knees. I bolted to his side. It looked like the lightning bolt had hit him directly in the back.

"Jonah, wake up!" Imogen tried shaking him awake, tears in her eyes, but he didn't respond. I worried he'd suffered some kind of cardiac arrest. That lightning bolt had hit him with all it had.

Squeaks barged her way through and nudged Jonah, but he still didn't stir.

Jake was there almost as soon as Imogen was. He stooped next to Jonah and studied his features, as if trying to remain calm and assess the situation, but it was clear that even he was at a loss for what to do. His breathing was ragged as he stared down at Jonah's body, eyes nearly paralyzed with fear.

Sophia's hands were over her mouth. She shook her head as she hushed, "I didn't mean for this to happen. I should've caught it."

"It's not your fault," I forced out, but only because I felt like it was mine. I'd interrupted the spell— though at the same time, maybe Sophia would've been at the receiving end of that lightning bolt instead. This had been a bad idea all around.

There were footsteps behind us. Luana knelt by Jonah's side and pushed Imogen out of the way, fear in her gaze. Imogen fell to the side. Luana hurried to put her hands over Jonah's heart. Esis scampered off Julian's back and helped her, laying his tiny paws on top of her hands. Sierra fluttered off Luana's shoulder and landed on Jonah's nose, aiding her help in the process.

Everything seemed frozen in time for a few horrible minutes. I didn't know if their healing magic was going to work.

Then Jonah's eyes opened, and he coughed. A sigh of relief echoed around the group as we watched Luana and Esis' healing magic clear away the burns, giving him fresh new skin. Jake helped Jonah slowly sit up, and Sierra fluttered off his nose. He took a few more ragged coughs before he looked around, dazed.

In a thin voice, he rasped, "Huh. Shouldn't have given it so much juice."

Luana ran her hand along Jonah's back as she helped him stay upright.

Imogen's lip was trembling. "You idiot! You know better than to try something like that!"

Before Jonah could say a word, Imogen made a noise that sounded like a sob before she whirled to her feet. She stomped several feet away and turned her back to us. Sassy nudged at her ankles, but Imogen ignored her.

Jake's hand shook. He held it up to Jonah's face and gently cupped his cheek, turning his head so that Jonah was looking directly at him. Jonah became still as Jakes' eyes searched him, like he was trying to figure out if Jonah was really okay.

"I think you've shown me quite enough. You need rest." Jake's voice was thick and rough as he dropped his hand from Jonah's skin. He sounded like a commander now, not a friend. Sabor clacked his beak in agreement.

Jonah's head hung low. He was totally embarrassed about messing up in front of Jake.

Luana signed a few words, and Sophia said, "Luana's right. The important thing is Jonah's okay. We can work on his Storm Lord powers another time."

"This went too far." Jake's tone was so firm, everyone else seemed scared to speak. He hefted Jonah into his arms, one arm under his back and the other beneath his knees, rising quickly to his feet.

Jake cradled Jonah close to his chest, and Jonah let out a small noise of alarm. Jake carried Jonah's weight all on his own, until he settled Jonah onto Squeaks' back. Jonah's cheeks were absolutely burning.

Squeaks carried Jonah back to the house. Jake then helped Jonah onto the couch, carrying him in that same intimate position again before putting him down.

Jonah spread out and put a hand over his eyes. Though he'd been healed, the lightning strike still took a lot out of him. Squeaks lay beside him and nipped at the edges of his fingers.

Once Jonah was situated, Jake stood at the door with a stoic expression. His voice was impassive as he stated, "I'll be back in the morning to assess your condition. Get some sleep, soldier."

Jake whirled around on his heel, and he and Sabor swept out of the house like they couldn't wait to get out of there.

The moment Jake left, Jonah groaned dramatically. "I made myself look like a complete *ass*," he complained.

"You just got carried away. I'm pretty sure Jake's still impressed. You were throwing lightning around like it was nothing," I offered.

"Yeah, until I totally *toasted* myself," Jonah whined.

Sophia nervously played with her hands. "I'm sorry I wasn't ready to catch it. You getting hurt was my fault."

"Nah, Sophia. I could've redirected that lightning at something else. I just panicked last minute." Jonah sighed heavily. "Now the guy I like is going to think I'm a total dumbass."

"Hey, if he's been working with you for any amount of time, he already thinks that," I joked. Jonah groaned again.

"Jake seemed to leave in a hurry." Sophia frowned, like she didn't approve.

"Well, *duh*. He doesn't want to involve himself with a loser like me," Jonah moaned.

"Hey, losers are cool. Requirement of being part of the Reject Team," I offered.

Luana smiled. She liked that.

Imogen let out a scathing noise. "Isn't it obvious? Jake blames himself. He thinks he was a distraction, and that's why you messed up."

Jonah's eyes grew in clarity. "Really?"

"Obviously," Imogen muttered. "I bet he's beating himself up right now. It was his idea in the first place to go down there and mess around."

Imogen's tone was resentful. It implied if something bad *had* happened to Jonah, she would've blamed Jake.

Jonah smacked himself in the forehead, then winced. "Ow. Great. Now he's really going to hate me *forever*."

"That's very drastic," I added flatly.

"He's not going to hate you." Sophia knelt by Jonah's side. "I just don't think he could handle seeing you hurt like that."

Jonah huffed a piece of hair out of his eyes. "This is going to make work awkward as *fuck*."

Squeaks chortled in agreement, and Sophia subbed cheerfully, "Well, you could always suck his dick. I bet that would cheer him right up."

Jonah shot Sophia a glare. "Right. Like I'm going to give a blow job to my commander just to smooth things over."

"Works for us," I said, and Jonah moaned louder as Sophia giggled.

There was a knock on the door. I thought Jake had come back, but when I opened the door I saw my brother, along with Stevie and Cade.

Ezra and Stevie were fucking attached at the hip. You never saw one without the other. As usual, Stevie had one of her signature bows in her hair. It was blue and matched the dress she was wearing.

Ezra seemed particularly somber. "Hey, do you mind if we hang out for a bit? I've got... uh... stuff on my mind," he said lamely.

Ezra's chief hood ceremony was tomorrow. I knew it'd been weighing on him heavily since Dad's funeral, but he looked worse than ever. There were huge bags under his eyes, and his shoulders sagged. It was like he was dreading dragging himself down to the river tomorrow to perform the ritual.

"If you need help preparing, I've got your back," I offered. "Just tell me what you need."

Ezra shrugged. "I just don't want to be alone right now. I figured we could have a party or something. Get my mind off it."

Ezra acted like he was going to his own funeral, and not a ceremony to make him leader over all of Toaqua. He should be meditating and concentrating on what he had to do, not trying to find a way out of it. My Dad was gone. The Water tribe needed him.

But my brother was not me, and we worked in different ways, so I said, "Sure. Come on in."

I noticed none of their Familiars were with them. I gave a curious look and Stevie said, "Arabelle, Dyami and Nihoni are playing by the ocean. They have a thing for hide-and-seek."

I couldn't imagine Dyami *hiding* anywhere, because he was so fucking huge. Ezra stopped when he saw Jonah lying on the couch. "Woah. What happened to you?"

"Lightning bolt got out of hand," Jonah mumbled.

Sophia smiled. "Well, look at the bright side. At least you got some attention from your man. He totally babied you."

"He's not my man," Jonah said wistfully.

I gave a scoffing sound. "Jake was carrying you around like you guys were on your honeymoon."

"He was not!" Jonah burst.

Stevie fluttered her eyelids. "Jonah, Jake is *totally* into you. He's changed since you've come around."

"Really?" Jonah raised his head, like he couldn't believe it.

Stevie nodded, the bow in her hair bobbing. "Yep. He can't stop talking about you. It's so freaking cute."

Jonah pressed his hands to his stomach, as if to try and stop his insides from doing backflips. "It's so hard to believe," he confessed. "I've never had someone who... I don't know, actually likes me."

Fuck Renar a million times over for giving Jonah issues. One of the many reasons I figured that prick needed to be removed from the picture permanently.

Sophia put a hand on Jonah's. "You need to get used to it, because Jake definitely likes you for you."

"He's also a closet freak, if any of you knew." Stevie giggled. "He puts on a clean persona in public, but from what I've heard, he's into some pretty dirty shit between the sheets."

You might as well have told Jonah Christmas was coming early. A huge grin spread across his face, and he twisted into the couch pillows, trying to hide it. This was his personal dream come true.

Ezra sat on the couch opposite Jonah and pulled Stevie onto his lap. "He's not the only one who can be filthy, baby." He nipped at Stevie's neck, and she squealed.

"Please don't have sex on my couch," I complained, and everyone laughed.

Cade broke into a smile, but his attention was obviously on Imogen. She hadn't moved from her place in the kitchen, nor looked at him since he'd walked in.

Luana signed quickly, and Sophia said, "Luana wants to play a game."

"Truth or Dare!" Stevie burst, and she giggled when Ezra tickled her sides.

"Are we ten?" I asked, but Sophia scooted over as I sat down next to her to join the circle. I pulled her onto my lap, too, and she smiled as she curled up against me.

"Don't be such a wet dick. It's a classic," Jonah stated.

Even Imogen left the kitchen and sat against Squeaks near the couch next to Jonah, though it was pointedly far away from Cade. Stevie's eyes glimmered as she bounced on Ezra's lap.

"I want to go first," Stevie burst. "This is my favorite game."

Imogen smiled. "I've got one. I dare you to... put chocolate syrup on a pickle and eat it."

Noises of disgust went up amongst the group, but Stevie got off Ezra's lap, opened the fridge, and rummaged through it. I nearly gagged when she ate a whole pickle smeared with the thickest chocolate sauce we had.

"Easy," Stevie said. "You guys are weak."

"Stevie's a truth or dare champ," Ezra noted. "She'll never turn down a bet."

"Ezra, truth or dare?" Jonah started.

"Dare," he stated confidently.

"Stick ice in your boxers," Jonah threw out.

Ezra's mouth dropped open. "Are you serious?"

"Are you gonna chicken out?" I teased.

Ezra gave me a hardened look. "No."

Stevie grabbed a handful of ice from the kitchen. She gave it to Ezra, who looked totally unhappy. I snickered as Ezra shoved the ice into his boxers and immediately started gasping.

"That's fucking cold!" he whimpered. "My dick's gonna be three sizes smaller than normal!"

"That might be a good thing," Stevie offered playfully. Sophia snorted, and the rest of the group chuckled. Ezra took deep breaths, though a smile played at his lips.

"Don't ever ask me for dare." Jonah wiggled his eyebrows. "I always come up with the worst ones."

"Okay, Cade. Truth or dare?" Sophia asked.

"Truth," Cade responded.

"Fucking pussy," Jonah added. Cade gave him the finger.

"Truth, huh? Hm..." Sophia's eyes got bright. "Okay. If you could trade lives with anyone in this room, who would you pick?"

Cade sat back for a moment and considered the question before his eyes went to me. "Definitely Liam," Cade said. "He's the happiest."

"Fucking ancestors, no one has ever said *that* before," Jonah cracked. Ezra died laughing.

"I mean it," Cade protested. "He's got his girl. That's all a guy ever wants."

Imogen stiffened.

My hands threaded through Sophia's hair, and she laid her head against my chest. I felt honored. "Well, thank you, Cade. That's actually kind of nice."

"It's the truth." Then Cade's gaze darkened, and his attention turned toward Imogen. "But I'd also like to change lives with Imogen. So she doesn't have to live with what I did to her."

Awkward. Not the right time to bring up something like this. We were playing a game, for fuck's sake. This was supposed to be fun.

Imogen's face contorted into a snarl, and Sassy's fur visibly bristled. "Cade, can we not fucking talk about this for *five minutes?*" she snapped.

The room got quiet. Nobody said anything. Cade looked down, almost as if he was ashamed he'd brought it up. Imogen smoldered from her seat on the floor, and the group didn't dare to try and calm her.

It was Luana's turn, and my turn to ask the question. I decided to hurry it along, to break the tension. "Luana, truth or dare?"

I was starting to pick up on a little sign language, and I moved my hands as I asked the question. Sophia had been teaching us how to use sign language, so we could communicate more easily with Luana. Luana made the sign for truth, and I asked, "Who do you like most in this room?"

Luana tapped her chin in thought. Then she smiled, and began signing. Sophia translated. "She says she likes me, because we have a common understanding. And Jonah makes her laugh," Sophia went on. "But she also thinks Ezra and Stevie are cute together, and Cade is really sweet. You're like a big brother, Liam. You make her feel warm and welcome. Plus, she likes that you like basket weaving. It's one of her favorite hobbies."

"You told her?" I asked, surprised. Luana nodded eagerly.

"Yes. I told her that today." Sophia gazed fondly at me.

I gave Luana a soft grin. It was nice to find somebody who liked the stuff you did, and basket weaving was definitely one of those fringe things not a lot of people were into.

"Dude, you're still doing that?" Ezra teased. He snickered, obviously thinking it was lame.

"Go fuck yourself, Ez," I snapped.

"But—" Sophia began, breaking our little spat. "Luana said the person she likes *most* is Imogen. Because she thinks they have a lot in common."

Imogen's eyes grew wide. She slowly sat up. I thought she was about to thank Luana for the compliment, until I heard the nasty tone emitting from her lips. "How can you say you like me? You don't even know me. You don't know any of us."

Luana's mouth dropped open in shock. A couple people gasped— both Sophia and Jonah looked horrified.

"Im, that was fucking rude," I started. I don't think Imogen heard me, because she kept carrying on.

"I don't even know why she's here. She's new to this group. It's not like she went to school with us," Imogen rambled. "She doesn't belong here."

Fucking dammit. I'd tried to ask something safe, and it'd resulted in this.

Luana was visibly tearing up. I didn't know if she'd caught everything Imogen had said, because a lot of words couldn't be lip-read, but she'd caught enough that it had hurt her feelings. Jonah turned his head away, like he was embarrassed how Imogen was acting.

Sophia simmered. I felt her temperature rise by a few degrees as her skin boiled against mine. Stevie and Ezra glanced away, not sure of what to do.

Cade looked a couple seconds from breaking down. He probably figured this was his fault for setting Imogen on edge.

All right, that was enough. Sophia scooted off my lap as I stood up. "Imogen, can I talk to you? *Outside?*" I demanded.

Imogen huffed like a bratty teenager. She jumped to her feet and rolled her eyes as she stomped out the door. Sassy followed her, her tail dragging along the floor. Jonah tried to remedy the situation by asking Ezra another dare. As I entered into the cool night, the door snapping shut behind us was a reminder of Imogen's harsh attitude.

I didn't know how to handle this. The rest of us were adjusting pretty well to life in the Anichi village, but Imogen was still imploding.

Imogen crossed her arms as she faced me. "Going to lecture me, *Mom?*"

"Fuck yeah, I am," I started. "Im, what's the deal? Why are you acting cold toward Luana?"

"Why are you guys defending her? We don't know her. We can't trust her," Imogen shot out.

"That's total bullshit. She's harmless. She's been nothing but sweet and kind since we got here. Her dad took us in. We'd be on the streets if it wasn't for her," I argued.

"That doesn't mean I'm going to kiss her ass like the rest of you," Imogen shot out.

I rolled my eyes. "You're being dramatic. Out of all the people who've treated us like shit, she's the one person who's welcomed us with open arms. You should be grateful."

Imogen let out a hollow laugh. "Grateful? I want to go home!"

I heard what she was really saying. She wanted to go back to Kinpago. She wanted to go to Orenda Academy again, go back to a time when she and Cade weren't having problems.

But that was a false reality. We were here now, and we had to make the best of it. "I don't know why you have such a problem with Luana. You guys are a lot alike."

Imogen's arms tightened against her body. "Yeah. She's a better version of me, right? No wonder it's so easy for her to take my place."

"Take your place? What the fuck?" Where was this coming from?

"Jonah and her are practically glued together whenever she comes over. I know it won't take long for the rest of you to do the same," Imogen quipped bitterly.

Something Imogen didn't say, yet that I knew immediately was true, resonated in the back of my mind. Whatever she said, Imogen saw Jonah as *hers*. She was already being forced to share him with Jake, which she couldn't say anything about, because she knew Jonah liked Jake and she wanted him to be happy.

But it was unacceptable to Imogen for Luana to swoop in and take away what attention Jonah had left to give— even though that wasn't the case at all.

"There's enough room for everyone. Just because Luana is our friend now doesn't mean she's replacing you," I argued.

Imogen shook her head and stared at the ground. "Yeah. Right."

I sensed Luana wasn't the real problem here. "You don't have an issue with Luana. You have a problem with Cade," I stated bluntly. "This all stems from you guys not getting along. Why don't you get back together and work it out?"

"Did you and Sophia get back together right away after you tried to kill her and she lied to you about Esis?" Imogen snapped.

Fair point. It'd taken five months for us to get over our shit and forgive each other, and I hated to admit it, but Imogen and Cade's problems were even worse.

But we *did* get back together, and that was the main point. "Sophia and I came out on the other side, though. We worked through our issues. You guys can, too."

Imogen gave a cruel laugh. "Worked through your *issues?* Come on, Liam. You two still haven't sorted out your shit. What happened to you guys talking about your problems? Because since we left home, it doesn't seem like either one of you are doing anything but avoiding the problem."

That fucking stung. I didn't think it'd been that obvious to everyone else. Shit, Sophia and I needed to get it together.

"We're working on it, and that's our business." My tone was getting a little heated. "And what lies between you and Cade is yours, but you keep dragging it into the entire group! It's bringing everyone down."

"Liam, he *broke my heart.*" Imogen's voice cracked, and she put a hand against her heart as if she could actually feel it cracking. "I have never been in this much pain before in my entire life. It feels like I'm dying, and there's nothing I can do to make that pain go away."

Sassy's ears drooped at Imogen's admission. I'd been in that position before. It fucking sucked.

But it did get better. It wouldn't have, though, if I hadn't faced my problems.

"You can't keep running from this," I insisted. "You're putting yourself through hell."

"I can't help it." She wiped her face. "If Cade is the one who's supposed to love me the most, and he did something like this to me, who's to say the rest of you won't betray me, too?"

I was completely astonished. "That's never going to happen. We're your friends. It's not the same as being in a relationship."

"I don't even know if I want to *be* with Cade anymore." Her lip wobbled. "He hid that my brother was alive and faked his death. I have a hard time believing anyone who could do that to me really loves me."

"Do you think there's someone else out there for you?" Ancestors, it seemed ridiculous to think of her with someone other than Cade.

"I don't know!" She pulled at her spiky hair. "I just don't want to get hurt again."

I was going to blurt out the automatic answer that wasn't true, but I held myself back. Cade or Imogen could both die in this war. Not to mention Cade had put the cause before Imogen once, so who's to say he wouldn't do it again? She wouldn't last a second time if he gave her up twice to play war hero.

And that's exactly what she was worried about.

I understood where she was coming from. I'd have a hard time trusting Cade, too.

But if there was one thing I learned. If you were meant to be together, Fire, Water, Earth or Air couldn't keep you apart. If Imogen and Cade were meant to be, nothing either of them did or said would prevent them from being together.

Yet Imogen still needed time to figure out if this is what she wanted, and I wasn't going to push her. Not when it had been Cade who had fucked up.

"Look, you can be mad at Cade. You have that right," I began. "But don't take it out on Luana. She didn't do anything wrong."

Imogen was seconds away from crying. She turned away from me and said through a thick voice, "Just leave me alone, Liam. *All* of you need to leave me alone."

Imogen ran off. Sassy darted after her. I watched as she disappeared into *Hok'evale's* streets. I thought about going after her, but the village was safe, and she obviously needed time to cool off.

The door opened behind me, and my brother slipped out. He leaned against the wall of the house. "You shouldn't be too hard on her."

"Well damn, Ez." Imogen's attitude was seriously making it harder than it already was to adjust here.

"I had a hard time forgiving Cade too, after I learned he was still alive," Ezra started. "Believe me, I was *pissed.* Imogen wasn't the only one who punched him. We had a go round like you've never seen. Water and rocks were flying everywhere."

I chuckled. "I would've liked to see that."

"It was rough." Ezra's shoulders sagged. "Shit, man, he's supposed to be my best friend and he let me believe I watched him die. That's fucked up."

Ezra shook his head. "But that's the thing. This cause was so important to him he was willing to give up his own happiness and hurt the people he loved. If we're gonna win this thing, we all need to make sacrifices. Imogen will come around in her own time. I did."

I certainly fucking hoped so. I didn't see any other alternative. Secretly, I worried Cade had done permanent damage to Imogen's soul that no Spirit magic could ever repair.

Dawn seemed to come early the next morning. I woke up right away with energy in my veins— couldn't really explain it. It seemed like the very air was different, charged with some kind of magic that told me everything was going to be different. I'd prayed to the ancestors I didn't wake up sick on this day, and I didn't, thank fuck. I took it as a sign that things were gonna go well.

Ezra's chief hood ceremony wouldn't be held until sunset, but there was a lot to do. I had to get the feast ready for later, and organize what was needed for the ceremony itself. As I did the work, it felt like someone was almost whispering in my ear... but I couldn't hear what was being said. Something heavy weighed on my shoulders, and I couldn't shake it off. Yet it was a good kind of weight, a comforting one.

As weird as it sounded, it seemed like there were people I couldn't see surrounding me, preparing me for whatever was to come tonight.

I had just managed to get the final preparations in place before we had to get ready to leave. Ezra was already waiting at my house. We'd be going together.

"Hey," he said dully as I entered. He was wearing a deerskin jacket and pants, a beaded shawl in a dark blue color draped around his form. He stared at the floor, seemingly sinking under the weight of his clothes.

None of it looked like it suited him. He seemed out of place.

"Are you ready for this?" I asked.

Ezra scoffed. "No."

He didn't offer another word. I chewed the inside of my mouth and hoped to the ancestors he could pull this off today. If he couldn't, Toaqua would be without a chief, and our line would end. Then the whole Water tribe would eventually die out.

I think Ezra understood how drastically important this was. I just don't think he wanted the responsibility.

My clothes were already laid out for me on the bed. As I was Ezra's second, and would be helping him perform the ceremony, Mom had made me a shawl of my own. The shawl was beaded with traditional Toaqua designs of the ocean, in all different shades of blue. She'd also sewn me a deerskin, fur-lined jacket similar to Ezra's, with matching pants and beaded moccasins. The fur hood hung over the shawl as I draped it around my shoulders.

This was an important day. It once would've been my day. But now it was Ezra's, and because of that, I wanted to support him all the way. I held no resentment toward my brother for taking what should've been my position. I wanted the best for our tribe, and that meant being behind Ezra no matter what.

"You look handsome." Sophia smiled as she watched me exit our room.

She straightened the shawl that was on my shoulders and brushed it off before she stood back. She was wearing a blue beaded dress that had the same pattern as my shawl. It had been Mom's the day Dad had become chief. She insisted we needed to match.

Esis had on a feathered necklace. He gave a twirl, his eyes growing at the sight of the beads on my shawl. The little guy loved shiny things.

"And you look beautiful." I leaned down and gave Sophia a quick kiss.

Jonah made a gagging sound. "Can we go? I want to get to the party."

Both he and Imogen were wearing simple deerskin outfits, though they had a few beads scattered in from the colors of their Houses. Sassy had on a feathered headband, while Squeaks wore purple paint smudged across her feathers.

"I just want to get this over with so I can get some sleep." Imogen rubbed her face. Her eyes were bloodshot, and she seemed distant. She held tightly to her stomach, as if she felt ill, and shivered once.

Imogen was never one to turn down dancing with Jonah. She was acting... off, but she was probably still upset about last night.

"Imogen's right. Let's do this." Ezra rose from his chair, and we followed him outside.

Julian and Dyami were both waiting for us. Julian was wearing a beaded blue collar that matched Dyami's. He gave a welcoming chirp, and I ran my hand over his head as we walked down to the ceremony site.

The ceremony itself was to be held in a wide river underneath the span of the mountains. Ezra was silent as we walked out of the village and into the trees. He seemed broody— he broke off ahead and walked alone. Dyami closely followed, bobbing his head. It was like Ezra was weighing some momentous decision and he needed advice.

Dyami must've suggested something, because up ahead, Ezra started. He gazed at his Familiar like whatever he'd said was impossible, and glanced back at me before setting his eyes forward.

"Hopefully the next time we have a big celebration, it'll be for our wedding," Sophia said eagerly. Esis cheered in her arms.

A jolt went through me. She was right. We were in a safe place. There was nothing holding us back from getting married, save for actually planning the wedding.

"I guess that's true, huh," I marveled. "Once we set a date, I'll be counting down the days. I can't wait to be Liam Henley."

She tripped, and I went to catch her. "Huh? Why would you take my name? I want to be Sophia Mitoh." Sophia's nose scrunched up, and Esis chittered in agreement.

"In many Hawkei households, husbands take the names of their wives instead of the other way around," I explained. "It's considered modern for a woman to take a man's last name if they're Elementai."

"Why? I don't get it." Her eyebrows knitted together.

"The Hawkei are a matrilineal society. We trace our ancestry through our mothers, not our fathers," I explained. "That's why chiefs are called by their last name and chieftesses by their first, so people don't get confused and you have the same family line of daughters taking a chieftess's name over and over."

"Oh," Sophia said. "But what about Ezra?"

"He'll be called Chief Mitoh, until he's married, then he'll switch to his wife's last name," I explained. "It's the Toaqua way."

"Hm. I mean, that's great for him, but that's not what I want," Sophia said. "I've always dreamed of changing my last name. So I think we should make an exception and keep your last name for the both of us."

"My dad took my mom's last name. It's tradition," I argued.

Sophia snorted. "Like we're very traditional. We've gone against everything the tribe ever stood for."

Julian grumbled, and I said, "That's true, but it doesn't have to be that way."

"I'm willing to compromise. But I've always had a certain dream in my head on what I wanted my family to look like, and I want our kids to have your last name," she argued.

"Why are you worrying about it now?" I asked. "Having kids isn't something that's going to be easy for us. It's a long way off."

Sophia stuttered. "I'm just saying— I think taking your name connects me to you. I always liked the idea of there being a *man of the house.*"

She made it sound like some sort of... sexual thing. This shit probably turned her on. "I didn't know you were so tied to gender roles."

"Fuck *gender roles.* It sounds so negative," Sophia spat. "It doesn't matter what gender we are. I just want you to lead the family, and I want to nurture. It feels right to me."

"Why can't we do that with your name, though?" I asked.

"We could. But at the same time, I feel your name is more Hawkei. It would tie our children more strongly to our heritage. This is what I want," Sophia said firmly. "I'm a strong, independent woman who wants her man to take the lead. This is the modern age. I can have both."

She'd convinced me. Not like I was going to win the argument, anyway. "All right. If it's that important to you, we can fuck tradition and you can take my last name."

Sophia smiled and hugged Esis. "Yay."

I chuckled. "Fucking yay."

For as much as she wanted me to be the man in our relationship, I don't think it was a secret who really wore the pants. Ancestors, I was going to be such a *yes, dear* kind of husband.

But that didn't bother me. Anything to make her happy.

Just before we got to the river, we found Luana waiting for us. She was wearing a white deerskin dress that tied around one shoulder, a feather in her hair and no shoes on her feet.

Stevie was with her, but instead of her dress matching Ezra's, it was made in a totally different design. I didn't get what was going on. Why didn't Mom give the dress to Stevie instead of Sophia? But I figured Stevie and Ezra weren't engaged yet, and Sophia and I were, so the rules were a little different.

Luana signed a hello, welcoming us to the ceremony. Her smile was genuine when it hit our eyes, even when she looked at Imogen... though Im's gaze darted away.

Luana led the way, and the trees parted as we came to a rocky bed underneath the span of a great mountain. The river directly across from us was at least twenty feet wide. It ran along the edge of a huge cliff and twisted behind a large rock face.

The entire Toaqua tribe... or what was left of it... was gathered around the area. Hundreds of people had their eyes on Ezra as he approached the river.

Baine was waiting by the water. He wore plain deerskin clothes and held a wooden staff in his hand. The staff had the Toaqua symbol carved into the top of it, and beads and feathers were wrapped around the top of it. Baine would be standing in place for my father today. This was the last thing he had to do before he set out on another expedition.

Seeing the staff made me cringe. It'd been my father's staff, and his father before him, and so on. The staff was hundreds of years old, and had been passed down from son to son for generations. Baine had rescued it from Serpent Assembly before he left Kinpago.

All of this was a harsh reminder that Dad wasn't here. He was supposed to pass the chief hood on to Ezra. It was how it always had been done, but since Dad had died before Ezra had graduated Orenda Academy, someone needed to take up the role in his place.

As we came near the water, leather drums began beating a sacred song. I watched as my mother placed incense on a stone altar near the water. Katie and Christian held on to Jackson, though their eyes were focused on me. Sophia's family gave us a polite nod.

Sophia, Imogen, Jonah, Luana and Stevie stood back as Ezra and I proceeded toward the river. Dyami and Julian remained close to us. As the drums kept beating, Baine raised his voice.

"I bring forth the son of the Water chief. Today, we ask the ancestors to accept his leadership, and guide his soul as it ascends to a higher purpose," Baine spoke.

He gestured to me. I reached for the bowl of green war paint on the altar and smudged it under Ezra's eyes carefully before I smeared it on Dyami's feathers, then stepped back. Green was a symbol of new beginnings for the tribe, and with the arrival of the new chief, it meant a fresh start for all of us.

Ezra had gone completely white. Dyami had an intense look that obviously signified he wasn't done speaking... and with every silent word, Ezra got paler and paler. I worried he was going to be sick.

*Come on, bro. Don't back out now.*

Not that he could. There were several qualities that made a great chief, and they were personified by the ceremony. Once the ceremony began, the contender could not speak, as silence showed you were willing to listen to your people and the ancestors. Ezra couldn't talk from this moment on; otherwise, it'd break the entire ceremony.

"A chieftain is always strong, and brave in times of danger. The son of the chief will now prove his strength and courage by demonstrating the power of his magic," Baine said.

Ezra swallowed. Dyami let out a cry as Ezra walked into the water, the river coursing up to his knees. As the river rushed past, Ezra raised his arms, and water began rising in two columns beside him.

There were several parts to the ceremony, and each one was difficult. Ezra had to prove that he had stronger Water magic than anyone else, and make the formation of the *Lisla Atsahmun*— the Rising Eagle— to show that he was worthy of leadership.

It was magic only chiefs could perform. If Ezra failed this part of the ceremony, it'd end before we even began.

Ezra's face contorted as he attempted to perform the spell. He was struggling, but I didn't know if it was with the water. It seemed more like he was fighting *himself.* The columns grew, but they didn't merge together like they were supposed to. The magic seemed weak and frail.

Fuck. He wasn't going to be able to do it!

My heart swelled with hope as the two columns began inching toward each other. Maybe this could work. Maybe Ezra could pull this off.

Then Dyami let out another coo, and it was like his whole face changed. Ezra glanced back at Stevie. She gave him a kind smile before she mouthed, *it's okay.*

With that permission from Stevie, Ezra dropped his arms. The two columns crashed back into the river, sloshing water onshore. Whispers and noises of shock broke out amongst the tribe. I was so stunned it felt like my heart had stopped. The drums halted completely. The sound was so abrupt it shook me to my very being.

Ezra stared at his reflection in the river for a few moments before he shook his head. As the crowd gasped, Ezra ducked his hand into the water and washed the green paint away. Dyami scrambled into the water. Ezra furiously washed the green paint off his feathers as if he couldn't stand to look at it.

Baine didn't know what the hell was going on. "Uh…"

"I forfeit," Ezra said, and the tribe broke out into panicked cries. "I forfeit the chief hood. This isn't where I belong."

My stomach bottomed out. I literally felt sick. It was almost like he'd failed the ceremony on *purpose.*

"Ezra," I said in a strained voice. What was going to happen now? If Ezra wasn't going to be chief, who would? Maddie was gone, and she couldn't be a chieftess anyway, as she was already a *naderei.* Katie and Christian were too young. We were in the middle of a war. The Toaqua tribe needed a leader *now.*

My little brother walked on shore. He had eyes only for me as he clapped a hand on my shoulder and spoke. "It's always been you, brother."

Ezra reached out and took the green paint from the altar. He held it up to me, as if asking if I was ready.

Wait. Was he suggesting what I think he was?

I took a step back and shook my head. "No. I— I can't do this. I'm not worthy. The tribe rejected me years ago. I—"

"This is your right. You're firstborn," Ezra said firmly, compassion melting from every word. "This is what you've been preparing for your whole life. And you know damn well I'd follow you anywhere."

Discontented murmurs broke out amongst the tribe. Baine stood there with his mouth hanging open. Most people mirrored him.

Mom, though, only wore a gentle smile. Out of all the people in the Toaqua tribe, my mother was the only person who didn't seem surprised.

My thoughts flickered to Sophia's dress, and I realized— my mother's intuition had predicted this all along.

"Ez, you've got to—"

"Liam." Ezra shrugged and smiled. "You know this isn't me."

He was so right. This wasn't what he wanted for himself.

*But this is always what you've wanted*, a small voice I hadn't let speak for a long while whispered. It felt so good to listen to.

A part of me wanted Ezra to reverse all this, go straight back in the river and try again. But he couldn't. He'd already broken the ceremony pact by speaking. He wouldn't be accepted as chief now. It was already too late.

Ezra shook his head. "I wouldn't be a good leader. I can't put everyone ahead of myself." He laid a hand on my chest. "But *you* can. It's what you've always done. You deserve to be chief. And our people deserve someone like you."

My mind was working overtime. Dad had taken the chief hood away from me... but I could get it back. There were no Water Elders here to stop me. I could make a council of my own.

Yet how could I? I didn't have a Familiar. Without one, I couldn't complete the ceremony.

A growl at my side answered that for me. Julian could stand in for Nashoma. I had a companion now.

But would it be enough for the ancestors to accept me?

My eyes searched the crowd until I found Sophia. She came forward without me even having to ask. Esis chirped loudly, like he was insistent I hurry up and do it already. Imogen and Jonah's expressions seemed unsure, but not Sophia's... she had that fiery look about her that I loved, the one she always got when we were about to do something that was meant to be.

"Do you think this is the right thing to do?" I asked Sophia. She was going to be my wife. I valued her opinion more than anyone else's here.

"I can't give you the answer. You have to feel it in your heart," Sophia replied. "If this is what you want, you need to accept your fate. Don't do it because you think the tribe needs you. Do it for *you*, because you want this. Because I know more than anyone this was your first love in life. Your people."

I swallowed down a lump of nerves. "I'm not sure I'm strong enough."

We were talking about the entire tribe, here. I didn't know if I had the capability to lead them during a war, to be responsible for everyone like that.

"You can't take a leap of faith if you have a parachute," Sophia said kindly. "This is your destiny, Liam. The only thing you can do is trust, and jump."

She always knew the perfect thing to say. I faced the Toaqua tribe. As I scanned the various faces, I caught sight of so many people I knew. These people had jeered and hated me after Nashoma's death. I'd faced nothing but shame and dishonor from them over the past two years. Could they really accept me as their chief?

"I won't do this unless it's with the blessing of the tribe," I announced. "I don't want to lead people who feel like they have to follow me out of obligation. I want to lead those who've decided I've earned the right to."

Mom came forward. "I think we all agree that you've long past earned your place," she said softly. "This is your birthright. We will be behind you all the way."

Katie and Christian clapped, while Jackson gave a yawn. Well, at least he didn't care either way. I waited anxiously for someone to speak up, but no one did. No one would go against the widow of the former chieftain.

Their silence was all the confirmation I needed. It said they'd be willing to follow me no matter the consequences.

Everyone was waiting on me. Shit, it was making me anxious. My mind scrambled as I wondered what to do, but there was only one clear answer.

Could've used a bit more preparation. Like we ever did anything unless it was last minute.

Fuck it. *Here goes nothing.*

I nodded to Baine, who had the proudest look on his face. He placed a hand on my shoulder, like Ezra had done, and squeezed it tightly as a father would.

"It is time." Baine bowed his head, and the drums started up again. I turned to Ezra, and he applied the green paint to my face. He smeared it across Julian's scales, and the red dragon chortled like this was his personal day as we strode toward the water together. Now that the green paint had been applied, I had to be silent until the ceremony's end.

I took a deep breath, and my hands circled the water. Two columns rose, just like Ezra's, but this time, the water twisted together as it met in an arch above me. I could hear gasps as I shaped the water to my command. Julian watched, his scales sparkling as the spray hit his scales. The water twisted into multiple different stands, hundreds of them that I had to keep aloft, all at the same time.

Yet this was easy for me. It was like something I was meant to do all my life. Twisting the strands together in a difficult pattern was just like basket weaving. Bewildered shouts grew behind me as I shaped the water to create a dynamic, beautiful portrait of an eagle spreading its wings wide. The portrait was fifty feet long, and just as high. I moved the water so that it looked like the eagle was flying, moving its wings in flight, and the astonished cries grew louder. The water rushed through the multiple avenues I created, making the eagle look alive.

I only dropped the eagle back into the river when my arms were burning and I couldn't hold it up anymore. As I walked onto shore, the Toaqua tribe stood back in awe, like they couldn't believe I'd pulled it off. Even my friends seemed impressed.

Not Sophia. Her look was nearly gloating as she watched me proceed to the altar. It was like she couldn't wait to rub it in everyone's faces that they were wrong about me.

You know, I really loved that she was Koigni.

I stopped at the altar and picked up a knife.

"A chief is always generous. He is a servant above all other things, and is willing to lay his life down for the tribe," Baine continued. "The first-born of the chief will show his compassion by bleeding freely for his people."

Sophia winced as I cut my hand with the knife, but I barely felt it. I knelt down and cut the bottom of Julian's paw. I worried I would hurt him, but the dragon acted like he didn't care at all. I then turned toward the face of the mountain. Back home, we had a rock wall where all the chiefs of the past had placed their bloody palms and left a mark. There was no such thing here, so I left my handprint on the side of the mountain instead. Julian placed his cut paw on the rock and placed a mark beside me, chortling in a pleased way.

"A chief is always faithful. He listens to the ancestors, and accepts their guidance as he leads the people of the tribe into a new life," Baine continued. He stepped away from the altar, giving me full access. Ezra stood back — not far enough away he was removed, but close enough I could feel his encouraging presence cheering me on.

Shit. This was the fucking part I was most worried about. I'd been rejecting the ancestors for the past few months. I'd said horrible things about them and doubted my faith. I'd all but hated them, cursed their names, and now I was asking for approval from them to lead the Toaqua tribe. *This is where my big mouth gets me. Never say never, Liam.*

I still didn't know if I was ready to forgive them for my Dad's death, and for putting the people I loved through so much pain. But the time for that was past. If I was going to become chief— *become chief, what the fuck*— I had to make amends with the ancestors for everything that happened, and for my past mistakes.

Julian laid a paw on my shoe and made a low song in his throat. I decided to pull myself together and show the world I still had balls. I used flint to light the incense, then called upon my magic to guide a stream of water into an empty bowl beside it. The beating of the drums grew louder, and singing voices appealing to the ancestors swelled around us. While the embers were burning, I grabbed tightly on to them and tossed them into the air.

The sky lit up. The sunset became more vibrant and altered into a painting of red, orange, and yellow. Every Familiar from every Water chief that had ever lived danced through the sky, their deep voices crashing through the twilight as eagles, bears, wolves, deer, bison, turtles and fish came down from the heavens and upon the earth. The colors bled through the clouds as the Familiars touched upon the ground. As their forms hit earth, they changed.

In their place appeared a line of men. The line trailed down the river in both directions as far as the eye could see, and was endless. Each of the chieftains were adorned in traditional Toaqua clothing, and gazed at me with stoic expressions I couldn't read. Each of the spirits were transparent, like ghosts, though their outlines clearly shone as the rushing water shimmered against their forms.

The ancestral chieftain standing closest to me was my father. He was only a few feet away, the water rising to his ankles. It was a complete shock seeing him as an ancestor, and not as I remembered. He remained expressionless, like all the other chieftains, but at his appearance I felt my face drain of color and tears rise to my eyes.

Standing beside him was my grandfather. Both had been such great chiefs. How could I ever hope to be as great as them?

Moments passed, and the singing went on as the line of chieftains stared me down. My throat became raw, and a tightness pressed down on my chest as I struggled to breathe. My hands almost shook as I stared them down.

This was it. Either they'd accept me, or they'd turn their backs on me and reject my claim. There was nothing else I could do in this moment to prove myself. They were going over the choices I'd made in my life. If they weren't good enough— if I wasn't a good enough choice— all this was over.

An animal broke its way through the line of chiefs. He floated through the spirits and drifted over the river until he came upon a rock that inclined over the water. The noble black wolf held himself high, where his gaze connected with mine and made my knees go weak. All the chieftains looked to Nashoma, as if waiting for his answer.

Nashoma tilted his head downward in a gesture that told me I'd finally accepted who I was. It was at that moment rain began pouring from the sky, coming down in waves, soaking my clothes.

And as he bowed, the line of chieftains did as well. They bent slightly and dipped their heads as if greeting an equal— welcoming someone worthy of their ranks. My dad and grandfather both nodded, and as they did so, the chieftains changed back into their Familiar forms. The music ended as the ancestors vanished, taking the colors with them— and any doubt I had that this wasn't what I'd been born to do.

The rain continued to fall down in a torrent. As the ceremony ended, I turned around slowly. This was a dream or something. It couldn't be real.

Baine offered my father's staff to me. I took it. As I gripped it tightly in my hand, I felt a warmth flood through me I couldn't explain. It was like all the wisdom the ancestral Toaqua chiefs had flowed into me in this moment. I had finally become one of them.

The faces that gazed back at me were full of reverence and respect.

"We welcome Chief Mitoh!" Ezra shouted, and he knelt to one knee.

Baine followed his lead. Mom got down on one knee, and Katie and Christian whispered in excitement as they went to bow.

The crowd behind them kneeled in unison. Hundreds of Toaqua got to one knee and bowed their heads, echoing Ezra's chant. The Familiars they were with, no matter how big, also bowed alongside their Elementai.

Imogen knelt. She slapped Jonah's leg, who seemed like he couldn't believe it. When Imogen smacked him again, he snapped out of it and quickly knelt.

As *Chief Mitoh* rang out over and over, something hit me. They weren't talking about my father. They were talking about *me*.

Holy shit. I'd actually done it. I was... I was chief! All these people were bowing to *me*.

Julian growled pleasantly, like everyone was sucking up to him personally. My eyes caught Sophia's. She gave a gentle smile. Esis had jumped to the ground and prostrated himself out flat on his face, like he was worshipping some kind of king.

Sophia knelt down, but instead of going down on one knee, she took two. She sat back on her feet and placed her hands in her lap, tilting her head downward so that it looked like she was praying.

Her offering seemed so intimate and humble. Even though there were hundreds of people here, what Sophia had done seemed reserved just for *us*.

I walked to her and held out my hand. She took it and gracefully got to her feet as the cheers died down.

People rose to their full height. I took a breath. I wasn't sure what I was going to say, but I needed to say *something*.

"I know I'm not the chief you expected," I cried out over the sound of the downpour. "But I hope that I will become the chief you deserve!"

A roar of praise and applause went up amongst the tribe, and I pulled Sophia close. Through the raindrops coating her eyelashes, she looked at me in a way she never had before.

I'd achieved my dream. Everything I'd ever wanted was right here in my grasp. I was no longer a boy— I was Chief Mitoh, and this was a new beginning. For all of us.

# sophia

## TEN

iam... a chief. I'd be damned if I didn't think that was sexy as hell. Over a week had passed since his chief hood ceremony, and I still got tears in my eyes every time I thought about it. It was so beautiful and touching. And that hot-as-hell Toaqua chief... he was *mine*.

I stirred awake on Sunday morning. A beam of sunlight shone through the window and landed on my face. I could feel the warm weight of Esis curled up on my belly. Julian had gotten too big for the bed and slept on his own bed in the corner of the room now. I reached over for Liam— but he wasn't there.

My eyes shot open, only to see Liam's face above my own. He sat on the edge of the bed, beaming down at me. I gave a start, but I quickly relaxed. I reached out and ran my fingers across his arm.

"What is it, *Chief Mitoh*?" I asked. A light smile touched my lips when I called him that. He insisted I keep calling him Liam, but something about referring to him as *chief* turned me on.

"Don't you know what day it is, *pawee*?"

I tilted my head to the side. "Sunday?"

Liam smirked. "Yes, but it's also June twenty-first."

"Already?" I asked. I had forgotten.

Liam held up a cupcake. It was decorated with white frosting, and a red and blue candle burned in the center. "Happy birthday, *pawee*."

I set Esis aside on the bed and pushed myself to a sitting position. "It's your birthday, too," I reminded him.

Liam shrugged. "Doesn't mean I can't treat you. What are you going to wish for?"

"I can't tell you," I teased. "Then it won't come true."

Liam gazed at me dreamily. "I know what I wish for."

I pressed my hands over my ears. "Don't tell me."

Liam chuckled. "I won't."

I dropped my hands into my lap. "Will you blow it out with me?"

"But it's your cupcake," he argued.

A smile spread across my face. "Our cupcake."

Liam hesitated a moment, then said, "Our cupcake."

Together, we leaned forward, and we blew out the candle together. I got a warm and fuzzy feeling when we did. We did everything together these days.

Liam pulled the candle out of the cupcake and licked the frosting off the bottom. "Just so you're prepared, Jonah's been planning us a party."

"Ancestors," I groaned. "He wanted to throw you a bachelor party complete with dick suckers and male strippers, right?"

Liam chuckled. "Sounds about right."

"What about Imogen?" I asked.

Liam bit into the cupcake before offering it to me. I took a bite as he said, "She seems to be coming around."

"Party planning is a good distraction for her," I said. Liam and I didn't need a birthday party, but if it put Imogen and Jonah back on good terms, I was all for it.

When I got out of bed, the house was quiet. Imogen and Jonah were both gone with their Familiars, but there was a whole feast laid out on the table. Esis scrambled up the chair and sat on the booster seat we'd got him. He started digging into bacon and eggs immediately. Julian tried to wedge himself into a chair, but he was getting too big.

I turned to Liam. "Did you do this?"

He took my hand. "I might've had some help from Imogen. The good news is we have the house to ourselves all morning."

I smirked and wiggled my eyebrows. "That is *very* good news, Chief Mitoh."

Liam groaned. "Can we stop it with the chief thing?"

I shrugged. "You're going to have to get used to it eventually... Chief."

Liam pulled out a chair and offered it to me, but I didn't sit down. Instead, I stepped up close to him, so our chests were only inches apart. I stood on my toes and pressed my lips to his. Warmth pooled in my belly as his ocean scent surrounded me. Liam parted his lips, and my tongue grazed across his bottom lip. I reached up and wrapped my arms around his neck and pressed my full breasts against his chest. Liam's hands trailed down to my ass, and he squeezed. My panties suddenly became *very* wet.

Liam drew away and took a deep breath, like he'd been holding it for the last minute. "Aren't you going to eat?"

My eyes trailed down his torso. Even with a t-shirt on, I could see the definition in his muscles. "I was hoping something else was on the menu..."

"Soph, the food's going to get cold," Liam insisted.

I glanced to Esis, who was scarfing down bacon like it was candy. My stomach twisted at the thought of all that grease, and suddenly I wasn't very hungry at all. Meat was disgusting to me lately. The smell of it always made me nauseous.

"Esis has that covered," I said.

"But I worked hard on this," Liam protested.

I snickered as I pressed my lips to the corner of his jaw. "Liar. Imogen did it. Are you really choosing food over sex right now?"

Liam stilled. "Fuck, when you put it that way..."

Liam swooped me into his arms and pressed his lips passionately against mine. He whirled me around toward the living room. I tried to be sexy by jumping onto him and wrapping my legs around his waist, but all it did was send him off balance. We went tumbling onto the couch. I yelped, and Liam started laughing. Esis barely noticed. He just glanced at us to see if we were watching him, then scarfed up our share of the bacon.

Liam lay on top of me, laughing. "Did I crush you?"

I shook my head, though to be honest, it was kind of hard to breathe under his weight. But I didn't care. "Being crushed by you would be the best way to go."

Liam rolled his eyes, but I barely saw it since I took his face in my hands and pulled his lips back to mine. His hands roamed all over my body, making me feel all hot and fantastic. I arched my back when he grabbed my breasts. I gasped when he squeezed too tight, and he quickly drew away. For some reason, they were really sensitive.

"Did I hurt you?" he asked.

"No," I assured him. "I... I liked it. Touch me again, Liam."

He must've noticed I used his name instead of calling him Chief Mitoh, because he got this hungry look in his eyes... like it turned him on. When he pressed his hips up against mine, I could tell.

Liam and I started making out again, and before I knew it, all our clothes were off. Liam reached for the afghan on the back of the couch and draped it over us.

"Ready?" he asked breathlessly, positioning himself above me.

I couldn't help but snicker.

His face fell. "What?"

"Jonah's going to freak when he finds out we did it on the couch," I laughed.

Liam scoffed. "Like he wouldn't do the same thing."

"Ew," I groaned.

"Well, he and Jake aren't together yet, so I guess we're the ones who get to break it in," Liam teased.

I shimmied my shoulders and snuggled deep into the cushions. "Then by all means, Chief Mitoh, break it in."

Liam didn't wait for a second invitation. He slammed into me like he meant to *break* the couch. I gasped and held on to the cushion, squeezing tighter and tighter as he moved inside of me.

"Fuck, Liam!" I moaned into his shoulder.

He chuckled lightly. "You like that? There's more where that came from."

"Yes," I gasped. I shoved the corner of the afghan into my mouth to keep from crying out. He went so deep it bordered on the edge of pain— but felt so good at the same time.

Liam wrapped an arm under my leg, pulling my knee to my chest so he could go deeper. I gasped over and over again and he rocked me hard.

"Sophia, you're so hot," he whispered. Tingles spread across my neck as his cool breath brushed my skin.

"Thanks," I told him breathlessly.

"No," Liam said. "I mean literally. You're so... hot."

I realized that my skin was burning, heat rising with the Koigni fire that burned inside. I opened my eyes to see Liam was sweating. The way he gazed down at me with nothing but pure love in his eyes... it was my undoing. I burst into a glorious orgasm. Liam wrapped his arms underneath me and curled into me, finding his release at the same time.

We both lay there panting, but I wanted nothing more than to go at it again. "Let me know when you're ready for another go," I whispered.

Liam chuckled. "Give me a moment to catch my breath."

"You're not allowed," I teased. "I want to go for a record."

Liam cocked an eyebrow at me. "Is that so? What will we have to look forward to on our wedding night, future Mrs. Mitoh?"

"Fuck, Liam," I breathed. "You can't say stuff like that to me and expect me *not* to jump you."

"Sure I can," he teased.

"No, you can't," I argued.

Just to prove it, I wrapped my arms around him and forced him to roll over. We made a slow fall onto the floor. I arched my back and rode him like my life depended on it, moaning as he ran his cool hands over my breasts.

We went at it like animals for at least another two hours, eventually moving it to the bedroom while our Familiars took over the living room to play. Liam couldn't go as long as I could, since it tired him out, so I ended up doing a lot of the work, which I was totally fine with. Pleasing him totally turned me on— and I was hornier than hell.

After lying in bed for a while, Liam turned to the clock and said, "We should probably get going. We don't want to be late for our own party."

"They can wait for us. Come back to bed," I protested as Liam started to get up.

Liam rolled over and kissed me, but he gave a half-hearted groan at the same time. "Soph, I don't know how much I have left in me."

I wiggled my eyebrows. "That's what I'm here for."

"No, like, *literally*," Liam said. "I don't have any left in me."

I frowned. "Fine. Can we at least fool around in the shower?"

"Geez, what's with you, you horndog?" Liam teased, poking me in the side.

I shrugged. "I just really love you."

Liam kissed my nose. "I really love you, too, *pawee*. I think after that it's pretty clear."

I snickered. "I'm just saying, in case it wasn't..."

Liam sat up and threw the pillow at my face. "Let's get you a shower... a *cold* shower."

I grumbled as I got out of bed. I was totally horny lately. It was like no matter how much we had sex, I was never satisfied.

Liam and I showered, dressed, and ate a cold breakfast before heading down to the beach with our Familiars. It was a beautiful day, and I was dressed in a pretty flowing sundress. Liam and I walked hand-in-hand through the magical streets of *Hok'evale*. For once, it felt as if nothing bad could touch us.

When we got to the beach, there was a big *Happy Birthday* sign hung from the porch of Haloke's house. Jonah and Ezra were playing beach volleyball with their Familiars, while Stevie and Luana sat on the sidelines.

They were only half paying attention to the game. The rest of their attention was on the crystals in front of them. It looked as if Luana was trying to teach Stevie a little about transference.

Amelia and Trace were splashing in the water with Christian and Katie. My parents and Haloke sat at one of the picnic tables and chatted, while Jackson played at their feet. Imogen lay on a beach chair. She wore big sunglasses and looked like she might be sleeping, except she was stroking Sassy's fur at her side. Cade was at the grill, and Arabelle eyed the beef patties with interest. Esis smelled the scent of cooking meat and tried to jump out of my hands, but I held him back.

"Hold on," I whispered, ducking back around the corner of the house before anyone saw us.

"What's wrong?" Liam asked as I put Esis in his arms.

"Nothing," I said with an evil grin. "I'm going to have some fun first."

I felt when I turned invisible, because the warmth of the sunlight bent around me. Liam peeked around the corner of the house and snickered as he watched my footsteps in the sand.

"Five-four serving," Jonah announced.

He threw the volleyball in the air and served it over to Ezra's side. Ezra bumped it back to Jonah's side, and Jonah sprinted toward it.

I stuck my foot out in front of him, and he face-planted into the sand. The volleyball bounced a few feet in front of him, and Squeaks ruffled her feathers. She shot him a glare as if to blame him for missing the ball.

Jonah jumped to his feet and dusted off his shirt, then cleared his throat. "I meant to do that."

Ezra rolled his eyes. "Sure, you did."

Meanwhile, Stevie was clutching her stomach and laughing from the sidelines. Luana held her hand over her mouth, but her shoulders shook in laughter.

"Five-five serving," Ezra announced.

While the ball soared over to Jonah's side, I ducked under the net and stood on Ezra's side. Jonah bumped the ball to Squeaks, who hit it over the net with her head. Dyami hit the ball with his wing, and it bounced off the net and back toward Ezra. Ezra dove for it and bumped it up, then I jumped and spiked it over to Jonah's side.

Jonah looked ready, but he was quickly taken off guard when the volleyball picked up speed. It bounced in the sand, and Jonah shot a questioning glance over to Ezra.

"What the hell, man?" Jonah demanded. "We said no elements."

Ezra shot him a confused look. "Hey, I'm not the one with Air power."

Jonah pointed to the volleyball. "Then explain that—"

He sighed and scanned the volleyball court, looking totally unamused. "All right, Sophia. You can come out now."

I couldn't contain my laughter. I doubled over and became visible again. Liam stepped out from behind the house with our Familiars, and all three of them were laughing. Amelia and Trace had stopped in the water to look at us, and they both began laughing as well.

Jonah pressed his lips together and flipped me off. "Screw you, Sophia."

It only made me laugh harder. "Now, now, Jonah. We both know neither of us would enjoy that."

That got Jonah to crack a smile, though he turned away from me like he wasn't willing to admit the comment amused him. He returned to the boundary line and announced, "Those last two points didn't count. We're back to five-four serving."

Ezra groaned but agreed.

I glanced to Amelia, but she looked like she was having fun showing Christian and Katie magical tricks in the water. I turned to my friends and was about to sit by Stevie and Luana when I saw that Imogen hadn't even noticed us joking around. I wondered if she was in one of her moods again. If so, I'd only make things worse by sitting by Luana. I didn't get why Imogen didn't like her.

Luana patted the sand beside her to invite me over, but I signed that I was going to sit by Imogen. She nodded in understanding.

I lay down on the chair beside Imogen. We faced the volleyball game, so I could watch as Esis and Julian joined. Poor Esis was going to get crushed by that volleyball, but I'd given up on trying to stop him from playing sports, as he was always so insistent about it.

Liam left our Familiars at the volleyball court and went to talk to his mom. Seeing him play with Jackson in the sand just about made my uterus cheer. I could've jumped him right there on the beach if his family weren't watching.

Usually, it upset me to see Liam with a baby. It reminded me of all we've never have. But my perspective had changed lately, and I enjoyed watching him with his baby brother. It was all too adorable.

I turned to Imogen and nudged her in the shoulder. "Hey, Im."

Imogen startled. She sat straight up and lifted her sunglasses to her head. I expected her to look all grumpy and down like usual, but her eyes lit up when she saw me. "Sophia, when did you get here?" she squealed, looking thrilled to see me. It was such a change from her usual mood lately that it caught me off guard. A party must've put her in the right state of mind.

"Just now," I said. "You didn't see me messing with Jonah?"

She shook her head. "I must've dozed off. But you're here! Happy birthday!"

Imogen reached over and drew me into a hug. I held on a little longer than normal, because it felt nice to hug her again.

Imogen drew away. "So, what have you been up to lately? I feel like we haven't talked in ages."

*No, because you've been shutting me out.*

I shrugged. "Same old, same old. Luana and I have been working on shields, light, and invisibility. I'm starting to understand the transference technique better, but I haven't done it yet."

Imogen scoffed and lay back on her chair, covering her eyes with her sunglasses again. "Please. I bet she's not even that good at it."

My stomach sank. Okay, so maybe Imogen *wasn't* in the bright mood I thought she was.

"Lay off her, okay?" I demanded. "She's helping me get better so we have a chance when we go up against the Elders."

"Whatever," Imogen said.

My mouth hung open. *What the hell?*

I was about to say something when Cade's voice sounded over the beach. "Food's done!"

I wasn't very hungry, but at least it gave me an excuse to walk away from Imogen. She was kind of being a bitch. I didn't get her lately.

"Ooh, food," Imogen said brightly, like she hadn't even noticed her weird behavior. "I'm starved."

Imogen went on ahead of me, and I followed behind her to the four picnic tables set up by the grill. Liam and I sat by each other, while everyone scrambled to take a seat. The Familiars sat off to the side, where there was food laid out on a long table for them.

Amelia plopped down next to me and threw an arm around my shoulder. "Happy birthday, sister."

"Am!" I complained, shrugging her off of me. "You're all wet!"

She looked to Trace across the table and wiggled her eyebrows. "I will be later."

Trace turned bright pink. I slapped her in the shoulder. "There are *children* here!"

She glanced around, but Christian and Katie were seated a few tables down. "They didn't hear."

"Donuts, anyone?" Jonah asked, holding out a box of donuts to everyone. Liam and I had just eaten breakfast, but those frosted donuts looked delicious.

"I'll have one," I said.

Jonah held the box out to me, and I took a long one covered in white frosting. I bit into it—

And I started gagging.

A fatty, rotten taste filled my mouth. I spit the bite out in the sand. Liam rushed to pour me a glass of lemonade, while Jonah doubled over laughing so hard he couldn't even breathe.

"What the fuck is in that, Jonah?" I demanded while I wiped my lips with a napkin.

"May..." Jonah gasped. "Mayonnaise."

"You're pure evil." I threw my donut at Jonah's face, and it smashed straight into his mouth and exploded. Mayonnaise coated his beard. He stopped dead in his tracks, but everyone else burst into a fit of laughter.

Jonah reached for the napkins. "I try, babykins. I try."

"Settle down, settle down," Haloke insisted gently. She looked better than she had at the funeral, but still, I worried about her. She wasn't back to her old self yet, and I wasn't sure she would ever be. "Liam, would you do the honors of saying the prayer?"

Jonah sat beside Imogen. Everyone bowed their heads and reached out to hold hands.

I was a bit nervous. The last time we'd asked Liam to pray, he'd totally freaked out on us.

But the chief hood ceremony must've changed him, because he recited the prayer without complaint. "Ancestors," Liam said. "We thank you for this beautiful day with our friends and family. Bless this food and keep us safe. *Akotee et veni.*"

"*Akotee et veni,*" everyone repeated.

I was secretly relieved. Liam must've made his amends with the ancestors. I was happy about that— his faith meant a lot to him. I couldn't imagine him without it, honestly.

I squeezed Liam's hand from under the table, because I could tell he was nervous leading the prayer.

"I didn't know what to say," he whispered under his breath. "It was usually my dad's job."

"You did fine," I assured him.

It got really quiet as people started to dig into their food. The tables were full of endless options. Some were traditional Hawkei foods like corn and beans, along with a sweet fry bread for dessert. Others were the usual summer cookout dishes I remembered from home, like hamburgers and potato salad. Liam, of course, went straight for the fry bread.

I nibbled on things here and there, but I was more focused on listening to the light chatter around me. It felt really nice to have all my friends and family in once place on such a lovely day.

"Hey, Jonah," Liam said when he finished his first piece of fry bread. "Where's Jake today?"

Jonah's shoulders slumped from across the table. "Running late. He has some work to do."

Imogen nudged him in the elbow. "*Somebody's* disappointed," she teased.

Jonah shot a glance around the tables. "Announce it to the world, why don't you?" he mumbled under his breath.

The next table over, Luana signed to him, and Jonah burst into laughter. He'd been picking up what he could so he could communicate with her.

Imogen's eyes darkened. "What'd she say?"

Jonah patted Imogen on the shoulder. "Nothing, babykins. She just says you're right."

Imogen poked at her food and covered the side of her face with her hand so Luana couldn't read her lips. She mumbled under her breath. "Well, fuck you."

Jonah laughed, but it was nervous laughter. We all got kind of uncomfortable after that.

Luckily, we were saved by Jake. He rounded the house and pulled up a chair at our picnic table, while Sabor pranced off to the Familiars' table.

"I hope I'm not too late," Jake said. "I'm starving."

Jonah rested his chin on his fist and gazed dreamily at Jake. "Trouble at work, boo?"

Jake sighed. "All I ask is for *one* day off."

"What's wrong?" I asked.

Jake began piling his plate high and took two hamburgers to start. "Oh, come on. I don't want to trouble you guys on your birthday."

"What if we can help?" I offered.

Jake lifted his gaze from his food and frowned at me. "Can you help with a drug problem?"

Liam's brow furrowed. "There's a drug problem in *Hok'evale?* How could anyone living here turn to drugs? This is Peaceful Valley."

Imogen gave Liam this look of total unamusement. "You're forgetting the shit half the people living here have gone through. There are a lot of refugees who've gone through hell and back, who want some kind of escape."

"True," Liam admitted. "How bad is it?"

Jake bit into one of his burgers. He got ketchup on the side of his face. He wiped it with a napkin, but Jonah looked at him like he wanted to lick it off himself. Ancestors, could he be more obvious?

"Well, we don't know where it's coming from, exactly," Jake said. So someone has to be trading with them. We don't know who, and it's starting to become a real problem among my soldiers."

"Problem how?" I asked.

Jake took another bite, then he glanced at Haloke and the kids and he lowered his voice so only those of us at our table could hear. "A couple of the privates started on it because it boosts their powers for a while. They thought it might help us go up against the Elders, but they didn't tell me about it. I only noticed when they started getting irritable and aggressive toward each other."

"It can't be all bad," Imogen argued. "I mean, if it boosts their magic, maybe it's good. And it's not like anyone has *died* from it, right?"

Jake shot her a dark look, as if she couldn't even begin to understand how dangerous it was. "Not yet, but like most drugs, overdoses are possible. People have died. Black Ivy— or nightshade, as it's called on the streets— isn't the Hail Mary it's been made out to be. I can't have my soldiers fighting amongst themselves. And the withdrawals are even worse..."

"What withdrawals?" Imogen asked curiously.

"It screws with your magic big time," Jake explained. "Makes it super addicting. I'm starting a whole rehab program to get my privates off the damn thing. Problem is, none of them will tell me how it's getting into *Hok'evale.*"

"We'll help you any way we can," Jonah offered.

Jake sighed. "Thanks, but I'd like one day to forget I'm a commander. Can we relax?"

No sooner had Jake said it that Luana gasped. It was so abrupt that everyone stopped to turn to her. She'd totally frozen up, though her lips quivered. I jumped out of my seat and rushed over to her. I signed to her, but she didn't react, so I took her by the shoulders and shook her.

*What's wrong?* I demanded.

Her eyes glazed over, and for a second, I thought she might be choking. Sierra fluttered over and landed on Luana's shoulder. That snapped her back to attention. She started signing to me so quickly that I could barely make out what she was saying.

*Someone's trying to get through my protection shield!* Terror was written all across her face.

*The Elders?* I asked.

She shook her head. *I don't think so. There aren't that many.*

My heart hammered. *How many?*

*Eight,* Luana answered.

Shit. It wasn't exactly an army, but if eight Defortai knew where we were, there had to be more coming.

"What's going on?" Amelia demanded.

Jake answered for her. "She says someone's trying to get through her shield."

"Fuck them!" Jonah jumped out of his chair. "We can face the bastards."

He lifted his hands to the sky, and storm clouds started rolling in.

"Jonah, wait!" I cried. "Let her finish."

*Any Familiars?* I asked her.

*Yes,* Luana said. *Four Elementai, four Familiars.*

I didn't know how she knew all that, but she must've sensed their magic against her shield.

*Can you tell which kind?* I asked.

*All Koigni,* she answered. *A dragon, chimera, basilisk, and... a kirin?*

I gasped, and my heart pummeled against my rib cage.

"What?" Imogen demanded. "What's she saying? Someone translate!"

I ignored her. My hands shook fiercely as I signed to Luana. *Let them in.*

*Are you sure?* she asked.

*Yes.* I'd never been more certain. *They're my friends.*

Luana's eyes went wide. *They're a mile down the beach.*

I took off running in the direction Luana pointed. I was mixed with so many emotions that I forgot to explain to everyone else what was going on. All I knew was that I didn't have time to waste. Sand kicked up at my heels, and I lost my flip flops along the way, but I didn't care.

"Sophia, wait!" someone shouted from behind me. It could've been anyone. I couldn't tell.

My legs protested as I ran faster, and my lungs started to feel heavy. It'd been a long time since I'd worked out, and I wasn't in the same shape I was last semester.

"Sophia!" someone yelled again.

I skidded to a halt in the sand as the shadows of a dragon and chimera came into view. Tears welled in my eyes and spilled over my lids. I was so happy I couldn't contain it. I started waving my arms.

"Down here!" I yelled.

Amelia caught up to me, and Jonah slowed behind her. Liam, Imogen, Jake, and Luana weren't far behind, along with their Familiars.

Amelia grabbed my arm and gasped for breath, while Kiwi landed on her shoulder. "Sophia, what in the name of the ancestors is—"

Amelia broke off when the dragon and chimera swooped down from the sky. Two people sat on each of the creatures' backs, along with a smaller Familiar with each one.

I ran up to the blue dragon. "Vanessa! I can't believe you're here—"

I cut off when Vanessa slid off Aisha's side. She barely looked anything like I remembered. Her belly was flat instead of round from pregnancy like the last time I'd seen her. She looked skinnier than I ever remembered, and her eyes were hollow and sunken in. Dirt coated her face, and her clothes were tattered and ruined.

I glanced to Bren, Lindsey, and Miranda. They all looked equally worn — like they'd just walked through a blazing inferno to get here. Bren had a huge cut above his eye, and dry blood was crusted in the wound.

I gaped at them, and my stomach turned hollow. Several other people came up behind me, but I didn't turn to see who had followed.

I swallowed the lump in my throat. "What happened to you guys?"

Lindsey slid off Aisha's back and crossed her arms. "The fucking Task Force happened. But we made it!"

She came forward to give me a hug, and before I knew it, everyone was embracing. I wrapped Vanessa tight as tears began to stream down my face, then I hugged Miranda. Liam shook Bren's hand and gave him one of those one-armed hugs guys give, and Jonah did the same.

Esis had followed. He approached Bren and bowed to him, like he was asking if it was okay to heal him.

So much was happening at once— everyone all talking over one another — that I couldn't take it all in. I drew away from Miranda and wiped my eyes.

"Where's the baby?" I asked Vanessa. "I want to meet him."

Tears entered Vanessa's eyes, and her bottom lip quivered. It was like an arrow through the heart. I knew without having to ask that something terrible had happened. She barely held back a sob as she spoke.

"That's why we're here," Vanessa said softly. She looked fractured, like she was barely holding herself together. "I went into labor during the battle of Orenda Academy. After I gave birth, the Task Force found me, and took our little Xavier. They're not just taking Biyami kids now— Oleander's taking the children of anyone he considers a threat. We've been trying to get him back, but we've achieved nothing except almost getting arrested. We need your help."

I gasped. Their child was missing!? I couldn't imagine anything more terrifying. I froze up so quickly I nearly forgot to answer. Just picturing what they were going through made me sick.

"Of course," I answered automatically, snapping back to attention.

Lindsey wiped her nose. Everyone had gone silent to listen to their story. "Things are really bad in Kinpago, Sophia. Biyami's basically bending over now that they've taken all the kids."

My guts sank. The child camps had haunted me for months now, but it sounded worse than I could ever imagine.

"How many children have been contained?" I asked, my voice wavering.

Vanessa opened her mouth, but she couldn't find the words. She curled into Bren's chest.

"Seven hundred, at least," Lindsey answered for her.

My mouth hung open. Jake had told me we needed further intel to save the children. Intel we didn't have and had to work carefully and patiently to get. It wasn't going to be easy getting Xavier out.

I swallowed the lump in my throat. "You know I want to help you, but if Xavier's being kept in those camps, we're going to need an army to set him free."

Jake stepped forward. "Luckily, you have access to one of those."

Bren eyed Jake up and down, looking curious. "Who are you?"

Jake held out his hand. "Jakob Weatherby, commander in chief of the resistance."

Bren looked more than happy to shake Jake's hand. "Ah, so *you're* the one Alric spoke so highly of."

Jake nodded proudly. "The one and only. So, what can you tell me about these camps?"

Lindsey and Miranda exchanged a glance, but it was Lindsey who spoke. "Well, Miranda and I have been in and out of the camps all summer. Alric's last request for us was to join the Task Force and go undercover. A lot of kids from Orenda were recruited after the battle, and we've been trying to help the kids as much as we can."

Jake looked impressed. "You know the layout?"

Miranda smirked. "A lot more than that, handsome."

Jonah shot her a look that said *hands off.*

Jake barely noticed. "Well, hello intel. Let's see what we can do to save those kids."

Vanessa exchanged a glance with Bren. "We just have the one kid."

Jake shook his head. "I'm not just talking about Xavier. We're busting them *all* out."

I HADN'T FELT MORE excited and nervous at the same time in all my life. Those kids needed us, and we were finally going to save them! It felt like I was finally living up to what everyone expected of me as the prophesied one, and this time, I wasn't scared.

After our friends arrived, we'd all ditched the party and followed Jake into the caves to strategize. My friends and parents had come along. Only Haloke and the kids had stayed behind.

Jake had a door at the back of his house that led into a huge cavern I'd never been in before. The ceiling was fifty feet high and there were doors in all directions, which I guessed were entrances from other high-ranking officers' homes. A metal balcony had been built along the perimeter of the room, which was where we came in.

The main part of the cave was down a level. It was set up with long, wooden tables, all covered in maps, blueprints, and other documents useful to the resistance. Several people were there already when we arrived, including Carter and his friend James, and their Familiars.

"We should go tonight," I insisted. The sooner, the better.

"Hold on," Liam said. "Let's think about this."

"I don't care when we go. Just tell me what to do," Imogen added.

"I'm going to fuck those Task Force members up," Jonah promised.

Everyone talked at once that I could hardly make out what they were saying. "I just want to be smart about this," Bren said. "I don't want my son to get hurt."

Lindsey spoke at the same time. "I'm ready to take the fucking Task Force down."

"Those kids don't have much longer," Miranda added.

"I'll help any way I can," Amelia said over all of them.

"I'm there all the way," Ezra offered.

"Can we calm down and listen to Jake?" my dad insisted. It was weird to see my parents so close to the resistance. Sometimes I forgot they'd been working with Jake for so long.

Esis shook his fist at everyone, like he wanted to be part of the argument.

"Guys, guys, guys," Jake insisted at the head of the largest table. "Can we just—?"

Everyone kept on talking at once. Jake's nostrils flared. He obviously wasn't used to being ignored.

A loud *bang* filled the cave when Jake slammed his hand down on the table. "WILL EVERYBODY SHUT THE FUCK UP!?"

The entire cavern stilled. Even Sierra, who was fluttering around above our heads, swooped down onto Luana's shoulder. The brush of her wings through the air was the last sound I heard before it went completely silent. All eyes turned to Jake.

He took a deep breath. "Now that I have your attention, I need anyone who's *not* part of my strategy team or the four newcomers to leave. We'll update you all with our plan of action shortly."

"But we want to help!" Amelia protested.

Jake pressed his fingers to his eyes, like he couldn't take any more of this today. "You will. But first, I need this place cleared of non-essential personnel."

Trace tugged on Amelia's arm. Imogen stayed put, since she'd been working with Carter for the last few weeks on strategy. Liam and I started to leave, but Jake stopped us.

"I need you two to stay," he said.

"But we're not strategy," Liam replied.

"You're a chief, and Sophia's been working on some ideas," Jake pointed out. "I need both of you."

Liam nodded in understanding. "Then we'll stay."

Half the people cleared out of the room. The rest of us sat at one of the long wooden tables. I sat between Liam and my parents, while Jonah and Imogen sat across from us. Bren, Vanessa, Lindsey, and Miranda took the seats on the end.

Jake leaned his knuckles onto the table and took a deep breath. "Carter, bring us up to speed. Where are we at?"

Carter grabbed a couple maps off one of the tables and reached over James' shoulder to set them on the table in front of us. "Professor Cheveyo's in Kinpago, feeding us information," Carter explained. "But getting inside the camps has been tricky."

"Not to mention communication is slow since the battle of Orenda Academy," my mother added.

Carter nodded. "Right. This is what we know so far."

"Can I see that?" Lindsey asked, and James pushed one of the maps over to her.

Jake eyed her curiously. "Are we close?"

Lindsey pressed her lips together as she surveyed the map. Miranda peeked over her shoulder.

"This section is wrong," Miranda said, pointing to a corner of the map.

"Right," Lindsey agreed. "They expanded this section a few weeks ago. They moved the infants to the south to make room for some of the older kids here."

"And these buildings are switched," Miranda added. "The bath houses are here, and this is the dining hall."

"Thank the ancestors they're still feeding the kids," Imogen said with a sigh of relief.

Lindsey scoffed. "If you can call it that. They give them just enough calories to live. And don't get me started on the bath houses. They're a nightmare."

"Okay, I want Lindsey and Miranda over on those tables with Carter, James, and the Henleys," Jake announced, pointing across the room. "We need your help creating a new, updated map."

As the six of them hurried off to start drawing up new maps, Jake turned to me. "Sophia, last time we talked, you had a couple ideas in mind. Let's discuss them."

"Maybe we need to restart," I suggested. "A lot has changed since I came up with those plans. They say there are at least seven hundred kids in those camps now. If any part of my plan is going to work, we're going to need to split up into teams. Our distraction is going to have to be massive, and everything else is going to have to move insanely fast if we're going to get out of there. We'll need more than one way out."

Jake nodded, looking thoughtful. "You're on the right track, Sophia. You mentioned dragons?"

"Well, that was my initial idea," I said. "But I think we can go bigger than that. You've got your boats, and we have the caves."

Jake turned to a chalkboard and started writing down ideas. "Yes, we've discussed all those options."

As Jake began to write more things on his list, Imogen's face grew more and more worried. "Hold up. If we get too complicated, we're not going to be able to get in there for at least another week. We need to do this *now!*"

I half agreed with her and half didn't. If we went in without a clear plan, we were going to get ourselves and the kids killed. Not to mention doing this would expose ourselves and accelerate the war if anything went wrong. We couldn't screw this up.

Jake turned to Imogen. "I thought you were good with strategy?"

Imogen's eyebrows shot up. "I also want to get these kids out of there."

"It's my job to make sure they aren't all killed on the way out, as well as prevent *Hok'evale* from being discovered," Jake said calmly. "So we're going to do this the right way. Make no mistake, Miss Ahnild, none of us will rest until we save each and every one of those kids. We leave within the week."

I stood in front of the mirror, frozen. The Spirit Totem hung from around my neck, and my hair had been pulled into a tight bun at the base of my skull. I'd thought so long about getting those kids out of the camps that I couldn't believe the day was finally here.

Esis sat on the vanity and reached out to me. He wore a tiny black jumpsuit and a miniature cap Imogen had sewn for him. He patted my hand with his paw, as if assuring me everything was going to be all right. I had no choice but to believe him.

I didn't want Esis coming. I worried about him because he was so small, but we also needed him. He had the power to heal, and something told me we needed as much healing power as we could get tonight.

Liam stepped into the room. He wore black cargo pants and a matching t-shirt, just as I did. Julian stood behind Liam, his scales coated in black paint. It was the best way to conceal ourselves in the darkness.

Liam stepped up behind me and ran his hands down my arms. "You okay?"

I steeled my nerves and turned to him. "I will be, once those kids are out."

Liam brushed his fingers across the side of my face. "Hey, just think, you get to see Adriel tonight."

My heart leapt at the thought. Adriel had been my foster kid in my parenting class last semester. We'd formed a strong bond, and I missed him terribly. There were a lot of other children in those camps I knew, too, ones from the group home and others from the daycare at school. I wanted all of them to be safe.

I wrapped my arms around Liam and pressed my head against his chest. "I don't want to split up."

The plan was to have multiple teams. The first were the scouts, who'd already gone ahead. The next was the distraction team, who would get the attention of the guards while several different extraction teams would sneak into the camps and break the children free. The extraction teams would work on getting the kids out of Kinpago, while the distraction team kept the guards busy, and burnt down the camps so they couldn't be used again.

Liam had been chosen to lead the Toaqua soldiers on the distraction team, as he was chief, while I was picked to be on an extraction team, as I was one of the few people who knew some of the children inside the camps. We had planned this so the Elders would believe it to be a Biyami protest, therefore keeping *Hok'evale* a secret.

It was a good plan, but unfortunately, it meant Liam and I needed to separate.

Liam sighed. "*Pawee*, we talked about this. I'm chief now. I have responsibilities. I need to lead the distraction team, and you need to get the kids out. They'll trust you."

"I know," I whispered. "But I'm going to be worrying about you the whole time."

Liam took my hands in his and drew away to look me in the eye. "I'll be thinking about you, too. But we'll make it."

I nodded in agreement. "We have to. The ancestors didn't get us this far only for us to fail."

"Then what are you worried about?" Liam asked.

I swallowed. "I don't know. I just have this... horrible gut feeling."

"It's just nerves," Liam assured me. "You want to do this, right?"

"Absolutely," I replied without hesitation.

"Then you've got to stay strong," Liam told me. "I know you have it in you, *pawee*. Those kids mean so much to you."

"They do," I agreed. "I'd do anything for them."

"Then you have nothing to worry about," Liam said.

I paused for a few moments, letting his words sink in. "You're right. I shouldn't worry. I just need to get in, get those kids, and get out."

Liam kissed the top of my head. "There's my strong Sophia."

I took a deep, calming breath. "I'm ready, Liam. And whatever happens tonight... I love you."

He pressed his soft lips to mine, then said, "I love you, too, *pawee.*"

Liam and I joined Jonah, Imogen, and their Familiars in the living room, then left to meet up with Jake at the largest cave entrance in the entire valley. The sun had dipped below the horizon, and the canyon was cast in shadows. There must've been a hundred soldiers at the cave entrance. Some of the soldiers I recognized from Kinpago, like Riley and Trevor. Others were civilians like us who'd been recruited for this particular mission, like Amelia, Trace, and Luca.

Bren was all suited up and looked ready to kick some Task Force ass to get his son back. Vanessa stood beside him, but she was only there to say goodbye. She was too fragile right now to come along. Lindsey and Miranda were at her side, hugging her and assuring her they were going to get Xavier back.

Ezra cracked his knuckles, and lightning crackled across Dyami's feathers. Stevie was close by, but she'd opted to stay behind at Ezra's request— though I overheard her complaining about not coming along. Luana was ready and would be joining Liam on the distraction team. Cade watched Imogen from a distance, though he didn't say anything to her. They'd be on the same team, despite Imogen's protests. Something told me Cade had pulled a few strings to be with her— so he could make sure she was safe.

Jonah ran his hands down Dyami's wings and snickered like the lightning tickled him. He gathered a ball of it in his hands and tossed it from one hand to the other.

"Oh, yeah," he said proudly. "Let's see what the Task Force thinks of this."

Imogen stood close to Jonah, arguing with her teen brothers, Soren and Roland. "You're not coming," she insisted. "You're too young."

"We want to help!" Roland snapped at her.

"We can fight just as good as you," Soren argued.

"You're not even bonded yet!" Imogen cried. "Do Mom and Dad know you're here? Go home!"

Soren and Roland didn't budge until Trace stepped in and demanded they return to their parents. I saw my parents next to Amelia and approached them. Liam followed beside me, holding my hand.

"Hey, you guys," I said softly.

Mom turned from Amelia and pulled me into a hug.

"I thought you weren't coming," I said.

Mom drew away. Her eyes brimmed with tears, but it was obvious she was trying not to let it show. "We're not. You know we prefer to work behind the scenes. We wanted to say goodbye."

Dad wrapped an arm around Mom's shoulder, but he looked to me. "We can't believe you two are doing this. Can't say I ever thought either of you would grow up to join the military."

"Really?" Amelia teased. "I've always been tough, Dad."

Mom sniffled. "He just means... it's dangerous out there. If it were up to us, you wouldn't be going."

"Well, we *are* going," I said. "Those kids need us."

Dad's features softened, and he shared a similar solemn look as Mom did. "We're so proud of you, Sophia. Of *both* of you."

Amelia chuckled. "Please. *She's* the chosen one. I've done nothing."

"That's not true," I argued. "You got me the totem."

She shot me a pointed expression. "The *ancestors* got you the totem."

"You're going to save those kids, too," I pointed out.

Amelia smiled proudly. "Of course I am."

"All right, everyone!" Jake's voice boomed across the crowd. "Let's head out!"

"I'll see you on the other side, *pawee*." Liam squeezed my hand, then kissed me.

I said goodbye, and before I knew it, Liam was jumping onto Dyami's back with his brother. Julian wasn't big enough to ride yet, but he would fly alongside Dyami to fight with us.

Several people took to the skies with their Familiars that were too big to fit into the caves. There were several dragons, hippogriffs, a chimera, and a thunderbird, along with a few other flying creatures. I had to ask about one of them, and Amelia explained it was a *minokawa*— a large dragon-like bird from Filipino lore.

The rest of us followed Jake into the caves and didn't stop until the tunnel came to a T. He placed two fingers in his mouth and blew a shrill whistle.

Moments later, the soft sound of slithering along the cave floor met my ears. I stumbled back a few steps as a huge serpent came into view. It was at least five feet in diameter and took up half the tunnel. I couldn't even tell how long it was, as its body stretched deep into the tunnel beyond. It had a long nose and miniscule eyes, like a mole, but a long, thin body and the scales of a snake. It was mostly black, and shimmered a dark green in the light of the military's flashlights.

"My team will go first in case we run into anything in the caves," Jake announced. "The rest of you will follow behind. Let's move."

Jake stepped forward and climbed atop the snake's back with ease. He squeezed his knees behind its neck and held on to its scales to stay secure. Several of his men joined him, until he gave the signal and the snake took off down the tunnels. It slithered so fast that it was out of sight within a few moments.

Once it disappeared down the tunnel, another serpent came forward and stuck its head out of the neighboring tunnel. It waited patiently. I suspected there were plenty of other snakes waiting to haul us all to Kinpago like a subway train.

The rest of us climbed atop the snakes. They were tall, but a man in my group helped hoist me up. I thought the snake would feel slippery and unstable, but I straddled it comfortably. Esis settled between my legs and held on tightly. The creature took off. I was surprised by the speed. We moved so fast that strands of hair whipped out behind me, but I never felt like I was going to fall off. It felt like we were moving at least fifty miles an hour.

I didn't actually know where *Hok'evale* was in relation to Kinpago— since we'd been knocked out when we got here— but it only took a half hour to get there with the speed of the snakes. When we dismounted the snakes and emerged from the caves, it was dark out. A quarter moon should've been shining above us, but thick clouds had already moved in, blocking out all light from the sky.

We split up into several groups on the ground, and everyone moved quietly. I was in a group of about ten soldiers, led by one of Jake's higher ranking officials— an older Yapluma guy named Anton. He was accompanied by a boar with leathery wings. Amelia and Trace were the only two people I knew in my group, since my friends had been assigned to others.

We reached the edge of the trees, and Anton crouched down low. Shadows from the lights in the camps crossed his face as he brought a finger to his lips, signaling us to stay quiet.

My guts sank as I scanned the camp. It was tucked into a valley, and we couldn't see Kinpago or the ocean from here. Hundreds of yards of chain-link fence with barbed wire on top surrounded what looked like a military camp. There were dozens of large canvas tents in rows, along with a couple of larger tents that must've been the dining hall and Task Force headquarters. Several large lights like those that lit football fields towered above the perimeter. We could see Task Force members roaming between the tents, carrying noxite guns. Others stood atop lookout towers that had been twisted out of trees and were obviously built by Nivita. The sound of a child's cry could be heard several acres away at the other side of the camps.

Car doors slammed in the distance, then someone said, "Take 'em away."

We all froze as the gates to the camp opened and a military vehicle drove out. Esis clung tightly to my shoulder as his eyes followed the moving Humvee. It passed only twenty yards from where we were hiding in the trees. I noticed the cargo space in the back was piled high with something. At first I didn't know what it was. I thought maybe it was just garbage—until I saw the shadow of a limp hand hanging out of the back.

I threw my hands over my mouth to keep from throwing up. Amelia gasped under her breath and turned to pull my face to her chest. "Don't look, Sophia," she whispered in my ear.

But it was too late. All the bodies had already taken shape in the night. Children of all ages lay slumped lifelessly atop one another. One of the precious children's heads was rolled back in my direction. The little girl's pigtails swayed back and forth. Her lifeless eyes were clouded over, but I could've sworn they looked straight at me.

*Fuck the Task Force! Fuck the Elders!*

Trace's hands curled into fists. He looked like he was about to stir up some serious Nivita magic, but our commanding officer gestured for him to stay put. Amelia kept a tight hold on me, but I couldn't stop shaking. My skin heated in rage.

The air around us cooled as the storm rolled in further. Soon, lightning crackled across the sky. A light rain trickled down through the trees onto us, and the raindrops sizzled on my skin. Amelia noticed and began controlling the water above us to keep us dry. Inside the gates of the camp, the rain pounded down so hard we could barely see the lights anymore. Task Force members shouted to each other through Jonah's storm as they tried to use their elements to calm the wind. But they were no match against the Storm Lord and his army of Yapluma soldiers.

Amelia could tell I was losing patience, because I was shaking more and more as the seconds ticked by. Esis cracked his fingers from my shoulders and positioned himself to fight.

*Crack!*

Lightning split through the sky and connected with the ground inside the camp. The deafening sound of thunder made the ground beneath my feet shake. Through the downpour, we could see the flames as they began licking into the air, consuming the headquarters tent. Task Force members began running across the camp to help put out the fire ignited by Jonah's lightning. But with a Koigni team on the other side helping accelerate the flames, it was no use.

As soon as the Task Force members scattered, our commanding officer gave the signal. Two Yapluma on our team waved their hands, and their Air power knocked two Task Force members out of their lookout towers. The lights shining on the camp shattered as debris flew into them. When all Task Force members were out of sight, we started forward.

Once we got to the perimeter of the gates, Trace threw up his hands. A huge mound of earth shot upward beneath the gate, and the metal twisted and groaned under the assault. The earth fell flat back into place a second later, but the gate was still twisted, leaving us a space to duck under and get inside.

It seemed that the gates were more about keeping the kids inside than keeping anyone else out, because they weren't particularly strong. The Task Force couldn't use noxite chain-link, or it'd render their own magic useless.

We entered behind a row of tents. We were mostly concealed, but I wasn't naive enough to think we'd gotten rid of all the Task Force members. My eyes darted both ways, and I noticed a Task Force member appear from the other side of one of the tents. He saw us immediately and aimed his noxite gun at us.

Amelia reacted instantly. She gathered water from the air and formed it into a ball. It went flying toward the Task Force member and slammed into him so hard he was knocked out cold.

Suddenly, a loud, shrill noise cut through the storm— the sound of an alarm. I could hear the sound of the Task Force marching through the dirt on the other side of the tents. People began shouting at each other, and the sound of children crying met my ears.

"Go, go, go!" Anton shouted.

We ran toward the front of the tents to take the Task Force out. There were two dozen Task Force members on this side of the camps. Everything happened so fast. Elements began flying faster than I could process them. Water swirled upward from puddles on the ground, and whirlwinds whipped through the camps. Trace and other Nivita made roots grow from the ground, tripping Task Force members or holding them in place. Trace slashed his hand through the air, and one of his roots whipped a Task Force member so hard in the face it knocked his helmet off. Trace's fennec fox Familiar, Maxwell, jumped forward and sank his teeth into one of the Task Force members' legs. I heard a woman's voice cry out.

The Task Force fought back just as brutally with their own elements. As Anton used his Air power to knock a Task Force member on his ass, another used earth to throw rocks at Anton's face. Koigni shot fireballs at our team members, but each of them were lucky enough to dodge them.

A Task Force member raised his gun at Amelia, but Kiwi flew forward and knocked the gun out of the guy's hands. Amelia dove into the mud to grab it, then shot the guy in the leg. He cried out in pain before he slumped to the ground, unconscious.

Across the way, the fire consuming the headquarters tent was so large that the flames must've been at least fifty feet high. A screech came from the skies, and I looked upward to see a sparkling dragon swooping downward. It let out a fiery breath, lighting the dining hall aflame.

The earth rumbled beneath our feet, and I froze in place. I didn't know what had happened. All I knew was my body wouldn't let me take another step forward.

Esis crawled off my shoulder and grabbed me by the face, bracing his legs against my chest. He slapped me with one of his paws, trying to snap me back to attention.

It suddenly occurred to me that I was standing in the middle of the fight without making a single move. Slowly, I raised my hands, just to test them out. I aimed my palms at one of the Task Force members, but no Fire came out.

My stomach dropped to my toes, and my lips quivered. I felt completely hopeless in that moment. What the hell was wrong with me?

I ducked back behind one of the tents, where no one could see me. I crouched into a ball, curling my knees to my chest. My throat closed up, and I couldn't breathe. I gasped for breath as rain soaked my hair and dripped down my face. I tried to control the light around me to make myself invisible— if just for a moment to recover— but my heart raced so fast I couldn't keep control. My body flickered in and out of view. It felt like I was having a heart attack.

Esis shook me again, but I barely felt him. I didn't even realize I was rocking back and forth. All I saw was the swirl of roaring flames in front of my vision. All I heard was the sound of dragons in the sky.

*Fuck, no! Not now!*

It was the riots all over again. It was the battle of Orenda Academy. If I moved, I could die— just as all the people who'd fought before me.

A sob bubbled up in my chest as faces of those we'd lost flickered across my vision. Ben. Marcee. Liwanu. Alric. My grandparents.

I had to save those kids, but I just couldn't add another face to the list of the fallen.

Esis chittered and tugged at my hand, yet I'd gone as still as a statue. Every muscle in my body felt like it was made of rock, and I seemed to weigh six hundred pounds.

Fuck, I thought I could do this!

Tears began falling down my cheeks. They felt hot in contrast to the rain. I forced my hand to move, though it'd never felt so heavy, and I clutched the Spirit Totem around my neck.

"Ancestors, please!" I cried, squeezing my eyes shut tight. "Help me do this. I don't want to be afraid anymore."

I needed to be brave. My friends thought I was brave— Liam thought I was brave.

But I wasn't. I was nothing, because as much as I wanted to, I couldn't move from this spot. I was a total coward.

"Sophia," a gentle male voice said.

I gasped as my eyes shot open. *No way* was that voice real.

My grandfather was dead.

But there he was, standing in front of me and holding on to my grandmother's hand. The two of them weren't quite solid, and yet, they seemed so real I thought I could touch them. They looked down at me with gentle expressions. The rain dropped straight through them.

My bottom lip quivered. "What the—? Am I hallucinating?"

Grandma shook her head. "You asked for our help, Sophia. And we came."

Holy shit. Tears streamed down my face harder, but for a different reason this time. I couldn't believe they were here!

Esis stilled and turned to them. He bowed reverently, and the two of them bowed back.

"I— I miss you so much," I told them.

"Sophia, there isn't time," Grandpa said in a rush. "You must get up and fight!"

My whole body shook. "I— I'm trying! But when I get out there, I just freeze. I can't control it."

"You must," Grandma said.

"How?" I sobbed.

Grandpa knelt to my level and looked me straight in the eye. "You must stop fighting against yourself, Sophia. Accept this war, and you can end it."

"Accept it?" I balked. "How can I accept what they're doing to these kids?"

"You will find a way," Grandma whispered. "For only through acceptance can you stop what's happening. Ignorance and denial will only increase the hate. Find the courage to stand up to it."

"Fight, Sophia, and don't look back," Grandpa encouraged. "You're going to see something that's horrible, but you need to keep going."

"Something horrible? What do you mean?" I asked, desperation filling my tone.

"It's time," Grandma said urgently. "Go, Sophia! And know that we will always be in your heart. Our spirits are all around you."

Then just like that— they vanished. It was like they hadn't even been there at all. But it also felt like they left something behind— hope.

*Accept this war. Stop fighting against myself. What does that even mean?*

Esis stood on my knees and took my face in his hands again. His fur was soaked and stuck to him, but when I looked into his eyes, there was more clarity there than ever. Esis gave me this look I couldn't explain. It wasn't one of tough love like I was expecting. It wasn't like he was trying to tell me to push past my blocks and pretend they didn't exist.

It was a look of compassion— one that said he was by my side no matter what.

And that's when it hit me. The trauma would never go away. The riots happened, and I couldn't pretend they were all part of some horrible nightmare. People I loved died at Orenda Academy, and nothing I could do would bring them back.

I couldn't rewrite what had happened to me or keep pushing the memories aside. Because the more I pushed, the more the memories pushed back, and that's what kept me from moving forward.

And I couldn't keep running away. That would only make the memories worse. I had to summon what courage I had, and face them without backing down.

I wrapped Esis in my arms and bowed my head, pressing my nose into his wet fur. Horrible, fiery images flickered behind my lids. This time, instead of pushing them out of my mind, I embraced them. I watched the flames burning down the Blessing Tree in Kinpago Square. I felt the rumble of the earth as the buildings crumbled down around me. I relived the moment of Ben and Marcee's death with reverence— and then I did it all over again with the Orenda Academy battle.

Thick smoke filled my lungs, though it was only just a memory. Liwanu's voice echoed in my ears. Alric's body burned in front of my eyes. My grandparents lay on the forest floor, and the horror of it all came rushing back, gutting me to the very core. But with it came something else.

*Acceptance.*

I was a victim of trauma, but I— and only *I*— got to decide what I did with that trauma. I wasn't going to hide it away anymore. I would let the memories come as they please— and I would cherish that through it all, I learned how to be a fighter. It was okay that my grandparents were gone, because they were in a better place. They fulfilled the duties they had to the ancestors. It was okay that we were forced out of Orenda Academy, because we found the resistance instead.

And whatever happened here tonight, it would be okay— because I was going to save those kids.

The sound of the fight came back to me, and children's screams met my ears. I regained control of my body again and leapt to my feet. Esis scurried to my shoulder and pointed forward. I sprinted around the side of the tent to see our team was still fighting Task Force members, though they'd taken over half of them out. Amelia and Trace were already ushering kids out of one of the tents. A Task Force member aimed a gun at Anton's Familiar, but I threw a force field around the boar, and the noxite dart dropped out of the air. A solid ball of light shot out of my palm. It slammed into the Task Force member's chest, and he was blasted backward.

I stood there in shock for a moment, unable to believe what I'd just done. My light had solidified enough to make a firm impact, and I hadn't struggled with it at all.

I didn't take too long to dwell on it, because I had work to do. I turned to the nearest tent, but a Task Force member jumped in front of me. Before I could use my elements, they flipped their visor up. I stumbled back, surprised to see Mia's eyes staring back at me.

"Sophia, it's me," she said in a rush.

My insides flared with rage, and I raised my hand. A ball of light shimmered in it. "Get. The. Fuck. Out. Of. My. Way."

Mia's eyebrows knitted together. "You don't understand, Sophia. I want to help. It's the only reason I'm here."

I eyed her up and down. I didn't have time for this shit. "You're Task Force!"

"I'm also *pregnant!*" she reminded me. "Are you still going to hurt me?"

The light in my hand dimmed. I hated Mia with everything I had in me — and yet I couldn't harm a pregnant woman. It went against everything I stood for.

"I really do want to help," Mia insisted. "I've been slipping the kids food when I can, and I bring them books and toys to play with when the other Task Force members aren't looking. I've *changed*, Sophia. I really have."

"You left Micah?" I asked in shock.

Mia glanced to her feet and bit her lower lip. "N— no. He's the father of my baby."

"Then you haven't changed at all," I snarled. "You're just trying to stall me."

"Sophia, I swear—" Mia said, but I cut her off.

"You really want to help?" I asked. "Then get the fuck out of here, bitch."

Mia's eyes shimmered, but I had more important things to do than try to save the bitch who nearly got my fiancé executed. I shoved past her and ducked into the nearest tent.

Twenty-five terrified children huddled together in a corner of the tent. I expected to see cots set up for each of them, but there was nothing more than a few blankets thrown on the ground. Defortai didn't even have the decency to provide a canvas floor. The kids had literally been sleeping in the wet grass.

I turned my attention to the kids instead. They were all very young— between the ages of four and six. Their hair was caked in dirt and looked like it hadn't been brushed in months. A couple of them had visible bruises on their faces. Most of their clothes were torn, and some were wearing over-sized t-shirts that clearly weren't meant for children. The oldest boy stood at the front of the group, his arms spread out like he was protecting the others.

"You want them, you'll have to go through me," he said bravely.

I rushed over to them and bent to their level. My heart broke as I watched them quiver in fear. "I'm not going to hurt you. I'm here to rescue you."

"How do we know we can trust you?" the boy demanded.

"Sophia?" a young girl squeaked.

The children parted to allow a girl to step forward. Though her face was full of dirt and her eyes were sunken in from malnourishment, I recognized her.

"Camila?" I asked. She was from the daycare.

"You know her?" the older boy asked Camila.

She nodded.

"I know her, too," another boy added. He peeked over someone else's shoulder. I realized it was Josiah, another one of the boys I cared for.

My guts twisted as more familiar faces came into view. I recognized a couple from the group home as well, but I didn't see Adriel anywhere. He must've been in one of the nearby tents.

"You can trust me," I told them. "I'm going to get you out of here."

The children didn't need much more explanation than that. They all jumped at the idea of escaping, but I pressed my index finger to my lips.

"Shh..." I instructed, and they quieted to listen. I looked them straight in the eyes and spoke firmly. "There are a lot of you and only one of me. To get out of here safely, I need you to stay quiet, keep close, and follow all of my instructions. Do you understand?"

They all nodded in unison, except for the oldest boy, who hesitated.

I turned my attention directly to him. I knew if I didn't get him on board, things could go terribly wrong. "What's your name?" I asked gently.

He didn't answer.

"You want to get out of here, don't you?" I asked.

Slowly, he nodded.

"I bet you have family back home you want to get to," I added.

He nodded again.

"Look, I'm not the Task Force," I assured him. "I'm a member of a group who stands against the Task Force. I've sworn myself to do whatever it takes to get you back to your families. So, are you with me?"

The boy swallowed. "Will I get to see my mom again?"

His eyes watered. All I wanted to do was promise him the best outcome. But I couldn't make a promise I couldn't keep. I didn't know if his mother was dead or alive.

"We will try our best," I said.

"Then I'm in," he stated. "And I'm Colter."

"Come on, Colter," I said. "Let's get you somewhere safe."

Esis chittered proudly as the children followed behind me. Esis took the back of the group, to make sure we didn't lose anyone. I created a force field around us as we exited the tent. Turns out, we didn't really need it. The camp was quiet in this corner, as all the Task Force members had been taken care of. Mia was nowhere to be seen. Anton noticed me leaving with the kids and sent me a thumbs-up, then went off to help the rest of our team with the other nearby tents.

War continued on the other side of the camp. The flames were so large by now they must've been consuming other tents. The fire cast shadows across the side of the mountain. A large screech sounded through the air, and I looked up to see a dragon with at least ten kids on its back spiraling out of the sky. My breath stalled in my chest when I saw a large arrow like a harpoon sticking out of the dragon's chest. It was probably made of noxite, too. None of us had known the Task Force had these sorts of weapons. The dragon faltered, still beating its wings in an attempt to get away.

We didn't have time to stick around and witness the damage. It wasn't something I wanted the kids to remember, anyway.

"Quickly," I instructed, ushering the kids in the opposite direction.

We faced no more Task Force members when we left. The children and I slunk through the darkness and back through the opening in the gate I'd come through. They followed me through the forest as I led them to the nearest cave opening. The kids moved slowly, but I made sure no one got left behind. I kept scanning the forest, expecting the Task Force to jump out from behind a tree at any moment, but they never did.

We reached the cave opening, and I ushered the kids inside. When I got there, Amelia and Trace, along with several other soldiers from our group, were rounding up kids. Esis crawled back onto my shoulder.

"Fifty-six... fifty-seven—" Amelia cut off when she saw me enter the caves with my kids. She breathed a huge sigh of relief. "Ancestors, Sophia! You got out. Where's Anton?"

"Rounding up another group," I told her.

"Good," she said in relief. "He should be here soon. The second he arrives, we're out of here."

"I'm here," a voice sounded from behind us. Anton rushed into the cave with his boar Familiar at his side. A group of kids followed behind, and two other soldiers took up the rear. Anton took a quick look around at the kids and counted up his team. "Everyone's here. Let's go."

"Everyone?" one of the soldiers balked. "What about Kreshawk and Denver?"

A shadow crossed Anton's face. "They didn't make it."

The soldier's head dropped, and Anton started into the cave.

"Wait!" I cried, glancing around at the children. I didn't recognize all of them, but there was definitely one familiar face missing. "Where's Adriel?"

"Who?" Anton asked. He sounded irritated, like he didn't have time to wait around for anyone.

"Adriel!" I cried. "My foster kid. He was supposed to be with this group!"

"Look, we can't go back for just one child," Anton snapped. "We have to get these kids out of here!"

It was clear he was grieving for his team members, but that wasn't an excuse to leave a kid behind.

"Adriel has autism," I told him. "He could've gotten lost in the woods. He could be confused and alone out there."

"We can't go back now!" Anton demanded. "We're leaving."

"Fine," I snapped. "You leave. I'm going back."

I turned on my heel and stomped toward the cave entrance.

"Don't go out there! That's a direct order!" Anton commanded, but I kept walking.

"Wait! Sophia!" Amelia cried.

"Stay with the kids, Am!" I called back to her as I broke into a run. "I've got this."

Adriel didn't like new people. I feared that if Amelia came with me, it'd scare Adriel off. It was probably why he'd gotten lost in the first place.

I hurried off into the trees. Esis jumped off my shoulder, then started swinging through the treetops. He landed in front of me and stopped dead in his tracks. I slowed behind him, listening to the sounds in the woods. I hoped to hear Adriel crying, but I couldn't hear anything over the sound of Familiar roars and children's shouts back in the camps.

Esis stood on his hind legs and sniffed the air. He pointed to his right, and my heart lifted. He ran so quickly that I could barely keep up with him. He was nothing more than a blur in the forest. I sprinted after him, my heart hammering quickly.

Esis stopped abruptly, and I skidded to a halt behind him. He looked over a deep ravine and let out a sad squeak.

"What is it, boy?" I asked as I approached. "Is it Adriel—?"

My words halted on my tongue as I reached the edge of the ravine. My guts felt as if they were trying to force their way out of my throat, and my heart pummeled against my ribcage. It was a ditch carved into the earth— and it was filled with something awful.

I saw the bodies first, and then the stench hit my nose. I pinched my nose tightly, because the smell was enough to make me puke. The pile of bodies— Elementai and Familiar— seemed to span forever. I couldn't tell where it ended. There were so many corpses in the pit— so many rotting bodies at various stages of decay.

I shouldn't have done it, but my curiosity got the better of me. I had to make sure what I was seeing was real and not just shadows I was making into images in my mind. I lifted my palm, and my Anichi light shone across the ravine.

I gasped as lifeless eyes stared up at me. At the top of the massive pile, I saw the young girl who'd been carried away in the Humvee when we arrived. But that single pile of kids we saw earlier was just the beginning. I couldn't tear my eyes away as I began walking along the top of the ravine and looking into the faces of the dead. I feared what I would find, but I needed the confirmation nonetheless. The further I got away from the fresh bodies, the more grotesque they became. Some of the bodies were bloated and their faces unrecognizable. Others had flesh rotting off their skin. Tiny white maggots squirmed through holes in people's faces.

One of the bodies was missing an eyeball. It was replaced by a dark hole that sent a shiver down my spine.

That's what sent me over the edge. I doubled over and spewed my guts.

When I stood back up, I could still feel bile rising in my throat. I held my mouth closed.

The ravine wasn't just full of children, either. There were just as many adults as there were kids, and there were piles upon piles of Familiars.

I stopped in my tracks when I came upon the body of a woman. Children had been stacked on top of her, but her face appeared through the sea of corpses. Her features were pale and swollen. I hardly recognized her. But there was something about the way her hair had been tied at the base of her neck. The carcass of a hummingbird thrown next to her was all the confirmation I needed.

It was Miss Evangeline, the head of the group home. Her body must've been dumped here months ago.

An invisible force slammed into my gut. I *knew* they'd been executing people. Liam saw it the night of the Orenda Academy battle. Was I so naive to think they'd actually kept some of them alive?

To be honest, part of me had hoped.

But they'd never been *arresting* Biyami in the first place. They'd been marching them to their graves.

It was clear what they were doing with the children. Anyone who stepped out of line met the same fate.

I moved my light over another group of bodies, and my knees buckled beneath me. Esis stood at the edge of the ravine and began crying. Tears streamed down my face, but I didn't dash them away. I let them fall freely as I gave a wretched cry of grief.

Beneath us lay Adriel's body. His eyes had been pecked out by vultures, and his mouth hung open. He looked in shock— as if asking why this had happened to him.

"I'm sorry," I whispered softly. "I'm *so* sorry, Adriel."

A soft breeze rustled through the trees. At least Adriel hadn't had to face the camps. They'd killed him right away. It was better that he was in the Ancestral Lands with the others.

Except—

I suddenly realized he *wasn't*. Adriel was an orphan. He had no family that cared about him. The one person that did— Miss Evangeline— was gone. If no one had done a funeral for these people, they were stuck here.

*I can't let that happen.*

I let tears continue to fall until I felt I had none left in me. Finally, I wiped them away. I folded my hands in reverence and bowed my head. Esis did the same at my side.

"Adriel, Miss Evangeline, and all the others who have been laid to rest in this cruel, inhumane way, I pray for you," I whispered. "I pray that the ancestors will have mercy on you. The tribe will not forget you."

I didn't know if this would work, but I had to try. It was one thing for the Task Force to murder so many innocent people. It was pure evil to damn them to walk the earth for the rest of eternity. They deserved to be in the Ancestral Lands.

I stood. I thought I'd cried as much as I could, but tears dotted my cheeks once again. My stomach felt hollow as I raised my hand. Heat flowed through me, and for the first time in months, Fire ignited in my palm.

I hesitated. For a moment, I thought of continuing down the ravine to see what other faces I might find. But I knew what would be there— the bodies of those we lost in the Orenda Academy battle. Somewhere in this ditch laid the bodies of my grandparents, and probably, Liam's father.

Seeking them out would be nothing short of torture, and I'd already said goodbye to them. They'd already moved on.

It was time the others got to as well.

My voice carried out over the ravine. "*All te torten, ei reldeya ve. Deya naan un beingo te ancestras te Ancestra Teryah.*"

*All the forgotten, I release you. Go forth and join the ancestors in the Ancestral Lands.*

I was no longer afraid of my Fire. Fire was destruction, but it could also give life. Bring warmth. Bring peace. I could use my flames for good, not evil. Fire was what had allowed humanity to survive, and it was what would set these poor people free.

Being Koigni wasn't a curse. It was a gift. Though the flames had destroyed Orenda Academy, they'd also kept me alive so many times. Fire had rescued the people I loved. The Elders had used Fire for hatred, but my flames would come from love and light.

I dropped my fire into the ravine, and flames licked high. Warmth blazed through my chest as I commanded the flames to spread and grow bigger. It wasn't the dangerous kind I'd shied away from. It was... peaceful.

I couldn't explain how I knew it, but I could've sworn that as my flames rose into the sky... I could feel the spirits of the dead rising, too. As I watched the flames lick around Adriel's body like a motherly embrace, I could almost hear his soul saying *thank you.*

Esis turned away from the flames and wrapped his arms around my leg. We stood there for several minutes, watching the fire spread across the ravine. I got hotter and hotter as the fire grew to epic proportions, but I didn't take a step back. For the first time, I felt like my Fire was actually fixing something instead of destroying it, and that was marvelous to watch.

A loud screech sounded above us. Esis and I both snapped out of it to look upward. My heart lurched when I saw a giant bird soaring above us, lightning crackling at the end of its wings.

*Dyami!*

Dyami cried out again, but he'd already disappeared from sight. Julian should've been with him, but I hadn't seen him. Dyami's cry faded... then came the horrible sound of a crash in the distance. My heart stopped.

*Liam!*

"Esis, we gotta go!" I shouted, scooping him up into my arms.

Esis clung to me tightly and cried out as I started sprinting through the forest. It was obvious he was just as worried about Liam as I was.

When we emerged from the trees, we weren't anywhere close to where we'd been when we got the kids out of the camp. We were way on the other side, where the fight was still going on. From here I could see a sliver of the ocean through the valley. Fire blazed on the water, its light glistening across the ocean waves. The boats we'd brought to transport some of the kids were on fire!

*Where the hell was Liam!?*

I heard the cry of a dragon. It sounded a lot like Julian, so I went running in the direction of the sound. I found my way through the gates where one of the other groups had broken through. Esis screamed in my ear and pointed in the direction I thought we heard Julian.

Jonah's storm had lifted, but the fires he had started continued to blaze. In the distance, I saw the headlights of the Task Force's Humvees rushing away. It didn't look like they were running— more like they were chasing someone down.

I rounded one of the tents and skidded to a halt. A lone man lay on the ground, groaning and clutching his chest. A large scorpion circled him, panicking.

"Luca!" I cried, rushing over to him.

Fire had singed his shirt, leaving a gaping hole in it. Beneath his shaking hands was crusted, raw skin. It was red in most places and peeling off of him, but some parts the burns were so bad the skin was black.

"Sophia!" Luca gasped.

My heart beat wildly as I knelt to his level to inspect his injuries. "It's okay. Esis will heal you."

Esis jumped out of my arms and placed his hands on Luca's skin.

"No, Sophia!" Luca insisted breathlessly. He shoved me. It wasn't very hard, but it seemed to take all his strength. "You have to get out of here. He could come back any second!"

"The guy who did this to you?" I asked. "Luca, I'm not leaving you! Esis is going to heal you."

Esis began working his magic, but I knew it would take a long time. Burns were particularly difficult wounds to heal.

"We'll get you walking," I promised him.

"Forget about me," Luca insisted. "Save yourself!"

Esis hesitated.

"No, Esis," I told him firmly. "Heal Luca."

A chilling, sinister laugh came from behind me. "He's right, you know. You should've left."

Every muscle in my body tensed. I turned to see Logan standing there.

Rage tore through my belly as I remembered what he did— how he tried to rape Isabella. He wore a Task Force member uniform, but his helmet was nowhere to be seen. His face was covered in dirt and soot, and his hair stood up at all angles. Pure, unadulterated hatred marred his features. His lion Familiar bared its teeth beside him with a similar look in his eyes. The lion was still missing chunks of hair from when I burned him last semester. It chilled me to the bone that Logan's Familiar was still following him around, because few Familiars joined their Task Force Elementai.

"I guess that's the difference between you and me," I stated. "I don't abandon my own."

Logan chuckled. "You're right, Sophia. You and I are very different. Why don't we finish what we started?"

Logan jumped forward. Instinctively, I threw my hands up and created a force field in front of me. Logan slammed into it, but his Familiar took a different route. The lion jumped over my force field and landed on the other side of us. It bared its teeth and growled at Luca. I threw my other hand behind myself to expand my force field, but the lion had already attacked. Before I expanded my force field around all of us, the lion had leapt inside of it. He swiped his paw at Dominique, Luca's Familiar, and she went flying to the side like she was nothing more than a ragdoll. The lion took another swing, and his paw slammed into Esis. My poor Familiar was knocked several feet away before he came to a sliding stop.

The lion's jaws clamped around Luca's throat so fast that I didn't have time to react. All I could do was scream. Luca opened his mouth, but his cries were quieted as the lion clamped his sharp teeth together. Blood squirted out of Luca's jugular, spraying warm, thick liquid across my face. Esis screamed and jumped on me. The whole front of his body was covered in blood.

Logan's Familiar shook its head back and forth, ripping flesh off Luca's body. Luca's eyes stared lifelessly to the sky. I saw the emptiness in them and knew he was gone. The lion had moved so quickly that neither of us had a moment to defend him. In moments, Dominique had quivered and curled up on her side, dead.

Anger so hot rose within my body that I could smell the scent of my clothes beginning to singe. I shot to my feet and whirled toward Logan.

"You asshole!" I screamed. "You fucking bastard!"

Logan held his palms up and wiggled his fingers in a "keep 'em coming" gesture. "That's right, baby. You know what I am."

I drew my force field back, so that it contained Logan's Familiar inside of it but allowed Esis and me to step out. The lion growled as it was trapped within the prison, unable to escape.

"You fucking demon spawn!" I screamed as I formed Fire in my palm. I shot it straight at Logan, and it came streaming out like a fire torch. He jumped out of the way and rolled across the ground.

"Think I'm scared of a little fire?" he taunted as he got back to his feet. "I *am* Fire, sweetheart."

Logan shot a fireball at me, but I caught it in my hands and threw it to the side. It should've hurt like hell, but right now, I didn't feel much of anything but the raging anger coursing through me. After everything Logan had done— trying to rape Isabella, threatening to rape me, and killing Luca — I wanted him to die. I bet he had plenty of blood on his hands working for the Task Force. Ancestors knew he didn't have a noble mission when he joined them.

It was only a second after I tossed his fireball to the side that I realized it wasn't an attack— it was a distraction.

In the split-second I dealt with the fireball, Logan had reached for a pistol on his hip. His hand snapped upward, and he pulled the trigger.

I tried to jump out of the way, but I wasn't fast enough. A sharp pain shot across my leg, and numbness began to spread. I yanked the noxite dart from my leg, hoping I was quick enough to reduce the damage. Esis's paws were on me in an instant, trying to work the noxite out of my system.

But it was already too late. My knees buckled beneath me, and I fell to the ground, numb all over. I couldn't raise my hand to shoot magic at Logan. I was paralyzed, except my eyes followed him, and I found I could move my tongue.

Once the noxite dart hit me, my force field died, and the lion walked free. I tried to turn invisible, but it didn't work.

"What is this?" I demanded, though it didn't come out as firm as I intended.

Whatever Logan had shot me with wasn't like normal noxite. If it were, I'd have passed out by now. This was enough to immobilize me but not knock me out completely.

Logan laughed and stepped forward. He swung his foot out, and it connected hard with Esis' stomach. I'd have seared the motherfucker when he kicked Esis out of the way, but I couldn't move. Esis squeaked in pain when he landed in the dirt not far from me, his eyes slowly closing as he passed out.

"It's nothing more than a diluted serum I came up with myself," Logan practically sang. "Works really well on girls like you. Now, how about we find ourselves some privacy?"

Logan reached for my ankle and started dragging me behind him into one of the tents that was still intact.

"Get off me," I insisted, but it came out sounding like a mumble.

Logan let out a deep belly laugh. "On the contrary, I'd like to do the exact opposite."

Logan dropped me, then knelt to the ground at my feet. Nausea rolled around in my gut when he spread my immobile legs and pressed himself against me. I was too numb to feel his erection, but I knew it was there, and it made me want to hurl. There were clothes between us, thank the ancestors, but I knew if I didn't figure out a way to fight back, there wouldn't be for long.

*No, no, no, this isn't happening.* I couldn't let this happen. I begged my muscles to move, but they wouldn't. I forced my Fire to the surface, but it was totally blocked. I even tried to summon my Anichi powers, but I couldn't find an ounce of peace within me as Logan's weight settled on top of me. The only thing I seemed to be able to do was cry.

Tears streamed out of my eyes and down my face. Hopelessness swirled around in my belly and felt all-consuming. I hated that I couldn't fight back.

"Now, now, Sophia," Logan taunted, pressing his slimy lips to the base of my neck. "Don't cry. There's no reason to go messing up a perfectly beautiful face."

Logan reached out a finger and ran it down my cheek. When he pulled away, Luca's blood coated the tip of his finger. He smirked proudly and placed his finger into his mouth. He sucked on it and rolled his eyes back, like the taste of blood pleased him.

*Sick fuck!*

"Mm..." Logan moaned in pleasure. "Sophia, you're ten times hotter like this. Covered in blood."

"Screw... you," I slurred.

Logan smiled, but it churned my guts so hard I could barely call it a smile. There was no emotion but pure evil behind it.

"Gladly," he teased. Logan leaned down again and ran his tongue across my face. He licked up the blood and smacked his lips. "Mm..."

The noxite might've knocked out my magic and left me immobile, but it didn't slow my heartbeat. I could feel it pounding against my chest like it was about to rip through my rib cage.

*Ancestors!* I cried in my mind. *Help me!*

"Now, for the good stuff," Logan said. He reached down between us, and I heard the sound of his zipper dropping.

Tears poured out of my eyes faster. *No! Ancestors, I beg of you. Don't let this happen! Help me!*

"Relax, Sophia," Logan whispered. "This will be fun."

For a moment, I thought that the ancestors had abandoned me. I'd already asked for their help once tonight. Would I be so fortunate to be granted another blessing?

The sound of the tent ripping opening met my ears, and it sparked radiating hope inside my chest. My eyes darted in the direction of the entrance, but I couldn't see past Logan's broad shoulders.

Then the voice came, and it was like I'd taken my first breath after being on the verge of drowning. "You're right."

Logan's head snapped in the direction of the voice, though he didn't get off of me. I heard the sound of quick footsteps, then saw a shoe swing out of nowhere and connect with Logan's stomach. He went flying off me and rolled across the dirt.

My heart melted when I saw Liam standing above me. Rage knitted in his features. He kept his angry gaze on Logan.

Liam lifted his hands. Rainwater from outside seeped under the canvas. It gathered in the air above him, an undeniable threat. "I'm going to have a *lot* of fun killing you."

# Liam

ELEVEN

There was no fucking feeling at all. I couldn't think. I couldn't hardly breathe. All that coursed through me was pure, primal instinct, and a need to protect my own. All I understood was that Logan was on top of Sophia, he was going to violate her, and for that, I was going to send him straight to hell.

Logan looked up at the sound of my voice. When I saw that his pants were undone and he was kneeling between my future wife's legs, I became a fucking lunatic.

The water ball burst out of my hands sent Logan flying. The blast slammed straight into his chest. Logan was thrown backward, smashed against the wall of the tent. He crumpled to the side, and I ran forward. I knelt beside my fiancé and scooped my arms underneath her. She was dazed, looking around like she barely knew what was going on.

My first priority was to get Sophia the fuck away from him. She couldn't move her limbs. She limply hung in my arms as I carried her out of the tent.

"Liam," she whispered. The word was thick and slurred.

That fucker had drugged her. Every painful punishment I could think of would never be enough.

"I'm here, baby, hold on."

Logan's lion Familiar was waiting for me outside the tent. I'd heard the sound of Sophia screaming and came running without paying attention to my surroundings. With Sophia in my arms, I couldn't use magic. The lion gave a running start, limbs bent as he prepared to crouch.

Julian came swooping in at the last minute. My dragon landed on Logan's Familiar mid-jump and crushed him to the ground. Julian's claws pinned the lion to the dirt, forcing him to stay put. Though Julian was smaller than the lion, he was still stronger, and the lion screamed in fear as Julian's fangs dove downward. Blood spewed through the air, and the lion gave agonizing roars of pain as Julian delivered blow after killing blow. The lion's blood soaked Julian's mouth and dribbled down his neck as the dragon tore Logan's Familiar to shreds.

Dragons were vicious in protecting their territory. And Julian had staked a claim on me.

I put Sophia down next to Esis. He'd been knocked out, and was just now coming around. Esis meeped in alarm as he watched me wipe the hair out of Sophia's eyes. She was still completely loose and fragile.

"Esis, get to work," I told him. Esis placed his paws on Sophia's hands in an attempt to get the noxite out of her system. As her head lolled, I heard a panicked cry.

"Akua!" Logan shouted. He'd pulled himself out of the tent, though he was bent over in pain. My water blast had definitely broken his ribs and probably shattered some internal organs. Even from here, my Water magic could sense his blood hemorrhaging inside his body.

The lion gave a dying gasp. Logan darted forward in a vain attempt to rescue his Familiar, though the act was slow and futile.

As Julian finished Akua off, I got up and blocked Logan's path. He gave a gasp as my hands latched on to his head.

"I hope the ancestors make you pay in the next life," I breathed. "If they don't, I will."

So much rage was pumping through me I couldn't contain it anymore. I twisted my hands, and in one fluid movement, I heard Logan's neck snap.

His body went limp, and I dropped him carelessly to the ground. He stared up at the sky blankly, as if in shock.

Julian left the carcass of the lion. Blood dripped from his scales, and he gave a low sound as I sneered coldly at Logan's corpse.

I never thought I'd be able to do that. I'd killed people with my elements before, but never with my bare hands.

This war was making a monster out of me.

I turned away from the body coldly. Fuck Logan. He'd deserved it.

There was no telling how many other girls he'd assaulted. And Sophia had almost been his next victim.

Now that *he* was dealt with, I turned and ran to Sophia's side. An expression of fear shone on her face. Esis had gotten rid of the noxite, and she'd witnessed what I'd done. She scrambled away, her back hitting a tree as I approached.

"Soph, it's me." I dropped to my knees at her side, but she moved away. She nearly flinched when I reached out to her. Esis' tail fur was on end, and he gave a little warning noise to back off. Julian made a few pleading noises.

She was terrified of me. That was a given. I'd been pretty fucking scary two seconds ago. Now she knew what I was capable of.

I should've killed Logan months ago when I had the chance. Now that I hadn't, I'd just given Sophia more trauma.

"*Pawee*, I'm not gonna hurt you," I said, in a voice that was as soothing as I could muster.

Her lip trembled. A few tears ran down her cheeks before she crawled to my side. She buried her head in my shoulder and cried. I turned her away from Logan, so she couldn't see his body.

"It's going to be all right," I said. I rubbed her back before I gently helped her to her feet. Esis scrambled onto her shoulder. Her whole body shook as she put her head into her hands. I had to help her remain upright.

"Let's get out of here." I put my arm around her shoulder and guided her into the trees. Her face was pale. Despite the tears pouring from her eyes, they looked vacant. She was in total shock.

"How— you—?"

"I went looking for you," I said. I knew she was asking why I'd shown up in this area of the camp. "The distraction team was clearing out. I ran into your commander in the caves. He said you disobeyed orders and took off," I said. Not a surprise— that was Sophia. "I couldn't leave without making sure you got out."

"S— sorry." She sniffed, and Esis patted her cheek.

I'd been furious with her for taking off before, but I couldn't muster an ounce of outrage at her now. "Why'd you come back, *pawee*? You were supposed to leave with your group," I asked.

"I went back for Adriel," she sobbed. "I— I found him— he's— the trenches—"

My stomach dropped. She didn't need to explain what had happened. I knew she'd found Adriel in the mass graves near the camps. We'd discovered a few of our own. The graves were everywhere.

Adriel had been like a son to her. Finding his decaying body— I couldn't imagine what that had done to her.

"I'm so sorry, Sophie." I gave her a tight hug. Another sob emitted from her. Esis and Julian both dropped their heads. "Let's get you back."

We didn't say another word as we ventured toward one of the cave entrances. I just tried to hold her. No words I could say would make this better right now, and I doubt she could process anything even if I could.

Yellow feathers flashed in my vision as Ezra landed Dyami in front of us. "Where the hell have you been?" I snapped. I'd lost Ezra sometime in the fight earlier. He'd flown off on Dyami to who knows where.

"We found Maddie," Ezra said breathlessly, with no other explanation. Sophia's eyes widened, and my breath caught.

"How?" I demanded. "Where is she?"

"I interrogated one of the Task Force," he said. "Oleander's keeping her and Drew somewhere in the north wing of the castle."

Something told me Ezra's *interrogation* hadn't fallen short of torture. "Are you sure about this?"

"He could've been lying, but if he's not, we can't leave Maddie there," Ezra insisted. "We have to rescue her."

I looked at Sophia. She needed me. I couldn't leave her now.

But my sister needed me, too. Maddie wouldn't last much longer under Oleander's imprisonment, if she hadn't succumbed already. "I have to take Sophia back," I told Ezra. "I'll meet you near the edge of the greenhouses. Don't go on without me. That's an order from your chief, not your brother."

Ezra nodded. "I'll be there."

He and Dyami took off. The moment they were gone, Sophia shifted. "I have to go with—"

"No, you don't. You're going home," I said forcefully.

Sophia hiccupped. "But I—"

"Soph, you're in no condition to fight. If you try to help me, someone's gonna end up getting hurt." I took my hand and wiped her tears away. "Those kids need you. They've got a lot of stuff to work through back in *Hok'evale*. Someone's got to take care of them."

"But you— need—"

"I'll be fine. I've got people to help me. I won't be able to save Maddie if I'm here worrying about you. I need to know you're safe, so I'm not distracted," I insisted.

Her shoulders sagged in defeat. She knew I was right. I guided her back on the path. When the cave entrance came into view, I saw two women with their Familiars standing outside it— Lindsey and Miranda.

"What are you guys doing here? You were supposed to move on with your group," I hissed. For the love of the ancestors, could none of these people follow orders?

"Our squadron went on ahead with the kids, but we stayed behind because we wanted to make sure Sophia was safe," Miranda stated. Sophia made a small sound, and I stroked her hair.

"Where's Bren?" I asked, noticing he wasn't with them.

"We don't know," Miranda said miserably. "One minute he was at our side, and the next he was gone."

I hoped to the ancestors he was all right. Lindsey was particularly observant. Her eyes widened as she took in Sophia's appearance. She was covered in blood and dirt.

"Sophia, what happened to you?" Lindsey asked kindly.

"Logan," I said sourly, as an explanation.

Miranda's hands went over her mouth.

Lindsey's face contorted in horror. "Oh, Sophia. Did he hurt you?"

"I got there before he did. We don't have to worry about him anymore," I stated bluntly.

Sophia opened her mouth, but no words came out. She gaped for a few moments and shuddered.

"Can you guys take her back?" I asked. "And make sure she *stays* there?"

"We'll take good care of her," Lindsey noted. "You have our word."

Miranda tried to pull Sophia away from me, but she clung to me like a cat. I turned Sophia around.

"I can't leave— you." Sophia struggled to get the words out.

"You're the most precious thing in my life. I won't lose you. I'll kill every motherfucker in this place if someone tries to attack you again." I squeezed her arms. "We can't have that happen. It's not worth exposing the resistance. Go, and be safe."

Sophia nodded. Her fingers slowly drifted away from mine as Lindsey put her arm around Sophia's shoulder and guided her into the cave. Miranda followed closely, as if to stop Sophia if she turned around. Esis waved goodbye. Once they were gone, a weight lifted from my chest.

Sophia was safe. Now I needed to focus on saving my sister.

Julian and I hurried down to the greenhouses. I couldn't believe that the camps were so close to the school all this time. Along the way, several figures stepped onto the path. I nearly flung a water ball at them, but hesitated when I saw that it was only Jake, Jonah, Imogen and Luana.

Luana had blood streaked across her face. She'd opted to leave Sierra behind, as the luna moth would be too fragile to take into battle. The rest of them looked just as bad, and the Familiars were covered with gore. Sassy was in her kitsune form, and though Luana had healed her, the remnants of injuries were still streaked across her fur.

"What are you doing?" Jake hissed. "The mission's complete. We need to leave immediately."

"What's Imogen doing here?" I asked. I didn't get it. Imogen was part of one of the extraction teams. She shouldn't be with the diversion group. What was more, Cade had been on her team, and I didn't see him here.

Imogen's tone was blunt and cold as she replied. "My team was decimated. The kids, the soldiers— almost everyone was killed on our way out. Cade took the few survivors on ahead, but there was a fight, and we got separated. I came back for all of you."

She sounded like a robot. Jonah put a hand on her shoulder, but Imogen barely registered it. Goosebumps rose along my skin. What had Imogen been forced to endure out there?

There were seven extraction teams total. I didn't know how many had made it out. "Where are we at, Jake?" I asked.

"The Toaqua boats that were taking two of the teams were exploded by Task Force," Jake stated. "I'm sorry, Liam."

Guilt plagued my entire form. Good Toaqua had been on those ships. They'd signed up to help because I'd asked them to. "What about the others?"

"The extraction team that was using dragons lost all their Familiars. They and the kids were shot down," Jake said heavily. "So far, we believe that four teams made it. The rest are all gone."

Four hundred kids saved, out of seven hundred. The others were all dead.

I tried to shake off that harrowing statement and get back to business. "We found my sister. She's being held at Orenda Academy. My brother and I are breaking her out."

"We can't risk exposing ourselves," Jake argued. "We're operating under the ruse that this is a Biyami protest. If the Task Force finds out that the Anichi are still alive—"

"My sister's a *naderei*. She's invaluable to the cause, and if you want the help of the Toaqua tribe in this war, it'd be best to appease me," I growled.

"I understand that you're chief, but this is putting us all at risk," Jake stated calmly.

"I'll take a small team. I'm not leaving here without my sister," I snapped.

Jake sighed. "Fine. Ancestors be with you. I need to work on getting the rest of my soldiers out."

"I'll come with you, Liam," Imogen added, in that odd voice of hers. "You'll need help."

Luana nodded, signaling she was joining us as well.

Jake's gaze flashed to Jonah. "I assume you're going with him?"

"Always," Jonah pledged. "I'll never abandon my friends."

"I figured as much." Jake cupped Jonah's cheek lightly, before he stated, "Stay safe, soldier."

Jake and Sabor ducked into the trees. I put a finger to my lips, to tell everyone to be quiet, before we continued on our journey.

Just before we got to the greenhouses, I heard a rustling in the leaves. I gave a warning, and we all ducked down. My pounding heart slowed in relief as a friend emerged on the path.

It was Bren. He'd come running out of the trees with a small bundle in his arms. I noticed a tuft of black hair, and a couple of features that resembled Vanessa's. It had to be his son.

Bren jumped when we came out of the bushes. "Where've you guys been?" he whispered. "Task Force are everywhere."

"We're rescuing my sister. She's in the castle," I hushed back.

"I can help," Bren instantly said, before his eyes flashed to the baby in his arms.

"Dude, get your kid out of here. Your wife needs you," I said. "We have this handled."

Bren nodded. "Stay safe, Liam."

I hoped to the ancestors that was the last person we ran into. We needed to be quiet now. As promised, Ezra and Dyami were waiting just outside the greenhouses. We crouched in the cover of the foliage and looked up at the castle.

It felt like my soul was dying as I gazed at the remnants of Orenda Academy. Most of it was in complete wreckage. Blackened stone from the fire lay in heaps of rubble that were piled up twenty feet high. The towers were toppled over, and every plant in the garden was shriveled up. The greenhouses were on the ground in tatters, and glass was strewn everywhere. Nothing was alive.

It was nothing like I'd remembered it. The only surviving part of the academy was the northwest wing, where a singular tower and a few halls still stood.

This had been my home, and the greed of evil people had left it entirely destroyed. I honestly didn't know how much more we could lose.

"I've been sweeping the perimeter," Ezra said lowly. "It looks like they're using the castle as a holding cell for prisoners, though for some reason, it's not heavily guarded."

"Which means the people here are being held under coercion, not force," I stated. I looked up. "If the northwest wing of the school is the only part that's left, Oleander could only be holding the prisoners in a few places."

"The Nivita and Koigni dorms," Jonah said. "I got you."

"The Koigni dorms are on the second floor. They're the closest. We should start there," Imogen offered.

No other decision was needed. We strode forward, where we'd be exposed on the grounds. I was on edge, expecting Task Force to jump out of the rubble and shoot us any minute. But the only sound was the wind, the only sights the shadows. It was completely eerie.

"This is creepy. There really is nobody here," Jonah said as we slunk around the ruins.

"Something's up," I muttered. I'd say it felt like we were walking into a trap, but that wasn't it. Campus had never been so empty before. I knew it was summertime, and there weren't any classes going on, but I knew Oleander was holding people here. The fact that the place wasn't crawling with Task Force members meant Oleander felt he had this area entirely under his control.

We didn't see any guards until we entered the first-floor corridor where classes were held. Two Task Force members patrolled the halls, but we hid in an empty classroom. They passed us without noticing. We made sure to keep out of sight as much as possible.

Coming back here was gut-wrenchingly painful. The last time we'd walked through these halls, they were going up in flames and people were dying. That one horrible night had ruined so many years of happy memories.

Luana tapped Jonah's shoulder. I knew enough sign language by now I understood what she asked. *Was this your home?*

"It was," Jonah said solemnly, signing back to her. Dyami gave a mournful coo. Luana looked around in shock, like she couldn't believe the wonderful stories we'd told her of Orenda Academy were about *this* place.

Students passed by our hiding places a couple of times, speaking in low tones and keeping their eyes down. Most looked Biyami, but I saw a few Defortai students in the mix. It didn't look like Oleander had allowed anyone to leave over summer break.

They were still keeping students here. It made sense they were imprisoning people our age. College kids were dangerous. They were young, rebellious, and often didn't have anything like spouses or children to lose. Look at what had happened when Oleander tried to take over the academy at the execution. He'd won, yeah, but not without a huge fight. Oleander would want to keep the young Hawkei here, to prevent them from creating another uprising.

As we climbed the stairs to the Koigni dorms, I still couldn't put my finger on what felt "off." I was about to ask if anyone had theories, before Ezra snapped his fingers.

"I've got it," Ezra said abruptly. "Have you guys noticed we haven't seen a single Familiar since we walked in here?"

Squeaks squawked, and it fell into place.

"Ezra's right. Where are all the magical creatures?" I asked.

Imogen drew Sassy close. "I don't know, but we should make sure that ours aren't next."

"We need to hurry." I increased my pace up the stairs, and the rest of the group followed. When we got to the Koigni dorms, each of us held an element in our hands. The Familiars crouched, ready to make an attack.

I pushed open the doors slowly. We walked into the dorms. It was dark in here, hardly any light. I heard rushing footsteps, and I pulled my arm back to release a water ball.

"Liam!" I was smacked into the wall behind me when someone tackled me full-speed. Julian growled, and I went to kick my assailant off of me—before I realized he was *hugging* me.

"Wyatt?" I gasped. Motherfuck, he was squeezing the shit out of me.

When he pulled away, my jaw fell open. Wyatt's face was blistered and raw, as if some Koigni had enjoyed burning off the skin on the side of his cheek and underneath his eye.

Yet he still smiled. "I'm *so* happy to see you, man." His voice wavered with relief. He grabbed my arm. "Come on. There's some people you need to see."

He led us to one of the dorm rooms. It was a tight fit getting everyone inside, and the room was dark. There wasn't a light anywhere, as if whoever was hiding in here was afraid they'd be discovered.

"Wyatt, what's going on?" A voice spoke up from the shadows. From somewhere in the back of the room, a light ignited in a Koigni's hand. It was Tabitha. She was scrunched in a corner with Lira, Maddox, and Sam.

"Oh my gosh! You guys are alive!" Lira shouted. She had a long cut along her face. Maddox was cradling an arm that looked broken, and Sam had two black eyes.

"What the hell happened here?" I asked. Imogen came forward to look at Sam's eyes. He winced when she placed her fingers on the swelling.

"Oleander took over the academy," Maddox burst through clenched teeth. "He's kept all the students that didn't escape prisoner inside the castle. We haven't been allowed to leave."

"What happened to your arm?" I asked Maddox.

"Haley," Maddox spat hatefully. "Oleander put her in charge of running the place. She likes to torture people in her free time. When she's not ordering the Fire Council around, of course. She was made Koigni chieftess. She passed her ceremony."

"Haley's a *chieftess* now?" I asked in disgust. That was always the one thing I'd prayed would never come to pass.

"Yep." Tabitha sneered at the thought. "And she makes sure we all know it by getting her kicks out of abusing the student body."

"Yeah. She did *this* to me," Wyatt said, and he pointed to his face. "I had the gall to tell her to stop picking on a First Year."

My insides curled in revulsion. I could hardly believe Haley's mother, who was an ancestor now, allowed Haley to pass her chieftain ceremony. But then I figured Koigni valued power over blood, and Haley exhibited the bloodthirsty traits the Koigni chieftesses valued most.

I clenched my hands into fists. "Well, you guys don't have to worry. I passed my chieftain ceremony. I'm the Water chief now, so you guys are under my protection."

"Huh, what? I thought Ezra was gonna do it?" Wyatt pointed at him.

Ezra shrugged. "My Familiar talked me out of it, thank the ancestors."

"You're chief? That's amazing! Congratulations, Liam!" Lira sang.

"You can congratulate me later," I said. "Right now, we need to get you guys out."

Luana came forward. She went to Wyatt and placed a hand lightly on his burn.

"Uh... who's your new friend?" Wyatt asked. Before he finished speaking, the burn on his face began to knit and heal. Wyatt gaped as his hands felt over the new skin. People gasped, and as Luana turned Maddox's way, he cringed.

"Who are you?" he yelped. Luana gave a kind smile in return.

"Luana's Anichi. She can heal. It's a long story," I hurried to explain.

Maddox cried out when Luana took his arm in her hands, but astonishment crossed his eyes when he began to feel Luana's healing magic work wonders. She healed Sam, Lira, and Tabitha. By the end, everyone was looking much more like themselves again— though completely bewildered.

"I'm guessing wherever you came from, there's more people like her?" Sam questioned.

"Sort of." I shrugged. My eyes wandered around the room. "Where are your Familiars?"

I regretted asking that question the moment it was out of my mouth. Lira started crying. Wyatt put his arm around her, looking close to tears himself. Sam nearly let out a sob, while Tabitha just stared at the floor.

"Oleander took them," Maddox said. "Remember when my Familiar was taken a couple of months ago? After the battle, Oleander separated all of us. He took our Familiars, and after they were abducted, no one ever saw them again. He's holding all the magical creatures somewhere secret, though nobody knows where, not even the Task Force. He had a specialized squad team take them away. Oleander said that if we want our creatures to stay alive, we'd better cooperate."

That was why all these people were here. All of their Familiars had been taken away, and they were afraid if they left, their companions would be killed.

"They have to still be alive, or we wouldn't be here," Lira gasped through tears.

"But where?" Maddox asked. "What kind of place is strong enough to hold powerful creatures like unicorns, dragons, and all the others? What kind of a cell could contain a creature that has magic?"

I wasn't sure, but it had to be more than Elementai magic, that was for certain. "We'll get your Familiars back. But right now, you've gotta come with us."

"But if we leave, Oleander might kill our Familiars," Lira spoke up. "What if it's not worth the risk?"

"It is risky," I agreed. "But if you stay here, there's *no chance* of getting your Familiar out, ever. If you leave, we might find a way to save them. Isn't dying better than being separated from your creature?"

Squeaks nudged Jonah lovingly, and he threw an affectionate arm around her.

Sam came forward. "Liam's right. I can't live another day knowing I'm doing nothing to find my Zaria. If Oleander kills her as punishment for me leaving, I'll die too, and at least we'll be together in the Ancestral Lands."

Lira nodded. "I'm in. We get out of here, and then we go looking for our Familiars."

Muttered agreements ran throughout the group. Wyatt looked down to Julian at my side. Julian puffed a ball of smoke to say hello, and Wyatt was like, "Uh, dude... did you bond again?"

"Another long story," I stated. "One we can go over once we're out of here."

"But you didn't come for us, did you?" Tabitha's eyes narrowed. "Why are you here?"

"We're looking for Maddie. Do you guys know where my sister is?" I asked.

Sam and Lira looked at each other. Wyatt purposefully averted his gaze from me. I felt my stomach churn. Were we already too late?

"Well?" Jonah subbed. "Come on, we don't have all day."

Tabitha was the one who had the courage to speak up. "She's being held in the Nivita dorms upstairs. She's heavily guarded. Oleander makes... personal visits to her every day."

I felt bile rise in my throat. I didn't dare to ask what that meant.

"What about Drew?" Imogen asked. "Is he with her?"

"Drew..." Wyatt sighed. "He's a goner, man."

My heart sank. "Are you sure?"

"We don't have any confirmation he's dead," Tabitha hurried to say. "But the last time we saw him, he didn't look good."

I couldn't give up on the kid. He was Maddie's boyfriend, and she cared about him. I felt obligated to save him if possible. "If we can get Luana to him, he'll be fine," I rushed to say. "We need to save Maddie, though I don't think we can take you guys with us. There's already too many of us as it is. We'll be caught."

"I can get these guys back to base," Imogen said surely. "I know the way back to the tunnel."

"Let me go with you," Jonah offered. "I can back you up."

"No." Imogen shook her head. "I know you want to protect me, but Liam's going to need help getting past those guards. And face it, Jonah, when people see you casting lightning, they start running."

He couldn't argue with her. "You stay safe, okay?"

"We won't get caught." Imogen hugged Jonah tightly before she waved a hand. "Come on, guys. I know the way."

We parted at the staircase. Imogen led the others away, while Jonah, Ezra and Luana followed me. The Familiars crept carefully. Even Squeaks was quiet, which was a miracle.

As we passed one of the classrooms, we heard a noise. I started, thinking it was the Task Force, but paused when I realized it was more like the sound of someone crying out for help. Gurgling and gasping could be heard from just beyond the door.

"Do you guys hear that... choking sound?" Jonah asked. He raised an eyebrow, and Squeaks ruffled her feathers.

Curiosity overtook, and I chanced opening the door. My body sagged in relief when I saw that, miracle upon miracle, we'd run into Drew. His wrists were chained to the wall, and both arms hung limply above his head. His legs were broken, and his face was so beaten that I couldn't recognize him. I wouldn't have known it was him if he wasn't wearing the same t-shirt he had been on the day of the execution.

He looked worse than shit, but he was still alive. What luck. The ancestors had to be on our side tonight.

Except there was a big problem. "He's choking on his own blood!" Ezra shouted. Blood dripped down Drew's chin and dribbled on his shirt. His face was slowly turning blue.

Luana dropped beside him. She placed a hand on his shirt, ignoring the gore. Drew gasped and struggled to breathe as the Spirit magic worked. Luana's face contorted, and we all held a breath. Healing magic only went so far. What if this was something Luana couldn't fix?

Then Drew took a breath, and we all relaxed. He coughed up more blood until finally, his breaths became even. Luana worked on healing his legs while Dyami and Squeaks took their beaks and broke the chains holding Drew hostage. When Luana passed a hand over Drew's face, the swelling faded, and he looked more like himself again— minus some cuts and bruises Luana hadn't the energy to fix.

Luana sagged on her knees. She was tired. She'd done a lot of healing magic tonight.

"Drew. How are you feeling?" I asked gently as I knelt beside him. He was still reeling. Probably from shock.

"I'm alive. That's what matters." He steadied himself on Luana. "I was praying they'd bring an Anichi when they came looking, though I wasn't sure if I believed they were still around. Alric was right all along."

"How'd you manage to survive this long, bro?" Jonah asked curiously.

Drew was still catching his breath. "Oleander's jealous of me— because I have Maddie's attention," he started. "I stayed alive for her. He's pissed I haven't died off yet. He let his Task Force generals toy with me for weeks. Those sick bastards have got a craving for violence. I'm pretty sure I survived out of spite."

There was a tiny clicking sound in the opposite end of the classroom. Squeaks' head went up. She cooed a low note, and Drew looked to the side.

"It's okay, you can come out," Drew said kindly.

From underneath a desk stumbled a tiny Familiar. He was bigger than he had been the last time I saw him— three feet tall now— and his feathers were streaked with soot, but there was no denying who it was.

"Baby?" I asked in amazement. It was the baby hippogriff with only one wing that had been Adriel's friend. Somehow, he was here.

"He kept me alive all this time." Drew scratched the hippogriff's head. "He's been bringing me things to eat. Rats and stuff. I used what little magic I had left to cook them, though my fire couldn't break the chains."

Jonah's nose wrinkled. I reached down and stroked Baby's feathers. "He must've got out of the camps somehow after they killed Adriel," I mumbled to myself. Baby rubbed his head on my leg, and Julian gave a resentful note.

Squeaks pushed Jonah out of the way as she ran toward Baby. She clicked her beak a couple of times. Baby's head tilted this way and that, and Squeaks bent her head down to nuzzle Baby's feathers. Baby pushed himself against her legs, and Squeaks dropped a tender wing over him, chortling. It was like she'd resigned to be the hatchling's mother.

"Aw, Squeaky, you're gonna make me cry," Jonah sniffed. She chirped in response.

"I don't know how he got here. He just showed up one day," Drew added. "He did what he could to help, though I told him to hide when the generals were kicking the crap out of me. I think he was just looking for a friend."

As Drew wiped his face, I noticed a couple of his fingernails were missing. This kid had been through hell.

"Well, you've proven to me you've got balls," Ezra stated. "Welcome to the family, bro."

Drew groaned and held his head. I stood up. "We're looking for Maddie," I began. "If you want to stay here until—"

"Maddie?" Drew cut me off. He got to his feet almost immediately. "If you're looking for her, I'm coming with you."

I hesitated— the kid still looked dead on his feet, but after what he'd experienced, I knew now there wasn't a damn thing he wouldn't do for my sister. And because of that, he'd earned my respect. "Okay. Stay close."

The Nivita dorms weren't far. Drew leaned on Ezra for support, while Squeaks kept Baby under her wing, protecting him. Luana walked by my side, but I could tell she was weary. Jonah brought up the rear with Dyami and Julian.

Finally, the wooden doors of the Nivita dorms came into view, alongside the balcony that stood beside. But there was a problem. A host of Task Force were stationed outside of it, all standing on alert. We ducked around the corner. My mind worked overtime as I came up with a plan.

I wasn't fucking around. Time to bring in some powerful magic. I nudged Luana. She nodded, and a bright light exploded in her hand. She jumped out from around the corner, and the Task Force was immediately blinded by her light. Dyami and Julian spread their wings. While the Task Force was incapacitated, they went in for the kill. Task Force members screamed as Dyami's claws and Julian's teeth ripped them apart.

Just before Luana's light faded, Jonah fired off a lightning bolt. It emitted from his hand and landed between the Task Force members, sending a dozen flying off the balcony. They screamed as they fell to the first floor below, until their voices went silent.

The rest of the Task Force didn't chance it. They dropped their noxite guns and ran off. I kicked their weapons to the side as I threw open the Nivita doors.

The Nivita dorms looked completely different. Once, they bloomed with all kinds of beautiful and colorful plants. Now everything inside was dead, rotting from the lack of care from Nivita magic, long turned to dust. It was as if winter had come inside and killed everything.

A woman stood in the middle of the barren room. She wore a beaded dress in red, green, and blue colors. Silver bells hung around her waist, and a robe with an intricate pattern hung on her shoulders. Both the skirt of the dress and the arms of the robe had long leather tassels. On the woman's head was an intricate headdress, adorned with feathers and jewels. Her face was painted white, Hawkei symbols written across her cheeks in black ink, lips painted red.

As the woman looked up, my jaw fell open. Tears beaded her eyes. "Liam. Ezra."

Holy shit. I hadn't recognized her, but it was *Maddie*.

She sobbed as I launched myself at her. As my arms encompassed her, I realized that Maddie was incredibly thin. She'd lost weight in the time she'd been missing.

"We were always gonna come for you," Ezra said, and he gave Maddie a tight hug. She could barely compose herself as Ezra held her.

As I looked her over again, it struck me that Oleander had dressed Maddie in a traditional *naderei* ceremonial outfit. My guts twisted. What an insane, deranged, degenerate fuck.

"Mads," Drew gasped out. He shuffled into the middle of the room. Maddie's jaw dropped open. Tears formed in her eyes as she looked him up and down.

"Drew. Oh my gosh." She immediately flung her arms around his shoulders. He held her back before he bent down to give her a kiss. Maddie didn't give a shit about the blood, either. She kissed him back, and though Ezra rolled his eyes, I let them have their moment. They'd definitely deserved it after all they went through.

"Are you okay?" I asked her. There was something haunting about Maddie that hadn't been there a few months before. It hung off her body like a warning. I could feel it radiating off of her, and it was disturbing, to say the least.

"No. But I will be." Maddie took a deep breath. "I take it you guys found the resistance?"

"Yes. We're taking you there. Mom and the others are waiting,"

At the mention of Mom, Maddie's eyes shone with hope. More than anything, she looked like a girl who wanted her mother.

"Why are you dressed like this, Mads?" Ezra asked. He scowled at the tassels hanging off of her.

"*He* makes me wear this. If I don't look presentable at all times, I'm punished." Maddie wiped her eyes. "Oleander parades me around like his little doll."

"Did he touch you?" My voice barely concealed rage. If Oleander dared to do a thing to my little sister...

Maddie shook her head. "He didn't, but he was going to soon. I could see it in his eyes."

Maddie put her face in her hands and turned away from me. "Liam, you don't understand what he did to me. He tried to force me into visions. The experiments—"

She cut off. In a deathly low tone, I asked, "Experiments?"

Maddie refused to say anything further. Drew put his arm around her. "Can we just get out of here?"

I wanted to find out what exactly Oleander had put her through, but now wasn't the time. Task Force members could show up at any moment. "Follow me."

Bodies of police lay immobile as we left the Nivita dorms. Maddie remained close to Drew. Luana, Jonah, Ezra and I created a circle around the two of them, along with our Familiars, to keep them safe. I heard the sound of boots marching, and Maddie gasped, but we clung to the wall and ducked into another classroom as a unit ran by. Once they were gone, we started taking the stairs two by two down to the main floor. Drew was slow going, but Maddie helped him along. I almost thought we were going to make it out of here without another fight.

"How'd you manage to keep Oleander happy?" Ezra questioned. I sent him a harsh look to tell him to shut the hell up, and he obeyed, but Maddie responded anyway.

"I made up some bullshit about how he was going to be the greatest High Chief in all history." Maddie rolled her eyes. "He bought it, at first, but I think he's getting suspicious I'm making stuff up. You guys got me out just in time."

"That guy sure is obsessed with prophets, isn't he?" Jonah asked.

"He's trying to use me as some sort of weapon. He's obsessed with knowing the future. He can't stand to think he's going to lose power," Maddie spat bitterly.

"And is he?" Jonah asked curiously. I cringed, because that was a mistake.

Maddie completely flew off the handle. She rounded on Jonah, fists clenched, and all but screamed, "What, do *you* want to use me for my powers, too? You think I know everything? Do you think I'm just some sort of *fucking* fortune cookie!?"

"N— no," Jonah stammered. He hadn't meant to be offensive. His cheeks tinged with pink.

"Don't you think if I knew how this was going to end I would've told you by now?" Maddie cried. "Is that all I am to anyone? A way to get answers? Put a coin in the vending machine and Maddie will answer?"

"Mads, keep your voice down," I pleaded. Maddie quieted, but the rage in her eyes was clear to see.

Jonah gaped. "I'm sorry."

Maddie simmered. "It's fine," she stated bluntly. "Let's keep moving."

Drew remained stiff. I myself was shocked. Holy shit. Maddie had never spoken like that to anyone. What the hell had Oleander done to her? Ezra was similarly shocked.

Luana frowned. It was like she could sense what was going on with Maddie, but didn't want to tell anyone.

"Everything will be okay once we—" My words stopped abruptly when I saw someone at the bottom of the stairs, waiting for us. We all froze. A cruel, feminine laugh echoed all around us as fire ignited on the torches lining the walls.

I'd always hated Haley— but something about her was different, and in a terrible, awful way. The side of her face where her mother had burned her was red and angry. Vicious burn scars ran up the side of her cheek and over her eye, making it look like her very skin was on fire.

Haley was wearing a ceremonial Koigni headdress and red robes that had flames embroidered up the sides. Oh, she was milking being chieftess, all right. Couldn't even take off the chieftess robes and wear day clothes like a normal person.

But it was off. The headdress was tilted to the side, and the Koigni robes were stained and torn. Her usually perfectly straight hair was tangled, and mascara stains ran down from her eyes. The lipstick was smeared on one side— like she'd taken the tube and painted it across the side of her face.

Haley was a stuck-up bitch. No way she'd slack on looking anything but absolutely perfect. As she walked toward us, a laugh bubbled up from her throat. Her eyes bugged out of her head, and she tilted it slowly to the side.

Aw, fuck. She'd become completely unhinged. Haley was always a little crazy, but after her mother's death, she'd gone full-on psycho. Just fucking great.

Her Familiar, Anwara, hovered overhead. Flames dripped from her feathers in warning. But they looked alone. No one was with either of them, which meant Haley was outnumbered.

As much as I despised her, I didn't want to hurt Haley tonight. I already had too many sins on my hands I wasn't sure the ancestors would forgive. "Out of the way, Haley," I warned. "This won't end well for you."

Haley stopped abruptly when I said her name. "That's *Chieftess Haley* to you, Mitoh," she sneered. "Show some respect, you Biyami ingrate."

"You need to watch who you're talking to," I seethed. "You're looking at the new Toaqua chief."

Haley let out an insulting guffaw. "You're fucking joking. *You?* They picked *you?*"

"Yeah. We did pick him," Ezra said loudly. He drew himself up and added, "And I suggest you don't challenge my brother unless you want to get your ass kicked."

"Shut up, Ezra, before I ruin that pretty boy face of yours," Haley snapped.

Haley's eyes wandered to Luana. She took in her white hair before giving a loud snort. "Huh. More freaks." Haley cackled. "It's like you guys collect them."

"Move out of the way, Haley," I boomed. "I won't keep asking."

Haley ignored me. "Where's your little girlfriend? I'd love my chance to see Henley writhe."

She was baiting me. I wouldn't fall for it. "This is your last warning." I raised my hand, and water began gathering from the air to form a ball in my hand. "If you think of calling for help, like Madame Doya—"

"Doya's been gone for weeks, you stupid prick," Haley snapped.

That was a surprise. I tried not to let it show on my face, but Haley saw, and she rolled her eyes. "Wherever you guys are hiding, they must be shit with intel. Oleander and I are running the show, as he promised me. It's a reward for killing my mother."

"You're sick," Jonah burst. Squeaks tucked Baby closer to her.

"I don't regret murdering her," Haley bit back. "She was an old crone who got what she deserved. If she was strong enough, she'd still be here today. But she's not, so the Koigni empire belongs to me."

"The Hawkei belong to no one, Haley. We've always been a free people," I argued.

Haley shrugged. "Times have changed. Oleander won't live forever. And once he dies, the entire tribe will be mine."

Talking to her was useless. Haley viewed people as things, and that's all they were to her. Tools to use to get what she desired.

But that was the difference between her and me. I wanted to be a chief in order to serve my people. Haley wanted to be chieftess because she got off on having power.

"Last chance, Mitoh. Hand over the *naderei*, and I won't burn your face off." Haley raised her hand, and a fireball ignited within it.

Julian growled. He planted himself in front of me, spreading his wings and putting his fangs on display.

Haley's eyes flickered from me to him. She knew something didn't add up, until she decided she didn't care. Haley threw back her head and laughed. The mad sound made a shiver roll up my spine. "A Water chief who has a *Fire dragon* as his companion? That doesn't make any sense."

"Neither does this!" Instead of tossing the water ball at Haley directly, I launched it at her feet. The water splashed over her shoes, creating a puddle. Haley looked down, and she began laughing hysterically.

"Are you kidding me? Is that all you've got?" Haley raised both her hands and started blasting off fireballs. Drew knocked Maddie to the floor and crawled over her body, to shield her from Haley's magic. Ezra and I flung ourselves to the side. Luana created a shield, and the fireballs bounced off the edge. They went soaring back at Haley, who had to duck. Anwara flew in circles, trying to avoid the flaming inferno her Elementai had created.

"Now, Jonah!" I shouted. Jonah sent out a burst of electricity from his fingers. The bolt connected with the water puddle, which was still soaking Haley's shoes.

The water conducted. Haley gasped as electricity jolted through her body, and I smelled burning hair. Haley slumped to the ground, and Anwara gave a cry. The phoenix fluttered to the ground and cast up desperate looks, as if begging us to help.

Maddie panted as Drew helped her up. "Is she... dead?"

"It wasn't enough to kill her," Jonah breathed. "Just knock her out."

"Maybe we *should* kill her." Ezra proceeded down the stairs, toward Haley's limp body. The look in his eyes said he was considering murder.

"No," Jonah said sharply. "It's not right to take a life when you can spare one. Even if it's Haley."

Damn Jonah and his philosophy. His morals might bite him in the ass one day. Luana put a hand on Jonah's shoulder, as if to say she agreed with him. Ezra sent a pleading look at me, but I shook my head, and he frowned.

We'd regretted leaving people alive before— Logan, for example. I hoped sparing Haley's life wasn't another mistake.

I thought Anwara might try to fight us, or take revenge when we walked by, but all she did was cry out for us to help. Her black eyes shimmered as we turned our backs on her and walked away. Her lonesome phoenix song echoed all the way down the hallway as we left the castle.

It crushed me. Whatever Haley did, Anwara never deserved any of this.

Drew collapsed when we got into the trees. Maddie broke down, but Ezra and I lifted him onto Dyami's back and told him to hang on.

It was a long walk back through the tunnel. My body was no longer running on adrenaline, and I'd pushed myself way beyond my limits today. Every part of my body was sore and crying out for some relief, though I said nothing and pushed on. I was totally going to be stuck in bed for the next two days when we made it back to the village.

Hey. I was chief. Still sick, though.

I worried I was moments from passing out, too, until we heard the sound of slithering in the cave. Jake had sent us a cave snake, to get us the rest of the way back through the tunnels. I almost cried with relief when I sat down. Dyami, Julian and Squeaks, along with Baby, were forced to walk behind us, but at least I didn't have to make the Elementai walk any further.

Luana fell asleep against Jonah on the way back. Drew and Maddie also drifted off. Ezra remained awake, his arms crossed. He stared at the floor, like the decision to let Haley go still bothered him.

It was a bumpy and painful ride— because, you know, we were riding a giant snake and it was still a fucking tunnel— but at least I didn't have to walk a step further.

When we emerged from the tunnels into *Hok'evale*, morning had come. I woke everyone up, and as we dismounted, I heard the sound of relief all around us.

The snake had taken us through a tunnel that led straight back to my mother's house on the beach. Imogen, Sophia, Mom and my other siblings were all waiting, along with Jake.

Squeaks chirped when she saw Sabor. She opened her wing, and Baby hugged her side as Sabor looked him over. The male hippogriff puffed out his chest and expanded his feathers. Baby lifted his head, trying to copy him. The Familiars, who were all more resilient than us, did the same— Esis, Dyami and Julian mimicked Sabor as if playing a game, though Sassy kept her distance and licked at her paw in an absent-minded way.

"Oh, my baby," Mom said, and she kissed Maddie's cheeks again and again. She reached out and brushed Drew's hair back. As if this was an ordinary day and nothing at all had happened, Mom said, "It's lovely to see you, dear. Don't worry about your accommodations. You'll be staying with us."

"I hope you've got condoms," Ezra mumbled with a snicker. Nobody else had heard him, but still, I whacked him in the side. Now wasn't the time for jokes. He rubbed his abs and sent me a glare.

As Jonah came close, Jake's features loosened. "Glad to see you made it home," he said in a gruff way, which was manspeak for not wanting to show your emotions.

*Oh, for the love of the ancestors, just kiss him already,* I scorned inwardly at Jake, but he didn't make a move. Instead, he put a firm arm around Jonah's shoulder and squeezed. Jonah brightened, like he hadn't been tired at all from the fight.

Sophia rushed into my arms. I held her, but she didn't cling to me. Her expression was clearer than a few hours before, which meant she was doing better, but I wasn't a fool to think she was completely okay. Yet she smiled when I looked at her, which meant things would be better again... for now, at least.

Imogen hung back from all of us and watched as Luana teetered. She really was beat. Imogen acted like she wanted to help Luana, until Luana looked at her and Imogen glanced away.

"Let's get you all inside. Breakfast is waiting. You must be starving," Mom said in that gentle way of hers. The smell of pancakes wafted out from the open window. My stomach rumbled. My plan was to devour a stack of pancakes, return home, and shower until I literally couldn't stand anymore. I wanted to collapse into bed. Seriously, I didn't want anyone bothering me for at least a few hours.

Which was impossible, because I was chief now, and I was quickly learning one wasn't a chief unless you had somebody up your ass twenty-four seven.

The Familiars lounged outside on the porch as we stepped inside the house. Once we were in the living room, Maddie seemed to realize she was still wearing Oleander's dress. Her eyes went wide. The group froze as Maddie tore the headdress out of her hair and flung it to the floor.

"Get this off me!" she screeched.

The sound of fabric ripping could be heard as Maddie yanked at the robe and forcibly removed her dress. She'd scratched at her skin in an effort to tear the robes off, and it bled. She furiously grabbed at her garments in a craze, eyes mad with a fever to get them off. She didn't care that all of us were standing right there. She cried as the dress fell to the floor until she was standing on just her underclothes.

"Maddie." Mom pulled her into another room and shut the door.

Maddie's deranged screams, along with the sounds of Mom trying to calm her down, could be heard as they echoed around the house.

Drew stared at the pile of clothes with a blank expression. It was like he couldn't comprehend what had just happened.

Ezra tugged on Drew's arm. "Come on, man. You need a shower, and I've got some clothes."

Drew followed Ezra like a zombie. Sophia stooped down, picked up the *naderei* regalia and tossed it into the fireplace. She ignited the clothes, and the robes crackled as her Fire quickly overtook them.

Jonah, the savior he was, immediately distracted everyone by rushing to the kitchen. "Who wants pancakes? I'm starved."

People gathered around the breakfast table and made small talk while Jonah distributed pancakes. Sophia tugged on my arm, and I followed her onto the patio.

"Who made it back?" I asked quietly the moment we were alone. I hoped to the ancestors she didn't have any bad news.

"Everyone we know, save for Luca and his Familiar," Sophia said quietly. "Riley got hurt, but he'll survive. The resistance lost some people, but not many. We got very lucky."

The weight that was always tightening my chest lately loosened just a tiny bit more. "Okay. Where do we stand now?"

"All the people you got out of Orenda— Wyatt, Lira, Tabitha, Maddox, and Sam— they're working with James and Carter to make a team, to start looking for the missing Familiars." Sophia sighed. "Though it's a long road ahead. No one has any idea where Oleander's taken them, and we have no leads. It could take months to locate them."

"We'll find them, Sophia." We'd promised to end the child camps, and we had. This was just another step to bringing down Oleander and the other Elders.

"I hope so. It seems no matter how far we come, there's always one more thing to do," she said hopelessly.

Esis had moved on from playing with the others and was chewing on her shoelace, but Sophia barely noticed. Her eyes were locked on the ocean.

"Everyone's back together, that's what's important," I said. "We just have to start over, and not look back."

Sophia said nothing. She crossed her arms over her chest and turned away from me, keeping silent.

She was doing it again. Not keeping secrets, but keeping her distance.

Sweeping our issues under the rug, because that was the only way she knew how to deal.

What had happened with Logan painfully brought everything into the light. And I was sick and tired of running from it. Sophia and I had promised each other we'd handle our issues together. And it was about time we did.

We had to end this, once and for all. This distance between Sophia and I wasn't serving us. If we were going to make it through this war, we needed to be united.

I only knew one way.

# sophia

## TWELVE

I thought that everything would be better once we saved the kids, but deep down in my gut, I *knew* something was wrong. Where had Oleander taken the missing Familiars? Why weren't we able to save everybody? How many more people had to die?

The worst part was I couldn't bring myself to talk to Liam about it. It felt like there was a wall between us. Every time I opened my mouth to say something, the words didn't come out. I just wanted to confide in him, but I didn't want to hand over the weight of my problems to him. We should be happy about the kids we *did* save... not dwelling on the parts we couldn't change.

The following morning, I woke to the feeling of lips on mine. I relaxed into the kiss and wrapped my arms around Liam's neck.

"Mm..." I moaned.

Liam tried to push away, but I held him down.

"Stay," I begged.

He chuckled. "I can't, *pawee*. I have chief duties before the class I'm teaching today."

My eyes fluttered open, and I faked a pout. "Do you *have* to?"

"Yes," he stated flatly.

I rolled over and groaned. "I guess that means I have to get to my class, too."

"Actually, no," Liam said. "Luana came by early. She's giving you the day off."

"Really?" I asked. I could use the rest— but I also wanted to practice my powers.

Liam nodded. "But I have one request."

I raised an eyebrow. "What's that?"

Liam sighed. "Will you go visit my mom?"

I sat up straight. The way he said it worried me. "Yeah, of course. Is something wrong?"

"No," Liam said quickly. "Well... yes. I mean, you know how she's been since my dad died. She could use some company. But it's not about that. She wants to talk to you."

"Oh, no," I said. "Is this some sort of *don't break my son's heart* lecture?"

Liam laughed. "No, the exact opposite, actually. Don't worry about it. You'll have fun."

"I hope so."

Liam took my hand in his and brushed his lips over my skin, then planted another kiss on my lips. Esis made laughing noises from beside us. He turned his back to us and wrapped his arms around his body, acting like he was making out with someone.

"Oh, real mature, Esis," Liam quipped. He nudged him. Esis tumbled over and did a somersault on the bed. He squeaked and shook his fist at Liam. Liam laughed and stood. "I'll see you after work. Love you."

"Love you, too."

Liam left with Julian, and I got up to take a shower. Once Esis and I were ready for the day, we headed outside and took a walk to the beach.

The door to Haloke's house was open when I arrived, letting in the cool morning breeze. I knocked lightly on the door frame and stepped inside.

"Hello?" I called.

No one responded, but I heard voices coming from one of the bedrooms. I followed the sounds down the hall and found Ezra, Stevie, and Haloke in Jackson's nursery. I could hear Christian and Katie playing in one of the other bedrooms.

Haloke pressed the back of her hand to Stevie's forehead. "Are you *sure* you're well enough to take him for the day?"

Ezra bounced Jackson in his arms. "I can handle them both."

Stevie swatted at him. "Please, I don't need *handling*. I'll be fine. I'm not contagious."

"Are you sure?" Haloke pressed. "If you feel unwell, you should lie down."

"Please, Haloke, I'll be—"

Stevie started coughing uncontrollably and covered her mouth with her elbow. She didn't look too well. Her eyes were red and puffy, and her lips pale. I'd seen Liam like this one too many times.

"Okay, maybe I'm not feeling the best," Stevie admitted. "But we really do want to spend time with Jackson."

"No, this was a bad idea," Haloke said, reaching for Jackson in Ezra's arms. "I'll take him. You rest, dear."

"I can help," I offered from the doorway.

Everyone looked up, and Stevie's eyes brightened. "Sophia, you see Liam like this all the time. Would you tell Haloke I'm fine?"

Stevie pressed her hand to her mouth and suppressed a cough. I felt really bad for her. All she wanted was to push through her illness and have a normal day. But I couldn't lie. She looked awful.

"You're right," I agreed. "I *have* seen Liam like this, and I know that it's just going to get worse if you don't take care of yourself."

Stevie gave me an irritated glare.

"I'll help with Jackson," I told them. "You go work on feeling better."

"Thanks, Sophia," Ezra said, placing Jackson in my arms.

Jackson clung to my shirt, and I bounced him on my hip. "It's no problem. I'm here to help."

"We'll be back for him as soon as Stevie's feeling better," Ezra told Haloke before he and Stevie left the room.

Haloke looked somewhat relieved, though I didn't know why. It was almost like she couldn't bear to be separated from Jackson... but it was obvious she needed the break. Her short hair was a mess, and she looked like she'd aged years since she'd left Kinpago. She wore a long skirt and a shawl around her neck, yet didn't look at all put together.

I turned to her. "Are you okay?"

She offered a light smile. "Of course, Sophia. I'm actually glad you're here. There's been something I've been meaning to speak to you about. How much time do you have?"

I shrugged. "All day."

Her eyes softened. "Perfect. Help me with breakfast, will you?"

Haloke led me to the kitchen, and I put Jackson in his highchair. "What is it you wanted to talk to me about?"

I knew Liam told me not to worry, but I couldn't help it. I didn't know what Haloke wanted from me.

Haloke pushed the dirty dishes on the counter aside and brought out a clean bowl. She turned to me. "There's a tradition in the Hawkei tribe,

Sophia. When a woman becomes engaged, it's customary for the mother of her fiancé to hand down her wisdom through a custom called *wife training*. I want to help you prepare for your marriage."

I breathed a sigh of relief. That wasn't so bad. "I'm all ears."

Haloke smiled genuinely. "Let's start on breakfast then, shall we?"

While she gathered ingredients, I found myself clearing out the sink and filling it with soapy water. I didn't even realize I was washing her dishes until I was a few dishes in. I just wanted to help, and she seemed to really need it right now.

Haloke spoke while the two of us moved around the kitchen. "In traditional Hawkei culture, it is the wife's duty to take care of the family. I know things aren't as traditional anymore and you may choose to take a job outside the home, but there's something to remember about marrying Liam."

Haloke set a bag of flour on the counter. I sensed the heavy conversation was about to start already. I set a clean plate in the drying rack and paused.

"What's that?" I asked.

Haloke took a deep breath. "Liam is a chief," she began. "He is the father of the Toaqua tribe. Which means that as his wife, Sophia, you will be the mother of the Water tribe, and be responsible for everyone in it."

Holy crap! I didn't know why that hadn't ever occurred to me. I knew what I was getting into with Liam— that I had to take care of him and support him as chief. But I never realized I'd have to take care of the Water entire tribe.

"Oh. Well, that's..." I couldn't find the words.

It was a large responsibility I wasn't sure I was ready for. Did it make me want to marry Liam less? Absolutely not. But it definitely gave me something to consider.

"But... I'm Koigni," I spat out.

Haloke placed a gentle hand on my shoulder. "I know. And so does the rest of the tribe."

"Do they accept me?" I questioned. Koigni and Toaqua were about as opposite as opposites could get.

"They are trying," she admitted. "We are all hoping for a future where the Hawkei can unite. You have taken care of Liam thus far, and because of that, they have not outright rejected you. You were born into a Toaqua family, and that helps tip the scale in your favor. But there are some who... doubt you because you are Koigni. They are waiting for you to prove yourself. That will come as you care for Liam. Being the wife of a chief is a full-time job, *shantee*," Haloke said, using the Hawkei word for *wife-in-training*.

"I know," I told her, but maybe I didn't. I knew Haloke worked really hard as a mother and a wife. She was one of the best moms I'd ever met. It just took her saying it to realize I'd be in the same position one day. Maybe not as a mother, but as the wife of a chief.

I heard what she was saying. If I wanted to marry Liam, I was going to have to accept that my marriage— and my commitment to the tribe— came above everything else. And the thing was, I was totally fine with that.

"I want to do the best I can as Liam's wife," I told her.

Haloke smiled. "Then let's begin."

I dried off my hands, and Haloke began teaching me a new recipe. "This is Liam's favorite," she said.

"Fry bread?" I guessed.

She shook a finger. "Not just *any* fry bread. This is his grandmother's secret recipe. It has just the right amount of fluff and the perfect crispness. He'll eat this for breakfast, lunch, and dinner if you let him."

I laughed. "That sounds like him."

"I have no doubt your kids will be just like him," Haloke said as she started mixing the ingredients. "So we're going to practice this recipe until you perfect it."

My stomach dropped at the mention of kids. I shifted my weight uncomfortably between my feet. "Um... you know Liam's sterile, don't you?"

Haloke's expression didn't change. She simply looked me up and down playfully and teased, "That doesn't mean you won't have children."

I furrowed my brow, unsure of what she meant, until I realized she must've meant adoption. "You're right, I guess. We could still end up with kids someday."

Haloke began kneading the bread. She didn't look at me, but she wore a knowing smile on her face. I wasn't sure what it meant.

Haloke showed me how to fry the bread and how to ensure the oil was at the proper temperature. She had a natural touch for cooking, while I managed to burn a few pieces and undercook the others. By the time we ran out of dough, I'd only managed to perfectly fry one piece. Jackson nibbled on fry bread while Haloke and I sat down to eat.

"There's much to learn about marriage, *shantee*," Haloke said. "It's not just about supporting Liam emotionally, but also taking care of the home and the children."

"That's the easy part," I said, biting into a delicious piece of fry bread. "It's the rest that I'm worried about."

She tilted her head to the side. "How so?"

I took a deep breath. It was weird talking to Haloke about her son, because there were things you just didn't say to your parents. "Liam... um... he can be a little closed off, and sometimes that's hard to deal with," I admitted. "I just want to help, but I don't know how. I'm worried he won't open up to me as chief because he doesn't want me to worry."

Haloke's features softened. "Liam is a lot like his dad in that way. He would rather take your burdens than let you take his. Marriage is all about being a team, which means you have to share that burden equally and not let him do it all by himself. It is the only way to lighten the load on both of you. When you are the wife of a chief, the chief has to be strong for the tribe, and the wife has to be strong for the chief. If the chief isn't taken care of, the tribe will fall apart."

My stomach twisted. I wanted to do all that for Liam, but I didn't know how. "How did you get Liwanu to open up to you?"

Haloke looked deep in thought. "I remained open with him," she finally said. "As *you* open up, so will he."

I nodded in understanding. Liam and I really needed to work on that.

"Is there anything else you can tell me about Liam that will help?" I asked.

Haloke dove into a huge explanation on Liam's personality. Most of it I already knew, though she told stories from his childhood that made me smile— like how Liam used to place all his stuffed animals in a circle, wear a blanket as a robe, and pretend to be chief and hold a council meeting. Ezra would join him and pretend to be an Elder. It was so cute that I could barely stand it.

Haloke spent the rest of the day teaching me how to care for the home and giving me tips on cleaning, shopping, and childcare that I never knew before. It was a lot to process, but I was grateful for the guidance. After her lessons were finished, I stayed and helped her clean up the house. Esis played with Jackson and kept trying to put on his socks.

It wasn't until late afternoon when Haloke took my hand and said, "Come, Sophia. I have something for you."

Haloke led me into her bedroom. I sat on the bed while she opened the top drawer in her dresser. She pulled out a thick, colorful piece of fabric and turned to me. I gasped when I realized I recognized the pattern.

Tears pricked at my eyes. "Is that...?"

"The blanket Liam made you," she finished for me. She held it out toward me, her hands shaking.

I took it and wrapped it around my shoulders. "I didn't know you saved it."

She nodded solemnly. "I didn't get much from the house, but I got what mattered."

I ran my fingers down the woven threads, admiring Liam's beautiful work.

"There's one more thing." Haloke sat beside me on the bed, cupping something in her hands, though I couldn't see what it was. "I think you should take this, Sophia."

Haloke pressed a cool object into my hands. I looked down to see it was a small compass, though it didn't have the cardinal direction markings on it.

Haloke noticed me eyeing the compass and hurried to explain. "This has belonged to the wives of Toaqua chiefs for generations. This compass will always lead you to what you need when you're lost— even if what you need is not what you were expecting."

My heart lifted. "It's enchanted? Like the Arcanea compass Oleander used at our execution?"

"No," Haloke said firmly, like Oleander's compass was an insult compared to this. "This is a Toaqua heirloom blessed by the ancestors themselves."

I half expected it to point me in the direction of the *Azaimperiai*, but the needle just spun in a circle— like it couldn't decide which direction I needed to go.

"Take care of it, Sophia." Haloke placed her hand over mine, wrapping my fingers tightly around the compass. I was so touched that she trusted me with it that I barely got the words out.

"I will," I whispered.

Haloke took a deep breath. "One more thing before you leave, *shantee*. You have spent all day learning how to care for others, but there is one person you must care for above all else. If you don't care for her, you cannot care for your family."

"Who?" I asked.

Haloke's eyes twinkled. "Yourself."

A silent beat passed between us. Her words cut through me, because I knew how much she'd been struggling with that very thing lately.

"You must be the wife you want to be *before* you get married," Haloke added. "Only when you know who you are and what your limits are can you effectively care for those around you."

I spoke softly in an effort to be helpful. "But Haloke, *you* haven't been taking care of yourself."

She blinked a few times, like it came as a shock. Her mouth hung open, as if she intended to defend herself but couldn't. I knew she was trying to be strong for everyone else, but it was wearing on her.

I took her hands in mine and looked her straight in the eyes. "You don't have to worry anymore. *I'm* the wife of the chief now. You don't have to be strong for the tribe, because I'll do it for you now. I love you, Haloke."

She drew me into a hug. "Oh, Sophia. I knew Liam made the right choice since the moment he brought you home."

WHEN I RETURNED HOME, Imogen and Jonah were the only ones there. They were sitting in the living room, flipping through magazines. Imogen wore a multi-colored maxi dress, though I noticed her wardrobe had significantly toned down since we arrived in *Hok'evale*. It probably had something to do with the limited fashion options in town.

"This tulle would be *perfect*," Imogen said, pointing to a picture.

Jonah leaned over and gasped. "Absolutely!"

Squeaks lay nearby and nodded along, like she agreed with them. Baby was curled up beneath her wing. I'd never seen Squeaks lie so still.

"Perfect for what?" I asked, stepping further into the house.

Imogen looked up from the magazine and scowled. "Out late with Luana again, huh?"

She sounded less than pleased, which ticked me off.

"No, actually," I snapped. "I was having dinner with Haloke for my *shantee* training."

Imogen's cheeks blushed pink. Esis jumped out of my arms and scurried up the back of the couch. He sat next to Sassy and peeked over Imogen's shoulder.

Jonah sat up straighter. "We were just going over ideas for your wedding!"

I sat on the edge of the couch and looked at the magazine. Good Lord. The picture showed a woman in a dress made of nothing but tulle. It was so puffy she looked like a marshmallow, and I could barely see her face. "Look, you guys. You can help with wedding planning, but I'm not wearing *that*."

Imogen chuckled. "We were looking at the *aisle* decorations. Want to help?"

"I was actually going to ask you guys if you wanted to visit some of the kids tonight," I replied. "My parents are fostering three of them, and I thought it'd be nice to play with them."

"Three kids?" Jonah balked. "That's a lot."

I tilted my head at him. "Don't you want to be a schoolteacher?"

"A *college professor*," he clarified.

I shrugged. "There are a lot of kids who need fostering. My parents are doing what they can. What do you guys say?"

Imogen hesitated. "Maybe we should wait for Liam. He said he had something to talk to you about tonight."

"Where is he?" I asked.

"Chief duties," Imogen stated. "He should be home anytime now."

"Well, I guess it wouldn't hurt to look at some wedding ideas while we wait," I said.

Imogen bounced in her seat and flipped to the front of the magazine. "Okay. I was thinking a cave wedding. It'd be *so* much fun to decorate, and we could light candles all along the floor. I could make some pretty neat cave formations— like ice sculptures, but Nivita-style."

"*I* thought we should do it on the beach," Jonah said. "You know, since Liam's Toaqua."

Imogen punched Jonah in the shoulder. It was supposed to be light-hearted, but he rubbed his shoulder like it actually hurt him. "You're just scared of caves, chicken."

Jonah scowled at her. "Since when did you start making fun of me?"

Imogen smirked. "Since you said we couldn't have their wedding in a cave."

"You know what?" Jonah replied. "I'm the Storm Lord. I bet I could make the entire guest party fly. We could have a sky wedding."

"I prefer to keep my feet on the ground, thank you very much," Imogen argued. "Why don't you save it for your wedding to Jake?"

Jonah's face fell. "We'd have to be *dating* for there to be a wedding."

I could hear the sorrow in his voice, so I spoke softly. "Why *aren't* you two dating? You obviously like each other."

"You think so?" Jonah asked hopefully. "Jake couldn't possibly like me."

Imogen snickered. "He *totally* has the hots for you. I've told you that a million times."

Jonah scrunched up his nose. "Yeah, but..."

"But what?" I questioned. "You should ask him out. Nothing's ever stopped you before."

Jonah sighed. "Yeah, but before I was just screwing around. With Jake... I don't know. I think it could turn into something serious. I've only had one serious relationship before, and it... it wasn't good."

"Jake is *nothing* like Renar!" Imogen spat Renar's name like it was a curse, and Sassy hissed.

Jonah shifted uncomfortably on the sofa. "I know. But I didn't think Renar was bad in the beginning, either."

"I don't understand," I said carefully. "Are you... scared?"

Jonah shrugged, looking more and more uncomfortable by the second. "Now that you say it, I guess I am. I want it to go really well, but what if Jake... what if he's not everything I imagined?"

The room had gone really quiet.

"Jonah, you have nothing to be afraid of," I told him. "Renar's with the Elders. Jake's with the resistance. They're polar opposites."

Jonah ran his hand down his beard, and he wouldn't meet either of us in the eyes. "That's not what I meant. Mine and Renar's problems went beyond that."

Imogen stared at Jonah wide-eyed— like she could sense there was something he'd never told her. "What do you mean?"

Jonah dropped his gaze. "Look, there's something I never told you guys that you should probably know."

Imogen's features softened, and she placed a comforting hand on Jonah's shoulder. "What is it?"

Squeaks came up behind him and rested her beak on his shoulder. She looked really sad, like she wanted to comfort him.

Jonah blinked a couple times, but his eyes still sparkled with tears. "The first time Renar and I..." He cleared his throat. "The first time we *did* it, I wasn't ready."

My guts sank, and Imogen threw a hand over her mouth. "You don't mean...?"

Jonah swallowed. "I'll spare you the details. What you need to know is Renar... he..."

Imogen's lips tightened. "What'd that low-life do?"

Jonah swallowed. "Renar drugged me, and he raped me."

Imogen and I gasped in unison. My hand shot over my mouth, and my stomach dropped to my toes. I knew Renar was a total asshole, but I never knew he'd taken things that far. Sick images flashed through my mind, and I was suddenly taken back to the camps. I could still feel Logan's weight on top of me. I felt like I might puke. I closed my eyes and shook the images off.

At least I'd been saved before anything could happen. Jonah hadn't been so lucky. I felt awful for him.

Imogen's hands curled into fists. "That motherfucker. I'll kill him for you, Jonah. I really will."

"No," Jonah said quickly. "That's not why I told you. I'm not out for revenge. Renar took advantage of me, and I know what he did was wrong. I just don't want to fall into that again with someone else... you know?"

"Jonah, I'm so sorry." My knees shook as I stood and crossed to the other side of the couch to sit next to him. I pulled him into a tight hug. I couldn't change what had happened, but the least I could do was let him know I cared. "You didn't deserve that."

"No shit!" Imogen shot to her feet. "No one deserves that— especially Jonah. He has the heart of a fucking saint!"

Imogen grabbed a throw pillow off the couch and started punching it like it was Renar's face. "I'll gouge his eyes out! I'll slit his throat!"

"Woah, Im!" Jonah cried, holding his hands up. "Calm down."

"Calm down?" she balked. "After what you just told me? No way!"

"I just want to move past it, okay?" Jonah said softly. "Please let it go."

Imogen eyed him a moment, and she must've decided he meant it. She dropped the pillow and returned to his side. Her tone softened— which was really weird with how she'd been raging a moment ago. "We're here for you. Whatever you need."

Jonah squeezed us both. "Thanks."

Imogen sniffled. "I just don't get why you stayed with him."

Jonah frowned. "Honestly, I don't get it either. At the time, I thought it was normal. I thought everything that happened was somehow *my* fault."

"It wasn't," I told him. "You know that, right?"

Jonah nodded. "I do now. As for Jake, I know he's not like that. I don't think he's going to hurt me. I just want to make sure he likes me for *me* first, and not just because I'm throwing myself at him... you know?"

"We understand completely," Imogen said.

Jonah sighed in relief. "You girls are the best," Jonah replied.

Just then, we heard the sound of the front door opening. Liam walked in, Julian right behind him. We all sprang apart, but we wiped our eyes at the same time. It was pretty obvious we were having a moment.

Liam stopped in his tracks. "Am I interrupting something?"

Jonah cleared his throat. "No. Im and I were just going to visit some of the kids. They'll love Baby."

"Oh, um, okay." Liam stumbled over his words as Imogen and Jonah made a quick exit, their Familiars on their heels. Baby frolicked behind Squeaks like he was excited to get out of the house. Esis stared after them longingly, then jumped off the couch and slipped through the door behind them.

"Esis!" I called. I hurried to the door and opened it.

Jonah gave a thumbs-up. "Esis is good. He can tag along."

I hesitated in the doorway. "Are you sure?"

"Pft." Jonah waved his hand. "For sure. The kids will love him."

Liam opened the door wider. "In that case, can you take Julian, too?"

Julian wagged his tail like a dog at the offer. Jonah whistled to him. "Come on, boy."

Julian sneered at Jonah before he went chasing after the other Familiars. Within moments, Liam and I were left alone. Liam cleared his throat and took a step toward me.

I shifted my weight when I faced him. "Imogen said you wanted to talk to me?"

Liam looked to his feet. "Yeah, I do."

My pulse quickened. "Uh, oh."

"No," Liam said quickly. "It's not like that. It's good... kind of."

"O-okay," I stammered. I already had a feeling I knew what he wanted to talk about, and I wasn't sure I was ready for it. "There's something I need to tell you, too."

He tilted his head in question. "Is everything all right?"

I sighed. "Well, for one, I just got some very disturbing news about Jonah."

Liam frowned and looked deeply disturbed. "Is it about Renar?"

"You know?" I asked.

Liam nodded solemnly. "Yeah. He opened up to me about it last semester. Pretty disturbing, isn't it?"

My heart twisted. "Absolutely. I feel awful for him."

"I know. Me, too," Liam admitted. "I wish we could change it, but we can't."

"I know. All we can do is help him through it."

"He's doing better," Liam said. "I think being in *Hok'evale* has made a difference for him. And being around Jake."

"That's good." I played with my hands. I didn't know what else to say.

Knowing one of your best friends had been raped was awful. I was still trying to fathom it had happened.

"So, what else did you have to tell me?" he asked, changing the subject.

I was glad for the distraction, because it was hard to think about what Jonah went through. "I wanted you to know that I saw my grandparents," I told him.

Shock crossed his features. "You what? In the pits?"

"No, thank the ancestors," I said quickly. "I sort of had a panic attack in the camps. They came to me and told me I had to face my trauma. They basically told me I was going to find the pits and that I had to keep going. Seeing them and hearing them again... it really helped me."

"Wait... they *spoke* to you?" he asked.

"Yeah," I replied, like it wasn't a big deal.

"You heard them?" he repeated.

"As clear as I hear you now," I stated. What did he not understand?

Liam pressed his lips together. "That's so strange. You shouldn't have been able to talk to them unless they were your spirit guides."

I shrugged. "Maybe they *became* my spirit guides when they died."

Liam looked deep in thought, like he didn't know if such a thing was possible. After a few moments of contemplation, his shoulders fell. "I don't know how you spoke to them, but I'm glad they helped you, and that you're doing better."

I offered a shy smile. "What was it you wanted to talk to me about?"

Liam hesitated, then wrapped me in his arms. He was so warm and comforting that I couldn't help but relax into him.

But he didn't say anything, and that frightened me. After a few moments of silence, I drew away. "Liam, you're scaring me."

Tears brimmed his eyes. My stomach twisted. "Ancestors, tell me you still want to marry me."

"Yes, of course!" he answered instantly. "It's not that. It's just..."

He ran his thumb over the back of my hand. "I love you so much, and I can't handle you being distant all the time."

"Me? Distant?" I balked.

Liam winced, like he'd caught what he said and knew it wasn't right to put all the blame on me. "You're right, *pawee*. We've *both* been distant lately. I know we don't want to burden each other, but if we're going to be married, we're going to have to carry our burdens together."

The knot in my chest softened. "Your mom said something similar. She said marriage lightens the load."

Liam pushed my hair out of my eyes and stared at me in admiration. "She's exactly right. I'd do anything to carry your burden, Sophia, so you wouldn't have to."

"And I you," I told him.

Liam wrapped me in a hug and kissed my forehead lightly. "That's the part we're good at. It's the opening up we need to work on."

"Okay," I told him. "I'll try to tell you stuff more often."

Liam shook his head. "It's more complicated than that."

I tilted my head up to look at him. "What do you mean?"

Liam took my hand. "Let's take a walk."

Liam didn't tell me where we were going. I was partially curious, but also worried. I was much better at avoiding difficult conversations than having them. But the truth was, I knew Liam and I had to work through this before our wedding. It was like Haloke had said. I had to be the wife I wanted to be before I married Liam, and I wasn't walking into our marriage holding on to our issues. Liam knew it, too.

Liam led me down the beach far away from the houses. We entered a narrow cave opening tucked back into the rocks. It would've been almost impossible to find if you didn't know where it was. When I stepped inside, I gasped at the vast beauty of the cavern. We stood on a rocky platform that was lined with endless candles. A small pool filled the other side of the cave, and light shone in through a hole in the ceiling. A beautiful waterfall cascaded down through the opening and into the pool. It shimmered a beautiful blue in the evening light. Above us, cave salamanders sat suctioned to the cave ceiling and glowed all different colors with luminescent magic.

"Liam, this is gorgeous," I told him, spinning around to take it all in. "And the candles... how did you... when did you?"

Liam pulled me to the center of the room. "It's a blessed cave. Luana told me where to find it. I was late getting home because I was setting it up for us."

"Setting it up for what?" I asked. "Is this like, a date?"

Liam chuckled lightly, but it sounded forced. "It's actually a ceremony, *pawee*."

I eyed him curiously. "What sort of ceremony?"

Liam held my hand and stared deep into my eyes. "It's a cleansing ceremony. I think it's time we finally face our problems. I want to enter into our marriage on the right foot."

"So do I," I told him, feeling the truth of it deep in my heart.

"Then will you do this with me?" he asked gently.

His question hit me right in the feels. Liam wasn't demanding I do this. He wasn't saying he wouldn't marry me if I didn't. He was giving me a choice— a chance to make things right between us. He was putting the future of our relationship in my hands. *That's* how much he loved me.

"Of course," I told him.

"You'll need to strip down, *pawee*."

I smirked at him. "Getting to the good stuff already?"

Liam rolled his eyes at me. "Believe me, this isn't the good stuff. It's part of the ceremony."

My heart dropped in my chest. "Oh... is this going to hurt?"

Liam shook his head. "Not physically."

"Emotionally?" I asked carefully.

Liam took a deep breath. "That depends. How much do you have to work through?"

I dropped my gaze. "A lot," I admitted.

"If you don't want to do this—"

"I do," I assured him, cutting him off.

"This ceremony is all about vulnerability," Liam explained. "We have to open up to each other completely. Are you ready to do that?"

"Yes." I reached for the hem of my shirt and pulled it over my head. "Tell me what to do, and I'll do it."

I tossed my shirt aside. Liam eyed me up and down a moment. He must've decided I was being honest— that I wasn't backing out of this— because he turned and walked over to a bag that was sitting at the side of the cave. He reached inside and pulled out five small jars. Each was a different color— red, yellow, green, blue, and purple. He wandered to the edge of the pool and lined them up in a row.

"What are those?" I asked as I kicked my pants aside.

Liam began undressing. "Ceremonial paints. They're often used in war."

I stepped forward, completely naked. "Is that what this is? A war between us?"

Liam dropped his pants and shook his head. "No, Sophia. Not unless you want it to be."

"I don't want to fight with you, Liam."

"I don't, either."

Liam stood in front of me stark naked. It was a little chilly in the cave, but that was the only thing that bothered me. Standing here nude out in the open like this in front of Liam felt natural.

Liam led me closer to the paints and instructed me to get down on my knees. He knelt across from me and began unscrewing the caps to the paint. I watched in wonder as he controlled the sparkling water from the pool and placed a small amount into each of the jars. The water inside swirled, creating a thick, colorful paste.

Neither of us spoke. I just watched, but my pulse quickened. There was something spiritual about being here in this blessed cave, kneeling across from Liam and being completely exposed. He knitted his eyebrows in concentration and stuck the tip of his tongue out of his mouth. My mouth went dry, but I kept my eyes ahead and focused.

When Liam finished mixing the paints, he lifted his gaze to meet mine. "*Pawee*, are you prepared to expose all your inner feelings, to speak your undeniable truths, and to embrace your vulnerability like you never have before?"

I swallowed, and my heart hammered. Liam and I were both good at shutting down when we thought it might hurt the other. But I couldn't keep it in anymore, not if I wanted to be his wife. And by the ancestors, I wanted to be his wife more than anything.

Liam dipped two fingers into the green paint. He lifted them just above the bosom of my breasts, and they hovered there. His fingers quivered, and his voice shook. "Green, the color of new beginnings— the color of forgiveness."

I jumped a little when Liam pressed his fingers to my chest and began wiping the paint across my body. It was really cold.

"Sophia, I forgive—" Liam's words halted on his tongue. He hesitated, like speaking them aloud was just too painful.

He dropped his gaze from mine, and his eyes roamed over the paint spread across my skin. He got a deep contemplative look in his eyes. For a second, I thought he was about to drop out of the ceremony. My breath caught, but before I could ask him if everything was all right, he cleared his throat.

"Sophia," he whispered softly, looking deep into my eyes. "I forgive you for burning me in the battle of Orenda Academy. And I forgive you for preventing me from saving my father."

Tears welled in my eyes. I *knew* he held it against me. He had every right to. But hearing him say it out loud made my stomach turn to knots.

"I'm so sorry, Liam," I whispered, my bottom lip quivering. "I only did it to save you. If I hadn't stopped you—"

"Shh..." Liam pressed a painted finger to my lips. His eyes watered, and he swallowed. "You don't have to explain. I mean it, *pawee*. I forgive you."

I gaped at him. "But... what I did was..."

*Terrible. Unacceptable. Vile.*

"I know why you did it," Liam said. "We'd all be dead if I'd gone to save my dad. You made the right choice."

I didn't realize how much of a relief it'd be to hear him say that until he did. The knot in my stomach loosened ever so slightly. "You think so?"

Liam nodded. There was no sign of dishonesty in his eyes. He truly forgave me for what I did.

Liam took my hand and guided my fingers into the green paint. "Your turn, Sophia."

I lifted my fingers and shifted on my knees. My mind raced, but I didn't know what to forgive him for. He hadn't done anything wrong.

My fingers hovered above his skin. "I don't have anything to forgive you for."

Liam shook his head gently. "You don't have to forgive me. You just have to open up to me."

I nodded in understanding and pressed my fingers to his skin, spreading the green over his chest. "Then... I forgive myself for burning you. And I forgive myself for the mistakes of my past."

The thought felt heavy at first, because I knew what I'd done was wrong. But saying it out loud made the weight lift. I think I needed Liam to forgive me of that for me to forgive myself. Now that it was out there, I felt like we could finally move past it.

I drew away from him, and Liam went for the next color. He lifted a blob of blue paint to my skin and began to run a line down my arm. "Blue for grief," he said softly. He kept his eyes on the paint as he let his heart pour out. "Though I don't love her, I never got over what Mia did to me. She backstabbed me twice, and sometimes I worry I'm going to get hurt again. I don't want..."

Liam took a shaky breath. "I'm scared that you're going to change your mind and leave."

Tears pricked at my eyes. I searched his features and saw pain laden deep within his eyes. It was one of the things he kept behind the stoic mask he often wore, and it tore me to pieces to know it'd been there all this time.

All I wanted to do was take it from him so he wouldn't have to feel this way ever again.

"I would never leave you," I assured him.

"But you did," he reminded me. "We broke up once, and I'm scared that one day you'll regret getting back together and ask for a divorce."

It broke my heart to hear him suggest it. "I never wanted to break up with you, Liam. It's *always* been you. I will *never* leave you."

"I can't seem to convince myself of that," he breathed. "Sometimes it's just easier to pull away than risk getting hurt again."

I placed a hand to the side of his face. The crease between my eyebrows deepened, and a lump grew in my throat. "I'm marrying you, Liam. I will *never* hurt you again."

Liam placed his hand over mine and closed his eyes. He took a deep breath. When he let it out, his features softened. "I believe you, *pawee*."

*Thank the ancestors.* Liam glanced down to the paints, signaling it was my turn. I dipped my fingers into the blue paint and ran it across his skin.

"Though I've said goodbye, I'm still having a hard time with my grand-parents' death," I admitted. "They were so kind to me, and I didn't get enough time with them."

Liam took my hand in his. "You must be grateful for the time you *did* have with them, *pawee*."

"I know." People kept telling me that. "I just wish sometimes they didn't have to go." My voice wavered as my tears threatened to spill over. "But it's okay, because I know I'll see them again someday."

"You will," Liam assured me. "Those we love are always all around us."

Liam dipped his fingers into the red, and my heart started to pound fiercely in my chest. Red was the color of fire— the color of anger.

Liam's fingers trembled as he brushed the paint over my other arm. "I'm angry at the ancestors. I'm angry that they allowed me to get sick, and that I'm never going to get better."

"You don't know that," I said softly.

"Yes, I do," he stated. "I know there's never going to be a cure. Not for me."

Liam stared at me with a pained expression. Tears began to spill over his lids and fall down his cheeks. I reached out my thumb to wipe them away, but he gently pushed my hands away.

"Don't wipe the tears, Sophia," he said. "Just let them come."

Liam wept. It killed me to see him like this. Liam wasn't the kind of guy who let me see his pain— not even when he was fighting with every ounce of strength to push past his chronic pain and fatigue. This was so different that it scared me.

"Liam?" I whispered, reaching out to him.

His shoulders shook, but he remained bowed. "I'm never going to get better," he cried. "It's just not possible with my illness. I'm going to be stuck like this forever. It's only going to get *worse*."

"Then we'll find a way to deal with it," I assured him, rubbing my hand over his back.

"I don't want to do it anymore," he sobbed. "Some days, it's just too much."

"I know." I desperately wanted to take his pain away. "Whatever you need— whether it's treatments or just support— I will be there to help you."

Liam lifted his head. "Are you sure you know what you're signing up for, *pawee*? You'll have to take care of me for the rest of your life."

"I know," I told him. "And I'm okay with that, because you're worth it."

"You'll resent me," he claimed, tears dotting his cheeks.

I shook my head. "No, I won't. This is *my* choice, Liam. I'll be there for you through all the doctor appointments, the pills, the treatments... I'll cook you soup on days you're too sick to get out of bed." A sob caught in my chest, and I sniffled. "I'll do all your laundry and give you baths, because I know you're too tired to do all that by yourself."

Tension built in my face, and my eyes started to heat. My voice shook. "I'll help to dress you when you can't stand. I'll hold you up when you're on the verge of collapsing, and when you fall, you'll fall into my arms. And when we're old and gray and you're in a wheelchair because you can't take the fatigue any longer, I'll push you down the beach, and we'll sit next to the water so that you can look out over the ocean you love. I'll help you weave your baskets because—"

The sob building in my chest finally broke, and tears began to stream down my face and fall to the cave floor. "Because I love you, Liam, and you deserve to enjoy every beautiful day on this earth as much as I do."

Liam's tears slowed. "*Pawee...*"

I wasn't finished. I spoke between the sobs. "And if the ancestors choose you before me... I'll let you go, because I know that— I know that you'll be with Nashoma and you'll be happy."

Liam sniffled. "Do you really mean all that?"

I nodded firmly. "I do."

"Then I have to believe everything is going to be okay. You'll be there with me," Liam said.

"Always," I whispered, taking his hand in mine.

Liam squeezed me back. "Then maybe the ancestors did me a favor. If I had never gotten sick, I never would've found you."

I blinked away the tears. "The ancestors work in mysterious ways."

Liam took a deep, calming breath. "You keep saying I need to take care of myself, and I think I finally understand. I'm going to be living with this my whole life. I need to find a way to manage it. And accept that it's a part of my existence."

"And I'll help you figure it out," I promised.

He let out an exhausted breath, but with it, he seemed lighter. With that, I sensed Liam was finished with the red paint. So I dipped my fingers into it and ran the paint across his arms.

I swallowed. "I'm angry at the Elders. I'm angry about all the lives they've taken. I'm angry that their greed for power led to the riots and the deaths at Orenda Academy. I'm angry at Oleander for his plans to execute us and for keeping all our friends prisoner in the castle. I'm angry at Logan for what he tried to do to me. I don't know how to *stop* being angry about everything they've all done."

"You have to decide how to direct your energy," Liam said. He ran a finger through the paint on one arm, then another finger over the paint on the other. In his hands, he rubbed together the red and blue paint, creating a beautiful purple hue. "If you redirect your anger, you can turn it into something else."

"Like... determination?" I asked thoughtfully. "Leadership? Innovation?"

Liam nodded. "Don't focus on what the Elders and Oleander have done. Focus on what you can do to change it."

"We will... together," I stated. "We'll change everything. I don't want to be angry anymore. I want to be..."

I paused for a moment to think. "I want to be compassionate," I decided. "I want to take care of the people the Elders have hurt."

"That's my Sophia," Liam whispered.

Liam turned to the purple paint next. He ran a line across my stomach. "Purple is the color of self-love. I vow to open up to you. I won't keep drawing away and holding things in. I'll tell you when I'm not feeling good and when I'm hurting. I can't take care of myself on my own, but being honest with you *is* something I can do to ensure I get proper care."

"That means a lot, Liam," I told him. All I wanted to do was help, but I couldn't help if I didn't know when and how he needed it. This was a huge step forward.

I smeared purple paint on his torso next. "Lately, I've felt like I don't really know who I am, because I don't know who my real parents are. I don't even know where to start, since we've found nothing in the Anichi records. It's possible I'll go my whole life without knowing. I don't want to go that long without knowing *myself*."

Liam eyed me with a sympathetic expression.

"I guess what I'm saying is, if I'm going to learn how to love myself, I have to accept that I don't need to know my lineage to do it." I didn't realize any of this until I said it out loud. "Whoever my parents are, it doesn't define me."

"You're right," Liam said. "They don't hold a candle to my Sophie."

A smile touched the corner of my lips.

Liam reached for the yellow paint, but hesitated. He pushed the yellow paint toward me, as if he wasn't quite ready. "You go first."

I dipped my fingers into the yellow paint. "What does yellow mean?"

"Acceptance," Liam said.

I pressed the paint to his cheeks. My heart hammered as I considered my options. What was I struggling to accept? The riots? My grandparents' death? No, that wasn't right. I was working on those, but there was something deeper in my gut I couldn't seem to shake.

I gasped with the realization. "I accept that you and I will never have children together."

My tongue went dry as I spoke the words. It was a hard pill to swallow, because it was something I wanted so much one day. But I was finally starting to feel like it was okay that we'd never have kids of our own. I'd considered adoption as our second option— but that was wrong. No child should ever be a backup plan. I didn't want to adopt a child unless I wanted them fully, not sought them as a replacement for something I couldn't have. And to be honest... I wasn't quite ready to let go of the hope of having a biological child of my own. So I had to accept the reality that I may never be a mother at all, and be at peace with it.

I wiped another glob of paint on Liam's other cheek. "I accept the role of your wife— of being the wife of a chief. I will become the mother of the Toaqua tribe. They will be my children, and I accept that it will be enough for me."

Tears streamed down Liam's cheeks, mixing with the yellow paint. He placed his thumbs into the paint and pressed them to my cheeks, but he didn't move from there. He froze, his hands shaking.

I reached up for his wrists. "It's okay, Liam. Take your time."

Several moments passed before he spoke. He closed his eyes and took a breath. "I accept that I may end up in *Aiya Nocshun.*"

My heart gave a start. It killed me that he still worried about this after the last time we spoke of it. "Liam, why would you think you'd end up there?"

"I've done bad things," he stated. "I've made so many mistakes in my life. I don't think the ancestors can keep giving me second chances."

My stomach sank. He was talking about the people he'd killed. But it'd been necessary. He'd killed Professor Fawn to spare her, and killed the Task Force and Logan to save me. He wasn't heartless.

"That doesn't make you a bad person," I told him.

"It does," he argued. "Bad people are people who've done bad things."

"Bad people have evil in their hearts," I countered. "They do bad things to serve an evil purpose."

"Who gets to decide what's evil, though?" Liam asked. "Murder is evil, isn't it?"

I held on to him tighter. "Have you ever done anything against your principles, Liam?"

He looked deep in thought as he contemplated the question.

"You took Fawn's life to save her," I reminded him. "It was an act of mercy. You killed Logan to save me. You do *everything* to serve other people. You're nothing like the evil that has plagued Kinpago. You're not on the same level as Logan or Haley or Oleander. They hurt people only to serve themselves. You do what you have to do to serve others. See the difference?"

Liam's lips trembled as he nodded.

"I refuse to believe the ancestors would think you're unworthy of the Ancestral Lands," I added. "They accepted you as their Toaqua chief. Would they do that if they thought you were a bad person?"

Liam blinked away the tears. "I guess you're right."

"You have nothing to fear," I told him. "The ancestors have already accepted you as you are. Someone as beautiful as you could never end up in hell."

Liam wrapped me into a hug and accidentally knocked the yellow paint over with his knee. Neither of us rushed to pick it up. We just sat there in the embrace, drinking each other in and letting the yellow paint spread across the floor beneath us.

I squeezed him as tight as I could and inhaled his scent. "Liam, I don't want to fight with you anymore."

"Me either." His voice cracked.

"Whatever happens moving forward, we're a unit," I told him.

He squeezed me back tighter. "Agreed. We'll fight against our issues together instead of against each other."

Tears began streaming down my face again, but they were warm, wonderful tears. I felt the last of the weight lift from my body, and a sense of peace settled in my stomach.

"I love you, Liam," I whispered.

"I love you, too." Liam drew away, but he took my hand in his. He stood, and I gazed up at him. "Come on, *pawee*. We're not done. We have to wash our confessions away— so they can't weigh us down anymore."

Liam helped me into the shallow pool. We walked into the middle, until we were waist deep. Water cascaded down through the open ceiling and fell onto our heads like a cool shower.

Neither of us spoke. There was something incredibly spiritual about the silence. Liam's hands roamed over my arms, spreading the trickling of water over my skin. I did the same to him. The paints ran down our bodies and swirled into the water beneath us, creating a beautiful, breathtaking work of art that twisted and swirled in a beautiful display.

The more I cried, the lighter I felt. As the paints swirled across the pool and away from us, I felt like my breaths became deeper and more peaceful. We could finally let go.

Liam pulled me to his chest. We stood there, taking in the moment like nothing else mattered. His skin was warm against mine. Right now, I didn't even care about the cold water falling down my back. It was all wonderful— every little piece of this ceremony and this cave. I truly felt like we'd been blessed.

I tilted my head up and pressed my lips to Liam's mouth. He moaned, and I felt the water swell around me. His magic pressed against my back-side, pushing me into him. I felt his erection harden against me.

"You feel that?" Liam asked, pressing his hips into mine.

I beamed. "I do."

"I love you this much and more— all day, every day," he said.

"Show me," I told him breathlessly.

He tilted his head to the side in question.

"Show me just how much you love me," I repeated.

"I love you to the Ancestral Lands and back," he said.

Then he cradled the back of my neck and brought his lips down onto mine. He kissed me like he'd never kissed me before. It felt as if our bodies were melting into one another, becoming a single soul.

I moaned as I wrapped my legs around his waist. The water around us swelled even higher. Liam thrust upward, and I gasped. I tilted my head back as he thrust upward again and again. The waterfall poured over my face and down my breasts, and though it sizzled on my hot skin, it felt amazing.

Liam continued moving inside of me as I clung to him. He made sounds of pleasure that made me go crazy. I ran my fingers through his hair and massaged his scalp while his hands roamed down my back and across my ass.

"Liam," I whispered, though my eyes remained closed. "I'm so happy right now."

"I've never been happier than when I'm with my *pawee*," Liam whispered.

I grinned and finally opened my eyes. "Then you're going to be happy for a long time, because I'm not going anywhere."

At that, Liam increased his speed, exploding into an orgasm. He held on to me and sagged as he finished. Something told me he was controlling the pool to help keep himself upright.

I giggled. He opened his eyes, pure bliss written across his face. "What is it?"

"Don't I usually go first?" I teased.

He smirked. "Sorry. I got carried away."

"Don't apologize," I told him. "I was only joking."

His lips curled into a smile. "I'm going to have to do something to make up for this, huh?"

I shrugged, feeling a rush of exhilaration run through me. "What do you have in mind?"

"Lie back," he said.

Liam guided me onto my back in the water. I started a little when he pulled away from me and left me there to float. I thought I'd start to sink, but I didn't.

"It's okay," he assured me. "I've got you."

Liam used his magic to keep me aloft. I tilted my head back into the water and completely relaxed as his magic swirled around me. Liam guided my body beneath the waterfall. I gasped when water started pounding down hard on my clit.

"Liam!" I cried.

He inhaled a sharp breath, and suddenly, the water pouring over me stopped. I looked up to see he was using his magic to redirect the waterfall.

"Was that not okay?" he asked gently.

"It was *great!*" I told him.

He beamed. "Then lie back and relax."

I did as Liam instructed and relaxed into the water again. The waterfall returned to its normal flow and rushed over my clit. Liam pressed his fingers into me.

Sizzling energy built up inside of me, tingling all the way down my fingertips. My moans echoed off the walls of the cavern as Liam worked wonders inside of me with his hands. Then the energy exploded— providing me with a sweet release.

I exhaled a deep breath and lay back in the water. Liam lay beside me, using his magic so we'd float together. It was like we were resting on top of a smooth, cold bed. I reached one arm beneath him and laid the other on his chest, resting my head on his shoulder, using my Fire to warm the water around us.

"This is nice," I whispered blissfully.

Liam kissed the top of my head, sending tingles down to my toes. "No, *pawee*. It's perfect."

LIAM and I stayed in the cave until well past dark. We eventually figured we should get dressed and return home before everyone started to worry. By the time we arrived, Imogen and Jonah were already asleep, and Julian and Esis were curled up in the corner of the room.

That night, I had the most incredible dream.

*I walked through the halls of a large house. It reminded me a lot of Liam's house back on his family island, but it was laid out differently. There was all sorts of Hawkei art on the walls, including the exact collection of arrowheads that hung in my grandparents' house.*

*In the distance, I heard the sound of a child calling, "Mommy! Mommy, come look!"*

*I opened the front door, and from the sky flew a beautiful beast— a red dragon with a rider on his back. I couldn't see his face from here, but the rider had long black hair and wore regalia worthy of a chief.*

*"Look out the window, pumpkin!" I called. "Your daddy's home."*

I startled awake that morning. Liam must've already left for work, because neither he nor Julian were anywhere to be seen. He must've said goodbye to me, but I'd been too tired to remember. By the silence in the house, Imogen and Jonah must've left as well.

Esis stretched from where he'd slept on my belly. He patted my stomach, and in that moment, something hit me. I sprang straight up in bed.

What day was it? How many periods had I missed now?

I'd accepted it wasn't going to happen, but what if...?

Esis eyed me with a sympathetic expression.

"You know something, don't you?" I accused.

He just kept looking at me without responding.

I took a deep breath, and my hands began to shake at the thought of taking a pregnancy test. Holy crap. Was I really going to find out today if I was *pregnant*? I'd been in denial about it for weeks. The thought of having a baby, right now, in the middle of a war, was just too... scary.

The weird thing was, the thought didn't scare me anymore. Now that Liam and I had gone through the cleansing ceremony, everything felt different. If I was, if I wasn't— it didn't matter. Because Liam and I would be fine either way.

"I guess it's time to start being honest with myself," I spoke aloud to Esis.

He nodded firmly.

Liam deserved to know if his baby was growing inside of me, and I wanted to find out, too. I stood from the bed and ran my hand over my belly. It hadn't really changed, but I swore there was the smallest bump there. Maybe I was imagining things. I didn't want to get my hopes up. But I was finally ready to figure out for sure.

Esis and I took the short walk to the convenience store to pick up a pregnancy test. I was so jittery that I practically ran all the way home. I fumbled with the package for a few moments in the bathroom, and nearly dropped it. My heart rate quickened. I was about to piss myself before I was ready.

Esis sat on the edge of the tub and crossed his fingers for me.

"Here goes nothing, buddy," I told him.

I closed my eyes when I put the cap back on the test and waited. I paced back and forth in front of the sink, waiting impatiently for the two minutes to pass. My mind raced. Did I want this? Did I want this *now?*

How was this possible? Would I be okay if the test turned out to be negative?

Esis chittered, and I opened my eyes. He was standing on the counter next to the sink. He pointed down to the pregnancy test proudly.

My heart slammed against my rib cage as I reached out for the pregnancy test. I blinked a few times, unsure if what I was seeing was real.

*One line.*

"It's... it's negative," I told Esis flatly.

But... how could that be? I was hormonal as hell. My boobs hurt. I'd been puking for a month straight. Was it really all part of the stress like I convinced myself of for so long?

I sank onto the toilet lid. Disappointment washed over me. It was so heavy I could hardly breathe. I should've been relieved, because I couldn't exactly raise a baby in the middle of a war, but I wasn't.

I was heartbroken.

Tears pricked at my eyes, and I wiped them away. I thought I'd be okay with this— and I *would* be. But after my dream, I just woke with this sense of positivity, like today was the day.

Who was I kidding? I was only twenty years old. I didn't need to worry about having kids now.

But to be told I'd never have them... it didn't matter if someone had said that to me when I was thirteen or fifty-five. I'd still feel devastated that I couldn't carry my own baby in my womb.

Wow. I didn't know how badly this would hit me.

Esis frowned and dropped his gaze. He kept his hands behind his back and rubbed his foot back and forth across the countertop.

I wiped my nose. "Not gonna lie, buddy. I'm pretty disappointed. It's for the best, I'm sure. But I guess there's just a little part of me that thought—"

Esis pulled his paws from behind his back, and he held up a second pregnancy test.

I grabbed for it immediately and sprang to my feet. My heart hammered, but for entirely different reasons.

*Two lines!*

I squealed, then threw my hand over my mouth. Tears began to stream down my face, and I braced myself against the countertop. This feeling of euphoria was unlike any other. A year ago, I'd been told I could never have the one thing I wanted— a child with Liam. Now here I was, staring down at a positive pregnancy test. It was like the ancestors had bestowed upon us a blessing unlike any other.

"Esis, what'd you do?" I demanded, placing the negative pregnancy test at his feet.

Esis looked up at me with a guilty expression. He pointed to himself, then squatted down like he was on a toilet.

"You peed on it when I wasn't *looking!*?" I squeaked.

Esis threw his paws over his mouth and snickered.

"You were testing me!" I realized. He'd tricked me, so I'd admit to myself how I actually felt about this. Familiars could be little shits sometimes.

"Esis, seriously, that wasn't funny." But I laughed. I was too thrilled to scold him for real.

"I'm pregnant," I said aloud, testing the reality of it on my tongue. It hardly seemed possible. I couldn't believe it myself. "Holy crap, Esis. I'm preg— wait."

My guts sank as the reality of it hit me. "Ancestors, what is Liam going to say? And what if the Elders find out? They'll try to hurt our baby."

Esis lifted his paws and shrugged, as if questioning if other people's opinions really mattered. Of course I cared what Liam thought, but the Elders could go screw themselves. I'd do anything to protect this child.

But... I was the chosen one. Would I put this baby before saving the tribe?

I knew the answer before I finished asking the question. To think what the Elders might do to my child was terrifying, but they wouldn't touch my baby. I wouldn't let them.

"How far along do you think I am?" I mused.

Esis shrugged, then made a butterfly with his paws.

"Sierra?" I asked. "You think we should ask Luana?"

He nodded.

"You're right," I said. With her healing magic, she could probably tell. "Let's go see if the baby's healthy."

Esis jumped onto my shoulder, and we hurried out of the empty house together. I kept the positive pregnancy test tucked in my bag, because it felt really special. I never thought I'd see one myself. It meant the world.

Esis and I found Luana in our usual meditation space in the caves. We were actually a little late for our daily session. She was running her fingers through the water when we arrived, while Sierra fluttered close by.

She stood, and instant concern crossed her features. *Are you okay?* she signed.

*Better than okay,* I told her. *Can you diagnose a pregnancy?*

A wide smile spread across her face. *I thought you'd never ask.*

I furrowed my brow. *You knew?*

She beamed. *Since the day we met. I didn't mean to find out. My Spirit magic told me.*

I recalled when she used her healing magic to assess my health— to see why healing was so hard for me.

*Why didn't you say anything?* I asked.

*I thought you didn't want anyone to know,* she signed. *You didn't know yourself?*

I shook my head.

She wore an expression of regret. *I'm sorry I didn't say anything.*

*That's okay,* I assured her. *Do you think you could check if my baby's healthy?*

She nodded, then guided me toward the sofa in the corner of the cavern. I lay on my back, and Luana knelt down beside me. Esis stood at my head and began massaging my scalp.

Luana placed her hands gently over my belly. Warm, tingling healing magic filled me. I felt completely at peace, but it still felt so surreal.

After at least a minute, Luana pulled away and started signing to me. *Congratulations! You have a healthy baby growing inside of you!*

*You mean it!? I* asked. *It's really okay?*

She smiled. *Perfect, as far as I can tell.*

Tears of happiness filled my eyes. *How far along am I?*

*Fourteen weeks,* she answered. *Which is why I'm surprised you didn't know. You're already starting to show.*

It was hard to explain to her why I'd waited so long. Hell, I could hardly make sense of it myself. I had been so scared to find out, I'd lied to myself for months. I had been terrified... but I wasn't anymore.

*When am I due?* I asked.

*Christmas Eve,* she told me with a soft smile. *Congratulations, Sophia. You're having a Christmas baby!*

I was so excited I couldn't hold it in. I squealed, and flung my arms around her neck. She embraced me back with a laugh.

Luana and I talked for a long time after that. I confided in her about how Liam was sterile and I never thought this was going to happen. This seemed like a miracle.

Then something crossed my mind. *Could the baby have Liam's disease?* I asked her, worried.

*It's possible. But I can't diagnose it yet. The disease doesn't usually become active until young adulthood,* she answered.

I didn't want my baby to suffer, but I knew everything would be okay either way. This baby would be so loved.

I spent all day learning about prenatal health from Luana. She tried to show me how to use my Anichi powers to check the baby's heart rate, but I couldn't manage it.

*We'll try another day,* she told me at the end of our session. *Get lots of rest and take care of yourself. You're going to need it.*

*Thanks. I will.*

I was beaming as Esis and I walked home. I practically felt like I was floating. Me, pregnant! I couldn't believe it.

When we got there, Imogen and Jonah were standing in the kitchen. They wore the same pointed expression, and both had a hand on their hips. Even Squeaks gave me *the look.* Sassy just sat on the counter with her head held high, like she knew something no one else did.

"Uh... what's going on?" I asked, cautiously stepping into the house.

"Sophia, what's this?" Jonah demanded.

He flung a pregnancy test onto the counter, but it went sliding off onto the floor. His face fell for a second, before going back into the pointed look.

My heart stopped for a second before I realized it was the negative test Esis had taken. Whoops.

"So you found Esis' pregnancy test," I said nervously.

"You can drop the act, Sophia," Imogen said. "We *know* you're pregnant."

I furrowed my brow. I wanted to tell them, but I'd been hoping to tell Liam first. "But that test was negative."

"Well, you're testing for a *reason,* aren't you?" Jonah questioned.

"Um... yes?" I said.

"So if this negative one is Esis', where's the positive one?" Jonah asked.

I balked at them. "How— how did you guys know I got a positive test?"

Imogen's stern expression melted away, and it was replaced by a wide-eyed gape. "*Oh em gee!* We were totally bullshitting you. You're pregnant?"

She held her arms out and came towards me before I could answer. Imogen let out a shrill scream. "Congratulations, Sophia!"

"Well, I guess the cat's out of the bag," I said.

Imogen pulled me into a tight hug, and a wave of emotions ran over me. I couldn't help it when a lump rose to my throat.

"Oh my gosh! You're going to be a *mommy!*" Jonah squealed. He wrapped both Imogen and me into a hug and picked us up, practically singing.

"You're squishing us!" I cried.

"Oh, sorry." Jonah set us back down, though he was totally gushing.

Imogen wiped her eyes and giggled. "Why didn't you tell us?"

"I didn't know," I told her. "I just found out today."

"Well, it wasn't hard to assume," Jonah said. "Squeaks and Sassy wouldn't say a damn thing, and we knew they were hiding something."

"Wait. They know?" I asked.

"Familiars can tell from the day of conception," Imogen said. "But they recognize it's a private thing, so they tend not to tell their Elementai."

Jonah jumped up and down. "I'm *so* glad we all know now! Having a baby around is going to be *so* exciting."

"Does Liam know?" Imogen asked.

"Not yet," I said. "I haven't told him."

"Ooh, so we're the first?" she asked brightly.

"Actually, Luana knows," I told her. "I had to go to her, to see how far along I am."

Imogen's face fell. "Oh," she said flatly.

I was about to snap at her, but Jonah quickly stepped in. "It doesn't matter who knows. What matters is that you're having a baby!"

I offered him a smile. "Yeah. Just don't tell Liam yet... okay?"

"Why not?" Imogen grumbled, crossing her arms. "You've already told everyone else."

"Because I want to tell him myself," I said firmly. "And I'm going to do it tonight."

# THIRTEEN

I f someone asked me what a Toaqua chief did, my response would be a *shit ton*.

Being chief meant I had to be available every day, no matter what time it was, just in case one of my people needed me. So far, I'd visited a Toaqua family on making funeral arrangements, taught a class, visited sick Toaqua in the Anichi hospital, signed off on a law the council had passed to outlaw fireworks on the beach after midnight so people could sleep (Christian and Katie's fault), and checked in with the foster families of the Toaqua kids we'd rescued from the camps to see how they were doing.

*After lunch*, I'd officiated a wedding and sentenced a Toaqua guy who'd gotten caught robbing a house. He was young and desperate, so I went easy on him and handed out community service. Around dinner, I'd met with Jake to discuss military strategy and organized tribal funds— or rather, what little funds Toaqua had after we'd been forced to uproot ourselves.

That was all in one day.

These weren't even the majority of my responsibilities. If we were back home in Kinpago and not at war, I'd be helping the other chiefs administer the federal programs from the U.S. government given to the tribe, like senior citizen projects, health management, education, housing, and a million other things.

It was hard work. I had a lot on my plate. But ancestors, I fucking *loved* it. This is what I'd been born to do. I could feel it in my bones. I'd never felt more happy and sure of myself. Life couldn't get more perfect.

For my last thing of the day... fucking finally... I had a council meeting around seven o'clock. Hopefully it'd end at eight and I'd be able to get home for a night off. That is, if someone didn't call me asking for help.

A part of me was worried how long my body could keep up. I could *not* keep doing these twelve-hour days. They were going to put me back in the hospital. I had only been chief for a little while, and I was already feeling run down. Soon, I was going to have to figure out how to work my career around my illness instead of against it. Fainting on the job wasn't a good way to show you were a strong chief.

I was beginning to see why my dad was so stern all the time, and kind of grumpy. This was a lot of weight to carry on your shoulders. If I didn't have Sophia, I didn't think I could do this.

But I did. And her support made all the difference.

The Anichi had given us a building of our own to use for Toaqua affairs. It wasn't much— just a few offices with a conference room we could use for meetings, but it would do. I'd composed my council of Baine, Madame Wells, Ezra, and Wyatt. Baine hadn't found anything in the underwater temple, but he was still exploring, taking trips for expeditions whenever I didn't need him. I'd had to twist Baine's arm to get him to become an Elder again, as he felt he'd failed the first time he was on my father's council, but when I told him I couldn't do this without his guidance, he'd caved. Madame Wells was all too eager to serve, and Ezra had jumped at the chance to be my second, though he insisted I didn't call him an Elder because he "didn't want to sound ancient."

Wyatt didn't get why I was asking him of all people to serve on my council, until I pointed out I felt like I could trust him, and allegiance was what I needed most to unite the tribe these days.

Except for Baine, we were all a bit young to be a proper Elder Council. There was definitely some wisdom and experience missing there. Hopefully youthful optimism and a determination to get shit done would make up for it.

"I think you should all be aware that intel has gathered some crucial information. Besides making himself High Chief, Oleander has also became chief of the Toaqua tribe in Kinpago," Baine began just as we sat around the council table. His eyes flickered to me before he said, "Well, he *thinks* he's chief, anyway. And the Toaqua left back home know no better."

"That's bullshit. Liam's the rightful chief. Oleander has no claim on the Toaqua tribe," Ezra spat. At his side, Dyami cooed in agreement.

"Settle down, Ezra," Baine said calmly. "The few Toaqua that still remain in Kinpago are committed to following his leadership. Against their will, of course. Most likely, he's threatening them with their lives. Rescuing them will prove difficult, if not impossible. At least until the proper time when we can expose where we are."

I shook my head. "Jake's not ready to expose the resistance. The Anichi Council made it clear that Sophia has to be ready to fulfill the prophecy before they come out of hiding. And she's not— not yet. She still needs more training."

"I understand your concern for your wife-to-be, but I'm not sure how much longer we can keep this up," Baine said in frustration. "Oleander believes that the liberation of the camps was a Biyami rebellion, but fooling him again won't be so easy. And now that Sophia's shown her face in Kinpago, Oleander has confirmation she's still alive. He's going to be looking for her, and it won't be long before he discovers she's here and that the Anichi are still alive. We need a contingency plan for *when* that happens, not *if*."

"Easy. Liam challenges Oleander to a chief's duel, and we end this," Ezra said.

"No, Ez. Not so easy." I frowned. "I'm sure my magic is strong enough to take Oleander down, but he has Skylis on his side. Julian's not big enough yet to battle a dracash. Chief duels involve Familiars too, not just Elementai. Even Valda lost against him, and she was an experienced dragon."

I reached out to itch Julian behind the horns, and he growled. Though he was just barely bigger than Squeaks now, he seemed eager at the chance to go head-to-head with Skylis.

"I believe the problem is we're still outnumbered," Madame Wells began. "Even with the Anichi tribe on our side, and all the refugees and the Biyami rebels in the village, those in Kinpago outnumber us two to one."

"But not everyone is going to fight for Oleander," Wyatt argued. "The only reason most people are still there is because they don't think they have any other option. Once we reveal ourselves, they'll come to our side."

"I think you're being too optimistic," Baine said. "Some Defortai in the tribe have gained comfortable positions and won't want to lose their status. Others won't want to risk fighting back, for fear of repercussions. Those brave enough to resist are probably already here."

"People will do what they have to in order to survive. Everyone is going to have to make the choice when the time comes," I began.

Julian laid his head on my lap, and I added, "Though we have a big problem. We can't even think about storming Kinpago when so many of our Familiars are missing. Winning a battle when the other side has companions and we don't is impossible. We need our magical creatures."

"Yes, but where are they?" Wyatt smacked his hand on the table. "It's like Oleander up and made them disappear."

Looking for the missing Familiars had proved futile. Nothing had come up as of yet. Wyatt had been suffering without Tuskin. Drew and Maddie were more or less in the same state.

"Familiars can't vanish. Especially powerful ones. They must leave traces," Madame Wells argued.

"Something doesn't add up." Ezra crossed his arms and scowled. "We need more people on this case."

"How? There's no one left to spare," Baine argued. "We've got every last man and woman booked up with a job, and if you take people from one place and put them in another, the whole system falls apart."

"Chief, what do you want to do?" Wyatt looked to me.

The table went silent. I pondered the question as Julian rumbled.

"Finding our Familiars is of utmost importance," I decided. "We'll get by in other ways, but this is one area we can't slack on. I want all Toaqua intel devoted to finding these creatures. We'll get our information on Oleander from the Anichi spies."

There was a mutter of agreement from the council. We talked for an hour about it, and didn't get far. When I could tell this wasn't going anywhere, I called the end of the meeting, and we split up.

Baine went back to his house to prepare for another expedition— his last one had come up empty, and he'd been a rotten bastard to deal with ever since. I'd learned that if Baine had a successful exploration where he'd found another clue, he was on top of the moon, but ancestors forbid if he came back with nothing, because he was a total crab. Calling council meetings with him gone every other week was difficult, but right now we didn't have any choice, as finding the *Azaimperiai* wasn't something we could sacrifice.

Madame Wells swept off to wherever she went, and Wyatt more or less stormed out. He'd been in a bad way. His support on the council was helpful, but I knew he wouldn't be himself until he got Tuskin back.

Ezra and I walked back to the main village together. Julian and Dyami flew above, wrestling in the sky and smacking into each other. Those two

Familiars never had a greater time than when they were beating each other up for fun.

It was how Ezra and I had acted when we were younger. I could still remember the time I'd thrown Ezra off the couch and into the coffee table. He'd gotten me back by shoving me into a dresser. Dad had to break us up. Good days, those were.

As we came into town, I saw Stevie wave outside *The Falcon's Nest*, still in her uniform. Stevie worked there as a waitress. Ezra told me that was how they met— the first night he was here, he went out for a coffee by himself, trying to process everything that had happened. Stevie had served him, and they'd hit it off right away. They'd talked until her shift was over and ended up hanging out all night. They'd screwed on the docks in the morning while the sun came up, and barely parted since.

Ezra spared me no fucking details when it came to Stevie. He was fricking obsessed with the girl.

"Hey, baby." Ezra swept Stevie into his arms and kissed her on the mouth. "I've been thinking about you all day."

I was going to puke. Stevie tilted up a smile, but even as she did it, I could see she was hiding her pain. Fuck, did I look like that sometimes? No wonder people worried about me.

"And I've been counting the minutes until I could see you again," she responded. She ran her fingers through Ezra's hair, and I rolled my eyes.

"If you two are gonna bang, could you go somewhere private?" I complained.

Ezra snickered. Stevie tried to laugh, but it was more of a grimace. There were bags under her eyes.

Stevie hadn't been her chipper self lately, but I figured she was having a flare up. I was about due for one myself. As I was working all the time, this one was gonna hit *hard*.

"Hey, Ez, can you give me a hand?" Lani called. She was unloading a heavy box off a truck that looked like it was full of food.

"Sure thing," Ezra called.

Ezra rushed to help Lani. As they carried the box inside, Stevie turned to me. "Getting by?"

"Barely." I laughed. "How you feeling?"

"Do you even have to ask?" She snorted.

I lifted a smile. "No. Not really."

Stevie gave a sad sigh. "I don't want to be treated like I'm incapable, you know? I can still do things. I know people want to help me feel better, but babying me isn't going to help."

I nodded solemnly. I knew the feeling. I took a cautious step away and said, "Hey... you aren't contagious, are you?"

"No. Trust me, I'm not going to give you my cooties. I know how dangerous it is." Stevie coughed.

"You should probably take it easy," I began.

She leaned against the side of a cave wall and stared up at the sky. "You're a fucking hypocrite, pulling long hours."

"I know I can't keep doing that. I promised Sophia I'd take care of myself." And I meant it. Though my job complicated things now.

I crossed my arms. "Keep pushing yourself like this and you'll end up flat on the floor."

Stevie gave a giggle. "No way. *You're* going to pass out first. I call it."

"Fuck that. It's gonna be you."

Stevie scoffed. "My job is way easier than yours. I am *totally* going to outlast you."

"Okay, how about this," I started. "Whoever faints on the job first owes the other one twenty bucks."

Stevie smirked. "Deal. Prepare to be paying me big time."

Now I had an even better reason to stay well, because I really didn't want to give Stevie any money. She'd use it for her and Ezra's endless condom fund.

"I think you're underestimating me. You don't understand how much of a pro I am at not letting people around me know that *everything hurts and I'm dying,*" I started.

Stevie threw back her head and laughed. "Please. Your game is *weak.* If I do anything fun, it's like my body gets personally offended."

"I had double pneumonia for about a month and didn't admit it," I said with a shrug.

"Hardcore!" Stevie exclaimed. "You know, have you ever been to a party that you *really* didn't want to go to, and you end up feeling like shit and you're just like, *how am I going to vomit politely?*"

"Yes!" I exclaimed. I gave a loud laugh. "Fuck, chronic illness humor is the *best* humor."

"I made a sandwich this morning, then I made another one because I forgot," Stevie challenged.

"I have literally stared at the bathroom sink for five minutes and forgot why I was there," I admitted.

"I've pretended I was drunk so people didn't figure out I had brain fog."

"I've eaten stuff that I knew would make me sick later just because it looked good and I'd ceased to give a fuck."

"Ditto." Stevie put a hand on your hip. "You know, Ez told me you're a pretty good fighter. I've got some skills with Water myself. We should duel and see who taps out first."

"Sure. We'll just have to schedule a day where we're both not feeling like crap, which will be *never*," I cracked.

"Hey, the only one tough enough to kick my ass is *me*," Stevie stated. "So if you wanna fight, we can go. Just give me twenty minutes to walk across the room and it's on."

I couldn't hold it in anymore. I burst out laughing. "Make sure there are breaks included!"

Stevie broke out into a fit of giggles. She bent over her knees and held her stomach as she laughed. Her laughter made me lose it. I'm sure we looked like a couple of lunatics on the side of the road.

Ezra came back. His eyebrow was raised as he approached. Stevie and I were still laughing our asses off. Ancestors, there were freaking tears in my eyes. I was totally cracking up. I couldn't joke around like this with my friends, because they wouldn't get it. They'd think I had a death wish or something. But Stevie totally understood.

"Hey," I managed to say. "Let's make a *real* bet. We'll put in every week. The Elementai that outlasts takes it all."

"That's perfect!" Stevie snickered. "Whoever dies first loses all the cash."

"You're buying me a new house," I forced out. Ancestors, I could barely breathe.

"You'll be eating your words when you're watching me drive a new car around from the Ancestral Lands," Stevie gasped.

Ezra didn't like our morbid sense of humor. He scowled and said, "Neither of you are dying. Cut it out."

Stevie and I stopped cackling, but silly grins were still on our faces. Ezra wrapped his arm around Stevie's waist and said sourly, "Come on, let's go."

Ezra remained silent, but Stevie gave me a wink. Ancestors, she totally got what it was like. And Ez needed to lighten up. It wasn't like we were being serious. Joking around about being sick was one of the few ways to actually deal.

The summer sun was starting to set by this point. I caught sight of

Imogen and Jonah ahead. We met up with them on the path. Squeaks was wearing a black feather boa, and Sassy had a roll of red ribbon in her mouth.

"What are you guys doing?" I asked curiously. Imogen had a list and was checking off items, while Jonah carried a bag that already looked full of stuff.

"We're shopping for the cabaret," Jonah began. "Jake said we could have one. It can't be all doom, gloom and work around here."

That stupid cabaret. At least when it was over Jonah would stop talking about it. I can't believe Jake had approved this. There was too much to do with the war effort for us to be wasting time on frivolous things.

But... I'd bet Jonah could ask Jake to put on a circus and the guy would give it to him. Ancestors, Jake was already whipped. And I guess Jonah was right, in a way. We had to keep morale up somehow and cheer people up. Even though a burlesque show wasn't exactly what I had in mind.

"So did you talk to Sophia?" Imogen eyed me. Sassy's eyes shined, and it was like the both of them were waiting on my answer.

"Um, yeah, it's all good," I said. Even though the cleansing ceremony had been painful, it'd done its job. I finally felt like Sophia and I were past our issues. Imogen gave a grin that could light up the world.

"Well, congratulations, buddy!" Jonah slung his arm around my shoulder. "I'm really happy for ya. Can't tell you how ecstatic I am."

"Um, thanks," I said off-handedly. Why was he congratulating me again? I'd gotten engaged months ago.

Jonah's eyes welled with tears. "I honestly can't believe this is happening. It's just too much." He took a tissue out of his pocket and blew his nose, right in my fucking ear, the disgusting bastard.

"You can't say you didn't know this was coming," Imogen replied in a teasing tone, and she poked Jonah in the stomach.

"No, but... ancestors, my little boy's all grown up!" Jonah cried.

He ruffled my hair, and I pushed him off of me. What was with Jonah? He'd never been so happy in his life.

"Would you calm down? We haven't even set a date yet for the wedding," I snapped. I mean, Sophia and I probably should've by now, but there was a lot of shit going on.

Jonah gave a laugh. "Well, you'd better hurry. The wedding's going to have to be moved up pretty quick, seeing as how Sophia's got a bun in the oven."

Time itself halted in place. It was like everything in my life came to a screeching stop, and my blood ran cold. The molecules of my being froze, and I went rigid. If there was life around me, I didn't take notice. I don't even think the *planets* moved. He didn't just say what I think he did... did he?

"Wha... what?" I stammered. My tongue felt thick in my mouth.

"Like you don't know." Jonah clapped me on the back. "I'm so happy you're gonna be a father, man. Really thrilled."

He was joking. He *had* to be joking, right?

"Hold on. Sophia's having a baby?" Stevie questioned. I nearly gagged.

"Yeah, we found out today," Imogen said, as if she was talking about the *fucking weather* or something. "She just told us now."

"Hey, why didn't I know I was going to be an uncle?" Ezra asked accusatively.

"I don't think *he* knew he was gonna be a dad!" Stevie rebutted.

Everyone in the circle turned to me. A slight verge of shock crept across Jonah's face as he saw my panicked expression. My hands were fucking shaking, too.

Imogen's face fell. "Wait. Liam, did Sophia tell you yet?"

I made a couple murmuring sounds, but nothing else came out. My mouth gaped. Jonah's and Imogen's faces went pale.

"Aw, man." Jonah's shoulders fell. "I spoke too soon."

"*Jonah!* You weren't supposed to tell him!" Imogen smacked her hand against Jonah's stomach.

"How'd you guys find out before he did?" Ezra all but shouted.

"We discovered a pregnancy test today. Sophia just found out this morning. She said she was going to tell Liam when he got *home*," Imogen whined.

"Well, they have sex all the time, what did they think was gonna happen? You know how many times I've had to block out their incessant fucking? Walls are thin around here," Jonah whined, and Squeaks clicked her beak.

"He's gotta be in shock," Stevie added. Imogen snapped her fingers in front of my face, but they didn't register.

"Oh no. I think we broke him," Jonah said quietly.

"Why can't you two ever keep your big mouths shut?" Ezra raged, and he shoved Jonah backward.

"Don't blame me. Jonah's the one who can't keep a secret!" Imogen hissed.

"I'm sorry! I got too excited!" Jonah profusely apologized.

I barely registered their bickering. I didn't hear anything else anyone was saying. My mind was going way too fast. I was counting up days, because I still didn't think this was possible. When was the last time she'd had her period?

I couldn't remember. It had to be... *fuck. Before we left Orenda Academy.*

"I have to get home." I stumbled out of the circle, my tiredness forgotten. I broke into a sprint in the direction of the house.

Someone called my name, but I didn't look behind. I fucking *ran*. The house wasn't that far away, but every step seemed like it took a thousand years. Julian noticed I'd lost my marbles and came soaring after me, crying out to ask what was wrong.

This couldn't be real. I couldn't have kids. Perot told me that himself.

*Perot could've lied*, a voice in the back of my head said. *Fuck.* Fuck, fuck, fuck! I wasn't ready for this!

But dammit all, I wanted it. I wanted it *so bad*. And I didn't think I could handle it if someone told me this was some kind of sick joke, or if it didn't turn out to be real after all. I couldn't get my hopes up if this was all a dream. But I had to know.

Months ago, I'd had nothing. Now all my dreams had been dumped in my lap— marrying Sophia, becoming chief...

Being a father.

*Wake up! Everything you've ever wanted is here.* Life had been kicked from stationary to full-speed, and there was no turning back.

I more or less threw the door open. It slammed against the wall and swung on its hinges. Julian landed and staggered into me, trying to catch his breath.

Sophia jumped. She was in the living room. It looked like she'd been pacing. Esis was sitting on the edge of the couch. He grumbled, like I was being rude and this wasn't a fucking emergency. Sophia had her hands enclosed around something I couldn't see.

I stood in the doorway, and she stared at me. Neither one of us said anything.

I crossed the rooms in a few strides and lightly held her elbows. "Sophia, is it true? Are you pregnant?"

Her big brown eyes stared back. She didn't respond. Instead, she unfurled her fingers. In her hands was a pregnancy test.

Two little lines. Who knew that such a small thing would change your life forever?

"Sophia." I embraced her. She let out a sob, and I fell to my knees. I couldn't help it. Sophia dropped with me. I felt tears pour from my eyes and run down my face. This was a miracle. This couldn't really be happening to me. To *us*.

Sophia cried tears of joy against my shoulder. I took her head in my hands and brushed her hair back. "You're incredible, you know that? Just fucking incredible." I kissed her tears away.

Julian curled around us, while Esis put a paw on Sophia's leg and crooned.

"I worried you'd be upset." Her hands stroked up and down my arms, though all hint of worry had faded away.

"Why would you think that? Soph, you don't understand. I never thought I'd be lucky enough to have kids." My voice was thick with emotion. It was like something that had been forcibly torn away from me had been returned as a precious gift. Unrestrained elation passed through me. I'd been through so much pain in my life, but nothing, *nothing* could compare to this joy.

"Guess you're not sterile." She let out a choked laugh.

I chuckled. "Guess not." My hand fell to cup the back of her neck. She put her forehead against mine and just breathed.

My thrilled heart was skipping beats. "This complicates things a bit."

Sophia giggled. "Just a little." She sighed. "Though I wish it wasn't in the middle of this stupid war."

"Fuck the war," I said instantaneously. This was happening whether we were ready or not, and I knew automatically that I'd do anything to protect this baby from it.

Sophia pulled away from me. The hand that wasn't holding the pregnancy test clutched mine. "I've suspected for a while now. Though I didn't want to admit it to myself. I was in denial."

"Ancestors, I'm such an idiot," I said, realizing. The mood swings. The constant throwing up. The never-ending fucking horniness. How hadn't I caught on?

"How did you find out? I wanted to tell you myself." She frowned in disappointment.

"Jonah," I responded.

She rolled her eyes. "Of course."

I trailed my fingers over her skin. "So, how far along are you? Do you know anything?"

"I went to Luana right after I found out. Her healing power could sense

I was pregnant, but she thought I knew. She told me my due date was Christmas Eve," Sophia squealed. She was practically glowing with the admission.

"Holy shit! You're already three months along?" I cried. Now I felt like a real jackass. This gave us hardly any time to prepare.

"Don't blame yourself. I should've faced the music sooner." She looked down to Esis. "We must've conceived sometime in April, though I don't know when..."

A beat passed, until we both said together, "The waterfall."

I smacked myself in the head. "Should've realized that." We'd had sex right after I proposed. Unprotected sex, to be exact. Which made babies.

"I don't think Luana was the only one who knew," Sophia said. "Remember how protective the Familiars were of me the night of the Orenda Academy battle? I think they understood."

She glanced at Esis. "Though I don't know why *he* didn't tell me, the little stinker. We can't talk yet, but he could've interpreted something."

Esis chittered.

"He probably wanted you to be ready," I said. "Can you imagine what it'd be like if we'd found out you were pregnant while on the run?"

*You were pregnant.* The words seemed fake coming out of my mouth.

Sophia snorted. "Yeah, that would've went well. I guess it's good he let me find out on my own."

Sophia's eyes narrowed as she thought of something. "Liam, I think your dad knew."

"What?" My eyes widened. "How could he?"

"He was acting weird before we saved you from the execution. He wanted me to stay behind in case I got hurt. Tatum must've told him," Sophia blurted.

*You need to take care of your family, understand? That's what's impor-*
*tant now. They come first.* My dad's final words to me came rushing back. Everything my dad had said to me before he died... and in my dreams... made sense now.

The fact that my dad knew I was going to be a father made me want to crumble all over again. *He knew.* That's why he'd sacrificed himself for all of us— for Sophia. He wanted his grandchild to live on.

Sophia dashed the tears on my cheeks away. "Your dad gave us the greatest gift he ever could. Thanks to him, we're going to have a family."

"Yeah," I all but wept. "I guess the ancestors know what they're doing after all."

She nodded, before her face darkened with horror as she thought of something. "Liam... your dad wasn't the only one who figured it out. Doya acted disappointed in me before we fought. She hesitated to attack when Naomi cried out. Naomi must've told her!"

A cold, dark weight settled in my stomach, chasing the joy I felt away. If Doya knew Sophia was pregnant—

"Liam, what if she comes after us? What if she's told Oleander I'm pregnant? She could hurt our baby!" Sophia said.

"She's not gonna lay a hand on my kid," I snarled, and Julian hissed beside me. "We're safe here, Soph. Even if Doya knows you're pregnant and she's out there looking for you, she can't find us here. The Anichi village is safe."

Sophia settled, but a bit of terror set in her eyes. She shivered. "I can't let her find us."

"She won't, Soph." I wrapped my arms around her torso and held her. "I'm never going to let anything happen. To you or our child. I'll die for you first."

Sophia sniffed. "Don't do that."

"I'm serious. Whatever you need, I'll give it to you. I mean it, Sophia. I won't have you go without. You and this baby are so precious to me."

One of my hands fell, settling against her middle. A thrill of momentary passion went through me. "You know... I didn't notice before, but you've got a small bump," I said. I passed my hand over Sophia's stomach lightly. It was slightly raised, giving me the confirmation that this was actually happening.

"I am starting to show, aren't I?" Sophia laid her hands on her belly. "Good thing we found out now, because I wouldn't be able to hide this much longer."

Sophia looked at me in a way she never had before. "I want to thank you, Liam. You made this all possible for me. I've wanted to be a mom ever since I could remember. You fulfilled my dream."

That statement made me go all soft inside, but I was still feeling so vulnerable that all I could squeeze out was a joke. "Don't thank me. You're doing all the work. All I had to do was fire."

Sophia laughed. "You're mature."

I smiled, but another terrifying thought hit me. The baby was inside of her, but, I mean, it had to come *out*. "I'm kinda scared for you to give birth."

Sophia made a *pshing* sound and waved her hand. "Women give birth all the time. This might be my first baby, but I think I can do this."

"I know you can." Though the thought of putting her through that much pain was excruciating to me. Even though I knew my mom would be there to help her, I didn't want anything to go wrong. I wanted to be by Sophia's side through every moment of it.

I stood and helped Sophia to her feet. "You wanna know what we're having?" I whispered.

She cocked an eyebrow. "It's a little early to find out if we're having a boy or a girl, isn't it?"

"Dragons can tell," I reminded her. We'd sexed Julian while he was still an egg last semester with help from the ice dragons. "If you want to know now, Julian can tell us."

Sophia's expression lit up. "I don't think I can wait a moment longer."

"Neither can I."

There was a pathway in the back of the house that led out of the cave systems and into a small garden. Julian and Esis followed us down. When we got there, I stepped aside and gestured to Julian. "Okay, Jules, do your thing."

Esis scattered out of the way, and Julian drew a breath. When he breathed fire, he didn't shoot it into the sky. Instead, his fire formed a circular wall around Sophia, boxing her in and protecting her on all sides. The fire blazed spectacularly, and in that moment, nothing felt real.

Dragons shot fire into the sky when the child was a boy, and made shields when the child was—

*A girl.* A little Sophie.

It was everything I'd ever wanted.

Our faces lit up at the exact same time the fire wall died down. "We're having a *girl!*" Sophia screamed and jumped on me. I caught her and spun her around. Esis clapped while Julian puffed smoke rings into the sky. She kissed me, and when I kissed her back, the sensation was totally different than anything I'd ever felt before. The feelings we held for another had completely transformed and changed into something new and extraordinary.

Ancestors, we were going to be *parents.* It was absolutely freaking nuts.

"Oh my gosh! I wonder what she's going to be like. What she'll do," Sophia gushed.

"If she's anything like you? Drive me crazy," I cracked. A daughter was everything I'd secretly dreamt of, but if she was anything like her mother, I was going to have my hands full.

Sophia grew quiet. "Is she going to have magic at all?" Sophia questioned cautiously. "I mean... people always say that interbred children are weaker. I know we don't *think* that way, but what if it's the truth? And if she does have magic, what'll it be? Fire or Water?"

I decided I didn't care. "Doesn't matter. We'll love her no matter what she is. Koigni, Toaqua, who gives a shit? All I care about is that she's half of me and half of you."

Sophia softened at that statement. I could tell she was contemplating something... Julian nudged my back, and I asked, "What's on your mind, Soph?"

She chewed her lip. "I have a name," Sophia whispered. "I'd always had favorites picked out since I was a little girl. Julian was my boy's name, but I could never convince myself to let my daughter's name go. Just in case."

"What is it?" I asked. My heart rammed against my ribcage. I was dying with anticipation.

Sophia held her breath. "I always thought... Ava-Marie."

"Ava-Marie." It sounded so beautiful. Elegant and timeless. "I love that. Ava-Marie Mitoh."

"I've looked up the meaning a million times. It means *life of the sea*," Sophia said.

"You couldn't have picked anything more perfect." Ancestors, it was like this was meant to be or something. I was going to ride this high all the way until my daughter came into this world, and I'd breathe for her every moment after.

*My daughter*. The very words seemed blessed. This was better than winning the Elemental Cup, better than winning the trial. Better than anything.

Esis cleared his throat, and Sophia tapped a finger to her lips. "We should probably move the wedding up. I want to be married to you before Ava's born."

I felt shivers creep over my skin when she said our daughter's name. "You think?" I chuckled. "We need to get on this thing. Before you get too far along. I bet my mom could throw a wedding together in a couple of months."

"Before the end of August," Sophia confirmed. "I need to still be able to dance at my own wedding, or Imogen will never forgive me."

That gave us two months. This would be a shotgun wedding to remember. We were jumping into things, but Sophia and I never did anything at less than full-speed, so might as well go feet-first.

I took Sophia's hands in mine. "I think we should tell everyone about the baby as soon as possible."

"I don't think we have much of a choice." Sophia grinned. I could tell she was counting down the minutes until she could spew the big news.

"I'll get everyone around at *The Falcon's Nest* tomorrow night. We can tell them there," I said confidently.

"That sounds just perfect." Sophia kissed me on the cheek. "I love you, Liam. You've made me so happy."

My insides coiled with pleasure. "You've made me happy too, *pawee*. More than you'll ever know."

When we came back to the house, Imogen and Jonah were waiting for us. Squeaks was perched on the edge of the couch, Baby snuggled against her. Jonah sat on the floor. Sassy and Imogen were bustling around, putting away stuff for the cabaret. It looked like Imogen had a scrapbook on the table, though I didn't know what for.

"Well?" Jonah asked as we entered. Squeaks' eyes were wide.

I shrugged. "Oops."

A wide grin spread across Jonah's face. "I knew it. Your pull-out game is weak, bro."

"*Ee!* This is so exciting, you guys!" Imogen cried. She hugged me, then Sophia before she burst, "I can't believe this is happening!"

"Yes. Nice to know you've conceived a child out of wedlock. Good job," Jonah teased, wiggling his eyebrows.

"Nice to know you're such an *ass*," I shot back at him.

"You're happy though, right?" Imogen's eyes nervously darted between us. "You're excited to be having a baby?"

"Seriously, Im. I couldn't be happier," I told her.

Imogen relaxed. "Well, that's good news. I was worried you'd have a meltdown."

"Did he react badly?" Sophia asked.

"Not badly, per say," Imogen said fairly. "Just surprised."

"Yeah. He gaped like a fucking fish." Jonah did a shitty impersonation of me, and Sophia laughed. I scowled and sent him the finger.

Just then, there was a knock on the door. Jonah got up to open it. It was Jake. He held a bouquet of flowers in his hands— purple tulips.

Ah. So *this* was why Jake had been in such a hurry to leave our meeting earlier. Jonah stood stock still, while Jake cleared his throat.

"Hey," Jake started. His eyes remained fixed on Jonah as he said, "I wanted to ask you something."

Jonah made a couple squeaking sounds. Squeaks hissed, and she head-butted his shoulder.

Jonah blurted out, "If you needed to tell me something, you could have sent a lieutenant. You didn't have to walk all this way."

I almost face-palmed. Ancestors, Jonah was such a dumbass. Jonah seemed to realize what he said was stupid, and he blushed.

Jake said, "This isn't about work. It's about... us."

I didn't know there was an *us*. Apparently, Jonah didn't either, as his cheeks got even redder.

"I'll, uh, meet you outside," Jonah stuttered. He followed Jake and shut the door behind him.

Jonah had acted like he wanted some privacy. So, naturally, the three of us clustered against the doorway and listened in. Our Familiars pressed beside. Julian nearly toppled me over trying to get through.

"These are for you." I heard the rustling of wrappings as Jake handed the bouquet to Jonah. "You said they were your favorite."

Jonah's astonishment was clear. "You bought these for me?"

Jake paused. "Well... why not?"

Jonah didn't say anything back. Not right away. Then Squeaks chirped, and he said, "What did you want to ask me?"

Jake's boots scuffed the ground. "I wanted to know if you'd like to get coffee sometime. On me. As more than friends."

The silence was deafening. Nothing could be heard for long moments. I was certain Jonah was going to wuss out.

"Say yes, Jonah!" Imogen whispered. Sophia eagerly nodded, as if she could say yes for Jonah herself.

"Um... yeah. I think that would be nice," Jonah said timidly. Squeaks chortled in joy.

I heard Jake give the slightest sigh of relief. "We could go for a ride afterward," he suggested. "I know a grove not too far from here the hippogriffs would enjoy."

"That sounds really fun," Jonah admitted. "I'd love to."

"Friday? I'll pick you up at eight."

"Yeah. That'd be awesome," Jonah replied, stumbling around his words. "Eight it is."

I heard Jake's boots again. He was moving closer to Jonah. Imogen dared to peek out the window. She nearly screamed. "Ahh! Guys, *he kissed him!*"

Sophia squealed in excitement. The doorknob turned, and we all scattered. Imogen and Sassy went back to the kitchen, while Sophia and I pretended to cuddle on the couch— though we'd fallen while running to it and ended up in a weird position, limbs sticking out everywhere.

Jonah didn't notice, or suspect. He walked in with a dazed expression. Imogen's look was coy as Squeaks skipped behind him into the dining room.

"So, what'd he want to ask?" Imogen taunted.

"Hm?" Jonah responded as he put the tulips in a vase. He'd barely heard her ask the question. His mind was somewhere else.

I smiled as I put my hand on Sophia's growing belly. Things really were changing fast around here.

I'D TOLD Ezra to get everyone around for a spur-of-the-moment dinner the following night at *The Falcon's Nest*. The restaurant was packed with people. I didn't know just how many friends and family members we had until they showed up at our request. Most people figured it was about the wedding, so no one thought it was weird.

Vanessa and Bren were in a corner booth with Miranda and Lindsey. When I caught Bren holding his child, my heart gave a start. To think that would be Sophia and I soon. Absolutely incredible.

Sophia and I stood at the head of the room. Julian was at my side, and Esis perched on Sophia's shoulder. I cleared my throat. The thirty or so people in the room fell silent as everyone looked at us.

"We have an announcement to make," I said. "Sophia and I have decided to move the wedding up. We'd like to get married as soon as possible."

"What's the big rush?" Wyatt asked.

I looked to Sophia. "You want to tell them?"

Sophia wrapped her arms around my middle as everyone went quiet. "Liam and I are expecting a little girl."

The room absolutely exploded. Screams of delight and surprise were everywhere. There was applause, and *congratulations* thrown in from everywhere.

Mom got to us before anyone else. She leapt out of her seat and flung her arms around both of our shoulders, hugging us tightly. There were happy tears in her eyes.

"This is such a blessing!" Mom bawled. I'd never seen her so freaking happy in my life. "A grandchild! I can't believe it! This is a sign from the ancestors."

"What do you mean?" Sophia asked, tilting her head.

"Sophia, the Hawkei tribe believes that when one spirit leaves this earth, another comes to take its place," Mom explained. "That you are having a child so soon after my husband's death shows that his soul will be close to hers, and walk beside her in this life."

Sophia glowed. As Mom stepped aside, Vanessa squealed. With her infant son cradled against her, she offered Sophia a one-armed hug. Miranda and Lindsey piled on after that, wrapping Sophia in a tight embrace. Their Familiars, Evelyn and Medusa, wrapped around her, too.

"Congratulations, dude." Bren gave me a handshake, and Kingston let out a happy growl. "Prepare to get no sleep."

"I hardly do as it is anyway," I said with a casual shrug.

"You have no idea." Bren laughed, like I was completely clueless on what was coming.

"Get out of my way!" Amelia had been at the back of the room, but she'd barreled her way through to get to Sophia. Bren almost hit the floor as she shoved him aside. Kiwi squawked in surprise. Amelia squeezed her sister so tightly that she choked.

"Amelia, I can't breathe." Sophia gasped for air as her sister put her down.

"A baby!" Amelia screeched. "This is the best news ever!"

Sophia faced her adoptive parents. Her mother looked thrilled. She wiped a tear away from her eye as she gave Sophia a kiss on the cheek. Meanwhile, Sophia's dad gave me a weird look that made me feel pretty awkward. I mean, he *looked* happy, but his expression clearly told me he was irritated I'd gotten his daughter pregnant before marriage.

Katie handed five bucks to Christian as Sophia and I passed. "Told you he'd knock her up before the wedding," he whispered with a giggle.

I rolled my eyes. There was a whole line of family and friends waiting to congratulate us.

I shook so many hands and hugged so many people. It felt like there was another person waiting to praise us the minute I stopped talking to another.

One person who didn't seem very happy was Professor Perot. He still smiled, but his grin wasn't as big and welcoming as the others. Worry hung behind his gaze, and I couldn't understand why. Baxtor stood on the table, his feathers a little ruffled.

As I shook Perot's hand, he said, "Congratulations, Liam. Though I'd hoped we'd talked about your options first before this day came."

Options? I didn't understand what he was talking about. I was still riding high on the elation this was happening at all. "It was pretty unexpected. Guess I'm not sterile after all, huh?"

Perot frowned. "I'm sorry, Liam. I fabricated the evidence for your case so you and Sophia would get off without charges. I didn't realize I'd forgotten to tell you your sperm was perfectly viable. I'd been in such a hurry to leave Kinpago, it'd completely skipped my mind."

I was shocked. He'd *forgotten*? That was a pretty important thing not to tell someone, wasn't it?

But I couldn't be angry at him. I was too thrilled. "It's all right, Professor," I told him sincerely. "It all worked out."

Perot gave a sigh. "I'm happy for the both of you. But I'd like to see you as soon as possible. Let's make an appointment for the end of next month."

Perot left before I could agree. He seemed like he wanted to talk to me about something else, but was holding it off until later.

Ezra flung his arm around my shoulders. "Looks like my big brother is gonna be a dad. And a girl! She's gonna have you wrapped around her little finger."

I gave a smile. "Probably."

"Why not? Sophia already has his balls in her purse," Wyatt spoke up, and everyone laughed.

Stevie watched Perot as he walked out the door. She seemed bothered by whatever had scared off Perot, but she didn't say anything about it, just told me congratulations like all the others.

Jonah stood on top of the bar. "All right, my two besties in the whole world are getting hitched and having a kid! It's time to *party*!"

There was a resounding cheer, and just like that, Squeaks ducked behind the counter and began passing out beers.

"I'm keeping a tab!" Lani shouted, but no one listened to her.

Everybody got drunk. Like *really drunk*. I stayed away from drinking, because Sophia couldn't and I didn't feel like it was fair to her. The kids played with the Familiars, and Vanessa and Bren stayed sober for their kid. Stevie turned down anything offered to her.

Everyone else? Wasted. Hours passed, and the booze kept on coming. Wyatt and Ezra couldn't walk. Dyami had to drag both of them around. Lindsey and Miranda were singing inappropriate songs, and Trace and Amelia were going overboard with the PDA.

Even my mom got a little tipsy. I don't think I'd ever seen her have anything more than a few sips of wine every now and then, so it was funny to see.

Jonah, to my surprise, hadn't had more than a few beers. He was usually the one who got the most trashed at parties, but Jake had shown up halfway through, and the two of them had spent most of the party cozied up together in a booth at the back.

Cade hugged Sophia and I. "Congratulations, you guys." He truly seemed happy for us, but still, there was a sadness in his eyes he hadn't gotten over. He hadn't enjoyed shots with my brother earlier, which was worrying.

Ezra was Cade's best friend. He should be partying with him, not sitting here feeling guilty about stuff that happened in the past.

Though it was hard to avoid when his mistakes kept getting shoved in his face. Imogen had avoided Cade all night. She shot dagger eyes at him as he spoke to us from her place at the bar.

"Thanks, Cade," Sophia said, obviously trying to redirect things. "Do you think you could help us with the wedding? I know you're probably busy, but since we're on such a tight schedule, we're going to need a lot of hands."

Cade opened his mouth to reply, but Imogen got there first. "Why are you asking *him*? He doesn't care about us," she quipped snidely.

Cade turned toward her slowly. "I care a lot, Imogen."

His tone was flat. It clearly implied he was getting tired of dealing with her shit. Imogen wrinkled her nose and snapped, "You have a funny way of showing it."

Cade's voice began to rise. "I don't deserve your forgiveness. But the least I want is respect!"

"You don't deserve *anything* from me," Imogen snapped.

Sophia tensed at my side, and I tried to contain my temper. This was Sophia's big announcement. Couldn't Imogen and Cade resist ruining it with their drama, just for one night?

Jonah had noticed the fight and ducked out of the booth with Jake. He came rushing over and placed a hand on Cade's arm. "Can you guys not make a scene?"

People were staring. Jonah dragged Cade away, and Imogen turned back to the bar. I felt completely lost. Imogen hadn't had much to drink, only one wine cooler, so her behavior couldn't be excused by that. Had being around Cade put her in that bad of a mood?

Chief Cauac stepped forward, Luana beside him. Cauac puffed out his chest. "This is wonderful news to hear, Chief of the Water tribe. I come to you as an equal and congratulate you on this gift from the ancestors."

"Thank you, Chief of the Spirit tribe," I responded, as was the custom. "It was unexpected, but we're excited."

"The Anichi Council has spoken," Cauac went on. "Due to your bravery rescuing the Hawkei children from the camps, we have unanimously decided to gift you your wedding, free of charge. It will be nothing elaborate, as we only have so much to spare— but it is what we can offer, as gratitude for your commitment to the tribe."

"Thank you so much, Chief," Sophia breathed. "A simple wedding is perfect. We don't need much. This is a great gift."

Cauac nodded stoically. "I am happy for you both, but be warned, prophesied one. Our enemies are closing in. We will not go to war until after you have given birth to this child. But once you have given this child life, you will be expected to give yourself over to the tribe. Use this time for preparation wisely."

Luana scowled, like this wasn't the right time for her father to be bringing this up. As Cauac walked away, Luana signed something to Sophia, and it made her break out into a fit of giggles. Luana made a stern impression of her father's face, and Sophia laughed harder.

The party lasted until midnight. A few people stuck around to help the four of us clean up, including Luana, Cade and Jake. Ezra *tried*, but he was passed out in a booth. Stevie lovingly stroked his hair as his head lay on her lap. Esis polished the tables, while Sassy and Julian piled up dishes.

I expected Squeaks to binge-drink like normal, but she hadn't had one. Baby seemed to be her number-one priority. She taught him how to pick up bottles while Sabor watched, moving tables so Jake could sweep under them.

Sophia was picking up, but I took the glasses out of her hands and lifted her onto the counter. "None of that. Let me do it."

She snickered. "It's a bit early to be babying me."

"You're not going to lift a finger for the next six months," I scolded. "You need to get plenty of rest."

Sophia rolled her eyes. "I'm pregnant, not incapacitated. Pregnant women work all the time. Even up until birth."

"Not my Sophia. You can work on your Anichi magic until the baby comes, but nothing else," I said sternly.

Sophia scoffed, like I was being ridiculous. To the side, Imogen shook her head in disgust.

What the hell? Was Imogen *jealous* Sophia was getting all the attention? No. That couldn't be it. That wasn't Imogen.

Cade noticed as he was cleaning off tables. His eyes lingered on Imogen for a moment before he went back to what he was doing.

This went beyond Cade. I felt Imogen was just using him as a scapegoat.

Luana came forward. She jostled Sophia's arm and opened her palm. Inside was a small bracelet, white in color. It was made of small stone ruins and the fragments of white seashells. It looked like Luana had made it herself. She slipped it on Sophia's wrist and signed to her.

Sophia's cheeks warmed. "Thank you, Luana." Luana nodded, and Sophia ran her fingers over the bracelet fondly.

Imogen had seen Luana give Sophia the bracelet. Her hands shook, and her eyes slowly welled with tears. I didn't get it, until I realized that Sophia was wearing Luana's bracelet instead of Imogen's. Imogen had given Sophia a charm bracelet at the Elemental Ball. Sophia had lost it in the battle of Orenda Academy. It'd gone up in flames in the Anichi dorms, like everything else.

I hoped to the ancestors Imogen didn't take it like she was being replaced. But apparently, she did, because Imogen sneered, *"Please.* What a cheap gift."

Luana had her back turned to Imogen, so she couldn't read her lips to see what she said. But Sophia could hear her, and she cringed.

"Is there something you wanna say, Im?" I asked. Her bratty behavior was getting on my nerves.

Imogen threw down the trash bag she carried. *"Yeah,* actually. Sophia doesn't need to be sitting there like a queen while the rest of us act like her slaves."

"I asked her to," I snapped. There wasn't even that much left to clean up. We were almost done.

Imogen snorted. "Just because you worship the ground she walks on doesn't mean the rest of us have to. So she's pregnant. Big fucking deal. She doesn't deserve an award for getting knocked up."

I reeled back. I never thought something so cruel would come out of Imogen's mouth. I had known Imogen for years, and it was like she'd turned into a completely different person overnight. On the other side of the restaurant, Cade stared at the floor.

Jonah stepped in. "This is Sophia's day. Let her have a moment," he insisted.

Imogen sneered. "What do you know, Jonah? You've got a new boyfriend now, so you don't need me anymore."

Jonah flinched. "We're just seeing where it goes," he said quietly.

She put her hands on her hips. "Yeah, right. I know how you are. Your mind goes blank every time a guy walks into the room."

Jonah cowered away, like Imogen had actually hit him. Jake came forward and took Jonah's hand in his. "What's between us is our business."

Sophia hopped down from the bar and faced Imogen. "Why are you being so nasty lately?" Sophia accused. "You were thrilled I was pregnant not two hours ago. Now you're acting like you're pissed about it. You've done a complete one-eighty. Is something bothering you?"

"Yes!" Imogen shouted. "But you wouldn't notice. You're too busy hanging out with *other people*."

Luana ducked her head and went to leave, but Sophia grabbed her by the wrist. "No, Lu. Stay."

Sophia rounded all her fury on Imogen. "If you can't be supportive, you need to fucking leave."

"Gladly." Imogen whirled around and stomped out of the restaurant. She slammed the door on her way out.

Sassy darted after her, and Squeaks tilted her head curiously. The rest of us stood in shocked silence.

"I'm so sorry," Jonah apologized to Jake, profusely embarrassed. "She's my best friend. I swear she never acts like this."

Jake grimaced, but he said, "It's all right. Some people have a hard time adjusting to life here."

"This isn't normal!" Sophia insisted. She ran a quick hand through her hair. "Something else is going on. It has to be. She's not telling us something."

"Jonah, do you know what's up with her? This is becoming a problem," I stated.

He shook his head. "I don't know what's bothering her. She's shutting me out lately. I can't get her to open up no matter what I do."

I took a deep breath. I turned to Cade, who was still standing alone at the end of the room. "Cade, you've gotta talk to her," I said in exhaustion. "This has gone on long enough."

"I've tried!" Cade rebutted. "She won't let me. I can't get a word out. I'm giving her space."

"Her behavior isn't your fault, but it is connected to what's between you guys," I said. "You two need to work it out."

Cade shrugged miserably. "Okay," he said, but he didn't seem too confident.

As we finished up, I boxed Sophia off in a corner so we could talk privately. I lowered my voice. "I don't want you getting stressed out about Im," I said. "It's not good for you. Or the baby."

Sophia was still fuming. "I'm sick of her bullshit! I know she doesn't want to be here. But we don't have any choice! What is up with her lately?"

"I have no idea." Whatever Imogen's problem was, I had a bad feeling it went far deeper than any of us realized.

# sophia
## FOURTEEN

Imogen was my best friend, and I hated to see her so upset. I tried to talk to her, but whenever someone came close with anything less than a friendly expression, she stormed off into another room. I didn't know what to do but let her come to me at her own pace.

A few weeks later, a letter arrived. I walked into the kitchen, my hand resting on my swollen belly. It was Saturday, so I had the day off, but Liam had already been gone for hours. That was the thing about being a chief. As a tribal leader, he rarely got days off. I worried that the long days were taking their toll on him, but he really seemed to enjoy the work. Since he learned that I was pregnant, he seemed in a better mood overall, which seemed to help his symptoms.

"A letter came for you," Imogen announced in a bored tone when I finally came out of my room.

She picked it up off the table and handed it to me. She was knee-deep in magazine clippings for the cabaret. Ever since she stormed out the night of our pregnancy announcement, she'd put all her effort into Jonah's cabaret rather than the wedding. I felt like it was her way of saying, *Screw you, Sophia,* but at least she was doing something to keep herself busy. The last thing I wanted to do was fuel her anger at me. To be honest, I didn't really understand what she was mad about.

Sassy lay at her feet, her chin resting on her crossed paws. She looked really depressed, which I figured had to do something with Imogen. Esis scampered over to Sassy and started massaging her back.

339

I opened the letter and read it.

"What is it?" Imogen asked without looking up from the picture she was cutting out. She tried to sound indifferent, but I heard a hint of bitterness in her voice.

"It's from Haloke," I told her. "She's invited me over for lunch."

"Oh. Well, have fun," Imogen huffed. She didn't sound the least bit genuine.

My initial reaction was to be offended. I mean, how could Imogen have a problem with *Haloke*? She was the sweetest woman, and she was going to be my mother-in-law.

But there was something else on Imogen's face, something that felt like a knife nicking my heart. She seemed hurt that I would leave her alone while Liam was at work and Jonah was... ancestors knew where. Probably hanging with Jake.

"Do you want to come with?" I offered.

Imogen finally looked me in the eyes. I thought I saw a spark of happiness in them. "Sure. Let me clean this up."

I helped her pile her magazines away, and we left for Haloke's with our Familiars at our sides. It was a really nice day, and the August air was warm. Imogen didn't say a thing, just walked quietly beside me with her gaze locked on her feet.

"Hey, Im," I said cautiously. She could try to run away from the conversation, but there was nowhere to hide right now. "Do you want to talk about it?"

Her gaze snapped upward, but her expression gave nothing away. "Talk about what?"

"You know..." I didn't know how to put it. "Everything. I know you don't like it here in *Hok'evale*—"

"*Hok'evale* is fine," she countered, but I knew it was a lie. She'd voiced her opinion on *Hok'evale* multiple times.

"I know things have been hard since Cade—"

"I don't need a lecture on Cade," she snapped.

"I wasn't going to give you one," I assured her.

She quickened her pace, and I realized I wasn't going to get much out of her. All I could do was continue along on this waiting game.

Imogen and I arrived at Haloke's. She practically dragged us inside the house, as she was so happy to see us.

"Come, sit!" Haloke encouraged. "Lunch is ready."

Haloke seemed brighter than she had weeks ago. I think the news of our daughter sparked something inside of her that hadn't been there before. The house was clean, and her hair was tied neatly into two short braids at the side of her head. Jackson kicked and cooed from his highchair. Even he seemed happier.

"I hope Sassy and I aren't intruding," Imogen said.

Haloke waved her hand. "Not at all. I always make extras in case of guests."

Haloke went over to the cupboard to pull out another plate. "Kids! Lunch!"

The twins came running down the hall screaming at each other. I laughed as Katie chased Christian around the kitchen table.

"Children, please," Haloke said. They nearly ran into her and knocked the plate out of her hand.

They stopped, and Christian pointed a finger at Katie. "She's tormenting me!"

"I am not, you twerp!" As if to prove a point, Katie grabbed a glass of water from the table and splashed it at her brother. It covered the front of his pants.

"Look what she did!" Christian cried.

Haloke huffed. "Christian, go clean up. Katie, take this to your sister."

Haloke handed her a plate piled full of food. Katie groaned, then took the plate and headed off down the hall. My stomach sank at the thought that Maddie still wasn't joining the family for meals. She really had it rough with Oleander, and it was going to take her months— maybe even years— to recover.

I sat beside Jackson.

"Well, shall we?" Haloke asked.

Christian and Katie returned a few minutes later. They initially sat next to each other and kept pushing each other, until Haloke made Katie move to the other side so they couldn't fight.

"Mm..." Imogen gushed as she bit into the casserole. "This is delicious, Mrs. Mitoh."

"Oh, it's simple," Haloke said, before diving into how she made it. I swore my eyes started to cross as she explained, because her idea of *easy* was far from mine. It was obvious I really had to step up my cooking game if I was going to match her skills.

"Sophia, what do you think about another *shantee* lesson after lunch?" Haloke asked.

I shrugged. "I'm up for it, but..."

I glanced over to Imogen, whose eyes had darkened.

"Only if Imogen gets to help," I finished.

Imogen smirked as she placed another bite in her mouth. She seemed pleased to be invited.

"Of course," Haloke said brightly. "It will actually be good for both of you, because today's lesson is going to be a little different. It's not a *shantee* lesson, per se. More like... a birthing lesson."

"Ancestors!" Katie cried, throwing her hands over her ears. "Do you have to say that word at the table?"

Haloke shot her a look of utter confusion. "What word?"

"Birth," Katie gagged. "Makes me think of gross things."

Christian started laughing. "Birth, birth, birth, birth—"

"That's enough," Haloke said calmly.

Katie pushed her plate away. "I don't think I can take another bite."

Haloke rolled her eyes, like she'd never had to deal with such a drama queen before. "Please clean up your plate if you're done."

Katie and Christian both moved so quickly to clean their plates that I wasn't sure they were quite clean by the time they put them in the drying rack. The two ran off to play.

"So, where do we start with this birthing thing?" I asked.

"Well, first things first is how to recognize the difference between false labor and actual labor," Haloke said while she fed Jackson.

"Ooh, I heard about this in my biology class in high school," Imogen said, sounding brighter than normal. "They're called Braxton-Hicks contractions, right?"

Haloke nodded. "Yes. They're not as painful as real labor contractions. It more or less feels like you can't breathe."

Jonah would have a hell of a time giving birth, then.

"So how do you know it's real labor and not false labor?" I asked. "I thought your water broke and you were rushed to the hospital."

Imogen threw her head back in laughter. It almost felt like she was mocking me. "This isn't Hollywood, Sophia. It's not like you see in the movies."

I eyed her. "Have you ever *seen* anyone give birth?"

"No, but I read about it," she said, like she was a total know-it-all.

Imogen usually knew her stuff, but I wasn't sure how much I trusted her on this. I mean, she'd never *given* birth.

"Let's go over some breathing exercises and positions after we clean up," Haloke suggested.

I took another bite. "Sounds good."

After Haloke put Jackson down for a nap, we went to her bedroom. I was shocked to see a creature inside organizing Haloke's dresser. It was the size of a child, with long limbs and opposable thumbs on its hands and feet. It reminded me of an orangutan in size and stature, except instead of fur, shimmering blue feathers covered its entire body. Its facial features were baby-like, with huge eyes and a tiny mouth and nose. The creature wore an apron and carried a bin of cleaning supplies.

"Um... Haloke, what is that?" I asked.

The creature continued to move around the room, tweaking things here and there.

"This is Beatrice," Haloke said. "She's a britnai— a type of Anichi primate."

Imogen gasped. "I read about them! They were known as Anichi house-keepers. They love helping."

"Yes," Haloke confirmed. "She came to us a week ago and hasn't left since."

"Does she get paid?" I asked.

"Oh, no," Haloke said. "Britnai see payment as an insult. They just want to be of service. In fact, she'll be a very good companion to have at the birth. They make excellent birthing assistants."

At the word *birth*, Beatrice looked up from her cleaning supplies. Her eyes immediately went to me. She stared at me for a second before walking over and pressing her ear to my belly.

I stilled. "What's she doing?"

Haloke laughed. "She knows you're pregnant."

Beatrice pulled away, then grabbed my hand. She had a surprisingly tight grip. I laughed as she dragged me to the bed and made me lie down. She reached into her bin and pulled out a clean wet rag and draped it over my forehead. She patted me on the shoulder, then grabbed her bin and walked out of the room.

"Ancestors, Beatrice is adorable," I said. Esis huffed from beside me, like he *owned* the word.

"Beatrice is something," Haloke said. "Anyway, shall we sit?"

We sat cross-legged on the floor and took deep breaths.

"Your breath is sacred, Sophia," Haloke said. "Each breath you take is a gift from the ancestors. It will be especially crucial to honor your breath during labor. It is helpful in managing the pain."

"I thought Esis might be able to help with that," I admitted, glancing over to him.

Haloke got a very worried look in her eyes. "Oh, no. We do not use Spirit magic during birth."

"Why?" I tilted my head to the side.

"I asked the Anichi the same thing when I arrived. As they explained, the body is not meant to heal during labor," she said. "Spirit magic disrupts the body's natural processes, and in labor, it can do more harm than good."

"Roger that," I said. "Totally natural birth it is."

Haloke took me through various breathing exercises. They mostly involved me counting my breath to get through each contraction.

After we finished with the breathing exercises, we moved on to learning various positions that were supposed to relieve the pressure during labor. I had to be honest... it was kind of weird doing them in front of her. I mean, I'd been in some of these positions with her son, and some of them just seemed way too sexual. There was a lot of spreading my legs.

I think Imogen noticed my discomfort right around the time Haloke had me squat in front of her while she held me under the arms, which was supposed to widen my pelvis and use gravity to get the baby out. Esis squatted at my feet, like he was practicing with me, but he looked ridiculous. Sassy shot him a disgusted look from where she observed on the chair.

Imogen snickered. "Maybe *I* could try being the partner. I mean, I'm Aunt Im, after all. I'll probably be there when the baby's born. I can help."

She shot me a nervous glance, and I smiled back at her. "Of course I want you to be there, Imogen."

She beamed.

"Perfect," Haloke said brightly. "I want to show you two something that should really help relieve some of the pressure. Sophia, I'm going to have you lie on your side on the bed. Imogen, you're going to wrap your arm underneath Sophia's leg."

The two of us hesitated, but Haloke raised an eyebrow as if to ask what we were waiting for. We got into position. Esis scurried onto the bed and copied how I lay. Once Imogen's arm was under my leg, we didn't really know what to do.

"Okay, now hook your elbow under Sophia's knee," Haloke instructed. "Pull up toward her chest... pull, pull, pull... widen that pelvis."

I snickered as Imogen awkwardly followed Haloke's instructions. She was practically on top of me. If she weren't on her knees, we'd be spooning.

I didn't care, because it was Imogen. I was just glad she'd taken over before Haloke demonstrated this position.

Imogen laughed and teased in a low whisper, *"Widen that pelvis, Sophia."*

I started laughing harder. "Ancestors, Im."

She snickered. "Is this how you and Liam conceived?"

"Shut up!" I hissed, slapping her playfully in the arm. It was so good to laugh with Imogen again.

"Okay, girls," Haloke chuckled under her breath. "Let's get back on track."

Imogen gasped between laughs. "You're right, you're right. It's not funny. What do we do next?"

"You're going to press on Sophia's pelvis, right about here." Haloke pointed to a spot behind my hip. "That will open everything up and—"

She was cut off by the sound of the doorbell. "Excuse me."

Haloke went off to answer the door, while Imogen and I continued laughing.

"Is it okay if I press on your butt?" Imogen snickered.

I chuckled. "Go ahead."

Imogen pressed down on my pelvis, but she more or less was groping my ass. "Feel anything?"

"It feels like you're trying to feel me up," I teased.

Imogen fake gasped. "I would never."

We both burst into another laughing fit, but she stopped dead. I followed her gaze to the door, where I noticed Haloke and Luana were standing. Imogen and I shot apart.

I quickly signed to Luana. *We were just practicing birthing positions.*

*Cool,* she replied. *I'm very familiar with them. Perhaps I can help?*

"Luana came looking for you," Haloke explained. "She and Sierra have attended many births, and I thought she might be able to help."

Imogen crossed her arms and shot Luana a dark glare.

I hesitated, because I didn't want to upset either of them. "Um... yeah. That sounds good."

I signed to Luana that she could help, and she walked over to the side of the bed, cutting in front of Imogen. Sierra fluttered over to land on Esis' horns. Imogen's bright demeanor shifted quickly. I knew she didn't like Luana, but I couldn't figure out why. Was it the language barrier? Did it make Imogen uncomfortable?

Well, she was going to have to get over it. They were both my friends, and I wanted them to get along.

*Imogen was doing it wrong,* Luana signed to me. *You have to press here to get the pelvis to widen.*

Luana placed gentle hands along my lower back, and I could feel my hips widening. It really did help take off some of the pressure.

"Wow, that actually feels good," I said.

"What?" Imogen demanded, crossing her arms. "What'd she say?"

"She said you were doing it wrong," I translated, without thinking about it.

Imogen scoffed. "I'm *learning.* That's what this whole thing is about, isn't it?"

"Yes," I said, rather sternly, still signing for Luana. "We can learn from Luana."

Luana glanced between the two of us.

"What does *she* know?" Imogen practically growled.

Haloke didn't seem to like Imogen's tone any more than I did. "Luana's apprenticing as a midwife. She's attended over a dozen deliveries and is the only certified medicine woman *Hok'evale* has."

"O-oh," Imogen stumbled over her words. "I didn't know she was *certified.*"

Luana signed to Imogen, but Imogen scowled back— like she thought it was rude for Luana to wave her hands in her direction.

"She says you should try again," I told Imogen.

Imogen hesitated.

"Come on, Aunt Im," I encouraged. "I want you at the delivery. Let's learn this together."

She dropped her arms to her sides. "Fine. What do I have to do?"

Luana guided her forward, then took her hand and placed it on my pelvis. The two of them pressed down together, and I felt the pressure relieve.

"That's perfect, Im," I told her.

"Really?" she asked, sounding excited.

"Really," I said.

Luana drew away and signed, *Good job.*

Imogen looked to me. "What'd she say?"

I smiled softly. "She said you did a good job."

Imogen looked flustered. "Oh, well... I'm a fast learner."

For the first time in... forever... I saw a spark in Imogen's eyes when she looked at Luana. It made me think that with a little work, the two of them could actually get along. They just needed to find something to bond over.

An idea suddenly struck. "Hey, what do you guys think about going wedding dress shopping today?" Surely they'd have to bond over wedding planning.

"What, right now?" Imogen asked.

"Yeah, we could all try on dresses and then go out to dinner," I suggested.

Imogen shot a look at Luana, like she wanted to go as long as *she* wasn't coming.

"Come on, Im." I reached out and took her hand. "I can't go wedding dress shopping without my Maid of Honor."

Imogen's jaw dropped, and her eyes sparkled. "I— I'm going to be your Maid of Honor?"

I smiled. "If you say yes."

"Of course!" she squealed. Imogen made a big deal out of hugging me, but I didn't miss the look she shot Luana, as if to say *take that.*

"What do you think, Haloke?" I asked. "Do you want to help me find my dress?"

She looked happy to be invited along, but she declined. "No, I have the kids. But you girls have fun."

"We don't have to leave right now," I offered. "I want to learn more about labor."

Haloke waved her hand. "Nonsense. We have plenty of time. Besides, the wedding is coming first. We'll do *shantee* training later."

I wondered if Haloke could sense the hostility between Imogen and Luana.

On our way to the dress shop, we ran into Jonah and Squeaks. Jonah already had a pile of shopping bags in his hands. His face lit up when he saw us.

"*Oh em gee*, Im," he gushed. "You will not *believe* the boots I just found. They were on sale!"

Imogen's jaw dropped dramatically. "How could you go shopping without me?"

"I didn't mean to," he defended. "I was on my way back from Jake's and saw them in the store window."

Imogen raised an eyebrow. "And the other bags?"

Jonah ducked his head. "I sort of... got carried away."

He shoved the bags toward Squeaks, who begrudgingly took them in her beak. He draped his arms around Imogen and Luana's shoulders. "So, what are my girls up to?"

Imogen's lips tightened when he said *my girls*. She obviously didn't like that he was including Luana. The expression only lasted a split second before she raised her head proudly. "We're going dress shopping. Guess which one of us is going to be the Maid of Honor?"

Jonah gasped and threw his hands over his mouth. "Dress shopping!?"

He threw me a glance and teased, "I thought *I* was going to be Maid of Honor."

I laughed. "Do you want to come with?"

"Do I ever!" he exclaimed. "There's a dress I saw in the window you *have* to try on."

"I'm going to go out on a limb and say if it's in the window, it's probably out of my price range," I told him, which he got really disappointed about.

The four of us and our Familiars stopped at a small shop called *Unicorn Bridal*. A really puffy dress took up the entire window display. Glowing butterflies danced around it, as if they'd been hired to draw the eye. It *was* really pretty, but it wasn't *me*.

*It looks like a pastry*, Luana signed, and I laughed.

"I was thinking the same thing," I said aloud while I signed back to her.

Imogen placed her hands on her hips. "Whatever she said, tell her *I* like it."

*Imogen's in a bad mood today*, I signed to Luana instead.

She shot me a sad look.

Sierra fluttered above Sassy's head, then landed on her nose. Sassy barked playfully at her, then rocked her head back and forth like she was giving her a ride. Imogen's features soured. I turned to Jonah. "Sorry, but I think we're going to go in a different direction."

"Fine," Jonah huffed. "But you're not going to find anything as beautiful as this."

We entered the store, and the first thing I noticed was the live unicorn behind the counter organizing tiaras. Its fur was a shimmery white, and its horn was a glossy gold that matched its eyes.

A woman strolled out from behind the aisle of dresses. "Hello. Can I help you find anything today?"

"We're just browsing," I told her. "Is it okay if we try a few things on?"

"Of course," she said brightly.

She asked us a bunch of questions about my preferences, dress size, and wedding date before explaining the layout of the store.

Finally, she said, "Feel free to take a look around. I'll get a dressing room ready for you."

Imogen and Jonah immediately ran for the largest, poofiest dress in my size.

"She *has* to try this one!" Imogen said, pulling it off the rack.

Luana eyed them for a moment before turning to me. *What do you want?*

I shrugged. I hadn't really thought about it much. *Something simple, I guess. Maybe some lace and with a sweetheart neckline.*

*Let's start here.* Luana pointed to a row of lace dresses, and Sierra fluttered over to her first choice. Esis scurried over and buried himself under the dress, then lifted his arms up over his head like he was trying to get it off the rack.

I chuckled and pulled the hanger down. When I turned around, my heart leapt into my throat. A giant creature that hadn't been there moments ago stared down at me. My heart rate settled as I took in the beautiful beast. It had the body of an elk and the antlers of a moose. Its fur was a soft pink color, and its antlers had white velvet all over them that looked like snow. It bowed its head to me.

"Well, hello there," I said. I reached out and petted its nose.

The creature huffed, then bowed its head again. I looked to Luana, and she laughed.

*He wants to take the dress for you,* she told me.

Luana took the dress out of my hand and hung it on the elk's antlers. Then she took a few more dresses off the rack and hung them next to that one. Once his antlers were full, the elk walked off toward the dressing room. I watched it as it went.

*What is it?* Luana asked.

*I never get tired of seeing new magical creatures,* I replied.

Jonah came up behind us then, his arms piled so high with dresses that I couldn't see his face. Behind him, Squeaks carried at least five dresses on her back. "We're good to go," Jonah said. "You're going to *love* these."

We ended up with so many choices that they took up almost all the racks outside the dressing room. I ran my hands down Jonah's first choice, which was nothing but endless tulle. "Um, I might need help getting in and out of these things."

Imogen took a quick step forward. "As Maid of Honor, *I'll* help."

Imogen and Esis accompanied me into the dressing room. Outside, we could hear Luana and Jonah laughing, though we couldn't hear what they said. In the mirror, I could see Imogen frowning while she helped me into my dress. I wanted to say something, but I didn't want to ruin our day.

Imogen zipped me up in the back. "How's that?"

I ran my hands across the bodice. "It fits, but..."

"But what?" she asked.

I grabbed the skirt and lifted it. There was so much poof I didn't even get it an inch off the ground. "But there's just so much fabric. I'm going to trip over it."

Imogen puffed the skirt. "We'll get it altered. It'll be fine. How does it *look?*"

I eyed myself in the mirror. Honestly, it was a disaster. The dress only had one sleeve, and there were puffy flowers all along the skirt. It was asymmetrical, and it looked like a cat had attacked the skirt. I hated it, but what would dress shopping be if I didn't humor Jonah?

"Let's see what Jonah thinks," I said.

Imogen opened the door. I gathered the skirt, but the more I picked up, the more fell out of my arms. I was trying desperately not to step on Esis, since he'd gotten lost somewhere at my feet.

"Where's Es—?"

*Squeal!*

I took a step, and my foot connected with something hard. Esis went flying out from under my dress and rolled on the ground, coming to a stop at Jonah's feet.

"Oh my gosh!" I cried.

Esis got to his feet and shook his head, then stopped dead when he looked at me. His eyes widened, and his jaw dropped.

Luana shot me a grimace, but Jonah covered his mouth like he was about to cry.

"It's perfect!" he gushed. "Don't you love it?"

*No.*

I stepped out of the dressing room and turned to the big mirror outside. "Well, it's just the first one. We have lots of other choices."

"Are you kidding?" Jonah asked, coming up behind me. "This one is perfect. Throw out the others! All you need is a veil, and— wait, I'll show you."

Jonah whistled, and out of nowhere came these tiny silver hummingbirds. They carried a veil and gently placed it atop my head.

I laughed as the birds fluttered away. "Wow, I feel like Snow White."

"See?" Jonah asked. "Isn't it perfect?"

If anything, I liked it less the more I looked at it.

"Why don't we try the next one?" I suggested.

I tried on at least a dozen dresses that Jonah and Imogen had picked out for me. Each one was more poofy and ridiculous than the last. I tried on a dress that had huge fabric layers that looked like seashells, another that was all puff around the middle and tight at the ankles so I looked like a walking marshmallow, and one with sleeves so big they covered my face.

When we finally got to the dresses I liked, I was so sick of trying them on that I didn't like any of them.

"None of these work for me," I complained.

*You'll find something,* Luana encouraged. *We just have to keep looking.*

*The wedding is at the end of the month,* I reminded her. *We don't have a lot of time left.*

*Does anyone you know have a dress you can borrow?* she asked. *As a backup?*

I sighed, feeling frustrated.

"Is she upsetting you?" Imogen asked. "I can ask her to leave."

"No, Im," I said quickly. "That's not it. I think we should just take a break and look at bridesmaid dresses instead."

Imogen's eyes lit up. "I know the perfect one!"

I changed back into my normal clothes, and we went to the bridesmaid section to look for dresses.

"I'm thinking strapless and tons of fluff," Imogen said as she made a beeline for one of the dresses.

"Sounds perfect," Jonah agreed.

*I'm not a fan of strapless,* Luana told me.

Neither was I.

Imogen grabbed a dress from the rack, but her face fell when she saw Luana and I talking to each other. Her eyebrows fell over her eyes.

"What is it now?" Imogen complained. "She doesn't like it?"

"Not really," I admitted.

Imogen scoffed. "Well, it doesn't matter, because she won't be the one wearing it."

*Oh, shit. Here we go.*

"Actually," I said cautiously. "I was thinking she could be one of my bridesmaids. We should probably pick something everyone will like—"

"*She's* one of your bridesmaids!?" Imogen exploded.

I gaped at her. How could she be so mean about this? It was *my* wedding, after all. I could ask anyone I pleased to stand up there with me. Right now, Luana was looking like a better option than Imogen.

"How could you ask her?" Imogen raged. "You hardly know her!"

Was she serious? Heat flared across the surface of my skin. I'd held it in so long that I was about to blow my top. Imogen was being ridiculous.

"Luana and I spend tons of time together," I reminded her.

Imogen's nostrils flared. "Then maybe you'd rather *she* be your Maid of Honor!"

Imogen shoved the bridesmaid dress into Jonah's arms, then stomped away. Sassy hesitated a moment before hurrying after her.

"Imogen," I groaned, but it didn't stop her. I quickly abandoned Jonah and Luana and raced after Imogen, who'd already stormed out of the shop. "Imogen!"

She didn't look back. I ran down the street until I caught up with her, then grabbed her by the wrist. "Imogen, stop!"

She whirled toward me, her eyes filled with tears. "Why?" she snapped. "Why *should* I stop? You obviously don't want me around."

I was stunned. How did she come to that conclusion?

"What are you *talking* about, Imogen?" I asked. "Of *course* I want you around. I asked you to be my Maid of Honor, didn't I?"

"But you would *rather* have Luana, wouldn't you?" she bit. "You'd rather she came to your birth. You'd rather *she* stand in your wedding."

This was just too over the top, even for Imogen. I couldn't take it any longer.

"Imogen, you're driving me crazy!" I shrieked.

She blinked a few times, shocked that I finally snapped at her. After she had a moment to process it, she scoffed. "*I'm* driving you crazy?"

I pressed my fingers to my eyes, trying to calm the heat rising inside of me. "Yes. I've been letting this slide because I'm pregnant and don't want to cause drama, but I'm sick of it, Im. You've been a total bitch since we got here. You're mean to everyone around you for no reason, especially Luana. What did she ever do to you?"

"Open your eyes, Sophia!?" Imogen shouted, earning us a few stares along the street. "You're so wrapped up in your own little world that you don't realize you're hurting the people around you."

"*I'm* hurting *you*?" I scoffed. "How? What did I ever do to you? *Enjoy* myself?"

"Yeah," she snapped. "You're enjoying yourself with everyone but *me*. You're forgetting about me, Sophia. Every day, it feels like I'm losing you more and more. First you're getting married to Liam, then you find a new best friend. Now you're going to have a baby to take care of, and you'll forget about me entirely!"

Imogen started sobbing, and my heart began to turn to mush in my chest. I had no idea she felt this way.

"I don't want to lose you!" she cried, throwing her hands over her face to hide her tears.

I swallowed the lump in my throat. I wished Imogen had told me all this sooner, because I *never* wanted her to feel like this. It was untrue and irrational.

"Im," I said softly, stepping toward her. "You're not going to lose me."

I pulled Imogen into my arms, but she shoved me away.

"I already have, Sophia," she cried. "You should just forget about me."

"Imogen, stop it!" I demanded.

I took her by the shoulders and shook her. Finally, she looked at me.

"Im, I will *never* abandon you," I promised. "Yes, I'm marrying Liam, but that's not going to change anything between you and me."

She sniffled. "But the baby..."

"The baby is going to have a lot of fun with her Aunt Im," I told her. "And as far as Luana, yes, she's my friend, but there's enough room in my life for both of you. She's not replacing you. *You're* my Maid of Honor, and you *always* will be. Don't you think you could at least try to get along with Luana? She really likes you."

Imogen stared down at her feet. "I can't really talk to her."

I sighed. "I don't want any drama at my wedding. Consider it my wedding present."

Imogen huffed, but she didn't answer.

"Imogen," I begged. "Please believe me. We're besties for life."

"You don't know that," Imogen snapped. "Can you really look into my eyes and promise me that?"

"Would you believe it?" I growled, feeling even more annoyed with her.

"I don't know," she said in a clipped tone.

"The old Imogen would," I pointed out.

Her lips tightened. "What does that mean?"

"It means you're not acting like yourself lately!" I burst. "Tell me what's wrong so we can work through this."

Imogen rolled her eyes. "Whatever. Forget about it. It doesn't matter."

"Yes, it does!" I said.

"No, it doesn't," she argued. "This conversation's over. Don't worry, I'll behave at your wedding."

Then she whirled around and started stomping away.

"Wait, Im!" I called after her, but she didn't respond.

Though she had agreed to behave, I sensed this was far from over.

❧

LATER THAT WEEK, I visited my parents. They were staying in one of the small cottages near Jake's cave home. Though it had wooden sides and thatched roofing like the old Anichi huts, the inside was very modern, with running water and electricity.

"Sophia!" my mom cried when she opened the door. "It's so great to see you."

Mom dragged me inside and gave me a hug. It felt so good to be in her arms. A lot had happened in the last two years, but nothing beat my mother's hugs. She was warm, soft, and comforting— everything a mother should be.

"Sophia," Dad said brightly from the stove. "You're just in time. The cherry pie just came out of the oven."

My mouth was already watering. "I'd love some."

Mom was so happy to see me that she dragged me over to the table and made me sit while she got dishes out of the cupboard. I glanced around and noticed a few toys scattered from the foster kids staying there, but they weren't around, as they hadn't returned from school yet.

"Mom, I can get my own plate," I told her.

"Nonsense, honey," she said, waving her hand. "You're carrying our grandbaby. I don't want you lifting a finger."

It was nice that people treated me so kindly with the baby and all, but it sort of made me uncomfortable, too. I didn't want people thinking I needed to be waited on hand and foot.

Esis sat on his own chair next to me, waiting patiently for pie. He kept throwing nervous glances at Bruno and Oliver, who were curled up on the couch. It was like he was worried my parents' Familiars might steal his share of the pie.

Dad brought the pie over and set it in the center of the table. Mom passed out plates, and they both sat down.

"So, what brings you to our neck of the woods?" Dad asked while he served up the pie.

I shrugged. "Can't I come see my parents without a reason?"

Mom gave me a doubtful look. "There's always a reason."

I took a bite of pie, and I couldn't stop shoveling it into my mouth. It was my favorite. Apparently, the baby really liked it, too, because I was ready for a second piece right away.

"There *is* something I want to talk to you two about, but it's good news," I said once I swallowed.

"Oh?" Dad asked brightly.

"It's about my wedding," I told them.

Mom's eyes lit up, and she straightened in her chair. "We'll help any way we can."

"Yeah," Dad agreed. "If it's money you need—"

"It's not," I told them quickly. I didn't want them thinking I only came to visit for money. "I actually need someone to walk me down the aisle."

Dad's jaw hung open. It was like he never expected me to ask him, which was plain silly. He was my dad.

"What do you say, Dad?" I asked hopefully. "Do you want to give me away?"

Dad's eyes started to water. He dabbed them with a napkin. "I would love to give you away, Sophia. Liam's a fine man, and the chief of our tribe. I can't think of a better man to give you away to."

I got out of my chair and hugged my dad. "Thank you."

Mom smiled sweetly from beside him. "Mom, I was thinking you might be able to help, too," I suggested.

"Help how?" she asked, looking eager.

I took a deep breath. "Well, I couldn't find a dress I liked at the store. I was wondering... by any chance did you bring your wedding dress with you when you moved?"

Mom's eyes widened, and she placed her hand on her heart. "You want to wear *my* wedding dress?"

"I thought we could at least see if it fit," I said.

She gaped for a moment before finding her voice. "Yes, of course, Sophia! It's in a box in the closet."

Mom didn't even finish her pie before she started dragging me toward the bedroom. She pulled out a big box and helped me into the white dress. Esis whistled as soon as he saw it on me.

When I turned to the mirror, my heart melted. The dress was perfect in every way. It had long lace sleeves that fell to my elbows, beautiful bead-work on the bodice, and a light-weight skirt. It hugged my curves in all the right places, and seemed timeless. It was such a simple dress... yet it made me feel beautiful. I went speechless when I saw it.

Mom poofed the skirt out around my ankles. "It's a little dirty and wrinkled, but we'll get it dry-cleaned. We can put your hair up, and— oh, look, here's my veil."

Mom took the veil out of the box and held it up behind my head. It was that moment that I knew with certainty that this was the one. Tears pricked at my eyes.

Mom noticed. "Honey, what's wrong?"

I turned to her, my heart full. "Nothing, Mom. It's perfect."

A knock came at the door. "Can I see?" Dad asked.

"Come in," I told him.

Dad opened the door, and his shoulders sank. He couldn't take his eyes off me. "Sophia, you look... there are no words."

I chuckled lightly. "Thanks, Dad."

I gestured him over, and the three of us wrapped each other into a group hug. Tears of happiness rolled down my cheeks. I was so lucky to have these two wonderful people in my life. I didn't know who I'd be if they hadn't raised me. I drew away and wiped my eyes.

Mom fanned her face. "Don't cry, honey. Now I'm going to cry."

"It's okay," I laughed. "They're good tears. I'm just so happy that I get to do this with you guys."

"What do you mean?" Dad asked curiously.

My heart warmed just looking at them. "I know I hit a dead end with my birth parents, but that's okay, because I don't need another set of parents. I have you guys. And I'm really happy Betsy and Alan chose to give me to you. You guys have been the best."

I couldn't handle just standing there. I drew them into another hug.

"Sophia," Dad sighed. "We're so happy they chose us, too."

"We've loved every second of being your parents," Mom added.

I loved being their daughter, too.

I just hoped I could be as good of parents as they were, to mine and Liam's little Ava-Marie.

# Liam

## FIFTEEN

"Liam, hold on."

Sophia grabbed me as I was on my way out the door one August morning. Her grip on my arm was tight. She pulled me back and planted me so that I faced her. She wore a stern expression.

"You've been working almost every day since you became chief," Sophia protested. "You need a break. Before you crash and burn again."

I hated that as she said that, I wavered on my feet. I'd had a long, late night at the office and had gotten up early this morning. Not to mention I'd worked through a summer cold last week, which had only gotten better because Luana had spent all her magical energy healing me every day until I got better.

"There's stuff that's gotta get done. I can't just leave it," I argued.

"I know exactly how you are. You'll overwork yourself until you burn out, then you'll be stuck in bed for weeks and no use to anybody," she argued.

That much was true. That it hadn't happened already was a miracle. "I need to be of service. It's my job."

"You're becoming a workaholic, and it's worrying me." Her eyes narrowed, and her tone became stern. "I told you if you ended up in the hospital again, I'd kill you."

"I'm just trying to provide a good life for the tribe. And for you and the baby." I put a hand on her growing stomach. The baby was getting bigger every day. The amount of pride and love I felt whenever I looked at Sophia now was overwhelming. A warmth settled over me whenever I saw her and thought about all that was to come. We were going to be married in days now, and not soon after, our daughter would come into the world. It was so perfect it felt like this couldn't be my life.

I was desperately worried I was going to fuck it all up somehow.

"You can't help any of us if you're dead," she stated. "Tribe matters can wait for one day."

I slumped over. "All right, fine. I'll take the day off. But you've gotta let me go for now. I have an appointment with Perot."

"You're taking the night off, anyway. Your bachelor party's tonight," Jonah said as he walked by. He and Squeaks began raiding through the fridge. Imogen and Sassy were still sleeping— they hardly came out of their room anymore.

"Why wasn't I informed?" I asked.

"I wasn't aware that was necessary," Jonah replied.

Sophia kissed my cheek. "Just hurry back."

Julian was waiting outside for me. He was too big to fit in the house now, so he basically roamed around the village at free will and waited for me to come out. He gave a cheerful roar when he saw me and licked my torso with his forked tongue.

"Ugh! You gross ass." I slicked dragon slime off of myself and playfully punched his shoulder. Julian chortled like he was laughing.

Stevie was at Perot's house when I arrived. She was sitting on his desk and swinging her legs, a large yellow bow perched on top of her high pony-tail. Her Familiar pulled itself around the room and made chirping sounds. The griffin-hippocampus hybrid looked pretty silly sliding around on the floor with no water to swim in, but she seemed happy.

Stevie giggled. "Nihoni, you're so sweet."

The cypher chirped loudly. Julian tried to fit his head in the house and failed. He groaned when he got stuck. I had to push him back out the doorway. "Wait outside, dummy."

Julian groaned, but he did as he was told. As I shut the door, Perot came shuffling out of the back of the house with a collection of potion vials in his arms. Baxtor flew behind him with rolls of paper in his claws.

"Good to see you're on time. I just got done with Stevie," Perot replied.

"Bet my stats look better than yours," Stevie teased as I took a seat beside the desk.

"We'll see about that." I laid my arm on the desk so Perot could draw blood. Stevie and I's "Death Bet" had somehow become a thing since we'd spoken about it. It was like some sort of undisclosed competition between us had begun to see who was healthier or sicker.

Perot took my blood, then jotted some stuff down on his clipboard. "In any regard, you're better than ever. Things finally seem to be stabilizing. My research on Anichi magic has proven fascinating."

"Any process on finding a cure?" Stevie asked hopefully.

I cringed. Stevie was obsessed with discovering a permanent solution to this thing. Me, I didn't dare to hope. Learning how to exist with my illness and not desperately wish for some kind of miracle was the only way I got by. I was sure if I let myself believe there could be a cure, my whole life would get sucked up in the hope that I wouldn't be stuck like this forever and I'd forget to live at all.

Perot frowned. "No. I'm afraid that's out of our capabilities just yet."

Stevie hung her head. There. *That* was the reason why I refused to believe like she did. Constant disappointment was something I couldn't bear to live with. Acceptance was much easier.

"How are you handling your work schedule?" Perot asked, a hint of reproach in his tone. Perot hadn't exactly approved of me becoming chief. He thought the job was too hard on my body.

"I've been fine. Sophia's making me take the day off."

"Good. You need it." Perot frowned. He didn't seem happy these days. I don't know what had gotten into him lately. "There is something we need to talk about. I don't mean to damper your enthusiasm over your firstborn, but some things can't be avoided."

"What do you mean?" I didn't get what he was talking about. Luana was primarily responsible for Sophia's prenatal care and the health of the baby. I didn't think Perot had anything to do with it.

Stevie and Perot glanced at each other. Perot spoke gently. "Liam, you do understand. Your illness is genetic. This much we know from my research. There's a chance you've passed on your disease to your child."

My blood prickled as it became ice, and I suddenly felt sick. My stomach sank into a pit so low I didn't even know it existed. It was like the world itself narrowed around me and became sharp and defined. My breath hitched as time froze, and slowly, my mind comprehended the awful reality.

This couldn't be happening. But it was. I was so worried that I'd screw up our perfect little life.

I had fucked it up. I'd cursed a little girl to a life of pain.

Perot saw that I was starting to hyperventilate. "Breathe, Liam. It's not a sure thing."

It felt like I was choking down air. Stevie got up to give me a glass of water. I sipped at it, and it shook in my head. The cypher at my feet looked up in alarm.

"You didn't think it could happen?" Stevie asked curiously. I shook my head. She took the glass of water from me before I could spill it all over the floor. That's why she hadn't been happy at the baby announcement. She knew what this was like.

"I've worked out the math, and the probability is one in four. There's a seventy-five percent chance that your child is fine," Perot said firmly.

"That means there's a twenty-five percent chance she's not," I gasped. Nobody in my family's line of recent memory had this disease. Somehow, some long-forgotten descendent of Anna Cedrick had passed Combined Magical Suppression Syndrome down to me. How could Ava-Marie be so lucky to escape this?

"I want you to know if she's ill we'll deal with it. We have Anichi magic now, and more information than we did when you started showing symptoms. My research is getting better every day. She won't suffer as you did," Perot insisted.

It didn't matter. I didn't want her to suffer at all. I leaned forward and put my head in my hands. The cypher licked my forehead while Stevie rubbed my back.

"It's just important to consider the possibility. We won't have a way to test her until she's older. She won't begin to show symptoms until she gains her magic. Most likely, you'll have a healthy baby," Perot said.

"I can't deal with this." I got up and left. I practically ran out the door. Stevie called for me to come back, but Perot said nothing.

If I gave my child my illness, I'd never forgive myself. I'd fucking hate myself forever for giving this shit to a child. No one should ever be subject to this. I wouldn't give this illness to my worst enemy. And I might've passed it on to my kid.

The only thing I could think would be worse than suffering through this myself would be to see a child of mine go through it. It would be my darkest nightmare.

Julian noticed I was fucked up the moment I walked out of the house. He made an alarmed noise and rushed toward me, shaking the ground.

I rubbed his forehead when he collided with me. "I just can't stop fucking things up, huh Jules?" I asked. My voice was thick.

"Liam!" Stevie came rushing out of the house. Her cypher pulled herself behind her and bellowed. She breathed heavily when she stopped in front of me. "Could you not run out like that?"

"What would you do?" I asked her. "How would you handle getting news like that?"

"I know. I can't imagine how you feel." Stevie shrugged helplessly. "With me having it, and the disease being in Ezra's bloodline, our chances are more like one in two. That's why we're so careful."

I hadn't thought about that. I felt sick inside. Stevie took a breath. "Look, maybe things aren't as bad as you think."

"Oh, really?" I asked sarcastically. "How so?"

"You don't even know if your daughter has it yet. You won't for years. And let's be honest, even if you *knew* she was going to be sick, would you go back in time and not make her exist at all?" Stevie asked.

"No..." I said slowly. "I'm not sure what you're getting at."

"Okay, then let me rephrase." Stevie's tone was blunt. "Sophia isn't twenty-four weeks along yet. Let's assume we know your kid's gonna be sick. Would you consider taking Sophia in to have an abortion?"

"No!" I replied, fucking horrified. "Of course not!" I wasn't going to get rid of my baby just because she might have my disease. CMSS was chronic, and it was awful, but it wasn't necessarily terminal.

"Then honestly, what's the big deal?" Stevie shrugged. "I'm sick, and it blows sometimes, but my life doesn't fucking suck. You're sick, but you're chief! Your life far from sucks. Yeah, our bodies are basically shit and there's a probability we'll die early, but does that make our lives any less worth living than anyone else? I'd rather have a short and badass life, even one that's painful, than a long and worthless one where I'm healthy and don't do anything meaningful."

She did have a point. Her logic was calming me down, but it still didn't help the guilt. "I just don't know what I'm gonna do if she's got CMSS. I can't watch her go through that kind of pain."

"Disabled people are just as valuable as healthy people. She can do just as much as anyone even if she is sick," Stevie said firmly. "I know this is awful, but you need to get over yourself, because if your kid is ill, she's gonna need you. Especially to teach her that this isn't something to give up on herself over."

If anyone else spoke to me like that, it would piss me off— but Stevie and I were on the same level. She could speak plainly about our disease and I would get it. "You're right, Stevie. Thanks for knocking some sense into me."

"You Mitoh boys can be really dense. I've had a lot of practice with your brother," Stevie said with a giggle.

"I can imagine." Ezra had a huge heart, but he wasn't the brightest. I waved goodbye and headed on my way back to the house. There was still a sickening weight in my stomach, but it felt lighter now. I just didn't want to break the news to Sophia.

She must've noticed my face was white when I walked in the door, because she put down the brush she was using to comb Esis and took my hands. "What's wrong?"

Esis chirped, and I said, "We should talk about something."

Her eyes darkened, as if this was a conversation long since coming. Esis hopped onto the pillows as we entered the bedroom, and I shut the door. We faced each other as we sat on the bed, and I tried to steady my voice. "I met with Perot. He... he said that there was a chance that I might've given my illness to Ava-Marie. One-in-four."

I expected her to freak out, but she merely frowned. "I thought about that. It was one of the first things I considered when I thought I was pregnant."

"And it didn't bother you?" I was surprised.

"What are we gonna do? We can't go back in time and change it. And if you think I'm getting rid of this baby, you're fucking nuts." Her tone was hard.

"I never said that. I wouldn't want you to." I looked down as I squeezed her hands. "I worry that if she is sick, you're going to blame me."

"I'd *never* do that." Sophia moved closer. "If Ava is sick, I'm gonna love her just as much as I love you. And probably even more."

My throat got tight. "I don't want her to be in pain."

"That doesn't make her any less worthy of life if she is," Sophia argued. "Humans spend their whole life trying to avoid pain, but you know what, Liam? I think a bit of pain actually makes life better. We've all been through so much, but look where we are today because of it. I don't think we'd be where we are if you weren't sick, and that's a fact."

I knew she was right. Even losing our home had turned out for the better— we'd found a new home, discovered the Anichi, and had hope now that the Hawkei could be saved.

"It just sucks to think of her feeling like I feel." My shoulders slumped. I wanted to break down just thinking about it.

"If it comes, we'll handle it," Sophia said firmly. "There's no point worrying about it until then. We're going to love her anyway."

"We already do." I hadn't met Ava-Marie yet, but I already knew I adored her in a way I hadn't anyone else— not even Sophia. It was a special kind of feeling reserved only for her.

Sophia started. She shifted on the bed a bit, and her eyes widened as Esis came running over. "Do you want to feel her kick?"

"What?" I'd never done that before.

"She's moving now. Here." She took my hands and placed them on her stomach. Underneath my palms I felt a firm pressure. Small prodding movements bumped against my fingers. Esis put his paws next to my hands so he could feel, too.

Tears rose. I had to choke them back. This made everything feel ten times more real. The kicking increased in intensity against my hands, and I laughed. "She's kicking the shit out of me."

"How do you think my ribs feel? The kid is always doing somersaults. She never quiets down." Sophia giggled.

"She's a little fighter," I murmured. Esis chittered, like he agreed with me. When Ava-Marie gave a particularly strong kick, I almost reared back. Reality had suddenly set in with how alive this tiny baby was. And I was lucky enough to be a part of her.

"That's not death, Liam." Sophia smiled and stroked my hair. "That's life."

Sophia and I spent a long day lazing around the house and doing nothing. It was kind of uncomfortable for me, because I'd been working endlessly all the time. It felt strange to have nothing to do, but it definitely had an effect on me, because by the time evening rolled around I felt a lot less stressed. We had the house to ourselves until nightfall. Jonah had taken off with Jake, and Imogen thankfully left before lunch to get the bachelorette party ready.

I still didn't know what was up with Imogen. I was certain that there was something else going on that she wasn't telling us, but with how explosive her attitude was lately, I was afraid to ask.

"You've been pampering me all day." Sophia laughed as I tickled her feet after I just got done giving them a full massage. "Isn't the point of taking a day off to relax?"

"Good thing I relax by spoiling you." I smiled.

"That doesn't count." She rolled her eyes before they wandered to the fridge. "I'm hungry again."

I chuckled. She'd just had a snack an hour ago. Now that the morning sickness was more or less done, Sophia was constantly hungry. "What do you want?"

"Erm... pickles, peanut butter, and bread," she responded. Esis clapped, like he agreed.

I didn't know what she wanted them for, but best not to ask questions. "Yes, dear."

When I brought them to the table, Sophia spread the peanut butter on the bread before she put the pickles between two slices and took a bite. I cringed in revulsion as her face melted, like she'd just eaten the most amazing thing on earth.

"Ancestors. I'm going to gag." I tried not to watch her eat it.

"I swear, it tastes good!" she insisted. Esis made his own nasty-sandwich and devoured it.

One thing I wasn't going to miss about Sophia being pregnant was her disgusting cravings. I'd caught her at midnight last week eating sugar cookies topped with garlic cheese spread.

"Don't get too crazy during the bachelorette party," I warned. "You're carrying precious cargo."

Sophia finished her first nasty sandwich and made another. "I'm not sure what we're doing. Imogen said it was a surprise. She did say she was bringing a penis cake, though."

I snorted. "How original. Who's all coming?"

"Imogen, Vanessa, Miranda, Lindsey and Luana," she said. "And I invited Stevie to come along, too."

"What about Amelia?" I knew she was a bridesmaid.

"She and Trace are out doing something for the tribe tonight. I didn't ask what," she explained.

The door burst open as if someone had kicked it down. Jonah, Jake, Ezra, Cade and Bren strolled in like they owned the place. Wyatt was one of my groomsmen, too, but he'd caught the summer cold and opted to stay home from the party, as he wanted to be well for my wedding.

"Are you ready to have the most epic night of your life?" Jonah challenged. I groaned, and Sophia giggled.

"Let's just get this over with." I couldn't imagine what Jonah had planned for the bachelor party. Sophia waved goodbye, and Jonah led the way down a path I'd never been before.

"So what exactly are we doing?" I asked as the village limits ended and we headed into the trees. The Familiars— including Squeaks, Sabor, Julian, Arabelle, Dyami and Kingston— all flew above us.

"You'll see!" Jonah sang. He gave a silly grin to Jake, who nudged him gently.

"For the love of the ancestors, no strippers," I growled.

"We can't go to the strip club. Sophia and the girls probably have a reservation!" Ezra quipped, and the guys roared.

I rolled my eyes. "I thought we all agreed to never mention that night again."

"Nobody agreed. We are all going to rub it in your face for the rest of your life that your wife likes boobs," Cade said as he flung his arm around my shoulders. I sighed.

Eventually, the trees parted, and we came to a long runway strip set in the middle of the trees. I tilted my head when I saw what was waiting.

A plane. Huh. This was interesting. It wasn't very big— just a small recreational aircraft. We climbed inside, and the Familiars outside scaled farther into the sky. There was a pilot, as well as some kind of worker in the middle of the plane. He welcomed us as the plane took off into the air.

I figured we were doing some sort of airline tour over the village, but when we got inside the plane, it was very bare bones— only a few seats littered here and there, and some small windows. I took a seat and watched out the tiny window as the plane climbed higher and higher, until we were at least thirteen thousand feet up. Ezra grinned, like he couldn't wait for what was coming.

"Can I have the groom come up here, please?" the worker asked. He was standing by a large sliding door that opened up the middle of the plane.

I got up from my seat. Cade and Bren cackled. Jonah was practically pissing himself with excitement. "Uh, sure. What am I doing?"

The worker didn't answer. Instead, he opened the sliding door. I felt warm air rush by my face, blowing my hair back and exposing the clouds. I went to take a step back, but he grabbed my arm. "Have a nice flight!"

Then he *pushed me out of the plane.*

I didn't have time to grab on to the side of the plane. One second, I was safely inside the plane, and the next, I was falling through the air at a high speed.

I went breathless. I couldn't scream. My heart was pounding, and my hearing went muted as nothing but the wind rushed by. I felt completely weightless as I watched the forest and the mountains below near at a terrifying rate.

Holy shit! I wasn't an Air Elementai. I didn't even have a parachute! I was going to be totally crushed when I hit the ground. He'd totally thrown me to my death!

A flash of red caught my eye. My heart tumbled in my chest as I saw that Ezra was falling not too far away. On my left, Cade had also leapt out of the plane. Bren was falling a short distance ahead. Ezra sent me a thumbs-up, like this was totally A-fucking-okay.

I spotted Jake and Jonah tumbling through the skies at a farther distance. Both of them looked completely content up here, and did tricks and flips as they fell. They manipulated the air so they flew through it like a superhero, performing loops and dives.

What the hell were they doing? Couldn't they stop flirting for five freaking seconds and save us? I tried to get their attention, but they pointedly ignored me. I desperately looked around for Julian, for any of the Familiars, but they weren't around.

Well, might as well make my peace. My friends had gone completely nuts and decided to jump out of a plane for no good reason. This is what I got for talking to crazy people.

As the ground neared, my heart beat even wilder. But then, from out of nowhere, something swooped underneath me and caught me. My weight settled on something soft and feathery. I felt a creature move under me as it dipped in and out of the air currents like they were waves.

I looked down. The creature that had caught me was like a fish— a *flying fish*. I watched with amazement as the creatures caught Bren, Ezra, and Cade. Jonah and Jake ignored them, as they didn't need a ride, flying in their own little world.

The creatures looked like string-rays, but with white feathers. They had long, flat fins, and tails that glowed white. And they could fly! They soared through the air like they'd swim in the water. Their fins-slash-wings glided effortlessly through the wind and over the horizon. I dug my fingers into the feathers and hung on as my creature turned toward the ocean, dipping lower and lower.

Our Familiars reappeared. Julian let out a greeting as he sailed beside my stingray-creature. Arabelle danced with Cade's ray, and Dyami tried to tussle with Ezra's mount, though the ray more or less ignored it. The hippogriffs stayed by Jonah and Jake, entwining their talons together like they were performing some sort of mating dance.

The ocean approached. The Familiars pulled off, and I realized that my ray wasn't going to quit diving. I held my breath as I felt the rush of the sea envelop me, and held tight. The feathers on its back melded into spines and smooth scales. The creature changed, continuing on its mission as it pulled me further underwater.

I saw a white glowing up ahead. Ezra's ray had followed me down. Ezra pointed, and our rays swam together toward the light.

My eyes widened when I saw that there were all kinds of Anichi water creatures down here. The glowing was coming from white sea lions, which had antlers like deer, and orca whales that were white and fuzzy all over. A pod of dolphins swam by, but they were anything but ordinary— long white ribbons of light streamed off of them, and swirling tusks like those of narwhals spiraled out of their heads.

This was incredible. To think there were so many magical creatures out there that the Elementai didn't know about. So many we even had yet to discover.

Eventually, I was starting to lose my breath, so I tapped on the ray's back to let him know it was time to go up. We surfaced. The rest of the party was already waiting on the beach. When I got to the shore and dismounted, the ray I had been riding changed again. His scales became feathers as he joined the other rays, and they sailed back into the skies once more, vanishing into the depths of the clouds.

Bren was wet, but being a Koigni, he couldn't hold his breath for long and probably hadn't dived as long as we had. Cade was similarly soaked, along with Ezra— but Jake and Jonah were completely dry. They'd probably stayed out of the water to make out or something while the rest of us were busy.

"Cool creatures, huh?" Bren asked as he shook water out of his ears. "I bet there's tons more down at the bottom. I'm almost jealous I'm not Toaqua."

"What were those things?" I asked. I didn't take my eyes off the rays until they were gone from sight. They'd been breathtaking.

"They're called stingsailers," Jonah replied. "They're Anichi-Toaqua type creatures that can fly and swim. I paid for all of us to take the tour."

"So... you thought it was okay to push me out of a plane without telling me it'd be okay?" I crossed my arms.

"Shut up. I knew you'd love it," Jonah replied. "You don't feel alive unless your life is in danger somehow."

He was right.

"Okay, I can't be mad at you for that one. That was pretty wicked," I admitted.

"Of course it was," Jonah replied confidently. Squeaks nipped at his hair.

"So where can we go get drinks? I'm way too sober for this shit," Ezra asked. Cade nodded in agreement.

"There's this really cool bar on the other side of town," Bren suggested. "Vanessa and I went there last weekend."

"A good a place as any!" Jonah hopped onto Squeaks' back and pointed. "Onward!"

As we headed back into town, Bren came by my side. "So. You ready to be a married man?"

"More than ever. This bachelor party is really something."

Bren laughed. "You should've seen mine. I didn't want strippers, but my buddies hired one anyway. She was aggressive. She jumped on my lap so hard she ripped my jeans and smashed my balls. It was rough."

"Ouch." I winced. "Yeah, glad we're not doing that."

"It made memories." Bren smiled wistfully before he frowned. "I don't have many friends left. The rest of my buddies didn't make it out of the fire. So I'm glad we're doing this. It's nice."

That was terrible. I'd more or less made Bren a groomsman because Vanessa was a bridesmaid, and she needed someone to walk with. I didn't really know him that well. Now I was glad I did, because he was obviously lonely after what had happened.

I didn't want to damper the mood further, so I changed the subject and said,

"How's parenthood?"

"It's harder than you could ever imagine and more incredible than you could ever think," Bren responded. "You'll get what I mean once she gets here."

"I'm not gonna lie, I'm kind of fucking terrified. I have no idea how to be a father."

"You'll learn." Bren shrugged. "I'm lucky. I have a son, and I already worry about him night and day. I couldn't imagine having a daughter."

No shit. This world was cruel to women. Now I had a little one of my own to protect. A million terrible things could happen to her, and I could only defend her so much.

"You might just have a daughter yet," I said.

Bren shook his head. "Not until after the war is over. Ness and I agreed it's too dangerous as it is."

"I'm with you there." We crossed into town, and I asked, "What do you do here, anyway? I rarely see you around."

"I was assigned to work maintenance on all the village buildings. It's all right, but I miss the *Hozho's* boiler room, honestly." He shrugged.

"I bet it was more interesting."

"I loved the job, but it was never a permanent position for me. I was just saving up so I could open a vintage car shop. I know cars aren't really useful in Kinpago, but I loved them." Bren's face lit up as he talked about it. "It was always kind of my dream to work on muscle cars and hot rods."

"That sounds really badass. I guess if I ever need something worked on, I'll come to you." I looked at the ground. "My dad left me his bike. I love that thing. I was thinking about doing some modifications on it, but I had to leave it behind when we fled."

"My dad died when I was young. Heart attack. It's been me and my mom for a long time." Bren stared wistfully ahead. "But he taught me how to tinker with stuff before he passed away. He had a Z/28 Camaro that he left me. It's still back in Kinpago. I hid it before the Task Force could confiscate it. Working on stuff is the only way I can get close to him."

"Wish I could feel that way about my dad." We'd shared the chief hood, but to be honest, most days it just felt like work rather than a connection to my father. All the things we used to do together— hunt, fish, work on the bike— I couldn't do anymore, because the war effort took up everyone's time.

"Your dad just died, huh? I'm sorry." Bren gave me a grimace. "The first few years are the worst."

"How'd you get through it?" Some days it didn't feel like I ever would.

Bren shrugged. "How'd you get through Nashoma? Didn't have a choice, did you?"

He was right. There was no going back— only forward. "I just wish he could've met Ava before he died."

"I wish my dad could've met my son. But in a way, they will. They're ancestors now. Their job is to watch over us. And they'll be waiting in the Ancestral Lands when it's our time."

"Which has not yet come." Ezra had been eavesdropping. He flung his arms around both of our shoulders and said, "We drink tonight, gentlemen, for tomorrow we die."

"Well, maybe not *tomorrow*." I chuckled.

"Unless we get alcohol poisoning," Bren cracked.

Very possible, with Ezra and Jonah in the drinking party.

The bar we entered was packed on a Saturday night. It was dark inside, lit only by the glow of pulsing strobe lights— at least, I thought they were strobe lights, until I looked closer and saw that giant chameleons were lining the ceiling. They were as big as iguanas, and shone with a different neon color every time the bass pulsed, giving the club a rainbow hue.

The bar was packed with velvet booths. In the middle was a light-up dance floor that seemed exclusive to Familiars only. A blue-tinted creature with the wings of an eagle, face of a fox and bird talons for feet shook its feathered mane at a dog who was at least five feet tall, with a spiky ruff around its head and white, curved horns. At the bar, a silver deer with ghostly horns poured drinks. A dragon-like creature that had the wings of a rooster acted like a bouncer, throwing drunks out the back with a discontented roar.

My eyes wandered, until I caught sight of Sophia and the girls sitting in a booth big enough for ten people near the dance floor. The rest of the group spotted them at the same time I did.

Bren faced me. "Guess we had the same idea."

Vanessa waved us over. The Familiars rushed onto the dance floor. Julian trampled over several others to get there first. Nobody was hurt, but a wolf that had a coat that looked made of leaves grumbled as it got up to leave after Julian knocked him down.

Squeaks was shaking her hindquarters as usual, while Sassy copied her by twirling her tail in the air. Esis was on top of Squeaks' head and trying to do the robot. Medusa had entwined herself around Evelyn, and the kirin was doing some sort of strange, twisting move. Aisha was swinging from side to side, but unlike Julian, she was polite enough to watch where she was going. Sierra fluttered her wings as she flew in circles over the entire group.

Squeaks and Sabor immediately started bouncing together. Sassy hopped onto Arabelle's back, and Dyami swayed with Kingston. Julian rumbled lowly in his throat when he saw Aisha, and the two dragons crooned.

"We didn't expect to see you guys here!" Vanessa yelled over the music as we squeezed into the booth.

"We went stingsailing!" Jonah replied. "What'd you guys do?"

"We took Sophia to this *amazing* spa. It was total relaxation," Imogen gushed.

I took a spot next to Sophia. "Did you have fun?"

"Lots. The spa was so cool. They had these miniature pudu fawns that gave massages, and monkeys with rainbow fur that painted your nails. The fawns were so tiny— they looked like piglet deer." She showed me her hand — she'd picked a light pink.

"I'm glad." As I looked around, I noticed that the bar was mostly run by the Familiars. A white leopard with antennas that looked like butterflies distributed our menus, while some sort of dog-reptile thing waddled by with a tray on its head. It was really ugly— a mix of a pug and Komodo dragon— but also kind of cute with its bug eyes and tongue sticking out.

"You guys are just in time." Imogen fished in her purse. She triumphantly held an object over the table like it was some kind of trophy. "The Purple Dildo of Shame!"

My jaw dropped. The purple dildo that Imogen had bought from the sex shop months ago was in her hand— the same one Sophia had used to smack Logan in the face.

"*That's* the one thing you saved?" I asked ludicrously. I thought that thing had gone up in the fire.

"It was already in the truck before we left!" Imogen squealed. "Jonah wanted it just in case!"

All eyes went to Jonah, and he put his hands up defensively. "I swear that thing's never been up my butt."

Jake laughed. Jonah went pink, and Jake put his arms around him to draw Jonah closer.

"What exactly are we going to do with that thing?" I asked hesitantly.

"Play a game, obviously," Imogen responded. "You pass this around and say the dirtiest thing you've ever done. The winner gets to keep the dildo for the rest of the night."

"That's not much of a prize," I debated.

"What are you talking about? That's amazing. Let's play," Jonah started. He took a deep breath. "I'll go first. I've—"

"Nope, *no*, I'll go first." I snatched the dildo from Imogen's hand before Jonah could scar us for life. "I ate Sophia out on the beach."

"Ooh, good one," Imogen said approvingly as Jonah pouted.

I handed the dildo to Sophia. She spoke and signed at the same time. "I might've given Liam a blow job in the library."

"What is it with you two and doing it in public places?" Ezra wondered aloud. Stevie was sitting on his lap, his arms around her waist.

"That's nothing." Miranda snatched the dildo from Sophia. "Lindsey and I did it on the rooftop of Orenda Academy at sunset. No clothes or anything. It was naughty." Miranda giggled.

"Very romantic," I commented.

"Yeah, until we got caught by Baine!" Lindsey burst, and both girls broke out laughing. Jaws dropped around the table.

"Oh my ancestors! That must've been mortifying," Sophia commented. She looked as if Baine walking in on us was a personal nightmare.

"It was more funny than anything. You should've seen his face as we were trying to gather our clothes. He was absolutely horrified. He turned his back and everything," Miranda gushed. She deepened her voice to do an impression of Baine. "*Ladies, I understand when passion seizes the moment, but please take hold of your carnal desires in a more private location.*"

Imogen spat out her drink. As the rest of us were dying, Lindsey took the dildo from Miranda and pretended to think. "Hm... I have to say... I was eaten out in a carriage once."

Sophia hunched over beside me. I nudged her. "Something you wanna say, *pawee?*"

Lindsey winked. "Hey, I think Liam and I can both agree, Sophia's good at oral."

Loud *ooohs* went up around the bar. Sophia went beet red and clapped a hand over her mouth. I had to laugh.

Bren and Vanessa both had the same answer. They'd done it in the back of Bren's Camaro.

When it was Luana's turn, she frowned and signed something to Sophia. I didn't know what she was saying, but I was pretty sure Luana was confessing she'd never done anything before.

It wasn't a big deal. As horny and open as this group was, nobody really cared if you were still a virgin. We didn't pick on people for stupid shit like that. What you did with your body was your business. Unless you made it everyone else's, which was what my friends were always determined to do.

Sophia looked up. "Luana's not comfortable with sharing."

"You can skip turns," Imogen said hurriedly. "It's fine."

Luana seemed relieved. Cade skipped his turn, too. I was certain the only person he'd ever screwed around with was Imogen, and he didn't want to bring up old times and start an argument between them that would ruin the party like it had the baby announcement.

"I'll go," Imogen said. She tapped the dildo against the table and said, "I got off in the greenhouses."

"*No,*" Jonah gasped.

Imogen winked. "I can be kinky all by myself."

Sophia snorted. Cade reddened— pretty sure that was an image he'd be picturing when he was all by himself tonight.

Jake didn't even flinch as he took the dildo and said, "I've practiced bondage for six hours straight. Among other things."

"Impressive," Imogen noted.

Jonah's eyes got huge. He turned to face Jake. "You didn't tell me you liked ropes."

"I like a lot of things." Jake grinned. Jonah swooned.

I gagged. Did this guy have his own personal sex dungeon? The straight shooters were always the weirdest.

"Threesomes are a lot of work. Not for me," Ezra stated as he passed the dildo to Stevie.

She rolled her eyes as she took it. "Sex in the ocean. Easy."

"With who, pray tell?" Jonah wiggled his eyebrows as he leaned forward.

"I've only ever been with Ezra. Between the two of us, he's the whore," Stevie stated.

"More experience, baby," Ezra cooed. He kissed Stevie, tongue and fucking all.

Ugh. They were so gross. By this time, our drinks had arrived, and we all agreed that Jake had won the game.

I'd just ordered a beer, but Sophia had gotten this insane non-alcoholic beverage that was crazy to look at. It was in a daiquiri glass, but had sugar dusted over the top. It was a white-and-red swirling concoction that sparkled when you stirred it.

"Try it." Sophia handed it to me, and I took a sip. It tasted like strawberries and cream. The tones in the room morphed from multi-colored to red as my eyesight changed due to the mixture of the drink. It was probably infused with some kind of magical berry.

Hints of conversation could be heard around the table. "Are you sure you want *me* to be the face of your cabaret, Jonah?" Miranda asked hesitantly. "I mean, not a lot of people would consider having a black girl as their lead."

"Girl, you've got the *best* singing voice this side of California!" Jonah exclaimed. He flung his arm out, and the drink he was holding sloshed out of the glass and hit Ezra in the face. "Of course I want you as my star!"

Miranda sighed. "Don't you think Lindsey would make a better star? She's prettier."

"I croak like a frog when I sing," Lindsey deadpanned as she took a sip of her wine. Ezra coughed up his beer.

"You'll do great, Miranda. I've heard you sing. You're incredible!" Imogen stated.

Miranda blushed. "Truth is, I'm only half Hawkei. My grandmother on my human side lives in Georgia. I stayed with her during the summer break as a kid. She signed me up for the church choir. You know, those big Southern ones you always see in movies?"

"And it gave you pipes blessed by the ancestors themselves," Lindsey finished. "You love to sing. You belong up on that stage."

Miranda smiled bashfully and entwined her arm with Lindsey's. "If you say so."

As the night lingered on, people started pairing off in their designated couples. Miranda and Lindsey slipped off to the backroom to do ancestors-knew what, while Ezra and Stevie remained curled up in their own little world. Bren and Vanessa went home early, as they needed to relieve the babysitter.

Cade left, too. It was almost a relief. The tension between him and Imogen was so thick you could cut it with a knife, and I'd been waiting for the both of them to go off like a ticking time bomb all night.

Jonah and Jake were on the dance floor with the Familiars. Jonah was totally eating up what Jake was laying out for him. The two of them were stuck together like glue.

Luana signed something to Sophia. Sophia said to Imogen, "She wants to say thank you. For not leaving her alone as the only single person."

Imogen frowned. Technically, she was single, too, but it was only because she wouldn't let Cade back in. Everyone knew they should be together.

"Sophia and I are friends first. We started out that way," I said to Luana.

"And we always will be." Sophia squeezed my hand and smiled. I gave her an affectionate look back.

"Do you *want* to be with someone?" I asked Luana, signing the question.

She shrugged. She didn't seem to know.

"Nothing wrong with that. You can be single and just as happy as everyone else. Sometimes more so." I took another sip of my beer. "Just do you."

Luana nodded enthusiastically. Jonah and Jake returned from the dance floor. Jonah chugged the rest of his mixed drink and teetered slightly. He was at his limit and about to go over. "I'm thirsty. I think I want another."

"Be careful," Jake said kindly. "You don't want to have too much."

Jonah blinked. "You know what? I'll just get water."

I was floored. Wow. Jake had talked Jonah out of getting plastered. No one had ever been able to do *that* before.

As Jonah reached the bar, Imogen rounded on Jake. "Okay, mister, I think it's time we had a talk."

"What about?" Jake's voice was calm and cool. He faced the four of us as if he had been expecting this.

"What are your intentions with Jonah?" Imogen put her hands on her hips. "I think you should come clean."

I cringed. This wasn't really our business, but at the same time, Imogen had the right to be concerned. Renar had destroyed Jonah. None of us wanted that to happen again.

Sophia rushed to explain. "Jonah's been through a lot," she said. "He's gone through some bad relationships. We don't want him to get hurt."

"He's already told me everything," Jake replied. "I know what happened."

"Really?" I widened my eyes. I didn't expect that.

"Yes. I know what that... *degenerate* did to him." Jake's tone when he spoke of Renar was so full of disgust and hatred. It made a shiver run down my spine.

"So you know why we're concerned," Sophia said. "We're not saying you're a bad guy, but Jonah has a fragile heart."

"His home life wasn't the greatest," I added.

"I'm well aware of what went on in his childhood. As I said, he's been open and honest with me, as I have been with him," Jake said.

"That's a big deal, though," I said. "You haven't known Jonah very long, but I've been his best friend my entire life. He doesn't open up to anyone. He plays off things like they don't bother him. If he's being this open with you so early, it means he really trusts you."

"We just don't want you abusing that trust." Imogen raised her eyebrow.

A muscle worked in Jake's jaw. "I will be blunt. I like Jonah. He's funny, sweet and kind. He makes me laugh. And his personal quirks are attractive to me. I know I come across as intimidating, and a bit stern. He helps me not to take life as seriously as I do. My only intentions with him are to make him happy."

"It's just…" Sophia sucked in a breath. "He got attached to you quickly. He really likes you. Don't let this go on if you're not serious."

Jake's gaze softened when Sophia mentioned how much he meant to Jonah. "Trust me when I say that I want to make this permanent."

That was a big fucking deal.

Imogen snorted. "You're moving a little fast, aren't you? You've only been dating a couple of weeks. I bet you've already gotten him in bed."

*Damn you, Imogen.* It was like she didn't have a filter these days. Luana sat awkwardly between us and played with her hands.

Jake's voice became cold. "No, actually. We're taking things slow. In fact, I don't plan on sleeping with Jonah until he's ready. Which is a long way down the road."

"We don't need to know details," I hurried to say.

"I know Jonah comes as a package deal. If I'm with him, his friends come with it. You're his family. And you have a right to be protective." Jake took a breath. "I just want you to understand that I'm trying to protect him, too."

"Then you have our blessing," Sophia said, before Imogen could speak. "Anyone who cares about Jonah that much is a friend of ours. Just please, be careful."

With Sophia's approval, Jake nodded lightly to us. He walked off and joined Jonah at the bar. He wrapped his arm around Jonah's waist. Jonah lit up and started gabbing about ancestors only knew what, which made Jake smile. Jonah had no idea of the conversation that had just taken place.

"I don't think we have to worry about him," I said.

"Let's hope not," Imogen grumbled. She sipped her margarita sourly.

Sophia grimaced. Luana put a hand on Sophia's knee, as if to say she knew Jake and he was a good guy, one we could trust.

Imogen might not be convinced, but I was. Jake was good for Jonah. He brought the guy discipline, something Jonah had never bothered with before, and structure. He was a safe choice. And maybe even something indefinite.

The way Jake was talking, it looked like Sophia and I weren't the only ones getting married soon.

# sophia
## SIXTEEN

"Sophia, wake up."

Someone shook me, and I stirred awake. I rolled over, expecting to find Liam beside me. Instead, Amelia's dark eyes stared back at me. I startled and sat upright in bed, nearly knocking heads with her. Glancing around, I realized I was lying in Amelia's bed in her cottage. My other bridesmaids— Imogen, Luana, Vanessa, Lindsey, and Miranda— stood at the foot of the bed, beaming. They all wore the same thin white bathing gowns, like someone might wear to a baptism.

Esis stood at my feet and threw his hands in the air. Tiny pieces of confetti rained down onto the blanket, and he made a long cheering noise, as if to say, *Surprise!*

The events of the previous night came rushing back. I'd stayed at Amelia's with my bridesmaids, as Liam and I agreed to spend the night apart before the wedding.

*Wait... holy shit!*

"It's my wedding day!" I blurted.

I could hardly believe it was true. I had to say it again for it to sink in.

"*It's my wedding day!*" I squealed.

Imogen started screaming, and the other girls quickly joined in. If someone next door heard, they'd probably think we were being attacked.

Imogen bounced on her toes and flapped her hands as she came to the side of my bed. She was super bubbly this morning. "You're getting *married*! And we're going to make you look *fantastic*! Liam's going to orgasm when you walk down the aisle."

"Ancestors, Imogen," I groaned. "Did you *have* to put that image in my head? My parents are going to be there."

A voice piped up from the other room. "Imogen's said far worse this morning!"

I glanced to Amelia. "Mom's here?"

She shrugged. "She and Haloke came to help you get ready."

"Imogen and Miranda already have hair and makeup covered," I pointed out.

Amelia smiled and tugged at my arm to get me out of bed. "Everyone needs to be with you this morning. It's tradition."

I crawled out of bed and stood beside Amelia. Vanessa held out a plush white robe. "Strip down and put this on."

I took it from her and looked down at the robe. "Oh. Is this the same thing we did at your wedding?"

Vanessa smiled brightly. "Sure is. You're okay with that, right?"

"Yeah," I said quickly. "You're all like family to me. I'm not shy."

Amelia leaned in and kissed me on the cheek. "We're ready when you are."

She started for the door, and everyone followed. Imogen winked at me, then closed the door behind her. The only one who stayed was Esis.

My heart pounded in exhilaration as I stripped off my pajamas and pulled on the fluffy white robe. It was really soft on my skin and felt nice. I still couldn't believe I was getting married today. I took a few moments to stare down at my engagement ring. It hadn't sunk in.

"Well, Esis," I said, beaming. "By the end of the day, I'm going to be Mrs. Sophia Mitoh."

Esis clapped his paws and cheered for me.

A knock came at the door. "What's taking so long?" Imogen called. "Did your water break?"

I rolled my eyes as I opened the door. "Very funny."

Imogen chuckled. "I *am* hilarious."

Haloke laughed from where she sat next to my mom at Amelia's kitchen table. They wore the same white dresses as the bridesmaids.

"All you girls have such a bright, beautiful friendship!" Haloke stood and came over to me, holding her arms out before pulling me into a hug. "It is the *best* way to start your wedding day."

I drew away from her and turned to my bridesmaids. "Okay, girls. Get your jokes out now, because no one's saying a word during the ceremony. I don't want to hear any dick jokes!"

I shot a pointed look between Imogen and Lindsey. Lindsey threw her head back and laughed.

Luana signed to me. *They've been making shotgun wedding jokes all morning.*

I placed a hand on my hip and looked to Lindsey. "You've been saying what, now?"

Lindsey poked Luana in the side, and the two girls chuckled under their breath. "Don't go telling on me now. All I said was we would've had more time to plan the wedding if it weren't for a defective condom."

I shook my head, laughing. "That'd be funny if Liam and I used them."

I realized what I'd just said in front of the older women, and my face paled.

Haloke tried to hide her smile. "Don't be embarrassed. Liwanu and I didn't use them either. It's how Liam was conceived."

"Same for Amelia," Mom piped up.

I swore even *more* blood drained from my face, which I didn't think was possible. "That's a little *too* much information for my wedding day, guys."

"Everyone relax," Amelia said, crossing her arms. "We all know this wedding isn't happening because of a broken condom. The real culprit is... Perot."

She smirked proudly at the jab.

"Or maybe because Sophia's such a horn dog," Miranda laughed.

Imogen's eyebrows shot up. "Believe me, those two go at it like bunnies."

"We do not—" I started to protest, but Vanessa cut in.

"Come on, it takes two to tango," she said. "Liam's got to be just as horny."

Luana laughed and signed to me. *Next thing you know, they're going to ask how you two conceived.*

As if she could read minds, Lindsey started talking before Luana finished signing. "Spill the deets, Sophia. How'd it happen?"

"Ancestors, you guys. Can we *not* talk about my sex life in front of my mother?" I said.

"It's not like I don't know you're sexually active," Mom replied. "I've kind of figured that one out."

I frowned. "Yeah, well, you don't need to know specifics."

"Okay," Amelia caved. "We're done. We all know you and Liam are getting married because you love each other and not because of the baby.

So, let's get you ready to marry the love of your life. Your carriage is waiting."

"Where exactly are we going?" I asked.

"To the river, of course," Amelia answered. "You must wash to be blessed by the Great Spirit before your wedding."

My heart fluttered. I'd spoken with my ancestors before, but never to the Great Spirit. I felt honored to be invited to connect with Him.

My bridesmaids surrounded me like they were security detail as we made our way outside. A carriage led by a blue alicorn waited just outside the door, and we all piled in, along with our Familiars. It was bigger than the carriages I was used to— almost the size of a bus. We fit easily, except for Aisha, who had to follow along outside. The carriage led us through town and into the woods, until we came to a stop at the river.

As I stepped out of the carriage behind my sister, I saw that the area she'd picked was very secluded. It was beautiful, too. Ivy grew up the side of trees, and butterflies danced above the water. The river was wide, but the pool below us was calm. Esis oohed at the flowers as he scurried out of the carriage.

Amelia held her hand out to me. I took it, but instead of leading me forward, she pulled me into a hug. "I'm so happy for you, Sophia. Are you ready?"

I'd never been more ready for anything in my life. "Yes."

I tugged on the string of my robe, and the fabric fell away. Luana took the robe and hung it on a nearby tree branch. I stood stark naked in the middle of the woods in front of eight different women and their Familiars, but I wasn't nervous.

*I was ready.*

Amelia helped me down the bank. Her thin white dress touched the water and got soaked, but she kept going. Once I was waist-deep in the water, the other women stepped in behind me. They left their Familiars on shore, but entered the water in their white dresses.

"Lie back in the water, Sophia," Amelia said.

I did as I was told, and I found myself floating there effortlessly. I assumed my mother was using her Toaqua powers to keep me afloat, because I felt light as a feather. I took a couple of deep breaths, enjoying the sounds of the birds above my head and the sun on my toes. My muscles relaxed and seemed to melt into the water.

My mom ran her soft hands ran through my hair, fanning it out through the water. I felt her put something on my head, and the sweet scent of vanilla hit my nose.

"Sophia," she said softly. "Today, you are a bride— not just for Liam, but for the Great Spirit."

She worked the shampoo through the ends of my hair. "The Great Spirit has blessed us with this water. As you wash yourself in it this morning, you will shed your past and become one with the Great Spirit."

I took another deep breath and relaxed even more. I couldn't explain it, but when she spoke of the Great Spirit, I swore I could feel Him here with us. His energy permeated deep into my heart, and I felt my worry melting away.

"You remember the story of the Great Spirit, yes?" Mom asked.

I thought back to the lesson Professor Lopez had given when I accompanied Liam to his Hawkei Legends class in my second semester. "The Great Spirit wanted to create life, so he split himself into four parts," I recalled. "Earth, Water, Fire, and Air."

"Yes," she confirmed. "And then each of *those* spirits created gods and goddesses from themselves. All were born from the Great Spirit. Sophia, today I call upon the Whale Spirit to bless you with courage. May you hold to courage even in times when it feels impossible. May you be courageous as a wife, a mother, and a leader."

A lump rose in my throat, but it was only brief. I swallowed it down, and peace washed over me. I felt at ease as the energy of the blessing touched every inch of my body.

Though my eyes were closed, I felt myself rotating through the water. It was ever so slightly that I barely moved a foot. My mother's hands left my hair, and I felt Haloke's hands on me next. She worked the shampoo into my scalp.

"I bless you with the power of Deer Spirit, Sophia," she said. "May you always be gentle with your family, your community... and your enemies."

"I will," I whispered as I spun through the water again.

Another set of hands landed on my head, and Amelia spoke from above me. "I bless you with the power of Lion Spirit, the god of strength. Remember your strength in whatever you do, Sophia, because it is never far away."

Imogen was next. She began massaging the shampoo into my hair, and I could hear her sobbing from above me. Her voice cracked when she spoke. "I call upon the Elephant Spirit, the goddess of creativity. May you go through life creatively. Dance, sing, and *enjoy* yourself."

Tears began to well in my eyes as I continued to move through the water to my next bridesmaid. I felt Luana's gentle hands touch my hair, and I opened my eyes to see her signing above me.

*I bless you with the Sloth Spirit. Be patient, Sophia. With others and yourself.*

I nodded to her and signed back. *I will.*

Lindsey washed my hair next and spoke gently as she swept the ends of my hair through the water. "I choose the Dolphin Spirit. May you be blessed with youthfulness— not just in your health and body, but in your mind. Stay playful. Connect with your inner child. Remember that you are young and free— no matter your age."

Each blessing they bestowed upon me was like another weight lifted off my body. By this time, I felt like I weighed a mere two pounds.

"I bless you with Eagle Spirit," Miranda said as she began washing my hair next. "May you have virtue, Sophia, and be willing to fly above whatever ails you."

Vanessa cleared her throat and started washing me. "I call upon the Salmon Spirit, the god of abundance— to bless you with a bountiful life, in the emotional and physical realms."

Tears began to fall down the side of my face and into the water. They weren't the heavy kind, though. They were happy and light. There was just too much emotion flooding through me now that I couldn't keep it all in. I felt each and every one of their blessings touch me like a warm blanket. I'd never been so connected to the Great Spirit than I had been in that moment.

I rotated through the water one last time, until my mom's hands landed on me again. She rinsed the shampoo out of my hair while she spoke. "The Great Spirit has blessed you, Sophia. You are now connected to Him, and Him to you. Hold these blessings in your heart, Sophia, for they will always be with you."

A final tear streaked down my cheek and landed in the water.

"*Akotee et veni*," I whispered. *Let it come.*

"*Akotee et veni*," my bridal party replied in unison.

I opened my eyes, and the force holding me up in the water fell away. My body sank, and I placed my feet on the bottom of the riverbed and stood. When I walked out of the water, I felt like a different person. I was weightless, I was bright.

*I was Kyra Koignichi.*

Imogen's eyes glistened as she handed me my robe. "Well, Sophia. Are you ready to get married?"

"Absolutely," I said, beaming.

Imogen smiled back. "Then let's make you the most beautiful bride the Hawkei have ever seen."

❧

Something must've happened between the time we left the river and the time we made it back to Amelia's cottage, because that was the moment shit started to hit the fan. Whatever blessings I'd received this morning apparently weren't in place until *after* the wedding, because whatever could go wrong *did* go wrong.

It started with the rain. Down at the river, it was beautiful and sunny, but by the time we made it back, dark clouds had rolled in. It was only starting to sprinkle when we got out of the carriage, but within five minutes, it was a full-on downpour outside.

"We can't have a wedding in the rain!" I cried as I stared out the window. The rain was so thick I could hardly see to the next cottage over. Rainwater ran down the street like little rivers. "Can the Toaqua do something about the weather?"

"Calm down, Sophia," Haloke insisted. She grabbed me by the shoulders and guided me over to a kitchen chair. "I'm sure it won't rain all day. Let's just wait it out, then we can decide what to do."

"*Technically,* you're not allowed to manipulate the weather," Imogen pointed out. "But I'm sure the Toaqua chief will make an exception for you."

She winked at me, then held up a makeup brush. "Close your eyes."

I sat there patiently while Imogen worked on my makeup, but my hands knotted in my lap anxiously. I tried not to focus on the sound of rain hitting the roof, but I couldn't help it. I really hoped the rain let up soon.

"There," Imogen said after a good twenty minutes. "You look ah-mazing."

She set her makeup brushes aside and held up a mirror. My eyes were so bright and big, and my lips were pink and plump. I looked like a super-model or something.

"Thanks, Im," I said. "I love it."

"Now it's my turn!" Miranda sang. She came over carrying a bag full of hairbrushes, clips, and hot tools.

"I'm sorry to duck out, but Jonah and I have some decorating to do," Imogen announced.

My jaw dropped. "But what about the rain?"

Imogen patted me on the shoulder. "You let your wedding planners take care of that. I'll be back soon."

"Okay," I said nervously. I didn't know how Jonah and Imogen were going to stop the rain, considering they weren't Toaqua, but I trusted them to come up with *something*... hopefully. Maybe the Storm Lord had something in mind.

Amelia noticed me shifting in my chair. "Don't worry about it, Sophia. You're the bride. You're not allowed to worry today."

"I just want to get married," I admitted as Miranda started brushing out my hair.

"And you will," Amelia promised. "No matter what happens."

It was easy for her to say, because we didn't know what the day had in store for us at the time.

As Miranda was finishing the last of the curls in my hair, the front door banged open. We all whirled around to see Jonah and Imogen stumbling inside. They were both soaked head to toe, and were dripping rainwater all over Amelia's rug. Squeaks and Sassy followed. Squeaks shook out her feathers and water went everywhere, sticking to the walls and ceiling.

Jonah clutched his palm with his other hand and sucked in a sharp breath. All the color had drained from his face.

My stomach plummeted to my toes. "Ancestors, what happened!?"

"Esis!" Jonah squeaked. "We need Esis."

I shot out of my chair. Luana and Esis both rushed over to Jonah. Luana reached for his hand, and he let her take it. As he pulled the pressure off his palm, blood started to drip everywhere.

Amelia gasped and ran toward the bathroom to get towels. Haloke rushed over and helped clean up the blood with her powers, then gathered all the other water on the floor and pushed it out the door.

"Imogen, what happened?" I demanded again. My heart pounded with worry.

Imogen turned to me and frowned. "You're not going to like it."

Jonah breathed a sigh of relief as Luana used her healing powers on him. "Much better. Can someone get me a coffee or something?"

He stepped forward and plopped onto the couch, almost squishing Lindsey and Medusa.

I placed my hand on my hip and tapped my toe. "How long are you going to keep us waiting?"

Imogen bit her lower lip. "Well, see... the venue... it's— it's flooded."

My heart dropped. "*What?!*" I squealed.

"Jonah climbed some rocks to see if we could hold the ceremony on higher ground, but... he slipped," Imogen admitted.

I whirled toward Jonah, fuming. "Why didn't you *fly?* You remember you can fly, right?"

Jonah gave me a sour look. "The rocks didn't look too high. I didn't know they'd jump out and try to *impale* me."

I sighed. "I'm glad you're okay but... did you guys figure anything out for the venue?"

"Well... we didn't get very far," Jonah said.

Vanessa hurried to my side and grabbed my shoulders. "Everything's fine. Jonah's healed, and they'll figure out the venue. What you need right now is a massage."

"A massage?" I balked. "We don't have a wedding venue! I'm supposed to be getting married in a few hours! I need to figure this out."

"No, you don't," my mother cut in. "We'll get it figured out, Sophia. You don't have to worry about a thing."

Vanessa dragged me into the bedroom. She cocked her head at the Familiars, and the smaller ones came rushing behind us to help.

"I was nervous on my wedding day, too, but you have to just relax," Vanessa said reassuringly as she waited at the door for the Familiars to filter inside.

Right before she shut the door, I heard Imogen whisper lowly to my mother. "Don't mention the missing rings to Sophia."

My heart stopped. I didn't hear her right, did I?

I grabbed for the door as Vanessa was swinging it closed, then stepped out into the main room. "*Missing rings?* The rings are missing!?"

Imogen grimaced, like she'd made a horrible mistake in letting me overhear.

"Eh... they're not... *lost*, per se," Jonah said. "Just... a little misplaced."

"*A little misplaced!?*" I shouted. How could this be happening? My blood was starting to boil. "This has to be some sort of bad omen."

"No, just a bad case of forgetfulness on Ezra's part," Jonah said. "He'll find them."

My head was starting to hurt. I pressed my fingers to my temples. "Is there anything else I should know?"

Imogen and Jonah exchanged a look, but neither of them spoke. The whole room had gone silent.

Jonah dropped his head. "Well, I got a call from the DJ this morning. He's sick and can't make it."

"Ancestors. Someone tell me the cake is okay," I insisted.

Imogen sucked a breath through her teeth. "The cake is fine, as far as we know. But the caterer…"

"Great Spirit," I breathed. "What happened with the food?"

Imogen frowned. "Well, a fight broke out between two Familiars at the restaurant this morning. All the appetizers they prepared last night are ruined," Imogen admitted.

My jaw dropped, and my eyes watered. I didn't know how much more I could handle. I was starting to wonder if the ancestors wanted this wedding to happen at all.

Amelia's hands curled into fists. She stepped forward and exploded. "That's it! Sophia, we have this handled. *You're* getting your massage. Everything will be ready when you're done."

"But Am!" I cried. I had to do something to help.

"No buts!" She pointed to her bedroom. "You're the bride, and you're not going to deal with this crap today. Mom, Haloke, I need your magic. Miranda and Lindsey, we need a couple extra hands. And *you* two." She shot a pointed look at Imogen and Jonah. "We need your wedding planning expertise. Luana and Vanessa will stay here with the Familiars and Sophia."

She turned back to me. "Trust me, sis. We have *everything* handled."

I literally couldn't argue, because everyone started moving all at once following the instructions Amelia barked at them. For once, I was actually grateful for my sister's bossy attitude.

Vanessa dragged me back into the bedroom. "Lie down and relax," she demanded, pointing to the bed.

I groaned. "Is there really nothing I can do to help?"

"There is," Vanessa said. "You can chill out."

I basically didn't have a choice.

*Everything will be okay,* Luana signed to me.

I lay on my back on the bed, being careful not to tousle my hair. Vanessa, Luana, and the Familiars surrounded me. My bridesmaids each took one of my hands and started massaging them. Medusa rolled over my legs. Her soft basilisk scales felt good on my skin, and her weight was just the right pressure to massage my muscles. Esis stood by my head and rubbed my temples, while Sierra blew soft puffs of air into my face with her wings. Kiwi rolled the curve of his beak along my feet, and Sassy kneaded her paws on my shoulders, along with my mother's Familiar, Oliver.

I took a deep breath in through my nose and out through my mouth, then repeated it over and over. I was starting to relax, but my mind raced worrying about the wedding. Would everything get done in time? What if the ancestors didn't want us to get married today? Did *Liam* still want to get married today?

I was starting to drift off when I heard the sound of the front door. I startled. A bunch of voices spoke all at once that I couldn't hear what they were saying. Vanessa, Luana, and I exchanged a glance, then got out of the bed to see what was up. My bridal party was back, along with Jonah, but they looked flustered and uncertain. Mom and Haloke hadn't returned.

"Is everything taken care of?" I asked.

Imogen turned to me, biting her lip. A moment later, her eyes brightened. "All taken care of!"

I could tell she wasn't being entirely truthful.

My face paled. "What's wrong?"

"Nothing," Amelia insisted. "Everything is great. Let's get dressed."

I wished I could say I stayed relaxed, but I didn't. There was this energy in the air that told me things weren't quite as perfect as Amelia said they were.

By now, we didn't have a lot of time until the ceremony started. My bridesmaids rushed to do their hair and makeup, and Jonah stayed around to help. I remained on edge. Everyone insisted I calm down, so I didn't say anything.

"Time to get in our dresses!" Imogen sang. She reached into the closet and pulled out her bridesmaid dress. Everything was fine until—

*Riiiip.*

The sound of tearing fabric met my ears, and my heart dropped. I whirled around from where I was combing out Esis' fur. Imogen stood frozen solid, her eyes wide and her jaw practically on the floor.

I closed my eyes, certain I couldn't take one more thing going wrong today. "Please tell me that wasn't what I think it was."

"It'll be fine," Imogen said, but I heard the uncertainty in her tone.

"Ancestors," I sighed, sinking down onto the bed. Luana rushed over and rubbed her hands over my shoulders. It was supposed to be reassuring, but all it did was remind me of the weight this wedding was putting on me today. "If one more thing goes wrong, I swear..."

"It's fine," Imogen insisted. "All that matters is you're getting married today."

"Imogen's right," Amelia agreed. She hurried to Imogen's side and lifted the hem of her skirt. I couldn't see the damage from here, because Imogen was standing in front of the dress— obviously trying to hide it— but I *did* see Amelia's face. She looked utterly hopeless.

"Mom brought her sewing kit," Amelia said quickly. She grabbed the dress and leapt into action again. "Lindsey, Miranda. Help Sophia into her dress, will you?"

"Please don't tell me *that's* ruined, too," I said sourly. I wouldn't be surprised, considering how this day was going.

"No, no, it's perfect!" Miranda said as she pulled the dress out of the closet.

"Let's get our beautiful bride dressed," Lindsey said, grabbing my hand and helping me stand.

Putting on my wedding dress should've been one of the happiest parts of the day, but it just made me feel sick. Everything had gone wrong this morning. I feared what might happen at the ceremony. At least the dress fit, which I'd been uncertain of with my growing belly.

"How is everything in there?" Jonah asked through the door.

I huffed. "It's all wrong!"

Slowly, Jonah opened the door. His features brightened when he saw me in my dress. "Oh my gosh, Sophia! What are you talking about? It's perfect!"

"No, it's not!" I insisted. Tears pricked at my eyes. Though Esis gazed up at me in admiration, all I felt was a sinking in my gut. My bridesmaids surrounded me, except Imogen and Amelia, since they were trying to fix Imogen's dress in the living room. I felt like there were too many people around me— like I was suffocating.

"What's wrong with it?" Jonah asked, stepping into the room.

"I don't know," I admitted. It all felt like too much.

Luana signed to me. *You just need to add your veil and jewelry. Then it will be perfect.*

I frowned, uncertain. "Okay."

Miranda helped put the veil in my hair, and Vanessa handed over a beautiful silver and turquoise necklace. I took the Spirit Totem off and set it with the rest of my things, then put on the necklace.

"Now for the shoes," Lindsey announced, holding out a beautiful pair of white flats. "Sit down. You should feel like Cinderella today."

I sat on the bed. Lindsey lifted the hem of my dress and took my foot. She started to slip the shoe on. "A perfect fit—"

She cut off.

"Are you fucking *kidding* me?" I wailed.

Lindsey tried to force the shoe onto my foot, but it wouldn't slip over the end of my heel. Her eyebrows scrunched together as she tried again to force it on.

"It's not going to work!" I cried.

This was the last fucking straw. I lost it. Tears started to stream down my face. I was sure it was ruining my makeup, but screw that. It was like this wedding couldn't get any worse.

Jonah's face paled, and he knelt down to grab the shoe out of Lindsey's hand. "This can't be right. These shoes were *perfect* when we picked them out."

He tried shoving them onto my feet, but all it did was crush my toes. "These can't be the right ones."

"They are," I sobbed. "I have pregnancy feet!"

Jonah scrunched up his eyebrows. "Um... a little birds and the bees one-oh-one. Your feet can't get pregnant, Sophia."

"Not like that, dummy." Lindsey swatted Jonah on the shoulder. "She's saying she's retaining too much water."

Heavy sobs rocked my shoulders. Vanessa and Luana shared a worried look.

"This wedding's a disaster!" I cried. "Liam's not going to want to marry me once he sees my big fat feet walking down the aisle. Hell, the way this day is going, we'll be lucky if he even shows up."

"He's going to show up," Jonah promised. "He loves you more than anything."

"He won't care about your feet," Vanessa promised. "You can walk down the aisle barefoot."

"How?" I growled. "The aisle is probably underwater. If Jonah's hand weren't healed, he'd be trialing blood down the aisle instead of rose petals. Imogen's going to be walking in front of me with a dress that's in two pieces. There's no food. There's no music. Who wants to bet the officiant's late, too?"

"Sophia?" Imogen stepped into the doorway. Her face fell as she regarded me. "What's wrong?"

"*Everything!*" I cried, hot tears rolling down my face. "I just... I need— I need some space."

I sniffled uncontrollably. Lindsey, Miranda, and Vanessa backed off, but Luana continued rubbing my shoulders. Esis came closer and snuggled onto my lap for comfort. Jonah shot a look at Imogen, like he didn't know what to do.

Three of my bridesmaids left the room, but Imogen stepped inside and closed the door. I felt like I could breathe better now that there were only three people and my Familiar in the room with me.

"I'm sorry," I said, wiping my tears.

"You have nothing to be sorry for," Imogen said reassuringly. She sat beside me on the bed and took my hand in hers. "You have every right to feel frustrated. This morning has been a shit show."

Another sob rocked my chest. "I don't mean to be a bridezilla."

Jonah set the useless shoes aside and stood. He placed a hand on his hip. "Trust me, sweetheart. You are *far* from bridezilla territory."

"B-but my s-shoes d-don't fit!" I wailed.

"Your shoes don't *matter*." Jonah knelt at my side and stared up at me, forcing me to look back at him. "You listen to me, Sophia. Everything you're worried about... none of it matters. To hell with the venue. Who needs food and music at a reception anyway?"

"It wouldn't be a reception without it," I mumbled.

"Yes, it will," Jonah said firmly. He reached up and took my face in his hands. "Look at me, Sophia, my best friend and *precious* bride. There's only *one* thing that matters today, you hear me? You are marrying the love of your life."

"Well..." I muttered. "I can't get married without rings."

"Yes, you can," Jonah reminded me. "And you *will*. Forget about the rings. Forget about Imogen's dress. She's not the one getting married today. You are marrying Liam, the love of your life and the father of your baby. And you're doing it surrounded by all the people you love most in the world. In a few hours, you and Liam will be bonded for life."

"I guess, but—"

"No buts," Jonah cut me off, shaking his head. "You and Liam are getting married today. Tomorrow, you'll laugh about everything that happened today, because everything will pale in comparison to the moment you say *I do. That's* what you're going to remember from today. And from then on, all that matters is your relationship with Liam, and your little baby girl. That's what's important. The rest of this day can suck it."

Jonah's words completely touched my heart. His reasoning made all the terrible things fall away. "You're right," I whispered.

Luana stopped rubbing my shoulders and shifted on the bed to sit next to me. *You and Liam are going to have the most beautiful marriage,* she signed. *And that's more important than any wedding.*

I sniffled and wiped the tears from my eyes.

Imogen wrapped her arm around my shoulder. "I just know all the bad luck is over, Sophia. Just wait until Liam sees you walking down the aisle."

A final sob broke out of my chest. "Well, he can't see me like this. My makeup is ruined."

Imogen gave me a friendly smile. "Good thing your makeup artist has a touch-up kit."

I chuckled under my breath, mostly to break the tension. "Thank you, you guys."

"That's what we're here for, baby girl." Jonah stood and held out a hand. "Let's get you aisle-ready."

Imogen and Jonah teamed up to help touch-up my makeup, while Esis fluffed my veil and Luana straightened all my jewelry. Finally, the redness washed from my face and I felt like I could breathe again.

"Ready?" Jonah asked.

I nodded. "I'm ready."

Jonah opened the door, and Esis scurried out in front of him.

"Da da-da da!" Esis sang.

All eyes turned toward me as I stepped out of the bedroom. Several screams of delight hit my ears. Lindsey, Miranda, and Vanessa practically swooned. Amelia got all teary-eyed.

"Do I look okay?" I asked.

"*Of course* you do!" Amelia cried. She spread her arms out wide and walked over to me. "You're the most beautiful bride I've ever seen."

"Absolutely," Vanessa agreed.

Everyone else quickly joined in. Amelia hugged me tight.

I smiled nervously. "Well, let's hope everything went well on Liam's end."

Amelia drew away and took my hand. "Everything is going to be fine."

"You keep saying that," I pointed out.

She smiled proudly. "That's because it's true."

Jonah cut in when Amelia stepped away, and he drew me into a hug. "Squeaks and I have to go get dressed. You've got this."

He kissed me on the cheek, and I blushed. "Thanks, Jonah."

"Your royal highness, the Storm Lord," he corrected playfully.

I rolled my eyes at him and smiled. "How could I forget? You never miss a chance to remind me."

He chuckled. "I'll see you at the ceremony."

"Jonah's right," Imogen said as soon as he and Squeaks left. "This wedding is going to be fantastic."

Within minutes, Imogen had finished sewing her dress, and she got changed. I couldn't even tell it was ripped.

All the bridesmaids matched. Their dresses were light blue floor-length chiffon gowns with thin straps on the shoulders and ribbons around the waist. The Familiars dressed up, too. Esis wore a black bow tie around his neck, while Sassy wore a flower to match Imogen's bouquet. The others had on some sort of scarf, tie, or flower around their neck to celebrate the occasion.

It was still raining outside, but Amelia used her Toaqua powers to push aside the rain so we wouldn't get wet when we piled back into the carriage.

My hands shook in my lap, but Esis brushed his tail across the back of my hands to soothe me. I closed my eyes, trying to stay calm, and didn't open them until the carriage came to a stop. I let out a shaky breath.

"Are you going to be okay?" Amelia asked.

I nodded. "I'll be fine. Can everyone just give me a minute?"

"Sure," she said.

My bridal party climbed out of the carriage, but I stayed inside with Esis. In the stillness of the carriage, I placed my hand on my stomach.

"It's going to be okay, little Ava-Marie," I whispered. "Your daddy and I are getting married today, and nothing— not rain, not rings, not music— nothing can stop that. We love each other so much, and we are so excited to share that love with you. This day isn't just for us. It's for you, too. Today, we become a family."

A single tear streaked my face, but it wasn't because I was scared anymore. I was overcome with joy that in just a few moments, Liam and I would start on a beautiful new chapter of our lives. I couldn't wait to see where it took us.

I opened my eyes, and my breath became steady. Esis sat on the seat next to me and stared up with big, hopeful eyes.

I nodded to him. "It's time, buddy."

My heart pounded in exhilaration as I exited the carriage. The first thing I noticed was that the rain had let up. A smile touched the corners of my mouth.

The bridesmaids and groomsmen crowded beside a tall rock structure, with trees all around it. It was the same rock Liam had placed his handprint on during his chief ceremony. We couldn't see the ceremony from here, but I knew it was just around the corner. Everyone stopped talking and mingling when I stepped out of the carriage. My mom and Haloke had arrived and joined them. They all looked at me with the same soft expression.

"Is something wrong?" I asked.

Ezra stepped up and offered a hand. My bare feet hit soft, moist ground.

"Everything's perfect." Ezra patted his breast pocket, as if to tell me the rings were safe inside. "You look beautiful, my soon-to-be sister-in-law."

I smiled, then turned to Imogen, Jonah, and Amelia. "Thanks for taking care of everything."

"What do you think sisters are for?" Amelia asked.

Before I could answer, Imogen stepped in. "Everything's right on schedule, Sophia. In a few minutes, the Familiars will take their seats. Then the ushers will seat the parents. After that, Christian and Katie will walk down the aisle and smudge the area. Then it's just like we practiced, okay?"

I nodded and looked around. "Where's my dad?"

"Right here!" He came walking around the side of the rock formation. "Sorry, just a few last minute decorations to take care of. We're all set."

"We are?" I asked, hope surging in my chest.

Dad's eyes softened as he looked at me. "Oh, Sophia. My sweet baby girl."

Dad reached out and hugged me. There seemed to be a lot of hugs going around today.

After a few moments, he drew away, and I noticed the tears dotting his eyes. "You look... You're..."

He sighed, before finding his voice again. "I'm honored you asked me to walk you down the aisle. Liam's truly a lucky man."

"Thank you, Daddy," I said, trying not to cry. "I wouldn't have asked anyone else to give me away. I love you."

Dad wiped his eyes and chuckled under his breath. "Who turned on the water works?"

Jonah stepped forward and placed a hand on my father's shoulder. "Mister Henley? It sounds like it's time."

My heart fluttered. I turned my attention to the ceremony. I heard the sounds of drums, whistles, and flutes playing. The Familiars were already walking off to take a seat— except for Baby and Esis. Baby wore a bag around his neck filled with white flower petals, and Esis held a small white pillow. Ezra tied the rings to it. My mom and Haloke were both arm-in-arm with one of the ushers. They waved as they were guided around the side of the rock formation.

My heart pounded. "Wow. I can't believe it's really here."

"You still want to do this, right?" Dad asked while Imogen lined up the wedding party.

I nodded to him. "Absolutely."

"Good," he said. "Because I can't imagine handing you off to anyone but our chief. Liam's a fine man, Sophia."

"I know, Daddy." I chuckled. "That's why I'm marrying him."

"Sophia," Imogen said, holding out my bouquet. "It's time."

I got all jittery as I took the bouquet from her and lined up behind her and Jonah. I barely had a chance to take a breath before Esis started forward. I wanted to smile and cry all at the same time. I couldn't decide which one, so I just did both.

Vanessa and Bren stepped forward next, followed by Miranda and Jake, Lindsey and Wyatt, Luana and Cade, and Amelia and Ezra. Finally, my Maid of Honor and Liam's Best Man were up.

Jonah turned around to wink at me. "You've got this, boo."

The moment Imogen and Jonah stepped around the side of the rocks, my heart started to pound so hard my legs shook beneath me. Dad noticed my arm shaking in his, and he placed a gentle hand on mine.

"It's going to be okay, Sophia," he whispered.

I mostly believed him, but part of me worried that I was going to step into the ceremony and everything was going to go wrong— like Liam wouldn't be there, or he'd take one look at me and go running. What if he wasn't at the altar? Ancestors, I was going to faint.

"To be honest, Dad, this wedding is scaring the shit out of me," I replied.

Dad squeezed my hand. "I was scared when I married your mother, too."

"So it's normal?" I asked.

He nodded. "It's your ancestors speaking through you. They're asking you to prove yourself. They're saying if you go through with this, even though you're afraid, you and Liam can get through anything."

"Okay," I said breathlessly. "Then let's do it."

I forced my legs to move under me, and we stepped out from around the rocks. The ceremony came into view, and I was nearly knocked off my feet.

It was everything I dreamed and more.

Rows of white chairs had been set up in a clearing next to the river— the same clearing where Liam had been named chief. A huge cliff face rose on the other side of the river, and vibrant green trees surrounded us on all sides. There were no physical decorations, but I couldn't have asked for anything better. Elementai from every house had come together to create the most beautiful scene I'd ever seen. Beautiful green vines had grown out of the forest floor and lined the aisle. Beads of water had been strung into formations that looked like ribbon. Toaqua somewhere in the crowd must've been controlling it, because it hovered in the air and connected one row of chairs to the next. Above our heads, Yapluma used their power to keep tea light candles floating in the air. Between them, raindrops hovered. Each raindrop spun so that they reflected the candle-light at different angles, making it look like diamonds sparkling above us.

The cry of a bird came from above. I looked skyward to see Squeaks flying overhead. Sassy was on her back, tossing rose petals down on us. They fluttered down to the ground gently, and I smiled in delight.

My eyes returned to the ceremony. My attention was completely stolen by the archway at the end of the aisle. One side was made with swirling water, and the other was a calm fire. The two elements met in the middle and swirled together effortlessly. I don't know how the Toaqua and Koigni controlling it had managed, but it was perfect— as if Fire and Water weren't as different as they seemed. They *did* mix, just as Liam and I did.

Finally, my eyes fell upon the most beautiful, amazing thing in the forest. *Liam.*

He stood in front of the archway in a black tux, his hands crossed in front of him. Julian was at his side, but I barely noticed the dragon. All I saw was the incredible, heart-warming face of my future husband staring back at me. When our eyes met, my heart swelled beyond anything I'd ever felt before. That soft, gentle look he gave me was everything. I felt every ounce of his emotions flowing across the space between us and settling deep into my heart. In just that one look, I heard everything he wanted to say.

*I love you, pawee.*

But it was more than that— so much more. These weren't empty words, or something said to make me feel better. The words weren't even said at all, and yet I could feel them the way I felt the air on my skin and the humidity in the air.

Liam Mitoh loved me, and he was aching to pledge himself to me— and I him.

At that moment, the clouds parted, and sunlight broke through. The beautiful golden light streamed through the forest and landed on my magnificent groom, highlighting him for all the world to see. It was like the ancestors themselves were reaching out to touch him.

I was sure the guests stood as I walked down the aisle, but I didn't notice. All I saw was Liam. For all I knew, we could've been the only two people in the world right then. He was my light, and I would walk down this aisle for eternity just to reach him.

All my anxiety from earlier washed away as a sense of peace touched me so strong it sent tears rolling down my cheeks. In that moment, there was no Earth, Water, Fire, or Air. There was only Liam— and he was all I needed to survive in the world.

I felt like I was floating down the aisle. I barely noticed I was walking. But somehow, I reached Liam.

"Take care of her," Dad whispered, before handing me off to Liam.

My shoulder shook as Liam offered me his elbow, but it was for all the right reasons. I looped my arm through his, and he reached up and wiped his thumb across my cheek. That soft, caring look never left his eyes.

"Why are you crying, *pawee?*" he asked gently. "Pregnancy hormones?"

I shook my head, and my voice cracked. "No. I just can't keep in how much I love you."

Tears welled in his eyes. "I love you, too, *pawee.* Let's get married."

Liam turned back to Julian, who stood in front of the archway. For the first time, I noticed a narrow table in front of him with a tall candle on top. Liam led me in front of it and took my hands as we faced each other. The forest went completely still, except for the sound of water flowing behind us.

Julian bowed his head and blew a puff of fire from his nostrils. The flames caught the wick of the candle. As soon as it was lit, the dragon stepped aside, and Baine came forward. Traditionally, the chief of your tribe officiated wedding ceremonies, but since this *was* the chief's wedding, we'd asked Elder Baine to officiate. I couldn't think of anyone better to marry us than our mentor.

Baine raised his hands to the crowd. "You may be seated."

An eagle cried from above us, and I looked upward. At first I thought it was Squeaks again, but her cry was louder. Instead of a hippogriff, it was a bald eagle.

I looked back to Liam, who was beaming. "I've heard eagles are a sign of luck."

Liam nodded. "They are, but it's more than that. It's a sign that my grandpa made it to our ceremony."

I squeezed his hands. "I hope all our grandparents made it."

"They wouldn't miss it for the world," Liam whispered. "Our ancestors are with us today."

Baine cleared his throat, and Liam and I went silent. "We are gathered here to honor the love and connection between two of our very own. Today, we break boundaries that have been in place for generations. In Hawkei tradition, one must marry within their own House to preserve their bloodline."

Liam leaned in and whispered to me. "Remind me again why we let Baine officiate."

I snickered under my breath. "At least he's not giving us sex advice again."

Liam winked at me. "Yet."

Baine continued, like he didn't notice our side conversation. "Today, Liam and Sophia prove that the lines we have drawn in the sand are of our own making— that we have the power to erase those lines. Today marks the beginning of a new era. No longer will we divide ourselves between Toaqua, Koigni, Nivita, Yapluma, and Anichi. With the union of these two great souls— who society has deemed opposites— Fire and Water will become one. We are one Hawkei. And with their deep love for one another, Liam and Sophia have paved the way for us to reclaim that title."

Tears welled in my eyes again. I half expected Baine's speech to be comical, but it wasn't. It made me realize that Liam and I had a larger purpose together— and that made me love him even more.

"To our chief of Toaqua," Baine said, nodding to Liam. "And our chosen one from Koigni." He nodded to me. "May the Great Spirit bless you and your future— and may no element separate you."

I beamed at Liam. *Nothing* could separate us. Not now. Not ever.

"Come forth and wash your hands," Baine said, gesturing us through the archway and toward the water. "Shed your past evils and your past loves."

Liam took my hand and led me forward. We stopped just past the archway, at the bank of the river. Liam flicked his wrist, and water spouted up from the river, allowing me to reach out and stick my hands into it instead of kneeling in the dirt.

Liam kept his voice low as he spoke for only me to hear. "This is our new start, *pawee*. Our past doesn't define us anymore. Not after today."

"Agreed," I said, feeling it deep within my bones.

Liam reached for my hands. As we clasped them together, he made water swirl around them, giving our hands one final wash.

Baine waited patiently until we finished. "Now for the Blue Paint Ceremony."

We stepped through the archway again and returned in front of Baine. He held out a ceramic bowl with blue paint inside.

"Blue is the traditional Hawkei paint color for weddings," Baine explained, loud enough for the guests to hear. "As you paint each other's hands, you are motioning to the Great Spirit your promise. In this, you vow that you devote your souls to one another. Even in the case of death or divorce, you will always be joined in the eyes of the Great Spirit, forever."

Baine lowered the bowl. "Do you, Liam Mitoh, pledge yourself to Sophia Henley, to have and to hold, in sickness and in health, for now and all eternity?"

Liam couldn't take his eyes off me. Even when he dipped his fingers into the paint and began to paint the backs of my hands with blue hearts, he didn't look away from me.

"I do," he stated. My heart fluttered so fiercely I thought it might burst.

"And do you, Sophia Henley, pledge yourself to Liam Mitoh, to have and to hold, in sickness and in health, for now and all eternity?"

I pressed my thumb into the blue paint and wiped it across the back of Liam's hands. My heart pitter pattered in my chest. "I do."

Baine set the paint aside and picked up an ancient-looking Hawkei vase. "May the tea of the ancestors bless you."

He held it out to us, and Liam took it first. As each of us took a sip from the vase, Baine raised his voice and explained the ritual to the guests. "In this traditional Toaqua wedding ceremony, it is said that if a couple drinks their tea without spilling, they will live a long and happy marriage."

I finished my sip and held the vase back to Liam, smiling. "Well, no one spilled. That's good news."

He beamed, like he couldn't contain his happiness. "There's no other option for us than a happy, healthy marriage."

"And now," Baine said. "The couple has elected to exchange their vows in a traditional Koigni fashion. If you will take your candle and light your fire."

Liam and I both reached for the candle Julian had lit, and Baine stepped aside. Next to us lay a pile of dry sticks. Together, we carried over our candle and lowered it to the kindling. The fire lit, and we handed off the candle to Imogen. Liam rounded the fire, and he held his hands over top of it toward me. I took his hands in mine, and we each crossed one foot over the other like we'd practiced at the rehearsal. We rotated counter-clockwise as Liam began his vows. He never once took his eyes off me when he spoke.

"*Pawee*, I vow to protect you from the rain. There's no storm that can come our way that we can't weather as one."

As Liam finished, we switched directions and began in a clockwise rotation around the fire.

"Liam," I said softly, my heart swelling as I stared into his eyes. "I vow to defend you from the Fire. No inferno can burn away our love."

We switched direction again. Liam's hands shook in mine. "The strength of the ocean flows through me, and I vow to share that with you every day from this moment on."

Tears welled in my eyes. I started to choke up, but I pushed past it. "The flames that burn within me are no longer mine, but ours to share."

Liam blinked his tears away. "I will calm any waves that threaten you, and comfort you in times of need."

Each time one of us spoke, we switched direction. The fire beneath us kept us warm, bringing us even closer together.

"I will keep you warm during the darkest nights and become a safe haven for your heart," I promised.

Liam smiled. "I will honor you like the river honors the sea."

"I will respect you with the gentle care it takes to sustain a flame."

Liam let out a wavering breath. "I will be loyal to you above all others, as the tide is loyal to the moon."

I couldn't stop the flood of tears rolling down my face. "I'm devoted to you, as my spirit is devoted to the ancestors. I love you, Liam."

"And I love you, Sophia," he said softly.

Liam stepped around the fire and pulled me into his arms. Neither of us could stop crying tears of joy.

"Now for the rings," Baine announced.

Esis scurried forward and held the pillow in his hands as high into the air as he could. He nearly toppled over with how bulky it was. It was bigger than him.

"Thanks, buddy." Liam wiped his eyes and bent to untie the rings. He took them in his hands and handed me his.

After a moment of hesitation, we both looked to Baine, and he nodded.

Liam took my hand and positioned my ring over my left ring finger. "Let this ring always remind you— Fire and Water mix *perfectly*."

My tears flowed faster as he slid the ring onto my finger. I choked back a sob as I took his left hand.

"I love you to the Ancestral Lands and back, Liam," I told him. "When you look at this ring, remember that it has no beginning and no end. That's my love for you."

I slipped the ring on his hand.

"You may now kiss the—"

Baine didn't get a chance to finish. Liam already wrapped his hand around my waist and dragged me forward. His lips swooped down to mine, and he kissed me so passionately that it felt as if the world had dropped beneath my feet.

And then... it did.

Liam spun me around as he kissed me. The whole crowd cheered, and my heart sang with joy.

I laughed as he spun me around. He beamed back at me as he set me down. "How does it feel to be my wife?"

"Same way it feels to be my husband," I replied playfully. "There are *no* words."

Baine came forward holding out a blanket— *my* blanket, I quickly realized. It was the one Liam had made for me, that Haloke had saved from Kinpago.

I shot Liam a glance. "What's this? We didn't go over it at the rehearsal."

He took my hand and smiled. "I wanted it to be a surprise. It's tradition."

Baine draped the blanket across mine and Liam's shoulders, wrapping it around the two of us.

Liam leaned over and whispered to me. "The blanket honors us and symbolizes our new life together."

I beamed. "I love it."

"Face the crowd," Baine whispered.

Liam and I turned to our guests, who were cheering gleefully. I couldn't stop smiling— until something deep within the forest caught my eye.

For a moment, I swore I saw a flash of red hair and the soft blonde coat of a lioness. But I must've been seeing things, because that only meant one thing— Madame Doya and Naomi had come to see my wedding.

My heart rate spiked for a moment before I reminded myself it was impossible. Doya didn't even know where to find *Hok'evale*. I must've been seeing things.

I had to be.

Baine's voice distracted me.

"I now present to you, Mister and Mrs. Mitoh!"

SEVENTEEN

The wedding procession was loud as we left the riverside and began the walk down the winding dirt path to the reception. The drums and flutes increased in intensity as Hawkei danced ahead of us with their Familiars, creating a loud wedding procession. I kept Sophia tucked closely to my side as the whoops and cheers rang out.

Sophia seemed a little troubled. Her eyebrows were knitted together, like she was thinking.

I nudged her. "What's up?"

"It's nothing. I just thought..." She shook her head and said, "I'm sure I'm imagining things."

"It does feel like a dream, doesn't it?" I asked. "You and I, married."

A soft smile graced her lips. "Yes. I can't believe that I'm your wife. We're finally starting our family."

She put a hand on her stomach and laughed. "Though it was like hell trying to get down that aisle, let me tell you."

"Jonah told me you were acting *very pregnant*," I said with a laugh. "Can't blame you. Everything went to shit at the wrong moment."

"It all worked out for the best. How did you spend your morning?"

"Yelling at Ezra about losing the rings," I said. "Then we tried to get the flood water out of the venue, but it wasn't going to work. We eventually found the rings just in time. Stevie had them, because she knew Ezra would misplace them."

The guests began filing into a clearing up ahead. Before the party got

403

started, I pulled Sophia aside into the trees, so we could have a private moment. Esis followed after us. "I have something to give you."

She giggled. "Always with the gifts."

"The first of many in the rest of our lives." I pulled a small jewelry box out of my pocket. "I want you to have this."

As I opened the box, Sophia gasped. Lying on the velvet was a copper key, outlined with green patina from age. The key's handle was shaped into a heart formation, a crown sitting in the center of it. It was as long as Sophia's forefinger, and suspended on a gold chain. Her eyes grew wide as her fingers caressed the key.

"I saw it at the bottom of the waterfall a long time ago. It was glowing, like it was some sort of magic," I said. "Remember when I proposed? When I dropped the ring in the pool, my magic grabbed this first. Imogen made it into a necklace for you. I'd thought it would be a perfect gift, since it came from the waterfall and that's our special place."

"Liam, it's perfect." Her eyes sparkled in that special way of hers as she observed the key. Sophia took off the silver and turquoise necklace and gave it to Esis. I looped the key around her neck and fastened the chain. It looked beautiful around her neck.

"Consider it the key to my heart." I took her hands in mine and squeezed them. "You'll have it always."

"Hey, where's the bride and groom?" Ezra's voice broke through the trees. "Can't start without 'em!"

"You would if you could," I grumbled as I took Sophia's hand and we left the trees. Esis handed the silver necklace off to Imogen as we came back onto the forest path.

Ezra wiggled his eyebrows. "Couldn't wait until the honeymoon?"

"Shut up, asshole. That wasn't what we were doing." I shoved him, and he snickered.

"I've got to hurry up and announce ya. Since the DJ is out, I'm subbing," he said. "Prepare for this reception to get filthy."

"Great." I could only imagine the kind of music he was going to play.

As we waited at the clearing's entrance, Ezra began announced the bridesmaids and groomsmen one by one, until it was our turn.

"And now, the moment you've all been waiting for! Please welcome the brand new Mister and Mrs. Mitoh!"

As Sophia and I entered into the clearing to a state of applause, my mouth dropped open. The clearing was surrounded by redwood trees. Yellow stringed lights hung in a crisscross fashion over the area. Wooden tables and benches carved straight from the trunks of trees gathered in an open square around the dance floor, which was made of hardwood. White wildflowers and candles were strewn out along the tables and in various places on the ground. Fortune Fairies hovered in the air, and a wall of ivy had been set up behind the bridal table at the head of the clearing. The bridal clearing had a twisted arch of roots over the groom and bride seats, and a three tiered white wedding cake perched on its own wooden stand at the corner of the reception. White Anichi birds with long tail feathers and shimmering wings perched in the trees and sang to provide music for the dinner. Their voices sounded like a string quartet.

Jonah and Imogen had really outdone themselves. This looked fantastic.

As we drew to the bridal table, Jonah did a twirling maneuver. "I present to you, your wedding, styled by the fashionable Mister Chanee and Miss Ahnild. Keep in mind we did all this in the span of, oh, say, a few hours. We refuse to accept payment; however, we'd be more than happy if you gave a tip."

Imogen stepped on his foot, and Jonah yelped. Sophia appeared delighted. She spun on the spot in wonder, trying to take it all in.

"You did an amazing job, you guys. You should think about doing this for real," I said.

"We'll be too busy planning Jonah's wedding next," Imogen teased. Jonah went pink before fluttering his eyelashes.

"Is there food?" Sophia asked anxiously.

"While you were finishing up getting ready, Haloke and your mom cooked like mad," Imogen said. "They got the main dishes done in time. It was nuts."

"But smells amazing." We sat down at the bridal table and were immediately served salmon, venison stew, corn, frybread, and squash. Esis started packing food into his chubby cheeks, while Julian groaned to save some for him. I cut into a bit of salmon with my fork and held it up to Sophia.

She lifted a curious eyebrow as she noticed everyone was looking at us. "Am I supposed to do something?"

"It's Hawkei tradition for a groom to feed his bride," I said. "It signifies he'll be a good provider."

"Oh." She leaned forward and took a bite.

Once Sophia swallowed, everyone else started eating. Friendly conversation permeated the area, though I noticed the Koigni had taken one side of the clearing and Toaqua the other, with our loved ones mostly in the middle.

I hoped everyone got along tonight. Today was supposed to be a day of peace.

When dinner was nearly finished, Jonah got up with a glass of champagne to make his speech. "As best man, I've known Liam for a very long time. Over fifteen years, as a matter of fact," he began. "And I can testify that he's never been very good at dating. Most women he just scared off. Turns out he just needed to find someone who's scarier than he is."

Laughter broke out amongst the guests, and Squeaks bobbed her head in agreement. Sophia smiled, and Jonah continued. "Sophia and Liam were obviously head-over-heels for each other right from the start, and though they tried to hide it, it was obvious to everyone who knew them. I personally couldn't be happier that my two best friends are hitched. Ancestors know they deserve it. They've taught us something about love I think we can all acknowledge— that no matter what stands against it, love will always persevere so long as two people are committed to weathering whatever storm that comes. And that's good, because if their kid is anything like either one of them, or ancestors forbid, like *both* of them, Great Spirit help us all."

The crowd laughed harder. Jonah turned toward Sophia and me. "Sophia, darling. Liam Baby. I love you both. Now keep making lots of cute babies."

*Awws* resonated around the clearing. Mom wiped a tear from her eye away at the end of Jonah's speech. He passed the microphone off to Imogen, and she slowly stood. She fidgeted on the spot.

"I tried for weeks to come up with words to express how I feel about you guys," Imogen said. "I came up flat, because words could never describe how I feel in my heart. So instead of talking about it, I thought I'd just show you."

Ezra and Wyatt carried a large trunk in front of the bridal table. They opened it, and Imogen reached in to hold up whatever was inside.

I became speechless. "My regalia."

My regalia had been ruined in the riots, but it'd been completely restored. New beads had been sewn along the parts that had been broken, and feathers that looked like they'd come from Squeaks replaced those that had been destroyed. The regalia was more elaborate than it'd ever been, though. The design on the back placed blue, grey and white beads in the formation of a powerful ocean, the moon shining over it while a black wolf waited on shore and a red dragon flew across the dark sky. The detailing on the regalia was so complicated, it looked like it had to be completed by a master. I hadn't thought my regalia was possible to repair, but Imogen had worked her magic.

"Your mother brought it when she fled Kinpago. I've been working on it since we arrived," Imogen said shyly. "I wanted your regalia to be worthy of a chief."

Sophia and Jonah looked similarly shocked. Neither of them knew about this. Tears rose in my eyes. "Im, you can't possibly realize what this means to me."

"I do, which is why I fixed it," she replied. "And I'd say you don't have to thank me, but screw that, because this thing was hell to work on."

Sophia laughed. Imogen looked at her and said, "It's time for your present, Sophia. It's not something physical, but something I hope you can cherish in your heart."

Cade came onto the dance floor, carrying an old acoustic guitar. Imogen faced us as Cade tuned the instrument.

"We wanted to give you guys something special before your first dance," Imogen said. "So Cade and I wrote a song that we think symbolizes your relationship. And we want to play it for you."

Holy shit. They'd written a song? How the hell had they managed to get along well enough to do this for us?

Cade started playing a smooth beat, and Imogen began to sing. All of her words were in Hawkei, and her voice swelled around the clearing as everyone looked on in awe at her voice. I'd rarely heard Imogen sing, but it appeared to be one of her many talents, as her powerful voice swelled over the clearing and made the Familiars hum along.

*We began like the start of a story*
*A fairy tale just meant to be*
*In a world without happy endings.*

*We didn't want to be in love*
*But love takes what it wants*
*And I knew all I wanted was you.*
*The world thinks we've gone insane*
*But if I'm insane, it's because of you.*

*The world tried to drive us apart*
*But it cannot keep us apart*

*I will always come back to you.*

*So stay with me, cherished one*
*I will bring you back to me*
*I will take care of you, cherished one*
*And I will keep you safe.*

*Stay with me, cherished one*
*Let our story continue forever*
*I love you, cherished one,*
*And I will always be beside you.*

Sophia didn't know what had been said, but with music, you didn't have to understand. You just had to feel. She knew the meaning even though she didn't know much Hawkei. She curled inward on my lap and looked at me while Imogen sang, as if I was the only thing she'd ever wanted in life and more.

As Imogen finished the song, thunderous applause broke out from the guests. She blushed and took Cade's hand to do a curtsy.

Imogen had really gone all-out with this wedding. It really showed how much she cared about us.

Cade's eyes had never left her the entire song. By the way he was looking at her now, I knew he felt the same way about her as I did about Sophia.

Imogen deserved to be as happy as Sophia and I were. I prayed to the ancestors she'd be brave enough to open up and give Cade another chance.

Jonah was furious. His hips swaggered as he stomped up to Imogen, poking her in the chest. "You. Bitch." He put a sassy hand on his hip. "Why didn't you *tell* me you could sing like that!? I'd have put you in the cabaret as more than a dancer!"

Imogen shook her head. "I'd rather do the costumes. Besides, Miranda's doing most of the songs, and she never gets a chance to be in the spotlight."

Jonah threw his head back and rolled his eyes in an extra-dramatic way. "Okay, I get it. I'm not mad at you or whatever. Ezra, let's party!"

Ezra gave a thumbs-up at Jonah's command and immediately started blasting dirty music from the speakers. The Familiars in the trees got spooked and scattered, while the guests stampeded onto the dance floor.

Julian's head shot up as his favorite song roared over the speakers. Tongue lolling out of his mouth, Julian romped toward the dance floor like an oversized, deadly puppy. His jumps from one place to the other caused mini-earthquakes. People struggled to keep their balance and screamed as they saw the charging creature.

"Dragon incoming!" Jonah bellowed, and everyone scattered. Julian knocked over several tables and benches before he skidded across the dance floor, which was smaller than he was.

I lifted Sophia off my lap and headed toward Julian. He cowered when he saw me coming— which I'm sure looked ridiculous, as he was twenty feet long and I was barely six feet tall.

"Jules, you're not tiny anymore! You need to learn your big ass can hurt people," I scolded.

Julian's eyes welled over, and his lip trembled. He gave a rather pathetic whimper as a plea for me to forgive him.

I rolled my eyes and scratched the area behind his horns. "You're such a baby."

When the guests were sure they weren't going to get trampled by a dragon, they slowly made their way back onto the dance floor. Ezra changed the song into soft music. I took Sophia by the hand and led her to the center so we could have our first dance.

As the song played, I spun Sophia around and held her close. All eyes were on us, but the feeling that encapsulated me made it feel like Sophia and I were the only two people in the world. She looked more beautiful than she ever had in white. If I thanked the ancestors a million times for sending her into my arms, it wouldn't be enough.

"Reminds you of the first time we danced at the Elemental Ball, doesn't it?" I asked.

Sophia nodded and blinked away tears.

"Soph, are you okay?" I immediately became concerned. Was something wrong?

"It's nothing," Sophia forced out. "I just never thought I could be so happy."

"Get used to it," I told her. "Our lives are going to get a lot more incredible from here on out."

I placed a hand on her growing stomach, and Sophia relaxed into me. I knew this was supposed to be the happiest day of our lives, but I already knew that as amazing as this wedding day was, it wasn't going to compare to the birth of my daughter. I almost wished she was here already, so she could experience this day with us.

Immediately after the song was over, Ezra switched the slow dance over to hardcore EDM. This was what everyone had been waiting for, as the crowd swelled around us and pressed in as Ezra turned the music up.

Jonah immediately took the opportunity to impress everyone. He did a breakdance in the middle of the floor while people cheered, before taking Jake's hand and dragging him into the circle. Jake danced rather stiffly— he wasn't very good at it— but when Jonah began grinding against him, he loosened up a little.

Lindsey and Miranda pressed their bodies into each other and swayed, while Amelia twirled with Trace. Luana couldn't hear the music, but she still danced alongside everyone else— I think she could feel the bass thump from the speakers, and enjoyed the vibrations just as much as everyone else enjoyed the music. I nearly fell over in shock when I realized Imogen and Luana had choreographed a dance together to one of the songs.

They must've practiced together before the wedding. Maybe Imogen was finally getting back to her old self.

I think Julian had the hots for Aisha. He was crooning as they danced together. The two dragons wove their heads back and forth like serpents performing a mating ritual. Aisha replied with low notes of her own, and Julian's tail wagged in delight.

Squeaks was brushing up against Sabor and leaning into him so heavily he nearly fell over. Usually, you couldn't get Squeaks away from Jonah at dances, but at the current moment, all she had eyes for was Sabor.

Was it Familiar breeding season around here or something? Something about weddings made everyone fall in love, even the animals.

Esis, who clearly had no lady friends to pursue, entertained the crowd by doing the worm before spinning into a pose. The guests cheered at his non-stop performance. Sassy stepped in and did some dance moves of her own, though the two Familiars started shoving each other to retain the spotlight.

After an hour of dancing, Sophia walked to the head of the dance floor to throw the bouquet. Amelia, Imogen, Lindsey, Miranda, Stevie, and Luana lined up behind her, their eyes fixed on the gathering of flowers in Sophia's hand. As Sophia turned her back to the group and prepared to throw, Amelia shoved her way to the front.

"Out of my way, bitches," Amelia growled. "That bouquet is mine."

Sophia threw the bouquet. It sailed in an arc. Amelia crouched down like a predator waiting to strike, eyes on the bouquet that was heading directly toward her.

Jonah came charging out of nowhere like an Olympic runner. His hand reached up, and he jumped three feet off the ground. Amelia's mouth dropped open in rage as Jonah caught the bouquet. As if he'd scored a game-winning touchdown, Jonah proudly held up the bouquet for all to see and did a victory dance. Amelia fumed, her face turning red as she stomped to the bar and demanded Trace order her another cocktail.

Sophia sat down in a chair for the garter removal. I stood in front of her as Ezra changed the music to something corny. I swear it sounded like what you'd hear in a bad eighties porno. Girls gushed in excitement. Sophia gave a nervous laugh and asked, "Uh, what's going on?"

"I will *never* do this again, so you'd better enjoy it," I said.

As Ezra turned the music up, my jacket slipped off, and I tossed it to the side. Her eyes grew wide, and people screamed as I undid the top buttons of my shirt and rolled my shoulders.

Yep. I was doing a sexy dance for her. Imogen and Jonah had insisted this was the only right way to do a garter toss, and I knew Sophia would be into it, so I subjected myself to humiliation in order to please my brand new wife. I gyrated my hips and swung my body as if some sort of porn star giving her a lap dance. I was sure I looked like a member of a boy band.

It was absolutely fucking ridiculous, but it made Sophia smile, so I could really give all a fuck of what anyone thought. And, what the hell, the crowd was enjoying it. I fell down to my hands and knees and lifted her skirt as I went under to remove the garter.

I took my time, though. I grazed my teeth against the lace thong she wore, and felt her stiffen as my lips pressed against her clit. Her legs shuddered as I took the garter off with my mouth, and I ran my fingers between her thighs as a reminder of what was to come.

Sophia was blushing when I came out with the garter. I gave her a wink as the groomsmen gathered to catch it.

"Good job, bro!" Ezra called out. "If being chief doesn't work out, I'm always sure you could be a stripper!"

I flipped him off. When I tossed the garter, Jake caught it. It wasn't a surprise, as he was taller than everyone else and merely had to lift his hand to snag it. He twirled it on his finger and wiggled his eyebrows at Jonah, who I swear fawned like a girl.

Like, seriously. Jonah held the bouquet he'd caught up to his face and everything. It was obnoxious.

As the music started up again, Julian knocked over one of the ivy walls while dancing with Aisha. He profusely apologized to Imogen, his grumbling moans being heard across the entire reception.

"It's fine, Julian," Imogen said quickly as she tried to get the ivy wall to regrow. She lifted her hand over the pile of leaves, but only a single ivy strand grew out of the pile. Her face became contorted as she struggled.

Huh. Im's magic looked really weak today. She must be tired from all this wedding planning. People were watching her curiously. Her cheeks reddened as she struggled to grow a single leaf.

"Here, let me." Cade came up beside Imogen and waved his hand over the ivy leaves. The wall regrew immediately.

If possible, Imogen turned even redder. She rounded on Cade. "Do you have to interfere with everything?"

"I was just trying to help," Cade offered.

Imogen gave a huff. "Well, I had it handled, thanks."

She stomped off, seeming a little miffed. Cade looked like he wanted to follow her, but he didn't.

I pulled my attention away from them and watched the other guests. Maddie had shown up to the wedding, but she didn't seem very happy. She danced with Drew a few times, yet she'd barely smiled all night.

I didn't know what we were going to do with her. I wanted my sister to be happy again, but she seemed to be in a place that none of us could reach. Not even a wedding could cheer her up.

I knew she missed Eirakari and was worried about her Familiar. As was everyone who had a missing companion. Wyatt seemed to be burying his sorrows in beer after beer. I wanted to make him feel better, but I knew nothing I could say would help.

We had to find those missing Familiars soon. Before everyone without them lost hope.

As the next song faded into another slow dance, I pulled Sophia close. There were a lot of couples entwined on the dance floor. Jonah was wrapped in Jake's arms, and Ezra and Stevie were currently making out by the speakers. Lindsey and Miranda, along with Vanessa and Bren, looked cozy.

Everyone seemed happy, thank the ancestors. I just hoped it lasted for the rest of—

"For the last fucking time, Cade, I don't want to dance with you!"

Fuck me.

Imogen stood at the edge of the dance floor, her hands balled into fists. Cade appeared miserable. Imogen's eyes were locked on him, but her face was blazing red.

Cade's voice was flat as he replied, "I just thought it would be nice."

"What do I have to do to get through to you? I want to be left alone!" Imogen shouted.

Ezra noticed that Cade and Imogen were making a scene and hurried to change the music back to something upbeat. But too late— the argument had already started.

Arabelle cringed against Cade's side, and Cade replied, "That's not how you acted last night."

The reception went dead silent. A vein in Imogen's temple twinged, and she said, "*Last night* was a mistake. You're a mistake. One I don't intend to make again."

Imogen ran off in tears. Cade looked close to crying himself. Ezra ducked in to save the day and spoke to Cade in low whispers.

Sophia went after Imogen, but I held her back. "No, Sophia. It's not your job to handle it. Not tonight."

Sophia gave a hesitant glance backward in the direction Imogen had gone. "But there's drama, and—"

"There's always drama at weddings," I said. "Let it go and enjoy the night."

Luana was chasing after Imogen. Sophia still seemed reluctant, but she relaxed into me and continued with the dance as if nothing had happened at all.

Jonah's attention was focused fully on Jake, though it was obvious he'd seen the fight, too. While they were dancing, someone came up and whispered something in Jake's ear. He frowned and pulled away from Jonah.

"Something up?" I asked.

Jake's expression was stern. "I've been told Black Ivy dealers have invaded your wedding."

"Oh, no." Sophia frowned. I shared her sentiment. The last thing we wanted was people getting high on nightshade at our reception.

Jake shook his head. "Not to worry. I'll find them and ensure they leave the premises."

Jake strode off. Jonah sighed in defeat and rolled his eyes. "Stupid fucking drug dealers, stealing away my man. Don't they know Jake *never* takes any time off? He deserves one night to himself."

"One night obsessing over you, you mean," I corrected.

Jonah tossed his hair over his shoulder and replied, "Well, we all know I'm hard to resist."

I glanced around the dance floor. Baine was getting down with Chief Cauac. Although Cauac was dancing in a more traditional and dignified way, Baine was pulling out all the worst dance moves out of the book. He varied between doing an awkward version of the sprinkler before transitioning into the running man.

I'm sure his moves were popular thirty years ago. Even so, more than one woman had her eye on him. The thought of my professor getting laid was really freaking gross, so I tried to block Baine and his shitty dance moves out of my head as much as possible.

Ezra had one too many drinks and was wearing his tie around his head. Dyami had gotten his head stuck in a tankard and was trying, unsuccessfully, to pull it out with Squeaks and Sabor's help. Wyatt had passed out on a bench, and Cade was nowhere to be found.

We were getting close to cutting the cake, but it seemed the reception had gotten out of control. Some older woman with gigantic breasts had noticed Baine's muscles, and had her claws in him by the punch bowl.

The woman ran her fingers up and down his biceps. "I'm impressed that a man of your age still keeps himself in good shape. It's very attractive."

Baine seemed uncomfortable. "I, uh… thank you, madame."

Ugh, I didn't want to hear this. I turned away. Still, I cringed as I overheard the woman whisper, "We should go somewhere more private. Somewhere I can truly appreciate those muscles in person."

Baine gaped, clueless on how to respond. Before he could, the smell of burning hair filled the clearing. I whirled around. The woman screamed as her hair lit on fire, erupting into a raging inferno.

Baine did the worst possible thing he could do and summoned the punch from the bowl. He doused the woman's hair in it, extinguishing the flames but leaving her soaked.

The fire had eaten away her hair down to the scalp. She wasn't burned, but it'd take a long time to grow back.

The woman put a shaking hand to her bald head and screeched. "Who's responsible for this?" she raged. She rounded on the Fire side of the reception, who'd frozen completely.

Suspicion immediately turned to the Koigni in the area. Things were a little tense. I knew everyone got along in the village, but a marriage between Fire and Water was still considered taboo, and the Toaqua were looking to blame Koigni.

Baine stepped in before any accusations could be thrown. "Now, now, it's all right. Just a little mishap. I'm sure some poor Koigni drank too much and had an accident. No harm done."

The woman huffed and stomped off. Baine blinked, then resumed conversation with Perot as if nothing had happened.

"Liam!" Sophia came running to my side, breathless. "Liam, it's Doya."

"What?" I was totally confused. Jonah heard the name and came by, curious.

"I saw her in the woods," Sophia hurried to explain. "She cast her magic and ran off."

"Are you sure? Doya's been missing for a while now," I stated.

"I didn't want to tell you this earlier, but I think I saw her in the crowd at our ceremony," Sophia said. "I shrugged it off, because I thought I was imagining things, but I'm certain I saw her this time. She and Naomi are here."

My gut tightened. Jonah's tone remained skeptical. "If Doya found *Hok'evale*, wouldn't she show up with an army and not alone?"

"I don't know. Someone lit that woman's hair on fire, and it wasn't one of our guests. I'm certain it was Doya," Sophia insisted.

"So... her grand plan is to ruin your reception?" Jonah seemed unimpressed.

"Maybe!" Sophia threw her hands up. "Who knows?"

"That doesn't make sense, though. Why would she come to our wedding and not attack us?" I asked.

"Maybe she wanted to see Sophia get married," Jonah suggested casually.

"Please. She hates me," Sophia said in a scathing way. "She has to have an ulterior motive."

"But if you saw her at the reception, and she did nothing, it could be true," Jonah suggested.

"Or she's been looking for us and she's going to run back to Oleander to tell him where we're at," Sophia insisted.

"I'm not sure," I mused. "When we spoke with Haley, she made it sound like Doya and Oleander aren't on good terms. I don't think Doya's working for him anymore. She might be in hiding like us."

"We can't trust Haley. We need to find Doya," Sophia said firmly. "What if she's trying to turn *Hok'evale* against each other, and put that lady's hair on fire to start a fight between Fire and Water?"

That was a valid concern. "I'll send out Toaqua to look for her," I said. "If she's here, she won't get far."

I ordered some men of the tribe to search the forest for Doya, while Sophia, Jonah and I searched the reception. We tried to remain inconspicuous, as not to alert our guests there could be an enemy nearby. I informed Chief Cauac, and he sent out Anichi to search as well, but an hour passed and we came up empty handed.

"She's not here, Sophia," Jonah said tiredly. "If she was, we'd have found her by now."

My wife was unconvinced. "Doya's a slippery one. She could've gotten away."

Jonah shook his head, but I turned Sophia to face me. "If she is here, we'll find her eventually. But I don't want this ruining our wedding night. Let's trust Chief Cauac to do his job. He's been keeping the village safe for years and won't let anything happen on his watch."

Sophia bit her lip, but she knew there was nothing else we could do.

It was at that moment when Imogen reappeared. A bright smile spread across her face. Her pupils were dilated, and her face red. She bounced into the circle and squeezed Jonah.

"Hey, guys!" she said in a chipper tone. "What'd I miss?"

Her mood seemed to be better. I bet she'd been at the bar all this time and must've had one too many drinks.

"Not much," Sophia said offhandedly. I didn't think she wanted to make Imogen upset again by telling her Doya was hanging around.

Imogen gave a girlish giggle. "What are we standing around for? Let's make this a wedding to remember!"

Imogen dragged Sophia back onto the dance floor. Jonah seemed a little perturbed, but slowly joined them.

As they danced, Sophia asked, "Um... I know this is none of my business, but did something happen between you and Cade last night before you spent the night at Amelia's?"

Imogen didn't flinch. "I went over there and we messed around. We didn't have sex or anything," she stated. "But it was a mistake. I'm over it."

I didn't believe her, but it wasn't like I could tell her otherwise. If Imogen and Cade were hooking up without any sort of commitment in place, that was bad news. It was obvious they couldn't be friends with benefits. They cared too much about each other.

But I couldn't stop them, and it wasn't my business, so pushed it out of my mind and hoped they'd come to their senses eventually.

For the rest of the dancing, Imogen was energetic and talkative. Cade seemed to be entirely forgotten. She spun with Luana, Sophia and Jonah in a delirious haze, riding some sort of euphoric rush.

Not everyone was as happy as Imogen, unfortunately. I heard shouting at the edge of the clearing. I was just about to ignore it, but did a double take when I realized that a fist fight had broken out. By the looks of things, it was between Toaqua and Koigni.

I immediately ran to break up the fight. It was only six or so guys going at it, and thank the ancestors they weren't using their elements, but a couple of people already had bloody noses.

Julian rushed onto the scene and roared, forcing the two sides apart. The men faced off, blood dripping down their faces and breathing heavily, like they wanted to go at it again.

"What the hell is going on?" I snapped. Out of the corner of my eye, I watched Sophia approach, but thankfully Maddie saw and rushed forward to drag Sophia away. She was the bride. It wasn't her responsibility to handle a bunch of drunk thugs.

"This whole wedding is *wrong*, chief," one of the Toaqua complained. "Toaqua should be with their own."

"They've already tainted pure Koigni blood!" a Koigni shouted. "The chosen one's bloodline has been poisoned with a weak half-blood child!"

My insides raged at what they were calling Ava-Marie. No child of mine would be considered less in our tribe, not when I was alive to say anything about it. "Anyone, Koigni or Toaqua, who dares to insult my daughter will fully experience my wrath. And I promise you, none of you want to tempt that."

"But, chief, you're not the same!" another Toaqua protested.

I knew this was going to cause trouble. Even though the tribe had welcomed me as their chief, they didn't approve I'd married a Koigni girl, or was having an interhouse child. "Sophia is my wife. You are honor-bound to accept her, as are *you*," I shot at the Koigni. "The ceremony has been completed. Sophia and I are married in the eyes of the Great Spirit. There is no undoing what has been done."

Resentful glares were sent by both sides. I wondered if there was ever going to be a halt to this endless conflict between Fire and Water. They were opposites. They were bound to have conflict.

But they could also work together better than anyone else could. Look at Sophia and I.

I was about to give a lecture on how the Houses needed to get along before Ezra came barreling in. He was a little tipsy, but not so drunk he couldn't defend me. The tie around his head was gone, and he looked severely pissed.

Ezra bunched his hands into fists. "Look, this is my brother's wedding, and I'll raise hell before I let anyone ruin it. So unless any of you want to throw hands with yours truly, I suggest you disperse."

"And me." Jonah came up to stand beside Ezra, and everything went quiet. There were a few muttered taunts, but the two sides broke off. No one was stupid enough to fuck with Jonah. He could pick up a fully-grown man and snap him like a twig with his bare hands. The brawlers went back to their designated tables, though shifty eyes and harsh words continued to be swapped.

"I should handle this," I began. "I'm chief. I have to make sure these people get along."

"Dude, you're the groom. This is *your* wedding," Jonah said. "Let me and Ez handle it. Go enjoy yourself."

I didn't want to walk away, but he had a point. This was our night. Somebody else could deal with the bullshit.

Sophia's eyes were downcast as I joined her and Maddie on the other side of the reception. Her voice was angry as she said, "Even after everything we've been through, they still don't accept us."

"So prove them wrong. You always have," Maddie said. "When the tribes see that both of you are united and are better leaders for your Houses than any other have been, they'll be forced to eat their words."

Maddie spoke as if she already knew. And maybe she did. I put an arm around Sophia and said, "Do you think we should cut the cake—?"

My words were cut off by a splattering sound. Sophia gasped. Squeaks had backed up into the cake table while flirting with Sabor, and her hindquarters had sent the cake flying. It landed upside down, smashed into a pile on the ground.

And... too late. Had a feeling that would happen eventually.

"Squeaks!" Jonah moaned. Squeaks ducked her head under her wing, as if to say she was sorry.

Esis came up chittering and shaking his fist. He scooped up a section of the smashed cake and tossed it at Squeaks, hitting her in the beak.

Sabor didn't like that. He took a chunk of the cake off the ground with his beak and dropped it right over Esis' head, covering him in frosting.

Sassy wasn't pleased that Esis was drowning in cake. She changed into a kitsune and used her vines to throw more cake back at Sabor, but it missed and hit Julian, smacking him right in the nose.

That started a war. Julian scooped up part of the cake with his tail and tossed it, chuckling as it hit Aisha. Soon, every Familiar in the place was tossing cake back and forth— except for Dyami, who was eagerly swallowing down any piece that was thrown his way.

"Should we do the last dance and head off?" Sophia suggested as we ducked the cake that was flying everywhere.

"Might be a good idea." I signaled Ezra to play the last song.

As the Familiars finished up the last of their cake fight (Dyami had eaten it all, so there was no more to throw), Sophia and I centered on the dance floor. The guests of the reception gathered around us in a circle. The guests linked arms and sang a traditional Hawkei wedding farewell as the waxing moon shone overhead.

Years ago, I'd never have thought this was possible. Yet dreams really did become reality, for here Sophia and I stood, bound for life, never feeling more loved than when the people in our lives celebrated our romance. So many had said, and would continue to say, that fire and water didn't mix. But we did, and what was more, Sophia and I belonged together. Our love would show the world what words never could. Our relationship was strong enough to conquer whatever stood in its way.

As the song ended, Sophia wiped away tears. The reception was over, but our night was just getting started.

"Now for the fun part." I poked Sophia in the side, and she giggled.

"While those two lovebirds are consummating their marriage, afterparty at *The Falcon's Nest*! Drinks on me!" Jonah yelled.

"Can he afford that?" Sophia asked as we walked toward Julian.

I made a sarcastic noise. "Probably not. Prepare to be giving him loans for the rest of your life."

"Let him have his fun. We'll only have one wedding." Sophia giggled.

"Damn right. I'll be dead before I give you up." I squeezed her tightly and kissed her neck. She let out a little noise of delight and called to Esis.

Julian stood proudly at the center of the clearing, a *Just Married* sign hanging around his neck. I wiped cake off his wing before lifting Sophia onto Julian's back. I'd never ridden Julian before, but he was big enough to fly on now, and I thought our first flight would be perfect on the night of our wedding.

Esis jumped onto Sophia's lap, and I swung myself on behind her. Julian spread his wings. Our loved ones waved goodbye as Julian rose into the air, and I clung Sophia tightly to me so she wouldn't fall off.

It only took Julian a few powerful strides to rise over the treetops. As we looked down below, the lights of *Hok'evale* glowed like fireflies underneath the branches of redwoods, gleaming against the side of the mountains.

Billions of stars littered the black night around us, covering us in a dark blanket like velvet. The inky blackness of the sea stretched beyond, and I could feel the power of the moon as her magic wrapped around us.

I'd never realized how strong of a dragon Julian was. He sailed over the air with ease, only having to adjust his wings a few times to find the right current. Every time he beat his wings, he soared higher, and soon we were feeling weightless as Julian dipped in and out of clouds, creating a peaceful atmosphere against the silent night. Esis climbed up Julian's neck and perched on his head, looking down as the wind brushed back his white fur.

The exhilaration felt in that moment was mystical, but not more than the fact that Sophia and I were finally alone. I ran my fingers over her breasts as we flew, and she pressed against me, rubbing her ass against the growing bulge in my pants.

As Julian descended, a cabin came into view. It was placed on a hill in the mountainside, a small lake circling the left side. The cabin was painted white, surrounded by redwoods. The cabin was Chief Cauac's personal vacation home, but he had offered it to us on our wedding night, as Sophia and I wouldn't get a honeymoon.

Julian landed outside of the cabin. I helped Sophia off his back while Esis eagerly ran toward the lake. He jumped in, doing a cannonball. Esis couldn't really swim, but Julian lifted him out and set him back on land before he could sink.

Julian and Esis became preoccupied with having a night swim in the pool outside the cabin. I took Sophia's hand and led her onto the porch. Inside, the cabin was spacious and open. The sliding glass window was open, exposing the cabin to the cool air outside, the sound of the waves crashing against the shore resonating inside the cabin. A breeze blew through the window, bringing in the smell of the sea. There was a jacuzzi inside next to a king-sized bed with white linens. White rose petals were scattered around the cabin, along with candles that hadn't yet been lit. Sophia waved her hand, and the candles ignited, casting the room in a soft glow.

Sophia lifted her dress and looked down. "I don't want to get the floor all muddy. My feet are so dirty."

I gave a low laugh. "Here, let me."

I got a bowl from the bathroom and filled it with water while Sophia sat down at the kitchen table. I grabbed soap, then got on my knees as I placed Sophia's feet into the bowl. I washed the mud off of her gently with soap, working slowly as she held the dress out of my way.

The intimate moment closed in around us. I thought that I wanted my whole life to be like this, serving Sophia. Intimacy wasn't about sex, but about being vulnerable, and trusting the person you exposed everything to would keep the secrets parts of you safe. Sophia knew the innermost parts of me that I'd never show to anyone, and because she'd treasured them, I'd live and breathe for this woman.

As her feet became clean I ran my lips up her legs, kissing her inner thighs and trailing my wet fingers over her skin. Sophia's breathing became intense as I teased her, and though she shifted uncomfortably in her seat, I continued my slow tantalization, drawing out each moment for as long as it could possibly endure.

When I placed a hickey near the area where her thigh met her core, she gave a loud moan.

"Had enough, Mrs. Mitoh?" I murmured. Damn, that was hot. I'd never get tired of calling her that. She was mine now, in a way she never had been before.

"Get this damn dress off of me," she breathed. I stood. As she rose, I began unfastening the buttons at her spine, though not as quickly as I normally would've. I untied the ribbons holding the dress together at an agonizing pace, enjoying how the rise and fall of her chest grew quicker and quicker.

"You're doing this on purpose."

"I like watching you squirm." As her dress fell off her shoulders, I had to wonder who was torturing who. Beside the lace thong, Sophia had a white see-through bra that pushed up her breasts and exposed her nipples. Sophia tossed her dress over a chair as she faced me. My dick immediately got harder than a fucking rock.

"Your turn." She raised a sultry eyebrow, and I began shedding clothes. Her eyes grew wide at my extended cock. I tossed the tux over her dress and scooped her up in my arms, carrying her to the bed. As I set her down on it, I rummaged through the side table drawer— I'd left a few things here this morning in preparation for this. I withdrew massage oil, and slowly began taking off her lingerie top, leaving only the panties.

I rubbed the oil all over Sophia's body. She sat on her knees as I caressed the oil over her skin, massaging her breasts and nipples gently while taking care to knead her back and any other sore muscles she might have. As she arched upward against me, I cupped her ass in my hands, and her mouth met mine in a fever as we passionately kissed. She reached out to stroke my dick. I became more aroused with each movement, quaking as her fingers roamed over my head.

Sophia's head lolled as she relaxed. I guided her to the edge of the bed and gave her a few pillows, so she could lean forward on them without feeling uncomfortable because of the baby. I then got back on my knees and began kissing her core, using my tongue to pleasure her as I sampled her sweet taste.

I satisfied her in a delirious haze, my passion only amplified by the sound of her delight.

She moaned, her fingers digging into the pillows as I brought her to climax. She leaned forward, offering more of herself to me. I stood and I slowly entered her from behind, grabbing her hips and moving in smooth thrusts.

I started slow, but the temptation to pick up speed was too much to resist, so I began plunging into her at a quick speed. Sophia's loud moans of pleasure nearly turned into screams, and I was glad we were in the middle of the wilderness where we wouldn't be heard. Even my own moans were growing loud, and as I came, I fell forward onto Sophia's body and wrapped an arm around her to hold her close, because she was the only thing keeping me anchored to this plane of existence.

Both of us were shaking. I held her for a few moments longer before I pried myself away, and even then, I had to put a kiss on her lips, in her hair.

Sophia fell onto her back. I slid beside her, and our foreheads touched without our own accord as we remained curled up in our own little reality.

Sophia's fingers threaded with mine. "Do you think things will be this perfect forever?"

It only took me a beat of thought. "No. Things are going to be even better."

That made her smile. After a few moments of recovery, I got up to fill the Jacuzzi. As the tub filled, I turned on the jets and made sure the water temperature was somewhat cool instead of hot. We didn't want the heat to hurt the baby.

"A bath sounds amazing after a long day," Sophia commented as she watched me uncap a bottle of bath gel.

"That's just what I was thinking." I went to pour in a bit of the bottle, but my hands were still wet, and the bottle ended up slipping out of my fingers, falling right in the tub. "Oh, fuck!"

I went to grab it, but by the time I got it out of the tub, the whole bottle had already emptied. Bubbles were exploding everywhere, getting bigger and more out of control by the moment. I scrambled to turn off the jets, but we already had a problem, as the tower of bubbles was taller than I was.

"Shit! Liam!" Sophia laughed. Within moments, the bubbles had started to foam out the side of the Jacuzzi. I used my Water powers to send the bubbles toward the bathroom, to contain them in the shower, but was quickly becoming overwhelmed.

Sophia scrambled out of bed to help me. Both of us were laughing as she waddled over and grabbed an armful of bubbles, trying to throw them in the kitchen sink but more or less just getting them all over herself— and the rest of the house.

It took twenty minutes to handle the bubble situation. By the end, we'd gotten it under control, but were covered in soap. "Oh, ancestors. Look at you." I wiped off hordes of bubbles off of Sophia's skin. She scraped away a pile of bubbles in my hair and blew them away, snickering as we watched them land on the carpet.

"First rule of marriage. Never let you handle bubble baths." She kissed me on the nose and carefully avoided the slippery bubbles on the floor. I helped her into the Jacuzzi, where we sat down in the middle and she rested against me. I turned the jets back on, and this time, we didn't have an apocalypse on our hands.

Sophia gave me her signature mischievous gaze. "You know, you got to have all the fun earlier. I think it's my turn."

Sophia sank her head below the surface. I let out a gasp as I felt her lips slide over my dick, moving back and forth as she sucked me underwater. Though we'd just finished having sex a half hour ago, I was already getting hard again. But this time, I'd drag it out even longer, and even when we were done, it wouldn't be enough to satisfy the desperate need we had for each other.

I was very sure we'd be awake until dawn.

# sophia

EIGHTEEN

The weeks following our wedding were unlike anything I'd ever dreamed. The end of August faded into September, which faded into October. For those few short months, I almost forgot there was a war going on outside our home.

All my attention was on my husband and the growing baby inside of me. Oftentimes, I'd place a hand over my heart— where the key Liam had given me lay next to the Spirit Totem— and I would thank the ancestors for the beauty and peace they blessed me with every day. The greatest blessing of all: our sweet baby girl, Ava-Marie.

Day by day, she grew bigger and bigger. Our precious girl made her presence known on every occasion, doing flips and kicking my sides like she already had plans to become an acrobat.

One morning, Liam and I woke, and my bladder was screaming at me. Ava-Marie had taken a particular disliking to it. I tried to sit up in bed, but I just... couldn't. I scrunched my brow and flexed my abs, trying to pull myself upright, but my body wouldn't move.

"Um, *pawee*?" Liam asked after he'd pulled on his shirt. "What are you doing?"

I started laughing. "I'm trying to sit up. Ava's so big now I can't do it."

"Are you serious?" Liam chuckled.

"Yeah, see?" I raised my arms in front of me and tried to use them to offset my weight, but I only got a few inches off the pillow and couldn't go any further. "I feel like I'm going to crush her or something."

Liam laughed and took my hands. "You're not going to crush her. She's safe in your womb."

He helped me sit up, then placed a gentle hand on my stomach. Ava-Marie was already doing summersaults this morning. Her heel pressed below my ribs, and she ran her foot along the top of my bump. A twinge came as she pushed herself up against my bladder.

I laughed as Liam and I felt her wiggle. "I think she's trying to tell me to make more room for her. I really have to pee."

"Do you need help?" he asked, dead serious.

I rolled my eyes and stood from the bed. "No. I'm not totally helpless."

"But you can't get out of bed by yourself anymore," he argued.

"I could if I tried," I replied. "I can roll over onto all fours, just not sit up from lying down."

Liam laughed. "By the end of this pregnancy, you'll be like a turtle. Once you get on your back, you'll never get up."

He threw himself onto the bed and imitated what I'd be like at nine months pregnant. I couldn't help but burst out in laughter.

I snatched one of the pillows and threw it at him. "Shut up. I will— oh, fuck."

Liam's laughter instantly died, and he stilled. "What?"

My eyes went wide. "I just peed a little."

I whirled around and waddled to the bathroom. Liam practically died of laughter, and Esis snickered along with him, though I wasn't sure he understood what was so funny.

When I came out, the house was quiet again. I went back into the bedroom and was a little shocked to see Liam had made the bed. He *never* made the bed.

The room was empty, and for a moment I thought he'd already left for work, until I heard the sound of his footsteps coming from the kitchen. I turned to see him carrying a pile of wet towels toward the bedroom.

I furrowed my brow. "What's going on? Don't you have to leave for work?"

"I'm chief," he said simply. "They'll wait for me. Lie down."

"What?" I asked.

Esis jumped onto the bed and snuggled in.

"Lie down," Liam repeated. "I want to take care of my pregnant wife."

"But I don't need—" I started.

Liam cut me off by grabbing my wrist and practically dragging me toward the bed. "Don't say it, *pawee*. You may not *need* it, but my pregnant wife *deserves* it."

I swooned at his gesture. Liam guided me onto the bed and fluffed the pillows behind me, until I was lying comfortably. He set the towels on the nightstand and laid them out over my skin on my legs, arms, and belly. They were really hot and felt amazing. Liam began massaging my feet, and Esis rubbed his paws over my hands. I rolled my head back and moaned.

"Aren't *I* supposed to be the one doing this to *you?*" I asked.

"*I'm* not pregnant," he teased.

"But you're sick," I pointed out.

"So?" he said with a shrug. "Doesn't mean I can't pamper my wife."

My stomach fluttered when he called me his wife. I didn't think I'd ever get used to it. "I love it when you call me that."

"What? My wife?" he asked.

"Yes."

"Well, that's what you are."

"And you're my husband," I added. "See how great it is to hear?"

He sighed blissfully. "It does have a nice ring to it, doesn't it?"

"Mm hmm." I relaxed into the pillow, and the room went silent for a couple minutes, until Liam spoke.

"So, how are the *shantee* lessons going with my mom?"

"Good," I told him. "I feel like I know what to expect during labor now, though your mom wants us to visit together so you know what to do. One of these days when you're off work we'll have to go see her."

Liam's hands moved from my feet and up to my calves. "I'll be fine when you're in labor."

"You'll have to take care of me," I pointed out.

"That's what I'm doing," he said. "You don't think I'm going to freak out over a little blood, do you?"

I peeked my eyes open and raised my eyebrow. "A little blood? The way your mom made it sound, it's going to be like World War III down there. I'm probably going to yell at you for putting this baby in me."

His jaw dropped dramatically. "Why would you do that?" he teased.

I shrugged. "I don't know. I'll be all hormonal and stuff. I can't be held accountable for whatever I say during labor."

"Are you *trying* to scare me?" he asked with a smirk.

"No, just trying to prepare you," I said. "Everything should be fine, though. I'm not even worried. Your mom and Luana will be here, and they're both pretty experienced."

"Hold up." Liam's hands stopped moving over me. "By *here*, you mean the hospital, right?"

"No," I said slowly. "I mean here, as in, I was thinking about having a home birth."

"A home..." Liam's mouth gaped open, and he bobbed it up and down like a fish. It would've been comical, if I hadn't recognized he was having some sort of emotional crisis right now. "Soph, you can't give birth here!"

"Why not?" I asked. "It's comfortable, it's roomy, and I won't have to deal with nurses I don't know sticking their hands in places I don't like. You don't trust your mom and Luana?"

"Of course I trust them," Liam said. "But I want you to have access to medical resources. What if you need pain killers? Or if the baby comes out and she isn't breathing?"

"We'll have all that here," I assured him. "Luana's been training at the hospital when she's not with me, remember? We can get all that stuff."

"But what about the doctors?" he argued. "I want all the best staff and equipment in *Hok'evale* readily available to you."

"Luana *is* the best *Hok'evale* has," I reminded him. "I want to labor comfortably. It will only stress me out to give birth in a place I've never been with people I've never met."

"Then we'll tour the hospital," he argued. "We'll meet your doctors."

"But I don't want new doctors," I told him. "I *want* your mom and Luana. They're the best midwives out there, and you know it."

Liam sighed. "Yeah, I guess. But I don't like the idea of you giving birth at home. You should be at the hospital where they can get you whatever you need."

I cocked an eyebrow. "Says the guy who wouldn't go to the hospital when he had *pneumonia*."

Liam ducked his head. He couldn't argue with that one.

I reached over and placed my hand on his. "Don't worry. You have a few more weeks to warm up to the idea."

Liam leaned over and brushed my hair away from my face, then gently kissed the top of my head. "We'll see what happens."

Translation: He wasn't changing his mind.

But neither was I. And guess who was pushing this baby out?

"I guess we will," I said.

I could hear Julian's wings flapping outside. He was obviously getting anxious that Liam hadn't come out to greet him yet.

"You should probably get to work." I suggested. "I have a training session with Luana soon."

"Do I *have* to?" he groaned playfully.

I shrugged. "Only if you want to stay chief."

Liam smirked. "They couldn't get rid of me if they tried."

"True. I'll see you tonight."

Liam pecked me on the lips. "I'll see you, *pawee*. Love you."

"I love you, too."

Liam helped me out of bed before leaving the room. I showered, got ready for the day, and left to meet up with Luana. I found her in our usual cave, sitting cross-legged atop a pillow. Her eyes were closed, and she took deep breaths while Sierra fanned her face.

My footsteps must've sent subtle vibrations through the floor, because she noticed my approach. She opened her eyes.

*Hello*, Luana greeted brightly. *Do you want to join me?*

*Absolutely*, I replied.

I took a pillow down from the shelf and sat across from her. Esis perched himself next to me and closed his eyes. Sierra settled on Luana's shoulder.

I always felt at ease in this cave. All my training sessions with Luana had taught me that this cave was a safe, sacred place. The lighting from the candles around us was relaxing, and I loved listening to the sound of the water trickle down the side of the rock. I took a deep breath in through my nose and out through my mouth.

We sat there for a long time, though it didn't seem that long at all. We always started our sessions with meditation, and it had helped me clear the clutter in my mind over these past few months. It took a while to get into it, but with practice and understanding, I found it more peaceful than anything.

Finally, Luana tapped my knee, and I opened my eyes.

*Do you feel that energy around us?* she signed.

*Yes*, I replied.

Though the cave was calm and still, I noticed energy everywhere. It was one of the things Luana had been teaching me in my lessons— to sit and observe, and feel the energy of the Great Spirit flowing through every object within reach. I could feel Esis' energy beside me, and the strong connection we shared. I felt my own magic buzzing inside of me. If I focused closely on Luana, I could feel the heat coming off her body, and I felt the beat of Sierra's wings. Energy moved through the cave floor, connecting us to the city outside.

*Which energy do you feel the strongest?* she asked.

*My own,* I said. *I feel my magic.*

She nodded proudly. *How much do you have to give?*

*I'm not sure I understand,* I admitted. *I could never use it all up. I'll always have more.*

She smiled, then reached behind herself to grab something. She placed whatever it was between us. When she pulled away, I saw it was a translucent red crystal.

*Can you give your magic to the crystal?* she asked.

I bit my lip nervously. We'd been practicing transference for months, and I still hadn't managed to get it.

*I'm not sure,* I told her.

Luana pressed her lips together thoughtfully. She grabbed the crystal and set it aside.

*Let's try a different approach. Place your hands on your stomach,* Luana instructed.

I did as she said, and my daughter responded by kicking me. I giggled lightly.

*She's kicking,* I told Luana.

She smiled sweetly. *What would you do if she stopped?*

The blood drained from my face at the thought. *I'd use my healing magic, of course! I'd try to diagnose what was wrong, the same way you do.*

*How?* she asked curiously.

I hesitated. I'd never actually done it before, but I'd watched Luana do it plenty of times. *I'd let my Anichi magic flow into her, then read the energy signature that's given back.*

*Exactly,* Luana agreed proudly. *Everything we do is an energy transfer, Sophia. When you eat food, it nourishes your body with energy. That energy travels through your bloodstream and to your baby. She grows out of the energy you give her. She responds with a kick, and that energy fills your heart, right?*

*Absolutely.*

*Everything we do is either giving energy, or taking it,* Luana explained. *But the beauty of energy is that it can be shared— for both good and for bad.*

*I'm not sure I follow,* I admitted.

Luana shifted on her pillow to get more comfortable. *When your daughter kicks you and you respond with joy, you* chose to receive that *energy. Every energy transfer— every interaction— is a choice. You either choose to give your energy or to receive it.*

*So, you're saying transference is a choice?* I asked. *Not merely strength or talent.*

*It is both,* Luana clarified. *You cannot lift a rock without the strength to do so. But if you nourish your body with energy and exercise your strength, you can carry that rock up a mountain.*

*I think I see where you're going with this,* I signed. *You'll never get the rock to the top of the mountain if you don't choose to pick it up first.*

Luana smiled proudly. *Exactly. I know you have the strength, Sophia. You have exercised your soul and are ready for this. All you have to do is choose to let go of the resistance that's blocking you.*

A few months ago, I might've snapped at her. Resistance? What resistance?

But she was right. I could feel my energy resist when I tried to channel my magic into a crystal. My first thought was that I doubted myself, but that didn't feel right. My magic was powerful. I didn't say that to be cocky— it was just true. I was capable of things the average Elementai wasn't— like conjuring lightning. So why couldn't I figure out how to do transference?

*Because I'm scared,* I realized.

It wasn't until I asked myself the question that it suddenly hit me. I loved my magic. It was a part of me, and I was a part of it.

But sometimes, it honestly scared me. I was already stronger than others, and mastering transference would only make me *more* powerful.

*I think I know where my resistance is coming from,* I told Luana.

*Tell me about it,* she offered kindly.

*I'm happy where I am,* I admitted. *I'm powerful, but I'm not too powerful, you know? I think I'm scared of pushing my boundaries and finding out just how powerful I am. I don't want to hurt anybody.*

*You won't,* Luana promised. *The more you learn about your power, the more you can control it. You must align your heart with your mind and accept the full extent of the power the ancestors have blessed you with.*

*Is that selfish?* I questioned. *To... hoard all this power.*

Luana shook her head. *The more power you accept, the more you can give, and the more you can help people.*

*That makes sense,* I told her. *If I had more power, I'd be able to heal.*

*Exactly,* Luana replied. *Once you figure out transference, healing should be easy. Like I said, it's all a transfer of energy.*

*Then I'll try again,* I suggested.

Luana smiled and handed over the crystal. The room went silent as I closed my eyes. I started by paying close attention to the vibrations and energy around me, then slowly turned my focus inward. First, I noticed the energy that Ava-Marie gave off, with her moving limbs and the magic that flowed through her. Then I turned my attention to my heart, where my magical energy concentrated. I visualized it flowing down my arms. When I felt the energy reach my fingertips, I felt an invisible force pulling back— resisting.

*It's okay,* I said in my mind. *My magic isn't going to hurt anyone. I want to help. I choose to release my magic, and I bless it with the goodness that's in my heart— and in my daughter's. This magic is no longer mine. It now belongs to this crystal.*

Luana and I had gone over mantras like this so many times before, but it wasn't until that moment that I felt it deep within my heart. I loosened my grip on the crystal, and I let go of my magic.

Energy flowed out of me. But instead of manifesting in the form of flames or light, the magic swirled into the crystal. I could feel the vibrational hum of energy in my hand, but it wasn't my own anymore. It was free and ready to be claimed by anyone.

"I did it!" I cried out loud, signing in excitement.

Esis jumped at my sudden outburst, then started clapping and cheering. Sierra fluttered her wings from Luana's shoulder.

Luana beamed. *Great job, Sophia!*

*I can't believe it!* I signed back. *All it took was letting go. It's so simple.*

*But it's not,* she argued. *You don't realize how far you've come. Letting go is simple once you know how, but just like carrying that stone up the mountain, you have to work up to it. You weren't ready before, but you are now, Sophia. You've done wonderful.*

I smiled proudly. *Thank you. You've been a great teacher.*

*You're a good student,* she replied. *Let's try it again.*

Luana had brought along an entire bag of crystals. We spent most of the morning practicing transference, until I found myself getting really tired. Beside me, Esis swayed on his feet, and I could tell I was starting to overexert both of us. I knew we needed to rest for our magic to replenish itself.

*I think I need a break,* I signed.

*I wondered when you might say that,* Luana replied. *You've done amazing today, Sophia.*

*Thank you.* I looked to our pile of crystals. There had to be at least a dozen, which I was really proud of. It meant more magic for the war we were fighting.

Luana and I took a break for lunch, and Esis and I felt better after that. We spent the rest of the afternoon discussing healing techniques, though I still couldn't do it.

*You're getting really close,* Luana said. *You'll figure it out soon.*

*I think so, too,* I agreed.

*Can I walk you home?* Luana offered.

*Sure,* I replied.

*I have to make a stop on the way, if that's okay.*

*That's fine.*

Luana didn't say where she had to go, but I noticed about halfway there that we were headed toward *The Falcon's Nest.*

*Are we getting something to eat?* I signed to her.

*Why?* she asked. *Are you hungry?*

I chuckled under my breath. *Always.*

She smiled. *Then you're in luck.*

Luana and I reached *The Falcon's Nest,* and she gestured me forward. I opened the door, and—

*"Surprise!"*

A chorus of cries came from behind the door. Esis and I both jumped so high we nearly fell down the stairs. My jaw dropped as I stepped into the restaurant to see my friends and family crowded around the nearest tables. A pile of presents were stacked on a table nearby.

"Oh my gosh!" I cried, holding my heart. "What is this?"

I looked around to see that everyone was here— my parents, Amelia, Liam's mom and his siblings, Imogen and Jonah, and the rest of our family and friends. Even Maddie and Drew were there, though Maddie looked really tired.

Liam stood from the nearest chair. He beamed proudly and said, "It's your surprise baby shower."

"What?" I gaped as he led me over to an empty chair. "I didn't know I got a baby shower!"

Imogen snickered. "That would ruin the surprise, wouldn't it?"

My heart warmed at the gesture. "Thank you, everyone."

I turned to Luana and signed. *That was really sneaky. I had no idea.*

She chuckled. *I'm pretty good at keeping my lips sealed.*

I burst into laughter as Luana took a seat beside Imogen. Imogen shot her a glance, but she didn't say anything or rudely ask what I was laughing about like she did sometimes. I barely had a chance to breathe before everyone started chatting.

"Congratulations, Sophia!" Mom cried as she came over to give me a hug.

I hugged her back tightly. "You guys didn't have to do this."

"Yes, we did," Dad argued as he followed behind Mom.

My eyes fell on the cake. It had pink frosting that looked like bubbles, with a cake topper made to look like a shower head sticking out of it and a tiny baby doll on top.

"You guys!" I sighed happily. "I *love* it. A *baby shower* cake?"

"Trace and I made it," Amelia said proudly.

"Thank you, everyone," I said. My voice cracked a little, but I tried not to let the hormones get to me. I was just really happy to have them all here to celebrate our baby.

Liam leaned over toward me. "Are you hungry, *pawee?*"

"Do you have to ask?" I teased.

"No, though I have to request your craving of the day. Pickles and mayonnaise?"

I blushed pink. "I was thinking a hot dog with ranch on top?"

"Coming right up."

As Liam got up to get me a plate of food, Jonah leaned forward. He dragged Jake with him, since Jake's arm was around his shoulder.

"Tell me, Sophia," Jonah said. "Would you have been upset about a cabaret show for your baby shower?"

My eyebrows shot up, and I chuckled. "Tell me you didn't plan a dress rehearsal for today," I joked.

"I wanted to!" Jonah cried. "But Lindsey and Miranda talked me out of it. They said they're not ready."

Miranda tossed her dark curls over her shoulder. "It was the only way to convince him. Apparently, *'a cabaret is not appropriate entertainment for a baby shower'* wasn't a good enough excuse."

"Wait," I said. "What kind of entertainment *did* you come up with?"

I glanced around. I noticed for the first time that a bunch of Familiars were missing from people's sides. My parents' Familiars were close by, as was Bren's chimera and Cade's *alebrije*. I assumed the dragons were outside somewhere. Sassy, Medusa, Evelyn, and Squeaks were nowhere to be seen.

"Where are the Familiars?" I asked, before anyone had a chance to answer my last question.

Esis put his index finger to his lips, as if to say it was a secret.

I shot him a pointed look. "Esis, do you know something you're not telling me?"

Esis put his little paws over his mouth, and his shoulders shook in laughter.

Jonah cocked his head toward the back of the restaurant. "Why don't you go get them, buddy?"

Esis' eyes lit up, and he jumped out of my lap. Jonah got up and followed behind Esis. Just then, Liam returned with a plate of food and set it in front of me.

"Where's Esis going?" I asked. "What's going on?"

Liam smirked as he sat, then ripped one of his dinner rolls in half and started eating it. Of course, that would be the only thing on his plate. "You're just going to have to wait and see."

I tried to follow Esis with my eyes, but he was so small that he quickly got lost in the sea of bodies.

About a minute later, I heard the sound of hooves and paws coming from the back, and the whole restaurant got really quiet. Suddenly, Jonah's up-beat music boomed from the speakers, and the parade of Familiars began.

I burst out laughing as Squeaks strutted through the doorway wearing a rainbow-colored clown wig. She bobbed her head to the music and tried to spin in circles, but after knocking an empty chair over and swatting Bren's drink out of his hand with her tail, she stuck to walking in a straight line. Baby waddled out behind her wearing a top hat. Medusa slithered into the room next. She wore a flashy purple dress that was more or less a big sock that covered the serpent's entire body. Sassy danced into the room wearing a tutu and a huge bow, and Evelyn followed behind her. The kirin wore striped pants on her hind legs and had a fabric puff ball attached to the end of her antler.

Finally, Esis twirled into the room. He shook his butt, then tried to do the moonwalk before planting on his face. He was barely down a second before hopping back up and saving his fall with a sick dance move I could only guess Jonah taught him.

I couldn't stop laughing when I saw what Esis was dressed in. He had on a polka-dotted vest and a red clown nose.

"Ladies and Gentlemen," Jonah announced over the music. "I present to you the latest entertainment sensation that's sweeping through *Hok'evale*. The fierce, the almighty... Familiar Six!"

People started clapping, before Jonah quickly added in a rushed voice.

"Now available for hire. This content is intended for children. Parties for eighteen-plus can find the good stuff down the street."

Jake roared with laughter, and Liam almost choked on his food. My stomach hurt from laughing so hard, and it only got worse as the Familiars continued dancing to the music. I was pretty sure it was meant to be graceful, but it came off looking like comedy inspired by a Charlie Chapman film.

By the end of it, Sassy must've had a bruised paw where Squeaks had stepped on it, Evelyn's pants had torn down the back, and Squeak's wig had flown off and smacked Cade in the face.

"Ancestors, you guys!" I cried as the Familiars returned to the back to take off their costumes. I was still trying to control my laughter. "That was hilarious. It was the perfect baby shower entertainment."

"Don't thank me," Jonah said as he returned to his seat. "It was all Squeaks' idea."

"Aww, she wants to be like you," I said.

Jonah puffed his chest out. "Well, she's got a long way to go."

"Jonah, you're so humble," Imogen cracked.

"It's a gift," Jonah sighed.

"Gifts!" Imogen cried. "Let's do presents!"

Before anyone could say anything, Imogen hopped out of her chair and grabbed a bag from the gift table. She shoved it in my direction. "Open mine first!"

"O-okay," I said, barely having a second to think about it.

"Shh..." Amelia hissed to get everyone's attention. "Sophia's opening presents!"

The room got really quiet, and all eyes turned to me. I reached into Imogen's bag and pulled out a wad of tissue paper, then peeked inside.

My heart fell when I saw what was inside. I pulled out a small, twisted tree in a green pot. It would've been beautiful, except all the leaves were brown and falling off.

"Um, Im... what's this?" I asked, holding it up.

The blood drained from Imogen's face. "W-what? It's not supposed to look like that!"

Imogen snatched it out of my hands and twisted it around to look at it from every angle. "I don't know what happened! I chose the *perfect* bonsai tree for Ava-Marie's nursery— so she'd think of me when she saw it. This is all wrong!"

"Where have you been keeping it?" I asked. "Maybe it's not getting enough sunlight, or it's too cold."

"I know how to take care of plants," Imogen snapped.

Trace shrugged. "Just use your magic and fix it."

Imogen sneered at him. "Easy for you to say."

Cade eyed Imogen from where he sat beside Trace. "This should be a piece of cake for you."

Imogen gaped at him for a moment before snapping out of it. She turned her eyes to the bonsai tree and concentrated. The leaves turned from brown to green, but the trunk was still sad and wilted.

"Are you okay, Im?" I asked in genuine concern.

"I'm fine," she snapped. "Sorry we can't *all* be at the top of our game at all times."

"But Cade's right—" I started.

"I know my magic's all over the place," Imogen growled.

"So's your attitude," I mumbled under my breath. Imogen was starting to show her irritated side again, and it was bringing down the whole party.

"I don't need to give you an explanation," Imogen said, before huffing and sitting back in her chair. She shoved the bonsai tree at her brother. "Here. You fix it."

Everyone stared at her for several long seconds, before Amelia hopped out of her chair and broke the silence. "Mine next!"

Amelia hurried over to the gift table, then handed me a large present wrapped in pretty pink paper. I opened it to find a bassinet inside. It came in a large flat package and wasn't put together yet, but there was a picture on the front, which showed it came with an attachable dragon mobile.

"Wow, Amelia!" I said. "I love it!"

"I knew you would," she raved.

The presents kept coming, and my heart swelled with gratitude. My parents had gotten us a really fancy baby monitor. Haloke gifted me a pile of gifts for the labor, like a soft nightgown, slippers, and aromatherapy oils. Jonah and Jake gave us a really fashionable diaper bag, and Miranda and Lindsey got me a gift card to the spa, along with a swaddle for the baby. By the end of the night, we had everything we could possibly need for our newborn.

*Did you get everything you wanted?* Luana asked while we were cleaning up.

*That and more,* I replied with a smile, but my smile quickly faded.

Something had been bothering me the entire party. *There's just one thing missing.*

She tilted her head in curiosity. *What's that?*

I glanced around, but no one was watching us. *I'd like Ava-Marie to know her real grandparents. I wish there was a way to find them so they could meet her.*

I'd tried using the compass Haloke gave me, but the needle spun each time I picked it up. Either it was broken, or the ancestors were trying to tell me something, because it never pointed in a single direction. Liam seemed to think it meant whatever I was searching for could not be found— or that perhaps it didn't work because I was no longer lost. I thought it felt more like the compass was telling me to wait... for what, I wasn't sure.

Luana's gaze dropped. *I'm sorry. I've looked in the Anichi Hall of Records, but our charts are incomplete. Most of our records were destroyed in the war, so our genealogy only goes back a hundred years or so. You're nowhere in the documents.*

*Have you tried looking for unnamed girls or missing children?* I questioned. *My name wouldn't necessarily be Sophia in the records.*

*I considered that and still couldn't find anything,* she admitted. *I'm sorry. I looked down every possible avenue, and I didn't find anything.*

*Thanks for trying,* I told her.

I frowned, but my disappointment ran deeper than that. I was hurt. Devastated, actually. The truth was, I'd come to terms with never meeting my birth parents, as painful as that was to accept. I'd long given up hope of ever finding my real mother and father. I didn't even know if they were alive or dead, and I had to live with that.

But I didn't know if I could accept that Ava-Marie would never know her own heritage. She'd never know my parents... *her* grandparents. If I could give my daughter anything, I'd want to tell her where she came from. But I didn't even know where *I* came from.

And I didn't think I ever would.

NINETEEN

"That's perfect! You're getting it."

I observed as the Anichi students hovered small white orbs around the training area, in the clearing underneath the rock formation. In last week's class, they'd struggled to conjure a ball at all. This week, it seemed like they were actually sustaining it.

Julian perched on a rock high above me, looking down at the class. His wings created shade over the group, which we really didn't need, as it was already chilly at the end of November.

I knew nothing about Anichi magic, but I understood how elemental powers worked, so I more or less tried to feel my way through my teaching sessions instead of standing there barking orders. It was just like teaching Sophia how to use her Fire, like I'd done so long ago. All I had to do was point my students in the right direction, and they'd managed to figure out most of the basics on their own.

We'd been working for months on learning how to intrafuse Anichi magic from magical creatures. So far, a few of the students could make small shields, and we'd been working on creating balls of Spirit magic for them to use in defensive battle. Some of the students could heal small cuts and bruises, but it was nothing like Luana could do.

Still, we'd come pretty far after starting with nothing. I felt like once we discovered how to get the Anichi their powers back, these kids would be way ahead of everyone else. Now I wanted to try something different.

"We've been practicing summoning our magic from the earth around us and magical creatures for some time now," I said. "Now I want to try something experimental."

"What do you mean? *Everything* we've been doing is experimental," Linus said. He was one of the kids at the top of my class, and though he was smart, he had a tendency to act like he knew everything.

Instead of explaining, I demonstrated. "Zoey, can you come up here, please?"

A Koigni girl that had bonded recently came forward. The Familiar at her side was an enfield, a creature with the head of a fox, the forelegs of a bird and the back legs of a wolf.

"What do you need me to do?" she asked.

"Throw fireballs at me," I suggested. "Don't worry— you won't hurt me."

She conjured a fireball in her palm and tossed it my way. I threw up a Water shield from the fountain nearby to block it, but instead of retaliating, I did something else. I focused my attention entirely on the Familiar at her side.

After concentrating, I felt a strong and steady connection between Zoey and the enfield. The fox-hybrid was giving her a steady magical supply that fueled her powers. I focused my attention on the enfield, like I did Julian. As I felt the enfield's magic coursing through her, I shut the connection to Zoey off, and instead, channeled the creature's magic into my own. My water shield grew three sizes, while Zoey's fireballs fizzled out in mid-air.

Zoey gasped. She waved her hand as if trying to pitch another fireball my way, but nothing appeared. The class stood silently in shock.

Her mouth dropped open. "I can't use my powers!"

"That's because I cut off your connection to your Familiar," I stated.

Surprised notes of alarm went up around the class. Most people seemed shocked.

"How did you do that?" Linus gaped.

"You know how we've been working on drawing energy from unbonded creatures and our environment? I just channeled the magic in Zoey's Familiar into myself instead of allowing it to flow into her," I explained.

"But how?" Zoey peeped. "That should be impossible."

"But I did it," I pointed out. "Which means some of you might be able to, as well."

"Teach us." Linus eagerly came forward. "If we can take the power of another person's Familiar, that means the Task Force won't be able to fight back!"

"You're thinking what I'm thinking," I stated. "The process is the same as drawing from any magical creature, or the earth, except that you've got to override the bond created by nature between an Elementai and their Familiar. If you focus, you should be able to feel the bond out and redirect it, like you would any magical energy."

"That's crazy. Nothing should be able to override the natural bond between an Elementai and a Familiar," Zoey protested.

"It's exceptionally uncommon. I don't know anyone else who can do it yet, besides myself," I confessed. "But maybe one of you can get a handle on it."

Linus was the first to try. He attempted to take Zoey's magic, like I had done, but she conjured a fireball without breaking a sweat. We worked through the line, though no progress was made— even though I demonstrated again and again, the students didn't progress.

We worked for hours and got nowhere. Except for me, no one was able to interrupt an Elementai's line of power.

"It seems like this is something only talented Elementai can do," I mumbled under my breath. I didn't like giving myself the formal label, but other people had called me that, and I wasn't so self-deprecating I denied I was in a different category. I was masterful of magic. A lot of people were good at it, or even great, but for this kind of advanced skill that wasn't enough.

The class seemed pretty discouraged, so I dismissed them. I wasn't in a good mood myself. My plan hadn't worked, which meant that it'd be useless in the fight against the Elders and the Task Force. If I was the only one who could cut off someone's powers, it wasn't much help. I couldn't go through a whole battle taking people's magic one by one. Not to mention it was hard to sustain. I think I could interrupt two connections at most before they began to drop off. This was totally useless.

I needed to clear my head. I went home and got some basket fibers before I started wandering, looking for a place to go. I hoped to the ancestors no one would bother me with chief stuff for an hour so I could think.

Finally, I found a secluded area in the redwoods next to a river, big enough for Julian to lay in. He came down from the skies and fit in through the narrow canopy, nearly knocking himself out of the air in the process.

I sat on a rock by the water and began weaving. I got frustrated and swore several fucking times, because I messed up, and had to start over three times before I finally got a rhythm down and maintained some sort of consistency.

I was making a cradleboard for Sophia, so she could carry Ava-Marie on her back. It was something I planned to give to her once the baby arrived as a surprise. Basket weaving was one of those mindlessly repetitive activities that soothed my mind enough to straighten out my thoughts.

I wondered if anyone back in Kinpago had mastered intrafusion. Was this what Oleander was doing? Taking power from Skylis, even though he wasn't truly his Familiar?

That explained why Oleander was so powerful currently when no one had heard of him before. I didn't think Oleander was a talented Elementai — but maybe he'd found a way around it.

Except I was worried. The Anichi students were progressing, but they were nowhere near ready for a fight. These kids weren't prepared to go to war— and the Elders were. I was desperately trying to make up for what the Anichi didn't have, but even so, it felt like a clock was ticking in the background, warning me we didn't have much time left.

I scowled as I continued working on the cradleboard. The baby was going to be here at the end of next month, and I didn't know when I was going to get a spare moment to finish this thing. As chief, I was always busy either dealing with something direly important, or stupid shit I couldn't care less about.

Wouldn't change it for the world, though.

Soft footsteps interrupted my process. Luana sat down next to me, and Sierra fluttered above her head. Somehow, she'd located me.

Luana held up a small deerskin bag to say she was working on something. I nodded, to show that it was okay to join me. She sat on the rock beside me and took out dozens of beads from the pouch. She began stringing them together as Sierra gave them to her, both of them humming a faint tune.

She held up the string of beads she was working on. I think she intended to add them to the cradleboard to decorate it after I was finished. I smiled. "That's really sweet, Luana. Thank you."

We worked in silence for a while. As I wove, she added the beads to the cradleboard by weaving them into the work with a few basket fibers of her own.

I was nearly done. Maybe things weren't as drastic as I thought.

I knew Luana was teaching Sophia later on that night. When she got up to leave, I followed her, so I could hide the cradleboard before Sophia came home.

It was a short walk back home. Once I'd put the cradleboard away in Imogen's closet, Luana held out a hand for me to take.

"You want me to come to Sophia's lesson?" I asked.

Luana nodded. She grabbed my wrist and guided me out the door. We walked to the beach, and I saw Sophia sitting on the porch at my mom's. Esis was building sandcastles not too far away.

Julian came down and did a belly flop in the ocean. Waves went everywhere, splashing onshore and ruining the sandcastle. Esis squeaked and shook his tail. As Julian came onshore, Esis beat his little fists on Julian's leg. They ran and played together as Sophia waved us over.

Sophia was eight months along. Luana said the baby was healthy, but small. Sophia still had a rough time getting around, though. Picking up things off the ground had become completely my responsibility, as she couldn't bend over at all— not to mention I had to pull her out of the bed lately, because she could barely manage to get up on her own.

Still, she was glowing. Her hands were placed softly over her belly as I sat next to her on the porch swing.

Luana pointed to the area underneath her eyes, commenting on the dark circles Sophia wore. She laughed.

"Ava hasn't been letting me sleep. She's been keeping me up most nights," Sophia said in a tired way. "She likes to jump around and lay right on my spine."

I only expected it to get worse. Sophia's attention turned to me. "How are you feeling today?" she asked.

I grimaced. "Not great." I didn't want to get into details.

Except it felt like all the muscles were ripping from my bones and I could definitely feel a cold coming on. I needed to be healthy when the baby got here. Sophia would need help.

But winter was on its way, and that usually meant a crap ton of viruses all season long that I wasn't good at fighting off. It wasn't the best time of year for me to be having a kid, but here we were.

Luana gestured to me and signed quickly. Sophia's mouth fell slightly open, and she signed back. "You want me to try my healing powers on Liam?"

Luana nodded eagerly. Sophia looked hesitant. "I don't know. We've tried that before, and it didn't work."

"Luana might have a point," I offered. "You couldn't before, but you've been training for months now. It might be possible."

Sophia blushed. "All I've managed to heal is a simple scratch. I don't know if it's going to work with you."

"Let's just try." I placed her hand against my chest. "Just see what you can feel. Like Luana did when I met her."

Sophia frowned slightly. "Okay." She closed her eyes and tried to concentrate. Nothing happened right away. Luana's gaze went from me to Sophia, like her magic could sense what Sophia's was trying to feel inside of me.

Sophia's expression was clear, until it suddenly changed. Her eyebrows knitted together, and she frowned. She recoiled away from me, holding the hand that had been touching me as if she'd been burned. She seemed shocked.

"What do you feel?" I asked. Luana signed the same question.

Sophia hunched her shoulders. "It's... not what I was expecting."

That was Sophia-speak for *you feel awful.* Tears beaded at the corners of her eyes. I think she understood for the first time just how sick I really was. Telling someone about it and describing it to them was a lot different than feeling it yourself.

Luana said something again, which caught Sophia's attention. I knew Luana wanted Sophia to try again.

Sophia sighed before she hesitantly laid a hand over my heart. Her lip quivered, and a tear leaked out as she touched me. I quickly brushed it away.

"Concentrate, Soph," I told her. "Look past it. I don't know what Luana's been teaching you, but try to use it to heal me."

Sophia took a deep breath. "Healing magic is the process of using someone's power inside of them to make the body do what it's supposed to. But you're hard, Liam. Your systems don't know *how* to work. It's like the information they need to function properly isn't there."

Luana's eyes narrowed, and she made a pushing gesture, as if telling Sophia to force it to. Sophia frowned, and I asked, "What's wrong?"

"She's suggesting I try to transfer some of my Anichi magic into your body— like intrafusion, but backwards. She says the healing magic will work to get your systems going again— basically like the magic is teaching your cells how to regenerate," Sophia said.

"Is that going to work?" I asked.

"I don't know. Let me try." Sophia closed her eyes once more. As she did, her hand began to glow white. I felt warmth begin to spread from where her fingertips touched me, and I knew it had worked. It was the same feeling I got when Esis healed me.

Except this was less of a warmth and more of a fire. A strong one, a fire that didn't hurt, but one that rather blazed throughout my internal systems with an intense passion. As I felt the fire spread over me, the pain in my back disappeared, and I felt the symptoms of the oncoming cold lessen. Fatigue that had been plaguing me for days vanished, and I felt completely refreshed— like I'd slept for days, gotten a massage and taken the strongest pain pills known to man.

Sophia's face lit up. "I did it!"

"You did, Soph!" I cried, and Luana clapped. I gave Sophia a tight hug — tight as I could, anyway, with the baby in the way. I stroked her hair back. "How do you feel?" I knew great feats of magic could leave Elementai feeling exhausted, and Sophia had just done something incredible.

"Honestly? No different," she said. "It was easy for me once I got past the initial shock. I think being pregnant has really helped me harness my Anichi powers."

"I feel fucking amazing," I said. "Well done, *pawee*."

Luana pointed to Esis, as if to say not to tell him, because he'd get jealous. The little kurble was on top of Julian's head and beating his paws into the dragon's temple. Julian yawned, like he was bored.

I got an idea. "Hey, you want to try healing someone else?"

"What do you mean?" Sophia tilted her head.

I knew healing magic had some effect on mental illnesses, and Maddie was in a bad place right now. Esis had cleared my head after my suicide attempt, and though it didn't work as well on physical ailments, I had a theory that consistent Anichi magic could at least help offset some of the symptoms. "Wait here."

I walked into the house and lightly tapped on Maddie's door. I could see under the crack it was dark inside her room. "Maddie. I've got something that might help."

"Go away, Liam!" Her voice was muffled and angry.

My heart fell. Maddie had hardly come out of her room since the wedding. She barely even talked to Drew now; the kid had buried himself in his job working with James and Carter in intel, to try and distract himself from the lack of Maddie's attention. Though she loved him, she was purposefully pushing him away for a reason I didn't understand.

Mom didn't know what to do with her. Neither did the rest of us. Maddie hadn't said a word about the strange "experiments" Oleander had forced her to take part in. Whatever Oleander had done to Maddie had taken a permanent effect. One more reason why I couldn't wait to kill the bastard.

"Just try. Please?" I begged.

"No. Leave me alone!"

I tried to open the door, but it was locked. I'd have to break it down and drag her out of there, which I didn't think would go well. I wouldn't push her into this if she didn't want it.

I sighed and returned to the porch. "Never mind," I said. "She won't come out."

Sophia and Luana frowned. "That's too bad," Sophia said.

Luana signed something, and this time I could interpret what it meant. *She'll come to us when she's ready.*

Not promising. But nobody could make me better when I had been in a dark place, either. I had to be willing to crawl out of it. Maddie needed more time.

"Let's go home. It's pizza night!" Sophia said in a chipper way, though I knew it was more or less to get my mind off my sister. "Imogen's making your favorite thing. Crust!"

I laughed. "Yeah. Wouldn't want to miss that."

When we got back home, Imogen was putting toppings on top of uncooked dough— except mine, of course, because toppings were gross. Sophia's was loaded with everything but the kitchen sink. Her pregnancy cravings had made her beg Imogen to put *eggs* on her pizza now. It'd totally gotten out of hand. Sassy was making pizzas for herself, Squeaks, and Esis, balancing pepperonis on her nose... though I think she ate more toppings than she placed, because the bag was half gone. Esis scurried onto the counter and rearranged the toppings so they were placed in a symmetrical order instead of all over the place. Sassy huffed, like she was offended.

You could order twenty pizzas for Julian and it wouldn't be enough. I could hear the beat of his wings outside as he flew away to go hunting.

Imogen finished Jonah's cheese pizza before she started placing basil pieces on her own— she loved margarita. When Luana came up to the counter, Imogen's eyes flashed upward. She pushed a small pizza toward Luana and began signing while she spoke. "I prepared your favorite. Ham, bacon and pineapple."

A huge smile spread across Luana's face, though Imogen more or less grimaced back.

Imogen's unpleasant look couldn't fool me. She wouldn't have made a pizza for Luana unless she liked her. The girl was having a hard time not letting her in, and ancestors, it showed. These days, Luana went everywhere Sophia did, and Sophia always had Imogen. I bet Imogen was secretly growing to like Luana, despite her best efforts to keep her at a distance. Imogen could act like she hated Luana all she wanted, but I wasn't buying the ruse.

As Imogen placed the pizzas into the oven, Jonah walked into the house wearing a stunned expression. Squeaks squeezed her way through. She danced on her hooves as Jonah sank down onto the couch in slow motion. He let out a very long, dramatic, and *loud* sigh.

He obviously wanted attention. "What the hell's the matter with you?" I asked, irritated. Sophia sat beside him on an armchair, while Luana took a spot on the couch.

"You'll never guess," Jonah teased. He played with the ends of his hair, and Squeaks copied his sigh from earlier.

"Well, we're waiting, so spill," I said.

"Jake said he wants to *wait* to have sex," Jonah said in a dreamy, distant voice.

I didn't get the tone. It was like Jake had asked him to go to Disney World or something.

"Isn't that a good thing? It shows he doesn't want to hurt you," Sophia asked. I was thinking the same thing.

"It's not just that. There was more," Jonah rushed to say. "Jake, well... he said he doesn't want to have sex until *after we're married.*"

Jonah said the words like he revered them. Imogen's jaw dropped, and Sophia reeled back, like she'd been given some kind of scandalous news. Luana merely smirked.

"Um, okay. Why?" I asked.

"I think he noticed I was uncomfortable the other day," Jonah said, with a bit of a frown. "We had this big, long talk today, and he said that... I don't know. He wants to show me I have value. That he really treasures me, and I'm more than what I can offer people. That when it's the right time, he wants to make this last forever."

Jake was really building Jonah's hopes up. He'd better pull through on all this bullshit, because if he didn't, me and him were going to have a problem.

"Oh my gosh. That's so sweet!" Tears beaded in Imogen's eyes, and she fanned them frantically with her hands.

"I didn't know things were that serious," Sophia said. Luana scoffed as if to say she didn't know Jake.

"I didn't either, but... he really likes me for *me*," Jonah said. "I mean, he still wants to fool around, but he doesn't want to go all the way until we make things permanent."

"*Have* you guys fooled around?" Imogen ate a chip and Jonah— no shit — turned pink. You'd think he was a freaking virgin.

"No. All we've done is made out," he admitted.

"In five months?" Sophia asked in surprise. I elbowed her lightly, to let her know that was rude. It didn't matter how long it took you to sleep with someone, or if you ever did. She knew that. She sent me an apologetic glance.

Jonah didn't notice. "Yes. And it's just been *dreamy. He's* been dreamy. This relationship is the best one I've ever been in, and we haven't even touched each other! I didn't think that was possible."

"Sure it is." I shrugged. "All the best relationships start out that way."

"Well, I thought you had sex with someone and *then* you started to love them," Jonah explained. "After you gave them what they want."

"No, Jonah." I shook my head. "That's not how it works."

"I know that now. I didn't know you could have feelings for someone without doing anything, but you totally can," he gushed. "I seriously have never felt this way about *anyone*."

"Well, congratulations on taking a vow of abstinence, because I couldn't do it," Sophia cracked. She slapped Jonah on the shoulder.

I snorted. That was a fucking understatement. The woman couldn't last three days without going on a hunt for my dick.

"It's *so* romantic. But also, so *frustrating*." Jonah collapsed against the cushions. "Do you know how long I've been dying to jump him? Now I have to wait until we say our vows. I'm going to get blue balls!"

"I'm sure blow jobs are still on the menu," Imogen quipped, and Sophia snorted. Luana let out a tiny giggle.

"A bit of abstinence will be good for you." I rubbed my eyes. Maybe Jonah would stop being such a perverted, intolerable horn-dog now.

Or he'd get worse.

Yeah. He'd probably get worse.

"Jake just needs time to stock his sex dungeon." Imogen laughed.

Jonah's eyes gleamed with interest, and he sat up. "Do you really think he has a sex dungeon?"

I thought about Jake. Military guy who had a control fetish? "Probably."

Jonah squealed. "This is *so* going to be worth the wait."

I groaned. "Please don't give me any images." For the love of the ancestors, I didn't know why we couldn't keep this shit private.

Sophia giggled. "Come on, Liam. You're just as filthy as the rest of us, you just know how to hide it."

I had to smirk.

"Ooh, so Liam's not such a prude after all, is he?" Jonah questioned in interest.

"Hey, he comes up with all the ideas in the bedroom," Sophia stated. I shrugged in agreement.

Imogen smiled. "It's so cute how you two are married. Now Jonah's next on the list," she said. "I guess *wedding bells* are ringing!"

Imogen meant to be playful, but I caught the bitter resentment in her tone. Her words came out in a snarky jibe. She was probably feeling left out again.

Imogen had plastered on a smile that showed she was trying, but was obviously fake. Luana reached out a hand as if to place it on Imogen's shoulder, until she thought better of it and recoiled.

There was scratching at the door. Luana stood and opened it. In walked the jaguar that was Chief Cauac's companion. Around the jaguar's neck was a note. Luana took it and unrolled it. As she read the note, she looked up to Sophia, then down to the letter again.

"What's up?" Sophia asked, curious.

Luana signed something, and Sophia said, "Chief Cauac has summoned me. He says he must speak with me. It's urgent."

"Want us to come with you?" I offered.

Sophia narrowed her eyes as Luana continued speaking. "She says it's best if I go alone. I won't be long."

Sophia left arm-in-arm with Luana, following the jaguar.

"What do you think the chief wants her for?" Jonah wondered.

"I don't know. It's weird he asked her to come alone," I mused.

"She's not alone. She's with Luana. We can trust her," Jonah said in a carefree way. Squeaks clacked her beak in agreement. Imogen rolled her eyes, but I ignored her.

"I wonder if Chief Cauac summoned her because he found something about her birth parents," Imogen wondered.

"Hopefully." Though I was sure it wasn't about that. We had no clues whatsoever on where Sophia had come from, and that was unlikely to change.

Jonah sighed. "Poor Sophia. I feel just awful for her, having this baby and not knowing who Ava's grandparents are."

"It's not easy." Heritage aside, my first thought was the downside of not knowing who Sophia's parents were meant we didn't know if they carried any medical conditions they could pass down to Ava-Marie like I did. It was terribly worrying.

"There's got to be an explanation." Imogen tapped her chin. "We've barely looked into this."

"We haven't had time," I said. "We're too busy trying to win the war."

"We've got time now." Without another word, Imogen slunk off to mine and Sophia's room. She opened the closet door and started ruffling through items, tossing clothes and boxes to the side. She pulled out a backpack that we'd taken on the road the night of the battle of Orenda Academy and started rifling through it.

"Imogen, you shouldn't be going through her things," I growled.

"Relax. I'm not trying to be nosy. I just want to help," Imogen insisted. Sassy stuck her head in the bag, but came up empty.

This invasion of privacy wasn't like her. The old Im wouldn't have done this, but the new Imogen didn't care anymore.

I was about to stop her before Imogen pulled out something from the backpack. "Ah-ha! We can start here."

From what I could see, Imogen held a photograph— one the three of us had never seen before. I think it came from Sophia's scrapbook, but she'd never shown us it. It was too personal. The scrapbook had gone up in the fire, but Sophia had managed to save this picture.

"How is that going to help?" Jonah asked.

"I don't know. We'll look at it and try to find clues," Imogen said crossly. She left the room and slapped the photo on the dining room counter. We huddled over it in a circle, inspecting it closely. In the picture were Alan and Betsy Weber, along with two college-aged girls tucked closely to their sides. All were wearing smiles and looked happy.

"It's just an old picture," Jonah said with a casual shrug. "This gets us nowhere."

The photo had gone through the ringer since we were on the run. Age had made it faded and yellow, and there were burn marks and holes in it from the various bullshit it had survived while we were fighting the battle and on the run.

At first glance, I thought the woman in the photo was Sophia, but a chill ran up my spine when I became certain the woman in the photograph was not my wife. There were small features that were different— but they were there. The woman in the photograph was strong and beautiful, but she wasn't Sophia Mitoh.

The most telling fact was Sophia didn't have green eyes. Or red hair.

"This mystery woman seems familiar somehow," Imogen said, pointing at her.

"I think the other girl in the picture is Lucy Greyson. She was Alan and Betsy's daughter," I said. "She was the one everyone thought was Sophia's mom, but she died in childbirth."

"If that's the case, this other woman in the photo *must* be Lucy's best friend. It makes sense that she'd give up her baby to the parents of someone she trusted," Imogen mused. "She *does* look a lot like Sophia."

"This mystery woman... that's gotta be Sophia's mom, then!" Jonah shoved the both of us aside to get a closer look, but I pushed him back.

We leaned so far over the photograph that I thought our breath might blow it away. As we observed the strange woman, I took in her sharp jawline, her perfectly manicured brows... even today, she never had a hair out of place—

But her nose was different. She must've changed it. That one small detail had been enough to hide the truth for years.

I put things together a second before the others did. My stomach bottomed out. Bile rose in my throat, and I inwardly cringed as my heart picked up speed.

No. It couldn't be possible.

It'd break Sophia's heart.

Imogen let out a great gasp. She flung herself away from the counter and waved her hands as if shooing away imaginary flies. Sassy yipped at her feet like she'd given her the idea.

"What? Did you figure it out?" Jonah asked, looking wildly around. Squeaks copied him, swiveling her head from side to side.

Imogen jabbed her finger at the photo. "How did Sophia overlook this? How did she not *recognize*—?"

"She doesn't look at herself every day like we do, Im," I said. My throat was parched, and my voice was hoarse. Of all the terrible things to happen.

"Anyone mind bringing the Storm Lord up to speed?" Jonah said crossly.

Imogen made an annoyed noise. She picked the photo up and held it in

Jonah's direction. "Is it really not that obvious? Who else do we know has red hair?"

Jonah's eyes widened. He looked at the photo again, then back to Imogen before he stated, "No fucking way. If that's *really* her, she must've had some work done, because she doesn't look like that anymore."

"We don't have any proof," I rushed to say. "A photo means nothing."

"Look at her, Liam! She looks just like her!" Imogen shoved the photo in my face.

I pushed it away. "Coincidence," I forced out.

Jonah played nervously with Squeaks' feathers. "Maybe she's not her daughter? Maybe she's a clone?"

I rolled my eyes at Jonah's pathetic attempt to remedy the situation. Jokes weren't going to help.

"You can't deny this! Neither of you can!" Imogen burst. "Sophia deserves to know."

I shook my head. "How can you even suggest that?"

"How can you suggest hiding this from her? She has a right to know who her mother is!" Imogen yelled.

My hands were shaking. "What are we going to do? We can't *tell* her that—"

"That Madame Doya is her *mother*?" Imogen screamed. "We have to, Liam!"

"Do you know how badly this is going to crush her? She's been working up a fantasy in her head that her parents are incredible people. How is she going to react when she finds out the woman who gave birth to her is a fucking psychopath?" I screamed.

Just then, the door opened, and Ezra walked through. He paused when he realized we were all shouting at each other. "Uh... hey."

I felt a twinge of annoyance at my brother. "Not a good time to stop by."

"Hey, your place is my place," Ezra said. He went to the fridge, took out the milk and drank it straight from the carton. Gross ass.

"Don't you have to be annoying somewhere else? We're busy," I stated.

"Hey, I just came by to celebrate," Ezra offered. "I can take the party elsewhere, but I thought you'd all want to join in, seeing as how you all hated the bitch as much as I did."

"Celebrate what?" Imogen asked, cocking her head.

"Haven't you heard the news?" Ezra asked. "Madame Doya has been found and arrested. She's been put into holding to wait for her trial. Her one request was to see Sophia in private. Probably to beg for mercy or something."

Ice filled my veins. *That's* why Sophia had been summoned moments ago. She was probably with Doya right now!

I didn't know what that madwoman was going to do to my wife and baby. I had to get to Sophia. "Where'd they take her, Ez?"

He noticed my balled fists and my harsh tone. He backed away. "Uh... why does it matter?" Ezra asked.

Imogen flung the photo at him. He caught it, and asked, "Why are you giving me this?"

"That's Sophia's mother," I forced out.

Ezra looked closer, then his hand went over his mouth. "Oh!" He staggered backward a few steps. "Oh *no*."

"Yeah. You see what we're dealing with," Imogen said.

"Ez. Where's. Doya?" I snarled.

"There's a holding cell near the temple. She's probably there," Ezra blurted out. He still seemed stunned.

I didn't waste any more time. I ran out the door. The door slammed against the wall. I hurried down the stone steps, where Julian was more or less napping on the ground below.

"Julian," I called, and his head snapped up once he heard my voice. I climbed onto his back and held tightly to his spikes, pressing myself to his form. "The temple. We have to get there right away."

He spread his wings and took off, flying over the village as quickly as his wings could carry us. As the cold wind blew back my hair, I shivered, but it wasn't from the chill.

I wasn't sure what kind of trick Doya had planned. But I did know one thing. Sophia might be Doya's daughter, but I was her husband.

And I'd make damn sure that woman would never hurt her again. Even if I had to do something drastic.

# sophia

## TWENTY

I didn't know why Chief Cauac had summoned me, and neither did Luana. The note didn't say much, just that I was needed urgently—and that it was best if I come alone. I didn't know why they hadn't summoned Liam, considering he was the Toaqua Chief. If something bad had happened, he'd be at the top of the call list. Which made me think either this wasn't bad... or was very personal.

The closer we came to the Anichi temple, the faster my heart beat. Ava-Marie kicked my stomach, like she too could feel my anxiety. I couldn't explain why my heart thumped like the rhythm of a drum. All I knew was I didn't think I was ready for whatever Chief Cauac had summoned me for.

Luana and I, along with our Familiars, followed her father's companion around the side of the temple and to the Elders' meeting quarters nearby. Chief Cauac stood on the steps outside, his hands casually crossed in front of himself. His eyes were soft, but his expression gave nothing away.

*Is something wrong, Daddy?* Luana signed as soon as we were within view.

Chief Cauac sighed and responded by signing and speaking at the same time. "It's too soon to say. Come, Sophia."

I hesitated as he held a hand out to me. "What about Luana?"

He frowned. "I'm afraid your presence has been requested privately. Luana and I will wait for you outside."

"What do you mean?" I asked. Chief Cauac placed a hand on my back and began leading me to a door on the other side of the building. "I thought *you* summoned me."

"I did," he replied. "But it's our prisoner who wants to see you."

"You have a prisoner?" My eyebrows shot up. Esis squeaked in equal surprise at my feet.

"She turned herself in today," Chief Cauac explained, stopping in front of a door I'd never entered before. "Her one request was to see you."

I racked my brain, trying to think of who he could be talking about. All my friends and family had either died or were with me in *Hok'evale*. My only other thought was Haley, and she'd only want to see me to kill me. She'd never turn herself in, though.

"Who are you talking about?" I asked.

Chief Cauac reached for the door and swung it open. I caught sight of the woman's fiery red mane a moment before he answered. "Madame Eleanor Doya."

My stomach bottomed out. I must've heard him wrong. Doya couldn't be here.

But she was— clear as day.

Beyond the door sat a small room with only four jail cells. There were small windows along the top of the walls with bars over them. They let in a small amount of light and cast sharp shadows across the jail floor.

The nearest cell housed a lioness behind noxite bars— Naomi. I could feel the noxite draining my energy the moment I stepped into the room. She lay on the ground, her ears drooping like she was ashamed to be locked up.

Madame Doya sat on a cot inside the farthest cell. Her red hair was tied into a frayed braid, and her usual smooth skin seemed worn down by stress. For the first time, I noticed age lines along the corners of her eyes. She wore one of her usual velvet dresses, with a cloak over the top. The hem of both were covered in dirt. She sat straight up with her shoulders back in a regal position, but something in her eyes had changed. When she looked at me, she did not narrow her gaze or look down her nose at me. In fact, it was just the opposite. Soft eyes filled with pain, regret, and sorrow met mine. They darted downward at my pregnant belly momentarily before she met my gaze again.

Part of me wanted to run away. This had to be a trap. But another part of me was curiously drawn forward. I had to know what she wanted to say.

"What is this?" I demanded as I stepped into the jail hall. There were bars between Doya and I, but I still felt uneasy. Esis followed at my side. "What could you possibly have to say to me?"

Madame Doya stood from her cot and came forward to the edge of her cell. "I've come to apologize, Sophia."

I scoffed. "Apologize? For what? Tormenting me when you were supposed to be my mentor? Turning your back on me when I thought I could trust you? Siding with Oleander? Killing Alric?"

I took another step into the jail. The main door quietly shut behind Esis and me. I had the urge to summon my Fire, but even if I wanted to burn Doya's ass, I couldn't with the noxite surrounding me, separating us.

"I'm here to apologize for all of it," Doya stated. "I did what I thought was the right thing."

"*Seriously!?*" I cried. "You sided with the man who started a war!"

"No," she said firmly. "I never wanted this war to happen— not like this. You have to understand that I made sacrifices in order to fulfill the ancestors' will."

"What will?" I demanded. "How do you know what they want? You did what you did to gain power."

"Yes," she confirmed. She didn't sound proud of it, but she didn't seem to regret it, either. "Only those in power are able to make change. You and I are not so different, Sophia."

Her words hit me like a punch to the gut. I went breathless.

"I'm *nothing* like you," I spat. "I won't kill for power."

"But you *will* kill to save the people you love," Doya shot back.

It was true. I'd do anything to win this war and save the Hawkei.

"The only difference between us is how we go about saving the people we love," Doya stated. "I thought I could protect people by being in power. I thought I could change the Elders' views. But the deeper I got, the harder it was."

"I don't believe you," I growled. "You killed Alric."

"Because Oleander was questioning my loyalty!" Doya roared. "Oleander asked me to kill him! If I didn't, I'd lose my place on the Elder Council, which meant I had *no* power to save anyone else."

I crossed my arms. "That's pretty bold of you to claim *saving* anyone. Name one person you've saved."

She gripped the bars to her cell and dropped her head. I'd never seen her look so vulnerable— and I still couldn't believe it. It had to be an act.

Slowly, Doya lifted her gaze and answered simply, "You."

My jaw dropped. Was she *serious*? In what twisted way had she convinced herself she *saved* me?

"What?" I gasped, practically laughing. "You've done nothing to help me. You almost killed me when we left the castle."

"I was trying to stop you," Doya stated. "I do nothing without good reason, Sophia."

"Then I want a reason," I snapped. "Why'd you try to stop us from leaving the castle?"

"Because I couldn't protect you from Oleander if I didn't know where to find you!" she burst.

The jail went really silent. I could hardly process the idea that she wanted to *protect* me.

"You may not realize it, but I have *always* protected you," Doya said. "When the Koigni Elders wanted to use you, *I'm* the one who led them astray."

My knees felt weak. Why would Doya do all that, just to turn around and act like such a bitch to my face? Was that another cover for the Elders? There were times when she was nice to me, when I thought we actually had a connection. Which was the real Doya, and which was the fake?

"If that's true, then what are you doing here?" I demanded. "Why aren't you in Kinpago using your position to overthrow Oleander?"

"Because..." Doya inhaled a deep breath, then dropped her shoulders and sighed deeply. "Because I'm *tired*, Sophia. I'm sick of fighting this war."

Weren't we all?

"Why not tell me this before?" I insisted. "Back at school, you could've said you were trying to protect me. I might've actually believed you then."

"I couldn't, because..." Doya trailed off.

I pursed my lips. "Because you're a cold. Hearted. *Bitch*."

Holy ancestors, that was like a thousand pound weight lifting off my chest. I hadn't even meant to say it, but I wasn't lying, either. I'd been thinking it since the day Doya humiliated me in front of my class by trying to make me light a candle with no knowledge of magic. It felt really good to finally tell her how I felt.

The jail went silent for a few moments before Doya said, "You're right."

*Excuse me?* Had I heard her right?

"I should've done better," Doya admitted.

I was so shocked I nearly forgot how to breathe. Esis pressed close to my leg, like her confession terrified him. It was like Doya had been body snatched and replaced by a clone.

Doya shook her head, and true regret crossed her features. "It's why I left Oleander to come find you, Sophia. It's why I was at your wedding."

"I *knew* I saw you in the woods," I growled. "What I don't get is why you care. Why start making your amends with me? Why attend *my* wedding?"

Doya held her head high, but her features softened. "What kind of mother would I be if I had missed my own daughter's wedding?"

The air left my lungs, and the world spun around me. What she was saying... no, it couldn't be possible.

And yet it made so much sense...

"No. You're ly— lying—"

I could hardly get the words out as the realization hit me like a bolt of lightning. Doya was really close to my grandparents. I had Koigni powers like she did. She spoke to me about becoming chieftess because I had Elder blood in my veins, and she'd always known.

It *fit*, but that didn't make it *true*.

And yet something told me it was. Call it intuition. Call it a message from the ancestors. I didn't know what. But I did know that my search for my birth mother was over.

I just hadn't pictured it ending like this.

My knees buckled beneath me. I gasped as I dropped to the concrete. Esis screeched and placed a healing hand on mine immediately. A moment later, the door behind me burst open.

"Where's that sorry excuse of a motherfucking—?" Liam cut off as he entered the room and saw me gasping on my knees.

I glanced over my shoulder at him, and his face paled. He rushed over to me. I could hear Jonah, Imogen, and Ezra shouting outside, along with the beat of Julian's wings overhead.

Liam knelt at my side and pulled me into his arms. I relaxed into him and finally felt like I could breathe again. Liam looked down at me and pushed my hair out of my face. "Talk to me, *pawee*. What'd she do to you?"

"N-nothing," I stammered. "She just said... she's my mother?"

I phrased it like a question. It was just too unreal to accept.

Liam frowned, but there was something in his eyes that was unlike the shock I expected. It was like he already knew.

I pushed myself up straighter. "Liam, she's lying. She has to be."

"I don't think she is, Soph," Liam admitted. "I never realized it before, but you actually have a lot of Doya's features. It's possible—"

I cut him off. "Don't say it."

"But it's true," Doya cut in.

Liam shot a disgusted look at her, then turned back to me. "Let's discuss this outside."

Liam started to help me to my feet, but Doya stopped him. "Wait!"

Liam let go of me to stomp closer to Doya's cell. "Wait for what?" he roared, getting close up to her face. "We've waited long enough, but you've come too late. Sophia wants nothing to do with you."

Doya watched me the whole time Liam spoke, then finally turned her narrowed gaze on him. "Why don't you let Sophia speak for herself? It's what Koigni women do."

Heat flared in my veins. "Don't you *dare* pretend I'm anything like you. I may be Koigni, but that's where the similarities end. My husband is right. I want nothing to do with you."

My guts twisted. How could this horrible woman be my birth mother? It seemed like some sort of sick joke.

I reached for Liam's arm. "Come on, Liam. Let's go. There's nothing more she can possibly say to me that will make this better."

Liam and I turned toward the door, but Doya's rushed words halted me in my tracks. "Don't you want to know who your father is?"

I whirled toward her, but hesitated. Of *course* I wanted to know who my father was, but right now, I feared terrifying disappointment. He might be like her. Maybe it was better if I didn't know at all.

Before I could answer, Doya reached into her cloak and pulled out a small leather-bound book. She reached through the bars of her cell and held it out to me. I didn't take it right away.

"I'm on your side, Sophia." She glanced back to the book, as if encouraging me to take it. "This is one of my journals. It explains everything you need to know."

I wanted to stomp out of there, just to show her she had no hold over me, but I still had so many questions.

Curiosity won out. I reached for the journal.

"Wait!" Liam cried. "It could be cursed."

Liam was right, but I hesitated. There was so much I still wanted to know.

"Please, Sophia, I mean you no harm," Madame Doya begged. "Just take it."

I eyed Doya a moment longer, searching for ill intent in her features, but I didn't find it. Cautiously, I reached out for the journal. "I want to know," I whispered.

Liam shot Doya a hard gaze as I stepped away. I walked to the other end of the jail, where I flipped open the journal to a page marked with a red ribbon. The entry was dated the same week I had arrived at Orenda Academy.

Liam wrapped a protective arm around my waist and looked over my shoulder. We both began reading.

*Dear Diary,*

*I thought that I could outrun my past. I thought that abandoning it that night would make sure it stayed in the past where it belonged. Eighteen years later, my past finally caught up with me.*

*Sophia Henley is a reminder of everything I lost, and I despise her for it with every fiber of my being. She doesn't know that her eyes look just like his. She doesn't know the reason I can't stand to be around her is because every time I look at her, I'm reminded of the worst moments I've ever endured. She doesn't know what she's done to me.*

*I can't say it's all her fault. Elliot played a part, too, though he doesn't know it. Even eighteen years later, I'd never once mentioned it to him.*

*Elliot Baine has always been a master of charm and confidence. One day of Hawkei History, and I was done for. I knew I should've stayed away. Forget the fact that he was twelve years my senior, my teacher, and that I was his student. He was Water, and I was Fire. Mixing the two was strictly forbidden.*

*All the more reason to chase him.*

*Elliot Baine was a forbidden fruit in every way, and if there's one thing I know about Koigni, it's that we will fight until our very last breath to get what we wanted. And I wanted to prove to the whole goddamn world that I could have Elliot Baine.*

*It started out with innocent tutoring sessions, just so I could get him alone. I was cunning. I was careful. I didn't strike right away, only lured him in. It only took a few months before I had him right where I wanted him, in a position he couldn't resist even if he wanted to. Elliot Baine was in love with me, and we didn't give a flying fuck what the Elders or the ancestors thought of it.*

*That first time I kissed him in his office was everything. I still remembered the feel of his hands on my hips, the way he kissed me back even though he knew it was wrong— even though he knew it could cost him his life.*

*"Eleanor," he whispered, drawing away. "We shouldn't."*

*I didn't have to speak. All I had to do was kiss him again, and he was back under my spell.*

*Our months of innocent tutor lessons turned into months of guilty pleasures. Of all the men that had crawled into my bed over the years, none of them could love me like Elliot. He loved me with an unmatched passion I had never experienced before, nor would ever experience again. Fire and Water didn't belong together, but Elliot and I did. I was sure of it...*

*Until the night he called it off.*

*"It's getting dangerous, Ellie," he told me.*

*I was still lying naked beneath his sheets. The sorry bastard had the nerve to fuck me first.*

*I ran my fingers down the side of his face, drinking in his features. I was so aroused that I was ready for another go. I climbed on top of him, and his breath quivered as my skin brushed against him.*

*"It's always been dangerous, Elliot," I pointed out. "That's what makes it fun."*

*I pulled the sheet up over our heads, but Elliot took me by the waist and rolled me off of him.*

*"This is serious," he insisted. "I don't... I don't think we should see each other anymore."*

*The room spun around me. I couldn't have heard him right.*

*"Are you... are you breaking up with me?" I demanded.*

*Elliot dropped his gaze and spoke so softly that I barely heard him. "Yes."*

*I sat upright in bed. "Tell me you're joking!"*

*He didn't respond.*

*"Tell me you're fucking joking, Elliot!" I shot out of bed and paced across the room. The Fire in my body raged. I needed to calm down. And fast.*

*I grabbed the first thing my hands could find. I held a vase over my head and smashed it to the floor.*

*"Ellie," he said, horrified. "Calm down."*

*"Calm down?" I snapped. "I can either break things, or set your goddamn house on fire. Which would you prefer?"*

*"Ellie, this has to stop," he said firmly. "People are starting to notice us. You have to understand, I'm only doing this to keep you out of harm's way."*

*"Yeah, well, maybe you should've thought of that before you fucked me six ways from Sunday." I grabbed my clothes and rushed out of the room.*

*"Ellie, wait!" Elliot stopped me in the hall.*

*I looked back at him, and I snapped. I raised my arm and a fireball formed, hovering in warning. "If all you wanted from me was some sauce on the side, you should've made that clear. You told me you loved me!"*

*His face fell in apology. Looking at him was too much. I whirled around and ran.*

*I've never stopped running since.*

*It took four months. Four whole fucking months to realize my body was changing. I'd attributed the fatigue and vomiting to symptoms of depression. It literally made me ill to lose the man I loved. I couldn't tell Lucy or Tony about it. They were starting a life of their own— married with a house in Kinpago. They even had a baby on the way.*

*I couldn't tell them about my own, the half-breed monster that was growing inside of me. I kept it from them for their own protection. If word got out, they'd be at risk for not reporting it. Elliot and I would be put to death, as would the child. I couldn't breathe a word of this to anyone.*

*So I didn't. Not my best friend Lucy. Not my parents. Not even Elliot.*

*As the months passed, I covered up with thicker and thicker clothing. By the end of my Third Year at Orenda Academy, I had entered my third trimester. It was impossible to hide any longer. I told everyone I was traveling for the summer, but instead, I rented an apartment in Kinpago and relied on delivery services to bring me what I needed until this was all over.*

*The night it happened, I was lounging on my couch when tight cramps spread across my belly. I went to the bathroom, thinking that was all it was. But the cramps kept coming, getting worse and worse each time.*

*"No, no, no," I cried to the silence as I realized what was happening.*

*I heard a pop, and warm water gushed out between my legs, soaking the floor. It suddenly occurred to me that I couldn't have this child here. I couldn't leave any evidence behind.*

*I left the apartment in the dead of night and walked into the forest, clutching my stomach the entire way. I walked until it felt as if my limbs might fall off, until I could no longer trudge on by sheer will. I fell onto my hands and knees as the contractions squeezed my body tight, blocking off my airways. I gasped for breath.*

*A moment of relief passed. I panted, pulling in as much air as I could. The forest spun around me as a wave of pain hit me once again. I curled up on my side, and the dirt stuck to my sweaty face. I cried out, begging the ancestors to make it stop. The urge to push came, and I did all I could just to get it over with.*

*When the child came, the pain melted away. I could suddenly see the world more clearly. I lifted the small body in my arms and pulled the child to my chest as tears soaked my cheeks. She didn't make a sound, and for a moment, I thought it was a blessing.*

*Then the first sound escaped her lips. I pulled her to my chest, right beneath my collar bone. I pressed her face into my night gown to muffle the sounds.*

*To smother them.*

*She was a half-breed. She would die by the Elders' hands if not by mine. The least I could do was make sure they didn't torture her first. She was so small. So innocent.*

*The child wiggled in my arms.*

*Tears continued to stream down my face. "Please forgive me."*

*A growl came from behind me, startling me. I dropped the child from my collarbone, allowing her to breathe. She sucked in air, but she didn't cry.*

*I turned to see a pair of golden eyes staring at me through the darkness. The moment I laid eyes on them, the whole world tilted on its axis and spun the opposite way. It felt like I was unwinding. The pain in my lower abdomen eased, as if it had never existed in the first place. I smelled roses and heard the sound of the harp playing in the distance. The taste of sweet banana cream filled my mouth.*

*The creature stepped forward, and her blonde fur transformed into bright orange flames. They burned all across her body, lighting up the forest around us. The fire lioness ducked her head, as if inviting me to reach out to her. I was so struck by her that I did just that. My fingers touched the flames, but they didn't burn.*

*"Naomi," I whispered. I didn't know how I knew her name, but it was like I'd known it all my life.*

*Naomi took another step forward and pressed her forehead into the child's chest. The child didn't protest against the red-hot flames. She relaxed into them, enjoying their warmth.*

*"She's Koigni," I realized.*

*There was no question about it. This child had Toaqua blood running through her veins. But she also had mine. She was my daughter, whether I liked it or not.*

*Naomi drew away, and the flames faded. She stared at me with sad eyes.*

*"I have to," I whispered to her. "The Elders would not let her live. I'm doing it to protect everyone."*

*Naomi shook her head, as if to say this wasn't the only way.*

*Tears ran down my throat as I struggled to hold them back. It felt as if I were choking. What was Naomi suggesting? I couldn't leave the child out here. That would be merciless. I couldn't just give her away...*

*Or could I?*

*Once the idea came to mind, it took root and didn't let go. Naomi helped me to my feet and steadied me as we walked for miles through the forest. I held my daughter close in my arms, so she would feel warm, so she would feel safe.*

*We snuck through the darkness of night through the Koigni village until we arrived at 1345 Firebrick Lane. We avoided the streetlights and slipped through the gate in the back. I raised my hand and knocked on the door.*

*Alan answered, and his face went stark white when he saw the blood on my nightgown. "Ellie? Dear ancestors! Betsy!"*

*Betsy was a midwife. I knew she could help.*

*"Betsy!" Alan screamed again as he guided me inside.*

*Betsy came running down the stairs. She was already in her nursing scrubs, with fresh gloves in her pocket. There was blood streaked on her shirt. She took one look at me and dove into medic mode. "In our room. Now."*

*I couldn't hold the tears back. I shoved the child into Betsy's arms. "Take her. Please."*

*Betsy held the child gently and guided me down onto the bed. "Alan, I need towels. Tony!"*

*I was sobbing so hard I couldn't process what happened next. Betsy began administering medication through an IV. I curled up on the bed and let the emotions wash over me, taking me away from the child I'd just birthed. It was almost as if it hadn't happened at all...*

*I woke hours later feeling disoriented. Betsy sat in a chair beside the bed, watching over me. I heard the sound of a man singing soft lullabies from the living room. Was that Tony?*

*"How did you know?" I whispered. I could barely speak after everything.*

*Betsy shook her head. "I didn't."*

*"But the medicine, the gloves, it was like you were prepared—"*

*My words stopped dead in their tracks. She was prepared, but not for me.*

*"Lucy?" I asked. "Her, too?"*

*Betsy nodded, but tears began to well in her eyes. "They didn't make it."*

*Betsy began to sob. She couldn't be serious.*

*"Lucy?" I asked breathlessly. "And her daughter?"*

*Betsy nodded. "She wanted a home birth. Complications arose, and..."*

*She cried so hard she couldn't finish her sentence.*

*I curled in on myself. I'd cried so much that I had no more tears to shed. I couldn't wrap my head around the news that my best friend was gone.*

*"We're going to tell everyone in the morning," she said— like she needed to give an explanation.*

*Footsteps padded down the hall. Tony entered the room carrying a small bundle of blankets. He stared down at it with hope in his eyes.*

*"I heard you talking," he said softly. "Would you like to hold her?"*

*"No!" I said quickly.*

*Tony hugged the child protectively. "Why didn't you tell us you were pregnant, Ellie?"*

*I rolled away from him and didn't answer. The answer was just too painful.*

*"Ellie," Tony said softly, in that tone he always used to keep me calm when my emotions rose too high.*

*"I can't do it, Tony."*

*"Of course you can," Betsy said. "I have resources that can help. If it's about finances—"*

*"I said I can't do it!" I snapped. I quickly softened my tone. "Take her for me, will you, Tony? You can raise her as your own."*

*Tony hesitated. "You mean... lie?"*

*"No one will know," I pressed. "They'll think she's yours."*

*Tony gaped at me, like he was half considering it.*

*"Ellie, maybe you should get some rest," Betsy suggested. "This isn't the kind of decision to make right now."*

*"I'm not going to change my mind. Betsy, you're like a mother to me. If I wasn't serious about this, I wouldn't be asking."*

*A man cleared his voice from the doorway and stepped into the room. I hadn't realized Alan had been listening.*

*"Whatever you need, Ellie," he said. "We're here for you."*

*Tony's eyes brimmed with tears. "If I'm going to take her, she needs a name."*

*I knew what Tony was doing. He was trying to get me to bond with her. I couldn't.*

*"You can name her," I said.*

*Tony stared down at the sleeping child. "We named our daughter Charlotte. Maybe we can give her Lucy's second choice. Sophia."*

*Damn it. Lucy and I came up with that name together.*

*"Whatever you want," I said, already trying to erase Sophia's name from my memory.*

*No matter how hard I tried to forget, that name would forever haunt me with what I'd just done.*

My knees quivered and my ears rang as I read the passage. This couldn't be real— Doya my mother, and Baine, my father? Liam and I exchanged a wide-eyed look of disbelief.

I whirled back toward Doya. "How do I know this is real? How do I know you're not lying?"

"What reason do I have to lie to you?" Doya asked.

"I don't know!" I cried. "A million, I'm sure. You could be Oleander's spy. You could be trying to get me to help you out of here. If Baine were my father, I'd have Toaqua blood. I don't."

If anything, my father was Anichi. We could at least confirm I had Spirit magic in my blood.

"You *do* have Toaqua blood," Doya claimed. "Mixed children always inherit the magic of their same-sex parent. If I wasn't telling the truth, I never would've turned myself in."

"But *why?*" I demanded. "Why are you here? This isn't like you."

"Things have changed," Doya snapped.

Liam crossed his arms and stepped forward, protecting me. "Changed how?"

Doya opened her mouth, but she hesitated. "I'd rather speak to Sophia alone."

"Anything you can say to me can be said in front of Liam," I insisted. "Answer the question. What changed?"

Doya pressed her lips together firmly, then answered carefully. "For one, you're carrying my grandchild."

Ancestors, I hadn't even thought of that. How could my precious Ava-Marie have *Madame Doya's* blood running through her veins?

My voice shook in anger as I glared at Doya. "You *just* admitted you tried to smother me as a child because I'm mixed House. Why would I believe you wouldn't try to do the same to my baby?"

Doya let out a shaky breath, as if I'd hit a nerve. "Because if I were to kill every mixed child in Kinpago... I'd have to kill myself."

The breath left my lungs. For a moment, I couldn't speak as I processed what Doya had just said. Liam was the first to compose himself.

"You're saying *you're* mixed House?" he snapped. It was obvious he didn't believe her, either.

Doya nodded.

"Then why didn't you fight for interhouse relationships!?" Liam snapped.

"I did!" Doya shouted. "Or don't you remember how I found Vanderbilt's son and presented him at your trial?"

It was true. She'd helped us win our trial. We wouldn't have without her.

"Your actions don't match up," I accused. "Why all the resentment against me if you're mixed House, too?"

"Because I didn't know," Doya insisted. "Not until I went looking for Sean Andre to save your case."

Her tone softened as she explained. It was so strange to hear her speak without firmness. "When I was young, just a toddler, my parents spoke of leaving Kinpago. I always knew there were other Hawkei out there, but I didn't know where. When your case came up, I went searching for them to help win your trial. I turned to my mother's journals and discovered that my father had come from *Hok'evale*— he was Anichi. He posed as an unbonded Koigni, in order to attend Orenda Academy to learn alchemy and bring the knowledge back to the tribe.

"My parents fell in love and had me, but my father's true identity remained a secret long after his death. I was able to piece together information from my mother's journal to find a secret passageway to *Hok'evale*, where Vanderbilt's son had been living for years. That is how I found him to bring him to your trial. It is also how I got through *Hok'evale's* shield to attend your wedding."

I couldn't stop my hands from shaking. Everything Doya said made so much sense. It filled in all the holes that hadn't made sense in the past. It explained why my Anichi magic was so strong— because it wasn't as far back in my lineage as I thought.

And yet, I couldn't wrap my head around her actions. I couldn't forgive her.

I went so weak that the journal fell from my hands. The cover flipped open, and an old, worn photograph fell out. I didn't care, until I caught sight of the woman's features. The air left my lungs as I bent down and lifted the photograph. In it a young, regal woman with flowing red hair smiled at the camera. She wore a floor-length dress that I recognized.

It was one of my ancestors— my spirit guides. *The woman in the red ball gown.*

"Who is this?" I demanded, shoving the photograph toward Doya's cell. "Why do you have a picture of her?"

Doya looked momentarily confused. "That's my mother, Viola. She died just before I went to Orenda. Why?"

Liam took the photograph from my hands. I could see recognition in his eyes. The first time I met my ancestors, Liam had been there to summon them. He remembered her.

"Doya must be telling the truth," Liam said. "Spirit guides are always our direct ancestors."

Which made Viola my grandmother. Doya wasn't lying.

Hot, angry tears pricked at my eyes. "Why not tell me all this sooner? You knew for *months* you were mixed House. You've known since the day I came to Orenda that I was your daughter. And you *lied*! You continue to lie and deceive— anything to serve your twisted, evil purpose."

Doya didn't deny it. It was almost like she agreed with me. "I admit, I let my shame consume me. I allowed excuses to treat you the way I did."

"You were mad at yourself and you took it out on me?" I accused, shaking my head in disbelief. My stomach knotted so tight I thought I might hurl. "You're a horrible, bitter woman, and you will *never* be my mother."

At that, I whirled around and stomped out of the jail. Esis followed close at my feet, and Liam exited behind me.

Once I was outside the jail, I felt a strong wave of heat rush over me as my Fire surfaced. Jonah and Imogen both said something, and Luana signed, but I couldn't hear or see anything. My vision blurred, and my ears rang. This had to be some sort of nightmare.

I stomped several steps away from the door, but my knees were too weak to hold me up. As angry magic swept through me, I felt my blood pressure suddenly drop. I lowered myself to my hands and knees to keep from passing out.

"*Pawee!*" Liam cried, coming to my side immediately.

"I think I'm going to puke," I admitted.

Esis put a hand on me, and the nausea eased immediately. I took several deep breaths.

"What happened in there?" Jonah demanded.

I just shook my head, letting him know I couldn't handle speaking right now. To say this was the shock of a lifetime was an understatement.

When I finally caught my breath, I looked up to Chief Cauac, whose eyebrows were knitted in concern. "What's going to happen to her?"

"She'll stay here until her sentencing," he answered.

"Good," I said breathlessly. It'd give me time to sort my feelings.

Finally, I turned to my friends. "Let's get somewhere comfortable. There's something Liam and I need to tell you."

We returned to the house with Jonah, Imogen, Luana, and Ezra in tow. Jonah kept insisting we tell him what was going on, until Liam snapped at him that he was going to have to wait until the two of us could catch a breath.

Finally, we settled into the living room, and I felt like I could breathe again. Liam sat next to me on the couch, his arms wrapped protectively around me.

"So, what happened?" Imogen asked carefully.

It took me a moment to say it out loud, because I still couldn't wrap my head around it. "It turns out... Doya's my mom."

I expected gasps to travel around the room and utter looks of shock, but nobody seemed surprised.

"Wait..." I narrowed my gaze. "Why aren't you all shocked and furious?"

Jonah bit his lip. "Well, we sort of... figured it out."

"What? When!?" I cried, my spine straightening. "You just *failed* to mention it to me?"

"Relax," Jonah insisted. "It was barely an hour ago."

Imogen lifted her hand and held out a piece of paper. "We looked at your pictures for clues, and we found this."

I took the picture from her. It was one of my grandparents that I'd saved from Lucy's scrapbook. But they weren't the only ones in it. Doya and Lucy stood beside them.

"We never realized how much you two look alike," Imogen said.

"I guess I can see it," I remarked, but my stomach sank, as this was another confirmation that Doya was telling the truth.

I looked to Liam. "I'm guessing you didn't figure out who my father is?"

Liam shook his head. "Do you want to tell them, or should I?"

"*Oh em gee*," Jonah gushed. "I'm guessing it's scandalous."

I cringed. "That's a bit of an understatement."

Imogen's jaw dropped. "It's not Alric, is it?"

All eyes turned to her. Jonah looked totally disgusted. "Sweetheart, he banged Perot for years. No way did he go anywhere near Doya."

"Well, I don't know!" Imogen cried. "He could be bi. It's the most scandalous Koigni relationship I could think of. She could've killed her baby daddy to cover it up."

I ran my hands over my belly. "The thing is, it *wasn't* a Koigni relationship."

Ezra's eyes got really wide. "Not Oleander. Please, ancestors, anything but Oleander."

Liam shook his head. "No, thank the Great Spirit."

I took a deep breath and spit it out. "It was Baine."

Jonah's jaw dropped so wide it was comical. Imogen started screaming so loud I swore the neighbors could hear it.

"Ew, ew, ew, ew!" Imogen cried, before slapping her hand over her mouth. "I thought Baine was *hot!* I thought *your father* was a total silver fox! Ew, ew, ew!"

Ezra had no words. He just shook his head in utter disbelief. "But... how?"

Jonah chuckled. "I think it's a little late for the birds and the bees talk, bro."

"No, but I mean, like... Baine?" Ezra looked a little disgusted.

*It's pretty weird*, Luana agreed.

"It actually explains a lot," Jonah cut in. "I mean, that's why Sophia's totally gorgeous. Both her parents are *fine*."

"And it explains why you were attracted to Liam," Imogen cracked. "You're totally hot for a Toaqua like your dad."

"Ew!" I frowned. "I don't like Liam because of Baine."

"Nah," Ezra agreed. "She likes him for... *other* reasons."

He made a rude hand gesture toward his package, which sent the room into a laughing fit.

"I can't believe it. He went from Buff Baine to Daddy Baine." Jonah snickered.

"Now you can *really* call him daddy," Ezra added, and everyone died of laughter— except Liam, who grimaced.

"Ew, gross!" I put my head in my hands. "That's so nasty!"

I'd always gotten a weird dad vibe from Baine, and never found him attractive— ancestors, now I knew why.

"Do you think Doya called him daddy?" Imogen wondered aloud, and she totally cracked up.

Everyone else lost it. Even Squeaks and Sassy were laughing up a storm. I wasn't sure if they actually found it humorous, or if they were trying to lighten the mood for my sake.

I still didn't know what to think of it, but I had to crack a smile.

I turned to Liam, who hadn't had much to say about the whole thing. "What do you think?"

"I don't know," he admitted. He looked grossed out. "All I can think about is Baine's shitty sex advice."

I started laughing.

Liam tapped his finger against his chin. "You know, that totally makes sense now. He went on and on about passion and makeup sex. He *had* to be talking about Doya."

"Oh, my god!" I realized. "He wanted to give us pointers on our *unique situation*. He was totally talking about Koigni and Toaqua banging!"

Liam cringed. "Ancestors. Once, he warned me you might try to burn my house down. He must've said that because Doya threatened to when he broke up with her."

I couldn't stop laughing. It felt really good to make light of this whole thing. "You think he would've said any of that if he knew I was his daughter?"

A silent beat passed between us, before realization hit.

"Wait... Baine doesn't even know," Liam realized. "Should we go tell him?"

I thought about it for a moment. My laughter had died, and a heavy rock settled in my gut. "I... don't know if I'm ready for that. I still need time to think about this."

Liam ran a finger down my arm. "Okay. We'll sleep on it."

Just then, the door burst open, and Cade came running inside. Arabelle followed breathlessly behind him. Imogen's eyes darkened the second she saw him.

"You guys!" Cade cried. "I just heard Doya—"

"Turned herself in and is being held in a holding cell near the temple?" Ezra cut in. "Yep. Beat you to it, bro."

Imogen rolled her eyes. "Someone *always* beats him to it. Usually it's me."

The room went really quiet, except for Jonah, who threw his hand over his mouth and sang, "Oooh."

Cade crossed his arms, and his nostrils flared. "Seriously, Im? You're going to bring this up now?"

She shrugged. "*You're* the one who came over. Usually it's hard to get you to come."

"That's it!" Cade shouted. "I'm sick of this, Imogen. What do you think the deal is? That I don't love you?"

"I don't know," she snarled. "Let's take a poll. Who here thinks Cade's impotent because he's not attracted to me?"

Esis started to raise his hand, but I didn't think he understood what Imogen meant.

"I'm not *impotent!*" Cade shouted. "I just want it to *last*. I want *us* to last."

"You made that *really* clear when you left me," Imogen said sarcastically.

Nobody said anything as we watched them implode at each other. They fought so much it was practically normal now, but they usually went off in private. This was a different level of shit.

Cade raked his hands through his hair. "We're really going to do this again? When are you going to start acting normal?"

"Do you even *know* me?" she screamed. "I've *never* been normal. I never *will* be."

"And that's what I love about you," he insisted. "But this isn't like you at all."

"That's because you haven't been paying attention!" Imogen cried, her hands balling into fists at her side. "None of you have!"

At that, she stomped off and slammed the door to her room, leaving Sassy behind.

"Whoa," Jonah breathed. "That was... intense."

Cade rolled his eyes, like he couldn't deal with her right now. "She does this all the time. We get in a huge fight, she storms off, and two seconds later she's all happy-go-lucky and wants my attention. I swear something weird is going on."

"Except she won't talk to anyone about it," I added.

"True," Jonah agreed. "I've tried, and she just shuts me down."

Sassy whimpered and stepped forward, nudging me in the leg. I bent to pet her. "What is it, girl? You want me to go check on Imogen?"

Sassy whimpered again. Her eyes glistened when she looked up at me.

"Just let her cool off," Cade said. "She'll come around. She always does."

I ignored him and stood— though Liam had to help push me up. "Sassy's right. Imogen needs to know we care. I'll go check on her." I needed a distraction from all this Doya bullshit anyway. Helping Imogen would take my mind off things.

I left the room and went to knock on Imogen's door. "Hey, Im. Is it okay if I come in?"

"No," she snapped.

I sighed. "Im, please. I'm just trying to help."

The door swung open, and Imogen stood in the doorway. Her hair was a mess. Her eyes were bloodshot, like she'd been crying on the bed, but her features were hard to read.

"You can help by getting Cade to leave," she suggested.

I sighed. "I'm not going to do that. You and Cade have to work things out. Come back to the living room, and we'll all talk about it."

Imogen scoffed. "What? Like a therapy session? I don't need help from you."

I took a step back. I was pretty offended by the accusation in her tone. "I *do* have some experience with relationships," I bit back.

"Sure, but you and Liam have been a train wreck for ages," she growled.

"*Excuse* me?" I cried. "Liam and I are perfectly fine."

"Yeah, *now*," she emphasized.

"Which is exactly why I can help!" I told her. "Liam and I have worked through our issues. There's a ceremony that might help you and Cade—"

"I don't care," she said in a clipped tone. "Whatever it is, I don't want to do it. Now, if you'll excuse me, I need some air."

Imogen pushed me aside and stomped toward the door. I was so shocked that I didn't move for a second, then I hurried behind her. The living room was full of voices layered atop each other as everyone tried to talk some sense into Imogen.

"Get out of my way," she snapped at Cade, who had placed himself between her and the door.

"Im, please just let me—" he begged, but he was cut off as Imogen twisted her hand. The viney plant next to the widow grew three times its size and curled around Cade's arms, dragging him back and pinning him to the wall.

What the hell? A few weeks ago, Imogen couldn't even revive a bonsai tree. Now she was doing crazy magic?

Imogen stomped right past Cade and through the door. Sassy scurried beneath everyone's feet to follow behind her.

"I've got this," I said to everyone as I hurried past them and left the house behind Imogen.

"Im, wait up!" I called down the path.

She didn't acknowledge me. With each step she took, she brushed her fingers across a different piece of foliage, and the plants died beneath her touch. She was farther ahead. I lost her around a corner, but it was easy to follow the trail of dead plants.

My pulse quickened. I was really frightened for Imogen right now. I'd never seen her use her magic for anything but growth and beauty. She was obviously really pissed— way more than I knew.

When I caught up with her, Imogen had stopped in a small park. She sat at the base of a large tree with her head in her hands. Sassy ran up to her and curled at her feet, but Imogen nudged her away.

"Imogen," I said softly as I approached. "Please talk to me."

"I can't!" she sobbed without lifting her head.

"Yes, you can," I insisted. "We're best friends. I want to help."

"You can't help!" she roared. Her eyes were red and dilated when she looked up to me. "Your life is fucking perfect, Sophia! You have Liam and Luana and Ava-Marie. I'm nothing to you."

Fuck, I didn't want to do this again. How could I show her how much she meant to me?

"Imogen, I love you so much," I promised. "You have no idea."

"That's not true!" Imogen shot to her feet, and she held her hands upward. I took a cautious step back as her magic began to shake the ground. Her eyes darkened— she was really starting to scare me. "If you really loved me, you'd know the truth! But you're all so wrapped up in your little lives that you can't see what's staring you straight in the face."

"Then *tell* me," I begged.

Imogen's eyebrows knitted together. The ground continued to shake, and roots tore out of the soil. The tree behind her twisted, and the branches rustled, sending leaves raining down around us.

"Look what I can do, Sophia!" Imogen cried as the tree uprooted.

Roots swung everywhere like vines. I threw my arms out to create a force field around me. Heavy roots whipped past me and slammed into the ground at my side. My heart hammered, and I seriously thought that Imogen had finally fallen off the deep end. But none of her roots touched my shield. They avoided me on purpose, like this wasn't an attack but a display.

And still, I feared for myself and my daughter. Imogen had never terrified me so much in my life.

"I don't get it!" I cried. "Your magic's been weak. How are you doing this?"

"Just because I'm not *special* like the rest of you doesn't mean I'm weak!" Imogen cried. "I'm powerful!"

"I know, but Im, you have to stop!" I cried as roots continued to swing toward my force field. "This isn't you."

Tears streamed down Imogen's face as she continued to control the tree. "I don't know how to be myself anymore."

"Then let us help," I begged.

"But I can't stop," she sobbed.

"Stop what?" I asked, ducking from another root that came too close to my shield.

"*The nightshade!*" she screamed.

My whole world seemed to stop. Though her magic raged around me, I felt timeless in my little bubble.

Imogen was using Black Ivy? How had I not realized it before? It explained *everything*— the irritability, the weakening magic when she was off it, the high when she was on it, and the strange surge of power she had now. She must've just taken it when she stormed off into her room.

I felt like the worst friend in the world for not realizing it. Then again, it wasn't something I'd ever had considered. The old Imogen never would've done this. She would've never touched drugs.

But times had changed. We all had.

Imogen dropped to her knees, and the roots returned to their place in the ground. Tears streamed down her face. Sassy tried to cuddle up to her, but Imogen didn't acknowledge her Familiar. "I just want to be happy," Imogen sobbed.

Finally, I dropped my shield, and I stepped forward. I reached out my hand to her. "I want you to be happy, too. I want the old Imogen back."

Tears continued to stream down her face. Even the high of nightshade couldn't cure her heartbreak right now. "You don't get it. The old Imogen is gone. All I am is nightshade now."

"That's not true, Im," I promised. I felt sick not knowing how to help her. "We can find the old you again."

She shook her head. "You still don't get it. Just forget I ever told you."

Imogen scrambled to her feet and started running.

"Wait! Im!" I tried to keep up with her, but she moved faster than I could. When I turned a corner, she and Sassy were gone. This time, there were no dead flowers to lead me to her.

In that moment, it was clear. Today I had gained a mother and father, but I had lost my best friend.

# Liam

## TWENTY-ONE

It'd already been a long day, and I had a bad feeling in my gut things were about to get even worse.

Imogen hadn't come back after she'd stormed out. We hoped she was at her parents, though we weren't sure. We never knew where Imogen was anymore. She was always running off and disappearing.

Sophia came back, though. She didn't say anything to anyone, just went immediately to her room. Cade and Ezra, sensing the tension, booked it. Jonah chatted with Luana while I went to the bedroom to check on my wife.

My heart sank like a stone in water when I saw Sophia crying on the bed. She was curled around a pillow and holding it, while Esis braided her hair. She was a total mess.

"*Pawee*, you gotta calm down." I sat next to her and rubbed her back. "This isn't good for the baby."

"It's been too much today," she sobbed. "I can't take it."

"I'm sorry about everything that happened with Doya. It's not fair."

"It's not even about Doya," she cried. "It's Imogen."

My worry intensified. If Sophia was more upset about something Imogen had said than the fact that Doya was her mom, we had a real problem here. "Did you guys get into another fight?"

"Yes. But it's worse than I imagined." Sophia let go of her pillow and sat up slowly, brushing hair out of her eyes. Esis grumbled when she ruined the braid he was making. "She... Imogen told me she was using Black Ivy."

My veins turned to ice and shattered. A sickening feeling entered my stomach as the world tilted around me, almost out of reality. "What? Are you sure you didn't misunderstand—?"

"No. She said she was using nightshade and all of us had been too ignorant to notice." Sophia gave another sob.

As much as I wanted to deny it, it was the only thing that made sense. Imogen hadn't been acting like Imogen, not since we got to *Hok'evale*. Substance abuse was the one thing that would make her change her behavior so drastically. What if Cade and her brother's betrayal, losing our home, losing everything, had been too much for her to handle, and she'd turned to drugs to escape?

"She said we should've noticed. Why didn't we?" Sophia's tears ran hard and fast. "She was right. This is our fault."

"It's not our fault, Soph. Even if she is using. We can't be responsible for Imogen's choices." I reached out and grabbed a tissue from the nightstand to wipe away her tears, and she took another to blow her nose.

"You say that now, but maybe if we had been better friends—"

"Nothing is going to stop someone from using drugs if they decide it's the only thing that's going to help," I said firmly. "We've all been wrapped up in our own lives, but we did it because we had to move on. We wouldn't have survived if we didn't. Imogen knew she could come to us for support, but she didn't. You can't put that on us."

Sophia sniffed. She was warring with my logic versus what was in her heart.

I never thought this would happen to Imogen. She was the bookish girl who was sweet and innocent, the girl who was at the top of her class and had more fun being in the library on Saturday nights than going to parties. Even when we had drank together, she'd never gotten wasted. I'd bet on my life she'd never do drugs.

Yet addiction always happened to the people you thought it would never touch. Even Imogen had a limit. She was strong, but she had a breaking point.

"Come on." I took Sophia's hand and dragged her upward. She stopped crying and wiped her face frantically, though it still looked puffy and red. Esis followed us as we headed to Imogen's room.

"Hey, guys. What are we doing?" Jonah asked as we passed him in the hall. Neither of us answered. Jonah saw Sophia's tear-streaked face and drew to our side without question. Luana had noticed the tension and remained near, though a little distant.

Sophia and I began going through Imogen's things. I searched the closet. Sophia went through the nightstand and searched under the bed. Esis even helped, scanning the top of Imogen's desk. Jonah stood in the doorway while Squeaks watched from behind him. Though he seemed stunned, he didn't stop us.

"Why are you searching Im's room?" Jonah asked immediately. Sophia and I didn't say anything.

Suddenly, Esis chittered loudly. He stomped his foot on the desk, pointing to the drawer.

I crossed the room and opened it. My gut twisted. There it was. The Black Ivy sat in three small vials, the liquid a purplish-blue color. It was placed in such an obvious spot it was almost as if Imogen wanted us to find it.

Maybe she had. And we'd all let her down.

Jonah let out a noise when he saw the nightshade. He knew what Black Ivy was. He'd done plenty of raids for it with Jake while working in the army. The note sounded devastated. He fisted his hands in his hair and took a few shocked steps backward. Tears beaded at the corners of his eyes.

Sophia's expression was crestfallen. Luana seemed less surprised, but very sad. Sierra's wings slumped on Luana's shoulder as the Black Ivy glimmered in the light.

Me? I was pissed.

"I fucking knew it." I'd *known* something was up with Imogen. I wished I would've followed my instincts and investigated earlier, before it ended up like this.

Jonah flew to explanations. "Maybe it's not hers. Maybe—"

"She told me she was using. She confessed while we were having an argument." Sophia pinched the bridge of her nose and closed her eyes. She was trying not to cry again.

"For how long?" I asked. I struggled to keep my voice even and not yell. "How long has she been using this shit?"

"I don't know, Liam!" Sophia's voice rose a few pitches. "She didn't say."

"Well, when did her behavior change?"

"Why are you asking me all these questions? I wouldn't know!" Sophia was getting frantic again.

Jonah leaned against the wall. He had a hand over his mouth and was silently weeping. Squeaks laid her head on his shoulder.

Luana tapped Sophia's shoulder and signed something. Even though I didn't completely comprehend, I got the gist. Luana was right.

"She must've found a dealer shortly after we got here," I murmured.

There were a few beats of silence. Sophia said, "I don't get it. Why didn't Sassy tell us? She had to have known."

"Familiars operate off free will and loyalty to their Elementai. Even if Sassy wanted to tell— and I'm sure she did— she won't interfere with Imogen's choices unless she's the one who wants to get help," I said.

"*You* had to have known." Jonah whirled on Squeaks, fists clenched. "You could smell the Black Ivy on her. You knew she was using for months and didn't tell me!?"

Squeaks made a clicking sound with her beak and stomped her hooves. Jonah's expression grew outraged. He crossed his arms and turned his back on Squeaks, fuming.

"What'd she say?" Sophia asked.

"That it wasn't her story to tell. She could've overdosed, Squeaks! She could've *died*. This is total bullshit!" Jonah roared.

Squeaks tossed her head angrily and shook it, stating she was insistent she'd done the right thing.

"That means... Esis. You knew, too." Sophia turned to the little guy, and he hung his head in shame.

"All the Familiars knew. But it's the same thing. Free will is their most sacred law," I stated. "They're our souls. They're supposed to guide us on our life paths, not interfere in our choices and tell us what to do. In their eyes, revealing Imogen's secret would've been wrong, like revealing Sophia's pregnancy."

"It doesn't matter. I'm getting rid of this right now." Jonah shoved past us. He grabbed the bottles of nightshade and stomped to the bathroom, where he poured them down the toilet. He flushed the nightshade down the drain and threw away the bottles, still shaking.

"That's only a temporary fix, Jonah. She can go get more," Sophia said weakly.

"No she won't. We won't let her," Jonah said.

I hated to tell Jonah this, but nothing could stop an addict from using if they were determined to. If Imogen was addicted to Black Ivy and she didn't want to get better, we couldn't help. This was on her. All of this was a desperate cry for help, but I worried Imogen had gone to a place we couldn't reach.

Though I knew we weren't to blame, a small part of me felt like we'd failed her.

"We have to tell Cade," Sophia whispered.

"I'll tell him," Jonah said viciously. "Then we're fucking fixing this."

Sophia and I gave each other miserable expressions. We couldn't fix anything if Imogen didn't want to.

Cade had his own apartment on the other side of town, and Jonah was determined to get there yesterday. He walked at such a fast pace that it was like jogging for the rest of us— and his long legs didn't help.

Sophia had a hard time keeping up. Her pregnant waddling would've been funny if the situation wasn't so dire. Luana took her arm and helped her powerwalk, while I kept an eye on Jonah up ahead.

All of us were panting when we caught up with him. Jonah pounded on the door. It was Trace who opened. He stood wide-eyed at Jonah's rageful expression. Jonah didn't wait for an invitation. He forced himself past Trace.

"Uh, come in?" Trace said. He stepped aside to let Sophia and I pass.

Sophia looked at me like she wanted me to control Jonah's wild behavior, but I wasn't about to get in the pathway of a raging bull. Jonah rarely lost his temper, but when he did, best to run the other way. Squeaks tried to squeeze in behind us, but when she couldn't, she just waited outside.

Cade's house was a typical bachelor pad. There was a widescreen TV on the wall, beer cans littering the area, and a ping pong table set up in the middle of the room. It was clean, for the most part, but felt pretty bare. I'd had a sad feeling he'd been waiting for Imogen to move in with him so she could decorate.

Ezra and Cade were playing ping-pong. Stevie sat on a nearby armchair and watched, while Amelia threw treats to Kiwi to get him to do tricks. Arabelle was curled up on a rug on the floor. She raised her head as Jonah's big boots stomped by.

Jake was there, too, thank the ancestors. He had a beer in hand and was messing with the stereo. I don't know why he'd stopped by, but I was glad he did, because he was probably the one person who could handle Jonah right now. He was currently blustering around like a raging tornado.

The ping pong game halted when Cade saw Jonah's face. He put the paddle down as he asked, "Jonah, what the h—"

"Did you know Imogen's been using nightshade?" Jonah was on the verge of crying again. The silence was deafening once he spoke the words.

Cade's face had gone completely white. "Huh?"

"We found Black Ivy in her desk. She told Sophia she's been using," Jonah said. "She's an addict."

Several people gasped, but it was nothing compared to Cade's reaction. He fell to his knees in shock. Arabelle darted to his side. Ezra ran forward and tried dragging Cade to his feet, but his limbs appeared to have become weak and frail. His eyes stared blankly, calculating all the signs over the past few months.

Trace put a hand on the wall to keep from falling like Cade had. Amelia immediately got up and put her hands on his shoulders to steady him.

Jake frowned. He was the first to say something. "This is very serious."

*Thanks, Jake, for stating the fucking obvious.* Sometimes the guy was a bit too stoic. Ezra guided Cade into a chair. His hands were shaking, but he said nothing— just stared ahead like he couldn't accept what was right in front of him.

"I thought the Black Ivy problem was under control," Amelia said, with a sideways glance at Jake.

"Mostly, but we haven't been able to keep all the suppliers from getting in," Jake said. "They prey on desperate people."

"And Imogen was one of those people. She was looking for a way out, and she thought this was the only way." Jonah completely broke. He crumbled. Everyone looked away at the sound of his sobs, except for Cade, who still appeared like he wasn't looking at anything. Jake immediately took action and placed two hands on Jonah's face, trying to get him to relax.

"Mom and Dad need to know," Trace said. He was almost in a daze. He shook his head slowly and said, "Maybe if we talk to her, something will change."

"I'll go with you." Amelia hurried after Trace, probably to make sure he made it home.

Jonah was so bereft that Jake had a hard time calming him down. He'd become distraught, babbling sentences that were hard to understand and didn't make sense. I wanted to do something, but what could I do?

"I'm taking him over to my place," Jake said, his hand on Jonah's shoulder. "We should meet up later to discuss this."

"Tomorrow," I confirmed. I glanced at Ezra. "You got him?"

Ezra glanced anxiously down at Cade. "Yeah... I'll stay the night."

I sure hoped so. Kid was freaking me out. Cade looked like he wanted to murder someone, or cry, or... both. Fuck, I didn't know.

"We need to go looking for her," Sophia protested. "She could be anywhere. I don't want her getting hurt."

"I'll launch a search party," Jake said. "The resistance police will track her down. The rest of you should return to your homes. It's best if we keep emotions to a minimum once we find her."

Sophia was more disheartened than ever. Her gaze remained on the floor. I put my arm around her and said, "Come on, *pawee*. Let's go home."

Luana sadly waved goodbye. The walk back was quiet. Neither of us said anything, not until we got back to our bedroom. Sophia turned toward me and said, "So what do we do now? We can't let Imogen keep doing this without saying something."

"Secret's out, *pawee*," I said. "We don't know where she is, and it's unreasonable to take action until everyone's had time to process. Let's get some rest. We'll figure it out tomorrow."

Sophia nodded somberly. I had to rub her back to get her to fall asleep.

My own sleep was fitful. I barely got a few hours in.

I woke up sore and aching. I gagged for a few minutes in the bathroom before I dragged myself to the kitchen and took some pills. I knew I looked like shit. I sent a message with Julian to let Madame Wells know I wasn't coming in today, and to handle matters in my absence while I dealt with things back home. Jonah still wasn't back from Jake's, and I hadn't heard from Ezra about Cade.

Around ten, Trace's Familiar stopped by with a note saying that the search had been called off. Imogen had spent the night at her parents. There, her family had confronted her about the drugs.

It hadn't gone well. She'd stormed out of there, too, and hadn't returned.

I knew she had to come back here at some point. She had nowhere else to go. When she did, we'd be waiting for her. I gave Julian more notes to deliver and set things into motion for later, hoping my idea would work.

Sophia didn't wake up until around noon. She sat up in bed and blinked at me. "What are we going to do about Imogen?" she asked quietly. It was the first thing out of her mouth.

"I have a plan," I said. "We need to stage an intervention. But we can't do it until she comes back, and Jonah still needs some time to chill out. We can't come at her if we're emotional. She won't listen."

"You're right." Sophia rubbed her eyes. "There's nothing left to do but wait."

Esis hopped onto her lap, rubbing his stomach. He wanted breakfast. Sophia handed him a granola bar that was sitting on the nightstand, but she didn't look hungry herself.

"In the meantime..." I began, not sure how this was going to go, "Look,

I've been doing a lot of thinking. I think you need to sort things out with Doya."

Sophia's expression immediately hardened. "*Sort things out?* Have you lost it?"

"It's eating away at you," I began. "As shitty as this information is, there's no getting around that she's your mom."

I stayed up all night thinking about this. As pissed as I was at Doya yesterday, I knew I had to be the voice of reason. I understood why Doya had done what she did, and why she came back. I felt Sophia deserved to have a clear head before she made any decisions about Doya that were permanent.

"She's no mother of mine," Sophia snarled. She got up from the bed and went to walk away, but I stopped her and made her face me.

"Soph, things were really bad between me and my dad for a long time. If I had a chance to go back and make amends, I'd take it," I said. "Doya's in trouble with the resistance. They could execute her for what she's done. You might miss your chance to put this to rest."

"Why do I think I care what happens to her?" she asked.

"Because like it or not, you share blood. You have a bond. I don't want you to have regrets, no matter where this ends up."

Sophia bit her lip anxiously— she was thinking. As much as she hated Doya, I knew she was scared about having remorse.

And like it or not, there was a child involved that had a connection to Doya as well. We had a responsibility to protect Ava-Marie from Doya if she was a threat— but we also had a duty to make sure she knew where she came from.

It kinda sucked being in the middle.

When Sophia's eyes met mine again, I took a breath and said something risky. "I never realized before how much you look like her. But now that I know, the resemblance... it's uncanny."

"Don't say that," Sophia snapped, and she pulled away. "I don't want to cringe every time I look in the mirror."

"She's a beautiful woman, Sophia. As are you."

"I don't care! I don't want to be anything like her."

"I know you don't want to hear this, but... you are," I stated. "You're like her in so many ways. The good stuff, anyway."

"There's nothing good about Doya!" Sophia shouted. "She's pure evil!"

"People aren't one way or the other. The world isn't black and white," I said.

"What good traits are there about *Doya?*" Sophia hissed. "I can't name one thing."

"I can. She's confident. She's determined. She's intent to have things her way no matter what she has to face. She's brave and not willing to back down, not even to someone stronger than she is. She sees things through even when most people would quit. Those are all good qualities that show up in you."

Sophia reeled back in shock, as if she was slapped. After a few moments, she stuttered, "I'm nothing like her."

"You are a little. Which isn't a bad thing."

"Doya is cunning and manipulative! I don't want to be like that," Sophia said. "I don't know how you can put this in a good light."

"That should mean something. I despise the woman, and I can still see the good traits that she passed down to you," I said. "You don't have to have a relationship with her if you don't want to. You could throw her out of your life forever, and you have that right. But if you did without figuring out what she means to you, you might feel like something is missing."

"Do you want that wicked crone around our child? Because I want to keep Ava far away from her," Sophia bit back.

I hesitated. "Well... yes and no."

"How can you even say that?" Sophia's tone was full of disgust.

"As much as we don't like it, Doya is her grandmother. Ava-Marie should at least get to meet her, to decide for herself. And I don't think we've gotten to see the real side of Doya, only the shield she puts up to try and keep you alive, and keep everyone else out," I said. "She might not be the villain we all make her out to be."

Sophia snorted. "She sure acts like it."

"Look. As much as I hate to be sympathetic towards Doya... her life collapsed around her just before she had you. Her mother just died. Baine threw her out, then she was pregnant with you all alone. Her best friend died the same night she gave birth. If all that happened, wouldn't you become bitter?"

Sophia bit her lip. "I guess if my mom died, you left me while I was pregnant and Imogen died too, I'd be devastated. I'd hate the world."

"Right. And as for everything she did to you— this isn't an excuse— she was trying to protect you. She needed to make you strong so you could survive the Elders. Think about it, Soph. Would you do the same for Ava-Marie if you had to? Because I think you would."

Sophia took a long pause before she ran a hand over her belly. "I'd do anything to protect my daughter and keep her safe. Even if she hated me in the end."

"Exactly. So don't be too hard on Doya. See things from her point of view," I suggested. "She pushed you, but it was because she cared. And all along, she really was on our side. She tried to manipulate the trial in our favor. She protected you against Chieftess Annette and the rest of the Elders. She did bad things along the way, but it was all for you."

"She did those things because she wanted me to fulfill the prophecy and become chieftess!" Sophia bit back. "She didn't give a damn about me."

"No." I shook my head. "No, Sophia, I don't think that's true."

"Why are you defending her? After everything she's done. You hate her." Sophia's eyes narrowed as her expression became stern, her mouth settling into a thin line. Ancestors, she looked *so* much like Doya when she did that.

"Because I'm a parent now. Or I will be, in less than a few weeks. I can consider how she would think. You have to be in the same position."

Sophia took a few moments in silence before she put her head in her hands. "You want to know the thing I hate the most about this? Even though I despised everything she did to me, once she explained herself, I could see her reasons why. I could see myself turning into a woman just like her if all that bad stuff happened to me. I *was* turning into her, when you and I broke up. The only thing that stopped me from becoming a terrible person was having people around me who loved me. She didn't have that. I feel sorry for her, when all I want to feel is anger."

"You're allowed to feel anything," I said gently. "But don't make any decisions on kicking her out of your life just yet. Try to get to know her as your mother, not as a tyrant, then decide what you want to do. If you really don't want her around Ava, I'll back you up. But I don't think now is the right time to make that decision."

Sophia looked away. "All those pictures in Lucy's journal… Doya was so happy and carefree. She was so silly and sweet… I often had the thought she was just like me. I always wondered what had happened to turn her so cruel."

"It was giving you up," I said quietly. I froze to think who Sophia would become if she had to give up Ava-Marie. A monster just like Doya had been, I was certain.

I'm sure we had the same thought. Sophia's shoulders sagged in defeat. "Maybe we're more alike than I thought."

Esis chittered. Sophia picked him up from his place on the end table and stroked his fur. "What are we going to do about Baine?"

I suppressed a shudder when she brought it up. I mean, Baine was cool and all, but the thought of him being my father-in-law was more than a little weird.

"We should tell him, Sophia. He deserves to know. Would you hold back on telling me about Ava, for twenty years?" I asked.

She twisted her fingers in Esis' fur. "I know. It's just awkward."

"Very," I confirmed. "But I'll be with you every step of the way."

"I think Doya needs to tell him," Sophia said slowly. "But we can be there."

"Then let's go get him."

Julian was more than happy to stretch his wings after being excluded from the drama yesterday. When we landed in front of Baine's house, I had to help Sophia off Julian. She could barely ride now, being eight months pregnant. She took a deep breath before she knocked on the door, though I more or less felt like barging in.

Baine opened the door. Despite it being the afternoon, he was still in his pajamas. "Ah, just the two I wanted to—"

"We know about you and Doya," Sophia said, without any leeway of an explanation.

The color drained from Baine's face. His mouth fell open, and he made a few incoherent noises. "I— uh— it's not—"

Baine took a few very deep breaths that expanded his chest. The man nearly started hyperventilating. Ancestors, it was good no one had ever figured it out, because if they had, Baine was shit at covering it up.

After a moment of trying to gather himself, Baine blurted, "I can assure you that whatever that woman said—"

"Cut the crap, Professor. We know you and Madame Doya were in a relationship. She told us," I said tiredly.

Baine's shoulders fell. He sighed, and admitted the truth almost regrettably. "It is true. Eleanor and I were involved, for a time. I can't say it wasn't serious, but I did have to end it. For reasons you both understand."

I got now why Baine had always remained single. The longing in his voice gave it away. He really loved Doya— and even after all this time, no one else could measure up.

"It's okay. We don't care," Sophia said. "But she has something to tell you, and I think that it's important you listen."

Baine fiddled with his hands as he nervously bounced on the spot. "I— I don't think that's a very good idea."

"Please," Sophia begged. "It's urgent."

Baine caved. "Very well. Let me put on something suitable and I'll come."

The sound of things toppling over and breaking could be heard once Baine closed the door, as if he was searching for something. We waited for him for at least a half-hour. I was getting more impatient by the minute. How long did it take him to put on some pants and a decent shirt?

Sophia held back a laugh as Baine exited the house. I tried not to groan. Baine had put on a bright pink suit that looked like it hadn't been worn since the nineties, with dress shoes and a white tie. His messy hair was combed back, and he wore a pink carnation in the pocket of his suit. He looked like he was going on a date instead of visiting his old lover in jail. Julian hissed, stomping his foot as if this was some great joke.

"Oh, ancestors." I rubbed my face and tried not to freak out. "Let's just go."

We had to walk, because Julian couldn't carry the three of us. Baine kept babbling the entire way, trying to explain himself.

"You two must understand," he began. "The advice that I gave you about being in an interhouse relationship long ago, I was merely trying to protect you. I didn't want you to end up like—"

"It's okay. We're over it," I said. "We know things didn't end the best between the two of you."

Baine hunched over. "It did not. Times were different back then."

I snorted. Things had only changed in the past year, what with Sophia and I's trial, and it wouldn't have been that way if we hadn't taken a stand.

"Interhouse relationships are legal, you know," Sophia started. "*Hok'e-vale* is a safe place."

Baine smiled slightly. "I'm very aware. Yet... I'm not sure it's possible."

Still, his eyes shined with hope. Was he hoping for some kind of reconciliation? It'd been over twenty years. I wasn't sure that Doya still wanted him, after what he'd done to her.

Not that it mattered anyway. I was counting on the Anichi crying for her head.

The Anichi standing guard at the jail let us pass. Doya was sitting with her head down in a corner of the cell. She shot to her feet when she heard footsteps coming. Even though all the grime Doya was covered in, her eyes still lit up when Baine came into the light.

How could I have missed that all these years? It was the same way Sophia looked at me. It was veiled and disguised... but still there.

After all these years, she still loved him. And by the way Baine looked at her, I was sure he felt the same.

Doya observed Baine's suit. She laughed and put her head against the bars. "Oh, Elliot... you kept that old thing?"

"Well, pink *is* your favorite color," Baine said. "And you picked it out."

"I was sure you wouldn't come," she said. "You abandoned me before. I considered this no different."

"I never abandoned you, Eleanor," Baine said. He seemed a little annoyed. "Teaching wasn't my passion; it was only meant to be something temporary. I desired to go back into the field. I stayed for you."

Doya's lip trembled slightly, but she disguised it with a sneer. "Well, you should've left the academy, to go on your little treasure hunts. I was perfectly fine without you."

"This isn't what we're here for," I said, interrupting the conversation. I faced Doya. "Tell him."

Doya steeled herself. Without emotion, she said, "I lied to you, Elliot. For twenty years, I lied. We conceived a child together. Sophia is your daughter."

Baine's mouth dropped open. He made a strangled sound, then clutched at his chest. His beady eyes darted from Doya to Sophia, noticing the resemblance, putting two and two together. His expression seemed calculating, adding up months. When the evidence became undeniable, his skin became clammy and turned ashen.

*Aw, shit. Ancestors, don't let this old man have a heart attack.*

Well, he didn't have a heart attack, but he more or less fainted. It only lasted for a few seconds— he'd come around by the time I'd knelt by him. Esis put a healing paw on his arm, and I fanned his face.

Baine opened his eyes and saw Sophia standing over him in concern. He reared back from her, like she was some kind of alien.

"Oh, please, compose yourself," Doya spat nastily as Baine clambered to his feet. He took a handkerchief out of his pocket and dabbed at his sweaty skin.

"How can this be possible?" he finally rasped. "I—"

"I'm certain you know how it came to be, since you decided to get one last fuck in before you threw me out of your life," Doya snarled.

Baine's face wilted. "I was *trying* to say goodbye!"

"Oh, *goodbye*, was it? You left me with quite a going-away present!" Doya shouted.

"How do I know this wasn't on purpose?" Baine questioned. "You could've planned this!"

"Says the man who whined endlessly about wearing a condom!" Doya bellowed.

Sophia grimaced, and I also made a face. Ew.

"Look, we don't need to hear graphic details," I began, but neither of them heard me. They were too busy arguing.

"I never wanted to leave you, Eleanor. Never," Baine snapped. "I did what I had to do to protect you. I wanted you to stay alive."

"You left because you were a coward," Doya snarled. "You were afraid of what the Elders would do. I cared not. All I wanted was you, damn what the Elders had to say. Yet you still chose your fear over me."

"You can't possibly assume that I would've left had I known you were carrying my child!" Baine burst.

"I did, because you have no spine," Doya seethed. "You began exploring right after the Toaqua riots, right after Sophia was born. You failed me time and time again."

"How was I supposed to know, Eleanor? You never told me!" Baine shouted.

"And what if I had?" Doya raged. "You wouldn't have done what I was willing to in order to protect Sophia and I. You didn't have what it took."

Baine appeared physically wounded by Doya's words. Doya's fingers whitened against the bars as she clenched them for dear life.

"It was I who sacrificed everything for Sophia, while you did nothing," Doya seethed. "I'm the reason our daughter is alive. If I'd left it up to you to take care of her safety, she'd long be dead."

"How can I know if she's really mine?" Baine asked.

Sophia's face fell. He'd given her a heavy blow.

Me, I wanted to hit him. How could he stand there and deny his child? It was something I could never do.

Baine saw the look on my face and rushed to explain. "It's not that I don't want her! I'm *proud* to be Sophia's father," he stammered. "It's only a surprise. I never thought of myself in that role. I've been a bachelor my entire life. I only wish there was proof."

"What proof do you need?" Doya snarled. "Do you think I was with another man in the time I was screwing you?"

"No, but I—"

"Look at her!" Doya cried. "She has your eyes!"

Baine caught Sophia's gaze and flinched. He hunched inward. "Yes... I suppose there is no denying it."

*Denying it?* This was going too far. I was seconds away from losing my temper and telling Baine the only worthwhile thing he'd done in his life was make a beautiful daughter, and even then, Doya had done most of the work on that.

But Sophia didn't take it offensively. She stepped forward and said, "I know this is a shock for most of us." Her eyes flashed toward Doya. "But we need to figure this out somehow. For the baby's sake. She deserves to be in a family where things are secure and she's loved."

Baine said nothing, but Doya drew herself up. "I will be here for this baby, Sophia. No matter what happens, you can *always* count on me to protect my granddaughter. She is my blood, and Koigni defend their own. Both you and the baby are precious things to me. I'll make sure you both have whatever you need."

Her tone implied I'd walk out like Baine had done and become a deadbeat dad or something. I resented it. But Sophia's gaze softened. Doya had never admitted she cared about Sophia before, and it struck something in her heart.

"She's your grandchild, too," Sophia said, turning to Baine. "She doesn't need you in her life, but she'll want you. The only question is if you want her."

Baine seemed contemplative— and a little scared. "I don't know what kind of a grandfather I'd be. Or even a father. I've never—"

"You were my mentor in the tournament. You've been my teacher for ages. You know me," Sophia begged. "Is it really that hard to accept me as yours?"

"You can't depend on him," Doya snapped. "He's not reliable."

Baine's expression soured. He stood upright as he looked Sophia in the eye and said, "If you are indeed my daughter, I have a responsibility to you and this child. I promise I will be here to help care for my granddaughter... and try to make up for my past mistakes."

Well, at least he was past his denial. But Doya wasn't convinced. She gave a sarcastic laugh and said, "Promises. More vows to break."

Baine's temper broke. His voice rose as he cried, "How could you keep this from me? My own daughter. This was *wrong*, Eleanor."

"Because I truly believed you would cast her aside, as you did me, or even turn her in," Eleanor said bluntly. "How could *you* love an interhouse child?"

"The same way I love you!" he bellowed.

It was the first time he admitted it, and it was in the present tense. Baine paused. His face reddened as he realized the gravity of what was said.

Doya's lip trembled again, and this time, she didn't bother to hide it. Her eyes welled, like she was on the brink of tears.

She made the same face Sophia did when she was about to cry.

"I think we've covered enough." I put an arm around Sophia's hip. "You both know now. Just understand that Sophia and I aren't going to let this affect our baby. So you both need to make up your minds on what you're going to do."

I guided Sophia out of the jail. Behind me, I heard Doya utter lowly, "Will you come back?"

There was an audible pause before Baine replied, "I don't know, Ellie."

I cringed. This was such a messy situation. I didn't want Sophia to get wrapped up in it.

Naomi rumbled as we walked by. It crossed my mind that a lioness was a very good Familiar for Doya. She'd do anything to protect her cubs, and ensure the lineage of her pride went on.

The sunlight was a welcome reprieve from the cold darkness of the cells. I sighed and said, "I think we've got proof now that interhouse children aren't weaker than others. You've got mixed blood in two generations, and you're the strongest Elementai I know."

"That's true." Sophia laid a hand on her stomach. "It makes me wonder how strong Ava will be."

Baine joined us outside. He looked at Sophia again and paled. He forced a nervous smile before he stated, "Ah... I um... I must prepare to go on another excursion. Excuse me."

He hustled off without a goodbye. Damn, he really was shit with interpersonal relationships.

"He's avoiding me," Sophia said bluntly.

"Yes," I admitted. "He probably needs time to process. We dropped a bomb on him."

"Do you think they'll get back together?" Sophia's tone was thoughtful as she nuzzled Esis.

"You noticed, too." I frowned. "I don't know. That all depends on what the Anichi Council does with Doya. She's not off the hook for her war crimes."

Sophia frowned. I knew this wasn't the grand family reunion she'd imagined in her dreams. She probably expected some big thing with a group hug and tears, but she wasn't going to get that with Baine and Doya.

Squeaks came trotting up the pathway, a note in her beak. I took it and read it quickly. "Jonah's home. We need to get ready for tonight. Go there and wait for me, please."

Sophia nodded. Julian escorted her back. Meanwhile, I decided that Baine and I should have a talk.

Or, more accurately, I needed to knock some sense into him.

I let myself in when I got to Baine's house, and nearly broke my neck tripping over a valuable artifact. Baine was hustling around, an open suitcase on the table. He tossed clothes and other shit into it haphazardly until it was fit to bursting. I was sure the old man hadn't folded laundry since the day he was born. His glasses were knocked askew, but it was like he didn't notice, or didn't care to fix them.

"You can't run away again," I started.

Baine jumped. He grew sheepish as he saw my eyes on the open suitcase.

"I beg your pardon, but I'm on a very tight schedule." Baine spoke quickly, voice bordering on irrational. "The *Azaimperiai* is very close. I can feel it. If I can find it, we may be able to turn around this war."

"This isn't about the *Azaimperiai*. This is about Sophia."

"You don't understand. I'm very close to cracking this mystery, and—"

"Look, I get you're terrified, but this isn't something you can walk away from," I said. "Burying yourself in your explorations isn't going to work this time."

Baine's shoulders sagged. "I'm well aware. But me, a father, Liam? I just don't think I'm capable."

"You got past all the hard stuff. It's not like you're going to be changing diapers." I rolled my eyes.

"No. This *is* the hard stuff, Liam. My child is grown. I missed my daughter's entire life." Baine's tone was full of regret. "Now she's a married woman about to have a child of her own. I'm concerned I'll just get in the way."

"Make it a priority not to miss any more of it." I crossed my arms. "Sophia has a dad. She was raised by the Henleys. But that doesn't mean she couldn't use another. You aren't going to mess up Sophia's life. You'll make it better."

Baine ran a hand through his peppered gray hair. It was wilder than ever. "How did you handle the news, when you heard you were going to be a father? How are you going to get by?"

I couldn't believe this. I was twenty-three years old. Baine was more than twice my age, and he was asking *me* for advice on how to be a parent, when I didn't even know how to do that yet?

"I don't know," I said. "I just... fucking roll with it, I guess."

"Roll with it," Baine mused, as if the words were sacred. "Hm... yes, I suppose I could *roll with it*, as the young people say."

"Congratulations, you're already acting like a dad," I said bluntly. "And even better, you already like making dumb jokes, so you're father— I mean —*farther* ahead than you thought."

Baine seemed ridiculously pleased with the praise. He straightened his glasses and fixed his askew tie. "This search I'm about to embark on is crucial. It can't wait. But I promise I will make amends with Sophia once I return."

"That's all I can ask for."

I wasn't very concerned with Baine's relationship with Sophia. I knew he cared about her, even before he discovered he was her dad. They'd work things out somehow.

Doya, though, I wasn't so sure. Before we dealt with Imogen, I needed to have a private conversation with her.

Doya looked up as the jail door abruptly slammed. Her eyes narrowed as she watched me stride. She didn't rise from her seat, as if to show that she didn't think I was worth her time.

"Why are *you* here?" Doya asked condescendingly. She got that tight-lipped expression she always did when I was in her presence.

I always wondered why she'd hated me so much. In the past few days, I think I figured it out. At the beginning of the year, I'd initiated a fight with Logan, and told Doya I was protecting what was my own.

Doya was venomous when she said Sophia wasn't mine. Now I understood. Doya considered Sophia hers, and I had taken her daughter away from her.

"I'm here to sort things out." I shoved my hands in my pockets. "Let's get one thing straight. You and I are never going to like each other."

Doya scoffed. "I'm sure that conclusion was momentous for your small Toaqua brain to fathom."

"But we *should* get along. For Sophia's sake," I finished through clenched teeth. Ancestors, she was already trying my nerves.

"I don't plan on you sticking around," she seethed. "Eventually, I'm certain Sophia will get tired of you."

"She married me. This isn't a phase. I'm staying with her, no matter what's to come."

Doya gave a cruel laugh. "It's not really your choice whether you stay or go, is it?"

What Doya said stung. No, more than that, it actually hurt. Which was tremendous, because I'd resolved not to let anything she said get to me after Nashoma died.

But she was right. "I can't stop living my life just because I have a disease."

"You *got my daughter pregnant* when you know you're on a time limit," Doya growled. "Like it or not, you're leaving behind a young wife and child."

I swallowed the lump in my throat. "My life expectancy is still up in the air. Any of us could die in this war."

Doya's tone was spiteful as she rose from her seat. "The cold, hard fact is my daughter will most likely have to bury you long before she grows old. And when you are gone, it is I who will be there to pick up the pieces."

"If you survive," I spat. "You're slated for execution."

"Foolish boy. I've survived far worse than this." Doya's gaze was cruel. "I've done unimaginable things to live. This is one more setback in a very long list."

This was getting us nowhere. "I came here to make peace."

"I wanted better for her!" Doya shouted. I could feel her anger as heat rolled off of her in waves. "My father was ill. He left my mother and I behind, to handle life on our own. That's not what I wanted for Sophia."

Things clicked then. I had a thought that Doya didn't really hate me at all. She hated the idea that I would die, and leave her daughter alone— like Baine had done to her. Like her father had done.

"It can't be helped. We're joined together in the eyes of the Great Spirit. What's done is done," I said firmly. "If you're so concerned, at least know she'll be taken care of if the worst happens. Widows of chiefs are always treated with reverence by the tribe. She and Ava will have their needs met."

Doya gave a sarcastic huff. "Your status means nothing. You could never be good enough for my daughter."

"At least that's something we agree on." I crossed my arms, and Doya's expression became mildly surprised. "I could never become everything that Sophia deserves. But regardless, she chose me. And I won't leave her until she demands my absence, if that day ever comes. I'm not like Baine. I didn't run away when things got tough. I was willing to die for her time and time again. That should prove to you I'm serious. However much you hate me, you can't deny that I love her."

Doya paused to consider. It was almost as if she was struggling not to like me.

Then she shook her head, as if convincing herself otherwise. "You're a Toaqua. They're all the same. Loose and spineless, like water. You can't understand the passion that burns within a Koigni. We'd do anything to save the ones we love. I can't understand why she would choose you of all people, instead of one of her own kind."

"Water can be gentle, but it can also be ruthless. I've killed for Sophia. I'll do it again if it becomes necessary."

Doya drummed her fingers against the bars. "Toaqua men have a way with women. They manipulate them."

"I didn't manipulate her into having a relationship with me. I was the one who tried to end it. But no matter what I did to separate us, it never worked. When two people are destined to be together, nothing can keep them apart."

Doya let out a cold laugh. "You're still young enough to believe in a naive thing like fate."

"I have to. Hope is the only thing that's kept us alive."

"You stole her away on a vague sense of *hope*," Doya spat. "She left Orenda Academy without me there to protect her."

"If she had stayed, she'd be dead. You know this."

Doya bit her lip and turned her face away. "I could've done something."

"You could've done nothing." My temper was rising, but I forced myself to remain in control. "I could've done nothing. Back there, we had no power. But here, she stands a chance."

Doya's cold gaze met mine. "You will not be able to control her once she becomes all she's meant to be."

"Neither will you. I don't think it makes me any less of a man to admit that scares me."

"You should be scared of her." Doya pushed away from the bars. "We all should."

There was a beat of silence, until Doya said, "I can only imagine the power her daughter will inherit. Three generations of interhouse ancestors running through her bloodline. We know now that kind of power does not inhibit a child; it perhaps makes them stronger."

A chill crossed over my skin, yet I suppressed it. "This is all speculation. None of us are sure if Ava-Marie will be Koigni or Toaqua."

"If you think your daughter won't be exceptional, you're dead wrong." Doya hugged her arms to her chest. "This child is a woman. She will most likely inherit a Koigni bloodline. Are you prepared for your firstborn to be a Fire child? She cannot inherit the Toaqua chief hood if she has no Water abilities, not to mention *your kind* has never given the chief hood to a woman."

"Perhaps it's time for things to change in the Toaqua tribe," I said. "If Ava-Marie wishes to pursue chief hood, then I will organize that for her. But if it's not her life's path, then it won't be forced upon her. The chief hood will be her choice, and the tribe will accept her regardless. She has the blood of all the Toaqua chieftains running through her veins. Gender has no standing on that."

Doya's eyes narrowed. "If you're alive to enforce such a radical position."

I rubbed my eyes. "Look, all I'm saying is, we should make a pact. Both of us have the same interests. Our main priorities are to keep Sophia and Ava-Marie happy and alive. We have a common goal."

Doya's face was contemplative. "I will make this deal with you, Mitoh. We will work together to protect them both. For some asinine reason, you please my daughter, so I won't stand in your way or continue to oppose your marriage."

Doya's tone turned dark. "But mark my words, if you hurt my daughter, there will not be a hole on this earth where I won't find you, and burn you alive."

"Great. Glad we had this talk." I took an impatient huff. "One last thing. I'd like to invite you to have Christmas with us. That is, if the Anichi Council decides to spare you, and set you free."

Doya's eyes widened. A hand flew to her heart. She kept it pinned there as she said, "I've... never spent Christmas with anyone. Not since my mother died, at least. It's always been Naomi and I."

What a sad thing to say. "Well, the baby is due to arrive on Christmas Eve. And Sophia doesn't say it, but I think she might want you to be there."

"Why would you invite me?" Doya's tone grew condescending, as if she thought this was some kind of trap.

"Because... like it or not, we're family. And I think Ava-Marie should get to know her grandmother."

Doya's face cleared. She clicked her nails against the bars and said, "Well, thank you for the invitation. Though I'm not sure if I will attend."

I'd probably be happier if she didn't show up, honestly, but the offer was out there. Holidays were going to be really weird with Doya hanging around.

If she survived her judgement.

&

I HAD QUITE a crowd of people waiting for me when I got home. Sophia and Jonah were on the couch. Jake stood behind them, rubbing Jonah's shoulders. Both Sabor and Squeaks were curled up on the rug, Esis on top of them. Baby was outside with Julian, as we thought it would be best he didn't witness this.

Ezra was in the kitchen, eating, as fucking usual. Trace was there, too, leaning forward on an armchair with his hands clasped. Amelia had a hand on his shoulder, as she was there for emotional support. Kiwi chirped on his head. I was pretty sure the dumb bird had no idea why we were all here.

Luana stayed against the wall like some kind of ghost, Sierra in her hands. Sophia had asked her to come, but it was clear she was a little uncomfortable.

"Imogen should be home any moment," Jonah said hollowly.

This was it. Time to get ready. "I think Sophia, Jonah and I should do most of the talking," I said. "The rest of you can back us up."

Heads nodded in unison. I glanced around. "Where the fuck is Cade?"

Ezra shrugged and took a massive bite of his sandwich. "I don't know, dude. When I got up this morning, he'd disappeared with Arabelle."

Cade knew we were doing this. It was critical he be here. Was he done with her now that he knew she was doing drugs?

Whatever. Cade wasn't my problem. I cared about Imogen.

The silence was awkward. The clock ticking on the wall seemed to grow louder with each second of impending doom. None of us knew how this was going to go. It was likely she'd explode. I feared Imogen would get out of control.

Jonah broke the quiet. "So how'd telling Baine go?"

Sophia sighed. "As you'd expect it to. He was in total denial, then when he couldn't handle the truth, he ran away."

"He's coming back, Soph. He said he'd fix things with you once he returned from his expedition," I said.

She blew a strand of hair out of her eyes. "I sure hope so."

"Honestly, we should've figured it out a long time ago. You're clueless, just like your father," Jonah said playfully. He was trying to make a joke to lighten the mood, but in the shadow of the dark situation we were in, it came out kind of harsh.

Sophia's mouth dropped open in outrage. "I'm not clueless!"

"Please, girl. You're always ten steps behind, just like Baine. It's *so* obvious now," Jonah purred.

Sophia looked at me to back her up— which was difficult to do in this situation. "Do *you* think I'm clueless?"

I knew better than to challenge a pregnant woman's ultimate wrath, but still, it was really hard to lie. "Uh... you're a *little* oblivious. But in an adorable way," I admitted.

Sophia's eyebrows knitted together as she gave me a frown. Esis scrunched up his nose.

"So what if you're slow on the uptake? It's one of your quirks," Jonah said.

Sophia gave a groan. "Great. You all think I'm stupid."

"You're smart. Baine's brilliant, and so are you," I said. "You both just... have a tendency to be in your own little world."

Sophia straightened up. "Well, *I* take it as a compliment. Baine's one of the supernatural world's best explorers. His... wandering mind could be mistaken for genius!"

Wouldn't go that far, but okay.

"Hey, you have your mother's temper, I'll give you that," Ezra said. "We all know better than to make you angry, cause watch out!"

"Not helping, Ez," I growled.

He shrugged. To my surprise, Sophia didn't take the Doya thing in a bad way. It more or less made her reflective. "Do you really think I'm that scary?"

"When you get mad? Hells yeah. Never scorn a Koigni female unless you want to get burned," Ezra said around a full mouth.

Sophia grinned, like the compliment thrilled her. Nobody could argue she had a fierce Koigni streak. "I *like* being scary."

"Well, I don't like it, so let's keep it to a minimum," I quipped. A couple people laughed— it eased the tension a little, which helped.

Then the door opened. The laughter died as Imogen stepped through the threshold. She had leaves in her hair and dirt on her clothes.

Her Familiar looked worse. Sassy's fur was dull, not as red as it usually was, and the fox crawled along as if it was exhausted. She dragged herself to Squeaks' side, where she collapsed with a great sigh.

Jonah looked at Imogen and almost started crying all over again, but Jake squeezed his shoulder, and he remained strong. Imogen glanced at him and quickly looked away.

"What's going on?" She asked the question, but she knew.

I stood. "Come sit down, Im. Let's talk."

Imogen hesitantly crossed the room and sat between Sophia and Jonah. She crossed her ankles and looked up, expecting a lecture.

I began. "Im, this has to stop."

"What has?" She was playing dumb. Her eyes were big and round, but I saw they were dilated. She'd taken a hit before she'd gotten here.

"The nightshade," Jonah spat. It was obvious he couldn't handle seeing her high. "We all know you're taking it."

Imogen immediately got on the defensive. "Of course Sophia told you," she sneered. "You can never trust her to keep a secret."

Sophia cringed, but Jonah wasn't having it. "Did you honestly think we'd *never* figure it out? Look at you! You're high right fucking now!"

"Jonah." I held out a hand, to tell him to calm down. He was making things worse by taking it so personally. He kept his mouth shut, but fidgeted in place.

"Black Ivy is dangerous. You can overdose so easily on the stuff. We don't want anything to happen to you," I said.

"Why do you guys give a shit? You hardly care if I live or die," Imogen snarled.

"We're friends. It's what we do." Sophia moved closer to Imogen, but she pulled away.

"Do you have any on you right now?" I asked.

Imogen's lip rose. "That's none of your business."

"Good thing we got rid of the rest of it. I dumped your entire stock down the drain," Jonah said nastily.

"What?!" Imogen leapt up from her seat. She ran to the bedroom, and we followed. She ripped out her desk drawer, and when she saw the drugs were gone, gave an angry cry.

"You had no right to go through my stuff!" She shoved Jonah, but he didn't go anywhere— just planted his feet and didn't move.

"You don't get privacy when you're using. Not here," I said. I was trying to maintain some sort of control, but already, things were getting out of hand.

"You're not the boss of me, Liam! We all share this house! You have some sort of god complex, running around telling people what to do all the time!" Imogen burst. She bolted around her room, throwing pillows and clothes around, looking for any Black Ivy she might've stored away. When she found none, her breaths grew ragged and panicky.

Jonah crossed his arms. "Well, I'm with him, and Sophia's with us, which makes you outvoted!"

"You just want to control me. All you guys ever do is tell me how to live my life!" Imogen shouted. "You guys think you're so perfect, but you're just controlling assholes!"

This wasn't her. This was the nightshade talking. Imogen shoved past me and went back into the kitchen. She pulled open the cupboards and started tossing things into a bag she'd grabbed on her way out of her room. Sassy curled against Squeaks, her ears back. Squeaks put a wing over the fox and cooed.

"What the hell are you doing?" I asked. She seemed nearly manic.

"I'm leaving. I don't want to live here anymore," she snarled. "I don't want to be in a place where I'm not appreciated."

"How do we not appreciate you?" Jonah had broken away from Jake and threw his arms skyward. "Do you want us to fall down and worship the ground you walk on?"

"You're so fucking dramatic, Jonah. And you know what? It gets old." Imogen threw the bag on the ground as she rounded on him. "I'm tired of being the little sidekick in this freak show."

"What are you *talking* about?" Jonah's tone was full of disdain. Imogen's face had gone so red I knew an explosion was coming.

"You're the Storm Lord. Sophia's the chosen one, and Liam's the chief of Toaqua. What am I?" Imogen started crying. Angry tears gushed out of her eyes so fast I was sure she'd repressed them for months. "You all have something special. And me? I'm worthless."

My heart dropped. Sophia whispered, "You're not worthless, Im."

Imogen huffed. "Oh, really? Because ever since we got here it feels that way. You needed me back at Orenda Academy. You don't need me here. Once we arrived, you replaced me with *her*."

Imogen pointed at Luana, and she cowered against the wall. I stepped in front of Imogen's accusing hand to shield Luana from her rage. "Im, we love you. If we didn't care, we wouldn't be doing this at all."

Imogen rolled her eyes. "Yeah, right. More like you just want to judge me for my life choices."

"Black Ivy isn't a life choice. It's life or death," Sophia protested.

Imogen gave a harsh laugh. "Nothing's going to happen. I have it under control."

"You're an addict," Sophia said gently. "You have a problem."

"And if I do? So what?" Imogen placed a hand on her hip. "It's my business, not yours. You need to butt out of my life."

Ancestors, we needed to fight for her. We needed to fight for her hard, harder than we ever had before. Nightshade was the cruelest thing we'd ever gone up against.

And right now, the nightshade was winning.

"You think you're not special? We couldn't have found the pieces of the prophecy without you," I said softly. "Where do you think we'd be without you, Im, huh? Cause I'll tell you. We'd be dead."

"You just keep me around so I can do your homework!" Imogen snarled. "You're not smart enough to figure this stuff out without me, so you guys put up with me to get what you want."

This time, it was Jonah who laughed. "Wow. That is really fucking stupid."

Imogen's nostrils flared. She clenched her hands into fists, but before she could respond, I stepped in.

"You're the one who saved us when we were on the run. You had a plan, put away money, had a place for us to live. None of us were smart enough to do that," I said.

"Big fucking deal!" Imogen gave another laugh, but this one sounded more like a sob. "You all have special jobs in the rebellion. You guys are all heroes. And what the hell am I doing? Growing food!"

"Yeah, that's not important. I'm sure we could win the war if we were starving to death," I replied sarcastically. "I guess working on the strategy team is useless too, huh?"

Sophia glanced at me, this time telling me I was the one who needed to calm down. I paused for a beat as a memory came back to me. A creeping horror twisted in my gut as I said, "Wait a minute. Were you high at our *wedding?!*"

"I was sober until that fight with Cade!" Imogen's form trembled. "That day I decided I wanted to get clean. I didn't have any nightshade all day, until we got in that fight."

"It was your choice to start taking nightshade in the first place," Trace grumbled sourly.

"You don't have the right to lecture me, *brother*," Imogen seethed. "You're the one who started it all, when you decided to fake your death. Everyone in my life walks out. You abandoned me. Mom and Dad abandoned me. The love of my life walked out on me when I needed him most. And he's not even here now!" Imogen gasped for breath. "He couldn't even be bothered to show up!"

"Then fuck him," I said. "Don't do it for him. Do it for the people who matter most. Do it for yourself."

"*Myself?* I hate myself." Imogen wiped at her eyes frantically. "I'd give anything to stop feeling like this and to be someone else. I wish I could snap out of it and stop, but I can't."

"Don't say that, Im. It's not true," I said softly. "You're a great person."

She took a ragged breath. "It's only a matter of time before you guys leave me, too."

"We aren't going to leave you, Imogen. I'd rather die," Jonah said. Squeaks chirped, to announce he was telling the truth.

"If I mean so much to everyone, why did no one see me when I needed them the most?" she asked. "I thought you guys would notice the first time I used, or the second, but you never did. I brought drugs into this house time and time again, got high so many times right in front of your nose, and not one person noticed."

"We noticed, we just didn't know what was wrong," Sophia pleaded. "How can we help you if you won't let us in?"

"I shouldn't have to ask! I've always been there for you guys. I tried to help you with your demons and get past your pain when we were in hiding, but it didn't work!" Imogen burst. "You didn't get better until you got to *Hok'evale*. Luana ended up helping you more than I ever could. Nothing I did helped you."

"Imogen, it wasn't like that," Sophia pleaded, but she sounded guilty. I didn't think she should be. Different things worked for different people, and just because Imogen hadn't been able to help Sophia with her PTSD and Luana had, it meant nothing. Imogen still cared, and that was the important part.

She didn't see it like that, though. And I didn't know how we could change her mind.

"Why couldn't you be there for me?" Imogen gasped for breath. "Turns out you're all too involved with your significant others to care about your friends."

Her gaze was directly aimed at Jonah. His face fell. Sophia stepped in to defend him. "If you'd just talk to us, we'd help. Imogen, you're my best friend—"

Imogen's voice rose to a screech. "Shut *up*, Sophia! You don't know anything about me. You just want to be a baby cannon for Liam."

"That's not fair," Sophia responded viciously. "You know it's my choice to be a stay-at-home mom."

Imogen snorted. "Yeah, some choice, relying on a man your whole life. We can't all be Mother of the Year like you. Sophia, patron saint of unexpected pregnancies!"

"I'm getting *so* fucking tired of you being jealous of me!" Sophia screamed. "You'd have what I have if you stopped being such a bitch and let Cade back in!"

"Maybe I want to accomplish something that's harder than spreading my legs!" Imogen yelled.

My. Mouth. Dropped. So did Sophia's. Both of us were temporarily lost for words. I couldn't believe she'd been so cruel.

But Jonah, queen of sass, wasn't about to let a comment like that slide. "Says the little virgin," he mumbled under his breath.

Imogen whirled around. "Excuse me? What did you just say?"

Jonah's gaze became cruel. "I think you need to get some action like the rest of us. You wouldn't act like someone pissed in your Cheerios."

"Take that back." Imogen's fingers curled, and the stone walls overhead began to crack. Debris and dust fell from the cracks, and the stone floor underneath began to shake. I was concerned the cave the house was built into would collapse at Imogen's wrath.

"*Enough.* We don't talk like this to each other." I stepped between the two and forced them apart. The cracks in the ceiling stopped spreading, yet Imogen and Jonah's eyes remained locked. Sophia took deep breaths and ran her hands over her stomach, trying not to cry.

I grabbed Sophia by the shoulders and dragged her to the side. "Soph, take a break," I growled.

"I'm not going to walk out now when this could be Imogen's last chance!" Sophia pleaded.

"We are *this close* to making it full term," I snapped. "I'm not going to have Imogen's bullshit trigger labor a month early because you're overly stressed. There are more than enough people here to handle this. Give yourself five minutes to chill out."

Sophia breathed deeply. "Okay." She quietly slipped into our bedroom and closed the door. I returned to the intervention... all had gone silent. Imogen had somehow ended up on the floor, kneeling to try and catch her breath. She was crumbling, like the weight of what she'd just said had crashed upon her.

I lowered my voice to a gentle tone. "Im, that wasn't okay."

"You don't know what it's like," Imogen sobbed. She wiped tears away with the heel of her hand. "I was feeling so miserable when we got here. So lonely. Cade betrayed me. My family betrayed me. Then we liberated the camps, and all those children were slaughtered in front of me. I had to watch those poor kids *die*, and I couldn't handle it. I needed you guys to be there for me, but how could I reach out? What with the wedding, and the baby... then Jonah got together with Jake, and I felt like I'd lost you all for good."

Imogen sobbed harder. "The night we got here, I went for a walk. This guy was on the corner... he said it'd make all my problems go away. And I thought... I'll just try it once, just to see if it helps. And it did. Nightshade didn't make me feel weird, or strange. It barely made me feel high. It just made everything feel like things were going to be all right again. It was euphoric. I hadn't been fine since Cade left. I'd been barely holding on. And every time I took a hit, I felt good. Even if things were bad, I just didn't care. I forgot all the horrible things we went through. The nightshade made it so I was in a good mood all the time, no matter what happened. I was always floating. And feeling fine is so much better than feeling like you're nothing inside."

"I understand. I really do," I said. "Remember when I almost jumped off that bridge? I felt like that for a long time. But I got better, and you guys were there for me. Now we're here for you, too. And you can get better."

"I'm scared to give it up. I'll lose my powers. If I stop taking nightshade, my magic might leave me for good. It's so weak now without it," she whimpered.

"If you keep taking it, you're going to die," Jonah pleaded. Trace nodded miserably beside him.

Imogen's face twisted. "Sometimes I think dying wouldn't be so bad."

Imogen wasn't backing down. Time to bring in the big guns.

I took a deep breath. "Im... if you keep doing this, I don't know if I can stick around to watch."

"What do you mean?" Strands of hair clung to her face as she looked up.

"I'm having a kid. She's gotta come first." I locked eyes with her. "I don't want someone on drugs around my daughter."

Imogen's mouth gaped. She couldn't believe I said that.

"Liam's right." Sophia came out of the bedroom. She took my hand as she came by my side. "I have to stand by my husband. If you're not getting help, not getting clean, you're putting my baby at risk. You can't be in my life if you're endangering Ava-Marie. I won't put up with it."

Imogen sought out Jonah. "You won't leave me, will you?"

Jonah's voice shook. "I don't want to."

"What do you mean?" Imogen asked quickly.

"I mean... if you keep using, you're gonna get kicked out," Jonah said quietly.

Imogen glanced to Jake. He remained rigid and impassive. "We have programs that can help you. There's a rehabilitation center here for night-shade addicts. It's proven that people can recover and lead full lives."

Imogen's expression was hard. "What if I don't want to go to therapy?"

"I'm afraid the policy is the same. Even for you." Jake crossed his arms. "We can't have nightshade addicts who refuse to be rehabilitated in *Hok'e-vale*. They're a threat to our security and compromise the safety of the rebellion. If you don't agree to attend our rehabilitation center, there will be consequences."

Imogen stared at the ground and said nothing more. I could see the decision weighing in her eyes. She was so addicted to nightshade she had to think twice if she was willing to give us up.

Then the door opened. Imogen turned on her knees. Cade had arrived. He appeared calm and collected, if not still hurt. I was kind of pissed at him for showing up late... until I realized that he hadn't arrived until now on purpose. He was holding off on showing up until he could go into this with a clear head. I bet he'd been outside the door the entire time, listening in to the conversation. Cade knelt by Imogen's side when he got to her and took her hands in his.

Imogen trembled. "Cade, I'm so sorry."

"I know you are, *chica*." Cade's voice wobbled slightly. "But this has to stop."

"I'm not ready," she whispered. "I'm not strong enough."

"You are strong. You're my Imogen." He squeezed her hands and brought them to his lips to kiss them.

A tear dropped from Imogen's eye and landed on the floor. "What if I can't?"

Cade took a deep breath. It looked like it took all the strength he had to say, "If you don't go to rehab— if you don't get help— we're done. For good. I can't keep doing this to myself, Imogen. Your behavior has been out of control. At times, it's been abusive. I'm not happy. And I can't put up with it anymore. If you go to treatment, I'll be by your side all the way. I'll walk to the ends of the earth to make sure you get better, because I love you. I love you more than I've ever loved anyone else. I'd die for you. I'd go to treatment in your place if I could. I'd take the withdrawals for you."

Cade took a deep breath. "But that's not possible. You have to put in the work. If you don't get help... I'm sorry. It's the end of you and me."

Cade's tone implied he meant it. Imogen's eyes darted from his to the floor in a long contemplation.

Finally, Imogen dug in her pocket. She took out a half-vial of night-shade and gave it to Cade, without any complaints.

Once she handed over the vial, she said, "I'll go, Cade. I'll go for you. For my friends."

Sassy rose from Squeaks' side and crossed the room. She slid into Imogen's lap to kiss her face. Imogen stroked her hand across Sassy's fur and whispered, "For me."

# sophia
## TWENTY-TWO

Imogen had promised to do better, and I could tell that she meant it. It took a huge weight off the entire group to know she was serious about recovery. It would take time for her to get back to her old self, but at least now we knew what was wrong and were in a better position to help.

She wasn't around the next morning, since she'd agreed to attend the live-in rehab program, which meant she'd be at the center for at least a month.

Liam left early. He had a lot of chief duties to catch up on from the day before, and it sounded like he had an important meeting to attend.

Jonah and I were left in our house alone with our Familiars when a frantic knock came at the door. Esis and I were eating breakfast, while Jonah was in the kitchen tossing raw bits of bacon to Squeaks and Baby while he waited for his coffee to brew. We exchanged a quick glance, as if to ask each other if we were expecting company.

The knock came again. Jonah dropped the package of bacon on the counter and rushed to the door. Squeaks immediately grabbed it, flinging bits of bacon all over the kitchen while she tried to rip the package open further.

Jonah opened the door, but I didn't hear anything. I tried to peek around him, but his shoulders were so big I couldn't see who was in the doorway.

"Slow down," Jonah insisted, while making motions with his hands. My heart leapt when I realized it was Luana.

"What's wrong?" I asked urgently. I pushed myself up out of my seat, but I couldn't manage to rush it these days with how big I was getting.

Jonah stepped aside and held the door open for Luana. "Something about Doya," he said. "She's talking so fast I can't understand."

Luana's eyebrows came together, and her breath came in ragged heaves as she signed quickly to me.

*The Anichi Council is making their final decision on Doya today!* she signed.

*Why didn't they tell me?* I demanded.

*They're not holding a public trial. There's no trial at all.*

*What do you mean?* My heart hammered. *They've already made a decision?*

*No,* she told me. *They're handing the decision over.*

*To who?*

*Perot.*

Oh, fuck. I knew instantly what that meant. The Anichi Council didn't want to make the decision themselves, so they gave the power to the person they thought deserved a say most— the man Doya had wronged in the most unthinkable way. She'd killed Perot's lover. He was going to choose execution for sure.

I couldn't let that happen.

It wasn't until that moment that I realized how I truly felt about it. At first, I didn't understand my feelings— not really. I'd watched Madame Doya murder Head Dean Alric in cold blood. A part of me wanted revenge for everything she'd done. But I didn't wish for her to die.

Something Liam had said that hit me in that moment. It came to me so strongly that it was as if my ancestors themselves were standing beside me, screaming into my ears.

*The world isn't black and white,* I recalled Liam saying.

And he was right. Nothing was black and white, hot or cold. For the first time, I actually believed Doya when she said she had a reason for everything she'd done. Standing in her shoes, I couldn't say what choices I would've made. I couldn't begin to understand it, but I didn't have to. I just had to trust this feeling in my gut right now.

I had to save her.

*We must stop this,* I told Luana.

*Follow me.*

I grabbed my coat and hurried out the door behind Luana. Esis followed.

"Wait!" Jonah called. "What's happening? Can I help?"

I turned back toward him. "Find Liam and tell him Perot's giving Madame Doya's sentence."

Jonah's hand went to his heart, as if clutching at invisible pearls. "But Perot will—"

"I know," I said firmly. "That's why I need to be there. She needs an advocate."

At that, I turned back toward Luana, and we walked as fast as we could toward the Anichi Elders' quarters. The door was shut when we arrived, but we could hear voices inside. I didn't wait for an invitation. I opened the door and stormed in.

"You can't do this!" I cried before I had a chance to assess the room.

Everything went silent as all eyes turned toward me. The Anichi Elders sat behind their stone meeting table with their companions at their sides, but they weren't the only ones there. Liam and his Toaqua Council were also present, along with representatives from all the other Houses.

I noticed the solemn look on Baine's face. He was supposed to be leaving for another expedition, but he'd stayed for Doya. Perot was nowhere to be seen.

Chief Cauac was the first to speak. "We can't do what, Miss Mitoh?"

I paused a moment, unsure of what my next move was. "You can't execute Madame Doya."

Liam stood and stepped toward me. "Sophia, calm down. That decision hasn't been made."

"But Liam, they're giving the choice to Perot!" I cried.

"I know," Liam said softly.

I heard the confirmation in his voice. "Wait. You agreed to this?"

Liam cleared his throat. "The vote was... split."

"He'll want her executed," I pointed out.

"We don't know that," Liam insisted. "Perot is being summoned as we speak. We'll figure things out once he gets here."

"Speak of the devil," Ezra muttered under his breath.

Just then, Professor Perot stepped through the open doorway. Jake was on his heels, like he'd escorted him here. Perot's gray hair was a mess, and he looked particularly anxious, as if someone had interrupted his morning nap. Baxtor ruffled his colorful feathers and stayed close to Perot's side.

"Perot, please!" I begged before anyone else could say anything. "You can't kill Doya."

Perot looked shell-shocked by my blatant protest.

"Miss Mitoh," Chief Cauac said. "Let's take a moment to discuss this, why don't we?"

Liam pulled me aside, while Perot stepped forward.

Chief Cauac folded his hands in front of himself. "Doctor Perot, as the council understands it, you have a personal grievance with Madame Eleanor Doya. Is that correct?"

"Yes, sir, it is," Perot said calmly, though I noticed his hands were shaking.

"Due to the level of Madame Doya's crimes, the council has decided to hand the sentencing over to you," Chief Cauac announced.

"Hold on," I argued. "Why should he be the only one to decide?"

Chief Cauac frowned. "Madame Doya harmed no one when she came to *Hok'evale* and turned herself in. Her worst crimes do not concern the Anichi. Seeing as we have no evidence to present and our council is in disagreement over her sentencing, we have decided to turn the decision over to someone else. Long ago, the Hawkei would consult those a criminal hurt most, as a true testament to the extent of their crimes, to decide their sentencing. We choose to revisit that tradition today. Doctor Perot?"

Perot looked shaken. "Well, I— I may need some time to think about this, Chief."

Chief Cauac nodded in understanding. It was clear he'd be at peace with whatever Perot decided.

I didn't need to convince Cauac of anything. I had to convince Perot.

"Professor, please," I begged. "Spare her."

Perot eyed me curiously. "Forgive me, Sophia, but I don't understand. It was my knowledge that you and Madame Doya have never been on good terms."

I bit my lower lip. "Well, no, but..."

"But...?" Perot cocked an eyebrow.

"But... she always did what she had to do to protect me."

Perot's spine straightened. His curiosity had piqued. "How so?"

I glanced down to my belly and ran my hands over it. It was hard to admit Doya had helped me in any way, but the more I thought about it, the more I realized just how much she had done.

I swallowed the lump in my throat. "Madame Doya gave birth to me."

Gasps traveled around the room. Perot's eyes widened in shock, like he couldn't imagine Doya being a mother at all.

"It's true. Doya is my mother— a fact I did not learn until recently," I clarified. "What she did to keep me safe was exactly what any mother would do. She gave me up to save my life, because she knew the Elders would kill me otherwise."

"Because you're the chosen one?" Perot asked.

"To be honest, I don't think she knew that at the time," I admitted. "But if she hadn't given me up, I very well may have died in the Toaqua riots— the night the Toaqua intended to kill me. The truth is, I'm mixed house— part Koigni, and part Toaqua."

Another chorus of gasps traveled around the room. People started whispering, until it got so loud I could hardly hear my own thoughts.

"Quiet!" Baine tried to calm down the council, but it didn't work. "It is true. Let Sophia explain."

The room went silent a few moments later, and all eyes turned to me. I glanced to Baine. He wore a somber but defeated expression.

"Do you want to tell them?" I asked him.

He nodded, though he looked nervous. "The truth is, I am Sophia's father."

We couldn't get the council to shut up after that. A few Koigni representatives got really angry, while Ezra and Wyatt were cracking jokes about Doya and Baine.

"That relationship had to be wild," Ezra said.

"She's gotta be a dominatrix," Wyatt agreed.

"Shut up," Liam growled under his breath. "Now is not the time."

Perot looked deeply contemplative. "Elliot... you and Madame Doya? Come to think of it... I should've seen that one coming."

Baine scoffed. "I could say the same about you and Alric. Our secrets aren't so unusual after all."

"No, I guess not," Perot said thoughtfully. "But I don't understand. Sophia's so powerful, yet she's interhouse."

Liam stepped in. "I think we all learned after our trial that mixed children are not as weak as they are made out to be."

"Yes, I suppose that's true." Perot turned back to me. "So, Madame Doya gave you up because you were mixed house?"

"Yes," I confirmed. "The Elders would've killed me if they found out."

Perot dropped his gaze. "I'm sorry, Sophia, but that is not enough to forgive what she did."

"No, it's not," I agreed. "What she did to Alric was... unforgivable. But I believe her when she says she had a reason."

Perot's hands curled into fists. "What reason could she possibly have?"

The room quieted again, as everyone seemed interested in the answer.

"She wanted to help the Hawkei," I said. I realized for the first time that I didn't just believe the things she had told me— I actually understood them. Life and death situations had a way of twisting your own worldviews. "She intended to gain favor on the Elder Council, because she believed that was the only way to make change."

"But she didn't," Perot argued. "She didn't change anything."

"She did!" I replied. "She *saved* me from the Elders. Chieftess Annette wanted to use me, then dispose of me. Madame Doya lied to the council to keep them from getting their hands on me. She sacrificed what she thought was the key to elevating her own House in order to save my life."

My breath grew ragged as I realized the truth of everything she'd done. "She burned a rapist to keep him from hurting me. She hid my lineage from me so the Elders wouldn't prosecute. I know that in the past, she craved power. But more than that, she wanted to protect me. It takes a deep, unconditional love to make those kinds of sacrifices for other people."

Perot tilted his head to the side. "You're saying she loves you, Sophia?"

I gaped at him. I hadn't realized it before. Deep down in my heart, the anger I felt for Doya melted away, and for a moment, I saw the truth through her eyes. "In her own way, yes. Madame Doya loves me. And she loves Baine, too."

I looked to Baine, who had tears beading in the corners of his eyes.

"Is that true?" Perot asked.

Baine nodded. "I hope so, because I love her, as well. Please don't kill her, Jacques."

Perot looked between me and Baine. The crease between his eyebrows deepened. "What do you believe will happen if I choose to pardon her?"

My heart lifted at the thought. "Honestly, I don't know. But I do know one thing. Madame Doya will go to the ends of the earth for the people she loves. That's the kind of passion and devotion *Hok'evale* stands for."

"I believe she will fight on our side," Baine added. "To protect Sophia."

Perot didn't answer. He pressed his lips together thoughtfully and shot a glance at his Familiar. I held my breath. I felt Liam stiffen beside me, and Baine wiped his forehead. He was starting to sweat.

Finally, Perot let out a breath and turned to Chief Cauac. "I've made my decision."

Chief Cauac cocked an eyebrow. "So soon?"

"Yes," Perot said confidently.

"Okay." Cauac nodded. "What will it be?"

I felt the whole room hold a collective breath. I didn't doubt some of the council members were hoping Perot announced Madame Doya's execution. But others looked uncertain. I took Baine's and Liam's hands in mine and squeezed them tightly, awaiting the answer.

"What Madame Doya did to me— to Caspian— is something I can never forgive her for," Perot announced. "She has wronged many people, both in this war and before."

My hands tightened. I didn't like the way his speech was going. They'd have the water tank ready for her drowning by this afternoon.

"*But,*" Perot said sharply. "Caspian would be damned if I stood here and strung this noose. I will not allow another unnecessary body to drop in this war. My only wish is to hear her apology. After that— consider her a free woman."

My heart swelled. There was something ironic about saving Doya's life, but I couldn't say I didn't owe her. She'd saved mine more than once.

It took Chief Cauac a moment to answer. I didn't think he expected Perot to pardon her. "So be it," he finally said as he stood from his chair. "Follow me, Doctor Perot. Let's get you that apology."

Chief Cauac led Perot and Baxtor out of the Elders' chambers and around the building to the jail. Liam, Baine, and I followed quickly behind them, but we were not permitted inside. We stood shivering in the cold and waited. I held Esis close, pressing my nose into his fur. Liam wrapped an arm around my waist, but none of us said anything. I think we were all worried Perot would change his mind.

Several other people from the Elders' chambered had gathered around us, though the crowd remained quiet and curious. While we waited, I heard the sound of hoofbeats, then a squawk. We turned to see Jonah and Squeaks approaching.

"Bro, I've been looking for you everywhere," Jonah said. "Looks like Sophia found you first. So, what's the verdict?"

"Perot's decided to spare her," I said. "But only if she apologizes."

Jonah winced. "That might take a miracle. Do you think she'll do it?"

"To save herself?" Liam asked. "I don't think even Doya has that much pride."

"She'll do it," Baine assured us, though he didn't spare us a single glance. He kept his eyes locked on the jail door, looking worried.

After what felt like two hours, the door to the jail swung open, and Perot and Cauac stepped outside. My heart pounded as the crowd began to murmur. I didn't see Doya behind them.

Chief Cauac lifted his hands to quiet the crowd. "A decision has been made. Eleanor Doya has confessed and apologized for her crimes, and Doctor Jacques Perot has accepted this apology. We have reached an agreement to her role in *Hok'evale*. She will be stripped of her Elder title and be accepted as a full citizen of our tribe. No one is to harm her."

Baine pressed his hand to his mouth, and his eyes sparkled with tears of relief. Liam squeezed me tight to his side. I finally felt like I could breathe.

Perot and Baxtor stepped aside, and Chief Cauac motioned Doya forward. "Miss Doya," he said. "You are now a free woman."

From out of the shadows, Doya stepped into the daylight. Naomi prowled at her heels. Dirt covered Doya's face, and her eyes looked sunken in. She had been totally worn down and defeated, but she lifted her chin in confidence.

It seemed that nothing could quite break this woman. She had a steel spine if I ever saw one.

Baine couldn't stop himself. He rushed over to Doya and swept her into his arms, burying his face into her shoulder. Liam and I exchanged a glance, shocked at the sudden display of emotion. I thought I'd seen it once before, the night of the Elemental Ball when they danced together, but I'd written it off. It was strange to see those two together like this, but it also felt *right*.

Baine set Doya on her feet. He helped steady her, and she stared up into his eyes. A beat passed where they were locked in each other's gazes.

I knew that look all too well. It was the same look Liam gave me just before we kissed.

For a moment, I thought that's exactly what was going to happen. Baine reached up to take Doya's face in his hands, but he had to go and screw it up. His unsteady fingers moved forward— and he poked her in the eye.

"Ancestor's cock!" Doya screamed, covering her assaulted eye with her hand. Naomi growled at Baine.

Liam rolled his eyes. "Freaking clumsy as hell."

Jonah burst out in laughter and tried to hide it by pretending to cough. Esis covered his mouth and snickered.

"I bet that's not *all* he'll be poking tonight," Ezra teased under his breath. Liam elbowed him.

"I'm sorry, Ellie," Baine cried. He tried to comfort her, but he only made it worse by stepping on Naomi's paw. When he tried to get closer to Doya to assess the damage, she lowered her hand and accidentally slapped him in the face.

"Ancestors," I groaned. Could these two *really* be my parents? "Someone has to go rescue them."

I stepped forward, and Liam followed. Esis stirred in my arms. I cleared my throat, and the two of them straightened. Doya wiped at her eye.

"Sophia," she said. "Perot tells me you're the one who advocated for my release."

I shrugged like it was no big deal, but I knew it was. "You saved me more than once. I thought I should return the favor."

Doya gazed at me with one of the softest expressions I'd seen her use. It was strange how gentle she was being with me lately, when she was still sharp with everyone else. I supposed it was her way of trying to right her wrongs with me.

The soft expression vanished a moment later, and she cleared her throat — as if she couldn't be seen showing emotion. "Well, serving as a carriage driver isn't exactly my idea of fun, but at least I'm alive."

"That's what they've assigned you to?" Baine balked.

"I'm not in a position to make demands," she reminded him. "The council will no doubt be keeping a very close eye on me. But now I am free to come and go as I please. And... if Sophia and Liam will allow... I am free to see the birth of my granddaughter."

Liam tightened his hold on my waist. "That's your decision, *pawee*."

I ran my hand over my belly. Ava-Marie kicked, like she was urging me to respond. "I'd like that."

I didn't know where the words came from. If you'd asked me weeks ago, I would've said Doya was the last person I wanted at the birth of my daughter. But now... now I thought it might be my chance to actually bond with her. Maybe now that she was free, we could get back some of the time we lost.

ACCEPTING Doya as my birth mother was a hard pill to swallow. To think we could make up both terrified me and excited me at the same time.

That night, I visited my parents to tell them the truth. I wanted them to hear it from me before the gossip spread across all of *Hok'evale*.

Mom and Dad had been playing a game of chess when I arrived. Their foster kids played in the yard. My parents led Esis and me into the living room, and we sat to talk.

"What's wrong, Sophia?" Mom asked. She had a way of always being able to read my moods.

Esis went to sit by my parents' Familiars. I knotted my hands in my lap. "I have something to tell you guys."

Dad sat on the couch beside me and leaned on the armrest. "It's a little late to tell us you got knocked up."

Mom swatted him in the leg, but I just laughed.

"It's not that," I said. "I found out who my real birth parents are."

The room went dead silent. Even our Familiars didn't make a sound.

It took my mom a moment to compose herself. "You did?"

"Yep. I don't think you're going to like it," I admitted.

"Do we know them?" Dad asked curiously.

I sighed. "Yes. It's Madame Doya and Professor Baine."

Mom and Dad gasped in unison.

"No... Elliot wouldn't," Mom mused. "Eleanor must've been a student! She was *years* behind us in school."

Dad shrugged. "Well, she is a very attractive woman."

Mom swatted him again, and Dad clammed up.

"Look, I don't want to know all the details about how it happened," I said. I already knew too much. Picturing Baine and Doya screwing was the *last* mental image I wanted in my mind. "But it's true."

"Madame Doya..." Mom's eyebrows knitted in concentration, like she was trying to figure out how Doya could possibly be my mother.

Dad eyed me. "I never would've guessed Baine, but he's a good man. I have to admit, if I were to share a daughter with any man, I'm proud to say it's with an Elder— one of the good ones, anyway."

"Ugh," I groaned. "Don't tell me *you* have the hots for him, too."

"Not *me*!" Dad cried. "Your mother's the one who crushed on him all through school—"

"Robert!" Mom snapped.

I chuckled. "So, you're not upset?"

"Sophia, honey," Mom said gently. She sat next to me until I was sandwiched between my parents. "We've always known you had other parents out there. We are not so naive to think you would never find them. It's shocking, yes. But..."

"But what?" I asked.

"But we've already prepared for this," she said. "We knew the truth might surprise us."

"So you're not... upset?" I asked.

She shook her head. "This is not something we can change. It just is."

I continued to knot my hands in my lap. "And what if I wanted to try to build a relationship with them?"

"Then *do* it," Dad encouraged. "Don't let us get in the way."

Mom rubbed my arm. "If this makes you feel better, then you have to do it. Just know that we're not going anywhere. We will always be here for you."

A smile touched my lips, and I reached an arm around each of them. "Thank you guys. You're the best."

Nothing would ever change that. They were my parents, and they always would be.

But I had other parents now, too. And I wanted to have some kind of relationship with them.

I just didn't know where to start.

Cool water splashed on my face, and I squealed. I sat in a chair on the beach with Liam and Jackson, my arms wrapped around myself to ward off the chill. Liam was in a t-shirt, since the cold December air didn't bother him. Jackson didn't seem to care either, as the calm ocean waves washed over his toes and he giggled. Esis watched the waves carefully, waiting for them to recede so he could run forward and grab as many shiny rocks as he could before high-tailing it back to dry sand when the next wave came in.

Liam snickered at me as he drew the water away from my face.

"Not fair," I teased.

He snickered playfully. "You look lost. What's on your mind?"

Two weeks had passed since Doya had been pardoned, and I was still trying to process everything that happened. I hadn't had a chance to talk to Baine yet, since he'd left on another excursion the moment Doya had been released. Things between Doya and I were still a bit stale. I could tell that she was trying, but she seemed to avoid me, too. I knew it would take time to break down the walls she'd spent two decades building up.

I shrugged. "Just thinking about Doya and Baine."

Liam lowered himself into the chair beside me. It was his day off, and we'd agreed to babysit Jackson to give Haloke a break. She was inside, helping Beatrice with housework and making sure Maddie was well. Liam's little brother was having a blast in the sand, and Liam had been twisting the water to make shapes for him.

"Do you think it will ever sink in?" he asked. "Because I still can't believe it."

I scrunched up my nose. "I know. Doya's so... harsh. And Baine's so... clumsy. They just don't seem like a couple."

Liam chuckled. "Don't get me wrong. I see where you get some of your personality traits. But seeing those two together... it's just so—"

"Weird," I finished for him.

I said it, and yet I wasn't sure I believed it. Those two fit together— not in the same way Liam and I did, but in an opposites-attract sort of way.

The sound of a door slamming caught both of our attention. We looked down the beach to see Baine coming out of his house. He didn't notice us as he started down the front steps and headed toward the ocean.

I glanced to Liam. "I didn't know he was back."

"Me, neither," he admitted. "You should go talk to him."

"What? Now?" I balked. "He looks busy."

Liam frowned. "*There's* the Baine in you talking."

I furrowed my brow. "What do you mean?"

"I mean you tend to avoid conflict when it doesn't stem from anger," he teased.

"I do not," I lied, but he was telling the truth.

"Come on, Soph," Liam said. "One of you is going to have to step up and talk first. And I think we all know it's not going to be Baine."

I took a deep breath and eyed Baine far down the beach. He stepped into the waves and started manipulating the water.

"Okay," I caved. "I'll go talk to him."

Liam kept an eye on me as I headed down the beach alone. Baine didn't notice my approach. He was standing ankle-deep in the waves, tossing dead fish to multi-colored porpoises with long fanned tails. They surrounded him, jumping in the shallow water and making clicking noises to get him to feed them more.

I cleared my throat from behind him. Baine jumped so high that he dropped his bucket of fish. The porpoises tried to swim forward and eat them, but they didn't make much headway in the shallow water.

"S-Sophia," Baine stammered as he bent to scoop up his half-empty bucket.

"Professor Baine." I nodded back to him. It felt really weird to call him that, now that I knew he was my father.

He paused a second, and his eyes went wide. "Dear ancestors," he muttered under his breath.

"What is it?" I asked.

Baine cleared his throat. "You just... when you say my name, you sound like her."

He had a note to his voice that seemed to question how he didn't see it before. "W-what brings you here?"

I shrugged, but we both knew the truth. We had to talk about how he was my father. "I was wondering if you found anything on your expedition."

Baine straightened his glasses, then reached back into the bucket and started tossing fish again. He didn't meet my eyes. "I, uh, eh hem. I haven't found the *Azaimperiai*, but clues continue to emerge. I'm getting quite close."

"That's good," I said. I walked over to a nearby boulder and sat on it. It was just the right size for me to rest on. "So, did you get much time to think about... us?"

Baine tossed a fish, but I must've startled him with my question, because his aim was totally off. He smacked one of the creatures straight in the nose. He winced, but didn't look back at me. "I had a few moments," he admitted.

"And?" I prodded, my heart hammering. "What do you think about being my dad?"

Finally, Baine turned around. His mouth bobbed open and closed like a fish. It looked like he wanted to say something, but didn't know how.

I straightened on the rock. "I can go first."

"Sophia, you don't have to—" Baine started, but the words had already started coming out, and I couldn't stop them.

"I've pictured for a long time who my birth father might be." I gazed down at my belly and started rubbing it, just so I wouldn't have to look him in the eye. It was easier that way. I supposed I got that from him. "For a long time, I believed it was Anthony Greyson. From the stories I've heard, he was a really great guy. He died for me in the riots, but I never got a chance to know him. When my grandparents told me it was all a lie, I created a picture in my head of this guy who gave me up to save me— because that was the noble thing to do. But I never thought I'd actually meet him. I assumed like Lucy and Tony, he was dead. But it turns out he's not."

Baine slowly walked over to me. "Sophia, if this disappoints you—"

My gaze snapped upward, cutting him off. "No, of course not. Just the opposite, in fact. You're alive, and I get a chance to actually meet you and... love you."

Tears beaded in the corners of Baine's eyes. I couldn't help it when my voice cracked. "You saved my life by mentoring me in the tournament. You're busting your ass to find the *Azaimperiai* for us. You are as noble as any dad I could ever ask for."

Baine's shoulders fell, and he came to sit beside me on the rock. "It means a lot to hear you say that. Mentoring you for the tournament— and seeing you win— was one of my greatest accomplishments. You are a truly gifted Elementai, Sophia. You have a big heart, and a sharp mind."

My heart swelled at the compliments.

He sighed before continuing. "All my life, I thought I would remain alone. But now... now I have a daughter— a family. If it should be anyone, I'm glad it's you."

Tears began welling up. "I'm glad it's you, too, Baine."

I threw my arms around his neck, and he stiffed for a moment before relaxing into it.

"Please, Sophia," he sighed. "Call me *pataa*."

"What does that mean?" I asked.

Baine smiled. "It's Hawkei for *dad*."

I RODE the high of my conversation with Baine for the next two weeks. He stuck around so he could be home for Christmas— or so he said. I'd noticed Doya's carriage parked at his house a few times when we went to visit Haloke, though I wasn't sure if they were merely talking or something else.

I think he was finally starting to face his past instead of running away from it.

Baine had come over to visit a few times and kept bringing presents for the baby— most of them ancient artifacts he'd picked up, because apparently my dad didn't know what shopping was. I figured it was his way of trying to make up for not being there for me.

Doya invited Baine and I to dinner on Christmas Eve. She didn't cook, so we ended up at *The Falcon's Nest*.

It was our first time out together as a real family. After I'd told Amelia the truth about my parentage, she'd said the idea of Baine and Doya together was *"stranger than water on a phoenix's ass."* I couldn't say I didn't agreed, but there was something oddly natural about it, too. I couldn't explain it.

Doya and Baine sat on the same side of the table. He insisted she try his shellfish and spooned it into her mouth.

A few people threw dark glances our way, and I knew they were aimed at Doya. Most people weren't happy she'd been pardoned, but she was doing her job and keeping out of trouble, and they couldn't fault her for that. All she had to do was shoot a sharp gaze back at them, and people cowered under the weight of her stare. I guess some things never changed.

"We were almost to the entrance of the underwater temple when a beast sprang from the shadows and jumped straight in front of Thalassa!" Baine was going on and on about his adventures. He used wild hand motions and the leftovers from his clams to tell the story.

I'd already heard this one three times, but Doya looked particularly interested. She leaned an elbow on the table and twirled her hair around her finger, biting her lip. She couldn't take her eyes off Baine. She was totally smitten. It was sort of weird to see her show any emotion that wasn't pure hatred. It was a welcome change, to say the least.

"He had the head of a shark and the tentacles of a squid, and he was as big as the temple itself," Baine continued. Each time he told the story, the shark-creature got bigger and bigger. Last time, he was only the size of a semi-truck.

"He had rows and rows of razor-sharp teeth," Baine said. "He bared them at my Familiar, but I assaulted him with my magic. Thalassa then whipped out her tail and severed his head before he could touch her!"

Baine snapped one of his clam shells in half to demonstrate.

"You're so brave," Doya praised, and she wasn't kidding, either. Her eyes darted down to his muscles, but he was oblivious to her flirting. Liam would've complained about it, but I thought their courtship was half endearing, half comical.

Baine turned his gaze to me. "Sophia, eat up."

I had a plate of steak and potatoes in front of me, but I barely ate a thing. Esis was scarfing down most of it, and what he didn't eat, he dropped under the table to Naomi. She was still distant and unsure of us, but she was starting to warm up to Esis.

"I'm full," I told him. "This baby isn't leaving *any* room for my stomach anymore."

"Yes, of course," Baine said. "How much longer to go?"

Doya and I exchanged a glance. Sometimes Baine could be so clueless.

"Elliot, she's due *today*," Doya reminded him.

Baine's eyes went as wide as saucers. "Today! Ancestors, we must prepare! Shouldn't you be getting ready?"

I giggled under my breath. "There's no guarantee. It's not like we have a set time. It could still be a week."

As if Ava-Marie could tell we were talking about her, she moved inside my belly. A nerve in my back twinged, and my stomach cramped, but I was used to the discomfort by now.

Baine straightened in his chair. "Yes, of course. I only meant—"

"Sophia!"

The door to *The Falcon's Nest* flung open. All eyes turned to the entrance as Liam ran into the restaurant, looking panicked.

Doya looked him up and down. "Can't you see we're trying to have a quiet family meal?"

Liam ignored her and wrapped me into a tight hug. "Thank the ancestors you're okay!"

My heart hammered, and my stomach dropped. Esis froze, and potatoes started falling out of his full mouth. "Liam, what's wrong?"

"It's the Elders," he warned, glancing between the three of us frantically. "The Task Force is trying to get through Luana's shield."

"*What?*" I gasped. "How did they find us?"

"We don't know," Liam admitted, shooting a glance at Doya.

"It wasn't *me*," she growled. "If you think Oleander doesn't have intel like your military does, you're sorely mistaken."

"Someone must've given us up." Baine's eyes were wild as he considered who the traitor might be.

"It doesn't matter," Liam decided. "They could be here any moment."

Baine shot up out of his chair. "We must fight!"

The entire restaurant heard our conversation, and they broke into a panic.

"Get somewhere safe!" a father commanded his wife and children.

"We're going to fry those motherfuckers," a Koigni guy growled.

Chairs screeched, and people spoke so loud I could hardly hear Liam beside me. Everyone rushed for the door, as if a fire alarm had just went off.

"Come on," Liam said. "We have to go!"

Liam took my hand, and I scooped up Esis. We hurried out of the restaurant with Baine and Doya on our heels.

Outside, the chaos had erupted as news spread. People rushed every which way, gathering their Familiars. The ground began to shake beneath our feet, and wind whipped by us as Elementai lost control of their emotions. I drew in ragged breaths as my whole body contracted in fear. They couldn't be here! Not yet!

Imogen and Luana stood to the side of the rushing crowd, with Sassy, Sierra and Julian. Luana was on her knees, her fingers pressed to her temples in concentration. Imogen had just left the rehab center yesterday—already, on her first day of recovery she was dealing with major stress.

"You can do this!" Imogen cried, trying to comfort her, though she knew Luana couldn't hear her.

"Liam, what's happening?" I shrieked, my voice rising several pitches.

"Luana's trying to hold her shield," he explained. "But there are too many Task Force battling it with their elements. We don't know how much longer it will hold."

"I can help!" I suggested. I could do shield magic, but not as well as Luana. I'd never created a shield large enough to encompass a house, let alone an entire town. But the least I could do was try.

"No!" Liam argued. "You have to get someplace safe. Doya, get Sophia to the caves! Baine, you're with me."

"Wait, Liam," I begged before he could turn away from me.

He placed a hand on either side of my face. "This is not your battle, Sophia."

"But what if you—?" I started, but my breath caught. Worry knotted like a knife in my guts, and cramps formed in my lower abdomen, growing in intensity.

"No what ifs," he insisted. "The only thing we need to worry about is keeping our baby safe. You need to get somewhere they can't find you."

"C-come with me!" I sobbed.

"I'm chief," he reminded me. "I have to protect the tribe. But most of all, I have to protect you and Ava."

He placed a gentle hand on my belly, and Ava kicked his palm. Around us, *Hok'evale* had gone into an uproar. The ground continued to shake, and angry Familiars streaked through the skies in search of their Elementai. But in that moment, it felt like Liam and I were alone— our little family blessed with a moment to say goodbye.

But I couldn't do it, because I refused to believe this was goodbye. Liam would come back in one piece— he *had* to.

And yet I couldn't stand here and allow my husband to walk into battle without me. Tears streaked down my cheeks, because I knew I had no choice.

"I love you, *pawee*," Liam whispered.

"I love you, too," I hiccupped.

"Take good care of her," he said, before planting a passionate kiss on my lips. I wasn't sure if he was asking me to take care of Ava-Marie, or if he was asking Doya to take care of me.

"Baine, it's time to go," Liam barked. "Jake will be waiting for us. Im, make sure Luana holds that shield as long as—"

Liam was cut off as a rock tumbled from the cliffside above and connected with the top of Luana's head. She grunted in pain, and Imogen let out an earth-shattering scream. The ground continued to rock around us as Nivita freaked out. Luana slumped to the ground, unconscious.

"No!" I cried.

I rushed over to her, but Imogen had already caught Luana and was cradling her in her arms. Sierra landed on her chest to begin healing, and Esis scampered to her side. Sassy turned into kitsune form and looked upward, like she could defend us from any other falling debris.

"Luana? Luana!?" I shook her, and she blinked a few times. The rock had barely been the size of my fist, but it left her dazed.

Above us, the sound of a dragon's cry echoed. Luana's eyes went wide, and we all looked upward to see a huge dragon streaking across the darkening sky.

Luana lifted her hands and signed weakly to me. *Sorry. I couldn't hold it any longer. They're here.*

My hands shook, and my stomach ached as I looked up to Liam. "Her shield has failed."

"Fuck!" Liam growled. "What are we going to do?"

"You're a chief," Doya snarled. "Isn't it your job to figure it out?"

Liam glanced around frantically, until his eyes fell upon two students running up the canyon toward the military base. "Linus! Zoey!"

The students halted in their tracks. The girl had a Familiar at her side. I guessed she was Koigni.

"Gather all the Anichi students you can find," Liam instructed. "It's time to put your lessons to work. We need as many Anichi as we can to create and hold that shield."

"But Chief Mitoh, we barely have any power," Linus protested.

"Then take it from creatures, the earth, the air, I don't care!" Liam barked. "We need a shield *now*. You can do it if you all work together."

He looked uncertain to me, but the students didn't catch it.

*Take these,* Luana signed to me. She reached into her pocket and pulled out three crystals. They were small white rocks she'd been transferring Anichi magic into during our training sessions.

"Wait, Liam," I said quickly, stopping him. I took the crystals from Luana and held them out. "Have them use these. It should help."

Liam handed the crystals off to Linus. "You've got this."

Linus saluted him and said, "We're on it, chief!"

As the students ran away, the chaos increased. "Liam, thank the ancestors!" Haloke ran out of the sea of people, holding her skirt up to keep from tripping over it. Beatrice, the Anichi primate who'd been serving as Haloke's housekeeper, followed closely behind. Her blue feathers were in disarray, and she looked worried, like she wanted to do anything to help. I remembered Imogen saying britnai were especially helpful creatures.

Liam's jaw dropped when he saw her. "Mom, what are you doing here? Where are the kids?"

"They've gone with a group of Anichi into the caves to hide," she said. "Beatrice and I want to help."

"The best way you can help is to take Sophia into the caves with the others," he said.

She nodded in understanding. "Anything to lend a hand."

"Everybody move!" Liam shouted.

My stomach tightened again as Liam rushed away. He mounted Julian, and the dragon took to the skies before I could process what was going on.

Down the street, a group of Anichi students had gathered. Anichi creatures joined them at their heels, until they'd formed a circle. The students joined hands, and they bowed their heads in unison. Each wore a similar expression of concentration.

Between the crystals and their lessons in intrafusion, it didn't take long for a white ball of Anichi light to begin forming. The ball hovered in the center of their circle for several moments, before growing too big to contain. My heart jumped as it shot upward toward the sky as if it'd just been launched out of a cannon. I watched in awe as it exploded high above our heads like a brilliant white firework. The light dispersed into the shape of a dome, encompassing *Hok'evale* in a protection shield once again. I didn't think it was as big or as strong as Luana's shield, but it was going to have to do for now.

And ancestors, I hope it held.

"Hurry," Doya said sharply to Imogen, Luana, and me. "We must protect the baby."

My heart hammered as Imogen and I helped Luana to her feet, but it dropped deep within my chest as I stood. I heard the sound of a light *pop* first, then felt the gush of warm water between my legs.

Doya was the first to notice I'd frozen up. "What is it, Sophia?"

I swallowed the lump forming in my throat. "I don't think we're going to make it to the caves. My water just broke!"

Haloke was the first to react. She reached out to Luana before gesturing for Imogen and Doya to follow. "Come, girls. We must get Sophia home. There's no time to waste."

My heart pounded out of control, and I gasped as painful contractions rippled across my middle. I'd been having them for a few hours now, I realized, but I'd written them off as cramps— now I couldn't deny the truth, as the agony increased with every new pulse.

I didn't want this to be my reality. This wasn't how I'd pictured my labor to go, but yet, I had no choice.

Liam was gone, fighting in a battle I had no certainty he'd come back from. I'd have to do this without him. This baby was coming, and it was at the worst possible time.

# Liam

## TWENTY-THREE

"Can't these stupid fucks take a break? It's Christmas."

I was complaining under my breath as we were in-route to combat Oleander's army. The Anichi students had gotten the force field back up, but the damage had been done, and the Elders knew where we were. With enough pressure, they could use their magic to break the force field down once again... unless we fought back and forced the Elders to go back where they came from.

Of course these assholes had to wait for the day of my wife's due date to try and pick a fight. I was majorly pissed. They were going to be eating teeth and blood once I got done with them.

A battalion of resistance fighters were already waiting for us on the beach. The Nivita there were constructing a huge wall of earth at least fifty feet high around the area, to stall any Task Force that made it to shore. Jake had arrived before us, along with a collection of Yapluma soldiers. He was commanding people left and right to their positions as battle preparations were hastily made under the light of the moon.

I did a quick glance around. Hundreds of Yapluma were sailing through the air, Toaqua surfing the waves beneath them. Koigni stood on the beach, creating a barricade of Fire. I saw Lindsey, Bren and Miranda charging the barricade with their magic, while their Familiars marched in front of it protectively. Behind the barricade, Cade was doing his best to add as much earth as he could to the wall with the aid of the other Nivita. Trace was helping him, but his hands shook as he cast his magic, throwing anxious glances at the ocean. Arabelle prowled before the earth wall, haunches rolling and teeth exposed as she growled a low warning at the sea.

I landed Julian on the beach and dismounted. Ezra slid off Dyami, and Jonah jumped off Squeaks as we approached Jake. Sabor flew high above him, his eyes fixed on the horizon for signs of the approaching warriors.

"Where are we?" I asked, getting straight to the details. There was no time to mess around when an army of Task Force could show up any minute.

"According to our spies, Kinpago isn't coming out in full force. They're only sending their best warriors. I'm certain they think the resistance is a small uprising and this will be an easy fight." Jake's expression hardened. "Little do they know we won't be so simple to defeat."

"So where do you need us?" I had an idea already, but I wanted to be sure.

"They *were* coming from the land, but since the Anichi have got the shield going again, the army has changed directions and is attempting to launch a surprise attack by air and sea. They'll be arriving from the west. Luckily, we have intel, so we know they're coming," Jake responded.

"What about Koigni and Nivita soldiers?" Ezra questioned.

"There won't be many. Oleander has kept the majority of the Koigni and Nivita forces back in Kinpago, to defend it if anything goes wrong. I'm sure he's concerned a surprise counterattack. He's been spooked ever since we liberated the camps and is implementing more security," Jake said. "He's playing it safe in the hope we'll be a pushover. This will most likely be an assault by Water and Air Elementai."

"So I'm guessing those are the people you need to send them packing," Jonah stated.

"Correct. We need Toaqua out in the water and Yapluma in the air on the front lines," Jake said. "They'll be our main defense against what's coming. If the Elders make it past us, they'll run into the Koigni waiting on the beach. The Nivita are our last stand. If their wall fails..."

Jake trailed off. We all knew what could happen then.

"I'll be with my men, commanding the Yapluma from the air. A commander's no good if he can't get his hands dirty," Jake noted.

"And I'll be right beside you," Jonah added. The two men entwined hands and Jonah gave Jake a reassuring smile, like he was certain it'd be all right.

"I'll command the Toaqua from the sea. We'll back you up," I said.

"Do you think this is going to work?" Ezra asked cautiously.

"We knew this day would come eventually. We've had these defensive maneuvers planned for decades," Jake replied. "Now it's only a matter of if we've come prepared."

"They will work," Jonah replied confidently. "Ain't no way they'll get through to *Hok'evale*."

I contemplated things quickly. "Maybe we don't have to fight."

"Uh, you crazy?" Jonah raised his eyebrow. "The Elders are coming to stick our heads in a place where the sun don't shine."

"Hear me out. There are plenty of Toaqua on the Task Force. I'm their rightful chief," I said. "If I ask them to stand down, they might follow. We'll outnumber them. The Task Force will either have to return to Kinpago or surrender."

"That's not going to work," Jonah argued. "I'm for peace as much as you are, but even if they want to follow you, the Toaqua working for Oleander are scared shitless of him. They'll do whatever he says just because they think there's no other way."

"I don't want to start my chief hood like this. Any leader who leads their people into war has failed them," I said.

"I apologize, Chief Mitoh, but if we're going to defend ourselves, there is no other way." Jake frowned. "You can make an attempt, but I'm certain this day will end in nothing but blood."

I knew he was right. But I at least had to try.

"What the hell are you doing here?" I heard Ezra snarl. I turned to see Stevie swing off of Nihoni as the griffin-hybrid swam up the beach. Stevie walked onshore with her hands on her hips, water dripping off of her.

"I'm here to fight," she stated. "What, did you think I'd just sit home and cower while you boys have all the fun? You stopped me from helping you liberate the camps. You aren't going to stop me from protecting my people."

"You're not going out there," Ezra said viciously. "You'll get hurt."

Stevie threw her head back and laughed. "I'm the one who'll be causing pain, I assure you."

"You've never been in a battle! You don't know what it's like out there. I won't let you risk your life!" Ezra shouted.

"And I won't let you risk yours! Not unless I'm out there with you!" Stevie insisted. Dyami gave angry caws, while Nihoni slapped her tail in discontentment.

It was the first time I'd ever seen them argue, but it was clear neither of them were budging.

"Ez, let her fight," I said. "She has just as much right to be here as you."

"But she—"

"Is sick? So am I. Let her fight for what she loves."

Ezra's mouth became thin. "Fine." He rounded on Stevie. "Stay close to me."

"If you can keep up," Stevie deadpanned.

"Ezra, I need my council," I told him. "I'm counting on you as backup if things go wrong."

He nodded. He clambered back onto Dyami as I mounted Julian, and Stevie got back onto Nihoni. She sailed below us as we flew our Familiars toward the center of the ocean. Jake and Jonah soared beside us on their hippogriffs toward the Yapluma air force, who was hovering over the line of Toaqua waiting in the ocean. The Toaqua soldiers were lined up for more than a mile, their Familiars churning the waters and making the ocean agitated.

I saw many familiar faces in the resistance below. I didn't want to do this, but I had no choice. I had to put some Toaqua at risk to save the rest of us. I wasn't a chief who desired to lead his people into battle unless there was no other way, and the resistance was backed into a corner.

The beach had been evacuated. The only people who weren't here were Maddie and Drew— who I'd instructed to stay in *Hok'evale*— as well as the women we'd left behind to help Sophia just in case she went into labor.

Ancestors, I prayed that wouldn't happen with me gone. There was too much on the line today. We either had to win this fight, or the resistance was done. There was no other option.

Baine was waiting for us out in the water. He was riding Thalassa, who seemed calm as she kept her gaze fixed on the horizon. Wyatt was also there, appearing incredibly alone as he kept himself aloft on the water's surface. I caught sight of Amelia and Mr. and Mrs. Henley working together to freeze a large wave, to form a third barrier to slow the army up.

"What's our orders, chief?" Wyatt yelled up to me as Julian hovered close.

"Hold the line. Don't let them get to shore," I stated. "And if they do get past us, hit them with everything you've got."

"Simple. I like it." Wyatt surfed across the ocean waves, to give my orders to the rest of the Toaqua and the Familiars forming the central battalion.

The skies began to darken. Lightning ignited across them as Jonah called upon the wind and storms to work in our favor. The Toaqua around me spread their hands over the water. Their magic worked together, and the ocean's crests grew larger, until they became tidal waves and even I was scared of their power. The Water Familiars hung back, so they wouldn't get caught up in their torrential fury.

Baine was more somber than I'd ever seen him. He clung tightly to Thalassa's horns as he watched the incoming storms. "This will be one of the greatest battles of our time."

"But it won't be the last." I was determined that the resistance make it through today, whatever it took.

We heard them before we saw them. A line of Task Force members approached from over the sea. Yapluma flew over the waters while Toaqua came cruising in across a huge wave that was the size of a tsunami. They came riding Water Familiars and soaring on creatures with wings that blocked out the skies. There had to be hundreds, both Elementai and Familiar.

A stone sank in my gut and dragged my hopes to the bottom of the sea as I watched their shadows grow. I'd been in battles before, but I'd only been trying to escape, survive. Now I was in an actual war, and I was fighting for something I believed in. I was the leader of my tribe, and my people depended on me to get us through this.

I wouldn't back down. I'd bring the wrath of the entire ocean if it meant protecting my little girl, who was due to arrive at any time.

"Baine, don't let them get through to your daughter," I told him as I watched the incoming line of soldiers sail closer and closer.

His eyes darkened. "They will have to take my life."

Thalassa rumbled in agreement. The opposing army slowed as they approached us, and the tsunami began to halt. They were less than fifty feet away when they came to a stop completely. The only sounds that could be heard were the lashing of the waves and the beating wings of Familiars pumping against the thunder.

Nobody moved. It seemed both sides were waiting for orders from their commanders. I urged Julian forward. As he hovered before the army, I took a deep breath to speak. I felt Jonah's magic encompass me to project my voice as I addressed the Task Force.

"People of Toaqua!" I cried. "You don't have to do this! You know my name. I am Liam Mitoh, firstborn and rightful chief of Toaqua. I have gone through the ceremony and been accepted by the ancestors. You know as well as I that Oleander has no claim on our tribe. I beg you, leave your place on the Task Force and join us. We will accept you into our ranks as one of our own. For too long, the Hawkei have been divided by hatred and bitterness. Let us unify into one tribe!"

I couldn't see the expressions of the people behind the helmets, but by the way their bodies tensed as they rode the waves, I knew many were shocked. They probably wondered how I'd been accepted to the chief hood, and why I had a dragon at my command.

"This is preposterous!" A hideous voice interrupted my speech. I saw at the head of the wave someone I truly despised.

Fucking Elder Malison. And Elder Poole. Oleander had sent them to make sure the job got done. I knew Malison's kraken and Poole's leviathan were swimming somewhere in the deep, waiting to strike. Malison remained vengefully rigid, his sneering gaze on me, while Poole cowered behind him. He'd been forced to come here, I was sure.

"Oleander is the chief of Toaqua! This boy has no claim to you," Malison told his army. "Blood is more important than loyalty to one family! His father betrayed our tribe, and his son turned his back on the ways of the Hawkei. We must punish them!"

"Massacre and genocide have no place in the Hawkei culture," I replied. "Oleander has destroyed everything. He's ruined our homes, our lives, even our faith in the ancestors themselves!"

My voice grew stronger. "But Oleander can't take any of that from you unless you allow it to happen. Choose to resist. Take a stand against what's wrong, and become the Elementai I know you are— the Elementai you were always meant to be!"

"If anyone moves, it'll be treason!" Malison screamed.

That was his favorite fucking word. And he loved to scream it at anyone who had the bravery to think for themselves.

A few very brave Toaqua had the courage to break ranks. Three took off their helmets— they tossed them into the ocean, and swam their Familiars to the opposite side to join us. No one else moved.

The majority of them weren't going to change sides. They were too afraid of Oleander.

Who was too big of a coward to be here, I saw. Neither he nor Skylis were anywhere to be found. It was great being a dictator when you could send everyone else to die for you.

With the betrayal of three mere Toaqua, Malison flew into a rage. His face turned red, and he flung out a crooked finger as he screamed, "Attack!"

The two sides converged. The tsunami came crashing down. Members of the resistance went flying everywhere as the wave crashed them deep into the sea. Julian flew above it. I hung on, and Jonah's lightning cracked across the night sky, striking Yapluma from the air. Thalassa gave a roar, and I watched her and Baine plunge headfirst into the tsunami with her jaw wide, slaying dozens of Task Force members as they met untimely ends between her fangs.

Everything became instant chaos. I'd thought there'd be some sort of organization to the battle, but no such thing existed. There was only blood and discord. It soon became a battle of whose magic was stronger as the Elementai warred to control the waves and the air.

Some Task Force members raised noxite guns. I began to panic. *No fucking way.* If they shot those into the crowd, and we lost our magic, we'd be fucking done for.

I raised my hands. I could feel the other Toaqua in the area controlling the water, but their orders to the ocean fell flat when challenged by mine. I was undoubtedly the strongest Toaqua here, and I'd show Malison exactly who he was dealing with. I commanded fifty-foot waves to rise, directing themselves at the dozens of Task Force members shooting into the oncoming resistance. They barely had time to look up before the waves smashed onto their heads.

Noxite guns and people went flying. The screams overheard were quickly doused as the Task Force was struck by the incredible wave. My magic felt it as people were crushed and drowned. Familiars struggled to get air, and failed. Toaqua tried to resist the wave, use their Water magic to find a way out, but my powers wouldn't let them. It kept them under until they gave up struggling, and I felt a collective breath of the Toaqua below me go out all at once like a candle.

I hated to do this. I didn't want to kill my own people. It fucking gutted me. I couldn't stand to accept the kind of monster I was for doing this to my own tribe.

Yet in war, we all had to make sacrifices. My humanity was a small part of that.

The Task Force members who'd managed to come up from the wave were immediately met with Julian's fire. Though I had reservations about slaying Elementai, Julian was a dragon, and he had no such restrictions. His fire encompassed the top-halves of the Toaqua struggling to breathe. I pressed myself to Julian's neck and hung on as he agilely flew through the skies, igniting the bodies of Task Force and Familiars all around us.

Jake and Jonah flew close to one another. Jake barked orders at the Yapluma resistance, who were, unfortunately, dropping like flies as they tried and failed to battle against the magic of the Task Force. Jake sent waterspouts spinning across the ocean, but they were combated and destroyed by Yapluma with their own Air magic. Jonah tried to make up for it, blasting off lightning bolt after lightning bolt with all the fury of the Storm Lord. Yapluma attempted to fly around and duck Jonah's hits, but most weren't quick enough. He sent plenty of smoking bodies, both Elementai and Familiar, plunging down into the sea, never to be heard from again.

Squeaks and Sabor had both gotten into fights with other hippogriffs. The birds clawed at each other in mid-air, going in for the kill. The male hippogriffs looked as if they were stallions battling for dominance. Sabor kicked his opponent in the head, and dazed his enemy just long enough to give a fatal blow to the spine. It wasn't seconds before another hippogriff was upon him, but Sabor was ruthless, fighting as if this was his territory and he would die to defend it.

Squeaks' opponent kicked her in the jaw and sent her spiraling down-ward toward the sea, but she recovered quickly, long enough to spin around just as her enemy attacked. As he reached forward to rip out her organs, she lashed out just in time and dug her beak into his neck, ripping out his artery.

The hippogriff gave a moan, then its wings failed. The creature crashed into the water, its blood spraying across the ocean and creating a dark maroon pool.

I spotted Carter flying Tiara over the horizon, directing her so she knocked Yapluma out of the sky. Amelia had joined hands with her parents, and the three of them combined their magic to create a deadly whirlpool. Task Force screamed as they were trapped within the powerful rush of water. Amelia's hair whipped around her face, and she bit her lip in concen-tration as the Henleys struggled to keep the whirlpool going against the command of the other Toaqua.

Madame Wells was riding her killer whale, who was skimming the surface of the sea. As the whale swam, Wells stood on his back and moved her hands in a circular motion. A column of water erupted at her command

and ricocheted toward the sky. She sent it spinning outward, and any Task Force unlucky enough to get in the way were immediately sucked into the column, unable to emerge again.

Wyatt looked like he was in a pinch. He was surfing the waves, sending jets of water out as fast as he could at any Task Force that approached, yet they were closing in.

I told Julian to go down. As I sent my hand flying outward, another wave came and submerged the Task Force chasing him. I reached out a hand, and he grabbed it. I yanked Wyatt onto Julian's back, and the dragon had to swing to the side to avoid getting hit by a Yapluma Air blast.

"This is a bit hairy, eh?" Wyatt cried out over the sounds of the battle. Though he'd shouted, I'd barely heard him.

"Just a bit." I shot a jet of water at the Task Force member who'd tried to cut me in half with his Air blast. He took it in the head, slamming down into the sea full force.

Stevie rode Nihoni through the rough waves, but the cypher handled the churning sea like a champ. She easily swam across the rushing sea effortlessly. Stevie raised her hands, and as Nihoni rushed by a group of Task Force, she created a water funnel with her magic. The funnel was twenty feet long, and just as high. It wrapped the Task Force within its waters, flinging them miles backward into the ocean beyond. Stevie created another funnel, and another, until she was manipulating ten at once. Stevie tossed the opposing Task Force and their Familiars far off into the horizon. She played the funnels like a puppeteer, making them move to her command with merely a flick of her fingers.

Ezra watched from Dyami's back, amazed, as his tiny streams of magic fizzled out. She was clearly showing Ez up. Ezra gaped as he saw Stevie perform spectacular feats of magic like some sea goddess, while she smirked in triumph.

"Glad she's on our side!" Wyatt said. I couldn't agree more.

The Henley's whirlpool was beginning to die down. Amelia was slumped over in exhaustion. She struggled to keep hold of her parents' hands. Their faces had long turned white. Someone needed to intercede, fast.

"Drop me over there," Wyatt said, pointing to the Henleys' whirlpool. Julian flew overhead, and Wyatt leapt downward. He surfed the waves and took position on the opposite side of the whirlpool. The whirlpool sputtered until it expanded again. Wyatt helped push it outward, to give chase after Task Force members.

With the aid of Wyatt's magic, the Henleys were able to get the whirlpool's strength up again and even expand it. But I worried they wouldn't be able to last much longer.

"Ez, they need backup," I cried out, pointing to Wyatt.

"We've got it. Just hold on!" Ezra jumped off of Dyami's back and landed in the sea. He looked upward. Dyami pumped his giant wings until he was level with the lightning crackling across the sky.

The thunderbird gave a loud cry that shook the air as he entered into the storm clouds. As he hovered in the air, Jonah's lightning gathered around his form, until the electricity was crackling off his wings and gathering into a ball at his chest.

Dyami opened his beak, and a beam of lightning emitted from it in a powerful blast. It struck a Task Force dragon, and the creature took the blow in the chest. The dragon cried out before its eyes rolled in the back of its head and it crashed into the sea, its body smoking from the blow.

Dyami continued to shoot at Familiars in the sky with lightning blasts from his beak. He used his long tail as a whip to fling bolts of lightning at the Task Force battalion. As they struck, the lightning bolts acted like bombs, exploding on impact and sending bolts of electricity whizzing through the water. Anyone near the explosions was killed instantly.

"That a boy, Dyami!" Ezra cheered.

I gave a quick glance over the battle to take record. The Task Force hadn't managed to advance. Holy shit, we were winning! We were holding them in place, and if we continued to do so, eventually Malison and Poole would have to give up.

I hoped. Poole was a coward, but Malison never gave up. The old bastard would die first before he surrendered.

Just as I was wondering where their Familiars were, a colossal roar broke through the rage of the fight. Julian screeched and lurched to the side. I had to grab hold of one of his horns to keep from getting flung off.

A massive tentacle had risen out of the water and was heading in our direction. One of the suction pads was almost as big as Julian himself. I steered Julian out of the way as the tentacle came crashing out of the sea. More tentacles began rising around us. I backed Julian off in horror as a giant red mantle rose from the deep.

The giant squid was at least three hundred feet long, a real monster. I watched in terror as the kraken's tentacles snatched dragons, griffins and pegasi out of the sky, snapping them like twigs as its large red eyes blinked without feeling.

The kraken had arrived. But it wasn't alone. Another creature jumped out of the depths, grabbing a peryton in its jaws to pull the deer down below. The second monster had a long neck, a flat face and fins that were ribbed with spines, sharp scales lining its massive body. Poole's Familiar— the leviathan.

As the leviathan crashed down, there was a rumbling sound from the ocean, and bubbles began rising. Many people screamed. Bodies were thrown from the water as a third creature came out of the depths, bringing all the fury of hell with it.

I didn't know what the hell it was— didn't even know what to call it— but I knew if we got close to the thing, it'd kill us all. It resembled a long, slimy grey worm. It had no eyes, and no other features, but what it did have was a very large mouth— and thousands of spinning teeth inside, which it displayed as the worm opened its mouth and roared.

There was an Elementai riding the sea worm's back, controlling the waves around it. The Toaqua made it so nobody could get through the water and to the sea worm.

Yet there was one creature strong enough to overpower the waves. A glimmering of sapphire scales shot past my vision, and I watched as Thalassa charged through. She roared as she dove forward, sinking her teeth into the sea worm's side. The worm gave a screech and attempted to divert its hundreds of spinning fangs in Thalassa's direction, but the sea serpent out maneuvered him, swimming underneath the worm only to rise up and toss him out of the water.

The worm went sailing, but the Elementai on its back held on. The worm regained its balance and slithered through the water toward Thalassa, who was waiting for it. She dove her fangs forward and back again, striking like a cobra as she delivered heavy critical blows to the creature.

Baine's teeth were gritted as he magically warred with the other rider. Both of them were attempting to make the ocean listen, but they seemed equally matched. The waves appeared confused, washing from this way to that as the magic manipulated them in different directions. Worse was the thrashing of Thalassa and the sea worm, which killed several people unlucky enough to be found in their path. Thalassa wrapped herself around the sea worm's body and squeezed, attempting to choke the life out of it. Yet Thalassa was only so strong, and though the sea worm couldn't get out of her hold, it also wasn't enough to kill the beast.

The kraken and leviathan began slaughtering. The water turned red with the onslaught of their attack as they ripped Elementai and creatures limb from limb. No one was spared— some were torn in half by leviathan teeth, others ripped apart by the kraken's tentacles. I watched, sick, as the kraken took a live man and deposited him in his beak, swallowing him whole.

These monsters could devastate the entire resistance army. We were losing this fight.

"We need to contain these creatures! Stop them!" Jake cried out.

Attention immediately turned to killing the three monsters. The resistance fighters abandoned holding back the Task Force and instead worked together against the kraken and leviathan. Familiars swarmed in from above, but their teeth and claws didn't even scratch the skin of the monsters — and more often than not, magical creatures were killed in the process. Fire from dragons bounced off the creature's backs like it was nothing. Not even Dyami and Jonah's lightning bolts were enough to hurt them. The lightning deflected, shooting off into the sky and causing more harm than good.

I tried and failed to intercede. As powerful as my magic was, my massive waves probably felt like a gentle massage as they rammed against the creatures over and over. Any ice we tried to create to freeze the creatures in place, they broke easily. It's like they were children playing with toys in the bathtub, and we had no say in our fate.

Malison and Poole surfed on a large wave nearby. Poole seemed grim, his mouth a thin line, but Malison was laughing over and over at the carnage like this was his own personal entertainment.

Thalassa had let the sea worm go and changed her strategy. She attempted to rip chunks out of the sea worm with her teeth to slow it down, while Baine used the water as whips to assault its rider. The rider had made a shield of water and was resisting Baine's blows, but the shield was barely holding up.

As Thalassa lurched forward again, the sea worm took an opportunity to strike. It's thousands of teeth latched on to Thalassa's neck, ripping all the way down to her shoulder. Thalassa screeched and tried to get away as blood poured from her scales, but the sea worm seemed to be some kind of parasite— it didn't want to let go.

Thalassa brought up her finned tail and smacked it against the head of the sea worm, over and over until the worm finally released his hold. As it did so, Thalassa gave a harrowing cry of pain that made my insides lurch. Baine's water whips fell back into the sea. He hurriedly bent down to examine the injury. A large portion of Thalassa's flesh was shredded, and it weakened her. She'd survive... as long as the sea worm didn't give her another blow.

Baine's face contorted in rage. He gave a cry of anger, and as he flung his hands outward, I saw ice spread over the ocean and lock the sea worm in its grasp. The Elementai riding it tried to intervene, but Baine wrapped a stream of water around him and froze that, too, so that his arms were pinned to his sides and he couldn't move.

Thalassa saw her opportunity and dived. She opened her jaw wide. The sea worm cried out as Thalassa's jaws dug into him viciously. I watched as she emerged victorious with the worm's heart in her jaws, which she swallowed in one gulp.

The Elementai on the worm's back sputtered and died. Baine's ice cracked and gave way as the sea worm sank downward. Thalassa reared her head, triumphant... though she seemed unsteady, and blood poured from the wound the sea worm had given her.

Out of the corner of my eye, I noticed the flash of Task Force helmets as a battalion sailed by. I turned on Julian's back, and watched in horror as the Task Force battalion— or what was left of it— snuck past us and arrived on shore.

I realized Malison's plan just as it had succeeded. The arrival of the sea worm, along with the kraken and the leviathan, were enough to keep the resistance fighters busy. We'd been tricked.

"Jake!" I cried out, but he already knew. The commander realized he'd been fooled just as we couldn't do anything to stop it.

The sea worm was dead, killed by Thalassa. But it was too little, too late. The kraken and leviathan still survived, and they were slaying anyone who got close.

What was more, Thalassa was wounded. She couldn't help us further without killing herself.

"They've broken through the line!" I heard Jake cry out. My heart plummeted. The Task Force Toaqua were using the ocean to quench the Koigni barricade. Lindsey, Miranda and Bren, along with the other Koigni resistance, rushed along the shoreline to keep the fire wall burning, but the flames noticeably shrank, as the Toaqua had an endless supply of water on the beach and the Koigni only had so much energy to keep the flames alive. Some of the Task Force managed to get past the fire barricade and were currently assaulting the earth wall the Nivita had put up. Even from here, I knew Cade was struggling as he and the other Nivita fought to keep the earth wall standing against the onslaught of both Air and Water.

It'd all been a trap. The Task Force had lured us into a false sense of security. Let us believe we were winning just long enough to get our guard down.

We were being overwhelmed. The monstrous Familiars were providing a great enough distraction that the Task Force was getting through. Even with powerful Familiars and incredible feats of magic, it wasn't enough to save the resistance.

Unless someone stopped their commanders. Malison and Poole were running this show. If they went down, the army would become disorganized. We might have a chance of winning this thing.

Of course, I'm sure they thought the same thing about me. Sucks for them I wasn't easy to kill.

I didn't want to take any more lives, but this wasn't going to end. There was no other choice. I had to end them.

But how? If I killed Malison and Poole, their Familiars would die, too, and the problem of the monsters would be solved, but the kraken and leviathan were protecting them. I couldn't get past the creatures and get close enough to kill them.

No Water power I had would end this. No matter how strong of an Elementai I was, *normal magic* couldn't stop this.

That's when it clicked. I had to stop fighting them like a normal Elementai. I had never been normal. I'd always been weird... unique. That was my strength. I was an exceptional Toaqua, and if I was going to take them down, I had to do it my way.

And I had to do it alone. So no one else got hurt. Before I became chief, I didn't believe one man could make a difference. Now I was going to see just how much of a difference one man could make.

"Get everyone out of the area," I shouted to Jake. "I'll handle this."

His eyebrows knitted together in confusion. "Are you suggesting what I think you are?"

"Take the resistance fighters and push the Task Force back from the shore!" I cried out. "I promise you I've got this!"

"*Are you crazy?!*" Jonah screamed. "You're not strong enough to take them on by yourself!"

"Yes, I am." My tone was firm. My eyes locked with his as I said, "Jonah, trust me."

I'd given him that same look in the Elemental Cup. I'd done it before in the Anichi temple, at the riots, in the battle of Orenda Academy. He knew I meant business.

He also knew there was no talking me out of it. Jonah gave a nod to Jake. His eyes were unsure, but I heard Jake call out, "Fall back! Stop the onslaught onshore!"

Jonah gave a hesitant look back at me as he flew after Jake to help the resistance. The only people who stayed nearby were Ezra, who refused to leave me, and Stevie, who refused to leave him. They rode their Familiars against the waves as they watched me fly Julian away.

"Liam, what are you *doing*?" Ezra cried out.

"Get yourselves out of the way!" I snapped. I ignored any further protests and advanced Julian toward the kraken and the leviathan. My shaking hands ran over Julian's scales as we drew within reach of the monsters.

"I'm gonna need your help, buddy," I told Julian. He grumbled a pact—he was not afraid.

Malison's greedy eyes fell on me, and a harsh, red hot band of hatred ran across my chest. He surveyed me with his lip turned up like I was some kind of filth.

Malison had been one of the people who'd killed my father. A thousand years of pain couldn't amount to the grief he'd caused me.

So I'd give it right back to him by taking away the one thing that could hurt an Elementai the most.

I couldn't stop Malison or Poole's hearts from here. They were too far away, and that kind of magic wouldn't work on something as powerful as the monsters they controlled.

But I didn't need to override the kraken's power, or the leviathan's.

I just needed to take it.

"What's he doing?" Poole asked nervously. The leviathan gave an anxious groan as Julian hissed a predatory growl.

"Most likely sacrificing himself, the fool. Giving yourself up won't save your pathetic little resistance!" Malison yelled.

"I'll give you one chance," I warned. "Stand down."

Malison threw back his head and cackled that hideous laugh again. "You're delusional. Finish them off!"

The kraken lurched forward, tentacles reaching for Julian and I. The leviathan leapt out of the water, jaws wide. I took a deep breath and held it in.

I focused all my intentions on the kraken. I reached out with my magic and felt the power coursing through its body. The amount of magical energy it had seemed vast and endless, more than any other creature. The same with the leviathan. No matter where my magic went, their power never seemed to end. Through it, I could feel Malison's connection to his Familiar, as well as Poole's, though it was noticeably weaker.

Geez, no wonder Malison had been able to creep around for so long. The kraken had enough magical power to keep the old bastard going for another hundred years.

I needed to redirect that energy. But there was no time to channel it slowly. This would take everything I got. I steadied myself, then anchored my powers to the kraken and the leviathan, connecting myself to them as I did to Julian.

I was worried the spell would backfire and the monsters would end up sucking all the magic out of me. But instead, the powers from the monsters burst forward like a broken dam and began flowing into me relentlessly, like a waterfall pounding into a stream. Taking all the kraken's power, and the leviathan's on top of it, should've killed me. There was nowhere in my body for all that magical energy to go.

But I was connected to Julian, and though we weren't bonded, his imprint still left an unbreakable magical tie. He was a dragon, a powerful magical creature, and he was strong enough to hold the energy I gave him. I sent the magical energy flowing down that tie to Julian, where it coursed through his body and nestled there, ready for me to use as a well when I drew from it.

The leviathan dropped out of the air in surprise. It landed on the water and floundered, trying to right itself but finding it barely had the strength to keep itself afloat. The kraken screeched, sinking into the depths and twisting its tentacles in uncontrollable pain. The monsters wailed as I continued to drain their powers away, making them weaker and weaker.

The wave that Malison and Poole created began to shrink. It became miniscule, then nothing at all. Malison flapped his arms against the water to keep aloft, while Poole swam frantically, trying to figure out what was going on.

"Poole! Restore the wave, you insolent weakling!" Malison hissed.

Poole raised his hand, but his face blanched when nothing happened. "My powers!" he yelped. "They're gone!"

"Ridiculous!" Malison tried to cast, but he also came up short. His wrinkled visage became astounded when the water didn't move at his command.

"What is the meaning of this?" Malison spat up water. "Explain yourself, boy!"

"I took your magic," I replied. "What power your Familiars gave you now resides in me."

Except I couldn't hold on to it for much longer, and neither could Julian. All that power had to go somewhere, and it was going *out*.

I could barely control what happened next. The magic came erupting out of me in a colossal burst. It exploded from Julian and I, and sent the ocean ricocheting into a shockwave. The very sound made my ears ring and go deaf. The sea spanned out below me until I could see the ocean floor miles below, and the sandy bottom. The magic burst created a crater there, and the water fanned out in a circular spout. My hair swept back, and my clothes rustled around my form. Julian spread his wings to stay in the air, though his body shook with the effort.

It was like we were in the eyewall of a hurricane. The kraken and the leviathan both got swept up in the magical blast. The head of the leviathan was decapitated by the wind and the water. It went sailing in another direction than the body. The kraken was carved to pieces by the magical explosion, ink gushing from its body and turning the ocean black.

I saw Poole and Malison get swept beneath the depths by the undertow. The last I saw of them was Malison's withered hand reaching upward as it fell beneath the waves.

Their magical energy faded from my body and returned to the ocean. It was then I knew that they were both dead.

After the blast was done, the ocean sloshed back inward, filling up the crater and returning the sea to its natural state. The waves crashed angrily, then became still.

Julian gave a moan. His head bowed, and his wings slumped. He went down. I felt the cold water swell around me as we both crashed into the depths of the ocean, slowly sinking downward into the inky blackness, where no light could be found.

My dragon and I floated toward the bottom. I tried to summon a wave to save us both, but there was nothing left in me. Draining the magical energy from the kraken and the leviathan had left me spent. It'd nearly killed me.

If it hadn't already.

Death was peaceful, and dying in water was the perfect way to go. I was so tired I forgot there was a family waiting back home for me. I didn't know if what I'd done had won us the battle, but I'd tried to save them. I'd tried so hard.

I only wished I could've saved my dragon.

Seen my wife one last time.

And by the ancestors... I wish I could've met my beautiful daughter. I hope Sophia told Ava-Marie about me. How much I loved her. That kid hadn't even taken her first breath yet, and already, she was my whole freaking world.

Or... what was left of it.

I closed my eyes, and the last thing I saw was Julian's red scales as they became enveloped by the totality of the darkness.

# sophia

## TWENTY-FOUR

I gasped for breath as contractions rippled through my abdomen. While Liam was down at the beach fighting off the Task Force, I was waging my own battle inside our home.

Outside, wind whipped by the window, and we could hear the roar of sea creatures in the distance. The voices of Anichi students trying to hold the shield could be heard from down the canyon. In the bedroom, it felt as if my body had betrayed me— like it was trying to rip me apart from the inside out. At first, all I felt were a few cramps, nothing more than I got on my period. But the pain quickly accelerated until I was writhing on the bed, waves of nausea washing over me.

*It will all be worth it when my baby girl arrives*, I thought to myself.

Four women surrounded me, but I barely noticed them moving around the room. All my focus had turned inward. I lay completely naked on my side, trembling on the bed.

"How long will this take?" I asked Luana. It must've been hours already, but I'd lost all sense of time. I didn't know how much longer I could do this.

Luana's eyebrows knitted together as she watched my lips move. Apparently, I wasn't speaking very clearly, because she didn't understand me.

"Every woman is different," Haloke answered. "Everything is progressing as normal."

I was about to reply, but another contraction came. The pain was deep in my abdomen, along my cervix, but it felt as if every muscle in my body contracted at once.

Imogen knelt beside the bed and squeezed my hand tightly. "Sophia, look at me. Keep your focal point. Remember to breathe."

I opened my eyes and kept them on Imogen. She took deep breaths and used her fingers to count the seconds to guide me. Without her, I'd probably forget how to breathe.

Finally, the contraction ended and I had a moment of reprieve, but I knew it would only last a minute before the next contraction came.

"She needs painkillers," Doya insisted as she came into the room with a tub of hot water. Beatrice followed behind with a stack of towels.

"Sophia has requested a natural birth," Haloke reminded her.

"We have Anichi powers on hand," Doya said, though I was too focused on making it through the next contraction that I couldn't read her tone. "Why not use those powers?"

"Because it can cause complications," Haloke answered. "When it comes to birthing new life, the body must break before it can heal."

Doya set the tub on the table beside Haloke, and the two worked together to spread warm towels over my body and rub my aching muscles. Meanwhile, Luana monitored my vitals, and Imogen helped me breathe through contractions.

Esis had gone into the living room to grab the throw blanket off the couch to provide extra warmth. He returned and draped it over my shoulders. He and Sierra were the only creatures in the room besides Beatrice. The others had stayed in the living room so they wouldn't crowd me.

Haloke rubbed my shoulder while I squeezed my eyes shut and tried to breathe through the pain. "Sophia, Luana's going to check your cervix now."

I nodded that it was okay, because I couldn't find the strength to breathe.

Luana placed a latex glove on her hand and gently reached inside of me. I barely felt her, as my focus was on other parts of my aching body.

"Luana says you're seven centimeters dilated," Haloke announced. "We still have a ways to go."

I groaned. I didn't know how much longer I could do this. It was unbearable.

"Is there anything more I can do?" Imogen asked. "Can I get you another pillow, Sophia?"

"Some water might be—" I started to say, but I gagged on my words. "Trash can!"

Imogen quickly grabbed the garbage, and I leaned over and puked. The scent of stomach acid assaulted my nose, which only made me puke again.

Loud gags filled the room. Esis scurried up to me and grabbed my face the second I stopped puking. Concern filled his big blue eyes, as if to ask if I was okay.

"I'll be fine, buddy," I assured him. "As soon as I stop feeling like I'm about to die."

I said it to make light of the situation, but Esis didn't read my tone. He took it seriously; like he actually thought I was on the brink of death. I felt his warm, calm healing magic flow into me before I could stop him.

"Esis, no!" I cried, but the damage was already done.

His healing magic flowed into me and rushed to the site of the deepest agony. For a moment, everything felt painless.

Then Sierra flew forward and dragged Esis off of me. She knew his healing magic would only make the labor worse. She was trying to save me.

The moment his healing hands left my face, the pain returned full-force. It came back stronger than ever— like a hundred pounds of bricks to my stomach. I gasped, but the air around me seemed so heavy I couldn't drag any of it into my lungs. I gulped in shallow breaths, but it didn't seem to help.

I screamed. My cervix contracted and expanded in painful tremors, and my whole body heated to the point where the hot towels on my legs started steaming. My womb spasmed, as did the muscles in my back. I arched my back and cried out once more. My heart slammed against my rib cage so hard it rocked my entire body.

Esis squealed in horror. Imogen screeched as I squeezed her hand with all my strength. Haloke began barking orders, while Beatrice cleaned up the trash can I'd puked into. I barely heard anyone. All I could think was my Fire was going to kill my baby— and yet I was in too much pain to voice my worry.

I squeezed my eyes shut tightly and tried to pull back my Fire, but another contraction started, and I couldn't hold back. My scream tore through the room. Sweat dripped down my face. I got hot and cold all at the same time, which only terrified me more.

"Liam!" I cried out, forgetting he wasn't there.

In desperation, Haloke cooled the water in the tub and tossed it over me, but it did nothing to cool my raging skin. The water boiled the second it hit me and turned into steam a moment later.

"Gaaaaaah!" I cried. Ava-Marie shifted inside of me. She pushed against parts of me that shouldn't move, like she was trying to find some way to escape the inferno of my womb. Tears streamed down my face— not because I cared about the pain, but because I feared for my daughter's life. "Help! Help my baby!"

"*Now* can we use Anichi magic?" Doya barked at Haloke.

Luana acted quickly. She forced my legs apart, then placed a hand inside of me to feel for the baby.

I forced my eyes open to look at her. My breaths came in shallow heaves I couldn't control, and my heart beat so fast I thought I might pass out. Blood covered Luana's arms all the way to her elbows as it poured out of me and pooled on the bed.

Luana's face fell. Her eyes went wide in a way that terrified me to my very core.

"Is she— okay?" I begged breathlessly.

Luana's hands were occupied, so she couldn't answer. It felt as if the weight of a thousand stones was weighing down on me in that moment. My baby had to be okay— she *had* to.

Imogen managed to tear her hand free of mine. She reached up to push my hair from my face, but she jerked back when she felt the heat on my skin. "Sophia, look at me. You have to calm down. Control your Fire. You've got this."

Tears streamed down my face. "No, I don't. I can't stop it. I can't control it."

I turned my gaze to Haloke. She was at Luana's side, her eyes full of worry. They didn't say it out loud, but I could tell something was very wrong.

"What's wrong?" I demanded. "Is she okay?"

"She's breeched," Haloke answered honestly.

*No!* My baby had shifted. She was coming out by her backend instead of her head. In such a position, she could die.

"There's more," I accused. I could see it in Haloke's eyes, and I could feel it within my womb. My daughter's energy had shifted. Ava-Marie wasn't herself.

Haloke placed a gentle hand on my leg. "You're going to make it, Sophia."

Tears poured from my eyes harder. "I don't care if I make it!" I sobbed. "Just save my baby girl."

"We will do all we can," Haloke promised. "But you, Sophia, are our priority."

Anger twisted in my gut. I couldn't believe that Haloke would choose *me* over her own granddaughter. I had already lived a full life. It was time Ava-Marie got to live hers.

Pain rippled through my abdomen and down my legs. I turned a hard gaze on Luana. Her gaze flickered to my face to read my lips. "You do everything to save her, okay? *Anything.*"

Luana nodded, but there was pain in her eyes— like she was about to lose a friend.

My vision blurred, and my head rolled backward.

Doya huffed and pushed Imogen out of the way. She took my face in her hands. Though my skin was hot and would burn anyone else, she was used to the heat and could take it. She forced me to look directly into her eyes while Luana and Haloke tried to move Ava-Marie back into position.

"Sophia, focus!" Doya demanded. "I'm going to take your Fire and cool you down."

I whimpered. The fear and pain were so intense I barely understood what she was saying. For a moment, my face cooled as Doya controlled the heat from my body and pulled it into her. A second later, she jumped back, like she'd been burned. She returned to my side after a split-second.

"Sophia, you have to let me in! Give your Fire to me. If you share it willingly, it will not harm me," she reminded me.

Sobs rocked my body, and I squeezed my eyes shut. "I c-can't!"

"You *can,*" Doya insisted. "You are the strongest student I've ever had. You created lightning as a First Year. You burnt the flesh from your hands to put a bully in her place. You fought alongside members of every House. You are a true Hawkei if there ever was one. And you are *my* daughter. You can do anything, Sophia. Do this for *your* daughter. Save her."

*Save her.* Of course I had to. I'd do anything to make sure she was all right. I would love her and protect her until the day I died.

If the ancestors willed it, that just might be today. And I was okay with dying— if it meant Ava-Marie lived.

"Take it," I told Doya.

She took my hands and squeezed tightly. It took every ounce of strength I had to manipulate my powers. I gathered them in the center of my chest, where my heart beat so rapidly my whole body quaked. I pushed the magic upward and outward, offering it to her freely.

Doya's hands squeezed tighter on mine, and she gritted her teeth. I'd never transferred magic like this before, but if I could share a fireball with another Koigni, I had to be able to share my heat— right?

Yet something about the pained look in Doya's eyes suggested it wasn't so simple. The heat seared her as much as it did me, and yet she didn't complain. It was as if this was her way of apologizing for everything that happened between us. She wasn't there for me before, but she was there for me now, in the moment I needed her the most.

The heat in my body began to recede. I gulped a deep breath, hoping it was enough to soothe my baby. I glanced back to Haloke, who was signing a question to Luana that I couldn't see.

"The heat's going away," I said breathlessly. "Is she—?"

I was just about to ask if my baby was okay, but then I felt it. When the heat spiked, Ava-Marie's heart rate increased. Now that we'd vanquished it, her pulse had plummeted. I could feel it the way I felt my own heart racing. My Spirit magic moved through her, and in that moment, I felt nothing. Everything just... stopped.

A beat passed where I tried to make sense of the total lack of energy between mine and my daughter's bodies. My own magic buzzed at a low frequency, but Ava-Marie's... I couldn't feel her at all.

"No!" I shrieked, my voice echoing off the walls of the house.

"Sophia, it's time to push!" Haloke instructed.

"She's still breeched!" I cried. I didn't know how I knew, but I could feel that she wasn't in the right position. "Luana, you do *anything*! You take my life and put it into this baby's! You hear me?"

Luana watched my lips move, then nodded firmly.

"Sophia, we're not—" Imogen started, but I cut her off with a loud scream as I pushed with the next contraction.

Imogen's terrified eyes widened, and she rounded the bed to take one of my hands. I gasped and squeezed Doya's hand on the other side. I squeezed so hard I swore I could've broken bones, but neither of them complained. On the other side of the room, Sierra held Esis back, and he wept as he watched helplessly.

Another contraction came. I cried out as I felt parts of me tear. Stinging pain radiated between my legs, and my bones were forced apart as Ava-Marie's body pushed them aside.

The contraction ended. I expected for a moment to see my baby girl, but she hadn't made it out yet. She was stuck. I'd never felt a pain so intense in my whole life— because the pain wasn't just in my womb. It permeated all throughout my body, deep down into my heart and soul like daggers tearing through every inch of me. My baby girl was almost here— and I'd already lost her.

"No!" I screamed. "Ancestors, please! Don't take her. Take me instead!"

Bargaining was all I had left. My energy had completely drained, and I didn't know if I could push another time. I'd do anything to save my baby girl.

"One more push, Sophia!" I heard Haloke say, but my vision was already starting to blur. The blood coated the mattress, my legs, the sheets. There was so much of it I'd fear I'd drown in it. I didn't think it was possible for a person to lose that much blood and survive.

Maybe it wasn't.

As the next contraction came, darkness began to close in all around me. I barely registered my own cries as I put every ounce of energy I had left into saving my daughter. I didn't want to leave Liam. I loved him so much. But I knew he would be okay, because he would have our little girl at his side. I could still save her.

I pushed with all my might, until I thought my body would give out...

Until it *did*.

The darkness completely consumed me. For a moment, there was nothing. I didn't feel my daughter slip out of me. I didn't hear the cries of her first breath. For all I knew, she hadn't taken a breath at all. There was just silence... just blackness.

And then I saw a light. It was a bright, brilliant light like that of Anichi magic, but it was so pure that I had to lift my hand to shade my eyes. All around me was black, except for the light far in the distance. Ahead of me, I could hear the sound of birds chirping, wind rustling through the trees, and the gentle trickle of a stream. It sounded still and peaceful.

I barely had a moment to take it in before I heard the sound of footsteps. Five figures stepped in front of the bright white light. I walked forward to get a better look at them.

The muscular man in front of me wore a feathered headdress, and he bowed reverently toward me. Beside him, a man in a cowboy hat bowed in a similar manner. Next, a woman with a red mane of hair and a corset ballgown curtsied.

*My ancestors.*

But they weren't the only ones here. The last two people standing in the light were... *my grandparents.*

Tears filled my eyes, and my heart warmed as I took them all in. They were here to guide me to the Ancestral Lands.

My grandmother stepped forward. Not Betsy, but my other grandma, the one whose DNA I shared— Viola Doya. She looked just like Madame Doya. I couldn't believe I hadn't seen it before. But there was a kindness to her eyes Doya's past had shadowed. I bet my grandmother had been a really good mom.

Viola reached a hand out toward me. She wanted me to come to her.

I started to take a step forward, but the sound of a newborn's cry stopped me dead in my tracks. I turned around and looked behind me, into the darkness. The baby was there, alone and crying out for her mother.

My heart broke as the cry continued, because I couldn't find her in the darkness. But I knew she needed me— and I needed her. Our souls were tethered, and I couldn't leave her.

I turned back to my ancestors. All of them held out a welcoming hand, beckoning me forward to join the ancestors.

But I couldn't move toward them.

"I'm sorry," I said. "My daughter needs me."

Betsy smiled first, like she understood. Then all five of them were smiling, giving me their blessing to return.

I bowed my head reverently at them. "Thank you."

Then I whirled around and raced toward the sound of my daughter's cries.

The darkness enveloped me again, but I continued to race forward until I could no longer feel my limbs. I didn't know where I was. All my senses had vanished until—

A sharp breath passed by my lips, filling my lungs. Beside me, Imogen was weeping over my bedside, and Doya was shaking me. Sierra glowed a brilliant white from above me. It was so beautiful and bright that it nearly blinded me. She fluttered her wings, aiming Anichi magic at my face like she was trying to force me to inhale it. Esis sat on my chest. Tears stained his white fur, and his healing magic warmed my heart.

The sound of my baby girl's cries could no longer be heard. Fear ignited in my chest as I worried I'd only imagined it.

Imogen and Doya shared a collective gasp as my eyes shot open. "Sophia, thank the ancestors—" Imogen started, but I barely heard her.

I sprang upright in bed, though it pained me to do so. Sierra and Esis must've worked some serious Anichi magic on me, because I felt significantly better than before, no longer on the edge of death.

"Ava-Marie!" I gasped, glancing frantically around the room. "Where is she?"

Luana and Haloke were hunched over the changing table. Beatrice walked away holding a wad of bloody towels. My heart leapt in worry. It was quickly soothed as Haloke turned around holding a small bundle of blankets. My daughter cooed, and my heart melted.

"She's stable," Haloke announced, eyeing her granddaughter with soft eyes. She walked over to hand her to me. "She's the most precious child I've ever seen, Sophia. Congratulations."

When I took my daughter in my arms, the world might as well have stopped spinning. In that moment, it was as if my daughter and I were the only two people in the world. We'd just fought the most intense battle together— and we'd won. Holding her was like holding on to the ancestor's magic itself. It was precious, fragile, and the most incredible blessing of all.

For the first time in my life, I felt all my elements swirl together as one. My heart swelled with Koigni passion, and my soul radiated the serenity of the Anichi. And then there was water— an element Ava-Marie and I shared. I could not control water, but Toaqua blood ran through my veins. With it came a stillness I did not know until now— like the stillness of a mountain lake blessed by the Great Spirit Himself. There was nothing in this life greater than that calm, perfect tranquility.

Ava-Marie looked like her daddy, with the same shade of black hair and a beautiful skin tone that was a few shades darker than mine. She kept her eyes closed, and she wiggled in my arms. She was smaller than I thought she'd be— at least half the size of Esis.

I brushed my finger across her soft cheek. I never thought I'd felt anything so smooth. She opened and closed her mouth, like she was trying to tell me something. I couldn't believe she was mine.

She was the tiniest, most precious thing I'd ever laid eyes on, and it warmed my heart to infinity and back. She wiggled in my arms and reached out her fingers and brushed them across my chest. That one simple touch tugged at my heart strings, as if she and I were spiritually tied and she had the power to influence my own elements.

I was so happy that tears began to stream from my eyes, and my smile turned into laughter. I was so relieved that she was okay.

Sobs racked my chest, but for once, they weren't out of anger, frustration, or pain. I wept for the love that flowed through my heart. My body could not contain it, and the tidal wave of emotions inside of me spilled over.

This is what I'd been waiting for. My whole life, I'd wanted her. I'd been through so much pain and so much grief, and she was my reward.

Nobody said anything. They just let me cry and admire my amazing daughter in silence. She was everything I'd ever dreamed she would be. People said Liam and I couldn't mix because we were Fire and Water.

But they were wrong. Fire and Water created miracles.

Our incredible little Ava-Marie was proof of that.

"You were right, Sophia," Doya whispered, leaning over to look at her granddaughter. "You and I are very different."

"How so?" I asked curiously, not taking my eyes off my precious baby girl.

Doya sighed. "You would do anything to protect this baby— even sacrifice yourself."

"I disagree," I said. "On that, we are very much the same. We would do things for our daughters others couldn't ever imagine."

Doya's features softened, and she smiled. It had to be the first time I'd ever seen her genuinely smile. "I see now why the ancestors chose you."

I stared up at her in shock. It was clear by the look on her face— she really meant it.

"Thank you," I whispered, before turning my gaze back to my daughter. She was perfect. "If there's anything the ancestors chose me for, it was to be Ava-Marie's mother. That's the greatest calling of all."

# iam

## TWENTY-FIVE

"**B**ro, you *really* need to stop being so dramatic."

I felt unstable, wet sand pressing against my body, and the ebb of the ocean washing against my feet. Slowly, I came to. The sky above me had gone clear as the stars faded, painted in colors of red and orange.

Sunrise. It was Christmas morning. We'd been fighting all night. I heard the sound of birds and smelled smoke, but everything else was quiet.

My head was pounding. I'd rarely felt weaker. Every limb ached, like someone was stripping off the muscles piece by piece then grating on the bones with a fine pick. I couldn't tell if the earth was spinning or if my stomach was. I definitely felt like I was going to puke.

I was going to suffer for what I did with a flare up from hell. But it was a small price to pay to get rid of Poole and Malison for good.

Ezra lay next to me, panting. I caught the sight of Stevie above us, her hands on her hips as she shook her head. All of us were soaked.

"You're a special one, Liam Mitoh." She reached out a hand to pull Ezra to his feet. He got up and shook the water out of his hair. Me, I stayed on the ground, because I worried if I tried to stand I'd collapse.

"I don't remember what happened." My heart was still pounding in my chest.

"Ezra dived in after you. He got you out, and I got you *both* out," Stevie clarified. "You passed out after you basically became a god. I'm impressed. Thought I'd win our little death bet for sure."

Ezra gave her a glare, but the memory of me falling into the sea sent an arrow straight through my chest. "Julian." I started, but I was too weak to get up.

"Relax. Dyami and Nihoni got him." Stevie shrugged casually.

I heard heavy footsteps. Julian peered over me, wide fangs on display in a grin. His tail wagged, like he was awfully pleased with himself. Dyami chirped at his side while Nihoni preened her feathers, looking proud.

It got to me how awfully silent it was. Only a short time before, the sounds of battle had been deafening. "Did we win?"

"Did we fucking win." Ezra let out a snort and threw his head back. "Dude, once you performed that crazy magic, they started *high-tailing* it out of here! The Task Force couldn't leave fast enough. They didn't get past the barricade, and once the resistance circled them on the beach, they didn't have anywhere to go. The ones that made it out aren't going to come back here anytime soon."

I sat up slowly. My stomach dipped with nausea at all the carnage displayed on the beach. Bodies, both Task Force and resistance. There were so many corpses that the sand had turned red. I watched, feeling sick, as resistance soldiers pulled carcasses out of the water.

We'd sacrificed people today to win this fight. But not as many as I'd feared. Our numbers weren't devastated.

"I think I'm in love with you," Ezra told Stevie as he wrapped her in his arms. "You were a badass out there."

"Hm. A badass." Stevie raised an eyebrow. "It's a good start, but not enough, I think."

"I'll worship you like a *goddess*," Ezra told her, and he peppered her neck with kisses while Stevie giggled.

Ugh. Fucking gross. These two were ruthless with the PDA.

"Can someone help me get up?" I asked crossly. "Otherwise, I'm not moving from this spot all damn day."

Julian tried to help, but only succeeded in kicking sand in my mouth.

"Geez, bro. You're so needy." Ezra whined as he untangled himself from Stevie to lend me a hand. As he helped me, I tried to get all the gore off of my clothes and dry off, but my magic just wasn't having it.

"Let me." Stevie waved her hand, and the blood and water evaporated off of our clothes, leaving us clean and dry. I was shocked she could still do magic after relentlessly kicking ass, but I'd bet anything her symptoms tomorrow would be just as bad as mine.

Baine was limping up the shore. He'd gotten a cut on his leg, but it didn't look deep.

"How's Thalassa?" I asked him immediately. I didn't see her in the ocean.

"Thalassa will be fine. She merely needs rest. She's gone to the deep sea to get some sleep and recover," Baine replied. "She's been in worse scraps before, I can assure you."

*Where the hell have you been exploring that she has to fight off giant sea monsters?* I had the balls to wonder.

"We should find Jake and get our next orders," Stevie said. "This is going to be a big clean up."

At the mention of Jake, I thought of Jonah. I hoped he was all right. We began searching the beach. I had to lean on Julian to walk as my strength recovered slowly. Baine turned in a different direction, to help a group of Toaqua carry off an injured Familiar.

With relief, I saw Jake and Jonah standing by a large rock up ahead. They were covered in blood and sea water, but looked okay. Sabor and Squeaks stood closely together, their heads touching. As we headed toward them, I saw Amelia and the Henleys. They sat on a log that had washed up on the beach and just stared out at the ocean. Kiwi, who I hadn't seen the entire battle, sat on Amelia's shoulder, head lolling. He was tired. Trace sat next to her for comfort.

Cade, Wyatt, Lindsey, Miranda and Bren were helping to clean up the beach, along with their Familiars. They all looked tired, but none seemed hurt. Although this had been a violent battle, none of our friends had been seriously injured or killed, which was a miracle in itself.

I didn't know how much longer we could keep pulling off miracles around here. Sooner or later, they had to dry up and our luck would run out.

"Well, if it isn't the hero of the day," Jonah quipped. "I bow to you, Chief of Toaqua."

Jonah made a show of grabbing my hand and kissing up my arm, which was annoying.

"Stop." I shoved him off. "It wasn't anything special."

"On the contrary, it was quite incredible," Jake replied. "I congratulate you on saving our ass."

"Not that I didn't help," Jonah said, batting his eyelashes. I rolled my eyes.

Jake chuckled lightly. "Yes. You did beautifully."

"What are the casualties?" I asked.

Jake's shoulders slumped. "We've lost a few hundred. It was better than I expected, but burying your soldiers is never something to celebrate."

"They died for us," Stevie said. "They knew what we're trying to create is worth dying for."

Jake straightened up. "Yes. And it's not over. We won, but they'll be back. They know we're here now and what we can do."

It would have to wait for another day. We'd take this victory, because we sorely needed it.

"Liam!" I heard Maddie call my name, and I gave a start. She was in the water, riding Menilly— my mother's kelpie— over the waves. Maddie seemed frantic, her hair a mess and eyes wild. She must've rode along the beach for miles to get here.

"Sophia's having the baby!" she blurted. Several people around me gasped. My exhaustion faded away completely as adrenaline took over and flooded energy into my limbs, making the pain I felt vanish. I didn't care how tired I was. That didn't matter now.

"Shit!" I didn't ask any more questions. I needed to be by my wife's side as soon as possible. I pulled myself onto Julian. He boosted me up with his nose before he spread his wings and took off flying, leaving the others behind.

Julian flew faster than he ever had before on the way back to *Hok'evale*. On the way, nervous thoughts kept running through my mind.

Was Sophia okay? Was she going to pull through this? What about the baby? Had anything gone wrong? Dammit, they needed me, and I wasn't there! Not that I could do fuck all but offer support, but I hadn't wanted her to go through this alone. Was I already too late to witness the birth?

All thoughts felt flat and went static as the house came into view. Julian landed roughly. I all but fell off and launched myself forward, staggering up the stairs.

I flung open the door. I expected to hear something— screaming, sounds of pain— but it was too quiet.

My lungs froze as my gut twisted anxiously. Something bad had happened, hadn't it? It was far too quiet.

Luana came out of the bedroom, Sierra fluttering around her. She was followed by my mother's britnai housekeeper. The front of Luana's dress was stained red, and in her arms, she held a bundle of sheets and towels... all covered in blood. Blood was a normal part of labor, right?

Except... there seemed to be a lot of it.

When Luana looked up and saw me, she beamed like the sun. Her smile made me relax just a little. Luana deposited the stained linens into a trash bag, then gestured for me to come forward and see.

I followed her into the bedroom. Sophia was lying on the bed, her front end propped up on a few pillows. Her face was whiter than a ghost, and her arms hung limply on the blanket. She seemed incredibly spent. Esis curled up on her shoulder sleeping, seemingly as tired as she was.

Her eyes fluttered weakly when she saw me. A thin smile crossed her ashen lips. "Liam."

"*Pawee.*" I rushed forward and knelt at her bedside. I grasped her hand — it was freezing cold.

Doya was kneeling at her bedside, stroking her hair. She gave me a harsh look, but said nothing. Naomi lay at the foot of the bed and gave a low growl, tail flicking.

"Are you okay?" I sensed something wasn't right. I rubbed her arm, and Sophia gave a long sigh.

"She'll be fine," Doya said calmly. As Sophia struggled to keep her eyes open, a question rose in my mind. Where was the baby?

Then... the most beautiful sound hit my ears. It was soft cooing. Little frustrated noises.

I heard the sound of footsteps and rose slowly. I let go of Sophia's hand as my mother entered the room. Imogen was behind her, almost dancing with joy. Sassy pranced in a similar style, like she was welcoming a princess.

"Sophia went into labor the moment you were gone," Mom said. "She just arrived not an hour ago."

I sensed there was something Mom wasn't telling me. But all of that fled my mind when I noticed the pink bundle she was carrying.

"Say hello to your daughter." Mom placed the smallest of babies into my arms, and everything changed.

My heart turned violently inside of my chest when I saw her. The baby was so small, no more than eighteen inches long, and was incredibly warm. She had soft brown skin, and a mess of black hair on her head. She wiggled in the pink bundle, looking up at me like I was the person she depended on most in the world. Every emotion, every moment in time that I'd ever experienced, hit me in that moment.

It was hard to believe she was mine, even though I knew she had to be.

Ava-Marie raised a hand and ran her fingers along my cheek, and affection for her exploded inside my chest. My love for her felt like a hurricane, overpowering and unstoppable. Nothing could get in its way. It was like the sky met the earth when I looked at her, and everything I'd ever done wrong in my life didn't matter. Any regret I'd ever had or mistake I'd ever made paled next to the ever-encompassing universe that was her. My daughter was an ocean, and I'd fallen so far in love there was no chance of ever coming up for air. Our gazes connected as she made those murmuring sounds all babies make, though hers were unexplainably better.

Ava-Marie's eyes were glittering— they almost looked like glass.

I started weeping openly. Didn't give a fuck who saw. Sophia's face melted as she watched me cry over her. Now that Ava-Marie was here, I felt like I'd known her my entire life. I couldn't fathom what life had been like without her, even though she hadn't been here yesterday.

"Ancestors, Liam! She looks just like you!" Imogen gushed.

I couldn't deny it. We did look a lot alike. But she was much prettier than I was. She had her mother's beauty.

"She's so tiny," I said, almost in wonderment.

"Five pounds, eight ounces," Mom said. "Smaller than average, but nothing to be concerned about. She's perfectly healthy."

I didn't want to let her go. She was mine. I couldn't imagine giving her up to anyone, ever. As she squirmed against me, something irreversible hit.

Holy shit. I was a father.

No matter what I'd suffered in life, it was worth it all for her.

I wanted to make her life perfect. I was scared, too— scared of what could happen to her, scared of hurting her or making a mistake. I couldn't understand how men could abandon their children. I'd cut my own heart out before I put this baby down. No matter what she did, I'd never give up on her.

So this is what love felt like. I'd loved before, but this was totally different.

"Oh my gosh!" I heard Jonah gushing behind me. He peered over my shoulder, eyes welling as he set sight on the baby. "What an *adorable* little thing!"

"Doesn't she look just like a doll?" Imogen asked as she crowded next to him.

There was snickering behind me, who I knew was Ezra. "She's cute. Too bad she takes after her dad."

"Shut up, Ez."

The baby started crying. I had a lot of experience with babies, because I had a bunch of siblings, but with my daughter, it was different. It's like I could tell what she needed.

"Do you want your mama?" I sat next to Sophia's bedside and placed Ava-Marie against her chest. Sophia cupped the baby close, and Ava-Marie began to calm down.

"You did so good, baby," I whispered as I rubbed Sophia's shoulder. "So good."

Sophia barely acknowledged me. She was too busy cuddling Ava-Marie to her chest.

"Mama needs her rest, and baby and daddy need to bond," Mom said, putting her hands on her hips. "Everyone out."

Doya rose, but I highly doubt it was because she was following my mother's orders. Doya did nothing unless it was of her own volition.

When we had the room to ourselves, Sophia looked up at me. "She needs to eat, but I need help. I'm too weak."

"I've got it." I helped Sophia feed the baby before she fell asleep. Ava-Marie stayed awake a while longer, wiggling in my arms and observing my features in curiosity.

Me, I couldn't keep my eyes away. We had everything already set up in the bedroom, so I changed her diaper and rocked her until she slowly fell asleep.

Ancestors, she made tiny snuffling noises when she slept. I really couldn't handle this. It was like emotion overload.

Hours probably passed, but I didn't connect with any of them. I'd seemed to step into a place where nothing else mattered and I was too wrapped up in my daughter's existence to be bothered with something as small as the passage of time.

After a while, there was a knock. Imogen entered quietly. She saw that Sophia and the baby were sleeping and whispered, "I can come back."

"No," I replied. "Stay."

Imogen entered. She stood above me and looked down at the sleeping baby in my arms. "Couldn't put her down once, could you?"

I laughed lightly. "No."

Imogen paused for a moment. "She was worth it," Imogen whispered as she observed Ava-Marie's face.

"What do you mean?" Her words were enough to make me wrench my gaze away.

"Sophia had a harder labor than expected." Imogen sent a worried glance at Sophia, but she was still out cold.

I frowned. "I wish I could've been here."

"It was a good thing you *weren't* here," Imogen said quietly. "We almost lost her. She was begging Luana to take her life and use it to save the baby."

The color drained from my face. "Really?"

"Esis used his healing powers, but when you use Anichi magic during labor, it speeds it up to a dangerous rate. She didn't have time to get ready, and then the baby breeched. Ava-Marie's heart rate went totally flat." Imogen's lip trembled. "Sophia went so still. I was sure she'd gone to the Ancestral Lands and we'd lost both her and the baby. I was trying to come up with what to say to you—"

Imogen put a hand over her mouth and didn't speak further.

My body had gone rigid. The thought of losing both Sophia and this precious baby—

"She'll be okay now, right?" The words were tight.

"Yes. But if we didn't have Sierra, she'd be dead."

My body trembled, but I didn't want to break down, because it'd wake the baby. "Take her."

Imogen lifted the baby out of my arms. I got up and knelt by Sophia's bedside once more. I stroked her hand lightly. Sophia's eyes slowly opened.

"Why'd you do that, *pawee?*" I asked. My voice was choked. "Why'd you try to give up your life?"

"Because that's what a mother does. I've been waiting for her my whole life," Sophia replied. "She's everything I've ever wanted. I wasn't going to let her go. Even if I had to die for it."

I blinked away tears. Because honestly, she didn't need to explain. If it came down to a choice, to sacrifice myself or Ava-Marie, I'd die a million times over.

"You are my miracle." I swept back Sophia's hair and cupped her head in my hand. She nuzzled against it and said nothing more.

The door opened again. Jonah was accompanied by Cade. They'd cleaned up from the battle, and were wearing new clothes. Jonah was carrying a Christmas bag, while Cade had a plate of food.

Cade beamed when he saw Imogen. "You look beautiful with a baby in your arms."

Imogen rolled her eyes, but there was still a smile on her face.

"Haloke said you should eat something," Cade said to Sophia. He put the plate down next to her bedside. Sophia picked up the sandwich and took small bites. Esis, who'd woken up, eagerly gobbled down his half.

"And look what I got! Her first Christmas present!" Jonah pulled out of the bag the biggest and poofiest pink newborn dress I'd ever seen. "When she wakes up, she *has* to try it on."

"When she wakes up," I said firmly. Anyone who woke a sleeping baby in this house was going to get my foot up their ass.

"Happy Birthday, little one," Jonah sang to Ava-Marie. "Can I hold her?"

"Go ahead."

I watched as Imogen transferred the baby into Jonah's arms. Ava-Marie looked comically small in Jonah's wide frame. She could almost fit in his hands.

Jonah stuck out his lip. "Aw! Now *I* want one!"

"You're going to need different equipment," Cade cracked.

"Ancestors, could you imagine Jonah in labor?" Imogen threw a hand on her forehead to imitate him being dramatic, and everyone laughed.

"She has the tiniest little nose," Jonah cooed. "I just want to poke it."

"Don't you dare," I warned, but at that moment, Ava-Marie woke up. Her mouth opened, and she kicked her legs, letting out a couple of grunts.

"Okay, back to daddy," Jonah said quickly, and he pawned Ava-Marie off like he was passing a football. He nearly dropped her. By the ancestors, if he had done that I would've lost my shit.

I took her quickly and scowled. "Be more fucking careful."

"I'm terrified of babies unless they're asleep. I don't know what they want," Jonah said.

"It's pretty simple. Food, sleep, to be changed," Imogen listed.

"Your own routine," Cade joked.

Jonah waggled a finger. "Hey, Jake and I are *not* into diaper play."

"Fucking gross." How did I know that was going to come up at some point?

I sat on the edge of the bed. Sophia lifted a hand to play with Ava-Marie's fingers as she ate. The room let out a collective *aw*.

"One day, that'll be us, *chica*," Cade said, and he gave Imogen a tight squeeze. Imogen smiled slightly and let Cade wrap his arms around her.

I felt happy for them. There seemed to be hope for their relationship after all.

Sophia finished her sandwich and put the plate aside. "Where's Haloke?"

"She's working on Christmas dinner for tonight," Cade said. "Along with... Doya."

Only my mom could deliver a baby and then cook Christmas dinner. The woman was a whirlwind. But Doya, too?

"She's cooking?" I asked. Ancestors, I hoped she didn't poison the food.

"Yeah. Guess she's staying." Cade shrugged. "This has been one weird Christmas."

"I'll say." A battle, a baby, and a totally new family, basically all in one day. You never knew what life was gonna throw at you.

Ezra called Cade's name from out in the living room. He gave Imogen's hand a squeeze. She closed the door quietly behind him, eyes knitted together in concentration.

"What's up, Im? Something's on your mind," I said. Ava-Marie squirmed in my arms, but as I jostled her, she began crying out. Sophia reached out for her. I handed her off, and the baby quieted again.

Imogen kneaded her hands together. "I don't want to ruin the moment. Or the holidays."

"But?" I pressed.

She sighed. "I hate to talk business, today of all days. But I think we have to. I had a lot of time to think while I was in rehab. And there's some things about the prophecy that just don't add up."

That got Sophia's attention. "What kind of things?"

"Well, prophecies are stories. They need to have an ending," Imogen said. "And the last piece is supposed to be the Air piece, but it just drops off from there. The Air piece says that the society will burn, and the Hawkei will go extinct. There's just no finality to it."

"Total Hawkei extinction isn't a finality?" Jonah questioned.

Imogen shook her head. "No. Not in the way it's worded. I had time to read books on prophecies while in recovery— I stopped reading after I started using. I lost so much time."

"What's your point, Im?" I asked.

"Prophecies always have a way out. A loophole, if you will, to avoid the warning that came before and restore things to balance. And there is no such loophole in the pieces we have so far."

Imogen tapped her chin. "I know we think the missing Koigni piece comes last, but I'm not sure we're right on that. I think there's something we're missing."

My heartbeat began to pick up. "And you think there's another part out there somewhere."

"Why wouldn't there be? There are five Houses. Why aren't there five parts to the prophecy?" Imogen questioned. "I know the Anichi tribe doesn't think there is, because Showana Harjo didn't give them a piece like the rest of the Houses, but maybe whatever she prophesied was only meant for one person to know."

"And that's why Showana would hide it," I said. "If it exists."

"Exactly." Imogen sighed and slumped over. "The thing is, I'm acting on a hunch. We have no proof. This could turn into a wild goose chase."

Sophia shook her head. "I think you're right. The prophecy hasn't sat right with me since we got here... we've just been too busy to pursue the idea there might be another piece."

"If that's true, where do we start?" Jonah asked.

"We already know we've gotten something wrong," I said slowly. "The Nivita piece said the weakest had to bend for our tribe to survive. But the weakest aren't the Biyami. The weakest are the Defortai— people like Oleander and the Elders, who harm the tribe to remain in power."

Sophia's voice grew stronger. "Showana said I had more to learn. That it was up to me to interpret the prophecy's meaning when I was ready. I think I get it now. We all believed the prophecy was about Koigni because they *wanted* you to believe that. The Koigni wanted the prophecy to skew in their favor, so they forced the interpretation on us. But we know the prophecy was never about Koigni; it was about Anichi. So why wouldn't Showana Harjo make a piece for the House the prophecy was about in the first place?"

My tone grew in excitement. "So that means... there has to be a Spirit piece. Nothing else makes sense."

The door opened again, and Maddie peeked her head through. "Mom wanted you guys to start getting cleaned up so we can open presents," she said. She looked at my battle-torn clothes and wrinkled her nose. "Preferably as soon as possible."

"It's actually a good thing you're here," I said. "We wanted to ask you a question."

"What's up?" Maddie crossed her hands in front of her. I hesitated. I didn't want to make Maddie mad by asking questions about prophecies, but she was a *naderei*, and we needed her advice.

"We've been thinking... what do you think the chances are that there's an Anichi piece to the prophecy?" I asked.

Maddie's expression was thoughtful. "To be honest... I'm not sure why there wouldn't be. I've looked over the pieces you guys have, and it seems unfinished in my opinion. There has to be more to the vision she had— a circle that makes everything complete."

"Do you know where she could've hid it?" I asked.

Maddie shook her head. "I don't— but maybe if I thought about it, I could come up with some theories."

Apparently, we had a revolving door on this place, because Doya was next to enter. All talk of the prophecy instantly shut down; we didn't trust Doya with such crucial information, which is why Sophia hadn't spoken to her about the missing Koigni piece yet. She might be trying to mend her ways, but she hadn't earned our trust one-hundred percent.

Doya was wearing an apron, her hair tied back. She looked rather motherly, which was *so freaking weird.* Maddie stepped aside, pressing to the wall to let her in.

"I've just come to see how things are," Doya said stiffly. If this was her way of checking in on Sophia, it felt rather formal.

"Things are just fine. Do you want to hold her?" Sophia held up the baby to Doya.

Doya's eyes darted down to the child. She seemed hesitant, before finally she held out her hands and took the baby into her arms.

I felt anxious while watching Doya hold Ava-Marie. I mean, the woman had tried to smother Sophia as a newborn. She was a cold-blooded killer.

Yet when Doya held the baby, her face softened like I'd never seen before. Her eyes took on a gentle quality, and Doya smiled— actually fucking smiled— for what I was sure was the first time in years. It wasn't a smirk or a nasty grin like I was used to seeing. This smile was authentic, and full of affection.

"You're going to be just like your mother," Doya said sweetly. The baby squirmed, and Doya placed a kiss on her head.

Holy shit. Maybe Doya could actually be... nice.

We were all caught up in the cute moment, until a loud *wham* smacked the wall and made all of us jump. Ragged breathing was behind me. I turned and saw that Baine had come charging in here like some kind of wild animal.

When Baine slammed the door, Ava-Marie started *screaming.* Like, full-out crying. I didn't even know a baby could be that loud. Holy hell, she had lungs. I thought my ears would shatter.

"I've made some headway. I—" Baine's words cut off as they were drowned out by the sound of Ava-Marie's wailing. He stood stock still, his eyes widening as he took in the image of the child.

"Oh, Elliot," Doya said with a sigh. "Can you please be more careful?"

Doya soothed the baby, and Ava-Marie's cries dropped to a low shriek. My instincts screamed at me to reach out and take her, but Doya seemed to have it handled.

Doya noticed my anxiousness. She gave me a kindly look and said, "I've got her. You're a good father."

I was floored. Had Doya seriously just given me a *compliment?* Seeing her daughter give birth must've changed her.

Ava-Marie's cries slowly dropped off as Doya rocked her gently. Baine stood overhead, his eyes alight with wonder as he took in the sight of her.

"In all my years," Baine breathed. "I've come across many treasures in my travels, but she is just perfect."

"Damn right she is," I growled, and I crossed my arms. Anything less than perfect would be an insult to my daughter.

"You're her grandfather. Hold her for a moment," Doya said, and she held out her arms.

Baine floundered. "Me? Oh no, I've never held a baby. I couldn't."

But too late, because Doya handed Ava-Marie off to him without caring what he thought. I stayed close, just in case Baine's clumsy ass managed to make a fumble.

Yet he didn't drop her, thank the ancestors. He was really still, like he was terrified to make a wrong move. Ava-Marie tucked her head against his chest, and Baine's mouth dropped open. It was like he couldn't believe she existed.

"You look very handsome with a baby in your arms," Doya cooed, and she stroked Baine's back lovingly. Jonah's jaw dropped, and he mouthed *what the fuck* behind them.

"Ah, thank you, Eleanor," Baine stuttered. He looked up from the baby and said, "I'm sorry I didn't get to experience this with you."

"We can make up for it with her," Doya said, and she squeezed Baine's shoulders.

Uh, what was going on? Were they getting back together or something?

I was getting kind of tired of watching Doya hit on Baine, so I asked, "You wanna tell me why you came blazing in here with your ass on fire?"

Baine looked to me. His expression became deadly serious as he said, "I've made a shocking discovery. One we don't have time to waste on."

"Well, tell us!" Sophia urged.

Baine took a deep breath. He glanced down at Ava-Marie, then at Sophia before he spoke. "I've found the *Azaimperiai.*"

# **END OF BOOK FIVE**

Continue on to read a special excerpt from Book Six: *The Soul Sacrifice!*

572

# HIDDEN LEGENDS

Read more from the Hidden Legends universe! Each Hidden Legends series takes place within the same world, but in separate and unique societies. Every series stands on its own, and they can be read in any order.

৯৯

## SHIFTERS, FAE, & SORCERESSES

University of Sorcery by Megan Linski

৯৯

## WITCHES, DEMONS, & REAPERS

College of Witchcraft by Alicia Rades

৯৯

## SUPERNATURAL PRISON

Prison for Supernatural Offenders by Megan Linski & Alicia Rades

৯৯

Never miss a new release! Join our newsletter at
www.hiddenlegendsbooks.com/fanclub/

# THE SOUL SACRIFICE
## CHAPTER ONE

### *Liam*

Running from a rolling boulder wasn't exactly how I pictured my new year to begin, but here I was, hauling ass to avoid being completely squashed under the weight of another booby trap— second one of the day, actually.

"Fucking dammit, Baine!" My breaths came in long gasps as I pumped my arms. The temple hallway was long and made of stone. There were no windows, and the only light we had came from a singular torch that Professor Baine was carrying. My eyes glanced everywhere for an exit, but I didn't see a spare door. The thunderous rolling of the boulder behind us grew closer and closer, picking up speed.

The hallway sloped downward. Eventually, the boulder would roll faster than we could run.

Baine wheezed for air. Though he was in shape from crawling around in temples lately, he was no spring chicken. Old man was starting to slow up.

My eyes focused on a door at the end of the hallway. If we made it there, we could escape— though it was still twenty feet away, and the boulder was right on our heels.

With a desperate glance back, I saw with horror the boulder was going to crush us any second. We didn't have time to make it to the door before the giant rock smashed us flat. My powers reached out for something, anything that could save us. Miraculously, the Toaqua magic flowing through my veins caught something.

There was an underground water system nearby, just beyond the wall that closed us in. We were in the bottom of the temple. It wasn't much, but it was our only shot.

I threw my hand in front of me like I was smacking something. The wall up ahead burst. A burst of water blasted open the brick on our right side and went clear through to the left.

As the wall exploded, I grabbed Baine and yanked him to the side. His torch went out as it splashed into the water. We ducked into the crevice the blast had made, though water continued to pour down through the hole I created and soaked our clothes.

We had to press together as the boulder rolled by. I held my breath. The rock scuffed us and ripped my pant leg, but it didn't hurt us. I heard the rock smash against the end of the hallway with a colossal *boom*, shaking the walls.

The water pouring from the hole I'd made trickled down the long hallway. It'd soon flood in here. Needing some reprieve, I pried Baine off and stumbled into the open space. I leaned over my knees and heaved, taking deep breaths.

I heard the sound of a lighter. Baine had lit another torch from his pack and held it high, so we could see. The water ebbed out of the hole, already filling up to our ankles.

One more mistake. One fucking more—

"Looks like we triggered another Nivita trap," Baine breathed. He leaned against the wall to steady himself and catch his breath.

"Oh, gee, no shit," I responded sarcastically. I spat and forced myself to stand up. "Guess that wasn't the right way, huh?"

Baine narrowed his eyes. "What are you implying?"

"I'm asking if you know where you're going." I sounded frustrated, but my patience was at its limit. I'd been away from my wife and newborn for a week and a half, and it'd been nothing but setting off traps and hitting dead ends with my dear old father-in-law.

"Of course I know where I'm going!" Baine said, flustered. "We can't be too far."

I'd heard that one before. When we'd gotten here, Baine had accidentally found a Fire wall Koigni trap and ended up burning his ass. *His literal ass.* I had to shield my eyes so I didn't have to watch him put cream on it once we were safe, as we hadn't brought any Anichi or healing Familiars along.

We'd had a week to recover after the battle in *Hok'evale* before Baine insisted getting the *Azaimperiai* was of absolute importance and the search had to begin right away. He told us the *Azaimperiai* could be found in the abandoned Anichi temple in Kinpago— the one where Sophia had summoned Showana Harjo to discover more about the prophecy. Baine had wanted to go alone, but all of us worried if we let something as important as this be left up to Baine, something would go wrong. We'd eventually harassed him enough that he agreed to take one other person. I more or less told him it was going to be me.

Lucky me, right?

"I sacrificed time with my daughter to be here with you," I spat. "I'd ask you not to waste it."

"You didn't *have* to come, you know," Baine said resentfully. "I work best on my own."

"I didn't trust you to come back with the *Azaimperiai* in one piece." I wiped my forehead. "Come on. We need to keep moving."

"*Excuse me?* I am in control of this expedition, sir!" Baine blustered.

He didn't have control of shit. As we wandered up the sloping hallway, I took deep breaths. I'd barely had time to feel well after my fight with the Task Force a few weeks ago, and my magic was still weak. Not to mention running around in this crappy temple and sleeping on hard stone wasn't doing wonders for me. My body was starting to give out. It wouldn't be long before I'd be forced to return to *Hok'evale* and get some rest. We had days left to find this thing, if that.

"I'm going to ask you again. Are you *sure* this is where it is?" I asked.

"Of course it is!" Baine exclaimed. "I wouldn't have brought us here if I wasn't absolutely sure."

Didn't put a lot of stock in that. "Let's go over what you know. You think the *Azaimperiai* is here because—"

"Because this is the only place it *could* be." Baine cut me off, his words an irritated jumble. "The Anichi would never hide the *Azaimperiai* in a place that wasn't sacred. They would consider such an object revered by the ancestors and want it in a location that honored it, and protected it from those who would try to steal it."

"And you're insistent it's in this particular temple."

"Correct. There are few Anichi temples left in the world, all of which I've explored— except for this one." Baine held up a finger. "I've never searched this temple because I considered it ransacked by the other Houses. Each House has traps set up here to prevent each other from investigating the temple; therefore, most of it has already been explored. I'd believed that if the *Azaimperiai* was here, it'd been long discovered by now. However, I had a thought. If the other Houses have put their mark on this place, why wouldn't Anichi?"

"And you think there's a hidden passage to a secret room somewhere containing it, most likely guarded by an Anichi booby trap."

"Yes. Nothing else makes any sense." Baine sounded so confident, like he'd bet his life on us finding the *Azaimperiai* today.

I just wanted to get the hell out of here, so I could see Sophia and my kid.

"And what if it's in one of the temples that's either disappeared or destroyed?" I asked.

Baine let out a breath. "Impossible. It must be here."

"You're going on a hunch," I argued. "You have no proof."

"Proof!" Baine exploded. "Of course I have proof. The *moglyn* Thalassa killed is all the proof we need."

*Moglyn* was the technical term for the sea worm we'd fought in the ocean battle weeks ago. It'd been a monstrous creature hundreds of feet long, with thousands of teeth. Thalassa had defeated it, but nearly lost her life in the process. According to Baine, *moglyn* were supposed to be extinct — which is why the appearance of this one was so strange. They only existed in underwater reservoirs beneath blessed ground— mainly, the site of Anichi temples.

The rider on its back had been bonded to it and was working for the Elders, which meant the creature had to come from somewhere around Kinpago. This was the only Anichi temple nearby, and Baine had a theory there was a *moglyn* pod in the temple near the *Azaimperiai*.

But it was just that. A theory. We had no definitive answers.

We left the hallway and entered into a giant amphitheater, one we'd been coming in and out of all week to use as a base. Baine put the torch into a holder and yanked out maps, propping them on the folding table we'd brought. I collapsed onto my cot and tried not to fall asleep.

My mind whirled. We'd been here forever. Was this actually going anywhere?

I heard a dragon's cry from above. It was Julian checking in. Julian was outside the temple, waiting for us to come out. He was hiding from the Task

Force in the forest around the temple, but still, it made me uneasy to keep him exposed for so long.

As Baine fussed over the maps, I said, "You've looked at those a million times. It's not going to change anything."

"Look, there's only one corridor we haven't tried." Baine circled the map and pointed. He walked over to me, shoving the map in my face. "*That's* where we have to go. If it's not there, we have nowhere else to look."

Thank the ancestors. Not getting the *Azaimperiai* would be really shitty, but at this point, I just wanted to go home.

We took another twisting hallway downward. I kept my eyes peeled, but luckily, we didn't run into any booby traps... yet.

Baine noticed my impatient stature. "I understand you're in a hurry to get back to your new wife, but she'll be there," Baine went on. He made a romantic, weird sound. "I remember what it was like to be young and in the honeymoon phase."

"I've been with Sophia for over two years." On and off, granted, but never stopped loving her besides.

Baine gave a *psh*. "Nothing when you've loved someone for a lifetime."

"You've barely been back with Doya for a month!"

That is, if he *was* back with her, which I was pretty sure he was. After we'd found out Baine and Doya were Sophia's biological parents, it'd all been very weird. They acted like a couple, but never really told anyone what they were. As far as I knew, the relationship didn't have any labels.

Baine didn't confirm or deny. Instead, he turned to his favorite topic lately, which was blithering on about how hot Doya was. "You know, some women only get more beautiful with age. Eleanor, for example. She's like a fine wine. Her hair's the color of wine. And her thighs. Eleanor has wonderful thighs, you know. I think that's my favorite part of her."

I gave a long, drawn out sigh. "Okay, I *really* didn't want to ask this, but you keep going on about it and I'm done with wondering. Are you and Madame Doya hooking up again?"

"What is *hooking up*?" Baine adjusted his glasses, confused by the phrase.

Fucking A. This guy taught college kids, for ancestors' sake.

"I mean, when I see her carriage parked in front of your house all the time, are you two doing unmentionable activities?" I asked.

Baine's face remained blank.

I facepalmed and shouted, "*Sex!* Are you guys banging again!?"

Baine frowned. "I hardly see why it's appropriate to ask."

"Well, you keep talking about her," I said crossly. He hadn't shut up about the woman since we'd been here.

"If it's so *dire* to know, then yes. We are *hooking up*." Baine puffed out his chest. "And I'm happy to report I've still got it."

"Fucking fantastic. Glad you float her boat."

We reached the end of the hallway. It was a dead end. There was no door leading to another place.

It was strange. Why would the Anichi build a passage to nowhere?

Unless this was a place only the Anichi were supposed to know about. I began looking for clues. I knelt to the ground, trying to find some sort of button or lever.

Baine stood back from the wall and surveyed it. He ran his hands over the bricks. "Hmm... there must be some kind of—"

Baine didn't finish his sentence, because he tripped over me. His boot connected with my face, and he went flying. I gasped as Baine kicked me in the eye, and I fell against the ground. Baine himself toppled over. As he landed, I heard a small *click*.

The wall before us opened. It was the hidden door we were looking for. Baine clambered to his feet. I remained on the ground, holding my eye. It was watering profusely and pounded in pain.

Baine beamed. "Look at that! We found the secret door!"

"Great. Only thing you had to do was blind me," I growled.

Baine scowled. "Quit being so dramatic. Come on."

I got to my feet and slowly drew my hand away from my eye, though it still watered and twitched. I didn't think Baine had given me a black eye, but it still hurt.

The secret door led to a large room a hundred feet across. The room was bare of artifacts or statues, unlike the other rooms in the temple. I searched for the *Azaimperiai*, but it wasn't there.

"Look," Baine stated. "The *moglyn*."

The giant worms slithered in and out of the open area, through holes connecting to the room. There were three or so, all differing in size. Though they were terrifying, they didn't seem hostile. They ate dirt and moved along the floor with no attention to us.

"We're getting close." Baine's voice picked up in excitement. "Hurry."

We took another twisting hallway, until it felt like we were at the lowest point of the temple itself. The ancient Anichi really wanted to hide this thing.

Finally, the tunnel ended, opening into a circular room. There was a white glow inside. As we entered, I saw that the white glow was coming from an Anichi shield. Unlike the others I'd witnessed, this one was visible. It wrapped around a tomahawk suspended in thin air, hovering tantalizingly before us, just daring us to take it. I wasn't sure how the shield remained in place with no Anichi here to sustain it. It must be some kind of deep magic.

Baine's eyes sparked with greed and desire. "The *Azaimperiai!*"

It was a short distance away, but there was a problem. A creature stood guarding it. The animal had fluffy white fur, long legs, a body and ears like a hare's, with big blue eyes and a thin tail that ended in a fan. It was at least twelve feet tall standing on its hind legs.

I think I'd learned about these at Orenda Academy. They were Anichi creatures, mammals called warbels. They lived underground, ate plants and were known for being more or less harmless. It was thought they were extinct, but as we had learned, most Anichi creatures had survived the war in years prior. I didn't think the creature would attack us.

Baine, though, didn't use his head. He was so amped up about getting the *Azaimperiai* he was willing to barge through anything in his way. Baine ran toward the creature, holding the torch aloft as a weapon and giving a wild yell. He went to swing it, but the animal turned around and whacked Baine with its massive tail.

Baine went flying and slammed against the wall. The torch skidded to the side.

Baine groaned. I walked over, trying to contain my irritation. "Calm down. It's not going to hurt us," I scolded. "It's just here to watch the *Azaimperiai.*"

"That thing?" Baine burst. He got up and shoved the torch in a nearby holder. The warbel gave a mew.

"Look around you. There's no Anichi to sustain the shield. That means the warbel is doing it," I said.

"That doesn't make sense. How did this particular creature survive decades to protect it?" Baine spat.

"It didn't. warbels live in colonies," I said. "There are probably more down here. I bet Showana Harjo tasked them with defending the *Azaimperiai,* and they've done it through the generations. We just arrived on this one's shift."

Baine huffed. "My life's work right in front of me, and I'm being prevented from obtaining it by an oversized rabbit."

I walked toward the shield. "We have to break it somehow."

But we couldn't get close. When we got near the shield, the warbel hopped in front of us, planting in our way and raising its tail as a warning. We tried to come at it from different sides, but the warbel was too fast. We couldn't get around it. Though the warbel didn't outright attack, it wasn't letting us through, either. We could use brute force, but that didn't mean the shield would fall, and there wasn't enough water in the air down here to be useful to either of us. Both of us carried a small canteen to in case of emergencies, but it wouldn't be enough to fight the warbel. I could stop its heart, but I didn't like killing things if I didn't have to, and the warbel seemed innocent.

"It's a puzzle, like most of the temple's traps," I said. "We just have to figure out the solution."

"And how, pray tell, do we do that?" Baine snapped. He was in a crabby mood.

I ran a hand through my hair as I thought, remembering my time in the temple with the group when we'd gone to speak to Showana Harjo. "Well, every House trap has a certain trait attached to it. The Toaqua traps are about leadership. The Nivita traps are about using intelligence, and the Yapluma traps are about mind games. Koigni traps center around bravery. We just need to discover what trait the Anichi trap is testing."

"Neither of us are Anichi. How do you expect us to come up with a solution?" Baine complained. He wiped sweat from his brow as he drank from his canteen.

"We'll find a way." My eyes were still fixated on the warbel, who tilted its head at me.

"It's useless. We might as well give up," he bitched.

"Okay, *Grandpa*." Now he was getting on my nerves. We'd found the thing he'd wanted so badly, and he wanted to throw in the towel and run away because we had an obstacle to face?

Baine sent me a glare. "You'll be old one day too, you know."

"Chances of that aren't stellar." I walked in a circle around the room. The warbel followed me, blue eyes keenly observing my actions.

Baine frowned. "Don't say that, Liam. You're a good man. You're kind, and caring, and you protect the people around you. You still have a long life to live."

"Personality traits don't extend your lifespan, sorry."

Baine blinked. "Have you considered the option you might not die as young as you think?"

That made me pause. To get the chance to see my daughter grow up— it was something I hadn't dared to dream of.

And there was a reason for that. I had a rare disease that was barely under control. My life expectancy was up in the air— and thinking about dying of old age instead of young in some hospital bed felt like wishing on a star. I'd already been in some bad situations because of my health, some of which I wouldn't have pulled out of without healing magic. I didn't know how many more times I could tempt fate and get away with it.

I sighed. "I'm counting my blessings by enjoying the years I've got. Nobody is ever promised anything. Especially not me."

"You need to stop this thinking that you're fated for an early death. It's not helping you in the long run," Baine stated. "Why, I'd thought years ago I'd be killed in some cave-in while exploring, and it hasn't happened yet! I've been through plenty of scraps and tight situations, and I've always survived. Perhaps you will as well."

I turned away. "Maybe."

"Liam." Baine proceeded toward me. "You're going to survive this war, and you'll have a long life afterward. You must accept that."

"Accept what? That I might, just *maybe*, last long enough I'll get to walk my daughter down the aisle? Don't get my hopes up." I dropped my head.

Baine put a hand on my shoulder. "We have to do our best with what the ancestors have given us. And I believe your time is far from over. You're not close to being done. You have many years ahead of you, and I want you to have faith in that."

His words brought me a small smile. If Baine believed I had more time than I had allotted myself, who was I to argue that?

He was right. I needed to stop putting myself on a time limit and start focusing on what mattered most— which was living. To constantly believe I was going to die young... I wasn't just hurting myself, I was being selfish by not considering other people. I'd done a lot of work breaking through my negative attitude over the years, but it still looked like I had a ways to go.

"Thanks," I replied. "I guess... I should stop being so hard on myself."

Baine nodded in agreement. The warbel gave a croon, and just like that, the light in the cave dimmed as the shield vanished completely.

Baine gasped. The warbel moved aside, and my eyes widened in shock. It hit me. Anichi's trait was compassion. Baine had broken the shield by being compassionate toward me— and I'd shown compassion by being kind toward myself.

"We did it!" I shouted. The warbel bowed its head.

Baine didn't waste any time. He ran toward the *Azaimperiai*, snatching it out of the air it suspended on. His gaze was revered, jaw dropped. He held the tomahawk like a holy object, completely sucked in to the historical significance of the artifact.

"I've got it," Baine whispered. "After all these years, I've finally got it."

I looked over his shoulder. It was just like what I'd seen in the drawings. The tomahawk was no longer than my forearm, decorated with feathers and still sharp. Small, unreadable runes, like the ones on Sophia's Spirit Totem, covered the handle.

It seemed like such a simple thing— but I wasn't fooled. I knew the kind of power that this object held, the power to control the ancestors themselves.

To be honest, it scared me. No one should ever have that kind of power, no matter what they intended to use it for.

Baine handed the *Azaimperiai* to me. The object was much lighter than I expected, though to my surprise, I didn't feel the pulsing magic within that it clearly held.

But this object wasn't meant for me. I wasn't Anichi, and I couldn't use it. The *Azaimperiai* belonged to Sophia.

As I gave the ax back to Baine, he stuck it securely in his pack. "Very good. Now let's get back home, so we can give this to Sophia, and she can use it to end this—"

The floor beneath us began rumbling. Dust fell from the ceiling, and bricks tumbled from above. Baine gaped, looking around as the circular room crumbled around us.

The trap wasn't over yet. The Anichi had set up a final test, just in case someone managed to get past the shield.

The warbel gave a nervous start and ran off. It hopped out the secret door, its long tail vanishing behind it.

"We have to get out of here!" I shouted, but my cries were already being swallowed up by the sound of falling stone. We made a run for it. The secret door was only a few feet away, but as we reached it, the door caved in, blocking off our only exit.

A huge rock hurtled from the ceiling and struck Baine in the leg. He gave a cry and fell to the floor, landing on his pack. His leg twisted at an odd angle, and he clutched at it in pain.

I dove out of the way of the falling rocks, dodging the debris and covering my head. Eventually, they stopped coming. The rumbling in the cave subsided and ceased completely, but by this time, there was no way out.

My heart pounded furiously in my chest. The one torch we had was starting to dim. Baine's leg was broken, and the oxygen within the room was slowly draining. Baine screamed as he held his broken leg.

"Julian!" I cried, but my shouts echoed back to me. I doubted my dragon could hear me through the heaps of stone piled over top of us. He could get us out, but only if he knew we were down here— and I didn't have a mental connection with him to alert him to our predicament.

There was no way out. We were completely trapped.

*Continue The Soul Sacrifice to experience the epic conclusion!*

# BONUS OFFERS

Find coloring pages, games, quizzes, and bonus content at www.hiddenlegendsbooks.com

Join *Orenda Academy of Magical Creatures* on Facebook to talk to other Elementai about upcoming books in the Hidden Legends Universe!

Never miss a new release! Join our newsletter at www.hiddenlegendsbooks.com/fanclub

Check out the *Academy of Magical Creatures Official Playlist* on Spotify!

# ABOUT THE AUTHORS

Megan Linski (left) and Alicia Rades (right) are two best friends and the authors of the *Academy of Magical Creatures* series. Both are USA TODAY Bestselling Authors and award-winning novelists for teens and young adults. Megan Linski is a disabled author who loves laughter, adventure, and fantasy worlds. She is a proud member of Koigni House. Alicia Rades is a mother who enjoys exploring paranormal realms and trying new recipes. She is a champion from Toaqua House. Both girls love nature, animals, sexy romances, and eating cheese.